Acclaim for John Katzenbach's

THE TRAVELER

"Fast, moving, and violent...The reader is swept along by the ever-mounting horror and by characters who burn with life. *The Traveler* has the qualities of a bestseller."

The New York Times Book Review

"*The Traveler* is a full-blooded psychological thriller....Mr. Katzenbach's attention to detail and his superb descriptive abilities make the book sizzle and crack with tension. The story sweeps to a genuinely shattering climax in a scene of devastating horror and suspense."

The Washington Times Sunday Magazine

"This muscular scary book seizes your interest rather than asks for it, and plunges you into the nightmare world of a crazed psychopath...high-voltage crime drama."

The Baltimore Daily Record

"A complex story of murder and revenge...it generates nail-biting suspense."

The Philadelphia Inquirer

"The suspense is gripping....Katzenbach has the touch of a master."

Milwaukee Sentinel

Also by John Katzenbach:

IN THE HEAT OF THE SUMMER*

FIRST BORN: THE DEATH OF ARNOLD ZELEZNIK:
   MURDER, MADNESS AND WHAT CAME AFTER

*Published by Ballantine Books

THE TRAVELER

John Katzenbach

BALLANTINE BOOKS • NEW YORK

Library of Congress Catalog Card Number: 86-25564

ISBN 0-345-34709-9

This edition published by arrangement with G.P. Putnam's Sons, a division of the Putnam Publishing Group, Inc.

Printed in Canada

First Ballantine Books Edition: February 1988

For Maddy

"Well, I never heard of the dev—of your claiming America citizenship," said Dan'l Webster with surprise.

"And who with better right?" said the stranger with one of his terrible smiles. "When the first wrong was done to the first Indian, I was there. When the first slaver put out for the Congo, I stood on her deck. Am I not in your books and stories and beliefs, from the first settlements on? Am I not spoken of still in every church in New England? 'Tis true the North claims me for a Southerner, and the South for a Northerner, but I am neither. I am merely an honest American like yourself—and of the best descent—for, to tell the truth, Mr. Webster, though I don't like to boast of it, my name is older in this country than yours..."

—STEPHEN VINCENT BENÉT
The Devil and Daniel Webster

CHAPTER
ONE

THE REASONS BEHIND DETECTIVE BARREN'S OBSESSION

1. SHE dreamt uneasily.

She could see a boat adrift, first in the distance, then suddenly closer until she realized that she was on the boat and surrounded by water. Her first thought was panic, to search about her and find someone to tell the important news that she was unable to swim. But each time she turned to look, her perch on the edge of the boat grew more precarious, and the wave action would sweep the small craft upward, balancing momentarily on wave edge, then falling away, sickeningly, bouncing her about, out of control. In her dream she looked for something solid to hold on to. As she seized the mast of the boat and clutched it with all the strength she could muster, an alarm went off, ringing, horrible, and she knew that it was the sound made when the boat sprung a leak and that she was moments from finding seawater lapping at her feet, tickling her with terror. The alarm continued to blare and she opened her mouth wide, ready to call or shout in fear for help, struggling as the boat rocked around her. In the dream the deck pitched abruptly and she cried out, as if to her sleeping self, Wake up! Wake up! Save yourself!

And she did.

She gasped wildly, spinning from sleep-state to wakefulness, sitting up suddenly in her bed, her right arm shooting out and seizing the bedstand, something solid amidst the vaporous fears of the dream. She realized then the telephone was ringing.

She cursed to herself, rubbed her eyes, and found the telephone on the floor by the bed. She cleared her throat as she answered:

"Detective Barren here. What is it?"

She had not had time to assess the situation. She lived alone, without husband, without children, her own parents long since passed away, and so the idea that her telephone would ring in the midst of the night did not hold any particular terror for her, as it would have for so many people who are unaccustomed to late-night calls and who instantly would have foreseen the telephone ringing in the darkness for precisely what it was: terrible news. And, being a detective by trade, it was not unusual for her to be summoned at night, police work by necessity often taking place beyond banking hours. That was what she fully expected, that for some procedural reason her capabilities as a crime-scene technician were needed.

"Merce? Are you awake?"

"Yes. I'm fine. Who is it?"

"Merce, it's Robert Wills in homicide, I . . ." He let his voice trail off. Detective Barren waited.

"How can I help you?" she asked.

"Merce, I'm sorry to be the one to tell you this . . ."

She had a sudden mind's eye picture of Bob Wills sitting at his desk at the homicide office. It was a hard, harsh, open office, illuminated with unforgiving fluorescent light that was always on, filled with metal file cabinets and desks that were colored orange and to her mind seemed stained with all the horrors that had passed so casually in confession and conversation over the desktops.

"What?"

For an instant she felt a rush of excitement, a kind of delicious fear, far different from the dream-panic in which she had been immersed. Then, as her caller paused, an emptiness formed in her stomach, a kind of vacuum sensation, that was instantly replaced by a rush of anxiety. "What is it?" she asked, aware that there was a touch of this new sense in her voice.

"Merce, you have a niece . . ."

"Yes, dammit. Her name is Susan Lewis. She's a student at the university. What is it? Has she been in an accident?"

But then the realization struck her: Bob Wills in homicide. Homicide. Homicide. And she knew then what the nature of the call was.

"I'm sorry," he was saying, but his voice seemed very distant and for an instant she wished she were back in her dream.

Detective Mercedes Barren dressed swiftly and headed across Miami's licorice late summer night toward the address she'd written in a hand she thought was possessed with someone else's emotions; she'd felt her own heart racing, but seen her hand steady, scratching numbers and words on a pad. It had seemed to her that it was someone else who had finished the conversation with the homicide detective. She had heard her own voice hard and flat requesting available information, current status, names of officers in charge, facts about the crime already known, options being pursued by detectives. Witnesses. Evidence. Statements. She persisted, trying not to be put off by Detective Wills' evasions and excuses, recognizing that he wasn't in charge, but knew what she wanted to know, and all the time thinking that she was screaming inside, filled to explosion with some beast emotion that wanted to twist her into a single sob-shout of agony.

She would not allow herself to think of her niece.

Once, as she steered the car up onto the interstate that cuts through the center of the city, blinded for an instant by the headlights of a semi-tractor trailer truck that had pulled in horrifyingly close, air horn sounding raucously, she had fought off the sudden fear of a crash and discovered that she'd replaced the sensation with a picture of herself and her niece some two weeks beforehand. They had been sunning by the pool in the small beachside apartment building where Detective Barren lived and Susan had spotted her service revolver sticking awkwardly out of a beach bag, silly and incongruous amidst towels, suntan lotion, a frisbee, and a paperback novel. Detective Barren thought of the teenager's response: she'd called the revolver "gross," which was, to the detective's mind, an absolutely apt description.

"Why do you have to carry it, anyway?"

"Because technically we're never off duty. If I were to spot a crime, I would have to react like a policewoman."

"But I didn't think you had to do that anymore, not since . . ."

"Right. Not since the shooting. No, I'm a pretty tame policewoman now. By the time I get to a crime everything is pretty much over."

"Yuck. Dead bodies, right?"

"Right. Yuck is right, too."

They'd laughed.

"It would be funny," Susan had said.

"What would be funny."

"To get arrested by a policeperson wearing a bikini."

They'd laughed again. Detective Barren had watched her niece rise and dive into the opaque blue pool water. She'd watched as Susan had effortlessly swum submerged to the far end, then, without rising for air, pivoted and snaked back to the edge. For one instant Detective Barren had felt a twinge of lost

3

youth jealousy, then let it pass, thinking, Well, you're not in such bad shape yourself.

The younger woman hung on the edge and asked her aunt: "Merce, why is it that you live next to the ocean and can't swim a lick?"

"Part of my mystery," she replied.

"Seems silly to me," Susan had said, slipping from the pool, the water glistening, flooding from her thin body. She continued: "Did I tell you I've decided to major this fall in oceanographic studies? Slimy fish for sure." She'd laughed. "Spiny crustaceans. Massive mammals. Jacques Cousteau, move over."

"That's excellent," said the detective. "You've always loved the water."

"Right." She sang, "Oh for a life of the sun, the sand, the deep blue sea and fish guts for me."

They'd laughed again.

She was always laughing, thought the detective, and she accelerated through the night. The explosive whiteness of the downtown night lights burst beside her, illuminating the edges of the great buildings as they rose up in the Southern sky. Then Detective Barren felt a great rush of heat in her heart, choking her, and she forced herself to concentrate on her driving, trying to wipe her mind free of memory, thinking, Let's see, let's find out, trying not to connect the scene she was heading toward with the memories in her brain.

Detective Barren turned off Route 1 and drove through a residential area. It was late, well past midnight and closing rapidly on dawn; there was little traffic and she had hurried, filled with the emergency sense of speed that accompanies any violent death. But a few miles short of her destination she slowed precipitously, until her nondescript sedan was barely crawling down the empty streets. She searched the rows of trim, upperclass houses for signs of life. The streets were dark, as were the homes. She tried to envision the lives that slept behind the ordered suburban darkness. Occasionally she would spot a light burning in one room and she wondered what book or television show or argument or worry kept the occupant up. She had an overwhelming urge to stop, to knock on the door to one of these houses with their meager sign of life, to stop and say, Is there some trouble that keeps you awake? Something that probes at the memory and heart and prevents sleep? Let me share.

She turned the car onto Old Cutler Road and knew the distance to the park's entrance was only a few hundred yards ahead.

The nighttime seemed to permeate the foliage; great melaleuca trees and willows hid blackness in their leaves and branches, stretching over the road like enveloping arms. She had the eerie sense that she was entirely alone in the world, that she was a sole survivor heading nowhere in the midst of an endless night. She could barely make out the faded white lettering on the small park entrance sign. She was startled when an opossum ran in front of the wheels of her car, and she slammed on her brakes, shuddering with fear for an instant, breathing out harshly when she realized that the animal had avoided the tires. She rolled down the window and could smell the salt air; the trees around her had shrunk in stature, the giant palms that rode the edge of the highway replaced by the tangled and gnarled branches of waterfront mangroves. The road curved sharply, and she knew she would be able to see the wide expanse of Biscayne Bay when she emerged.

She thought at first that it was moonlight glistening on the bay waters.

It was not.

She stopped the car suddenly, and stared out at the scene before her. She became aware first of the mechanical noise of powerful generators. Their steady rhythmic thumping powered three banks of high-intensity lights. The floodlights delineated a stage cut from the darkness at the edge of the park's parking lot, peopled with dozens of uniformed police officers and detectives, moving gingerly through the unnatural brightness. A row of police cruisers, an ambulance, white and green crime-scene search wagons were lined up on the fringe of the stage, their blue and red emergency lights throwing sudden strobes of color onto the people working within the parameters of the floodlights.

She took a deep breath and headed toward the light.

She parked her car on the rim of activity and started to walk to the center, where she spotted a group of men gathered. They were staring down at something that was obscured from her vision. She knew what it was, but this was an appreciation of experience, not of emotion. The entire area had been encircled with a three-inch-wide strip of yellow tape. Every ten feet or so a small white sign had been hung from the tape: POLICE CRIME SCENE DO NOT ENTER. She lifted the barrier and slipped underneath. The motion caught the eye of a uniformed officer, who swiftly moved to intersect her path, holding out his hands.

"Hey," he said. "Ma'am, you can't go in there."

She stared at him and he stopped. His hands dropped.

Exaggerating her movement by pacing it slowly, she opened her purse and produced her gold shield. He glanced quickly at it, then backed off rapidly, muttering an apology. But her arrival had been noted by the men in the center of the scene, and one of them quickly broke from the crowd and moved to block her.

"Merce, for Christ's sake. Didn't Wills tell you not to come down here?"

"Yes," she replied.

"There's nothing here for you."

"How the hell would you know?"

"Merce, I'm sorry. This must be . . ."

She interrupted him furiously.

"Must be what? Hard? Sad? Difficult? Tragic? What do you think it must be!"

"Calm down. Look, you know what's going on here, can you just hang on for a couple of minutes? Here, let me get you a cup of coffee." He tried to take her by the elbow and lead her away. She shrugged off his grip swiftly.

"Don't try to steer me away, goddammit!"

"Just a couple of minutes, then I'll give you a complete briefing . . ."

"I don't want a goddamn briefing. I want to see for myself."

"Merce . . ." The detective spread his arms wide, still blocking her vision. "Give me a break."

She took a deep breath and closed her eyes. She spoke in a clipped, deliberate fashion.

"Peter. Lieutenant Burns. Two things. One, that is my niece lying there. Two, I am a professional policewoman. I want to see for myself. Myself!"

The lieutenant stopped. He looked at her.

"All right. It will only be a few minutes now before the medical examiner completes his initial inspection. When they put her on a stretcher, you can come over. You can perform the official identification then if you want."

"Not a few minutes. Not on a stretcher. I want to see what happened to her."

"Merce. For Christ's sake . . ."

"I want to see."

"Why? It will just make it harder."

"How the hell would you know? How the hell could it make anything harder?"

A sudden flash of light burst behind the lieutenant. He turned and Detective Barren saw a police photographer moving in and out of position. "Now," she said. "I want to see now."

"All right," said the lieutenant, stepping aside. "It's your nightmare."

6

She marched past him quickly.

Then she stopped.

She took a deep breath.

She closed her eyes once, picturing her niece's smile.

She took another deep breath and carefully approached the body. She thought: Remember everything! Fix it in your mind. She forced her eyes to scan the ground around the shape she could not yet look at. Sandy dirt and leaves. Nothing that would produce a solid shoeprint. With a practiced eye, she estimated the distance between the parking lot and the location of the shape— she couldn't, in her mind, speak body. Twenty yards. A good dumping distance. She tried to think analytically: There was a problem. It was always easier if the—again her thoughts were staggered and mentally she hesitated—victim were discovered in the location where the homicide took place. Invariably there would be some physical evidence. She continued to scan the ground, hearing the lieutenant's voice behind her: "Merce, we searched the area very carefully, you don't have to . . ." But she ignored him, knelt, and felt the consistency of the dirt. She thought: If some of this stuck to the shoes, we could make a match. Without turning to see if he was still there, she spoke out loud, "Take earth samples from the entire area." After a momentary pause, she heard a grunt of assent. She continued, thinking, strength, strength, until she was next to the shape. All right, she said to herself. Look at Susan. Memorize what happened to her this night. Look at her. Look at every part of her. Don't miss anything.

And she raised her eyes to the shape.

"Susan," she said out loud, but softly.

She was aware of the other people moving about her, but only in a peripheral sense. That they had faces, that they were people she knew, colleagues, friends, she was aware, but only in the most subliminal fashion. Later, she would try to remember who was there, at the scene, and be unable.

"Susan," she said again.

"Is that your niece, Susan Lewis?" It was the lieutenant's voice.

"Yes."

She hesitated.

"It was."

She felt suddenly overcome by heat, as if one of the spotlights had singled her out, covering her with a solid beam of intense brightness. She gulped a great breath of air, then another, fighting a dizzying sensation. She remembered the moment years earlier

7

when she'd realized that she was shot, that the warmth she felt was the lifeblood flowing from her, and she fought with the same intensity to prevent her eyes from rolling back, as if giving into the blackness of unconsciousness would be as fatal now as it would have been then.

"Merce?"

She heard a voice.

"Are you all right?"

She was rooted.

"Somebody get fire-rescue!"

Then she managed to shake her head.

"No," she said. "I'm going to be okay."

What a silly thing to say, she thought.

"You sure? You want to sit down?"

She did not know who she was talking to. She shook her head again.

"I'm okay."

Someone was holding her arm. She snatched it loose.

"Check her fingernails," she said. "She would have fought hard. We may have a scratched-up suspect."

She saw the medical examiner bend over the body, gingerly lift each hand, and, using a small scalpel, gently scrape the contents under each nail into small plastic evidence bags. "Not much there," he said.

"She would have fought like a tiger," Detective Barren insisted.

"Perhaps he didn't give her a chance. There's severe trauma to the back of the head. Blunt instrument. She was probably unconscious when he did this." The doctor motioned at the pantyhose that were wrapped tightly around Susan's throat. Detective Barren stared for a moment at the bluish cast to the skin.

"Check the knot," she said.

"I already looked," said the doctor. "Simple square knot. Page one of the Boy Scout Handbook."

Detective Barren stared at the pantyhose. She desperately wanted to loosen it, to put her niece at rest, as if by making her look as if she were only sleeping it would be true. She remembered a moment when she was growing up. She had been very young, no more than five or six, and the family dog had been hit by a car and killed. "Why is Lady dead?" she'd asked her father. "Because her bones were broken," he replied. "But when I broke my wrist the doctor put a cast on it and now it is better," she had said. "Let's put a cast on Lady." "But she lost all her blood, too," said her father. "Well," the child in her memory said with insis-

8

tence grown of despair, "let's put the blood back in." "Oh, my poor little child," said her father, "I wish we could. I wish it were so simple." And he'd wrapped big arms around her as she sobbed through the longest of childhood nighttimes.

She stared at Susan's body and longed for those arms again.

"How about the wrists?" she asked. "Any signs of restraints?"

"No," said the doctor. "That tells us something."

"Yeah," said a voice from the side. Detective Barren didn't turn to see who was speaking. "It tells us this creep conked her before he had his fun. She probably never knew what hit her."

Detective Barren's eyes scanned down from the neck.

"Is that a bite mark on the shoulder?"

"Probably," said the medical examiner. "Got to check microscopically."

She fixed her eyes for an instant on her niece's torn blouse. Susan's breasts were exposed, and she wanted to cover them. "Swab the neck for saliva," she said.

"Did it," said the doctor. "Genital swabs, too. I'll do it again when we get to the morgue."

Detective Barren's eyes slid down the body, inch by inch. One leg was flung over the other, almost coyly, as if even in death her niece was modest.

"Was there any sign of laceration to the genitals?"

"Not visible out here."

Detective Barren paused, trying to take it all in.

"Merce," said the doctor gently, "it's pretty much like the other four. Mode of death. Positioning of the body. Dumping ground."

Detective Barren looked up sharply.

"Others? Other four?"

"Didn't Lieutenant Burns tell you? They think it's this guy the papers are calling the Campus Killer. I thought they'd told you . . ."

"No . . ." she said. "No one told me."

She took a deep breath.

"But it makes perfectly good sense. It fits . . ." And her voice trailed off.

She heard the lieutenant's voice next.

"Probably his first of the semester. I mean, nothing is certain, but the general pattern is the same. We're going to assign the case to him so the task force can work it—I think that's best, Merce?"

"Right."

"Seen enough now? Will you come over here and let me tell you what we've got and what we haven't got?"

She nodded. She closed her eyes and turned away from the body. She hoped that they would move Susan soon, as if by pulling her out of the underbrush and dirt that it would start to restore some humanity to her, lessen somehow the violation, diminish somehow the totality of her death.

She waited patiently next to the cars belonging to the crime-scene search specialists and the evidence technicians. They were all people she knew well, the night shift in the same office she worked. Individually, they all broke off from their duties within the yellow tape area and spoke to her, or touched her shoulder or grasped her hand, before going back to processing the scene. In a few moments Lieutenant Burns returned with two cups of coffee. She wrapped her hands around the Styrofoam cup he held out to her, suddenly chilled, though the tropical night was oppressively warm. He looked up at the sky, just starting to fade from dark, creeping gray light marking the edges of morning.

"Do you want to know?" he asked. "It might be better, all around, if you just . . ."

She interrupted quickly. "I want to know. Everything."

"Well," he started slowly. She knew he was trying to assess in his own mind whether sharing information with her would hinder the investigation. She knew he was wondering whether he was dealing with a policewoman or with a half-crazed relative. The trouble, she thought, was that he was dealing with both.

"Lieutenant," she said, "I merely want to help. I have a good deal of expertise, as you know. I want to make myself available. But, if you think I'll be in the way, I'll back off . . ."

"No, no, no," he replied quickly.

How simple, she thought. She knew that by offering to not ask questions she would get permission to ask every one.

"Look," the lieutenant continued, "things are pretty sketchy so far. Apparently she and some friends went out to a bar on the campus. There were a lot of people around, a lot of different guys hanging about. She danced with a number of different guys, too. About ten P.M. she went outside to get some air. She went alone. Didn't come back in. It wasn't until a couple of hours later, just about midnight, that her friends got worried and called the campus cops.

"Just about the same time a couple of fruits down here in the park just getting it on in the bushes over there stumbled on the body . . ." He held up his hand. "No. They didn't see or hear anything. Literally stumbled, too. One of the guys fell right over it . . ."

The body, she thought. It. She bit her lip.

"Girl disappears from campus. Body gets discovered in a park a couple of miles away. It wasn't hard to put one and one together. And we've been here since. Her purse had your name in it. That's why you were called. Your sister's kid?"

Detective Barren nodded.

"You want to make that call?"

Oh, God, she thought.

"I will. When we clear here."

"There's a pay phone over there. I wouldn't want to make them wait. And it's likely to be awhile before we finish . . ."

She became aware of the growing dawn light. The area was steadily losing its nighttime blackness, shapes taking form, becoming distinct as the darkness faded.

"All right," she said.

She thought how utterly mundane and hopelessly banal the act of telephoning her sister and brother-in-law was. For a second she hoped that she did not have a quarter to put in the pay phone's slot, then hoped that the telephone would be out of order. It was not. The operator answered with routine brightness, as if immune to the hour of the day. Detective Barren charged the call to her office. The operator asked her when someone would be there to confirm accepting the charges. Detective Barren told her someone was always there. Then she heard the electronic clicking of the number being dialed, and suddenly, before she was ready with the right words, the phone was ringing at her sister's house. Think! Detective Barren thought. Find words! And she heard her sister's voice, slightly groggy with sleep, on the other end of the line:

"Yes, hello . . ."

"Annie, it's Merce." She bit her lip.

"Merce! How are you? What's . . ."

"Annie. Listen carefully: It's Susan. There's been a . . ." she fumbled. Accident? Incident? She just barreled on, oblivious, trying to keep her voice a professionally calm, even, flat tone. "Please sit down and ask Ben to get on the line . . ."

She heard her sister gasp and then call to her husband.

In a moment, he joined the line. "Merce, what is it?" His voice was steady. Ben was an accountant. She hoped he would be as solid as numbers. She took a deep breath.

"I don't know any way of telling you this to make it easier, so I'll just tell you. Susan is dead. She was killed last night. Murdered. I'm sorry."

Detective Barren suddenly saw her sister, some eighteen years

11

earlier, immense with pregnancy, a week from delivery, moving uncomfortably through the oppressive July heat that hung unforgiving in the dry Delaware Valley summer to sit at her side. Detective Barren had tenaciously clutched the flag the honor guard captain had bestowed on her, her own mind black, empty, reverberating with the chaplain's words, blending with the crisp sound of the rifle volley fired over the grave. She'd had no words for any of the family or friends who'd sidled up self-consciously, wordless at the incongruity of someone as vigorous and young as John Barren dying, even in battle. Annie had settled herself onto the couch next to Detective Barren and when no one was watching, or at least when she thought no one was watching, had taken her sister's hand and placed it on her great stomach and said with heartbreaking simplicity, "God took him unfairly, but here's new life and you shouldn't leave your love in the grave with him, but give it to this child instead."

The child had been Susan.

For a moment, Detective Barren smiled at the memory, thinking: The baby saved my life.

And then, suddenly, swirling back into reality, she heard her sister's first sob of broken mother's anguish.

Ben had wanted to take the first flight to Miami, but she was able to dissuade him from that course. It would be simpler, she told them, if she made the arrangements with a funeral home to ship the body when the medical examiner finished the autopsy. She would accompany Susan's body back on the airplane. Ben had said he would call a local funeral home to coordinate plans. Detective Barren told them that they would probably hear from the newspapers, perhaps even the television. She recommended that they cooperate; it was much easier, she said, and the reporters would be less likely to get in the way. She explained that preliminary indications were that Susan was the victim of a killer who had prowled the campuses of Miami's various colleges the past year and that there was a task force of detectives assigned to the cases. Those detectives, she said, would be in touch. Ben had asked if she were sure about that killer, and she said nothing was certain but that it appeared to be the same. Ben had started to bluster, angry, but after spitting out a few words of rage, he'd stopped, lapsing into a continual stunned acquiescence. Annie said nothing. Detective Barren guessed that they were in different rooms, and that it would not be until they hung up and turned to face each other that full despair would hit them.

"That's all I can tell you for now," Detective Barren said. "I'll call later when I know more."

"Merce?" It was her sister.

"Yes, Annie."

"Are you sure?"

"Oh, Annie . . ."

"I mean, you checked, didn't you? You're certain?"

"Annie. I saw her. I looked. It's Susan."

"Thank you. I just needed to know for sure."

"I'm sorry."

"Yes. Yes. Of course. We'll talk later."

"Ben?"

"Yes, Merce. I'm still here. We'll talk later."

"All right."

"Oh, God, Merce . . ."

"Annie?"

"Oh, God."

"Annie, be strong. You'll have to be strong."

"Merce, please help me. I feel like if I hang up the telephone with you now, it will be like killing her. Oh, God. What is going on? Please. I don't understand."

"I don't understand either, Annie."

"Oh, Merce, Merce, Merce . . ."

Detective Barren heard her name fading. She knew that her sister had let the telephone slip from her hand to the bed. She could hear tears and it was like listening to a heart break. She remembered in high school watching a football practice; as she stood on the sidelines, one of the players had been struck awkwardly. The sound of the leg snapping had risen above the noise of bodies thumping together. She'd seen one of the other players get sick as the coaches and trainer rushed to the stricken boy. For an instant she expected to hear the same cracking sound. She held the telephone in her hand momentarily, then, gently, as if trying not to disturb a sleeping child, replaced the receiver on the hook. She stood still, listening to her own heart. She swallowed deeply, then flexed her arm muscles once, twice. Then her legs. She could feel the skin, muscle, and tendons stretch and contract. I'm strong, she thought. Be stronger still.

2. IT was midmorning before Susan's body was finally removed. Detective Barren had remained on the fringe of the crime scene, watching the orderly collection of evidence.

Uniformed policemen kept a steadily growing crowd of the curious far back, for which she was grateful. The Miami news media had arrived early, ubiquitously insinuating themselves into the scene. The television cameramen had photographed the activity while the reporters had busied themselves questioning Lieutenant Burns and some of the other detectives. She knew it was inevitable that one of the reporters would eventually hear of her connection to the body, and that it would become prominent in the retelling. She decided to simply wait for the questions.

She had turned away when two medical examiner's office technicians had gingerly slipped Susan's body into a black bag. She walked over to where Lieutenant Burns was standing, speaking with a pair of nattily dressed detectives in three-piece suits who seemed oblivious to the gathering muggy day's heat. When he saw her approach, he turned and performed the introductions.

"Merce. Detective Barren. I don't know if you know detectives Moore and Perry from county homicide. They head up this Campus Killer investigation."

"Only by reputation."

"Likewise," said Detective Perry.

They all shook hands and stood awkwardly.

"I'm sorry to meet under these circumstances," Detective Perry said. "I've been a fan of your work. Especially on that multiple-rape case."

"Thank you," said Detective Barren. She had a brief vision of a pock-marked face and misshapen nose. She remembered poring over some two dozen case files again and again until coming up with the link that had led to the arrest. The heavily muscled rapist always wore a stocking mask. Almost every victim said she was aware he suffered from severe acne on his back. A dermatologist had told her that people with acne on their back are generally scarred on the face as well. But she had thought the mask was to hide something else. She'd begun hanging out at the local gymnasiums and health clubs. More a hunch than a probable cause. At the 5th Street Gym on Miami Beach, a place where aspiring boxers' dreams mingled freely with the sound of speed bags thumping, she'd spotted a short, powerfully built lightweight, heavily pockmarked on the back and face, with a badly broken nose and a distinctive red scar that twisted down his cheek.

"Never underestimate intuition," said Detective Perry.

"Except it doesn't do much with a judge when you need a search warrant."

They all smiled hesitantly.

"So how can we help you?" Detective Perry said.

14

"Was there anything discovered underneath the body?"

"Nothing of obvious value. There was one odd piece of paper."

"What was it?"

"Actually a fragment. It looks like the top part of the type of tag they put on your luggage handle when you check your bags at the airport, only considerably larger. Some kind of tag, anyway." He held up his hand. "No, there were no markings on it. It was just the top quarter, the rest was torn away. Also, there was no way of telling how long it was there. She could have been put on top of it. Just a piece of trash, I think."

She thought of her niece lying amidst the refuse. She shook her head, trying to clear the thought.

"What are you going to do now?" Detective Barren asked.

"We're going to work the nightclub, see if we can find anyone who noticed someone talking with her, following her . . ." The detective looked at Detective Barren. "It'll take some time."

"Time is not relevant."

"I understand."

He paused.

"Look, detective. This must be impossible for you. I know that if it was one of my sisters I'd be going crazy. I'd want to blow the guy away myself. So, as far as I'm concerned, you can know whatever you want about the investigation, as long as you don't try to get in the way or do our job for us. Is that fair?"

Detective Barren nodded.

"One other thing," Detective Perry added. "If you get ideas, bring them to me directly."

"No problem," Detective Barren said. She wondered if she were lying. She thought for a moment. "One question. This is the fifth, right? What's the status of the others? Can you make somebody on an earlier case?"

The detectives hesitated, looking at each other.

"Good question. We got some leads. A couple of good ones. You come in in a couple of days, we'll talk, okay? After you get a little settled, huh?"

Condescending bastard, she thought.

"That's fine," she said.

She left the men still conversing and walked back to the evidence trucks. A thin, ascetic-looking man was checking the numbers written in black Magic Marker on plastic bags against a master list on a clipboard in his hand. "Hello, Teddy," she said.

The man turned to her. He had large bony hands that seemed

to flap about. "Oh, Merce. I thought you'd gone. You don't have to be here, you know."

"I know. Why does everyone keep telling me that?"

"I'm sorry. It's just that, well, no one really knows how to react. I guess you make everyone nervous. We're not accustomed to being affected by death, you know, and this, well, seeing you, makes it less a job, more a reality. Does that make any sense?"

"Yes." She smiled at him.

"Merce, I can't tell you how badly everyone feels for you. Everyone has worked real hard on the scene. I just hope there's something here that will lead us to the creep."

"Thanks, Teddy. What have you collected?"

"There's not too much. Here's the list."

He handed her the clipboard and her eyes scanned the page:

1. Blood sample area of v's head
2. Blood sample area of v's crotch (see diagram)
3. Saliva sample v's shoulder
4. Swabs v's genitals
5. Swabs v's shoulder (bite mark see diagram)
6. Dirt sample A (see diagram)
7. Dirt sample B (see diagram)
8. Dirt sample C (see diagram)
9. Fingernail sample v right hand (see diagram)
10. Same, left hand (see diagram)
11. Unknown substance/leaf
12. Possible clothing sample
13. Trace blood on leaf
14. Cigarette butt (see diagram)
15. Cigarette butt (see diagram)
16. Used condom
17. Used condom
18. Unused condom in foil (Ramses brand)
19. Beer can (Budweiser)
20. Coca-Cola can
21. Perrier bottle (6 oz.)
22. Unknown substance in tin foil wrapping
23. Unknown substance in plastic bag
24. Film box Kodacolor Instamatic film
25. Film box Kodacolor Instamatic film
26. Box end Kodak 400 black/white film for negatives
27. Used Cutter Lotion 5 1/2 oz.
28. Sea and Ski lotion 12 oz.
29. Crushed package (empty) Marlboro cigarettes

30. Woman's handbag (contents listed separately)
31. Woman's wallet (victim)
32. Woman's earring
33. Tag end paper color yellow origin unknown (under body)

"What about the condoms?" she asked.

He shook his head. "Merce, look at this stuff. It's the kind of stuff you find in any picnic area. The unknown stuff appears to be like tuna fish. And the condoms seem old, probably several days, just guessing. And look at the diagrams. Except for the skin and blood samples, all this junk was collected at least a couple of feet away. It's the kind of stuff you might bring along for a little time in the sun—not a killing in the middle of the night."

She nodded.

"Is this painful? Do you want to . . ."

"Yes."

"That's what I figured. Anyway, until we really get the stuff into the lab we won't know, but it seems to me and just about everyone else that she was dropped here. Probably the creep pulled his car up and just dumped her a little ways away. When we get the guy's car, that's where we'll put him away. There's got to be blood, skin, the works inside it. Can't hide that stuff. But workable evidence from this scene? We can hope, but I wouldn't count on it."

She nodded again.

"I'm not saying anything you don't know."

"That's right."

She handed the list back to him and stared at the rows of plastic bags, carefully lined up in the back of the wagon. She didn't really know what she was looking for.

"What's that?" she asked, pointing at one bag.

"That's the last item on the list. Some kind of yellow tag. It was found under the body."

He handed it to her. She searched through the clear plastic, turning the frayed piece of paper back and forth beneath her scrutiny. What are you? she wondered. What do you mean? What are you trying to tell me? Who put you there? She had the sudden urge to shake the small piece of paper viciously, as if she could force it to talk back to her. I will remember you, she said to the paper. She looked up at all the collected items. I will remember all of you.

She was overcome with how crazy she was. She put the plastic bag into the back of the wagon.

She thought she seemed silly. She knew that it would take some time to process the scene, knew the likelihood of some relevant piece of evidence was minimal. She flushed suddenly, turning around. She saw the detectives getting into an unmarked car. A police photographer was in the distance, taking long shots. The medical examiner's truck was pulling out of the rear of the lot; she saw the television cameramen lined up, getting a picture of the exit. She was overcome with a sense of helplessness, as if the carefully constructed police-veneer that had guarded her throughout the long morning was slipping away, as the crowd of technicians, detectives, and curious began to dissipate. She felt a sudden vulnerability, as if all she would be left with was her emotions. She caught a gasp forming in her chest, working its way up her throat. Breathing hard, she turned away and walked back to her own car, feeling the blast of built-up heat flood out as she opened the door. She quickly slid behind the wheel and closed the door. She sat in the broiling interior, letting the warmth penetrate her resolve. She thought of Susan. She thought of her dream. She wanted to scream to herself, as she had in the last moments of sleep, Wake up! Save yourself!

But she could not.

The lady in the flower store had eyed Detective Barren oddly and finally asked, "Is there some special occasion or event that these would be for?" Detective Barren had hesitated before replying, and the lady had continued, blithely, "I mean, if these are for a co-worker or secretary, then I might recommend one of these floral arrangements. Are they for a shut-in or an invalid? A bouquet like this would look nice. Someone in the hospital perhaps? We find that hospital patients love to receive small plants—you see, they enjoy watching the plants root and grow..."

"They're for my lover," said Detective Barren.

"Oh," said the woman, slightly taken aback.

"Is there something wrong?"

"No, it's just unusual. Usually, you see, it's the men who come in for flowers, roses generally, for their, uh, companions. This is a change." She laughed. "Some things never change in the world no matter how modern we get. Men buy flowers for their women friends and wives. Not the other way around. They come into the store and stand rather self-consciously in front of the refrigerated display, staring for all the world at the flowers as

18

if hoping there would be a sign, a something, that said: Buy me for your wife. Or girlfriend. And not young men, either. Young men today don't seem to understand the value of proper flowers. Sometimes I think we have grown too—I don't know—scientific. I mean, I expect they'll want to send computer-written Valentine's cards soon enough. But it's always men, dear, not women. No, I don't believe I've ever had a woman come in and . . ."

Detective Barren looked at the woman, who stopped speaking in mid-sentence, hesitated, then continued.

"Oh, dear," said the woman. "I'm making rather a fool of myself, aren't I?"

"A little," Detective Barren replied.

"Oh, dear," the woman said again.

"It's all right," Detective Barren said.

"You're kind," said the woman. The detective watched as she brushed a strand of gray hair off her forehead and composed herself. "I'll try again," said the woman. "How may I help you?"

"I'd like to buy some flowers," said Detective Barren.

"For someone special?"

"Of course."

"Ah, let me suggest roses. They are perhaps the least original selection, but the most trustworthy. And always loved, which, of course, is what we are buying flowers for."

"I think that would be nice," said Detective Barren.

"A dozen?"

"Excellent."

"I have red, white, and pink?" This was a question. The detective thought for a moment.

"Red and white, I think."

"Excellent. And some Baby's Breath to set them off, I would imagine."

"They look lovely."

"Thank you."

Detective Barren paid and the woman handed her the box. "I get a little crazy," said the woman.

"I beg your pardon?" replied the detective.

"You see, I end up spending most of the day talking to the flowers and plants. Sometimes I forget how to talk with people. I'm sure your, uh, friend will enjoy those."

"My lover," said the detective.

She clutched the flower box under her arm and tried to remember how many years had passed since she'd been to John Barren's grave.

The early September air had not even the slightest intimation of fall. Instead it hung heavy with residual summer heat, liar's blue sky broken with a few huge white clouds; a day for lazing about in August memories, ignoring the January inevitability of the Delaware Valley, with its snow, cold wind off the river, ice, and frequent visitations of what the natives called slush storms, an unfortunate mingling of ice, sleet, snow, and rain together in an impenetrable, chilling, slippery impossibility. One of those storms, thought Detective Barren with a small smile. She had been caught outside, battery dead, boots soaked. When she finally returned to her home, empty, cold, alone, she had vowed to start over somewhere warm. Miami.

She placed the flowers on the passenger seat of the rental car and drove out of Lambertville, across the bridge over the river to New Hope. The town, filled with the quaint, the precious, and the upscale, stretched out on either side of the river; in a few moments she had left it behind, traveling slowly through the warm afternoon, down a shaded road, toward the cemetery. She wondered for a moment why the family had ever moved closer to Philadelphia when it was so pretty in the country. She had a sudden picture of her father, learning of his appointment at the University of Pennsylvania, swinging her mother like some buckaroo at a square dance. He had taught mathematical theory and quantum mechanics; his intelligence daunting, his worldliness absent. She smiled. He would not have understood for an instant why she was a policewoman. He would have admired some of the deductive reasoning, some of the investigative tactics, some of the apparent precision of police work, but he would have been confused and dismayed by the truths of the profession and the ever-present rubbing up against evil. He certainly would not have understood why his daughter loved it so, though he would have admired the basic simplicity of her devotion: that it was the easiest way to achieve some good in a world filled with —in her mind she hesitated, as she had so often over the past few days—filled with creeps who kill eighteen-year-old girls suffused with life and promise and future and goodness. Detective Barren drove on, the warm memory of her father sliding away in the shadows, replaced by a sketchpad in her mind, and her imagination trying to draw in the features of a killer. She almost missed the entrance to the cemetery.

Someone had placed a small American flag on John Barren's grave, and for a moment she wasn't sure that she wanted it there. Then she relented, thinking, If this gives the local VFW some satisfaction, who am I to refuse it? That was what gravesites and memorials are for, she thought, the living. She could not look at the headstone and the parched grass that covered the plot and envision John below in a coffin. She caught her breath suddenly at a memory:

Remains nonviewable.

The coffin had a tag on one handle. It was probably supposed to be removed before she saw it, but she had seen.

In her unruly grief she had puzzled at the tag.

Remains nonviewable.

She had thought first, strangely, that it meant that John was naked, and that the Army, in a silly, foolish, masculine way, was trying to protect everyone from embarrassment. She had wanted to say to the men surrounding the coffin, Don't be so stupid. Of course we saw each other naked. We delighted in those moments. We were lovers in high school, in college, on the night he was drafted and in the hours before he took the bus to basic training, and constantly in the two short weeks of leave before he went overseas. In the summer, down at the Jersey Shore, we would sneak out after our parents had gone to bed and meet in the moonlight and roll naked in the sand dunes.

Remains nonviewable.

She'd considered those two strange words. Remains—well, that was John. Nonviewable—well, that meant she couldn't see him. She wondered why. What had they done to him? She tried to ask, but discovered that a young dead man's bride didn't get straight answers. She'd been hugged instead and told that it was all for the better, and told that it was God's Will and war was hell and any number of things that, to her mind, didn't seem to have a great deal of relevance to the issue. She had begun to grow impatient and increasingly distraught, which only made the military men and family men all the more frustrating in their denial. Finally, as her voice had started to rise and her demands grew more strident, she'd felt a hand clamp her arm tightly. It had been the funeral director; a man she'd never seen before. He'd looked at her intensely, then, to the surprise of her family, led her into a side office. He had sat her down, businesslike, in a chair across from his desk. For a moment he'd shuffled papers, while she sat, waiting. Finally he discovered what he was searching for. "They didn't tell you, did they?" he asked.

"No," she said. She hadn't known what he was talking about.

"They just told you he was dead, right?"

That was true. She nodded her head.

"Well," he said brusquely, then suddenly slowing, "you sure you want to know?"

Know what? she wondered, but she nodded again.

"All right," he said. Sadness crawled into his voice. "Corporal Barren was killed while on routine patrol in the Quang Tri province. The man next to him stepped on a land mine. A big one. It killed your husband and two others."

"But why can't I . . ."

"Because there wasn't enough of him left to look at."

"Oh."

Silence filled the room. She didn't know what to say.

"Kennedy would've got us out," the funeral director said. "But we had to kill him. I think he was our only shot. My boy's there now. God, I'm scared. It seems like I bury another boy each week. I'm so sorry for you."

"You must love your boy," she said.

"Yes. A great deal."

"He wasn't clumsy, you know."

"I beg your pardon?"

"John. He was graceful. He was a beautiful athlete. He scored touchdowns and he made baskets and home runs. He would never have stepped on a mine."

She thought of the old children's rhyme: Step on a crack, break your mother's back. Step on a mine, break my heart for all time.

Remains nonviewable.

"Hello, lover," she said. She took the flowers out of the box.

Detective Barren sat on the gravesite, with her back against the headstone, obscuring her husband's name and the dates of his life. Her eyes were lifted toward the sky; she watched the clouds meander across the great blue expanse with what she thought was an admirable purposelessness. She played the children's game of trying to guess what each cloud's shape was like; she thought of elephants and whales and rhinoceroses. She thought that Susan would have seen only fish and aquatic mammals. She allowed herself a pleasurable fantasy, that there was a heaven up beyond the clouds and that John was waiting there for Susan. The idea comforted her some, but she felt tears forming in the corners of her eyes. She wiped them away swiftly. She was alone in the cemetery. She thought that she was fortunate, that her behavior was decidedly ungrave. She felt a small wind that cut an edge off the heat, rustling in the trees. She laughed, not in humor but in sadness, and spoke out loud:

22

"Oh, Johnny. I'm almost forty and you've been dead eighteen years, and I still miss the hell out of you."

"I guess it was Susan, you see. You were dead and she got born and she was so tiny and helpless and sick. Boy. Colic and then respiratory problems and God knows what else. It just overwhelmed Annie, you see. And Ben, well, his business was just starting and he worked all the time. And so I just got caught up in it. Sitting up all night so that Annie could get a few hours' sleep. Rocking her. Walking her. Back and forth, back and forth. All those little baby tears, you see, all the pain and hurt she was feeling, well, I was feeling too. It was as if the two of us could cry together and feel a little better and I think if it hadn't been for her, I don't think I would have made it. You big creep! You had no right to get yourself killed!"

She stopped.

She remembered a night, crammed together in a small bed in his dormitory room when he told her that he had refused to submit his request for a student deferment from the draft. It wasn't fair, he'd said. All the farm boys and ghetto kids were getting slaughtered while the lawyers' sons went to Ivy League schools in safety. The system was unfair and inequitable and evil and he wouldn't participate in the evil. If he got drafted, so be it. If he passed his physical, so be it. Don't worry, he'd said. The Army won't want me. Troublemaker. Anarchist. Rabble-rouser. I'd make a lousy soldier. They'd yell charge and I'd ask where and why, and how come, and why not over there and let's take a vote. They had laughed at the improbable picture of John Barren leading a group discussion on whether to charge the enemy or not, arguing pros and cons. But her laughter hid a great misshapen fear, and when the letter that began with greetings from the president arrived, she'd insisted they get married, thinking only that she had to have his name, that it was important.

"Susan got better," Detective Barren said. "It seemed to take forever, but she got better. And suddenly she was a little girl and Annie was a little older and less scared of everything and Ben's job wasn't so hard and I guess it was okay, then, just to become Auntie Merce because she was going to live, and I guess I knew I was too."

Detective Barren suddenly choked on her thoughts.

"Oh, God, Johnny, and now someone's gone and killed her! My baby. She was so much like you. You'd have loved her, too. She was like the baby we'd have had. Doesn't that sound trite?

Don't laugh at me for being a sentimentalist. I know you, you were worse than me. You were the one that always cried in movies. Remember *Tunes of Glory?* At the Alec Guinness festival? First we saw *The Ladykillers* and you insisted we stay for the second feature. Remember? After John Mills had shot himself and Guinness goes a little crazy and begins to do a slow death march in front of the other men of the mess? The bagpipes were faint and you were sitting there in the theater with tears just streaming down your face, so don't call me the emotional one. And in high school, remember, when Tommy O'Connor couldn't shoot against St. Brendan's and he threw you the ball and you went straight up, the whole place screaming or holding their breath, championship on the line, thirty feet from the basket? Nothing but net, you said, but every time I brought that up, you started crying, you old schmooze. You won and it made you cry. I guess Susan would have cried, too. She cried over sick whales that beached themselves and seals that didn't have the sense to flee from hunters and seabirds covered with oil. Those are the things you would have cried over, too."

Detective Barren took a deep breath.

I'm crazy, she thought.

Talking to a dead husband about a dead niece.

But they've killed my love, she said to herself.

All of it.

Detective Barren showed her badge to a uniformed officer sitting at a desk, monitoring all the visitors to the Dade County Sheriff's Office. She took the elevator to the third floor and followed her memory to the homicide division. There was a secretary there who made her wait on an uncomfortable plastic couch. She looked about her, noting the same blend of old and new office equipment. There was something about police work, she thought. Even when things are new, they lose their shine almost instantly. She wondered if there was some connection between the grime of the job and the never-clean atmosphere of police offices. Her eyes strayed to three pictures on the wall: the President, the Sheriff, and a third man she didn't recognize. She stood and approached the unfamiliar picture. There was a small plaque beneath the portrait of a smiling, slightly overweight man with an American flag in the lapel on his jacket. The plaque was tarnished bronze. It had the man's name and the inscription KILLED IN THE LINE OF DUTY and a date two years earlier.

She remembered the case; he had been making a routine arrest, following a domestic that had been a homicide. A drunken father and son in Little Havana. A subject murder, the easiest of homicides: the father was standing over the body, sobbing, when the police arrived. He was so distraught that the uniforms simply sat him in a chair, without handcuffs. No one had suspected that he would explode when they tried to take him out, that he would seize a gun from a policeman's holster and turn it on them. Detective Barren remembered the funeral, thinking of the full-dress uniforms, folded flag, and rifle salute, so much like the one she had known earlier. But what a silly way to die, she thought. Then, thinking again, she wondered what was a useful way to die. She turned away swiftly when Detective Perry entered the room.

"Sorry to keep you waiting," he said. "Let's go to my office."

She followed him down a corridor.

"Cubicle, really. Work space. We don't really get a real office with doors anymore. This is progress, I guess."

She smiled and he motioned her toward a chair.

"So?" he asked.

"That's my question," she replied.

"Okay," he said. "Here's something." He tossed a sheet of paper across his desk to her. She took it and stared at a composite picture of a curly-haired, dark-complexioned man, not bad-looking except for a pair of deeply recessed eyes that gave him a slightly cadaverous look. But not enough so to throw one off, she thought.

"Is this . . ."

"Best we can do," he interrupted. "It's been distributed all over the city and all the campuses. It was on the television stations while you were at the funeral."

"Response?"

"The usual. Everybody thinks it looks exactly like their landlord, or the neighbor who happens to owe them money, or the guy that's dating their daughter. But we're checking them out slowly. Maybe we'll get lucky."

"What else?"

"Well, each of the killings has some distinctive features, but when you get everything settled they are pretty much the same. The girls have all been picked up at a mixer or a bar or a student union or a campus movie. Picked up isn't right. Followed out is more likely. No one has seen the guy actually snatch his victim . . ."

"But . . ."

"Well, no buts. We're interviewing people. We're doing background checks on all sorts of people—gardeners, students, hangers-on—trying to find some guy who has experience on all the campuses and is young and with-it enough to blend in."

"That could take a while."

"We've got a dozen guys working on it."

Detective Barren thought for an instant. She wasn't exactly getting the runaround, but nor was she getting the entire picture. And she perceived a sense of confidence in Detective Perry that didn't blend with a portrait of legwork, long hours, and frustration. She had the sensation of being humored. She also knew that she had to come up with the right question to open the right door. She thought for a moment. Then it struck her.

"What about assaults?"

"I beg your pardon?" Detective Perry said.

"So what you've been saying is that you've got a little bit of this, a little bit of that, but no makeable case out of the homicides. What about an assault? If this guy has been at this for, how long? A year or more, I'd guess, then he has to have had a few near-misses. Screwed up. Been surprised by another student when he tried to snatch a victim. Something like that, huh? You tell me."

"Well," Perry replied, drawing the word out. "That's an interesting idea . . ."

"Which I'm not the only person to think of."

"Well . . ." He hesitated.

"Don't bullshit me."

"I don't want to."

"Then answer."

He looked uncomfortable. He shuffled some papers. He looked around for help. "I wasn't supposed to be that candid," he admitted.

"I didn't think so."

"Can you back off? I mean . . ."

"Forget it," Detective Barren said. "I want to know."

"Okay, but I'm not gonna get too specific."

She nodded.

"Twice."

She nodded again.

"Twice the creep screwed up. Last time was the night before your niece got it. We got a partial license plate and a make."

"Have you got a name?"

"Can't tell you."

Detective Barren stood up.

"I'll go to your boss. I'll go to mine. I'll go to the papers . . ."

He motioned her to sit back down.

26

"We got a name. And he's got a tail. And when we got enough for a warrant, we'll let you know."

"You sure?"

"Nothing's certain. Look, the papers have been all over this thing and a lot of details have been in the press. So we're moving slowly, we want to make certain that we make this guy on a murder-one charge, not attempted assault. Hell, we want to make him on all five. That's taking some time."

"Do it right," she said.

Detective Perry smiled, relieved.

"That's what I figured you'd say."

She looked at him.

"Well," he said, "that's what I hoped you'd say." He stood up. "I want this creep to understand boxes. The first box is the one I'm putting together for him. Everywhere he turns, I'm gonna have an answer. No way he can crawl out. The second box is gonna be a nine-by-eleven on the Raiford Riviera . . ."

Death row, thought Detective Barren. She nodded.

"And you can guess what the last box will be."

She felt a momentary rush of satisfaction.

Detective Barren stood up. "Thank you," she said.

"You want to be in on it when it goes down?"

"Wouldn't miss it."

"All right. I'll call."

"I'll be waiting."

They shook hands and she walked out, for the first time in several days feeling hungry.

When she returned to her own office, two days later, after a hot, dirty day doing an inventory of car parts uncovered at a chop shop in the warehouse district, she found two memos on her desk. The first was from her own commander, listing a disposition of evidence gathered at the site where Susan's body had been recovered. The second was an autopsy memo from the medical examiner's officer. She read them carefully.

TO: Det. Mercedes Barren
FROM: Lt. Ted March

MERCE: That was a bite mark. But it was too ragged to make a distinct mold and is therefore not of high evidentiary value. Saliva breakdown from swab of the area shows normal enzyme values, but trace alcohol rendered it difficult if not impossible to come up with blood type. Guy must have had a drink or two. Booze always screws things up. Even just a beer or two. Anyway, I've sent the entire sample back over to the lab again and told them to try again. The two prophylactics recovered at the scene contained different sperm samples. Both had deteriorated considerably. Still, one was Type A/Positive, the other O/Positive. Further breakdowns are underway. No workable prints on anything so far, but they're going to try that laser evaluator on the soda cans. I'll let you know. Pretty much a total wash so far. Sorry. But we're going to keep trying.

TO: Detective Mercedes Barren
FROM: Assistant ME Arthur Vaughn
DETECTIVE: Cause of death of deceased white female, age eighteen, identified positive as Susan Lewis of Bryn Mawr Pennsylvania is massive trauma to the right rear portion of the occipital bone coupled with asphyxiation due to strangulation by nylon ligature around neck. (See autopsy protocol for precise cause.) Genital swabs negative. Acid phosphase test negative.

Detective: she was unconscious from the head blow when she was assaulted. She probably never regained consciousness when he strangled her. Sex act was premortem, however. But there were no signs of ejaculation. This could have been due to prophylactic device.

I'm terribly sorry about all of this. The autopsy protocol should answer any questions you have, but if it doesn't, don't hesitate to call.

Detective Barren put the two reports in her pocketbook. She glanced at the autopsy protocol, with its schematic diagram and pages of verbatim description of her niece's body, transcribed from the medical examiner's tape recorder. Height. Weight. Brain: 1220 grams. Heart: 230 grams. Well-developed, post-adolescent female American. No abnormalities noted. Life reduced to so many facts and figures. No way to measure youth, enthusiasm, and future. Detective Barren felt queasy and was thankful that the medical examiner in his compulsive thoroughness had neglected to send the autopsy slides.

On her way home from the office that night, Detective Barren stopped at a small bookstore. The clerk was a beady-eyed man who rubbed his hands together frequently, punctuating his voice with body motion. Detective Barren thought him a perfect reincarnation of Uriah Heep.

"Something to escape in? A novel, I suppose, an adventure, or a gothic horror story. A romance, or a mystery. What shall it be?"

"Real escape," said Detective Barren, "is substituting one reality for another."

The clerk thought for a moment.

"You're a nonfiction type, huh?"

"No. Maybe. I just don't feel romantic. But I want something distracting."

She left with two books. A history of the British campaign in the Falkland Islands and a new translation of Aeschylus' *Oresteia*. There was a gourmet shop down the street, and she indulged herself in a pasta salad and a bottle of what the counterman assured her was an excellent California Chardonnay. She would eat well, she thought, read a bit. There was a football game on the television that night which she could watch until she fell asleep. This was a secret passion. She smiled to herself; she hid her enthusiasm from her co-workers. They were threatened enough by her female competence. If she tried to usurp their game as well. . . . So she enjoyed in private. Buying single game tickets, sitting in the Orange Bowl end zone, or staying home and plopping down in front of her television by herself, her concession to her own gender represented perhaps by the glass of white wine in a cut-glass long-stemmed goblet rather than the can of light beer. But, she thought, she did dress for the occasion. If the Dolphins were playing, she would break out her aqua and orange tee-shirt and watch sweaty-palmed as any man. She recognized a level of foolishness in her behavior, but thought it harmed no one and she was comfortable with it. She thought of Susan, coming over one Sunday a year earlier and watching in almost open-mouthed amazement as Detective Barren, swearing frequently, unable to sit still, stalked around the living room of her apartment in obvious agony, relieved only by a forty-nine-yard field goal by the Dolphins' kicker in the waning seconds of the game. Detective Barren smiled at the memory.

"If only they knew. . ." Susan had said.

"Shh. Secrecy," her aunt replied. "Tell no one."

"Oh, Aunt Merce," Susan had said finally, "why is it I never know what to make of you?" And then they'd embraced. "But why football? Why sports?" the niece persisted.

"Because we all need victories in our lives," Detective Barren replied.

3. SEVERAL times over the next few days Detective Barren fought off the urge to telephone the county homicide detectives. As she went about her own business, processing other crimes, working evidence, she envisioned what was happening. She saw the tail working the killer, silently mirroring his movements while other detectives ran down his whereabouts, started showing his picture to witnesses, putting together all the minor pieces of a criminal case.

Some ten days after Susan's murder, Detective Barren was on the witness stand in a murder case; from the locations that shell casings had been discovered inside the house where a drug dealer and his girlfriend had been murdered, Detective Barren had reconstructed the entire crime. Her testimony was important, not crucial; consequently her cross-examination by the contract killer's high-priced attorney was more of a badgering than a blistering. She knew that she could not be shaken on facts; she was working hard, however, not to let the attorney so confuse the jury that the impact of what she had to say was lost.

She heard the attorney drone another question:

"So, because the shell casings were located here, you concluded that the killer stood where?"

"If you will refer to the diagram, marked into evidence as state's exhibit twelve, counsel, you will see that casings were discovered some twenty-four inches from the doorway to the bedroom. A Browning Nine-Millimeter ejects casings at a constant rate. Consequently, it is possible with a degree of scientific certainty to say precisely where the shooter was standing."

"They couldn't roll?"

"The rug in that portion of the room is a two-inch shag carpet, counsel."

"Did you measure it?"

"Yes."

The attorney turned toward his notes. Detective Barren fixed her eyes on the defendant. He was a wiry, small Colombian immigrant, uneducated save in methods and modes of death. He would be convicted, she thought, and within thirty seconds another would get off the next Avianca flight to take his place. Killers were the Kleenex of the drug industry; they were used a few times and then discarded unceremoniously.

Her eyes drifted up past the defendant, and she saw Lieutenant Burns enter the back of the courtroom. For a moment she connected him with the killer on trial. Then she saw him surreptitiously give her a thumbs-up sign.

Her imagination leaped.

She watched the lieutenant stride down the center aisle of the courtroom and bend over the barrier to whisper a few words into a bored-looking prosecutor's ear. He sat up straight, swiveled, and then rose to his feet.

Detective Barren looked at the lieutenant, who smiled at her, but only a small smile, just the slightest upturning at the corners of the mouth.

"Your honor," the young prosecutor said, "may we come to side-bar?"

"Is it important?" asked the judge.

"I believe so," replied the prosecutor.

The defense attorney, the court stenographer, and the prosecutor all walked around to the judge's side, where the jury could not hear them. There was a moment of conversation, then the three returned to their seats. The judge turned to the jury.

"We're going to take a brief recess now, then the state will continue with another witness." He looked at Detective Barren. "Detective, apparently your services are needed elsewhere. You are subject to recall, so please remember that you are under oath at all times."

Detective Barren nodded. She swallowed.

The judge frowned. "Detective, the stenographer cannot record a nod of the head."

"Yes, your honor. Under oath. I understand."

Detective Barren and the lieutenant hurried from the courtroom. As they passed through a sally port entrance and then through a metal detector, the lieutenant said, "They whacked the fucker about ninety minutes ago. He's at county homicide being questioned. They're doing his house and car now. Search warrant got issued this morning. Hell, you probably passed it on the way into court. We tried to reach you, but you were on the stand. So I decided to come get you myself."

Detective Barren nodded.

The two hurried outside. It was Florida fall, a subtle lessening of the oppressive heat of summer. A mild breeze caused the flags outside the courthouse to buffet about.

"Why'd they move on him?" she asked.

"The tail watched the creep buy two pairs of women's pantyhose last night at an all-night drugstore. He stashed them in a locker at the University of Miami, along with a ball-peen hammer."

"Who is he?"

"A weirdo and a foreigner. He's some sort of Arab. Kind of a

31

professional student, from what I've heard. Took courses all over the place. Registered with a bunch of different names, too. We'll know more soon." The lieutenant paused at the door of an unmarked cruiser. "You want to watch the questioning or the search of his place?"

She thought for a moment.

"Let's swing by his house, then go over to county."

"You got it."

The city washed past the windshield as they drove to the suspect's house. The lieutenant drove swiftly, not speaking. Detective Barren tried to fix a picture of the suspect in her head and was unable. She chided herself; good police work required one to draw suspicions and conclusions on the basis of fact. She knew nothing about this man, she thought. Wait. Absorb. Collect. That was how she would come to know him. The lieutenant slowed the car and took an exit for the airport. A few blocks shy of the airport, he turned onto a nondescript street. It was a place of small cinderblock houses, with mostly Latin and black families. Many homes had chainlink fences surrounding them and large dogs patrolling within. This was an urban normality; the largest of dogs lived in the fringe areas, the working-class neighborhoods that were so vulnerable to robbery, where both husband and wife went off to work each day. The houses were set back slightly from the street, but without foliage. The street was devoid of trees, even the palms that seemed everywhere in the city. Detective Barren thought it was a singularly uninviting place; in the summer the heat probably turned the entire street into a single hot, insistently dusty place where tensions and angers bred with the same intensity that bacteria did.

At the end of the street she saw police cars lined up around the last of the small brown houses. There was a truck from the dog pound. The lieutenant motioned at it. "Seems the guy had one loyal Doberman. One of the SWAT guys had to blow it away." An airplane, wheels and flaps down, passed frighteningly close overhead, drowning out in a huge flood of noise anything else the lieutenant was going to add. Detective Barren thought that if she had to listen to that sound with any frequency, she would have become a killer as well.

They parked the car and pushed through a small crowd of curious people who were watching the proceedings silently. Detective Barren saw a pair of homicide men she knew working the neighbors, making certain that they obtained any workable leads before the press was all over them. She nodded at the head of the team that was processing the house. He was a former street cop, not unlike herself, who had worked undercover a few too many times. In one of his last cases there had been a rather singular question about some drug money seized in a raid. A hundred thousand dollars in twenties and hundreds had been turned in to the property office, along with a kilo of cocaine. The defendants were two college students from the Northeast; they had told internal affairs that they had had more than a quarter million in cash when the raid went down, leaving some one hundred fifty thousand unaccounted for. A sticky situation that had resulted in the policeman being transferred and the two students receiving greatly diminished charges. The money was never recovered. Like many cops, Detective Barren had steadfastly refused to draw the obvious conclusion, preferring to believe that someone had lied and hoping that it wasn't the policeman. Still, she thought as she approached him, he was an extremely competent detective, and she was in an odd way relieved.

"How ya doing, Fred?" she said.

"Good, Merce. And you?"

"Okay, I guess."

"I'm real sorry for the reason you're here."

"Thanks, Fred. I appreciate your saying so."

"This is the creep, Merce. Stone cold solid. Just walk inside and you can feel it."

"I hope so."

He held the door open for her. It was cool inside the small house. She could hear the air conditioner blasting. Probably the detectives turned it up, she thought. Still, for an instant she shivered, wondering whether it was the sudden change in the temperature.

At first glance the house seemed typical for a student. The bookcases were made from gray cinderblocks and pine boards, and rows of paperbacks vied for space. The furniture seemed threadbare and modest, a couch with a faded Indian print covering it thrown over it to conceal a rend in the fabric, a pair of sitting chairs covered in plastic, a worn brown wood table scarred with cigarette burns. On the walls there were travel posters for Switzerland, Ireland, and Canada, all showing bucolic lush green settings. Detective Barren swept it all into her head, thinking so far it added up to nothing.

"Pretty ordinary, huh?"

She turned to the voice.

"Fred, show me something interesting."

"You just got to look a little closer. Check out the typewriter."

There was a typewriter on the brown table with a sheet of

paper in the platen. She stood over it and read what had been written:

unclean unclean unclean unclean unclean unclean unclean
unclean unclean unclean unclean unclean unclean unclean
God God God God God God God God God God God God
God God
Kill
I must wash the earth

"We also found his trophy box."

"His what?"

"Trophy box."

"I don't . . ."

"Forgive me, Merce, I forgot your connection." The detective paused. "Apparently he kept something from his victims. Or at least something from some of them. In the closet was a shoebox with a bunch of clippings about the killings, right up through the murder of your niece. There were some earrings and a ring or two also. Let's see, a woman's shoe and a pair of panties with a bloodstain on them."

He hesitated.

"It was the kind of box that guys like us always pray for on one of these. I don't know if there's something there that will link him positively to every one of the killings, but there's enough there to link him to some. And that means the sucker's nailed, solid."

She looked at him.

"I hope so."

"Believe it. No doubt about it. The damn thing is, I'll bet there's a couple of crimes this creep's done we didn't even know about."

He put his arm around her and started to lead her out.

"Don't worry. The search is legal. The evidence is there. The guy's probably copping out now. All there is to worry about is that weird note. He's probably whacko. Why don't you go see for yourself."

"Thanks, Fred."

"Think nothing of it. Don't hesitate to call, anytime, if you need to know something."

"I appreciate that. I feel better already."

"Great."

But she didn't.

She turned to Lieutenant Burns, who was waiting for her outside. "I want to see this guy. In the flesh."

She did not look back at the house as they pulled away.

At the county homicide office, she and Lieutenant Burns were escorted into a darkened room which had a two-way mirror which overlooked a second room. She shook hands with several other policemen who were assembled watching the questioning in the adjacent area. One man was operating a tape recorder in a corner. No one spoke. For an instant she was reminded of hundreds of movies and television shows she had seen. Someone offered her a chair and whispered, "He's still denying everything, and he seems strong. They've been at him for two hours. I give him maybe another five minutes, maybe another five hours. Hard to tell."

"Did he ask for an attorney?" She wondered.

"Not yet. So far, so good."

She thought of the typewritten note.

"Is he straight?" She asked the voice while looking at the suspect for the first time. He was a short, wiry-muscled man, powerfully built, like a lightweight wrestler or boxer, with wavy black hair and bright blue eyes, a combination that was oddly unsettling to Detective Barren. He wore jeans and an orange tee-shirt that celebrated the University of Miami's national football championship. To the detective, he seemed coiled; she watched the muscles on his arm flex. She thought how powerful that small arm was, and suddenly envisioned the short, chopping stroke of the hammer, an instant white flash of pain exploding into darkened nothingness.

"He's weird. Quoted the Koran a minute ago. Listen."

She concentrated on the three men in the interview room. Detective Moore was doing the questioning while Detective Perry sat, taking a few notes, but mostly fixing the suspect with an unwavering harsh glance, his eyes following each motion the suspect made, narrowing as the subject pontificated, equivocated, or evaded, narrowing evilly and threateningly as if angered to the point of violence by the lack of truth. Each time the detective shifted in his chair, the suspect moved uneasily. Detective Barren thought it a masterful performance.

"Tell me why you bought the pantyhose."

"It was a present."

"For whom?"

"Someone at home."

"Where's home?"

"Lebanon."

35

"What about the hammer?"

"It was to fix my car."

"Where were you the night of September eighth?"

"I was at home."

"Did anyone see you?"

"I live alone."

"Why did you kill all those girls?"

"I have killed nobody."

"So how come we found an earring belonging to a young lady named Lisa Williams at your house? And what about a pair of bloody pink panties just like the pair Andrea Thomas was wearing when some creep snatched her off the Miami-Dade campus? I suppose those were a present, too? And you've been a busy boy with the clippings, huh? Like to clip stories out of the newspaper, huh?"

"Those are my things! My special things! You had no right to my things! I demand their return!"

"Whoa, motherfucker. You ain't demanding nothing."

"You are a devil."

"Yeah, maybe, 'cause then I'll see your ass in hell."

"Never! I am a true believer."

"What? A believer in murder?"

"There are unclean people in the world."

"Young women?"

"Young women especially."

"Why are young women unclean?"

"Hah! You know."

"Tell me anyway."

"No. You too are unclean. Infidel!"

"Just me or all cops?"

"Policemen, all policemen."

"You'd like to take a shot at me, huh?"

"You are an infidel. The Book tells me that it is holy to kill an infidel. The Prophet says it is a passageway to heaven."

"Yeah, well, where you're going, fella, ain't much like heaven."

"It means nothing. It is only flesh."

"Tell me about the flesh."

"The flesh is evil. Purity comes from thoughts."

"What must you do with evil flesh?"

"Destroy it."

"How many times did you do that?"

"In my heart, many times."

"How about with your hands?"

36

"This is between me and my master."

"Who is that?"

"We have but one master who resides in the garden."

"How do you know?"

"He speaks with me."

"Frequently?"

"When he commands, I listen."

"What does he say?"

"Educate yourself in the ways of the infidel. Learn her customs. Prepare for the holy war."

"When does the holy war begin?"

The suspect laughed greatly, pitching back in his chair, opening his mouth wide, letting the snorts and whines of his voice flood the small room. Tears started to roll down his cheeks. He continued laughing for several minutes, uninterrupted by the detectives. Detective Barren listened to the sound and felt it rend her heart. Finally the suspect calmed, until only an occasional giggle slipped from his lips. He stared directly at Detective Perry, then spoke in an even, dreadful voice:

"It has begun already."

Perry suddenly pushed himself out of his chair and smashed both of his fists down hard on the table separating him and the suspect. The sound was like a shot and Detective Barren saw the men in the room with her stiffen.

"War on little girls, huh? Was fucking them part of the battle plan?"

The suspect stared frozen at the detective.

There was a silence.

When he spoke it was deliberate, awful.

"I know nothing about your unclean women."

He pointed a finger at the detective.

"I will not speak more to you."

The finger suddenly slapped down on a piece of paper in front of the suspect. Detective Barren knew it was a constitutional rights form. The suspect started to drum his fingers on the page.

"I do not have to speak to you . . ."

The finger drumming sounded like small-caliber pistol fire.

"I would like an attorney present . . ."

The rapping sound increased in intensity.

"Appoint one for me . . ."

The fingers curled into a fist and slammed on the table.

"I know my rights. I know my rights. I know my rights. I know my rights. I know my rights."

The two detectives stood, staring malevolently at the prisoner.

"You do not scare me," he said. "God is with me, and I fear none of your infidel justice. Bring me my attorney so that I may enjoy my rights! So I may delight in my rights! Do you hear? Sadegh Rhotzbadegh requires counsel, hah!"

The two detectives exited the room.

"I am a true believer!" he shouted. "A true believer!"

The suspect watched them go. Then he turned to the mirror and raised his middle finger. The tape recorder rolling silently in the corner captured another long, raucous burst of laughter before being switched off by a policeman who swore under his voice. Detective Barren stood up and sighed. At least, she noted, the man who killed Susan is easy to hate. And she took some comfort from that thought.

Time slid around Detective Barren's emotions.

She resumed her day-to-day routine, forcing the arrest of the Lebanese student into a location of diminished prominence. There was a difficult day when she went to Susan's dormitory room and packed all the books and clothes and papers away to send to her sister. She had come across a half-finished love letter to a boy named Jimmy, whom she had never met, that was filled with the mixed gushings of a young woman leaving her childhood behind so rapidly. She had read the words and connected them to a tall, gawky boy who'd stood self-consciously to the rear of the church during the service, and just to the side at the gravesite, unsure what his position was in the midst of the grief; embarrassed, the detective thought, as she herself had once been, at the idea of being alive, and horrified at the awkward sense of relief that speaks inside youth at moments of death, saying: At least my life goes on. Detective Barren read: ". . . I cannot wait for the year to get going. In midterm we are going on a week-long laboratory in the Bahamas. We take the research boat down and spend a week underwater. I wish you could be there to share it with me. I think about those last few nights and what we shared . . ." Detective Barren smiled. What had they shared? For an odd moment she hoped that her niece had known real passion and abandonment, given into desire completely. It would mitigate somewhat the violation of her last moments.

Then she had put the letter away. Reading it, she thought, was somehow unfair. But she had experienced a momentary pleasure, as if Susan had, if not been resurrected, at least for the barest of instants been restored. This made the detective feel a great sense of guilt, and she had occupied herself with the packing, setting

38

aside the letter and a few others like it for forwarding to the gawky boy.

Keep busy, she told herself.

Ten days after the arrest of Sadegh Rhotzbadegh she called Detective Perry at county homicide. It was late in the afternoon on a Tuesday, the day the grand jury usually met. He came to the telephone swiftly, apologetically.

"Jesus, Merce, I'm sorry I haven't called, it's just been so goddamn busy . . ."

"That's all right," she replied. "Did you go to the grand jury today?"

"Well, yes and no."

"Explain that to me."

"Well, yes we went to the grand jury and yes, we're expecting first-degree murder indictments today. But not on Susan's case and one other."

"I don't get it."

"Look, the MO was the same on all five homicides in Dade and one in Broward County at the community college there. He was taking a course up there in electrical engineering. Anyway, he had newspaper clippings of all six killings in his house. His blood type matches the blood from one of the semen samples found near Susan's body—but not the other. And there's the question of age on the sample that matches. His is a very common blood type and it was not possible to type it down much further. The best the lab could do was to get him into a twenty-five-percentile category."

"They couldn't eliminate further?"

"No. Same thing in the Broward case."

"So?"

"On one of the other Dade cases there's nothing, just the newspaper clipping."

"So?"

"Well, the bottom line is, we link him through jewelry, through the lingerie discovered at his house, through a shoe, which for some ungodly reason he kept, to three of the six homicides. Link isn't the right word. Nailed is more like it. So what it amounts to is this: we're clearing all the cases. But we're only going for three indictments. Now, we may introduce evidence of the others if it gets to a death-penalty phase of a trial—but that's down the line."

Detective Barren sat silently, thinking.

"Merce, I'm sorry. The point is, the guy's going to go away. Maybe the death penalty. Isn't that what counts?"

39

"Don't give up," she said.

"What?"

"What about his car?"

"It was clean except for an earring."

Detective Barren started to speak but was cut off.

"... No—I know what you're thinking. It belonged to one of the other girls. We haven't matched the earring found at Susan's body. If we could, well, bingo."

"Don't give up."

"Merce, we won't. We'll keep at it. But you know how these things work. I have to justify manpower and time to my superiors. They've cleared the case. We're going to get a conviction. The guy's history. My bureaucracy isn't any damn different from yours."

"Damn," she said.

"I don't blame you."

"I feel cheated."

"Don't look at it that way. Think of the people who commit murders and skate. C'mon, Merce, you know how unusual it is for us to make a case on some random killer like this creep. You got to be satisfied with seeing him do hard time for the cases we can lock."

"He never copped out?"

"Nah. He's too crazy smart for that. You know, one of his courses at the university was in constitutional law."

"He's not . . ."

"Not a chance. I mean, I'm sure they'll give the old insanity plea a ride, and I got to admit the guy's not playing with a full deck. Actually, it's more like he's shuffled a couple of decks together. I mean he's definitely not all there. But even if Allah was whispering in his ear to kill those girls, he sure as hell wasn't telling our boy also to rape them. That's not how Allah works, even on his bad days. And it sure isn't how some paranoid schizophrenic operates, either."

They were silent for a moment.

Detective Barren felt uncomfortable, as if the room had suddenly grown hot. She heard Detective Perry's voice on the line.

"Look, Merce, don't hesitate to call. If we get anything else I'll let you know."

She thanked him and hung up the telephone.

It was, she thought, completely unfair and unreasonable and precisely how the system of justice operates. She hated herself for being so familiar with the trade-offs and corner cutting that marks the legal system. That what had happened to Susan's murder was completely understandable from the policeman's point of view made her angrier. She was outraged with herself for understanding.

She could not sleep that night. She watched all the late-night talk shows and finally read Aeschylus until dawn, when, as the first few lights of morning crept into her apartment, she changed to reading the opening stanzas of the *Odyssey,* but even the classics could not settle her. She went to work early that day and stayed late, working feverishly on paperwork, redoing reports, analyses, and crime-scene workups, rendering her output as perfect as she could make it, until, finally, well into the evening darkness again, she went home and after stripping to her underwear and a tee-shirt, she put her pillow and a blanket on the floor and slept on the hardwood, thinking all the time that she wanted to know no comfort.

Liquid time enveloped her. She felt as if all her feelings had somehow been placed on hold while she waited for some sort of resolution to Susan's death. After the indictment for three first-degree murder counts was announced, Detective Barren went to the chief of homicide prosecution at the state attorney's office, reminding him, through her presence, that though uncharged with Susan's death, the Lebanese student still was responsible for it. She attended every court hearing, every meeting by the two young prosecutors assigned to the cases. She reviewed the assembly of evidence, considered it, then went and reviewed it again. She tried to anticipate areas of weakness that could be exploited by the public defenders that were charged with defending Sadegh Rhotzbadegh. She sent memos to the prosecutors with her every consideration, then followed up the memos with either a visit or, at the least, a telephone call, until convinced that the perceived gap in the case was closed. She knew that they found her behavior infuriating, especially in the pedantic way she would go over every aspect of the case. But she had also seen too many cases lost by lack of vigor on the part of the prosecution, lack of anticipation, and she was determined that this would not happen.

And when she had exhausted her mind and memory in constant review of evidence, she would go to the county jail, where the Lebanese student occupied a single cell in the highest-security wing. Past the electronic locking systems, down corridors gray with the crimes of men, through metal detectors and past a sign that declared: UNAUTHORIZED ENTRY TO WEST WING IS PUNISHABLE BY PROSECUTION. She would draw up a chair in the corridor outside the cell where the Lebanese student lived and simply watch him. The first time she did that, he'd laughed and shouted obscenities in her direction. When that failed to change her visage, he'd exposed himself. Once he grabbed the bars of the cell, spitting, raging, trying to reach through at her. Finally, however, he cowered, removing himself to a spot behind the toilet, occasionally peeking over the top to see if the detective was still there. She was careful never to speak to him, nor really listen to anything he might say. She let the force of her silence fill him, she hoped, with dread.

She told no one of those clandestine visits. And the jail personnel, fully aware of the reasons behind her attention, never logged her entry or departure on any official form. It was, the captain of the security unit told her in passing, the least they could do.

She attended the evidentiary hearing, when the defense tried to suppress the items seized at the student's house. She sat in the front row, eyes pouring onto the back of the student. She knew he could feel her gaze, and it was with great satisfaction that she noticed him wiggle in his seat and occasionally turn and meet the detective's glance. The evidence was not suppressed. She whispered, "Good going," to her friend Fred, the county detective, after he finished his testimony. "Piece of cake," he whispered back, striding out of the courtroom.

She attended a mental competency hearing for Sadegh Rhotzbadegh. She heard the defense attorneys argue that their client was decompensating under great stress, which, she was glad to note, the judge said was a normal state for someone facing the death penalty.

Months passed. Miami's winter arrived. The daytime light seemed to gain a new clarity, unburdened by harsh tropical heat. At night Detective Barren would sit on her porch and let the cool air wash her like a bath. She though of little save the upcoming trial; her only pleasure or release from the concentration on the case came when she would go to the old Orange Bowl, her end-zone ticket in hand, and stomp and cheer and wave a white handkerchief at the enemy as the Dolphins cruised through their schedule. When they lost the conference championship game on a bleak, New England sort of day, wet, steady drizzle and wind blowing in the open end of the stadium, chilling the shirt-sleeved crowd so unaccustomed to any weather other than warm, she felt an awful coldness inside. A fan's death, she thought. Losses are inevitable, yet terrible. To follow the game was always, ultimately, to know the wretchedness of defeat. That night she consumed almost an entire bottle of wine before sleeping. She

42

awakened with a headache, and thought that the team from Los Angeles was filled with Lebanese football players.

In the evening, a week before the trial date, she received a call from Detective Perry. He sounded excited.

"Merce," he said, "it's going down tomorrow."

"What?"

"It's guilty-plea time."

"No trial?"

"No. He's going to cop to the three cases."

"What's the deal."

"He gets to live. That's all."

"How much time?"

"The max on each. He does a mandatory twenty-five calendar, straight time, hard time, no gain time, no good time. All consecutive. Seventy-five years straight. Also he's gonna cop to some assaults, so the judge is going to add on some more time. He'll score a hundred easy. We can go up to Raiford Prison and dig his grave, 'cause that's where he's gonna die. He'll never get out."

"He should get the death penalty."

"Merce, Merce. He's in front of Judge Rule. The old bastard's had a dozen first-degree murder cases before him, including that biker-torture case, and he still hasn't fried anyone. You remember that case, Merce?"

"I remember."

"Cattle prods, Merce. Zippo lighters."

"I remember, dammit."

"Those guys are just doing twenty-fives."

"It still . . ."

He interrupted her.

"Sure, it pisses you off. It pisses off the other victims' families, too. But they're going along. Everyone's a little wary of the guy's insanity defense, too."

"Bullshit! The guy may be screwed a little tight . . ."

He interrupted her again.

"I know, I know. But those two guys defending him walked that guy who cut up his girlfriend with a hacksaw into a mental hospital last year."

"Yeah, but . . ."

"No buts. You want to take the chance?"

She thought hard for a moment. Before she responded, Detective Perry cut into her thoughts.

"And don't think for a minute that you could do the creep yourself. I know about all those jailhouse visits, Merce. Don't think it."

"He deserves to die."

"He is going to die, Merce."

"That's right," she said. "We're all going to die."

"Merce," Detective Perry said. His voice had softened. "Merce. Give it a rest. The guy's going away. He's history. It's over, understand? Don't make me make this speech. Hell, you probably know it by heart. You've probably given it a few times yourself. It's over. Over. Got it?"

"Over."

"Right."

"Over."

"Will be, at nine in the morning."

"See you there," she said, hanging up the phone.

Sadegh Rhotzbadegh seemed mouselike, timid, shivering, though the press of people jammed into the courtroom made the air thick, hot, and stifling. When he spotted Detective Barren sitting in her customary front-row seat he shrank close to the side of one of his public defenders, who turned and glowered at the detective. There was a stiffening in the courtroom as the judge swept in. An elderly man with a shock of white hair that gave him a slightly demented look, the judge surveyed the courtroom quickly, noting the lineup of victims' families and television and newspaper reporters, filling all the chairs and pressed up against the walls. It was an old courtroom, with pictures of distinguished judges staring down, now in utter anonymity, from dark walls.

"We'll take Mr. Rhotzbadegh first," he said. "There is, I believe, a plea."

"Yes, your honor." One of the young prosecutors had risen. "Simply put, in return for a guilty plea to all outstanding charges, the state will waive its pursuit of the death penalty. It is our understanding that Mr. Rhotzbadegh will then receive maximum terms on all counts, running consecutively. That would be a total of one hundred and eleven years."

He sat down. The judge looked at the defense table.

"That is correct," said one of the defense attorneys.

The judge looked at the defendant. The Lebanese student rose.

"Mr. Rhotzbadegh, have your attorneys explained what is happening to you?"

"Yes, your honor."

"And do you agree with the terms of the plea?"

"Yes, your honor."

"You haven't been coerced or forced to make this plea?"

"No, your honor."

"It is of your own free will?"

"Yes, your honor."

"You know that your attorneys had prepared a defense and that you had the right to confront your accusers before a jury of your peers and force the state to prove beyond and to the exclusion of any reasonable doubt these allegations against you?"

"I understand that, your honor. They were prepared to argue that I was insane. I am not."

"Do you have anything you wish to add?"

"I did what I did because it was written and commanded of me to do. This is what I am guilty of. In the eyes of the Prophet, I am blameless. I will welcome the day that he gathers me to his bosom and we walk together in the gardens."

Detective Barren heard the sound of reporters taking notes, trying to get all of the suspect's words. The judge broke in.

"That is fine, and I'm glad that your religious beliefs are a comfort to you . . ."

"They are indeed, your honor."

"Good. Thank you."

The judge made a small hand motion and the Lebanese student sat down. The judge looked out over the crowded courtroom.

"Are the relatives of the victims here?"

The room remained silent. Then an elderly couple sitting to the right of Detective Barren stood up. She saw another couple stand, followed by an entire family. She stood, too. The courtroom continued in fragile quiet and she noticed that Sadegh Rhotzbadegh's shoulders were twitching. Fear, she thought. He kept his eyes resolutely forward.

"Would any of you care to say anything for the record?"

There was a moment's confusion. Detective Barren's imagination flooded with words, about Susan, about what she meant, about what she would have become. Emotion gagged her and she sat down. But one of the others who had stood, a tall and thin, distinguished-seeming man wearing a well-cut blue pinstripe suit, strode forward. His eyes were red. For an instant he stared down at the defense table with a glance that seemed to suck the heat from the room. Then he turned to the judge.

"Your honor. Morton Davies, father of Angela Davies, victim . . ."

He hesitated.

"We have agreed to this plea because we understand that the system would sooner cheat us, who have suffered such loss, than it would this . . ." He stumbled, searching for a word.

". . . this refuse."

45

He paused.

"Our loss, your honor, our loss . . ."

And then he stopped.

His last word hung in the courtroom air, echoing in the sudden silence.

Detective Barren knew instantly why he'd stopped. Everyone did, she thought. How could one put words to the loss? She felt her own throat closing, and for an instant felt a kind of panic-sense that she wouldn't be able to breathe much more, certainly not at all, if he tried to continue.

He did not. He turned on his heel and walked through the room, through the doors to the rear, out to the corridor. There was a sudden flash of light as the television cameramen staked out in the hallway captured his grief. Detective Barren turned again to the front. Sadegh Rhotzbadegh had risen, his attorneys on either side. He was being fingerprinted and the judge was intoning the sentence, reading the counts off and pronouncing the maximum term. The years were adding up swiftly and suddenly the judge concluded and the two defense attorneys stepped aside, replaced instantly by two immense prison guards who firmly and deliberately began to lead Sadegh Rhotzbadegh from the court-room. She heard the judge declare a recess and disappear, black robe blurring, through a side door. The reporters were on their feet around her, and there were questions and answers flooding the air. One family pushed by, shaking their heads. Another stopped to inveigh against the system. Detective Barren saw the prosecutors shaking hands with a grinning Detective Perry. Then she stepped forward and watched the Lebanese student. He was almost to the prisoner's exist when he stopped and turned, eyes searching. They met with Detective Barren's, and they locked together for an instant. For the first time his eyes seemed, not scared, but filled with sadness. The two people looked at each other. He shook his head vigorously, as if trying to insist, trying to pass some negative of importance. She saw him mouth a word or two but wasn't sure what they were.

And then he disappeared. Swallowed up. She heard the door slam shut and lock.

She felt, then, a complete emptiness.

At first she did everything to excess. Accustomed to an easy two-mile run on the beach in the mornings, she upped it to five miles in forty-five minutes, aching and panting with lost breath in the aftermath. At work she pursued every aspect of each of her cases two or three times, precision and exactitude a comfort to her. She began to drink more, too, finding sleep elusive unless aided. A friend offered her Valium, but she used what she thought ruefully was the remainder of her good sense to turn down the drugs. She recognized that she was behaving exotically, desperately, and knew also that she was in trouble. Her dreams, when she could sleep, were fitful, filled with the Lebanese student, or Susan, or her own dead husband. Sometimes she saw the face of the man who'd shot her, sometimes her father, who looked at her curiously, tearfully, as if saddened, even in death.

She hated the idea that it was over.

She knew the procedure. Sadegh Rhotzbadegh would be sent to the classification center in mid-Florida, where he would get his physical and mental examinations. Then, in due course, he would be shipped up to the maximum-security unit at Railford, to begin his prison life, begin living out his days.

That he lived dismayed her.

In her mind's eye she replayed over and again the small shrug that had passed between them, trying to decipher, amidst the confusion and terror and madness, what he'd meant with that final shaking of the head.

She would lie in bed at night, thinking.

She would slow it, like fancy television camerawork, trying to separate each motion into a whole. His head bent first to the right, then the left, his mouth opening, words formed, but evaporating in the noise.

She took to spending time each weekend on the police range. It gave her some satisfaction to sharpen her skills with the standard issue .38 Police Special. The sensation as the weapon bucked and thrust in her hand was sensual, relaxing. She purchased a Browning 9-millimeter semiautomatic, a large, violent gun, and grew proficient with that, too. She went to Lieutenant Burns and requested a transfer out of crime-scene analysis and back to the street.

"I'd like to go back on patrol duty."

"What?"

"Take a regular shift. Maybe a beat."

"No chance."

"This is an official request."

"So? I should let you go out there and blow some purse snatcher away? You think I'm crazy? Request denied. If you want to go above my head, fine. If you want to go to the union, fine, but the bottom line's gonna stay the same."

"I want out."

47

"No, you don't. You want peace. I can't give you that. Only time can."

But she knew none.

She called Detective Perry.

"You know, Merce, we were damn close at the end to indicting him for Susan's murder. We had the newspaper clipping found at his house, and after the guy's picture ran in the newspaper a couple of students who were at the bar with Susan the night of the killing made him. They would have testified that they saw him there that night. Trouble was, they didn't see him with her, or follow her out, and one of the students distinctly remembers seeing the creep after Susan had to have disappeared. So we were close, but . . ."

"Can I have their names?"

"Sure."

She scribbled them down. She intended to visit them.

She thought often of the Lebanese student's head shaking. What, she thought repeatedly. What was he saying?

She lay in bed feeling blackness surround her. It was weeks after the sentencing; the tropical springtime with its great rush of growth and lushness had enveloped the city. Even the darkness seemed alive with resurgence. Suppose, she thought, he was trying to say, No, I didn't kill Susan. Don't be ridiculous. He hated you, she thought. He was mad as a March hare. Allah this and Allah that, he was seeking some kind of forgiveness. From her? He was too scared and too arrogant, an impossible combination. Then what was he saying? He shook his head, that's all. Forget it. How?

And then she was filled with an odd, disquieting fear, as if there were something very obvious that she had forgotten. For a moment her head spun and she turned on the light. It rended the nighttime. She padded across the bedroom to a small desk, where she kept all the copies of reports, evidence and notes from the investigation and solution of Susan's murder. Slowly she spread them about her. Then, carefully, thinking to herself, Be a goddamn detective, stop acting like a grief-stricken puppy, she began to search through them. Look, she said to herself. Find it, whatever it is. Something is there.

And there was. A small something.

It was in the evidence-disposition report from her boss.

Trace alcohol.

She read: ". . . Guy must have had a drink or two. Booze always screws everything up . . ."

"Oh, God," she said out loud to no one.

She ran to a bookshelf in the living room, pulled out a dictionary, and looked up "Shiite Moslem," but it wasn't enough of a help. She spotted a course catalog from the university that Susan had once left behind. She seized it and tore it open. She found Middle Eastern Studies on page 154. She underlined the department chairman's name and grabbed a telephone book. He was listed.

She looked at the clock. Three A.M.

She sat motionless for three hours, trying to blank out her fear.

Sorry, she thought, as the clock turned six A.M. She dialed the number.

"Harley Trench, please."

"God," said a voice clouded with sleep. "You've got him. No damn extensions, I told you all in class."

"Professor Trench, this is Detective Mercedes Barren of the City of Miami Police. This is a police matter."

"Ohmigosh, I'm sorry. It's usually students. They know I'm an early riser and they take advantage of me . . ."

She heard him collect himself.

"How can I help?" he asked.

"We have a suspect in an important case who is of Middle Eastern extraction. He claims to be a Shiite Moslem."

"Oh, like that horrid fellow who killed the young girls."

"Very similar."

"Well, yes, go on . . ."

"We need to know, well, we can exclude this fellow as a suspect in a case if we can show that he took a drink."

"You mean, like some alcoholic beverage."

"Right."

"A beer, or a glass of wine or a gin and tonic."

"Right."

"Well, that's a simple question, detective. If he's a sincere Shiite, like that poor crazed fellow said he was, not a chance."

"I beg your pardon?"

"A mortal sin, detective. No alcohol at all. Not through their lips. Not any time. It's a pretty widespread tenet of the fanatic Moslems and the reformists. A true conservative Moslem wouldn't touch a drop. Probably think the ayatollah himself would come after him. Now we're not talking about a Saudi, here, or a North African Moslem. But a real eye-rolling hostage-taking Shiite? No chance. Does that answer your question, detective?"

Detective Barren was silent.

"Detective?"

"Yes. Sorry. Just thinking. Thank you, it does."

Trace alcohol, she thought.

She felt dizzy.

She hung up the telephone and stared at the words before her. *Trace alcohol*.

Oh, God, she thought.

She saw the head as if in slow motion, shaking back and forth, insistent.

She raced to the bedroom and rifled through the papers until she came to an inventory of everything at Sadegh Rhotzbadegh's house. No liquor.

But he was at the bar, she thought. They saw him there.

But did they see him drink?

Oh, God, she thought again.

She got to her feet and walked into the bathroom. For a moment she stared at herself in the mirror. She saw her own eyes open in fear and horror. Then she was overcome by nausea, bent over the toilet and became violently ill. She wiped herself clean and looked back in the mirror.

"Oh, God," she said to her reflection. "He's still out there. I think he's still out there. Maybe, maybe, maybe, oh, God, maybe. Oh, Susan, oh, my God, I'm sorry, but he still may be out there. Oh, Susan, I'm so goddamn sorry. Oh, Susan."

A sob filled her throat. It burst from her lips like an explosion.

"Oh, Susan, Susan, Susan," she said.

And then, for the first time since the first phone call so many months earlier, she gave in to her sorrow, capitulating to all the resonances of her heart that she'd suppressed so successfully and was suddenly, completely, utterly taken over by tears.

CHAPTER
TWO
AN ENGLISH LIT MAJOR

4. THE glare off the highway filled the windshield, blinding him for a single second, and he pictured the way he'd stared across the table at his brother as his brother had said, "You know, I wish we'd been closer, growing up . . ."

He remembered his reply, quick, flip, but accurate: "Oh, we're closer than you think. Much closer."

Douglas Jeffers drove south thinking of the wan light of the hospital cafeteria that had caught his brother's face and made it lose its edge. The light, he thought, I always remember the light. He pushed down on the accelerator and watched as the scrub pines and bushes on the side of the highway seemed to pick up speed, rushing toward him.

America in a blur, he thought.

He spoke out loud to himself: "Ninety-five. Ninety-five on Ninety-five," and he goosed the accelerator again. He felt the surge of the car and he watched with some delight as the scenery fled past beyond the windows. He had the odd sensation that he was standing still and that the world was careening past him. He gripped the wheel tightly as the car shuddered, swooping past a tandem-semi-trailer truck, caught for an instant in the conflicting velocities of the two vehicles. He felt the wheel beneath his fingers twitch, as if registering a mild complaint or warning. But the engine seemed to him to be roaring in excitement, basso profundo, as it swept up the miles. He looked down at the speedometer and when the needle touched ninety-five, he abruptly took his foot off the gas until the car had slowed to a modest sixty-five miles per hour. He fiddled for a moment with the radio dial until he got a clear signal out of Florence, Georgia, country and west-

ern twangy-thump, thump. The deejay was drawling a request, a
tune "for all those striking school bus drivers in Florence, listening out on the picket line . . ." And he cued up Johnny Paycheck
singing, ". . . now you can take this job and shove it, I ain't
working here no more . . ."

Jeffers joined on the refrain and thought about the meeting
two days earlier with his brother.

He waited patiently at a small table in a corner of the hospital
cafeteria until Marty finished morning rounds and entered. "I'm
sorry I kept you waiting," the younger brother started, but
Douglas cut him short with a quick shrug of dismissal. They
made small talk for a few minutes, ignoring the clatter of dishes
and the voices that surrounded them. Fluorescent lighting filled
the room, giving both brothers a pale and sickly appearance.

"The light here makes everyone look pre-psychotic," Douglas
Jeffers said.

Martin Jeffers laughed.

"How long has it been?" he asked.

"A couple of years. Maybe three," Douglas Jeffers replied.

"It doesn't seem that long."

"No, not really."

"Busy?"

"Both busy."

"True enough."

Douglas Jeffers thought of his younger brother's laugh and
how rarely he'd heard it. His younger brother, he thought, was
prone to a quiet seriousness. Then, that was what one would
expect from a psychiatrist, even one that spent his days surrounded by the clanging noises and abrupt, disjointed screams of
a large state mental hospital.

"Why do you stay here?" he asked.

Martin Jeffers shrugged. "I don't exactly know. I'm comfortable here, the pay is good, there is the thought that I'm actually
doing something good for society . . . a lot of factors."

Penance, Douglas Jeffers thought.

But he failed to speak the word out loud.

My brother, he thought, sees too much. And, consequently,
sees little.

When his brother drank coffee, his little finger extended from
the cup, like some dowager aunt daintily drinking tea. His
brother had busy hands. He was forever plucking at the name tag
he wore on his white hospital coat, or seizing a pen from his
pocket, chewing the end for a few moments, then slipping it back

out of sight. When he was considering a question, he would often slip his hand behind his head and twirl his finger around a strand of hair. When the strand tightened sufficiently, he would reply.

"So, how's the shrinking business? Keeping up?" Douglas Jeffers asked.

"A growth industry," Martin Jeffers replied. "But only in numbers. It's always the same stories, over and over again, told in different tones and different language, but the same, only individualized. That's what makes it interesting. Sometimes, though, I envy the variety you have . . ."

The older brother frowned.

"It's not that different," he said. "In a way, for me, too, the stories are always the same. Does it really make a difference if it's Jonestown or Salvador or the Miami riots or the barrio in East L.A.? The misery is the same, whether it's a 727 crash in New Orleans or the boat people in the Philippines. One after the other. A tragedy a week. A disaster a day. That's all I do, really. I follow on the heels of evil, trying to catch a little glimpse of it before it heads off to some new location."

He smiled. He liked that description.

His brother, of course, shook his head.

"When you put it that way," Martin Jeffers said, "it sounds . . . unattractive. More than that, really, it sounds exhausting."

"Not really."

"You don't tire of it? I mean, I get angry with my patients . . ."

"No. I love the hunt."

His brother did not reply.

Douglas Jeffers looked ahead down the roadway and saw the two-lane blacktop shimmering with heat. The sun reflected harshly off the hood of the car, spinning light into his eyes. The road was empty ahead and he let his eyes wander, registering the colors and shapes of the Georgia countryside. Tall pine trees leaped up a hundred yards back from the breakdown lane, throwing cool shadows onto the earth. The shade looked inviting, and for a moment he longed to stop and sit beneath a tree. It would be pleasant, he thought, to do something simple and childlike. Then he shook his head and stared straight down the road, measuring the miles between his car and the dark hump on the highway ahead of him. A minute passed. Then another and he came on the rear of a station wagon. It was a large American wagon, filled with children, suitcases, the family dog, and parents. A tarp that covered the bags tied to the roof flapped in the wind. Douglas Jeffers' eyes met those of a young boy, who was sitting in the rearmost seat, his back to the front, as if ostracized by the rest of the family. The boy lifted his hand in a tentative way to Jeffers, and Jeffers waved back, smiling. Then he pulled out into the left-hand lane and accelerated past.

"Do you remember," his brother asked him, "the books we read when we were young?"

"Of course," Douglas Jeffers replied. *"The Wizard of Oz. Robinson Crusoe, Captains Courageous. Ivanhoe. The Hobbit and The Lord of the Rings . . ."*

"The Wind in the Willows. The Wonder Clock. Treasure Island . . ."

"Peter Pan. Just think happy thoughts . . ."

"And you can fly."

They laughed.

"That's what I call them," Martin Jeffers said.

"Who?"

"The men in my program. It's a hospital in-joke. The men in the sex-offenders program. We call them the Lost Boys."

"Do they know?"

Martin Jeffers shrugged. "They feel special enough."

"True," said Douglas Jeffers. "They aren't your ordinary types."

"No, not at all."

They were silent for a moment.

"Tell me something," his brother asked. "What is it that you like the best about photography?"

Douglas Jeffers considered the question carefully before replying. "I like the idea that a picture is indelible, with a pristine quality. Almost a sanctity. It does not, it cannot, lie. It captures time and events perfectly. When you need to remember, in your business, you need to delve into the past that is knotted by emotions, anxieties, tangled memories. Not me. I need to see the past, I can flip to a file, pick out a picture. Clear. Unencumbered. Truth."

"Can't be that easy."

But it is, Douglas Jeffers thought.

"I'll tell you what I don't like," he said. "It always seems that your best work is in the rejection pile. Photo editors always look for the best illustration of events. It is rarely the best photo. Every photographer has his private gallery, his secret stash of pictures. His own recollections of truth."

They were quiet again. Douglas Jeffers knew exactly what his brother was going to ask next. He wondered how he had held back so long.

"So why now?" Martin Jeffers said. "Why come visit?"

"I'm going on a little trip. I want to leave the key to my place with you. That all right?"

"Yes, but—where are you heading?"

"Oh, here and there. Back to some memories. I thought I'd revisit some past experiences."

"Can you stay for a bit? We could talk over old times."

"You will recall that our old times weren't so damn fine."

His brother nodded.

"Okay. But where exactly are you going?"

Douglas Jeffers remained silent.

"You won't say or you can't say?"

"Let me put it this way," he finally replied. "It's a sentimental journey." He mock-crooned the words. "To disclose the route would remove some of the, well, adventure."

Martin Jeffers looked perturbed.

"I don't get it."

"You will." Douglas laughed harshly. Heads turned at the sound. "Look, I just wanted to say goodbye. Is that so mysterious?"

"No, but . . ."

The elder interrupted. "Indulge me."

"Of course," replied the younger instantly. The two men walked down a hospital corridor in silence together. Light from a bank of plate-glass windows reflected off the white walls of the hospital, giving the two men a luminescent glow. They reached the hospital's main entrance and paused. "When will I see you again?" Martin asked.

"When you see me."

"You'll stay in touch?"

"In my own way."

Douglas Jeffers could see his brother was on the verge of asking more questions, but instead he bit back the query, keeping his mouth shut.

"Maybe you'll hear from me," Douglas Jeffers said.

The younger nodded.

"Maybe you'll hear about me."

"I don't get it."

But the elder shook his head and gave his brother a fake punch on the chin instead. Then he turned and started through the exit. But before walking through the doors, he turned, expertly seizing the camera from his shoulder bag and raising it to his eye in one fluid motion. He crouched, framing his brother quickly, then snapping off a series of shots. Douglas Jeffers lowered the camera and waved jauntily. Martin Jeffers tried to smile, and tentatively, awkwardly, lifted his arm in half-salute.

That's how he had left him. Douglas Jeffers laughed out loud remembering the look on his brother's face. "My brother," he spoke to himself, "sees but cannot see, hears but cannot hear."

For an instant he slid into sadness. Goodbye, Marty. Goodbye for good. When the time comes, take the apartment key and learn, if you can. Goodbye.

His attention was suddenly swept away by the sight of a police cruiser parked adjacent to a stand of trees. He quickly looked down at the speedometer. He was doing sixty-three. Then he thought, What difference does it make?

After Tallahassee, he warned himself, he would have to pay much more attention. The idea that his trip would be cut short by the accidental encounter with a police officer made him slow further. However, he thought a slow car draws as much attention as a speeder. Stick to the median. He reached down under the seat of the car and felt for the leather case he'd stuck in the hollow. It was where he'd left it. He pictured the short-barreled gun. Not as accurate as the 9 millimeter packed away in his suitcase, nor as well tooled as the Ruger semiautomatic 30-caliber rifle in a case in the trunk. But at close range it was very efficient. And it fitted nicely into the pocket of his jacket, and that was an important consideration. It would not do to wander about the campus with a gun bulging beneath his coat.

He passed a sign. The Florida border was ten miles ahead.

Closing in, he thought.

He felt a delightful rush of excitement, like awakening on the first morning of summer vacation. He rolled down the window and let the hot insistent Southern air blow through the car. The heat swirled around him, and into him, filling his bones with lassitude. He felt sweat start to form in his armpits and he rolled up the window again, letting the air conditioner take over.

He drove on, leaving the memory of his brother behind, concentrating on the highway, turning off the interstate and cruising through the Pan-handle on his way to the state capital. The trees, he thought, looked less stately, shorter, as if beaten by the heat, shrunken by the sun.

He found a motel about ten miles out of town. It was a run-down, forgettable place called the Happy Nites Inn. He started to remark on the spelling to the tired woman with stringy gray hair behind the counter of the small office building, but then thought otherwise. He signed with a false name, ready to provide proper identification, but she didn't ask for it. He paid in advance for five nights and took the key to the furthermost bungalow in the rear of the motel. He suspected that he would not be bothered there. No need even to ask. The rooms cost $18 a night and he got what he paid for. The bed was shaky, sagging, with gray sheets and a threadbare blanket. But for the most part, the room was clean, and, he thought, perfectly isolated. He slipped the weapons beneath the mattress, showered, and turned on the television, but he wasn't interested and within a few minutes decided to sleep.

As he lay in bed, however, indecision pummeled him.

He went over all the arguments that had filled his imagination for weeks. Once again he considered a history major. One of them would provide context, he thought, a sense of continuity, able to fit the actions into the larger scheme of things. But could they write? Would they have the necessary quick-wittedness to stay alert, instantly prepared to document what he had in mind? He hesitated. Perhaps a sociology major. They would have a better concept of trends and would see the statement in proper social perspective. But again he paused, concerned more about individual flexibility. He dismissed a psychology major out of hand; he would be forced to perform with a kind of clinical exactitude that he did not care for. It was easy to rule out the sciences and government. They would be dogmatic and probably uninformed. And he certainly didn't want to spend his free time talking politics. He knew, too, he didn't want a mathematician, or, for that matter, a musician or a linguist. They would be too wrapped up in their own particular specialities to appreciate the events.

His first instincts were probably the right ones: that he should seek either a literature major or a journalism major. Someone with an interest in journalism would be helpful; he would be able to discuss the many stories he'd covered, and in that way deflect some of the natural fear and anxiety. But, in the same respect, he reflected, a budding journalist might not understand the full picture, settling for an unfortunate recounting, producing a single-minded narrative of the events and missing some of the subtleties that he envisioned. What I'm going to do, he thought, could fill a book, so it is a book-child I must get. Someone from the English Department, he decided. He felt a surge of pleasure at having made the decision, recognizing, too, that his first feelings, after careful review and analysis, had been correct. But he hesitated again, cautioning himself, Be patient: a lonely, reclusive type would be disastrous. But someone too popular will be too easily missed. No bookworms, no cheerleaders. Choose carefully, he warned himself.

He felt a quietness sweep over him. Outside he could hear night sounds of bugs bumping against a window screen and far in the distance the high-speed wail of big trucks on the highway.

Stick to the plan, he thought. The plan is good.

He felt satisfied and within moments slipped into sleep.

Bright lights flooded through the windows of the McDonald's on the edge of the Florida State University campus in Tallahassee. He put his hand to the glass and felt warmth building on the outside. He was aware of the noise of the air-conditioning system, battling with the exterior, fighting against the heat rising from the bank of frying machines and the sizzling rows of hamburgers, lined up in military precision on the stove. Though it was morning, the restaurant was already crowded with students. He sipped his coffee and pored over the campus map, checking locations against a class schedule easily obtained from the university library before breakfast.

By his third coffee he had managed to isolate several promising courses in suitable locations. He packed the map and course catalog away in his briefcase. He checked his appearance in the mirror in the men's room before leaving. He straightened his tie and brushed his hair back. He wore a blue seersucker sportscoat and khaki slacks. No one would think twice about the dark sunglasses, he thought. Everyone on a campus in Florida wears sunglasses. He arranged the pens sticking from his shirt pocket and rumpled his jacket slightly, then took a paperback copy of John Fowles' *The Collector* from his briefcase and stuck it in his coat pocket, so the bookjacket title would protrude. He had purchased the book that morning and had carefully dog-eared the pages and bent the spine to make it appear well-read. He should have had the sense to bring his own copy, he thought. In the other pocket he stuck a sheaf of papers. He stared at himself, pleased. A graduate teaching assistant, he thought. Perhaps a young assistant professor, slightly befuddled by academia, greatly worried about tenure, but still friendly, outgoing, a little handsome and, most of all, harmless.

He set off for the campus. Confident. Excited. Pleased with his appearance, pleased with his plan.

But first, he thought, a spiritual stop.

He walked down a quiet, tree-lined street, passing an occasional knot of students, smiling, nodding to them as they swept past, searching for the address. He expected a sign out front, the way other sorority and fraternity houses were marked. It was an exceptional day; warm but not yet overwhelming, a relief from Florida's usual summertime. In its own way, he thought, the typical summer day in Florida is much like the dead of winter in the Northeast: in Florida, the heat creates the same oppressiveness, the same shut-in quality that the bitter cold does in the North. It is equally difficult, on the worst days, to travel abroad. In Florida one hides behind the air conditioning. He looked up at the sun, cutting across a cloudless sky, shading his eyes. He thought of Jack London and extrapolated: No, a man can't walk alone in Florida when the temperature rises . . .

Douglas Jeffers smiled to himself and paused beneath the dark branches of a tall oak tree. He stared across a green lawn at a white two-story wooden house, set back twenty yards from the sidewalk. Two teenage girls exited the wide front door as he watched, and he averted his glance, turning to look across the street until they passed. They were laughing together, and he doubted if they realized he was there. He looked back at the white house, studying the front. The house had many windows and a side exit. On the front lawn was a sign with two Greek letters. He read the letters twice to himself, then smiled inwardly.

Chi Omega.

Here we are, he thought. Here's where it happened.

His mind's eye envisioned the picture with professional swiftness.

Straight-on, he thought. Catch the light as it hits the left front quadrant. Simply a scrapbook shot, make it quick. Don't get noticed. He would have liked to wait for someone to walk down the path, or come through the door, which would have given the building a size perspective in the shot. But the person might notice, and that would be difficult. He framed the shot visually, so that a large oak tree on the edge of the closely cropped green lawn would provide a vertical measurement on one side. He moved a few feet to put himself slightly on angle. Quickly he checked up and down the sidewalk. Then he bent to one knee, as if tying his shoe, opened his briefcase, and grabbed the camera. He adjusted the speed and the aperture before removing the camera. Then, in a single, fluid, quick movement, he brought the camera up to his eye, pivoting toward the sorority house, focusing as he turned. He twisted the lens and snapped off a shot. The motordrive whirred and he punched the trigger again. Then again. Then, satisfied, he slid the camera back into the briefcase, actually tied his shoe, and stood up. He glanced about to make certain that no one had seen him and paced quickly down the street.

He walked swiftly for a dozen blocks, onto the campus, not stopping until he spied an empty bench beneath a tree. He settled on the bench, realizing suddenly that he was breathing hard, which he recognized came from excitement, not exertion.

"Did you get the shot?" he asked himself. In his imagination, his voice had the edge-of-desperation sound of a harried editor.

"I always get the shot," he answered himself.

"But did you get this shot?"

"Have I ever failed you?"

"Please, just tell me, did you get the shot?"

"No sweat."

He laughed out loud.

What a tourist, he thought. While everyone else who comes to Florida heads to Disney World or Epcot Center or treks to the Keys, you visit the site where . . . where what? He considered. Most people would look at a picture of the Chi Omega House on the campus of Florida State University and think of it as the location where two young women had been brutally murdered as they slept in their beds and a third badly injured. For a moment Jeffers considered the phrase: brutally murdered. It was journalese, a language with only the slightest connection to English. Murders were always brutal. So were beatings, except when they were savage. The clichés of the newspaper world created a type of safe shorthand—readers could absorb the words "brutally murdered" and not have to know that the killer was in such a frenzy that he'd severed one girl's nipple with a bite and clubbed another with an oaken branch like some berserk prehistoric man. Douglas Jeffers thought of the young women he'd seen walking from the house, laughing. He wondered for an instant whether at night she and her sorority sisters double-locked their doors, throwing solid deadbolts on memory. Jeffers pictured the house. He thought: They think of it as a place to stay, camaraderie for four years of college, but it's more, it's really a monument to something much more important: it marks the site where a prolific murderer started really to lose control and bring on his own end.

Jeffers remembered the short, wavy-brown-haired man he'd first seen on assignment in a Miami courtroom many months after the terrible night at the sorority house.

Idiot! he thought.

His mind segmented the memory into pictures. Click! The

killer turned. Click! The killer eyed him. Click! They stared each other, locking eyes. Jeffers wondered if the man could s past his own little stage-show. Click! The killer's mouth opened as he started to voice a word which evaporated into a slightly skewed, wry smile. Click! The killer turned back, smirking, glibly commenting on the trial work in front of him, angering the judge, alienating the jury, ensuring the inevitability of the result. Click! Jeffers caught that smirk, that dark edge of madness and fury, just before it was covered with sarcasm and arrogance. That was the picture he'd kept for his own file.

What a fool! he thought again.

Jeffers' stomach twisted with the memory. The papers had called him intelligent!

Jeffers shook his head sharply back and forth. What kind of intelligence can't control his own passions? Where was the self-discipline? Where was the thoughtfulness, the planning, the invention, in bursting in the dead of night into a crowded sorority house and savaging the occupants? Out of control. Enthralled by desire. Weakness, Jeffers thought. Silly, schoolboy indulgence born of conceit.

He remembered his own inner fury when his colleagues on newspapers and television had breathlessly marveled at the incongruity of an articulate, educated man who was a mass murderer. He looked like one of us. He talked like one of us. He acted like one of us. How could he be what the police said he was?

Jeffers spat, angry.

The truth was, Jeffers thought, he wasn't.

How simplistic. How foolish. So he was bright. So he was likable.

Well, does he like death row?

He deserves it, Jeffers thought.

First Degree Stupidity.

He rose from his seat, aware again of the increasing heat of the day. He decided to go over to the student union to eat some lunch before making his final reconnoiter and executing his plans.

The cafeteria was crowded, noisy, anonymous. Jeffers took his tray to a corner table and ate slowly, his map and course list spread before him, occasionally daring to look up and survey the melee of students. He thought that there was a nice symmetry in his behavior; he remembered the few months that he'd spent in college before dropping out to begin his career as a photographer. His time had been spent in much the same way as he was spend-

his time now. Alone. Quiet. Keeping to himself, watching, rather than joining. Listening rather than speaking. He remembered the awkwardness he'd felt, alone in his dormitory, separate from the easygoing welcome of the college community. It had been winter in the North, a frozen, regrettable day, gray-pitched and damp with the threat of snow, when he'd thrown his few clothes into a duffle bag, loaded his cameras, and stepped out to the edge of the campus, saluting freedom with his thumb, hitchhiking west across the nation. The memory of that trip made him smile: He'd sold his first photograph a week after starting out. He remembered sitting at a table in a soup kitchen in downtown Cleveland. He was alone, as always; one old derelict had tried to sit next to him, rubbing a knee against his beneath the table while spooning great gobs of greasy stew into his mouth and trying to behave with an ancient, encrusted nonchalance. Jeffers had hooked the man's leg beneath the table with his own feet and pulled suddenly back and to the side, twisting the derelict's brittle knee angrily. The leg creaked as the man grasped the table, about to shout out in pain, but stilled by Jeffers' quiet warning: "Say a word, scream, shout, anything, and I'll break it and you'll die out there this winter, huh?"

The man had swiftly crabbed away when Jeffers released him. A few moments later, just as he was sopping the last of his stew with a piece of doughy white bread, Jeffers had heard sirens, many of them, swoop down the street and come to a stop a block away. He'd grabbed his camera bag and jogged down to the scene of a two-alarm in a tenement. The families were passing children out the window to firemen, screaming, panicked, and Jeffers had shot all of it. But it was a picture of a fireman, icicles hanging from his coat and hat, clutching a terrified six-year-old in a blanket and carrying her to safety that he'd sold. The photo editor of the *Plain Dealer* had been skeptical, but had allowed Jeffers to use the darkroom. It had been a slow news day and he was anxious for a piece of art for the local break page. Jeffers remembered how careful he'd been, locked alone in the darkroom, mixing his chemicals with an abundance of caution, slowly souping the print until the image began to form. It had been the eyes that sold the picture, Jeffers thought, the benign mixture of exhaustion and exhilaration in the look on the rescuer's face in counterpoint to the accumulated terror in the child's. It was a very powerful picture and the photo editor logged it for the front page.

"Helluva shot," the photo editor said. "Fifty bucks. Where do we send the check?"

"I'm just passing through."

"No address?"

"The Y."

"Where are you going?"

"California."

"Everyone wants to go to lotus land." He sighed. "Free speech, free love, orgies and drugs, Haight-Ashbury and acid rock." He laughed. "Hell, doesn't sound so damn bad."

The editor pulled out his own wallet and handed over two twenties and two fives. "Why don'tcha stick around a little bit, take some more shots for us? I'll pay."

"How much?"

"Ninety a week."

He thought: Cleveland's cold. So he said it.

"Cleveland's cold."

"So's Detroit and Chicago. New York's a bitch and Boston is out of the question. Kid, you want warmth, head for Miami or L.A. You want to work, give it a ride right here. Hell, it's winter. Tell you what, I'll make it ninety-five and I'll buy you a parka and some long johns."

"What'll I be shooting?"

"No flower shows. No Chamber of Commerce meetings. Just more of what you did already."

"I'll give it a try," Jeffers said.

"Great, kid. One thing, though."

"What's that?"

"I'm gambling. This picture today, well, it turns out to be a lucky shot—I mean, I don't get more of the same—and well, bingo, you're back on your way to California. Catch my drift?"

"In other words, show me."

"You got it. You willing, still?"

"Sure. Why not?"

"Kid, with that attitude you'll go far in this business. And, one other thing. Cleveland's a blue-collar town. Get your hair cut."

He spent eleven short-haired months in Cleveland.

He remembered: An antiwar protester clubbed over the back by a hardhat carrying a two-by-four. Shot at 1/250, f-16, with a telephoto, from a block away. The grainy quality had accentuated the violence. A mob funeral, with a bodyguard exploding in rage at the collected bank of photographers and cameramen. He'd shot fast, ducking at the last minute, catching the black-suited muscleman swinging, teeth bared, 1/1000 at f-2.4 with high-speed film. Another funeral, flag-draped, a flyer who'd taken too much

63

flak over Haiphong and nursed his F-16 all the way back to the *Oriskany* and safety in the Gulf of Tonkin, only to lose power on his approach and die in the warm choppy waters before rescue could scramble to his side. The family had seemed resigned, Jeffers thought; there had been few tears. He'd caught them in a line, staring down into the grave, as if on parade, 1/15 at f-22, leaving the print a little long in the mix so as to bring out the grayness of the sky. He remembered, too, the stiffened, frozen body of a junkie, warmth found from a needle, who'd braved a February night outdoors and simply died. It had been by the waterfront; his shot had grabbed light from the Cuyahoga, reflecting an icebound world, 1/500 at f-5.6. But, as always, when he remembered Cleveland, he thought of the girl.

He had been in the darkroom, a small transistor radio that he'd purchased with his first paycheck playing in the corner, filling the room with Doors' harsh lyrics and sound. Every time he switched on the radio, "Light My Fire" had flowed out. He had spent two blistering summer days walking an early beat with one of the city's last foot patrolmen. He'd found the photos routine, too filled with softness. The policeman was popular, outgoing. Everywhere he went he was greeted, applauded, welcomed. Jeffers had snarled at the pictures. Where was the edge? Where was the tension? He wanted someone to take a shot at the cop. He prayed for it, and decided to spend another day on the street. Lost in the music, the darkness, and his plans, he'd barely been aware of the voice of the photo editor yelling for him.

"Jeffers, you lazy slug, get out of there!"

He'd carefully put his things down, moving deliberately. Jim Morrison was singing, "I know that it would be untrue..." The photo editor, he had swiftly learned, existed in two states: boredom and panic.

"What?" he'd asked, stepping from the cubicle.

"A body, Jeffers, one hundred percent dead, right in the middle of the Heights. A nice white teenage girl in a rich neighborhood very goddamn dead. Go, go, go. Meet Buchanan at the scene. Go!"

He had paced, oddly nervous, on the edge of the police perimeter, standing apart from the other newsmen and television cameramen who were waiting in a knot, joking, trying to learn a little, but mostly willing to wait until a spokesman or a detective came over to brief them en masse. Where's the shot? he'd demanded to himself. Moving right, then left, in and out of afternoon shadows, finally, when no one would notice, swinging up into a large tree, trying to get some clear vision. Stretched out like a sniper on a tree limb, he'd fixed a telephoto lens to his camera and peered down at the policemen working meticulously around the body of the young girl. He swallowed hard at the first sight of a naked leg, tossed haphazardly aside by the killer. Jeffers had strained to see, feverish, snapping off pictures, pulling the camera tightly on the victim. He needed to see her breasts, her hair, her crotch; he adjusted angle and focus and continued to fire the camera like a weapon, twisting it, manipulating it, caressing it to bring him closer to the body. He wiped sweat from his forehead and fingered the trigger again, swearing every time a detective moved into his line of sight, the motor-drive whirring every time he had a clear shot.

He'd kept those pictures for himself.

The paper had run three others: a shot of fire-rescue personnel bringing the body-bagged-wrapped victim out on a stretcher, a ground-level long-lens shot of the detectives kneeling over the body, which was obscured by their position save for a striking thin young arm, flung back from the torso, gently held by one of the policemen, and a picture of a tittering gaggle of teenage girls, drawn by fear and curiosity to the edge of the crime scene, staring out in tears and surprise as the body was carried out from the underbrush. He had liked the last shot the best, carefully approached the girls to get their names, sweet-talking the information out of them easily. The shot, he thought, spoke of crime's effect. One girl's eyes were wide in semishock, while the girl next to her had thrust her hands to her face, the eyes just peering over the edge of fingers stiffened with fright. A third girl's mouth hung wide, while a fourth was turning away from the vision. It was, the photo editor said, the best of the bunch. It ran outside, page one. "There might be a bonus," the photo editor said, but Jeffers, still suffused with excitement, thought that his real bonus remained developing in chemicals back in the darkroom, and, as soon as he'd seen the crop and the layout, he'd hastened back to his solitude.

He smiled.

He still had those pictures, almost twenty years later.

He would always have those pictures.

He heard laughter and turned toward a group of students sitting close by. They were teasing one of their own, who was taking it all good-naturedly. Jeffers could catch only snatches of the conversation, but it was about a term paper that the student had turned in, nothing of great import, a small, typical moment. Jeffers looked at his schedule and his map and decided it was time to start.

He cut rapidly across campus; it was just before one P.M. and he wanted to be in his seat before "Social Awareness in 19th Century Literature" started. He bounced up the short flight of stairs to the classroom building, sliding his sunglasses off as he entered the darkened hall, striding purposefully into Lecture Room 101 with a steady stream of students, some marching in singly, others in pairs. The lecture hall was filling rapidly; he quickly found a seat on the aisle, near the back. He smiled at the young woman sitting next to him. She smiled back, not breaking her conversation with a boy next to her. He looked about swiftly; there were a dozen or so conversations such as the one he was next to, just enough noise to crack the silence of the hall. To his right he spied a student reading a newspaper, another flipping through the pages of a paperback. Others arranged notepads in front of them. He did the same, trying to read something into some piece of behavior, a small movement that displayed an attitude which would signal to him a person's candidacy.

He spotted one girl, sitting alone, across the aisle and several rows down. She was reading Ambrose Bierce, bending head down over *In the Midst of Life*. Jeffers felt his eyebrows rise, thinking, What an extraordinary combination: the writer who may have sold his soul and a nineteen-year-old girl. Interesting, he thought. He determined to watch her during the lecture.

Sitting a few chairs away was another young woman. She was sketching lazily on a pad. Jeffers could just make out the skilled shapes that were forming beneath her pencil. He thought for a moment, excited, about the intriguing possibility of the sketch artist. He wondered if she could sketch with words. He thought: Someone who can re-create reality in art—perhaps a good selection. He decided to watch her as well.

At a single minute past one the professor entered.

Jeffers frowned. The man was in his mid-thirties, his own age, and glib. He started the hour with a joke about David Copperfield's narration of his own birth, as if that were some quirk of Dickens', some archaic piece of silliness. Jeffers suddenly wanted to rise and scream. Instead, he kept his seat, searching the auditorium for someone who failed to laugh at the professor's witticisms.

There was one who caught his attention.

She was sitting just off to his left. She raised her hand.

"Yes, Miss . . . uh . . ."

"Hampton," said the young woman.

"Miss Hampton. You have a question?"

"Do you mean to imply that because Dickens was writing for

66

serial consumption that he tailored his ideas and his style to fit the weekly newspaper form? Don't you think the reverse is true, that Dickens understood implicitly the points that he wished to make, and, using his considerable skill, fitted them into manageable segments?"

Jeffers felt his heart slow, his mind concentrate.

"Well, Miss Hampton, we know that the form was important to Dickens . . ."

"Form, sir, over substance?"

Jeffers wrote that down in capital letters and underlined it: FORM OVER SUBSTANCE?

"Miss Hampton, you misunderstand . . ."

Like hell, thought Jeffers.

". . . Dickens was, of course, preoccupied with the political and social impact of his work. But because of the necessities of form, we can now see limitations. Don't you wonder what his characters and stories would have been like if he had not been forced into the pamphleteer's role?"

"No, sir, I can't say that I have."

"That was my point, Miss, uh, Hampton."

Not much of one, at that, thought Jeffers.

He watched the young woman bend her head back to her notepad, scribbling some words on the page rapidly. She had dirty-blond hair which fell haphazardly about her face, obscuring what Jeffers thought was considerable natural beauty. He noted, then, that she sat with an empty seat on either side.

He felt his body quiver involuntarily.

He breathed in deeply and exhaled slowly.

Again, he thought, drawing in a great draught of air and letting it loose carefully, as if it were valuable. He surreptitiously placed his hand over his chest, speaking to himself: Be calm. You did not expect to find a biographer in the first class you visited. Caution, caution. Always caution. She has potential. Wait. Watch. He forced himself to study the other two young women he'd noticed earlier. He had a sudden image of himself as some small, dark, coiled beast, waiting, anticipating, curled in obscurity beneath a loose rock on a well-traveled path. He smiled, thinking with pleasure to himself: Progress.

CHAPTER
THREE
BOSWELL

5. AFTERNOON sun filtered weakly through the library window. It struck the notepad open on Anne Hampton's table, making the blue-ruled lines disappear, washed away in the glare. She looked down at the words she had been writing, staring so hard that the edges of the letters blurred and grew indistinct, the entire page becoming a floating, vaporous field. It made her think of snowfields in winter, back home in Colorado. She envisioned herself poised at the top of some long run, the sunlight exploding off the open expanse of snow, uncut as yet by skiers' trails. It would be early morning, the sun would hold no promise of warmth, just a single cold light flooding the white. She thought to herself about the way the reflection seemed to reach up, tangible, blending with the freezing air and wind, creating a world without edges, depth, or height, a solitary great white hole in the world, waiting for her to suppress that momentary hesitation that is the border of fear, and then plunge outward, down, dizzyingly thrust forward, feeling the cold sensation of flying snow bursting like shells around her as she cut through the deep powder.

She laughed out loud. Then, remembering where she was, clapped her hand across her face in mock embarrassment and sat back in her chair, looking out the window across the quadrangle toward a stand of palms that rippled gently as she watched. The palms, she thought, can find a breath of breeze even when there isn't one. They clatter their leaves together as if in greeting, feeling the slightest sway in the air, welcoming it, enjoying it, she thought with an odd jealousy, even when she was unable to detect the meagerest motion of relief in the summer's heat.

She looked back at the books spread about her. It must be easy to spot the literature majors, she thought. She separated her stack of books into two separate piles: Conrad, Camus, Dostoevsky and Melville on one side of her notepad, Dickens and Twain on the other. Darkness and light, she thought. She shook her head. She wasn't even reading half of the books and did not really understand why it was so important for her to tote them around in her backpack. But she did, packing them in every day, next to current assignments, as if the weight of great words resting on her back would somehow permeate her vision and motivate her behavior. She wondered if she had some unconscious time limit for carrying once-read works. She imagined that she could develop a rating system for literature; books that she carried about more than a month after completion were true classics. Three weeks meant a lasting greatness. Two weeks, probably should be hauled about for their themes, if not their execution. A week reflected perhaps a great character, but not a great book. Less than a week? Pretenders.

But, she thought, there is an odd comfort in knowing great words are close.

She sometimes wondered whether books were alive; whether, after shutting the covers, the characters and the places and the situations didn't change, argue, debate somehow, only to return to place at the moment the cover was flipped open. It would be fitting. She stared at the Camus, lying atop her dark pile. Perhaps, she thought, Sisyphus rests when the pages are closed. He sits, breathing hard, his back slumped up against his rock, wondering whether this time the rock will teeter at the top and then, miraculously, stick. Then, feeling the pages of the book open about him, he climbs to his feet, puts his shoulder to the rock, and, feeling the comforting coolness of the hard surface, flexes his muscles, gathers his strength, and shoves hard.

She was suddenly tempted to reach out and snatch open the book, to see if she could catch Sisyphus resting.

She smiled again.

She looked up and her eyes momentarily caught those of a man sitting across the room. He had been reading; she couldn't make out the title. He had looked up, it seemed, at the same moment. He smiled. She smiled back. A young professor, she thought. She looked away, out the window, for an instant. Then she let her eyes return to the man. He had returned to his reading.

She looked at her books. She looked at her notes. She looked out the window again. She looked back at the man, but he had disappeared.

She thought suddenly of her mother's complaint: "But you won't know *anybody* in Florida!"

And her reply: "But I don't *need* to know anybody."

"But we'll miss you . . . and Florida is so far away."

"I'll miss you. But I need time to get away."

"But it's hot all the time."

"Mother."

"All right. If it's what you want."

"It's what I want."

It wasn't hot all the time, she thought. Her mother had been wrong. In the winter there was an inevitable freeze, some wayward mass of cold Canadian air, lost in its pursuit of Massachusetts, tumbling down the midsection of the nation and landing squat and awkwardly on the Florida panhandle. It was a wretched cold, without any of the beauty or terrifying stillness of the Colorado mountains. It was simply irritatingly cold; the palms seemed to buckle, the buildings, lacking much in the way of insulation, seemed tenaciously to hold in the cold air. It was sweaters and overcoats underneath a sky that seemed to speak properly only of beaches. She thought it ironic that she had been far colder on a January day in Tallahassee than she ever had been at home.

She looked at the sunlight hitting her desk. Thank God for the summer heat, she thought. She was struck with the odd observation that in three and one half years she had failed to make a close friend, despite the warmth, despite the familiarity that it bred.

Pizza friends, she thought.

Beer friends. Beach friends. What-did-you-get-on-the-test friends. Did-you-read-the-extra-assignment friends. Will-you-go-to-bed-with-me friends.

Not too many of those, she laughed to herself.

But not for lack of people trying.

She pulled her notepad toward her and wrote: *Face it, you're a cold fish* in the margin. She was pleased. It was an easy association: cold fish and Camus.

She settled into her chair and continued reading.

It was dusk when Anne Hampton left the library and began to walk slowly across the campus. In the west the setting sun had turned the sky an astonishing purple, illuminating massive, stately cloud formations somewhere over the Gulf of Mexico. She thought how she loved to walk at that hour; the residual daylight seemed tenacious, seeking out form and shape and trying, against the oncoming dark, to give solidity to the world before acquiescing to the night.

70

Dying time, she thought.

She remembered the way it seemed that the last few fragments of sunlight caught on the diver's regulator when he emerged through the hole in the ice at her grandfather's pond, carrying her brother's form. The light had tumbled down from the bright aluminum apparatus of this odd marine creature, just hitting the little boy's encrusted features. Then she had lost sight; Tommy was surrounded instantly by firemen and rescue personnel, and all she could see was a dark mass being rushed up the hillside toward a pulsating red light. She saw his skates, the laces sliced, tossed aside. She pulled out from her grandfather's agonized grip and retrieved them.

Of course, she thought, as she walked along, he didn't actually die then; it was not until two hours later, amidst all the hum and buzz and beep of modern medical apparatus that he technically expired. The hospital's intensive-care unit was a wonder of lights, she thought; everywhere she had looked there was another light, filling every angle, probing every corner. It was as if by refusing to allow any darkness into the rooms, they could somehow stave off death.

She had caught sight of a physician's chart. It had an entry for Time of Death and the nurse had scribbled in 6:42 P.M. She had thought that inaccurate. When did Tommy die? He was dead when I heard the little spiderwebs growing in the ice surface below my feet. He died when I called out to him and he waved his arm at me in little-boy irritation and over-confidence. He died as he hit the water. She remembered thinking how undramatic it had been: one instant he was sliding along, arms pumping, the next, swallowed by this dark hole that had materialized beneath him, dying as the black cold enveloped him. His head did not bob to the surface even once. She had a sudden memory of the numb-cold pain in her feet as she ran, after stripping her own skates off, for her grandfather's house. Each step had seemed colder, harder, the snow deeper, more treacherous. She had fallen a half-dozen times, sobbing. She thought: I was only a little girl. And he was already dead then.

A warm breeze plucked at her shirt and she ran a hand through her hair. The sunlight had almost vanished; with it a sense of purpose and enthusiasm, replaced by a summertime lassitude amidst the evening heat.

No thin ice in Florida, she thought.

Not ever.

She cut through the campus, past knots of students making their way to meals, parties, studies, or whatever, and turned down Raymond Street, heading for her apartment. She filled her mind with the mundane, envisioning the stash of yogurt, cottage cheese, and fruit in her refrigerator, briefly considering stopping for a cheeseburger, then discarding the idea. Eat nuts and berries, she said to herself, laughing. She visualized her parents; both had a tendency to *size,* she thought. She hated the meals of mashed potatoes and steaks that inevitably hit the table before her on her rare visits home. They must think I'm anorexic, she thought. I'm not. I'm selectively anorexic.

She cut under the mercury vapor light at the corner of Raymond and Bond streets, marveling, as always, at the way the light turned her clothes and skin into a fluorescent purple. She had a brief vision of herself as the star of some 1950s horror flick; accidently exposed to a unique dose of radiation, now she would turn into . . . into what, she wondered. The Incredible Wallflower? The Fantastic Grind? The Phenomenal Serious Student? She heard raucous laughter pour suddenly from an open window, blending with a quick resonating chord from a stereo with the volume cranked up. Summer session, she thought, is the least serious of all the semesters. She preferred it, she realized; it made her own work stand out amidst all the people making up one failure or another.

She continued walking along, now humming a nameless snatch of music borrowed from the blasting stereo, until she turned onto Francis Street. She was two blocks from her apartment and she did not see the man until she was almost on top of him.

"Excuse me," he said. "Can you help me? I think I'm lost."

She started. The man was standing at the edge of a shadow, next to the open door of his car.

"Did I frighten you?" he asked.

"No, no, not at all . . ."

"I'm sorry if I did . . ."

"No, it's okay. I was just thinking."

"Your thoughts were elsewhere?"

"Right."

"I know the feeling," he said, striding forward. "One thought leads to another, then another, and before you know it you're in the midst of some tiny reverie. Sorry to intrude."

"Reality," she said, "always intrudes."

He laughed.

She looked at him closely in the meager light from a lamp a half block away. "Didn't I see you earlier today, in the library?" she asked. He smiled.

"Yes, I was there, catching up on some reading . . ."

She saw him study her own face.

"Aren't you the girl—I'm sorry, woman—with all the books? I thought you'd never get to leave if you had to read all those."

She smiled. "Some. Not all. Some were read already."

"You must be an English major."

"Bingo."

"Not that hard to tell, really."

"No, I suppose not," she said. "It's funny. I was just thinking that, earlier."

"See," he replied, "good instincts."

She smiled at him and he grinned in response.

They were silent for a moment. She thought the man handsome; he was tall, well built, with a sort of easy scruffiness about him. Probably just the seersucker jacket, she thought to herself. It adds a bit of rumpled familiarity to almost every man.

"Are you a professor?"

"Of sorts," the man said.

"But not from around here?"

"No. First visit. And I can't seem to find Garden Street: I've looked all over the place . . ." The man turned, first pointing up one way, then peering down the other. She thought for an instant that he was searching for something as his gaze lingered in each direction before turning back toward her.

"Garden Street is pretty easy," she said. "Two turns. Left at the corner, two blocks, then right. Garden Street intersects that street a couple of blocks down. I forget what it's called, but it's not very far."

"I've got a little map, not a good one," the man said. "Would you mind just showing me where I am exactly?" He smiled. "That of course is really a philosophical question, but this once I'd settle for the topographical."

She laughed. "Sure," she said.

She stepped next to him as he spread the map out on the roof of the car. He reached into his pocket for a pencil, talking to himself, really: ". . . now here is where I think I am . . ." And then a sudden "Dammit! Don't move!"

"What is it?"

"I dropped my room key."

He bent down. "Got to be here somewhere . . ." She started to bend down to help him look, but he waved her off. "See if you can't pinpoint for me where I am on that map." She stepped forward to the edge of the car and looked at the map. For an instant she was confused: it wasn't Tallahassee, but Trenton, New Jersey.

"This is the wrong map . . ."

She didn't have time to finish.

For one instant she looked down. She saw the man had a small rectangular device in his hand.

"Good night, Miss Hampton," he said.

Before she could move, he jerked her leg toward him and thrust the device up against her thigh. There was a crackling sound; an immense pain fled through her body; it felt as if someone had reached inside her and seized her heart and twisted it savagely. How does he know my name? she thought. Then she could feel her eyes rolling back and blackness sweeping over her. The crackling sound stopped and she thought: The ice broke.

And then she entered the darkness.

6. HER first thought upon reawakening was that death was not as she had expected it. Then, as her faculties came slowly into focus, she recognized that she was alive. Next she realized the pain; it felt as if every bone and muscle in her body had been straightened to its limit then hit or twisted. Her head throbbed and her thigh burned where she had been struck. She moaned slowly, trying to open her eyes against the pain.

She heard his voice, close but disembodied.

"Don't try to move. Don't struggle. Just try to relax."

She moaned again.

She blinked her eyes open, thinking that she must not panic, though fear was quickly overcoming the sensation of pain and covering her like a shroud. She gasped in air, hyperventilating. She heard the voice again.

"Try to remain calm. I know that seems difficult. But try. It's important. Think of it this way: If you remain calm, you extend your life. If you panic. . . . I know you're about to be hysterical . . . well, that would be hard for both of us. Take a deep breath and stay in control."

She did as she was told.

She opened her eyes and tried to assess her situation. There was only a small light, in a corner; the room was mostly dark. She could not see the man, but she could hear his breathing. She became aware, slowly, that she couldn't move; she was lying on her back on a bed, her hands roped together and fastened to the headboard, her feet tied to the baseboard. There was a little play in the bonds; she shifted about as much as they would allow, trying to see where she was.

"Ah, curiosity. Good. That shows you're thinking."

She was suddenly overcome by two swift emotions, one following the other without hesitation. First she felt an abrupt absorbing despair at her vulnerability, and she sobbed once. It was as if she had fallen from some great height and was tumbling downward, faster and faster. Then, as quickly as this sensation came, it retreated and she felt a burst of anger. I will live, she thought. I will not die.

Then, as this internal declaration suffused her, it was broken by the man's cold, even voice.

"There are many kinds of pains in the world. I am familiar with most of them. Don't test my skills."

She could not stifle the sob. She felt tears welling up in her eyes. She started to wonder what was about to happen, but managed to stop herself, thinking: Nothing good. But the words came out of her mouth as if spoken by someone else, some lost child.

"Please. Please let me go. I'll do whatever you want. Just let me go."

There was a silence. She knew he was not considering her request.

"Please," she said again. She was struck by how useless the very sound of the word was.

"Tell me what you want from me," she pleaded. Her mind raced over the possibilities, but she refused to put words to visions. She heard the man breathe out slowly. It was an awful sound.

"You are a student," he said. "You will have to learn."

She felt for an instant as if her heart had stopped.

The man hovered for the first time into view, just stepping past the shadows into the periphery of her vision. She craned her neck to see him. He had changed his clothes, replacing the seersucker jacket and khaki slacks with dark jeans and a black sportshirt. It disoriented her, and she had to look twice to make certain it was the same man. His face, too, seemed different; gone was the easygoing loose grin. He suddenly seemed to be all edges and angles. His eyes grabbed hers and she had the sensation of being tugged forward, helpless, by the rigidity of his gaze. She swallowed hard.

"Don't fight things," he said.

He paused.

"If you fight it only prolongs things. It's smarter to go along with the program."

"Please," she said. "Don't hurt me." She listened to herself speak. The words simply emerged, unbidden, plaintive, impotent. "I'll do whatever you want."

"Of course you will."

He did not take his eyes from hers. The absolute certainty of his words struck her a blow.

"Whatever I want."

He hesitated again.

"But that is a learned response. Conditioned. And the lesson has just begun."

He held up the small rectangular device so that she could see it. She twitched involuntarily, shrinking from the man. He pressed a button on the side of the device and she saw an electrical current jump from one pole to another. "You're already familiar with this," he said. She was suddenly acutely aware of the pain in her body. She let out a half-groan, half-sob. "Do you know that you can buy a stun-gun without a license in the states of Georgia, Alabama, Missouri, Montana, and New Mexico and at least a half-dozen others? They are also available through mail order, but that is more easily traced. Now, what reason would anyone have for one of these?"

He answered his own question.

"Except for inflicting pain."

She felt her lower lip trembling, and the quaver in her voice was new. "Please, I'll do anything, please."

He put the device down.

"It would hardly be fair," he said again, "after letting you experience it once, to use it again."

She sobbed, almost thankful.

Then she gasped as he thrust his face down close to hers.

He hissed: "But imagine. It was on its lowest setting when I hit you with it before. Imagine. Imagine how it would feel if I turned it up. Consider that pain. Did it feel like someone had reached for your soul and torn it from your body? Think of it."

She had a sudden vision of black agony. It swept over her. She heard the little-girl reply:

"Yes, yes, yes," she said. "Please, God."

"Don't pray," he said quickly.

"No, no, I won't. Whatever you say. Please."

"Don't plead."

"Yes, yes, of course. Yes."

"Just think."

"Yes, yes, yes." She nodded vigorously.

"Good. But remember. It's never far away."

"I'll remember, I'll remember."

His voice changed suddenly. He was solicitous.

"Are you thirsty?"

The word made her realize her throat was parched. She nodded. He disappeared from her sight. She heard a water tap running. He returned to her side with a dampened towel. He began to caress her lips with it. She sucked at the moisture.

"Isn't it fascinating how we can get so much relief from such a simple thing: a towel doused with water..."

She nodded.

"But... that the same thing which gives us relief can terrify us?"

As he spoke the last word, he suddenly pushed the towel down over her mouth and nose. She choked and gasped, trying to scream out, stifled by the wet towel. Oh, God! she thought. I'm dying! I can't breathe! She realized she was drowning and she had a sudden vision of her brother waving across the ice toward her. Her lungs felt as if they were being ripped from her chest. Her eyes rolled back and she twitched against the bonds, as her mind became a single black sheet of panic.

Then he released her.

She struggled for breath, filling her lungs desperately.

"Now relief," he said. He used the towel to dampen her forehead. She sobbed again.

"What are you going to do to me?"

"If I told you it would remove the mystery."

Sobs took over her body and she cried freely.

"Why?"

He ignored her, letting her cry for a moment.

The tears stopped and she looked at him.

"More questions?" he asked.

"Yes. No. I can't..."

"It's all right," he said gently. "I expected you to be curious."

He thought for a minute. Time seemed to hesitate with him.

"Have you ever read a story in the newspaper, a crime story, that suggests that maybe this thing or that thing happened to someone, but that it isn't quite clear, and your imagination has to filter through the euphemisms and analogies in order to come to an understanding? Have you?"

"Yes. No. I guess so. Please, whatever you want."

He looked at her angrily.

"Well, that's what's happened to you. You're caught up in one of those stories. You're a news event..." He laughed. "Only it isn't all written yet. And the headline remains to be invented. Do you understand that? Do you understand what I'm saying?"

She shook her head.

"It means you have a chance to live."

She sobbed. She did not know whether to be grateful.

Then he slapped her hard across the mouth and the room spun. She fought unconsciousness. She could taste blood on her gums and one tooth seemed to be loose.

"But it also means you might not. Keep that in mind."

He waited for a moment, watching the effect of the words on her face. She knew she could not hide the terror she felt. Her lip quivered.

"I don't like that," he said matter-of-factly.

Then he struck her again. His hand moved as if in slow motion toward her face. She was surprised that she felt the pain. She relaxed, wondering how she was able, and then this time she gave in to all the agony and passed out.

When she emerged from the nighttime of unconsciousness she was cautious to bite back the sound of hurt that was her involuntary response to the return of her faculties. She could feel how swollen her lip was and taste dried blood. She was still bound, and the pain in her joints and muscles had returned less sharp but with a throbbing energy that she feared.

She could not hear the man, but she knew he was close.

She breathed in slowly, fighting the pain, and forced herself to assess the surroundings. Without moving her head, she let her eyes scan the ceiling. There was a single overhead lamp with an exposed bulb, but it was out. She could tell that the room was small and she guessed that she was in a small apartment or motel room. Rocking her head slightly from side to side, she could see a few tacky furnishings and a window with its shade drawn. There seemed to be a small corridor just beyond the scope of her vision, and she thought that was probably the entranceway. She could not see where the meager light in the room came from, but guessed that there was an adjoining bathroom and that he'd left the light on. She could not tell what time it was or how long she'd been unconscious.

She realized with a sudden pang of despair that she could not remember the day or date, and she quickly tried to recall. I was working, she thought, on a Tuesday in the library. It is July. It is the end of July. The last week. There are only three more weeks in the semester.

Or is it four? She bit her lip and felt tears well up in her eyes. Remember! she screamed to herself. She could feel her mind spinning in agony over her inability to recollect the date.

How long have I been here? she cried to herself.

And then, as if he had been listening to her thoughts, the man answered:

"I control time from now on."

His voice seemed to carry a blackened finality to it and she could not fight off her tears. One sob slipped from her mouth, then another, until finally her entire body shook with despair.

He let her continue. She did not know how long she cried, whether it was minutes or hours. When she stopped, she heard him sigh and he said, "Good. Now we can continue."

Her body stiffened reflexively.

Out of the range of her vision she heard him rustling through a bag.

"What are you going to do?" she asked.

Immediately he was at her side.

"No questions!" he whispered savagely.

He slapped her.

"No questions!"

He slapped her again.

"No questions!"

He slapped her a third time.

It had happened so quickly that the pain and surprise seemed to meld together. "No, no, no, I'm sorry. . ." she said.

He looked at her.

"Any questions?" he asked.

She shook her head quickly.

He laughed briefly.

"I didn't think so," he said.

Again she felt her heart plummet with despair. She fought against a sudden rush of hysteria.

She heard a small clicking sound and craned to see what it was.

"It's exposure time," he said.

He held up a pair of surgical steel scissors.

The sensation of the blunt metal was cold against her skin. She shuddered, then listened. Then she moaned, thinking it had to be, Oh, God, I knew it. He was gently but steadily slicing through the denim of her jeans.

He cut first up one leg from ankle to waist, then the other. He carefully folded the pants back, exposing her legs. She shivered. She felt his hand reaching underneath her, pushing up on the small of her back, lifting her buttock off the bed, then releasing her as he removed the jeans. She heard him toss the tattered pants

79

into a corner. She closed her eyes and felt the scissors working with a terrible steady precision on her shirt. She felt her bra being removed and then the sensation of steel on her hips as he cut off her panties.

Again she sobbed.

In her mind she was filled with agony and embarrassment, exposed, trussed, and lost. The inevitability of what was about to happen to her seemed too dull, so obvious, so unavoidable; it was almost without fear for her. She thought, Just do it, please, get it over with.

She waited for him to cover her.

Seconds rolled into minutes and she became aware that she was cold. She shivered, her eyes still closed.

She could hear nothing except his breathing close by.

She was aware that the minutes were building.

She had a terrifying thought: My God! Suppose he can't? Suppose his frustration . . . then she bit her thoughts off and opened her eyes slowly. He was simply sitting next to her. When he saw that her eyes were open, he let his track down her body.

"You realize, of course, that I could do what I want?"

She nodded.

"Spread your legs."

She pushed her legs apart as far as the bonds would allow.

She heard the whirring sound of a camera motordrive, and behind her squeezed eyes the world suddenly went red as a flash exploded. There was another explosion, then a third. She opened her eyes slowly.

"All right," he said. He was returning his camera to a bag.

She tried to pull her legs back close, nervously.

"Are you going to . . ." she started, but her words were lost in the sound of another slap across the face.

"I thought we had learned that already," he said.

He hit her again.

She could not help the tears.

"I'm sorry, sorry, sorry," she said. "Please don't hit me again."

He simply looked at her.

"All right. You may ask your question."

She sobbed.

"Ask!"

"Are you, are you, are you going to rape me?"

He was silent.

"Do I have to?" he replied.

He put his hand on her crotch. She felt her skin shrink beneath his fingers.

Then he slapped her again. She gasped.

"I asked you a question. Don't keep me waiting."

"Oh, God, no, yes, I don't know, whatever you want, please."

"Good," he said.

He stood up and moved to the foot of the bed. She lifted her head off the pillow to watch him. He held up something small and it reflected the little light.

"Do you see what this is?"

She groaned. Her mind darkened.

"I have always," he said, "been fascinated by the simple razor blade. It could cut your throat with such subtlety that your first awareness of its work would be the lifeblood gurgling in your gullet."

Her eyes opened wide in fear.

His glance met hers. Then he slowly, carefully, lowered the blade and ran it along the tough skin on her big toe.

"Please," she started, but stopped when his eyes flashed at her. He moved to her side and touched the edge of the blade to her hip. She could not feel anything, but saw a small line of blood an inch or two long appear on her skin.

"Think of me as a razor blade," he said.

He moved up her body and slid the blade along her forearm, just on the edge of her peripheral vision. She could just make out the sight of another streak of blood. She felt herself spinning dizzily, trying to keep alert, in control, to scream, to do anything. Suddenly he was next to her face, and she could see the blade in his fingers. He slammed one hand down over her nose and mouth as he hissed:

"Shall I rearrange your face?"

And she spun into oblivion.

Anne Hampton woke gently, thinking to herself that she would make herself a slow breakfast, and a large one, indulging in eggs and toast and bacon, coffee, perhaps a Danish roll, and a leisurely reading of the morning newspaper. She thought that food and hard news would serve well to rid her of the nightmare that had plagued her, a dream vision of razors and madness. In half-sleep, she tried to roll from the bed, only to feel again the limit of the restraints that bound her. For a moment she felt confused, as if she could shake the sleep from her eyes and be done with this vaporous intrusion of nightmare on the solidity of day-to-day life. Then the tension in her wrists and ankles became real, and she realized that the thoughts of morning were the dream and she sobbed once in admission and defeat.

And then she thought of her face.

Her hand involuntarily shot toward her eyes, only to be stopped by the bonds. She tried to bend toward her hands: I need to feel! she screamed to herself. What has he done?

She felt an unruly, uncontrollable terror. Am I still me? her mind roared. She craned to look at the razor's cut on her forearm. To her immense fear, she couldn't feel a thing, though she could see where the blood had clotted into a thin brown scab. No pain, no sensation whatsoever. My face! What has he done to my face? She tried to segment her visage into parts: She twitched her nose, and it seemed to respond normally. She arched her eyebrows slowly, trying to feel the telltale hesitation in the flesh that might mean parted skin. She pushed her jaw forward, stretching the skin over her chin and lower lip. She was unsure, her lip was still swollen. She ordered her mouth into a smile, then a wide grin, feeling the flesh on her cheeks tighten and contract. She tried to wrinkle her forehead at the same time. Then she held this grotesque position, searching as if from behind, in the dark, like the blind man in a familiar room, aware suddenly that someone has shifted all the furniture from the positions he has so carefully and painstakingly memorized.

She was unable to be certain, and that frightened her as much as anything. She closed her eyes, praying silently that just this once she could open them and find herself back in her own room, surrounded by her own things. She squeezed her eyes tight and tried to remember her bedroom. She thought of the pictures that lined her bureau top: her parents, her grandparents, her drowned brother, the family's old sheep dog. She had a small box, an antique wooden hand-carved jewelry box, in the center between the photographs, where she kept earrings and rings and necklaces that were all worth considerably less than the box itself. She tried to picture the Christmas morning when she had unwrapped it and the hug and kiss she had bestowed on her parents in return. She tried to remember the smooth, satisfying texture of the polished wood. The scroll-like carving on the lid was especially fine and subtle, and she struggled to form the memory of the sensation in her fingertips when she ran her hand across the top.

But it seemed distant, as if something recollected from a wayward dream, and for the first time she wondered if anything that had existed so few hours earlier had ever been real.

She shivered, but not from the cold.

Where is he? she wondered.

She could not hear his breathing, but that told her nothing; she knew he was close by. She lifted her head to take in her surroundings in the same wan light that insinuated itself into the room. She did not see the man, but what she did see pitched her mind wildly and crashed into her heart with terror.

She slammed her head back down on the pillow and let sobs thunder through her body. It was then, for the first time, that she knew real violation.

He had dressed her.

She was wearing underpants, pants, a new bra and a tee-shirt.

She thought: I am a child.

And she cried out of control.

It was not for several minutes that she realized that the man was sitting in a chair just behind her head. As her tears slowed, he touched her lips again with a dampened washcloth. Then he carefully, gently, started to wash her face for her. He kept this up as she gained a grip on her fears; she concentrated on the sensation of the cloth against her skin, trying to be aware of any hesitation or pain that might signal his handiwork with the razor blade. There was none, and she allowed herself an inward sigh. She felt her muscles relax, and fought to maintain a rigidity, thinking that she must be prepared for anything. She became aware then that the discipline of her mind over her body had surrendered, that she no longer could order her limbs to perform, that somehow in the past hours, in the fear and tension, she had given up a part of her self-control. He started to speak then, softly, smoothly. She hated the sound of his voice but was unable to oppose its effect.

"Right," he said. "Relax. Breath in and out slowly."

He was quiet.

"Close your eyes and find your strength."

She thought: He does not mean that. He means for me to lose it.

"Listen to your own heartbeat," he said. "You are still alive. You've made it this far. You've made progress."

She thought of a hundred questions and bit each back.

"Just be quiet," he said.

She felt her breathing had stilled and that her heart had slowed. She hid behind her closed eyes, aware that he had stepped away from her side. She could hear him shuffling about a few feet away, then, just as quickly, he returned to her side.

"That's right. Keep your eyes closed," he said. His voice had a gentle lilt to it.

He stroked her forehead gently.

83

"Do you think I would hurt you?" he asked softly.

"No," she replied slowly. Her eyes remained shut.

"But you're wrong," he said, in his mild voice.

Light seemed to explode behind her closed eyes as he struck her. The sound of his hand on her cheek was sharp and awful, and she gasped back in mixed surprise and pain. Her eyes flashed open and she saw his hand drawn back for another blow, the only steady thing amidst a wildly spinning room.

She squeezed her eyes shut and tried to shrink into the pillow. "No, no, no, no, not again, please," she said.

And there was a silence.

In the darkness behind her closed eyes, Anne Hampton's mind spun wildly. For the first time she could think of nothing but pain, hating it, fearing it, longing to be free of it.

After a moment he spoke.

"I owe you another blow," he said. "Consider that."

And she heard him step away from the side of the bed, somewhere into what she was beginning to understand as the vast darkness of the little room. She remained behind her closed eyes, feeling abandoned completely, save for constant hurt.

She was no longer completely cognizant whether she was asleep or awake. The distinctions between fantasy and reality, between dream and alertness, had evaporated. She wondered momentarily whether the same barrier between life and death was becoming equally blurred.

The thought frightened her and she tried to encourage herself, thinking: But I am still alive. If he means to kill me, he would have already. He would have done it right at the start. He wouldn't keep me alive, keep up the pain, just to kill me in the end. No, he needs me. That need spells life.

And then, just as swiftly, the darkness of her mood returned, and she imagined that perhaps she was wrong. Perhaps he needed her only for what she had provided, a trussed victim. Perhaps he was simply building toward a climax, and, once reached, she would be, what? Dispensable? She tried to sweep the thought into a pile and deposit it in some closed container of the mind, but once envisioned, it grew until it came to dominate her imagination. She saw scenes as if from the evening news on television: a gaggle of cameramen, a squad of detectives, a milling mass of curiosity seekers all gathered around her naked form. In this vision she was trying to scream out to the crowd that she was alive, that she breathed and cried and thought, but she was ignored. To the mass of people, she was dead, despite her loud insistence to the contrary, and in this waking nightmare she saw herself loaded, frozen with fear, onto a gurney to be taken to a morgue. It was as if her screams of life were silent, soundless, disappearing unheard into the sky.

The man moved into the reverie and she saw that he was holding a revolver.

"I have other weapons," he said in his even tone.

For a moment she had difficulty determining whether it was the vision or reality. Then, slowly, she became aware of the dim light, the beige walls, the straps that held her, and she returned from the demimonde into the motel room.

"Pick up your hips," he said.

She did as she was told.

He put the gun down and as she held herself up, he pulled down the pants and panties that he had put on her, exposing her.

"A gun is an extremely cold thing," he said.

He placed the gun on her flat stomach. She could feel the weight and the chill of the metal. He let it remain there for a moment.

He picked up the gun. She watched him look at her, then at the weapon.

"If you wanted to destroy your identity, wouldn't you start by shooting yourself in the crotch?" he said.

He pointed the weapon between her legs.

"Oh, God, no!" she cried.

She heard the hammer click as he drew it back. She watched as he sighted down the barrel. She twisted on the bed wildly, fighting against the bonds as the man slowly took aim. She started to make small animal-like whimpers of protest, staring up at the black round hole of the revolver. It seemed to be gigantic, about to swallow her whole. She pulled hard one last time against the bond holding her, then slumped back in defeated acquiescence on the bed. She did not close her eyes; they remained fixed on the barrel of the gun. For a moment she thought she could envision the bullet coming out.

The man looked down at her, hesitated one moment, then pulled the trigger.

The hammer came down with a click.

"Empty," said the man. He pulled the trigger again. The gun clicked on another empty cylinder.

The breath fled suddenly from her body and she felt as if she had been pounded on the back. She gasped for air.

He watched her intently. Then he pulled from his pocket a

handful of live cartridges and slowly began feeding them into the pistol chamber.

She felt a wave of nausea overcome her.

"Please," she said, "I'm going to be sick . . ."

He moved swiftly to her head. The gun was tossed aside and she felt his hand beneath her neck, supporting her. He was holding a small plastic waste container. She gagged, but nothing came up. He put her head back slowly and quickly began to stroke her lips with the moist washcloth. She licked at the dampness and sobbed again.

"Pick up your hips."

Again she did as she was told.

He swiftly hiked the pants and underpants back up, fastening them deftly. He picked up the gun and showed it to her. "I am an expert at this, as well," he said. "But you knew that, didn't you?"

She nodded.

"In fact," he continued, "in modes and styles of death I am extremely well versed. Experienced. But again, I didn't have to tell you that for you to know it, did I?"

She shook her head.

"You are learning."

He looked down at her, pausing before continuing.

"You've read your Dostoyevsky, haven't you?"

She nodded. "Some . . ."

"Crime and Punishment? The Brothers? Notes?"

"Yes. And *The Idiot* as well."

"When?"

"Last year, in junior-year seminar."

"Good. Well, you remember what happened to the celebrated author before he was shipped off to the work camp in Siberia?"

She shook her head.

"He and the other condemned men were lined up against a wall before the Tsar's firing squad. Ready, yelled the captain, as the men stood trembling. Aim, he continued, as the men swiftly said their last prayers and stared out helplessly at their executioners. The captain's sword was raised, but before he could slice it down and yell the command to fire, a horseman thundered up, wildly waving a paper. It was the Tsar's pardon. Men fell to their knees in gratitude. Some babbled in instantaneous madness, their minds lost in that quick moment where they saw death. Several died anyway, their hearts too weak. And they were all shipped off to the camps. How did you survive in the camps?"

It took her a second to realize she'd been asked a question. Her mind fled back to the small room where she and nine other students had gathered to talk over the Russian's novels. In her memory she could see the sunshine reflecting off the flat green of the blackboard.

"By obedience," she replied.

"Good. Do you think the same is true here?"

She nodded.

He hesitated, looking carefully at her.

"Tell me, of all that has happened to you, what is the worst? What frightens you the most? What is giving you the greatest pain?"

He sat on the edge of the bed, waiting for her answer.

She was suffused with a wave of emotions and memories, thrown into despair by the question. She thought of the pistol he'd pointed at her crotch and fought against the bitter taste of bile in her mouth; of the electric savagery of the stun-gun; of the razor poised above her face; the drowning sensation that overcame her when he'd forced the towel down over her mouth and nose; or the arbitrary and capricious beatings he'd administered. Everything hurt, she screamed to herself. Everything terrifies me. And then she asked herself: Why does he want to know? Out of kindness—what kindness is that? She could not force herself to think carefully and rationally; the idea that she somehow held some power, some ability to affect the situation, dismayed her. And then she was swept with a new terror: Perhaps he wants to know because he will eliminate the others, leaving only the worst. Oh, God, she thought, how can I tell?

"Come on," he said with a small note of impatience. "What's the worst?"

She hesitated. Please, she prayed to herself.

"Well?"

"The razor." She started to cry. Tears flowed unchecked down her cheeks.

"The razor?" he replied. He stood up as she continued sobbing. He went out of her sight momentarily, then returned, holding the razor blade in his hand. "This razor?" he asked.

"Yes, yes, yes, please, God, please."

He held it closer to her face.

"This is what gets to you the most?"

"Please, please, please . . ."

He put the razor inches above her nose.

"Can't handle it, huh?"

She simply sobbed, her mind wasted with fear.

"Okay," he said simply.

She looked at him through the tears.

87

"Okay. I won't use the razor anymore." He paused. "Except to shave myself." He laughed. He looked at her and said, "You can smile. That was a joke."

She cried on. He said nothing as she sobbed minute after minute. Finally, when she started to regain some control over herself, he looked at her carefully and said, "Would you like to go to the bathroom?"

She was stunned again at the simplicity of the offer.

She nodded.

"All right," he said. He swiftly loosened her bonds. Before untying her wrists, however, he looked at her closely. "Do I need to explain the rules or do you think you already understand them?"

She was confused again. She did not know what he was talking about.

"No," he said. "I think you know how to behave. The bathroom is right there, around the corner. There is, of course, a small window, which will present you with a choice. To some, an open window might signify freedom. But let me assure you the opposite is true. There is only one way you will find freedom from me, and that is when I say you may have it. You should understand that by now. Still, the window is there. So the choice is yours."

He untied her wrists. She swung her legs to the side of the bed and tried to stand, but the blood rushed from her head and she was suddenly overcome with dizziness. She gripped hard on the bedstand, steadying herself.

"Take your time. Don't fall."

He had remained seated, not moving.

She stood slowly and felt the muscles throughout her body contract in pain. She took a small step, followed by another.

"Baby steps," he said. "Good."

She steadied herself against the wall with one hand, then the other. Using the wall as her guide, she stepped into the small corridor, then maneuvered into the bathroom. The light hurt her eyes and she shaded them. Her first thought was the mirror, and she forced her eyes open, the pain of it merely joining all the others that coursed through her body. She thrust her face up to the mirror and searched for wreckage. The lip is swollen, she thought, but that I expected. There was a bruise on her forehead which she could not recall receiving. Her jaw, too, was red and blemished from where he had hit her. But otherwise she was intact. She let out a sob of gratitude. Her hands shook as she ran water into the sink and splashed it on her face, washing some of the hurt away. She was suddenly aware of a huge thirst and she began to paw water into her mouth until she started to feel ill. She felt a wave of nausea, and she bent over the toilet and was violently sick. When she had finished, she reached back up and steadied herself on the sink. Again, she cleaned herself.

Then she looked up and saw the window.

It was open, as he had said it would be.

She allowed herself one brief fantasy of flight, then realized that he would be waiting on the other side. She knew this with absolute certainty. Still, she went to the window and placed her hand on it, as if hoping some of the slight cool in the summer night air would comfort her. She looked out at the blackness. He's there, she thought. She saw his shape moving, just on the periphery of her vision. She saw tree branches bend in the wind, but knew he was there, waiting. He would kill me, she thought, though the word kill did not form in her mind as much as a blackness of pain and hurt.

She suddenly thought: I'm taking too long! He'll be angry! She moved back swiftly to the sink, and, as quickly as she could, splashed another handful of water onto her face, then another into her mouth. Hurry! Just do what he wants!

She grabbed the wall again and staggered out into the motel room.

"I'm waiting," she heard him say.

She spun through the room to the bed. Without being bidden she slid back onto it, stretching her hands up to where he could bind them easily. She did the same with her legs, feeling the ropes tighten.

"Better now?" he asked.

She nodded.

"Do you want to sleep or would you like me to answer questions?"

She felt suddenly suffused with exhaustion, as if the trip to the bathroom had been some impossibly difficult peak to climb.

"Sleep, then," she heard him say.

She felt her eyes roll back.

He was sitting at the foot of the bed when she awoke. "How long was I . . ." she started to ask, but he interrupted her.

"Five minutes. Five hours. Five days. It makes no difference."

She nodded, thinking that he was right.

"Can I ask questions now?"

"Yes. This would be a good time."

"Are you going to kill me?" she asked. As soon as the words were out of her mouth, she regretted them.

"Not unless you make me," he replied. "You see, that hasn't changed. You still control your fate."

She did not believe that.

"Why are you doing these things to me? I don't understand."

"I have a job for you and I need to be certain that you will do it. I need to be confident in you. Comfortable, too."

"I'll do whatever you want. Just ask . . ."

"No," he said. "Thank you for your offer, but I need to know beyond your verbal assurance. You have to know the length of my reach. You need to know just how close you are to death."

He stood up and untied her hands from the bedstand, retying them together in front of her.

"I have to go out now. I will be back shortly. I don't have to remind you what is required of you."

He stepped away and started toward the door.

"Please," she said. "Don't leave me alone." She was surprised at the sound of her voice, and more surprised at the words that had blurted out.

"I'll be back shortly," he said. "You'll be fine."

She cried again as he went through the door. She saw a brief moment of darkness outdoors and she thought: It must still be night.

Alone in the room, she looked about her. Everything was as it had been earlier, but, with the man absent, it suddenly seemed more frightening to her. She shivered. She thought: This is crazy. He's the one doing these things to you. Then she grew more afraid, thinking, He didn't lock the door. Anyone could break in here and find me. She was suddenly scared that someone else would come in and rape her and it would be for nothing; it would anger the man, he would think of her as damaged goods and dispense with her like so much trash. She kept arguing inwardly, warring between two selves, one screaming at her for the wrongheadedness of her thoughts. He's the one! Get the gun! Kill him! Now's your chance!

But she remained rooted where she was.

Untie yourself! she heard herself say. Run!

Run where?

Where am I? Where can I go?

He'll kill me, she thought. He hasn't yet, but he will if I try to run. He's right outside the door, waiting. I won't make it ten feet.

No, run! Don't run!

She cried again to herself and tried to think of school, her family, her friends, her life. But they seemed terrifically distant, ephemeral. The only thing that is real, she thought, is this room.

She tried to comfort herself and found herself singing softly a memory from childhood: "Lavender's blue, dilly, dilly, lavender's green; When I am king, dilly, dilly, you shall be queen . . ." She remembered how she would sing the song to her younger brother and he would fall asleep. She felt tears welling up inside her. But he's dead, she thought. Oh, God, he died.

She put her head down on the pillow and waited for the man to return. She tried to make her mind a blank, but thoughts and fears kept intruding. She realized that she could no longer gauge time as it flowed around her, as if the man had somehow eliminated her ability to measure the moments that passed. Had he been gone an hour? Or five minutes? The silence around her was pervasive, the darkness, angry and threatening. She forced herself to listen for the noise of his returning, but she could pick no recognizable sound out of the blackness of the room. She raised her hands and covered her eyes, squeezing her eyelids tightly shut, thinking that she could at least retreat into her own darkness and perhaps find something solid there to hold on to. She tried again to think of something small, routine, and common, some item she owned that spoke of her existence, some memory that would remind her of her past and give her something concrete on which to struggle for her future. She thought of her parents back home in Colorado, but they seemed suddenly ghostlike. She forced herself to concentrate on her mother's face; in her mind's eye she built the features as one would paint a portrait. She fixed in her head the eyes, the mouth, the smile that should have been so familiar. Then she wondered whether the memory was all a dream, and she slowly opened her eyes.

She started suddenly, gasping.

The man was hovering over her.

"I didn't hear you come in," she said.

She saw his face set. He simply stared hard at her for a moment. "This is reality now," he said. Then he struck her with his open hand, hard. "Do you believe?"

"Yes, please," she replied.

He hit her again. She felt her body cloud with pain.

"Do you want to live?"

He hit her. She nodded furiously.

"I don't believe you," he said.

He hit her a third time.

"Yes, yes," she pleaded.

A fourth blow slapped her face.

91

Then a fifth, sixth, and seventh, in rapid succession, until the man was raining blows, using both hands, as if stoking the fire of her hysteria. She tried sobbing out "please" in the seconds between the blows, but finally, as his fists flew out of the darkness at her, she quit, raising her bound hands in supplication, letting her tears speak for her. He stopped only when he finally grew short of breath from exertion.

He sat on the side of the bed, resting as she cried quietly to herself. He spoke after a few seconds, his voice seeming distant, coming from someplace far on the other side of her pain and tears.

"You frustrate me," he said.

She felt his hands on her pants and suddenly he pulled them down, as he had before, exposing her.

"Are you listening to me?" he asked.

"Yes, yes," she said, opening her eyes and looking up at him. She saw he had the revolver in his hand.

"You're too much of a problem," he said, in his solid, matter-of-fact tone. "I had hopes for you. But I see you won't learn. So I'm just going to fuck you and kill you, which is what I should have done in the first place."

The words crashed through her agony and she rushed from her isolation to the moment. "Please, no, no, no, no, no, I'll do anything, give me a chance, just tell me what you want, what you need, I'll do anything, please, please, whatever you want, anything, please, no, no, no, please, please, give me a chance again, I won't be bad, I'll do what it is, anything, you just say it, please, I didn't realize, please anything, anything, anything . . ."

He stood by the bed, sighting down the pistol at her.

"Oh, God, please, please," she sobbed. She wanted to think of something different, to spend her last moment somewhere else, but all she could see was the terrifying barrel of the gun. She moaned as the seconds passed.

"Anything?" he finally asked.

"Oh, yes, yes, yes, please, anything . . ."

"All right," he said. "We'll see."

He stepped out of her sight for a moment, then returned. He was holding the electric stun-gun. He put it into her hand. "Hurt yourself," he said. He pointed to her crotch. "Right there."

It seemed to her then, suddenly, that all the pains she had endured to that point were insignificant. Her mind flooded with terror. She felt it choking her, as if, finally, all the things he'd done to her had fallen on her at once. But in the midst of this jumble of agony, she had one clear thought: Don't hesitate, she said to herself.

And she plunged the gun down against herself, trying in the same flashing instant to harden herself against the pain she knew was letting loose within her.

But there was none.

She looked up in confusion.

"Disconnected," he said.

He took the gun from her hand.

"A reprieve," he said. He laughed. "From the Tsar."

She started to cry for what seemed to her to be the millionth time in the past few minutes.

"There's hope for you."

He waited a second.

"I mean that literally."

He stepped back into the shadows and let her cry on unchecked.

Anne Hampton's first thought upon completing her tears was that something had changed. She was unsure precisely what it was, but she felt like some climber who had slipped on the glacier ice and spun wildly down into a crevasse until abruptly checked by a safety rope. She had the distinct sensation that she was spinning like a spent yo-yo on the end of a tether, aware that she was still in peril but safe for the moment. For the first time she allowed herself the thought that through compliance she might have a chance to live. She tried to picture herself, but could not. She remembered that she had had dreams and aspirations once, but she could no longer recall what they were. She allowed herself the recognition that she might be able to recollect them someday and in the same thought resolved to do whatever was required to remain alive. She looked up and saw the man staring at her face. He nodded as if signaling her that she was correct.

"We won't need these for a while, will we?" he said.

He undid the lines that had trapped her to the bed.

"Take off your clothes," he said.

She complied. She felt nothing as he searched up and down her body.

"Why don't you take a shower. You'll feel better," he said.

She nodded and started hesitantly toward the bathroom. When she reached the door, she turned back to look at the man, but he was sitting, absorbed, reading a road map in the dim light.

Hot water cascaded over her, and she thought of nothing save the sensation of soapsuds and warmth. She had not realized how cold she'd been. For the first time her mind seemed refreshed, empty, and at ease. She glanced at the open window, but only to see wan gray dawn light slowly slicing away the darkness.

She felt an odd sadness as she shut off the water, as if she had washed away something old and familiar. She dried quickly, wrapping one towel about her head in a turban, another around her midsection. She tried to hurry, but grew dizzy and had to grab the doorframe to steady herself. She saw the man look up. "Be careful," he said. "Don't slip. It'll be some time before you get all your strength back."

She sat down on the bed.

"It's almost morning," she said. "How long have I been here?"

"Forever," the man said. He stood and approached her. "Take this," he said. He held out a pill and a cup of water.

She started to ask what it was, then stopped herself. She swallowed the pill swiftly. He knew her thoughts.

"Just painkiller. Codeine, actually. It'll help you sleep."

"Thank you," she replied. She glanced over at the map. "When are we leaving?"

He smiled. "This evening. It is important that I get some rest as well."

"Of course," she said. She lay down on the bed.

He rummaged for a moment in the duffle bag that contained his weapons. He pulled out a pair of handcuffs. "These will be more comfortable than the ropes," he said. "Sit up." She complied. He cuffed one of her wrists, then fastened the other cuff to his own. "Lie down," he said. She rested her head back. He put himself next to her.

"Sweet dreams," he said.

Like spent lovers, they both reached out for sleep.

Anne Hampton awakened to the sound of the shower running. She realized quickly that she was handcuffed to the bedstand again. She curled up, as best she could, into the fetal position and waited. The towel she had wrapped around her midsection was gone and she was naked. For a moment she wondered whether the man would rape her when he came out, but the thought swiftly faded from her mind, replaced with a dull acquiescence.

She heard the shower stop and after a few moments the man emerged, drying himself. He was naked.

"I'm sorry," he said. "I had to take your towel. This is a cheap place; they're stingy with the linen."

She waited.

"No," he said, after pausing. "Time to get a move on."

She nodded.

"Good," he said.

She watched him pull on underwear, jeans, and a sweatshirt. She idly noted that he seemed extremely fit. He combed his hair swiftly, then sat on the edge of the bed and slipped on sweatsocks and running shoes. She waited for a command, as the man collected his things. She saw him thrust the stun-gun and the revolver into a small duffle bag. He pulled a small suitcase out from beneath the bed and she caught a glimpse of the seersucker jacket folded and put away.

"Back in a minute," he said. She watched him walk out the door. It was night. He returned in a moment. He carried a medium-sized red duffle bag that had several zippered compartments. "I'm sorry," he said briskly, "but I had to guess at colors and sizes. But I'm usually pretty good at this sort of thing." He uncuffed her completely and stood back, eyeing her.

The duffle was filled with clothes. There were khakis, jeans, a pair of shorts, a windbreaker, a sweater, and a sweatshirt. There were also two silk blouses, one a bright floral design, and a matching skirt. There was also a silk dress with a designer label. In one compartment there was a tangle of undergarments, in another, stockings and socks.

"Wear jeans," the man said. "Or the khakis if you prefer." He turned and handed her two shoe boxes. She did not see where he had been keeping them. There was a pair of dress sandals and a pair of running shoes. "Pack the dressy ones," he said.

He watched as she dressed.

"You're pretty," he said when she stood before him.

"Thank you," she replied. It seemed to her that it was someone else's voice that was speaking. She wondered for an odd moment who could have joined them, until realizing that it was herself.

He handed her a paper bag with the name of a pharmacy on it. She opened it and saw toothbrush, toothpaste, some makeup, a pair of sunglasses and a box of Tampax. She picked up the blue box and stared at it oddly. A disquieting fear moved through her slowly, triggered somehow by the box.

"I'm not having my . . ." She stopped.

"But you might, before we're finished," he said.

She wanted to cry then but realized she should not. Instead she bit her lip and nodded.

"Straighten yourself up and then we're going," he said.

She moved gingerly into the bathroom and started using the toiletries. First she brushed her teeth. Then she dabbed a bit of makeup on her face, trying to cover the bruises. He stood in the doorway, watching her.

"They'll fade in a day or so."

She said nothing.

"Ready?" he asked.

She nodded.

"First use the toilet. We're going to be on the road awhile."

She wondered where her modesty had disappeared. Again she had the sensation that it was someone else that was sitting on the toilet as the man watched, not herself. Some child, perhaps.

"Carry your own bag," he said.

She placed the toothbrush and other articles into one of the compartments. Then she hefted the bag up. It had a shoulder strap, which she placed over her arm. "I can carry something else," she said.

"Here. But be careful."

He handed her a battered photographer's bag and held the door open for her.

Anne Hampton stepped out into the night and felt the evening Florida warmth overtake her, crawling into her muscles and bones. She felt dizzy and hesitated. The man placed a hand on her shoulder and pointed her toward a dark-blue Chevrolet Camaro, parked in front of the small motel unit. She looked up for a moment and saw the sky filled with stars; she picked out the Big Dipper and the Little Dipper and then Orion. She felt a sudden warmth, as if she were somehow at the center of all the sky lights, her own brightness melding with theirs. She fastened on one star, one amidst the uncountable mass, suspended in the dark void of space, and thought to herself that she was that star and that it was her: alone, unconnected, hanging in the night.

"Come along," said the man. He had walked to the side of the car and was holding the door for her.

She stepped to his side.

"It's a beautiful night," she said.

"It's a beautiful night, Doug," he corrected her.

She looked at him quizzically.

"Say it."

"It's a beautiful night, Doug," she said.

"Good. Call me Doug."

"All right."

"It is my name. Douglas Jeffers."

"All right. All right, Doug. Douglas. Douglas."

He smiled. "I like that. Actually, I prefer Douglas to Doug, but you can use whichever you are comfortable with."

She must have looked odd, because he smiled and added, "It is my real name. It's important for you to realize that I will not tell you any lies. No falsehoods. Everything will be truth. Or what passes for it."

She nodded. She did not for one instant doubt him. She wondered idly why not, but then shook the thought loose from her imagination.

"There is one problem," Douglas Jeffers said. His voice had a sudden dark edge which frightened her.

"No, no, no, no problems," she said quickly.

He looked up at the sky. She thought he seemed to be thinking hard.

"I think you need a new name," he said. "I don't like your old one. It comes from before and you need something for now and from now on."

She nodded. She was surprised that she thought this a reasonable idea.

He motioned to the car and she sat in her seat.

"Seat belt," he said.

She complied.

"You're going to be a biographer," he said.

"A biographer?"

"That's right. You'll find steno pads and pens in the glove compartment. They're for you. Make sure you always have enough to get down what I say."

"I don't understand exactly," she said.

"I'll explain as we go along."

He looked down at her. Then he smiled.

"From now on you're Boswell," he said.

"Boswell?"

"Right." He smiled. "A little literary joke, if you will."

He closed her door, walked around the car, and climbed into the driver's seat. She watched him fasten his own belt and turn on the ignition. "Try your door handle," he said to her. She put her hand on the latch and pulled. The latch moved freely, but the door didn't open. "One of the nicer aspects of the design of the Chevrolet Camaro is that the door latches are remarkably easy to disconnect. So, whenever we stop, you wait for me to walk around and let you out. Got it?"

She nodded.

"I learned that in Cleveland, covering the trial of a football player who liked to pick up hookers, then expose himself. When they tried to get out, no go. That was what gave him the real kick."

Douglas Jeffers looked at her.

"You see, that's the sort of thing you need to get down."

He nodded toward the glove compartment.

She felt a momentary panic and reached out swiftly.

He stopped her. "It's okay. Just giving you an example."

He looked at her.

"Boswell, you see, takes down everything."

She nodded.

"Good," he said. "Boswell."

Then he put the car into drive and gently accelerated, slowly entering the darkness of the nighttime highway. She turned and looked back up at the stars. She thought suddenly of the childhood rhyme and spoke it to herself: Star light, star bright, first star I see tonight, I wish I may, I wish I might, have the wish I wish tonight.

To live, she thought.

CHAPTER
================================*FOUR*

A REGULAR SESSION OF THE LOST BOYS

7. OBSCENITIES crashed in the air around him, but he paid no attention. Instead, he pictured his brother sitting in the hospital cafeteria, grinning with an insouciance that he thought more properly belonged on an adolescent, but which on his brother's adult face had an oddly disquieting property. He tried to remember the regimen of his thoughts, but fixated only on the moment when he'd spoken in a foolishly heartfelt way, "You know, I wish we'd been closer, growing up . . ."

And his brother's cruel, cryptic, unfathomable reply:

"Oh, we are. We're closer than you think."

How close do I think? wondered Martin Jeffers.

To his right, two of the men's voices had steadily gained in volume, swiftly escalating in tone and content, reaching to the edge of rage. Jeffers turned and eyed the men, trying to assess the nature and quality of the dispute, wary, cautious, realizing that confrontation was an integral element of the therapy, but equally that these were violent men, and that he wanted no part of the savagery he believed them capable of inflicting on each other. He had the unusual thought that they were like some angry gaggle of old women, arguing less over some idea or real conflict than for the actual enjoyment of dispute. He decided to intercede.

"I don't think you're saying what you mean."

This was one of his usual comments. He knew that the men were frustrated by his oblique postures; for the most part, they were men of concrete ideas and sentiments. It was his desire to make them think, then feel, in the abstract. Once they could empathize, he thought, then they can be treated.

He remembered a professor in medical school standing before

an assembled class, saying, "Think of the experience of disease. Consider how it controls our senses, feelings, emotions. And then remember, no matter how capable a physician you think yourself, you're only as good as your last correct diagnosis." To which, a decade later, Martin Jeffers thought he would have added: And treatment, too.

Jeffers eyed the two men who were arguing.

"Fuck you, Jeffers," said the first, dismissing him with a half-hearted wave of the hand.

"Fuck yourself first," interceded the second. "And you'd better enjoy it, because you ain't gonna be fucking anything else for a real long time . . ."

"Look who's talking."

"That's right, you better look at who's talking, little man."

"Whoa. I'm shaking. Look at my hands. They're fucking shaking with terror."

Jeffers watched the two men carefully. He checked each for signs that the argument would prompt them from their seats. He was not terribly concerned about this particular argument: Bryan and Senderling went at it frequently. As long as they were trading insults, it was likely to remain verbal. Under different circumstances, Jeffers guessed, they would probably be considered friends. It was silence that worried him. Sometimes, Jeffers thought, they stop talking. It's not the silence of not knowing what to say, or being bored, or waiting for someone to say something. It was a silence forced by anger. Then it can be the eyes narrowing and fixing on the opposition that signals an attack, or sometimes just a subtle tensing of the muscles. Jeffers thought that he often spent his time looking for white knuckles on the fingers gripping the arm rests of the day-room chairs. There was once one man in the group, Jeffers remembered, who always sat on the front edge of a chair with his legs crossed in an X beneath him. When one morning the man unfolded his legs, Jeffers was already on his feet, moving to intercept the explosion that had arrived seconds later. Jeffers realized, as the months slid past, that he came to know each man in the group not only as a collection of memories and experiences, but with a recognizable physical posture as well. That there were twelve dossiers crammed with entries back in his office was to be expected; one did not qualify easily for the Lost Boys. It took two things: depravity and the misfortune to be caught engaged in it.

"Fuck you!"

"Fuck you right back!"

Obscenities were the currency of the group, scattered about

like so many coins of small denomination. He wondered idly how often he heard the word "fuck" each day. A hundred times? Surely more. A thousand, perhaps. The word no longer had any correlation with the sexual act for him. Instead it was used as punctuation for the group. Some men used "fucking" as others would use commas. He thought of the famous Lenny Bruce routine where the comedian started out by staring at the audience and querying, "I wonder how many niggers are here tonight," before moving on to spics, micks, kikes, wops, limeys, whatever, and ultimately by commonizing the insults so profoundly that they were rendered harmless and meaningless. Jeffers imagined that much the same process went on in the day room. The men used the word "fuck" with such frequency that it no longer carried any weight. It certainly had little to do with the crimes which they had pleaded guilty to, although each man was a sexual offender.

"Ahhh, the hell with you," said one of the men. It was Bryan. He turned to Jeffers. "Hey, doc, can't you straighten this dumb son of a bitch out? He still don't realize why he's here."

"Look, asshole," Senderling replied, "I know why we're here. I also know that we ain't going anyplace real quick. And when we do, it's gonna be over to the state pen to serve some real time."

Another man chimed in, first forming his mouth into a kiss, then smacking loudly enough to gain the room's attention. Jeffers looked and saw that it was Steele, who sat across the room and particularly liked to bait Bryan and Senderling. "And you know, sweethearts, how much guys like you are appreciated over there . . ."

The three men glared at each other, then turned to Jeffers. He realized that they expected some sort of response from him. He wished he'd been paying closer attention.

"You all know the arrangement here."

He was met with sullen silence.

The first lesson of psychiatric residency, he thought. When in doubt, say nothing.

So a benign silence filled the room. Jeffers tried to meet each man's eyes; some glared back at him, others turned away. Some seemed bored, distracted, minds elsewhere, some were poised, anticipating, eager. Jeffers momentarily considered the mystery of the group dynamic: there were twelve members of the Lost Boys, each man unique in the mode of his offense, typical in the nature of it. Jeffers was struck with the thought that the men all suffered from the same thing: once upon a time, in each man's childhood, they had been lost. Abandoned, perhaps, was a better

101

term. The rocky shoals of childhood, he thought. The darkness and cruelty of youth. Most people rise and grow and leave it behind, carrying their scars internally, forever, learning to adjust. The Lost Boys did not.

And the punishment they had wreaked upon the adult world was sorry indeed.

Twelve men. Probably close to a hundred reported crimes shared among them. Easily twice that number hidden, unreported, unsolved, unattributed, ranging from vandalism and petty theft to a rape, or two or a half-dozen, a dozen, a score or more. There were three killers in the Lost Boys as well—men who in the peculiar weighting system of the criminal justice system had managed to take lives that somehow were less valuable and therefore required less punishment, though Jeffers was hard pressed, sometimes, to understand the distinctions between a manslaughter and a first-degree murder, especially when viewed from the corpse's point of view.

The silence in the day room persisted and Jeffers thought again of his brother. It had been so typical of Doug, Jeffers thought. Call one instant, show up the next. Three years between visits, months between even casual telephone conversation, acting as if nothing were out of the ordinary. Drop his apartment key off with the usual impenetrable instructions. Typical.

What was he doing? Jeffers wondered. He returned to the meeting in his mind. But first he thought: What was typical of Doug? and felt a mild uneasiness at his lack of a ready answer.

He pictured his brother sitting across from him, sunlight caught in his shock of sandy hair. Doug, he thought, has this loose, flush, good-looking appearance, easygoing, relaxed, the kind of good looks that stemmed not from any striking physical feature but from a devil-may-care approach to life. For a moment he envied his brother the blue-jeans-and-running-shoes informality that accompanied the job of the professional photographer, resenting, momentarily, the quiet formality of his own profession. I am stiff, he thought. He envied his brother's out-of-doors life, surrounded by things that were actually happening instead of merely being talked about. Sometimes I cannot stand the constancy of small rooms and closed doors, suggestive comments and observations, and quiet, meaningful looks that make up my profession, he thought.

Then he shook his head, inwardly, and said to himself: Of course you can stand it. Not only that, you love it.

For a moment, though, he wondered idly what it was like to see life through a lens.

"Oh, we're closer than you think. Much closer."

Is it that different? he thought suddenly. Surely. He sees with an immediacy defined by the event, the moment. I hear the story told long after the fact.

He was dismayed by the quick realization that he could not remember his brother's first camera. It seemed that Doug had always had one, from grade school on. He wondered where and how Doug had acquired the first; surely not from their parents.

The only thing they gave out in substance was misery, Martin Jeffers thought.

The two brothers had never disagreed about that.

He suddenly remembered the night they'd been taken in, and wondered instantly why it had been so long since he had thought of it. He thought of the wild rain that had been driving against the police station windows rattling in the summer storm's wind. Night had surrounded the building, but the hard wooden bench that he'd sat upon, gripping tightly to his brother's hand, had been awash in artificial light. It had been late at night and they had been very young; not filled with Christmas Eve excitement over staying up late, but filled instead with a complete dread, aware somehow that they had been caught in some adult mystery that had taken place when their own little boys' eyes properly should have been closed and their minds captured by sleep; seeing something not meant for them to see at an hour not meant for them to be awake. His stomach tightened at the memory of looking up through the light at his first view of his cousin, face set, rigid and unwelcoming, remembering his first words: "Your mom's gone, which is as we expected for some time. You're to be with us now. Follow me." And the sight of that small, bent back, turning and leading them out into the storm. I was four, he thought, and Doug was six.

He tried to shake the memory loose, wondering why it was that they'd never talked about their real mother. He stared out the day-room window and tried to recall the features of her face, but could not. He remembered only that she'd lacked tenderness and seemed forever angry. She'd not been that much different from the cousin who'd become their mother. He saw her easily, wispy brown hair pulled back in a severe bun, contradicting wide lips covered in bright lipstick that never creaked into a smile. In the car, in the rain, the wipers making a dirgelike drumming sound, this new woman-mother had turned to them and said, "We're your parents now. I'm mom. He's dad. There won't be no talk about any other."

He remembered his own therapist asking once, "But what did happen to your real mother?"

And of his reply: "But I never really learned."

The therapist had been silent. A classic doubting silence; he'd used it himself a thousand times.

What did happen? he asked himself.

It was simple: She was gone. Dead. Run away. What difference did it make? They both had to work in their parents' drugstore. He had to clean the medicine bottles and keep the stacks of prescription drugs arranged neatly on the shelves, and he'd become a doctor. Doug's job had been to sweep out the darkroom and then mix the chemicals for the film-developing service and finally to do the developing himself, when he got older, so he became a photographer. It was simple.

We turned out fine, he said to himself.

But what did we become?

Nothing is simple.

He knew that. It was the first thing he'd learned in his residency. Things of the mind may seem clear-cut and direct, but they rarely stayed that way. If the formulations of psychiatry made sense—the theories and diagnoses and treatment plans— the realities of behavior always seemed to him strangely inexplicable. He understood why the Lost Boys were sex offenders, in a clear-cut clinical way, but he felt defeated by some greater why that eluded him. He could picture the physical strength it took to seize a victim by the arm and force her, but could not imagine the power of will that it also took.

He shook his head.

Doug understands realities, he thought. I understand theories.

He thought of his own life. I survived, he thought. Hell, we both did. We've done well. Damn well. Then he considered how extraordinary it is that one can acquire all the education and experience of human frailties and suffering and fail to be able to apply any of the knowledge to oneself.

He laughed at himself. You're a liar, he thought.

And not a good one.

He wondered why it was that his brother's visit stirred so many memories, then thought how silly a question that was; of course his brother's visit would prompt introspection.

He felt hot and realized that sunlight was slipping through the window and hitting his chest. He shifted in his chair, unsatisfactorily, then moved his chair slightly.

"You know what I hate the most," said one of the Lost Boys. "It's being treated like we're some kind of freaks in a sideshow, huh."

Jeffers looked up to see who was talking. His eyes caught a

glimpse of Simon, the hospital orderly assigned to keeping order among the Lost Boys. Simon seemed to be dozing in the sunlight, unaffected by the conversation. He was an immense black man whose build was well concealed by the loose-fitting white smock the orderlies wore. Jeffers knew, too, that he possessed a black belt in karate and had fought professionally as a kick-boxer. Simon's presence was the ultimate deterrent to violence.

"Freaks, freaks, freaks, that's what we are."

It was Meriwether speaking. This was one of the small man's favorite topics. Meriwether was a slight, sallow, middle-aged man who had owned a meager accounting business and who had pleaded guilty to the rape of a neighbor's daughter. It was only after entering the Lost Boys that Jeffers uncovered a compulsive affection for youth in the man. Meriwether was on the doubtful list: Jeffers doubted that the crime he was condemned for was his sole one, and he doubted that the program could do anything for him. Someday, Jeffers thought, he will cruise down some street and pick up some teenage boy who is more than he can handle and will get his throat cut for the pocket change. Jeffers refused to be ashamed by his unscientific guesswork.

"I can't stand the way they look at us," Meriwether said.

"At you," said Miller, sitting across the circle. Miller was a bona fide criminal in addition to being a rapist. He had twice killed men in barroom brawls, three times served prison terms for assault, robbery, and extortion. Jeffers particularly liked him for his straightforward approach to the therapy sessions. Miller hated them. He was, however, not on the doubtful list; Jeffers thought it possible that the man could learn not to be a rapist. What would remain, however, was a regular full-time criminal.

"You see, little man, they can sense something about you. Something slimy just beneath the surface. We all can, little man. We all can. Makes you think, don't it?"

Meriwether didn't hesitate: "Well, maybe they can sense something about me, but all they got to do is take one look at your face and they know, you know what I mean? They *know*."

Miller growled, then laughed. Jeffers appreciated the fact that Miller was unbaitable, although he wondered what force of restraint the man would have with a drink in him.

The other men sitting in the loose day-room circle laughed or smiled as well. Wright; Weingarten; Bloom, who seemed to prefer boys; Wasserman, who was the youngest at nineteen and had raped a prom queen who refused him a dance; Pope, at forty-two, the oldest, intractable, malevolent, gray-haired, with trucker's muscles and tattoos. Jeffers believed that he had committed far more crimes than the police suspected. He remained silent, mostly, leading the doubtful list. Parker and Knight completed the Lost Boys. They were a matched pair, acned, angry, in their mid-twenties, both college dropouts. One had been a computer programmer and the other a part-time social worker. They sneered at much, but, Jeffers thought, would eventually come to realize that they had a chance at a life.

The laughter faded and Meriwether jumped into the quiet.

"I still don't like it."

"Like what, little man?"

"We're not crazy. What are we doing here?"

Several voices jumped in quickly:

"We're here to get fixed . . ."

"We're here for the program . . ."

"We're here, you dumb fuck, because we were all sentenced under the state's sex-offenders act. That clear enough for you, slime?"

"Man, maybe you don't know what you're doing here, but I sure do . . ."

The last comment gained laughter. It subsided after a moment and Jeffers watched Meriwether wait until he had clear silence.

"You guys are stupider than I thought . . ." he started. There were hoots and meager catcalls. Again Meriwether waited. Jeffers noted the wry grin that the little man wore, clearly enjoying the center of the group's attention.

"Think about it for a minute, freaks. Here we are in a loony bin, but are any of us really crazy? If we were really criminals, don't you think they'd just lock us up? Instead they got us here in this carrot-and-stick world. Do the program, they say, learn to love right. Learn to hate what you were. Then we'll straighten you out and head back to the world . . ."

He paused, watching for effect.

"You know what gets to me? Everytime I walk through one of the psych wards everyone steps out the way. For me! It's enough to make you laugh, isn't it, Miller, you tough guy? But they know, don't they? They know."

He laughed.

"All of us here, inside, huh, way inside where we figure the skrink can't see, figures we're gonna beat this. We just hang on long enough and say the right things . . . well, we're gonna walk. They aren't going to be able to change me!"

He turned to Jeffers.

"Screw your aversion therapies. Screw your peer-group pressures. I'm smarter than all that."

"Is that what you think?" Jeffers replied.

Meriwether laughed.

"What a wishywashy question. Can't you see it's what all of us think deep inside . . ."

He thought. "Way inside. Way, way inside. Where you can't touch it."

Miller growled. "Speak for yourself, asshole."

"I do," said Meriwether.

The two men stared at each other and Jeffers thought again of his brother. He remembered how surprised he had been when he learned that Doug routinely robbed the drugstore's register for pocket money. He had thought that wrong, he realized, not because it was wrong to steal but because the consequences would be so severe if discovered. He recalled his brother's easy laughter and insistence that the money was only partially the reason.

"Don't you understand, Marty? Every time I take something I feel like I'm getting back at him. His precious money. A little here, a little there. It makes me feel like I'm not just a victim."

Doug had been thirteen. And he had been wrong. We were his victims.

He beat Doug, Jeffers thought. Why not me? He supposed it was his brother's insistent, obvious rebelliousness. Then he shook his head, thinking that was probably only partially true. Certainly Doug had been irrepressible, but there was something else, something further that their father had seen, which had catapulted him into red-faced anger and savagery.

"Little man," said Miller, "you piss me off."

"The truth," replied Meriwether, "always hurts."

"Tell me what you think is the truth," Miller said. "You know so much, you squirrelly little numbers runner, you tell me what you know about my life!"

Meriwether laughed.

"Let me think," he said. He eyed Miller like an appraiser looking over a cracked piece of goods.

"Well," he started slowly, aware that he had the entire group's attention, "you probably hated your mother . . ."

Everyone laughed except Miller.

"She loved everyone except you . . ."

Meriwether smiled at his audience and continued.

"And now, unable to punish her . . ."

The room laughed at the truism.

"You punish others."

Meriwether hesitated. Then, smiling to the audience, said, "Tah-dah! Basic truths illuminated!"

Miller did not smile. Jeffers found himself again trying to picture his own mother's face, but unable. When he spoke the word "mother" to himself, all he pictured was the druggist's wife, their cousin-mother, who would sit in the afternoons in a corner of the house, fanning herself, drinking tea, regardless of whether it was summer or winter.

"Keep going, hot shit. You're in a world of trouble already, might as well shoot the moon," Miller said.

Jeffers wondered briefly whether Miller would explode, then doubted it. He was too con-wise. If he feels he needs revenge, he'll take it at his convenience. He'll wait and bide his time; all cons knew that what they had in abundance was time, and the savoring of revenge could be as much enjoyment as the home-made shiv firmly wedged between the ribs itself. Jeffers scribbled a note on the daily session log to watch out for conflict between the two men.

"Well," said Meriwether, "how old was that last chick? The one you beat up and robbed in addition to, how shall we put it? Delicately, of course, ah, enjoyed. . . . Could she have been twenty? No, perhaps more. Thirty, then? No, still a mite shy. Well, forty? Lord, no, not close . . . fifty? Sixty? How about seventy-three years old? Bingo!"

Meriwether closed his eyes and sat back in his chair.

"Old enough, I daresay, to be your mother."

He was quiet before turning to Jeffers.

"You know, doc, you ought to pay me for doing all your work here."

Jeffers said nothing.

"So," Meriwether continued, "tell us, tough guy. How was it?"

Miller's eyes had narrowed. He waited until there was quiet.

"You know, mouth. It was perfect. It always is."

Miller paused.

"Right, freak?"

Meriwether nodded. "Right."

Jeffers stared around the room, halfheartedly hoping that a voice would be raised in opposition, but doubting he would hear one. He had come to realize that there were certain qualities the group could not frustrate, one being the idea of pleasure. He made a note for follow-up in each man's regular individual session. The group, he thought, only serves to reinforce the ideas imparted through the daily therapeutic sessions. Sometimes—he smiled to himself—the magic works. Sometimes it doesn't.

"Miller," Jeffers said, "are you telling the group that you con-

sidered the beating rape of a seventy-three-year-old woman a satisfactory sexual experience?"

He would not be so blunt with some of the others, he thought.

Miller shook his head.

"No, doc. Not when you put it like that," he sneered. "A
satisfactory sexual experience, whatever the hell that is. What I
was saying is—and freak there knows what I'm saying, don't
you, maggot?—is that she was there. I was there. It was just part
of the whole scene—nothing special."

"Don't you think it was something special to her?"

Miller tried to make a joke.

"Well, maybe she'd never had it so good . . ."

There was a smattering of laughter, which faded swiftly.

"Come on, Miller. You savaged an old woman. What kind of
person does that?"

Miller glared across the room at Jeffers.

"You're not listening, doc. I keep telling you, she was there.
It was no big deal."

"That's the problem. It was."

"Well, not to me."

"So if it wasn't such a big deal, what were you thinking of
when you did it?"

"Thinking of?" Miller hesitated. "Hell, I don't know. I was
worried she might be able to make me, you know, so I made sure
I crushed her glasses, and I was trying to be careful, didn't want
to wake the neighbors . . ."

"Come on, Mr. Miller. You left fingerprints all over the prem-
ises and you got caught trying to fence the old woman's jewelry.
What were you thinking about?"

"Hell, I don't know."

He crossed his arms and stared dead ahead.

"Give it another try."

"Look, doc, all I remember is being angry. You know, just
flat-out pissed off. It seemed like nothing had been going any
way except wrong. So I was definitely in a bad mood. And all I
remember really is being pissed off. So pissed off I wanted to
scream. I wanted to hurt somebody, you know? That's all, just
make someone else hurt. I wanted that real bad. I'm sorry the old
gal got in the way. But she was there, and that's what I wanted.
Got it? That do you okay?"

Jeffers leaned back. He thought to himself: I'm pretty good at
this for a newcomer.

"All right," he said. "Let's talk about anger. Anyone?"

There was a small silence before Wasserman, who stuttered, said, "S-s-sometimes I think I'm always angry."

Jeffers leaned back in his chair when he heard one of the men reply. "Angry at what?" There were only a few minutes left in the session and he knew that the group dynamic would take over; anger was always a fruitful subject. All the Lost Boys were angry. It was something they were intimate with.

He looked about the day room. It was an open, airy place, painted white, with a bank of windows that overlooked the exercise area. The furniture was old and threadbare, but that was to be expected in a state facility. There was a Ping-Pong table folded up against one wall, rarely used. Once there had been a pool table, but a pool cue in the hands of a psychotic patient one day had put two orderlies in the infirmary, so now there was none. There were magazines that flapped when a breeze found an open window, a television set that seemed possessed only to play soap operas and old movies. There was an out-of-tune upright piano. Periodically someone would step up to it and play a few notes as if hoping through some process of osmosis that it had come into tune. The piano is like the patients, Jeffers thought. We keep pushing at the keys, hoping to find a melody, usually discovering dissonance. Jeffers liked the room; it had a quiet, benign character, and it seemed to him sometimes that the room itself had defused trouble. It would be an incongruous place for a fight.

He could not remember a time he'd ever fought with his brother.

That was unusual: All brothers fight, why would we have been any different? But he was still unable to come up with a single memory of flat-out murderous brother-rage, the kind that suffuses one's entire being one instant then evaporates the next.

He remembered a time when Doug had pinned him to the floor, easily, arms twisted back; but that had been to prevent him from chasing after their mother, who was transporting their report cards to the druggist. He had failed a course for the first time—French—and had been ashamed. He remembered his brother's grip, which he could not break. Doug said nothing, just held him. He had not been certain what he was going to do: seize the report card, destroy it, he did not know. He simply knew that the druggist would be outraged, which he was. Locked for a week in my room each night. But next semester I got a B and the final semester it was an A.

"Hey, Pope!" It was Meriwether speaking. "Come on, Pope, you're a killer, Pope. Tell us how angry you've got to be to kill someone."

Jeffers waited, as did all the men in the room. This is a good question, he thought, perhaps not strictly from a therapeutic standpoint, but from curiosity.

Pope snorted. He had narrow black eyes and shoulders that were outsized for his small frame. Jeffers imagined him to be immensely powerful.

"I never killed nobody I was real angry with."

Meriwether laughed. "Awwww, come on, Pope. You killed that guy in the bar. You told us about it the other week. A fight, remember?"

"That's not anger. That was just a fight."

"He died."

"That happens. A lucky punch."

"You mean unlucky."

Pope shrugged. "I guess from his position."

"You mean you fought him and he died and you weren't even mad at him?"

"You don't understand so good, do you, wise guy? Sure, the dude and I had a fight. We'd been drinking. One thing came to another and he shouldn'a called me a name. But this ain't anything special. This happens in every bar every night. But I never been so angry at some man that I sat around sober and figured out a way to do him. You'd think you could guess at that."

This made sense to the group and they were quiet.

"I was that angry once," said Weingarten. He'd been silent most of the session, Jeffers noted. He was a greasy-haired exhibitionist who'd gotten carried away with his display in a shopping mall and actually grabbed a young woman. She'd fought loose, easily picked him out of a lineup the next day, and he'd landed in the Lost Boys. Jeffers doubted the program would have much success with him; he had just begun to escalate his deviant behavior. He probably remains too fascinated with his new vision to cut it out so early. The Lost Boys do not suffer from ordinary diseases. He had a sudden memory of the emphasis in medical school on catching disease early, before it progressed. Not so here, he thought. Here you had to catch the disease after it had formed and manifested itself fully. Then you tried to eradicate it. It was generally a losing proposition, he realized ruefully, despite the inflated rates of success that were created to ensure continued funding of the program.

"I mean I wanted to kill him and everything."

"What did you do?" Jeffers asked.

"In high school there was this one guy who was always all over my case. You know the type of guy that walks up to you in

111

front of everyone else and punches you real hard on the arm just to make you look bad. 'Cause he knows you can't hit him back? You know what I mean? A real jock. A real head case . . ."

"Look who's talking," said Meriwether.

Weingarten ignored him and continued.

"I was gonna just kill him, at first. My dad had a hunting rifle, he liked to go deer hunting, which I thought was real gross, but he never bothered to take me anyway. It had a real nice scope on it and I had the guy, one time, right in the crosshatches. Shoulda done it, too. But then I got smart and figured I'd just get him back kinda like he'd been getting me, right? Good and public, too. So I waited, figuring I'd get him back just before the big homecoming game. I'd get him suspended, you see, it was gonna be simple. The coach had a curfew and I knew this creep was always making it with this cheerleader. I just followed them out to the place where all the kids liked to park and waited. Wasn't too long before they was going at it. I watched for a bit, then snuck up and bam! Ice pick nice and easy in each tire. I knew they'd never get home in time. Bingo! He'd get suspended. The girl was the coach's daughter, you see. Foolproof."

"So what happened?"

"They didn't get in till four in the morning."

"Did the coach suspend the creep?"

Weingarten hesitated.

"He was the fucking fullback. All-county. Had a scholarship to Notre-fucking-Dame. It was the fucking homecoming game. What do you think?"

The Lost Boys all laughed and Jeffers joined in.

Weingarten laughed as well. "It was a good idea," he said. "At least the creep tore up his knee in the second quarter and kissed his scholarship goodbye."

"Whatever happened to him?" one of the other men asked.

Weingarten smiled. "Man, he was such a creep. He had to become a cop."

Laughter from the Lost Boys filled the day room.

His brother, Jeffers thought, could have been a terrific athlete. When he did play, it always seemed as if the ball would follow him. He was quick and coordinated and he had that odd strength, not muscle-bound at all, but stronger than the others. Doug always had that extra ability too, to be able to run all day if need be. He had unbelievable stamina. It came from anger. The more their parents encouraged athletics, the less Doug would have to do with them. It was another of his mini-rebellions. He remembered sitting in their room one night, lights out, listening to his brother talk about hatred. It had surprised him to know how deeply his brother felt: "I won't do anything for them," he had said. "Nothing. Nothing that makes them feel good at all. Nothing."

Now, Jeffers thought, he would say that such an attitude reflected a fundamental self-hatred. But his childhood memory was more powerful. All he recalled was the force of his brother's words in the dark room. He could not see his brother's face, but remembered instead the nighttime view through the window in their room, across the yard and out to the street, moonlight filtering through the trees. It was a modest house in a modest suburb that quietly contained all the anger within.

"The only person I was ever pissed off enough to want to kill was, man, my old lady." Jeffers looked up and saw Steele talking. "She complained, man, day and night. Morning, noon, afternoon. Hell, sometimes I thought she was complaining in her sleep . . ."

The others laughed. Jeffers saw heads nod.

"You know, it made no difference where we were or what we were doing. She just made me feel, uh, little, you know? Small."

There was quiet before Steele continued. Jeffers had a brief flash of the man's dossier. He had preyed on his own neighborhood, leaving his job as a plumber on lunch hours and finding housewives alone.

The room was silent.

"I suppose," Steele said, "if I could have figured out a way of getting back at her, I wouldn't be here."

Jeffers made a notation, thinking: But you did.

He glanced down at his watch. The session was almost over. He wondered for a moment why his brother refused to join him for dinner or overnight or any extended visit at all.

"It's a sentimental journey . . ."

What had he meant? He felt a rush of anger himself. Doug was capable of blistering directness one instant and unfathomable obtuseness the next. He felt a sudden empty feeling inside, wondering: How well do I know my brother? Then adding, as if by rote: How well do I know myself? He had a quick picture of the rest of his day: rounds. Several individual therapy sessions. Dinner alone in his apartment. A ball game on television, a chapter in a book, and bed. More of the same in the morning. A routine is a kind of protection, he thought. He wondered what his brother found to protect himself. And from what? That gets an easy answer, he thought. He looked around the room.

We protect ourselves only from ourselves.

"I follow on the heels of evil . . ." He smiled. That was Doug. A certain dramatic flair. For an instant he felt a complete jealousy. Then he let it pass, thinking: Well, we are who we are, and then felt embarrassed. Not much insight there, he said to himself. He wondered again: How close are we?

To his right, Simon the orderly stirred. He stretched and got to his feet.

He heard the men start to shuffle in their chairs and he thought of a grade-school classroom in the few moments before the recess bell rings.

"All right," Martin Jeffers said. "Enough for today."

He stood up and thought: Closer than you think.

Martin Jeffers watched the men as they rose and wandered out of the day room singly or in pairs. He heard an occasional laugh echoing down the outside corridor. When he was left alone, he gathered his notes and papers together, made a few entries in his daily log, and walked through the day room, feeling the warmth of the sunshine as it hit his back. The room was silent and he thought the session had been a success: no fights, no irreconcilable arguments, though Miller and Meriwether would bear watching. There had been a little progess, he thought. Perhaps Weingarten's story was something that could be followed up on. He resolved to bring up jealousy at the next session and shut the day-room door behind him.

The hospital corridor was empty and he moved swiftly past the entrance to one of the wards. He glanced in the window of the door and saw the same lethargic picture that he'd seen every day. A few people standing around talking, others talking to themselves. Some read, some played chess or checkers. So much of the time in a mental hospital is spent simply getting from one day to the next. The patients become expert at the practice of elongating time: meals were interminable. Activities were stretched. Time was wasted deliberately, passionately. It was not that unreasonable, he thought, for people to whom time had lost all urgency.

When he arrived at his office he discovered a note taped to the door: CALL DR. HARRISON'S OFFICE ASAP. Dr. Harrison was the hospital's administrator. Jeffers looked at the note, wondering what it was about. He unlocked his door and set his papers down. For a moment he stared about himself at the tired steel bookshelf sagging with papers, files, and textbooks. There was a calendar on the wall with pictorial scenes from Vermont. He had a sudden pleasurable memory: That was fun there, he thought. Fishing, camping. He remembered a trout that Doug had caught and thrown back, only to hear their father laugh. "It'll die," the drug-gist said. "Once you touch them, you wipe some of the fish slime off their bodies and they get cold and die. Can't throw a trout back, no sir." And then their father had continued laughing, pointing at his brother. Martin Jeffers wondered for a moment whether it was true. He had never checked. He felt an odd em-barrassment as he thought how he had gone through life believ-ing, from that moment on, that you couldn't throw a trout back into the water without killing it simultaneously. Doctor Harrison is a fisherman, he thought. Dammit, I'll ask him.

He picked up the telephone and dialed the administrator's ex-tension. The secretary picked up the phone.

"Hello, Martha. Marty Jeffers here. I got your note. What's on the chief's mind?"

"Oh, Doctor Jeffers," the secretary said. "I don't know ex-actly, but there's a detective here. All the way from Florida. Miami, she says, and she wants to talk to you . . ."

The secretary hesitated and Jeffers pictured palm trees and beaches. "I've never been to Miami," he said. "Always wanted to go."

"Oh, doctor," the secretary continued. "She says it's a murder investigation."

Jeffers wondered for a moment whether the trout knew, after it had been touched, that it was doomed to die; whether it swam off, searching out some lonely eddy behind a cluster of rocks to shiver itself to death, cruelly confused and betrayed by its own environment.

"I'll be right there," he said.

CHAPTER
FIVE

A SINGULAR PURSUIT

8. THE words echoed within her: *trace alcohol*.

At first she wondered whether her cheeks had been scarred by her tears in the same way that she felt her heart had been ripped and torn by her unchecked grief. She looked up at herself in the mirror, half-expecting to see permanent red welts on her skin, marking the paths her misery had flowed. There were none. She rubbed her eyes hard and felt a vast exhaustion enter her body, fatigue pushing aside and storming the barriers of resolve and perseverance and taking over inside her. She breathed out slowly, battling lightheadedness and residual nausea.

Detective Mercedes Barren wanted desperately to organize her thoughts, but was defeated by emotion. She gripped the edges of the sink and held tight for an instant, trying to clear her mind of everything, as though by creating a blank slate she could control what she thought and felt. She took a deep breath, and, moving with exaggerated deliberateness, turned on the faucets. She felt flushed and overheated so she ran cold water over her wrists, remembering it was her husband who had told her that this would cool her down quickly—an athlete's trick. Then she splashed water on her face and looked up again into the mirror, staring at her reflection.

I am old, thought Detective Barren.

I am thin, brittle, and tired and I am unhappy and there are creases in my skin, on my forehead, and in the corners next to my eyes that were not there not so long ago. She looked at her hands, counting the veins on the backs. An old woman's hands, she thought.

Detective Barren turned away from the mirror and walked

back into the living room of her small apartment. She glanced momentarily at the stacks of reports and file folders stuffed with statements, analyses of evidence, photographs, transcripts, psychological reports, and lists of items seized that formed into the paper substance of a criminal investigation. It was all piled haphazardly on her small desk. She walked to it and began idly to sort and arrange the documents, trying to impress reason on the mass of material. Susan's legacy, she thought, and again she bit back tears.

She wondered how long she had cried.

She went to the window and looked out at the pale-blue morning sky. It was cloudless and oppressively bright. It seemed to her that the air was filled with the reflection of the sun exploding off the expanse of blue sea so close to the city. It was a day without darkness, without even a taste of disorder, and this angered her. She put her hand against the glass of the window and felt the tropical heat. For an instant she wanted to draw back her fist and thrust it through the window. She wanted to hear the glass shatter and fall. She wanted to feel physical pain. She stopped herself when she became aware that her hand had balled itself into a fist, turned away from the window, and surveyed her apartment.

"Well," she said to herself out loud, "that's it, then."

She felt as though something had finished and something different was beginning, but she was not certain precisely what. She rubbed a tear away from her eye and took a deep breath, then another. There was a picture of her niece in a simple silver frame on top of the bookcase, and she walked slowly over to the picture and looked at it. "Well," she said again. "I guess it's time to start over." She put the picture down and felt a rush of sadness slip through her body, like a cool wind in the last few seconds before a hard rain. "I'm sorry," she said to herself. "I'm so very, very sorry." But she was unsure to whom she was apologizing.

The woman officer behind the reception desk at the Dade County Sheriff's Office was abrupt:

"Do you have an appointment?"

"No. I don't believe I need one . . ." replied Detective Barren.

"I'm sorry, I can't let you up to homicide unless there's someone expecting you. Who is it you want to see?"

Detective Barren sighed loudly, irritatedly, swiftly fishing her own gold shield out of her purse.

"I want to see Detective Perry. Right now. Pick up your phone, officer, and call his office. Right now."

The woman held out her hand for the badge. Detective Barren

handed it over and the woman carefully noted the shield number on a form. She handed the badge back and, without meeting Detective Barren's eyes, dialed the number for homicide. After a moment she spoke:

"Detective Perry, please."

There was a momentary pause.

"Detective Perry? There's a Detective Barren from City here to see you."

Another pause.

The woman officer hung up.

"Third floor," she said.

"I know," said Detective Barren.

The elevator ride seemed to take much longer than she remembered. She suddenly wished that there were a mirror available; she wanted to check her makeup, to make certain that all the outward signs of grief were properly concealed. She straightened herself self-consciously. She had selected her clothing that morning with far more care than usual, knowing that appearances were important when connected to what she was going to say. She had ruled out her dark blue and gray courtroom suits in favor of a simple, light-colored cotton blazer and khaki skirt. She wanted to seem loose, easy, and relaxed—informal. The jacket was cut stylishly large. Once upon a time, she had thought as she slipped it on, it would have been called baggy. Now it was oversize. But it was an excellent design to hide the shoulder harress which held her 9 millimeter. It was not her usual choice of weapons. Ordinarily she simply stuffed a short-barreled .38-caliber revolver into her handbag and forgot about it for the remainder of the day. But she had felt a wild sense of insecurity after she had dressed, had looked up suddenly at a sound outside her door, feeling the small hairs on the back of her neck stand. She had discovered herself strapping on the large automatic pistol without even thinking, and now she could feel its weight and bulk and she welcomed it.

The elevator doors rolled open with a swooshing sound.

"Hey, Merce! Over here!"

She turned and saw Detective Perry waving to her from a corridor. She walked toward him quickly. He was holding out his hand and she shook it. He gave her a little wave as well and started walking toward his desk.

"Come on—you want coffee? So how're you doing?" he asked, but, hardly pausing for an answer, he launched ahead. "You know, I was just thinking about you the other day. We had a rape-murder, the kid out in South Miami, right along the canal, you probably saw it in the papers, and all I could think of was that boxer you busted. Intuition won't get you a search warrant, isn't that how you put it? Anyway, I had this feeling, you see, that the killer wasn't really a murderer, right? I mean, it was a straight-forward rape all the way, but the kid's skull got fractured. She was unconscious when she died, the coroner says. I got to thinking maybe he didn't realize, you know? Maybe he didn't know how hard he hit her, right? So I got a couple of guys and a policewoman to dress up like a teenager, and we staked the place out last night—the same spot, can you believe, where the first crime took place, and bingo! Who should come walking up to our lady cop but some guy with scratch marks healing up all over his face. Wanna party? the creep asks. I got a party for you, the detective says back. Guy copped out finally after a couple hours of denials. You know something, Merce? We'd all be useless if the bad guys weren't so damn dumb most of the time. So, as you can see, I had a helluva night. Helluva night. Christ, the type of night that makes it seem worthwhile . . ."

He looked at Detective Barren before continuing.

". . . So here I am, finishing some paperwork before heading home to the wife and kids, and who calls up from the lobby? This I gather is not a social call, huh? Have a seat."

He motioned across his desktop to a chair and they both sat down.

"You're being real quiet," he said.

"Sounds like a good bust. A real good bust." It occurred to her that she liked Detective Perry and she was suddenly sad because she knew that he would not like her after they completed their conversation. "It helps," she said.

"What helps?"

"That so many of them are dumb."

He laughed. "No kidding."

He looked over the clutter of papers at Detective Barren.

"Merce," he said softly, "why are you here?"

She hesitated for a few seconds before replying in an equally soft voice:

"He didn't do it."

Detective Perry stared at her as silence surrounded them. Then he got up from his seat and walked about. She watched him carefully.

"Merce," Detective Perry finally responded, "let it go."

"He didn't do it."

"Let it *go*, Merce."

"He didn't do it!"

"Okay. Let's say he didn't. How do you know? How can you be sure?"

"Trace alcohol."

"What?"

"Trace alcohol. The bite mark on Susan's body was swabbed and saliva tests were run. They turned up trace alcohol."

"Right. I remember. So what?"

"He said he was a Shiite Muslim."

"Right."

"Sincere."

"Yeah, that's what he said. So?"

"Won't touch a drop of alcohol. Not a beer. Not a scotch. Not a glass of wine."

Detective Perry sat down heavily.

"That's it?"

"That's it for starters."

"Got anything else?"

"Not yet."

"Merce, why're you doing this to yourself?"

"What?"

"Why are you punishing yourself?"

"I'm not. I'm merely trying to find Susan's killer."

"We found him. He's in prison for the rest of eternity. When he dies he'll probably go to hell. He *will* go to hell. Merce, give it up."

"You're not goddamn listening to me! Trace alcohol!"

"Merce, please . . ." Defeat and sadness crawled into his voice. "I'm tired. I'm really tired. You know as well as I that this guy picked up half his victims in bars or student unions. You're saying he never had a beer? Bull! He was crazy, Merce! He was sick crazy. He'd have done anything, anything! to get his victims. The rest, all the religious garbage, that was just, I don't know, cover-up crap. Self-justification. Madness, hell, I don't know . . ."

Detective Perry rolled back in his chair.

"I'm tired, Merce. I shouldn't have to tell you of all people that that damn saliva testing will turn up trace alcohol if the creep rinsed his mouth out with mouthwash before committing the crime. Hell, you know that better than I do. You're the expert. You know."

"He didn't do it."

"Merce, I'm sorry. He did. He killed her. He killed all of them. You're going to have to learn to live with it. Please, Merce. Please learn to live with it."

Detective Barren looked at Detective Perry. She wavered for a moment, measuring all the sadness and discouragement in his voice. She thought how crazy she must sound. Then she thought, vaguely, in an undefined, vaporish way, of her niece and she toughened quickly.

"Will you help me?"

"Merce . . ."

"Will you help me, goddammit!"

"Give me a break . . ."

"Will you help me!"

"Merce. Get help. See the department shrink. Talk to your goddamn minister. Take a vacation. Read a book. Hell, I don't know, but don't ask me to help you."

"Let me have the file then."

"Christ, Merce, you've already got everything we had. I gave you everything before the guilty plea."

"You're not holding anything back?"

Anger flashed across Detective Perry's face.

"No! Goddammit! What a fucking question!"

"I needed to know."

"You knew already!"

They were both quiet, staring at each other. After a moment Detective Perry spoke again. His voice was slow and sad.

"I'm sorry you feel this way. Look, your niece's murder has been cleared by us. If you turn up some hard piece of evidence, well, you can always come on back and we'll take a look at it. But, Merce, it's over. At least it should be. I wish you'd see it that way . . ."

He hesitated before continuing.

". . . because you'd be much happier if only you'd realize."

She waited, to be certain he'd finished.

"Thanks . . ."

He shook his head and started to say something but she cut him off.

". . . No, I mean it. I know that you believe what you've said. And you've always played pretty straight with me and I appreciate that."

She looked at him hard.

"I know what you're thinking, but you're wrong. I'm not crazy. And a couple of weeks off thinking about it isn't going to change my mind. He's out there."

"I don't think you're crazy, Merce. Just . . ."

He couldn't find the word.

"It's okay," she said. "I understand your position." She stood up. "I don't mind," she said, "but I'm still going to go find Susan's killer."

She hesitated a moment.

"I'll let you know when I've got him."

She was not exactly certain what she was going to say to her own boss. That she didn't believe the Arab had killed Susan; that the killer was still at large; that she wouldn't rest until he'd been uncovered? Whenever she formulated the sentences to describe the situation she found herself in, it all sounded silly, melodramatic, and unconvincing. She thought: There is something ordinary and trite to revenge. It is a common urge that comes from uncommon circumstances. It carries a package of guilt with it, wrapped up and unavoidable. She knew it was wrong to desire it so, but she was unable to say precisely why.

The door to Lieutenant Burns' office was ajar. She knocked hesitantly, then slowly poked her head inside.

He was sitting at his desk. Spread in front of him were two dozen eight-by-ten color photographs. He looked up and smiled when their eyes met.

"Ahh, Merce. Just the person I need. Come in and look at this . . ."

She walked into the office slowly.

". . . Around here. Look at these pictures."

She stared down at the array of photographs. She saw a body curled in the fetal position in the trunk of a car. It was a young man who would have seemed to be sleeping save for a huge swatch of blood that covered his chest. Detective Barren stared at the pictures, struck with the odd peace that had fixed itself to the man's face. She picked up different-angled shots of the car trunk, seeing the same quiet, the same blood and tissue. She wondered idly what the young man had done to deserve his death, knowing the answer intuitively: Nine times out of ten, in Miami at least, youth and death translated into drugs.

"You know, Peter, what strikes me is he wasn't scared."

Lieutenant Burns eyed her cautiously.

"I mean, we know enough about the physiology of death to speculate a little. And this fellow seems, well, too comfortable. If you or I had been snatched, thrown into the trunk of a car, and driven out to . . . to where?"

"A rock pit in South Dade . . ."

"Right, some rock pit. And then blasted by a shotgun . . . it was a shotgun, right? I mean, the guy's chest is just about gone . . ."

"Twelve gauge. One shot."

"... Well, what I'm getting at is that we'd see the residue of fear all over him. Eyes would be open, probably. Face rigid. Fingers stiff. Look. The guy's hands aren't even handcuffed or tied. When you pulled him out, how much of him was left behind?"

"Some blood. Some tissue."

"Not a lot?"

"Medium amounts."

"And the car. It looks like a brand-new BMW, right?"

"Six months old."

"I bet," said Detective Barren, "that it belongs to some mid-level drug dealer. A ten-to-twenty-keys a month guy, not a real heavyweight."

"Right again."

"Did he report it stolen?"

"I'm checking on that."

"Well, this is off the top of my head, and only a guess of course, but if you were to ask me, I'd say the poor guy was shot somewhere else by someone he didn't expect to be unfriendly, if you know what I mean..."

Lieutenant Burns laughed wryly.

"... Then he was quickly dumped into the back of the car conveniently stolen a little while earlier, driven out to the rock pit ... where they knew we'd find him quick, not like out in the Everglades, and left there. It seems to me like some dim-witted Colombian drug dealer's idea on how to frame somebody in the competition. Perhaps someone's looking to start some bad blood between organizations and this is the first trump played. All speculation, mind you. But I don't know if I'd issue an arrest warrant for the guy whose car it is, either."

"Merce, you know why I like working with you?"

"No, Peter, why?"

"Because you think like me."

Detective Barren smiled.

"Everyone likes a yes-man. Or in this case, woman."

Lieutenant Burns laughed.

"Well, I agree with what you say about the crime. I had forensics do a test on the guy's sneakers. No rock pit sand at all. But there were some fresh grass stains. You see any grass in that rock pit? Didn't think so."

He stared down at the pictures.

"Merce, do you sometimes think the world belongs to the drug dealers? It makes me laugh, sometimes, when I think that they are the new entrepreneurs of our society. I mean, a hundred years ago, two hundred, people came over to this country, worked hard, put down roots, and bettered themselves. The American Dream. What's the American Dream now, Merce? A hundred-key score and a nice big brand-new BMW."

He stood up and gathered all the pictures together. "I'm getting to be too much of a pessimist. Well, anyway, I guess I'll take a little hike to homicide and talk to the detectives. Got to tell them what they're up against. Better call in narcotics, too, I suppose." He looked at her and sat down. "But first, what can I do for you?"

Detective Barren thought of the young man in the pictures and wondered why someone so young would be so silly as to get involved in the drug trade. No sillier than John Barren going to war over some foolish principle and dying and leaving her to face getting on alone. She felt a sudden rush of sadness for all the silly young men who died one way or another, followed quickly by a flash of impatient anger. How useless, she thought. How terribly useless and selfish. Someone, she thought, cried hard over this young man's torn body.

"Merce?"

"Peter, I need some time."

"Because of your niece."

"Precisely."

"It might be easier to talk to a counselor and stay on the job. You know, keep busy. Idle hands, they say, are the devil's playground." He smiled.

"I won't be idle."

"I mean, I just don't want you to go off and brood about in your apartment. What are you going to be doing?"

Finding Susan's murderer! her mind screamed suddenly. She bit back the words. She forced herself to sound diplomatic.

"You know, Peter, they were always unable to put together a prosecutable case against Rhotzbadegh for killing Susan. I don't want to imply I think the county guys didn't do their part. It's just, well, it makes me angry. I just wanted to poke around, see what I can come up with. Then maybe spend some time with my sister, you know, help her over this. She's still taking it very rough."

Lieutenant Burns looked carefully at her eyes. She didn't move.

"I don't know what I think about your poking around in the case. I think it's over. The other stuff, well, of course . . ."

"How much time can I have?" she asked. It makes no difference, she thought. I'll take forever. I'll grow old and gray and stiff and keep searching.

Lieutenant Burns opened a desk drawer and shuffled through a folder. He pulled out a sheet with her name written at the top.

"Well, you've got three weeks' vacation time and at least two weeks' compensatory time for overtime work . . . hell, make it three weeks as well. Then the department regs allow for leave under hardship circumstances. I could put you in for a leave, but it would be at reduced pay. Just how long do you think you'll need?"

She had no idea.

"It's hard to tell."

"Of course. I understand. I think." He eyed her, a bit warily. "Why are you wearing the cannon?"

"What?"

He motioned toward her jacket. "The elephant gun. What is it, a forty-five or a nine millimeter?"

"Nine millimeter."

"You need that to look at pictures?"

"No."

"So why?"

She didn't reply. Silence enveloped them. Lieutenant Burns looked down at the paper, then up at her.

"Leave it alone, Merce. It's over. He's doing hard time, which is how it should be . . ." He stiffened, his voice taking on a note of officialdom. "Here's an order: Stay out of the case. It's closed. All you're going to buy is more heartache. You want leave, fine, take it. But not to work. To recover. Got it?"

She didn't reply. He looked at her and his voice softened.

"All right. At least I gave you the official lecture . . ."

She smiled. "Thanks, Peter."

"But, Merce, for my sake, please, get yourself straight and get back to work. Okay?"

"That's what I'm trying to do," she said.

"Okay, take comp time first, then, if you need more, take vacation. After that, call me and we'll work something out. I'll have them send the checks to your house. On one condition."

"What?"

"See the department shrink first. Look, they're gonna make you see him when you come back, anyway. Trust me. All he's gonna say is take some time, two aspirin, and see him when you come back."

She nodded.

"Okay. That's it then." He rose again and picked up the stack of pictures. "You want to come with me to homicide? Those idiots usually take some persuading, especially when it means they're actually gonna have to go out and scare up some witnesses and evidence all by themselves."

"No, thanks," she said. The next time I see homicide, she thought, it will be to bring them a case.

She bit her lip. Or to turn myself in, she thought.

The visit with the department psychologist was as perfunctory as Lieutenant Burns had suggested it would be. She described to him a certain amount of restlessness, sleeplessness, inability to concentrate, and fits of depression. She told him that she felt guilty over Susan's death. She said that she thought she needed time to adjust to the loss. She listened to herself speak, thinking how easy it was to create a believable lie by mixing in some truth. He asked her whether she wanted sleeping pills. She declined the offer. He told her that she would probably be dogged by depression until she treated the sense of loss with therapy, but that he agreed some time off might be beneficial. He said he would fill out the proper departmental forms to provide her with a leave of absence for medical reasons, which would give her almost full pay. She wondered why everyone was concerned with money. Then he told her that he wanted to see her regularly after a month and scheduled an appointment. He filled out a card and they shook hands. She thanked him and threw the card away after closing his office door behind her.

It was all much easier than she had expected.

It did not take her long to clear out what she needed from her desk, despite the interruptions from the other members of the evidence-analysis section, who stopped and offered condolences, invitations, and friendship, which touched her. But she was excited, pleased, and anxious to get finished and out.

The heat was intense when she stepped through the doors of the city police department. The solid red brick of the building seemed to glow like hot coals. She breathed in slowly, as if afraid she would scorch her lungs, lifting her head and peering up into the sky, shading her eyes from the brightness. She felt for an instant as if she had been hit with a spotlight, singled out for observation.

But that sense passed and she felt a sense of anticipation, almost exhilaration. For the first time in months she could sense the depression sliding from her heart. I'm doing something, she thought. One foot in front of the other. One step at a time. She had a sudden memory of herself, rising in the midst of the nighttime darkness in her sister's home at the first mewings of baby pain and hunger. She remembered it as something of a ritual: Throw back the blanket, swing her feet out and into slippers in a single move, pluck the bathrobe from where she had spread it at the foot of the bed. "I'm coming," she would say, loud enough for the baby to hear, loud enough for her sister to know she was taking care of the problem and roll back into sleep. "I'll be right there, now hush, hush, hush," speaking the last words in a crooning midnight sleep lilt.

"I'm coming," she said out loud, but there was no one to hear her.

Then she hummed herself a tune as she walked down the steps.

9. THE first thing she did was purchase three cheap cork bulletin boards and a child's green blackboard. These she took back to her apartment and set them up next to her desk. She wrote SUSAN on a piece of masking tape and stuck it to the top of the first; RHOTZBADEGH on the second, and OTHERS on the third. The blackboard she set up in the center. She moved a bookcase out of the way, grunting as she forced it across the room to give her more space. She took push-pins and mounted a group of eight-by-ten color shots of the crime scene in the center of Susan's board. Then she put up the list of evidence seized and the statements of the two gay men who found her body. The Rhotzbadegh board filled swiftly too, with the evidence lists from his house and copies of the newspaper articles he'd clipped. She took a picture of him and placed it on the board, where she could watch it.

She felt an odd release in the activity. Be a detective, she thought. Make a case.

But first destroy the one they've got.

The inside of the student union at the university seemed cavernous and dark. It had not been difficult to find the people Susan had been with the night of her death. It was exam period and they were anxious to talk. To chatter, really. Anything, Detective Barren thought, to break the drudgery of studying, although their tanned faces spoke more of time spent in the sun than in any library.

"How are you certain?" Detective Barren asked one girl, a dark-haired young woman with the nervous habit of looking directly at a person while listening to their question, then letting her

127

eyes wander wildly about the room as she answered. Must drive her professors mad, thought Detective Barren. "How do you know that Susan disappeared by eleven P.M. that night?"

"Because we'd agreed we were going to leave by eleven. It was important, we each had an early class and we'd promised that no matter how good a time either of us was having, we were going to leave. It was going to be up to me to get her, you see, or her to get me. We were dancing and I lost sight of her. But at ten thirty I started looking hard and by ten forty-five I'd gotten the guys to help. Teddy even went out to the parking lot and all around outside. I mean, we couldn't have missed her, even in the crowd. I mean, Susan, you know, she always stood out, anyway. She couldn't hide, even in this place when it's packed. She was like that."

I know, thought Detective Barren.

"You didn't see her with anyone special, anyone you didn't know?"

"Well, the problem was, it was the beginning of the semester. Everyone was new. Everyone was a stranger. There were freshmen and new graduate students. There were some of the new faculty members, too, but they got out early. I mean, everything was new and exciting and friendly. But I didn't see her with anyone suspicious, if that's what you mean."

Detective Barren sighed and turned to another student, a huge, brawny young man wearing a tee-shirt. She wondered why he wasn't cold in the over-airconditioned room.

"You tell me how come you know Rhotzbadegh was here until midnight."

"I told the other detectives but I'll go through it again. It's simple, really. I had a date that was going to meet me at midnight . . ."

"Midnight?"

"Yeah. Sounds romantic doesn't it? It was just, well, she was taking this film history course and they had to go see some Russian guy's flick. Long, I mean, real long. She wasn't going to get out until after eleven. So we agreed to meet here. I squirreled down in a corner of the bar where I could keep an eye on the door. She was real pretty and I didn't want, I don't know, I didn't want her to have to be looking for me, you know. Too many single guys would be willing to help, if you get my meaning. Anyway, I get to talking to the dude sitting next to me. I mean, weird, right? Major-league weird. But kind of a goof, too, the way he was talking about girls and how wicked they are. But he'd say that, and I'd look at him, and then he'd laugh, and I'd laugh and I wouldn't take it too seriously. But still, I mean, it wasn't the kind of conversation you'd forget . . ."

Detective Barren looked up from her notepad. "What were you drinking?"

"Two beers. That's the limit. The team was still doing two-a-days and man, drink too much and you'll puke your guts out at practice."

The other students hooted. "More like two six-packs," said one. Susan's friend added:

"I saw you that night, Tony. You were ripped."

"Well, maybe a little . . ."

"Two beers is what you told the coaches, right?" Detective Barren said.

The young man nodded.

"What happened at practice the next day?"

"I got sick."

"Right. So how many did you really have?"

He tried to grin but it died quickly. "A bunch."

"How are you sure that this happened the night Susan disappeared."

"Because of the movie. It was only shown once."

"What was the title?"

He hesitated, then brightened. "It was about that battleship they had the revolution on . . ."

Detective Barren thought suddenly of a baby carriage bouncing down a wide flight of stairs. *"Potemkin?"*

"That's it!"

"But, Tony," the dark-haired girl interrupted, "I think that was the one they showed the next night. The night Susan disappeared they showed the war one, you know, with the knights and the ice breaks, that one. I think."

"I don't know about that one," he said.

"Alexander Nevsky," Detective Barren said. She sighed.

"Still, you're certain the suspect never moved from his seat."

"Pretty certain. I mean, I was dancing a bit. And I had to spend some time in the head. And you know, it was a party. You know, when some of the guys from the team came in, I had to get up and greet them . . ."

"So you weren't sitting next to him the whole time?"

"Well, not the whole time."

Detective Barren glanced at the young man's wrist. Great witness, she thought. Drunk. Willing to lie to his coaches and probably anyone else. Can't remember details. Probably can't remember what day it was. She looked at him again. I hope he makes the pros, she thought. No wonder his story was discounted by the county detectives. A grand jury would have laughed at it.

"Ever wear a watch?"

"Nah. Just get it stolen out of your gym locker."

"So you can't be certain what time it was."

"Well, not exactly."

"Okay, what did the suspect drink?"

"I bought him one. Tonic water. Like I said, weird."

"Anything else?"

"Just tonic water. With a lime twist."

"Go on."

"Well, not that much to it. He and I pretty much sat there, right until the stroke of midnight, when Cinderella popped through the door. And I grabbed her before the wolves jumped on, know what I mean? I mean, this place can get pretty rowdy some nights. What the dude did next, I don't know. The place was really getting down . . ."

Susan's friend smiled. "Susan knew that, you know. That's why she and I made the pact to split. If we'd stayed till midnight, let me tell you, this place is a zoo. We'd never have made it out alive . . ."

This was a joke and the other students laughed in shared familiarity.

"Susan didn't," Detective Barren said.

Some two weeks after taking her leave from the department, Detective Mercedes Barren drove through a blistering afternoon down to the park where Susan's body had been uncovered. It was summer and the heat rose off the highway before her, creating a wavy vaporous curtain. She thought to herself that she had reached a decisive position in her investigation. Days spent maneuvering about the University of Miami and reviewing forensic documents had convinced her of two things: Sadegh Rhotzbadegh was the natural, obvious suspect in the murder. He was at the scene of her disappearance, he had clipped the newspaper story of the murder, just as he had the others, the crime itself was performed in his style. All the other victims had been bashed and strangled. She thought to herself that if this had been her case, she would have devoted all her efforts to finding some noncircumstantial link between Susan and Rhotzbadegh. The tiniest of connections would have resulted in a first-degree murder indictment for sure. But Detective Barren was equally certain that he had not perpetrated the crime, primarily, she thought, because of the lack of some evidentiary link.

It's too simple, she thought.

She remembered the slight shake of the head.

Not him, she thought. Too obvious. Trace alcohol.

She frowned and mentally castigated herself: Find something!

She turned down the road to the park, which in the bright daylight seemed to have none of the malevolence she recalled from the night of Susan's murder. She rounded the corner to the main parking area and stared out at the opaque light bay waters that seemed to blend with the pale sky above in an endless enveloping China blue. There was no wind and the wavelets slid up against the shoreline, lapping at the gnarled mangroves, making a slight noise not unlike that of a faucet dripping. Detective Barren could smell cooking; there were families grilling lunch on open barbecue fires. The inevitable sounds of small children playing seemed distant, like background music.

She parked and hesitated, looking across the nearly empty parking area toward the underbrush and trees where the body had been hidden. Then, sighing, she got out of her car, locking the door, and started walking toward the spot. From the edge of the tarmac, she started counting. Susan weighed one hundred and eighteen pounds. She imagined slinging her niece's body over her shoulder. Fireman's carry. Deadweight is more difficult, more unwieldy. She thought how slight the Arab was, but knew that meant nothing; his arms were powerful. He could easily have carried her. But that meant nothing. She counted the distance in her head, one yard, two, up to twenty-two, before stopping and looking down at the sandy dirt. He'd already killed her, the detective thought, she did not feel the rudeness of this dumping.

He, she thought. Whoever *he* is.

But where? she wondered. The Arab's car was clean. Absolutely clean. Microscopic tests had been run on the rugs in the passenger area and on front and rear seat fabrics. Samples from the trunk, too, were put under a spectrograph. No blood. No hair. No skin. No residue of death.

Mentally she added that to her score sheet.

She bent down and felt the dirt where Susan's body had lain. Come on, she thought. Some cosmic message. Some idea. Something.

But she felt nothing.

All she was aware of was that it was hot. Children were playing. And Susan's murderer was outside somewhere.

"Nothing," she said. "Nothing at all."

She looked back down and had a sudden vision of Susan lying before her. She remembered with awful clarity the pantyhose biting into her neck, the swatch of blood behind her head, the violation of the haphazard way she had been flung to the ground, her legs akimbo, her sex exposed.

How cruel, she thought.

Then she shook her head.

There is something, she thought. Think. She considered the blunt trauma to the back of Susan's head. If I could find a weapon, she thought. Or the real location of the murder. Locations almost always speak of personalities. She went over in her mind all the forensic tests done on Susan's body. If I had a subject, she thought, maybe I could find something. She thought again of the pantyhose and an idea struck her.

She stood, turned rapidly, and returned to her car.

She noticed a small girl watching her. She had blond hair and an open, mischievous face. She was wearing a little girl's bikini bathing suit and that made Detective Barren smile. The child was eating a vanilla ice cream cone and it was melting about her, giving her shy grin a white outline. Detective Barren waved and the little girl half-waved back before turning and racing away. Trust no one, Detective Barren thought as she watched the little girl disappear amidst the trees and shadows, heading toward the beach and play area. Grow up and trust no one.

She had always hated visiting the morgue, not because of the bodies that were filleted there but because of the harsh bright lights which filled the rooms with an otherworldly glow. It seemed to her the light blended in some unusual way with the smell of formaldehyde and antiseptics which covered everything in the morgue. She preferred to think of death as something dark and private, which was the opposite of the atmosphere in the morgue, where people wandered in and out in a near constant parade. She watched from a corner of the theater as the medical examiner plucked various organs from a split body while talking into an overhead tape recorder microphone. His voice was monotonal until he found something that interested him, at which point it soared up an octave into a little boy's pitch. She saw the medical examiner root about inside the body, finally scooping a small shape from the bloody mass, and, raising it high into the light, he said in a delighted singsong, "See, detective, how small death can be?"

She didn't reply and he dropped the shape into a specimen container. ". . . In left coronary artery, at approximately three centimeters, one bullet fragment, nearly intact, apparently twenty-two or perhaps twenty-five caliber. This was the cause of death . . . impact severing artery, causing sudden massive loss of blood, shock, instantaneous heart seizure . . ."

He looked over his shoulder at Detective Barren.

"In other words he took it in the ticker . . . The news boys like the shoot-outs with machine guns and shotguns and all that fancy television stuff. But some things haven't changed in twenty years. You want to kill somebody coolly and professionally? A small-caliber bullet with a magnum load fired into the heart at close range. Or, if you need a variation, right here, at the base of the skull . . ." He tapped the back of his head with his index finger. ". . . A little pop! and your man's history. Or woman. No fuss. No mess. No people diving for cover. No innocent by-standers gunned down. No explosions. And, from my point of view, a big advantage. A little hole, right here . . ." He thumped his chest and the sound seemed to echo in the small room. "An Uzi or an Ingram makes a complete mess out of a person. No class. No class at all."

He looked back down at the shape on the slab before him.

". . . My kind of murder. No doubt about it. Simple. Direct and to the point, if you please, thank you, ma'am."

He shook his head and looked at Detective Barren. "I heard you were on a medical leave. What brings you around here?"

"I need to talk about . . ."

". . . Your niece. Right?"

"Yes."

"Well, what's the question?"

The medical examiner looked over at one of the orderlies who was replacing a shrouded body into a refrigerated container. "Hey, Jesús! Go get me file number eighty-six dash one eleven four, huh? Pronto, please. Susan Lewis is the name."

Detective Barren watched the orderly exit.

"He won't take more than a minute or two," said the medical examiner. "Still, what is it that's bothering you?"

"Susan was . . ."

"Asphyxiated. Cause of death was strangulation. Method of death was a pair of pantyhose around her neck. She was uncon-scious when it happened. You know all this. You were there and you saw the report."

"Knocked out by the blow on the back of the head?"

"Ahhhh, yes. Probably."

"You're not certain?"

"Well, the trauma to the back of her head was severe. It might have caused her demise in and of itself. But it always made me wonder." The orderly returned and handed over a manila envelope. "Right. Here it is . . ." He read momentarily. "Right. Left hemisphere . . . tissue loss . . . brain matter lost . . . well, what bothered me is that not much of the detritus from that blow was at the scene. I mean, there was just what you would expect from ordinary leakage from a wound that severe."

"I don't know that I follow . . ."

"Okay, she was hit, then strangled. Well, the theory of the case is that that Arab snatched her from outside the student union over at the university, banged her noggin, dumped her into his car, then took her to the park, raped her, strangled her, and abandoned her. But to me that simply didn't make sense."

"Why not?"

"Well, the blow Susan received on the head would have, as I said, killed her. Probably pretty promptly. There would have been a mess all over his car. A mess he couldn't clean up enough, realistically, to pass the spectrograph examination. And, if she had died while he was driving to the park, well, then the strangulation and the sexual congress would have been postmortem. Would have looked completely different. I mean, to a medical examiner it would look different."

"I think I see . . ."

"There was one other thing. Beneath the circular pattern the pantyhose made around her neck, I found a few slight areas of bruising."

"That's what I wanted to ask you about," said Detective Barren. "You mention those in one of the reports but not another. What were they? Could those have been finger-pressure bruises?"

"Well, yes is the answer to that question. But put me on the stand and ask me under oath whether those bruises were caused by a pair of hands and I couldn't testify to that, not to any degree of medical certainty. I mean, the marks were consistent with manual choking, but not conclusive. And they were just barely visible."

He hesitated before continuing.

"I hate this, you see. I much prefer things to fit together with the scenario the homicide detectives arrive with. If you add into the picture this manual choking, well, where? When?"

"Were you able to measure the distance between bruises?"

The medical examiner smiled.

"Good question. You always ask good questions, Detective. Yes. But only one possible combination . . ."

He carefully slipped off his surgical gloves and approached Detective Barren. "The problem, medically, is finding the right finger-and-hand positioning . . ." He put his hands around Detec-

134

tive Barren's throat. The medical examiner was a small, slight man, with mousy features and eye-glasses perennially perched on the end of his nose. But Detective Barren started at the strength in his thin fingers as they closed theatrically around her throat. "Here is your classic, Hollywood-in-the-nineteen-thirties strangulation, face to face. But see, if I'm a little taller" — he stood up on his tiptoes—"the angle changes. Or if you struggle, it changes . . ." The medical examiner kept moving his hands about Detective Barren's throat as he spoke. She watched him like a man would watch a barber he didn't quite trust shave him. ". . . And what about from behind? Changes things, too."

He dropped his hands.

"Five and one-half inches."

"From where to where?"

"My guess, and it is only a guess, I'd never, ever testify in court on this, is that the murderer's hands had to be at least five and one-half inches from thumb to index finger."

The medical examiner snorted.

"I hate this," he said. "Really. Sometimes I get so frustrated with questions."

"Do you think Rhotzbadegh . . ."

He cut her off.

"Of course I do." He stared at her. "Who else, tell me? The guy had desire. He was in the location. It pretty much followed his regular pattern. He killed her . . . that's certain, really, I'm sure."

"But?"

"But not exactly how they think it happened."

"Did you ever talk this over with them?"

The medical examiner snorted again.

"Of course!"

He turned and walked back to the corpse on the examining table. He looked down into the body before him, then spoke up. "The trouble is, there's no clear-cut indicator that it *didn't* happen the way they believed it did. And, really, what difference does it make? He did it, just as sure as I'm standing here breathing, and this young fellow is lying there dead . . ." He poked the body several times with his finger, as if testing to be sure he was right.

"But?"

"But. But. But. But I'm a man who likes things in order. This is the way the body works: take something away, and voilà! It no longer functions properly. Sprain the ankle and you'll start to limp. Take a bullet in the heart and you'll die. Things out of whack and out of line. Things twisted and things obscured. Hate it, really. That's why I like a good shooting. Dig around and bingo! There's the bullet. No doubts about it. He's dead. There's the reason. Can't stand loose ends . . ."

He hesitated again.

"You see, it makes no difference. And I may be off my rocker completely. That's what the prosecutor told me, anyway." He looked back over his shoulder at Detective Barren. "You know," he said with a touch of sadness, "that if you show two different medical examiners the same set of facts they will reach different conclusions? Every time. You can bet on it. We're the most contentious, disagreeing bunch. Everyone likes to think that, because we deal with the dead instead of the quick, we're not subject to the same vagaries of diagnosis, guesswork, what have you. We are."

He took a deep breath.

"Makes me sad."

The medical examiner seemed to be staring into the open chest of his subject. Detective Barren waited an instant before speaking.

"Five and one-half inches?"

"Right. For what it's worth."

She turned and started to leave.

"But it won't prove anything," he said after her. As she walked through the doors to the operating theater, she turned and saw the man bend over the remains, lost again in his work.

In her apartment that night, Detective Barren poured herself a glass of red wine, remembering the words of the clerk in the liquor store who'd assured her this California cabernet was the equal of those priced twice as high. She had not told him that she could barely taste the difference and liked to slip an ice cube into her glass as well. She had stripped off her clothes after the visit to the morgue and taken a long shower, scrubbing herself fiercely —pathologically, she joked to herself—to remove the lingering stench from the death room. You can't really smell it, she told herself as she had stepped from the shower, and then she had paused, sniffed the air, and finally said out loud, "Well, the hell you can't."

She stood in her room naked and sipped the wine, feeling the tinge of alcohol slide through her body. She breathed out deeply. For a moment she felt like staying naked, turning out all the lights and letting the darkness soothe her. The idea made her giggle and think that it had been a long time since she had done anything spontaneous and offbeat, anything that would remind herself that the world was not all murder and death. Then she shook her head and found a pair of shorts and an old Miami Dolphins tee-shirt from one of their Super Bowl years, which she slipped on.

She padded barefoot into the living room, carrying her wineglass and the bottle. She went to her bookcase and picked out a leather-covered photo album, then retreated to an armchair and, perching the glass on her knee, opened the book of pictures. There was one in specific she was searching for.

She flipped past snapshots of herself, of Susan and her parents, lingering momentarily over a few, a picture of a birthday party here, a graduation there. She was suffused with the warmth of memories, comforted. Finally she found the picture she wanted.

It was a simple five-by-seven snapshot of Detective Barren at age twenty-one, standing between John Barren and her father. She thought: The summer before we were married, the summer Dad died. She looked at the background, an expanse of blue-green waves rolling steadily and benignly against the Jersey Shore. In the picture the three were all in bathing suits, and Detective Barren remembered how the two men had teased her mercilessly about her inability to swim, yet her constant attraction to the beach. She thought about how she would lie, hours on end, reading on the sand in the sun, peaceful, relaxed. When it became unbearably hot she would take a child's red plastic water bucket down to the edge of the ocean and plop herself down in the damp sand, waiting for some slightly larger wave to send a small current of water shooting up the beach toward her. The foamy clear cool liquid would rise about her toes, curl around her buttocks, and refresh her. If need be, she would take the bucket, fill it in the shallow water, and unceremoniously dump it over her head. John would laugh and point and plead again for her to learn to swim, but not seriously, for he knew she wouldn't, regardless of how ridiculous she appeared.

She did not swim for the simplest of reasons.

She had been young, barely more than a baby at age five. She closed her eyes in the apartment and felt the familiar anxiety pass through her, just as it always did when this particular recollection came back. Her heart seemed to pick up its pace momentarily, the sweat on the back of her neck grow slightly clammy and uncomfortable, her stomach tense. She thought for an instant of the potency of fear, undiminished even as it traveled over the decades of memory. She had been sitting on the sand with her mother, her father had been in the surf, riding the waves in on the beach, then

137

dashing out again with the little boy's exuberance that he always displayed at the shore. Her mother had glanced at her and said, "Merce, darling, go get your father and tell him it is time to eat." It had been the meagerest of requests; even sitting in her apartment room, she thought it easy.

Detective Barren closed her eyes and with absolute sundrenched clarity remembered every step. She'd jumped up, and turned, and run down to the water, her eyes on her father as he turned and caught a large roller heading swiftly toward the beach. As she opened her mouth to call for him, she looked up, and in a frozen moment of utter terror realized that she had run right beneath a curling wave. The force of the water as it broke over her head knocked her onto her back, loosening all the air within her, stealing it from her little girl's chest. The water suddenly seemed dark green, then black, and it was as if the world had been blotted out. She had struggled hard, searching for the surface, and then suddenly something great and heavy had landed on her, holding her down farther, blocking her from reaching the sunlight. She could still remember with an expected uncomfortableness the sensation of sand scoring her back. Her mind had spun, her eyes clouded, her little lungs seared, her heart been clenched by darkness. She did not know really what death was, but thought in that incredibly brief, interminable moment, that it surrounded her.

And then, suddenly, she had been snatched from the blackness and lifted gasping into the sunlight.

It was her father.

His own ride had carried him directly over her. It had been he that held her down, he that raised her up.

She remembered a few tears, drying quickly in the hot afternoon. She had played safely on the sand that day. But at night, tucked into her bed, as the light had faded from the day and nighttime filled her room, she had cried bitterly and vowed never to trust herself to the waves, never to know the sensation of the ocean closing over her head, and never ever to go into the water again.

Stubborn, she thought. A stubborn little girl who kept her promise to herself.

She laughed. The little girl has not changed a whit in thirty-how-many years. And probably won't.

She looked at the picture again. She smiled. John had a sleek, muscular body which glistened as the ocean water caught the sunlight. She thought of the way her father would tease him about his hairless chest, sticking out his own, with its swatch of curly black hair, puffed up, mocking a beach body-builder.

They were such easy times, she thought.

She looked at her father's face. Sunlight was causing him to squint, just barely, giving his face an elvish look. It made her laugh out loud.

"What," she said to the man in the picture, "would you say about this case?"

Mathematics, her father would lecture in his best academic drone, prefers a steady procession of data to reach for an elusive conclusion. But this was not always the case: sometimes you could prove a theorem through an absence of contradictory information.

She suddenly felt a spasm of despair.

There would be no way to prove that Sadegh Rhotzbadegh didn't commit the murder of her niece.

Proving a negative. Her father would shake his head and smile. Now, that, he would say, requires some real intellect, some pure mathematical reasoning.

She felt that she wanted to scream.

Then she took a deep breath and a sip of wine.

She thought angrily about the concept of proof. Legal proof. Proof that stands up and is counted in a courtroom. Proof that clears murder cases. Evidence coupled with opportunity equals supposition of guilt, and finally an absence of alternative hypotheses amounts to a verdict. The hypotenuse squared is equal to the sum of the squares of the two remaining sides. Logic, she thought, is insidious. All logic points to the Arab. We live in a world that insists on accommodation. For every action there is an equal opposite reaction.

All instinct points away.

What did she have? A murder that happens not exactly as the investigators would want. A suspect who fits almost perfectly into the niche required of him—save for one or two critical details.

Start at the source of the dilemma, her father would say.

That was easy enough, she thought. And she knew where she would drive in the morning. She felt a rush of excitement and drained the remainder of her wineglass. She stared a last time down at the picture in the album resting in her lap.

Two weeks after her mother snapped the picture, the summer had ended. They had piled blankets, towels, umbrellas, and all the other traveling paraphernalia into their old bedraggled station wagon. The Labor Day weekend traffic had been horrendous, bumper to bumper at sixty miles per hour. She remembered the way her father had gripped the wheel, cursing mildly, complaining as the other cars swerved and swooped about them. An invitation to slaughter, was what he said. He said it every year when they packed up after the holiday and headed home. No wonder so many people die on the highway, he complained. They leave their brains at the beach. One hour slid into two, then three, and finally they turned up the street to their own home. She remembered her father adopting his best Charles Laughton accent and hunching over the wheel: "Sanctuary! Sanctuary!" he cried out as the exhausted family cheered. She stared again at the picture and in her mind's eyes saw them unloading the car and her mother turning to her father and saying, "Oh, there's nothing in the house for dinner, just run down to the corner store and pick up some hamburger." Her father had nodded, jumped back into the car, waving, be back in fifteen minutes.

But he wasn't, she thought.

She and John had been on the front lawn, hauling the stuff inside, and they'd heard ambulance and police sirens in the distance, looked up, thought nothing, and lifted another load.

Two drunken teenagers had run a stop sign and broadsided his car. He had been knocked clear across the seat and out and crushed as the vehicle rolled over him.

She smiled. He probably appreciated the irony of a mathematician becoming a statistic on Labor Day weekend fatalities. I still miss him, she thought. I still miss all of them. She looked again at the picture. She was standing between the two men in her life and they had each thrown an arm across her back. She remembered the moments before the snapshot had been taken: there had been a mock argument between boyfriend and father as to whose arm was going where on her back. They had loved each other, she thought, and I loved both of them. She felt a pleasurable rush of memory, as if she could feel the weight and pressure of those two arms draped across her shoulders and the warmth flowing from their bodies as she squeezed between them.

Sanctuary, she thought.

She closed the book and went to bed.

10. SHE was shading her eyes from the noontime glare and almost missed the small square green sign by the side of the road. It was set back a few yards farther than most roadside signs, which Detective Barren thought reflected a concession to distaste. No one wants a prison as a neighbor. It said: LAKE

140

BUTLER CLASSIFICATION AND EVALUATION CENTER F.S.D.O.C. NEXT RIGHT. There was a dusty black macadam road a hundred yards up from the sign. The road cut between two stands of tall pine trees, their needles turning a brownish green in the unrelenting Florida summer sun. Detective Barren slowly steered her car down the road, passing beneath a huge willow tree that threw shade down defiantly. The road curled around, across a brown field where some cattle grazed idly, contentedly, and Detective Barren caught her first sight of a cluster of low gray buildings that seemed to glow in the midday heat. She stopped the car to read a large black and yellow sign that dominated the side of the road: CAUTION. ANYONE PASSING OVER YELLOW LINE SUBJECT TO SEARCH. ANYONE CARRYING CONTRABAND INTO L.B.C.E.C. WILL BE PROSECUTED TO FULLEST EXTENT OF LAW. Painted across the road surface was a wide strip of yellow. Detective Barren accelerated gently, picking up her first sight of a twelve-foot-tall, barbed-wire-topped chain-link fence that surrounded the clutch of buildings.

Detective Barren parked the car in an area designated VISITORS and walked toward a pair of wide glass doors. Another sign informed her that this building housed the prison administration, although the word "prison" was not used. This was typical: We live in an enlightened age which is dependent upon euphemism, she thought. Thus, prisons are correctional facilities, manned not by guards but by correction officers, and prisoners are subjects. If we change the designation, somehow we believe the reality to be less evil and distasteful, though in actuality nothing ever changes. She stepped through the doors into the dark, cool interior, where she was blinded by the sudden shift in light. Her eyes adjusted slowly. Then she walked to a receptionist.

Within a few minutes she had checked her automatic with a uniformed security guard who'd eyed her with suspicion when she produced the heavy pistol and been ushered into a small office with the name and title of Arthur Gonzales, Classification Officer, on the door. It was a cramped space, filled with file cabinets, a small, cluttered desk, and two chairs. A window overlooked the prison's exercise area. Detective Barren stared out, watching a small cluster of men play basketball. They were stripped to their waists, and sweat made their bodies gleam as they maneuvered about the court. The window was closed to contain the air conditioning and Detective Barren could not hear the men. But she knew the sounds they were making, of sneakers pounding the cement surface and bodies slapping together.

She thought idly of her husband, who'd loved the game.

141

"There's a zone, Merce, a time, I guess, I don't know, but you get hot. It's like no other sport I can think of, but you just get possessed by this sense that you can throw anything toward the basket and it will fall. Hot. Electric, I suppose. It's hard to describe, but it sometimes seems that you can jump just a little higher, a little faster, and that the basket seems suddenly closer and the rim wider, and you know, you just know, that what you put up will slip in. It just happens, you see, in the course of the game. I don't know why. And then, just as the sensation arrives, it disappears. The ball starts to clank about and fall off. Your feet slow down. The magic evaporates. Maybe it passes on to someone else. You become mortal, suddenly, sadly. But the moments of immortality, Merce, they're something. It's as if you've been touched. Graced by some god of athletics. And until his mood changes and he plucks someone else out, you're on fire . . ."

She smiled.

He would take her to the outdoor courts on summer mornings and they would play against each other. At first he restricted himself to shooting only left-handed. Then she beat him one morning on a running, giggling jump-shot.

She smiled again, thinking how foolish men were with their games. Foolish but a little bit wonderful, as well. What she had liked about John was that the morning she beat him, he'd been the first to announce the event to her family. Without alibi, as well. Of course, the next day he'd suddenly shifted the ball from left to right and swooped past her. That was how he announced that the rules of their game were changing.

"Cheater!" she'd yelled.

"No, no, no," he'd replied. "Just returning to the proper balance between the sexes."

That night he'd been especially tender and tentative when he touched her.

Detective Barren shook her head and couldn't prevent the memory from making her grin.

She turned when she heard the door open behind her.

A rotund man in a pair of tan double-knit slacks and a white guayabera shirt entered. He stuck out his hand and said, "Hello, detective, how can I help you?" in a tone that told her that he no more wanted to see her or help her than he wanted to catch a disease. He instantly buried his head in files of paper, as if to indicate that her presence demanded only a portion of his attention. All detectives hate dealing with prison personnel, she thought. Because they always act like this. They are concerned with logistics and containment, who gets sent where and what bed does he occupy. Not issues of guilt or innocence.

She sat down opposite him.

"Sadegh Rhotzbadegh."

"He is one of my clients, yes . . ."

A new euphemism, thought Detective Barren.

"I would like to interview him, please."

"Is this another case like the ones he pleaded to?"

"Yes."

"And this is an official request?"

"No. Not really. Informal."

"No? Even so, I would probably counsel him to seek legal assistance before talking with you . . ."

Just whose side are you on? thought Detective Barren angrily. She kept her thoughts to herself.

"Mr. Gonzales, this is an informal inquiry. I believe Mr. Rhotzbadegh has been unfairly linked to a crime, and I think he can swiftly clear the matter up. He does, of course, have the right to an attorney. I will read him his rights if need be . . ."

She looked hard across the table.

". . . But you sure as hell don't have the right to tell him anything. Much less give him advice. Now, if you want me to talk to your supervisor . . ."

"No, of course, that won't be necessary."

He shuffled some papers quickly.

"Well?"

"Well, Mr. Rhotzbadegh is currently in his activities period. There is a rest time which follows, right before dinner. You can talk then . . . if he'll see you. He has the right, you know, to refuse . . ."

"But you're going to see he doesn't exercise that right."

"Well, I can't . . ."

"You sure as hell can. I didn't drive three and one-half hours just to have a convicted killer say, 'No thanks, not today.' You get him and bring him to a room where he and I can talk. If he wants to sit there and not say anything, well, that's his business and mine. Not yours."

"I can arrange for the room. But . . ."

"But what?"

"Well, we have just finished our evaluation and he's scheduled to be shipped out at the end of the week . . ."

"Yes?"

"Well, he's going to the psychiatric facility at Gainesville. We don't think he'd be safe in the regular population."

"You don't think he'd be safe!"

"Well, he's decompensated . . ."

"You think he needs to be protected!"

"That's the opinion of the evaluation and classification staff."

"So you're going to send him to some country club?"

"It's a maximum-security unit."

"Sure."

"Well, that's where he's going."

"I don't get it."

"Detective, if we send him to the state prison, someone will kill him. He's, well, no other word to describe it, he's obnoxious and near-psychotic. The other men don't like his religious mumblings. Or his conceited postures. Rapists have enough trouble in general population without these, uh, characteristics. What can I say?"

Detective Barren absorbed the news slowly. Her mouth was dry and her stomach churned. She shook her head.

"Just set up the interview room," she said.

Sadegh Rhotzbadegh's eyes darted about wildly as he entered the small office, almost as if he were trying to print the room's layout in his imagination. After this momentary assessment he brought his glance to bear on Detective Barren, who sat patiently at the small table in the center of the room. The table and two chairs were the only furniture. Rhotzbadegh stared at her, then took a sudden step forward, paused, and a stride backward, his eyes first reflecting anger, then fear, and finally settling on a confused compliance. He stood still, waiting for the detective to make some motion, which she did, waving him toward the empty chair across from her. He's gained weight, Detective Barren thought, and lost some of the wiry strength he had. Prison kitchen starches, she thought. Rhotzbadegh sat, shifting about in the chair, finally perching on the edge, balancing forward and eyeing Detective Barren. She met his glance and held it until he turned away. Then she spoke:

"First I want to inform you of your rights. You have the right to remain silent, the right to an attorney. . ."

He interrupted.

"I know those things. I have heard them many times and do not need to hear them again. Tell me why you have come to see Sadegh Rhotzbadegh! Why have you summoned him from his rest?"

"You know why."

He laughed.

"No, you must tell me."

"Susan Lewis. My niece."

144

"I remember that name, but it seems to be in a dream. Tell me more so that I may remember better."

"September. The University of Miami student union."

"This remains a mystery to me."

He laughed again, then continued.

"Why should I remember this person?"

He giggled girlishly.

"What reason do I have for remembering this person? Is she someone great, someone remarkable? Someone important, perhaps? I think not. Therefore there is no reason for Sadegh Rhotzbadegh to remember this person."

Rhotzbadegh leaned backward in his chair, relaxing, folding his arms across his chest and grinning in a self-satisfied fashion.

Detective Barren breathed deeply and locked her eyes onto his. She waited a moment before speaking, talking in a low, even, harsh voice: "Because if you do not start remembering, I will personally rip your face off, right here, right now."

Rhotzbadegh stiffened suddenly in his seat, immediately timid.

"You cannot do this!"

"Don't try me."

He bent forward, flexing his arm and showing Detective Barren the bulge of his arm muscle. "You think you have the strength . . ."

She interrupted, leaning forward eagerly.

"What do you think?"

She watched his eyes as they tried to measure the depth of her intentions. She narrowed her own glance until she was staring through slits, her face set. Rhotzbadegh suddenly sobbed and covered his face.

"I have nightmares," he said.

"You damn well ought to," replied Detective Barren.

"I see faces, people, but I cannot recall their names."

"I know who they are."

Tears started to form in the corners of his eyes and he rubbed at them.

"God is not with me. No longer, no longer. I am abandoned."

"Maybe he wasn't so damn pleased with what you were doing."

"No! He told me!"

"You misunderstood."

Rhotzbadegh paused. He produced a tattered handkerchief from a pocket and blew his nose three times hard.

145

"This," he said, in a tone suffused with despair, "is a possibility."

He wiped his nose vigorously.

"Still," he continued, "I will search him out again. I will learn his messages and find the true path. Then he will welcome me to his bosom in the garden, where I will reside for eternity."

"Great. I'm glad for you."

He didn't catch her sarcasm.

"Thank you," he said.

Detective Barren reached down into her bag and pulled out a simple child's schoolbox ruler. "Stick out your hand," she said. "Spread the fingers."

Rhotzbadegh complied. She held the ruler up to his hand. The distance between thumb and index finger was five and three-quarters inches. Damn, she thought. He could have made the marks.

"My hands reach out for God," he said.

"Let me know if you manage to touch him," she said.

Rhotzbadegh looked about the room again. Then he pushed back his chair and rose. He walked over and placed his back firmly against one wall of the interview room. Then, counting loudly, he paced the distance across, bumping up against the opposite wall as he said twenty-one. He executed a military-style about-face and returned to his seat.

"Twenty-one paces," he said, shaking his head as if in surprise. "Twenty-one full paces." He jumped up and leaped to the wall across from Detective Barren. Then he stepped off that distance, walking past the detective without glancing down.

"Nineteen paces!"

He returned again to his chair.

"My cell measures only nine paces by eight paces. I feel sometimes as if my heart has been caged."

He put his head in his hands and sobbed.

"They will not let me into the yard with the other men," he whined. "They fear for my safety. They think that I will be executed. I cannot sleep at night. I cannot eat. I think my food tastes of poison. They have put something in the water to make me drowsy and then they will come and kill me. I have to fight them at every step."

"The girls?"

"They are the worst. They come in my dreams and they help these men who would kill me."

"Who are they?"

"I do not know . . ."

"The hell you don't! Think! Dammit, I want some answers."

Rhotzbadegh lifted his nose in mock snobbery.

"These are my dreams. I do not have to share them with you."

Detective Barren stared hard at the little man but inwardly she sighed. Useless, she thought. His mind goes everywhere but where I want it. She reached down into her purse and took out a simple yearbook picture of her niece.

"Does she come in your dreams?"

Rhotzbadegh eyed the picture. He plucked it from the table and moved it close to his face, then held it out at arm's length. "This one, not exactly."

"What do you mean?"

"She comes in the dreams, but all she does is watch the others. She cries alone. It is the others who are my tormentors."

He leaned across the table conspiratorially, his voice low.

"Sometimes they laugh! But it is I who live and laugh last."

Detective Barren took the picture and held it up directly in Rhotzbadegh's line of vision. She raised her voice, demanding, insistent, frightening, mustering everything into a single question: "Did you kill this young woman?"

There was silence.

"Did you snatch her from the parking lot outside the student union at the University of Miami?"

More silence.

"Did you smash her head and take her to Matheson-Hammock Park and leave her there to die?"

He didn't respond.

Detective Barren lowered the picture and stared at Rhotzbadegh. She felt the hatred slip from her heart, emptying her of emotion. His eyes were filling again as he cowered at the anger in her questions. She felt no sympathy, nothing, just a need to fill a great vacuum within her.

She whispered: "Tell me!"

He lowered his face into his hands momentarily, then raised them. "I cannot say!" he sobbed. "I cannot say!"

He took a deep breath and swiveled in his chair as if rooted by agony.

"It seems to be a memory. It sounds like that which I would do. I remember the student union, with all the filth of dancing and alcohol and laughter. An evil place. God will someday cleanse it with a great fire. This I know. . ."

"The girl!" Detective Barren interrupted.

"I was there. The bodies surrounded me. This I know. But the rest . . ."

He shook his head.

"She comes in the dream, but I do not know her, not like the others."

"Why did you clip the story from the newspaper?"

"I had to keep a record! How else would God know that I had followed his wishes? It was proof!"

"For this one why did you need proof?"

"That is why I am confused," he cried. "I had my—my—my prizes from the others. But she I do not remember."

"When she comes in the dream, what does she say?"

"She says nothing. She stands aside and watches. I do not hate her quite like the others."

He paused.

"I need to sleep. God grant me sleep. Can you help me, detective, help me sleep? I am so tired. And yet I cannot. I must not. They come and torment my dreams. My enemies plot while my eyes are closed. I will not arise, one day."

He continued crying gently.

"This frightens you?" Detective Barren asked.

He shifted suddenly, throwing himself out of the chair and standing rigidly before her, his chest puffed out, his muscles flexed. His voice was no longer whining, but bellowing:

"Fear? Nothing frightens Sadegh Rhotzbadegh. I fear nothing!" He pounded on his chest. "Hear me! Nothing! God is with me. He protects me. I am afraid of nothing!"

Rhotzbadegh stared at Detective Barren. She let the silence lie in the room before replying slowly.

"You ought to be," she said.

It was late when Detective Barren finally reached her apartment. She had driven back from the classification center at a steady, minimal pace, letting other drivers swoop past her readily as she stuck doggedly to the speed limit. She felt a difficult emptiness inside her, an unruly, awkward sensation, as if the organs inside her body had shifted about somehow, slightly out of position. The thought made her smile when she considered how her friend the medical examiner would react. She easily envisioned his high-pitched voice reaching new sopranic levels as he sliced through her: "What's this, her appendix has moved! Her spleen has wandered! Her stomach has traveled! Her heart has packed up and moved away!" Detective Barren laughed out loud.

It was not so farfetched, she thought.

She remembered a visit, two years after John Barren's death, from a slender man who stuttered, but just slightly. He had been

148

a member of John's platoon, and he sat across from her in a restaurant and told her about her husband. He'd been very brave, the man said. Once, pinned down, he'd rushed out to bring back the wounded point man. They always did that, the VC, the man said. Bring down the point man. Then bring down the medic, because the medic always goes. Then bring down the men who owe the medic, which is everybody.

"John was the best of us," the man said.

She had nodded and said nothing. It was something she had known without being told.

"I just wanted you to know," the man said. He had risen.

"Thank you," she said, more for him than herself. "It helps."

She'd known it was a lie.

"I hope so," the man said.

He hesitated.

"I was the p-p-p-p-point man."

She'd nodded. "I guessed."

They had looked at each other.

After a brief silence she had asked, "What are you going to do now?"

He smiled. "It's back to the VA hospital for me. More surgery on the old guts. That's the trouble with getting wounded. Bullets tear the hell out of things. Army surgeons are great improvisers. They're like the guy everybody always knew in high school, the guy who could tinker around with any engine, fiddle here, adjust there, until he got the thing running okay. That's what they're doing to me. They've got intestines going north, digestive tract heading south. Pretty soon they'll get it all mapped out the way they want it."

"Then what?"

He'd shrugged. In her mind's eye, Detective Barren often pictured that young man's shoulders slumping against reality. Whenever she thought of the war, that was what she remembered: a wounded man shrugging at the future.

She wondered sometimes whether John would have been the same. He'd never had the chance to know disappointment. Never known frustration or denial or bad luck. He'd never been fired, never been rejected, never told to get lost, never told to take a hike. Never known loss.

Not like she had.

Detective Barren threw her notepad and briefcase on her small desk, kicked off her shoes, and went into her kitchen. She grabbed some lettuce, cheese, and fruit from the refrigerator. Rabbit food, she thought. She made herself a plate, then left it on her table. She went into her bedroom and dropped her skirt to the floor. She washed her hands and face, then padded out, half naked. She ate, trying not to think of Rhotzbadegh, trying not to fill herself with despair. She barely tasted the food.

He could have been direct, she thought angrily.

Dammit! Dreams! He sees her in a dream, but she doesn't torment him! What the hell does that mean? That he didn't kill her? Probably. Probably.

She smiled sadly, suddenly envisioning herself going to Detective Perry. Great news! she would say. The creep dreams! Clear-cut evidence that he didn't kill Susan.

She shook her head.

What a mess. What a hopeless mess.

She finished the salad and pushed the plate away. All right, she said to herself. Enough. Enough! Stop wasting your time with the Arab.

Clear your mind and start all over again.

She rose from the table and carried her dishes to the sink. She washed them carefully, dipping her hands into near-scalding water, gritting her teeth but making herself do it. She put the dishes away and went into her living room. She looked at the stacks of papers on her desk for what she thought was the millionth time. Maybe the billionth. It's in there, she thought. There is something in there.

"In the morning," she said out loud, "go to homicide and start pulling cross-referenced cases. Check out lists of known sex offenders. Go back to the school and find out if Susan had any enemies. Run the modus operandi through the NCIC computers. Maybe the FBI as well. Check for similar crimes after the Arab was arrested . . ."

She stopped and thought. She looked out the window.

"Out there," she said.

She smiled. You didn't think it would be easy. You didn't really expect to prove the Arab didn't do it and open the official investigation again. You're still on your own, and that's not terrible.

Not terrible at all.

She stared at the picture of Susan in the bookcase. Don't worry, she thought, I'm getting there. I'm getting there.

But her eyes were filling rapidly with tears.

She turned away and stared again out into the blackness of the tropical night. The sky was filled with the constellations, and Detective Barren saw one star burn brightly, shoot quickly across the void, then disappear.

"Oh, damn," she said. She felt tears flowing freely down her face, but she remained rigid.

After standing empty for minutes, she finally turned. Clear the mind, she thought. She walked to the television set and clicked it on. She was surprised to see a pair of local sports announcers talking animatedly on camera, and in the background she made out the Orange Bowl in downtown Miami.

". . . Well, this has been a pretty exciting start to the Dolphins' preseason," one announcer was saying. "We're getting ready to start the fourth quarter of the first exhibition game of the year, with the score tied at twenty-four and the Saints with the ball on their own twenty."

She had forgotten the start of the football exhibition season. "Not like you," she said, chastising herself. "Not like you at all . . ." She grabbed her glass of wine and settled in front of the television set.

"The ultimate in mind erasure," she said. "Come on, Fins!"

She watched in oblivious delight, letting the course of the game sweep away her thoughts and tears, comfortable, alone. The start of a new season, she thought. For them and me.

Midway through the fourth quarter the Saints kicked a field goal to go ahead by three. A minute later, a rookie running back for the Dolphins dropped the ball on his own thirty-yard line. This resulted in another Saints' field goal, and they led by six points as the game started to dwindle away. But as the game hurried toward its conclusion, the Dolphins rallied. Biting off chunks of yardage, they progressed down the field, until with less than a minute to play, they reached the Saints' one-yard line. It was fourth down and the game was in the balance. "Come on! Dammit! Get the ball in there!" She smashed her fist into her open palm. "Come on!"

She watched as the quarterback approached the line. "Over the top, dammit! Just smash it over the top!" Both teams were bunched up, awaiting the blast at the center, strength against strength. She loved it. "Just bash it in there!" she yelled.

Suddenly the two lines converged and Detective Barren saw the quarterback spin and hand the ball to a halfback flying toward the middle. There was a great crash, and the crowd noise swelled in anticipation. Then the stadium shook with sound as the crowd jumped to its feet, shouting out a great cry. Detective Barren, like the thousands in the stadium, rose up in half-cheer, half-cry, because she, like they, saw that the quarterback had not given up the ball, but had only faked the handoff and was now churning desperately, alone, without protection, for the corner of the end zone. Simultaneously, the Saints' outside linebacker, a large, violent man, was bearing down on the quarterback, angling sharply so that they would meet just shy of the goal line, in the very corner of the playing field. "Go! Go! Go!" shouted Detective Barren, her voice blending with the wall of crowd noise coming through the television set. "Put your head down!"

And this the quarterback did.

As he flung himself across the goal line, he was slammed by the linebacker. Both men flew into the air, rolling violently into a crowd of photographers assembled on the goal line for pictures. The cameramen dashed out of the way like scurrying geese, trying to avoid the flying bodies. The crowd roared, for the umpire had flung his hands skyward, signaling touchdown, and Detective Barren leaned back, not thinking, just letting the idea of victory fill her.

The announcers were babbling excitedly.

"That was some collision on the goal line, right, Bob?"

"Well, I think that was a gutsy call by the rookie quarterback and a tough way to learn about life in the National Football League. He took an all-pro shot."

"I hope those photographers are all right . . ."

"Well, I suspect that linebacker for the Saints probably ate a couple of them . . ."

Both men laughed, then paused.

"Tell you what, let's go down to Chuck on the field. He's with a couple of photograpers now. They had a real close-up view of the touchdown, didn't they, Chuck?"

"That's right, Ted. I'm standing here with Pete Cross and Tim Chapman of the Miami *Herald* and Kathy Willens of the Associated Press. Tell us what you saw, guys . . ."

"Well," said one of the photographers, a sandy-haired man with a beard, "we were all lined up to get the over-the-top shot, you know. And the next thing we see . . ."

The young woman interrupted. ". . . The next thing we see is these two fire-breathing players heading our way, and . . ."

"I had to grab Kathy," said the other, a curly-haired, barrel-chested man. "She was shooting with the motordrive and I thought they were going to run her over . . ."

"It can be pretty dangerous down here on the sidelines, huh?" asked the announcer.

"No worse than covering your average war or revolution," said the young woman.

The television picture held then, close-up on the three photographers. Detective Barren was listening idly, wondering whether she had ever met any of the cameramen on any of the crimes she had been assigned to.

And then she sat up sharply.

"Oh, God!" she said abruptly.

She fell to her knees in front of the television.

"Oh, God! My God!"

"That's the story from the sidelines. Back to you, Ted . . ." said the announcer.

"Hold it!" screamed Detective Barren. "Stop!"

She clawed at the sides of the television set.

"No! Stop! I need to see!"

The announcers were continuing to talk and the teams were lining up for the extra point. Detective Barren was unaware of the crowd's cheer as the kick sliced through the uprights. She shook the television set and cried, "No, no, no! Go back, go back!"

And then she slumped back and thought of what she'd seen.

Three photographers standing in front of a camera.

A slight gust of wind. Just enough to ruffle the hair.

Or to make their press credentials flap around their necks.

A wide, thick, yellow paper tag with the words OFFICIAL PRESS FIELD PASS embossed on it.

Detective Barren scrambled in panic across the floor to her desk. She pawed in desperation at the papers, speeding through her files of evidence until she came to the list of items discovered at the scene of her niece's murder. There were thirty-three items that had been identified, isolated, and seized by the crime-scene technicians. But it was only the last that she was interested in.

" . . . Tag end paper color yellow origin unknown (under body)."

"Yes," she said out loud. "I think so."

She gasped in air.

"Yes," she said.

She sat down hard on the floor and rocked, holding the paper list in her hands not unlike a woman holding a baby, remembering the piece of paper she'd inspected months earlier.

"I think so," she said.

In the morning she went to the dirty property office warehouse in downtown Miami. The clerk was reluctant to battle the stacks of boxes gathering dust in the cavernous interior. An angry man, unpleasant, scowling from the moment Detective Barren walked through the door, he first demanded a court order, then a letter from some superior officer. He finally settled for a handwritten authorization by Detective Barren, who kept smiling and acting nonchalantly throughout the man's wheedling complaints. The clerk was a wide man, with the no-neck appearance of a person who spent his free time grunting in a weight room. His shirt-sleeves were pushed up high on his arms, revealing a pair of elaborate dragon tattoos, and when he wielded a piece of pencil, snatched from behind his ear, she thought he would break it with the strength in his stubby fingers. She trailed after the clerk, trying not to anticipate, not to prejudge, but with her heart racing and a growing stickiness beneath her arms.

It took nearly an hour to find the right cardboard containers.

"Closed fucking cases, lady," the clerk complained. "Closed fucking cases means sealed fucking boxes. I don't have to do this, you know."

"I know, I know. Officer, I realize this is a special request. I can't tell you how much I appreciate your cooperation."

"Just so you knows I don't have to be doing this," he insisted.

"I understand," she replied.

All the boxes were coded with a simple numerical procession. The first digits represented the year the crime was committed, followed by the case number assigned by the various investigative squads. Robberies, burglaries, rapes, homicides, and other crimes were mingled together in a lazy, haphazard fashion that represented more the distinction of being a closed case than by any design. She ran her eyes up and down the stacks, thinking that if she opened any one, some tragedy would fall out, followed by someone's heartbreak or someone's terror.

"Jesus, I knew it. It's at the fucking top. I'll go get the fucking ladder."

She waited motionless while he retrieved the box.

"Now, you gotta sign this if you're gonna open it . . ." He thrust a preprinted form at her, which she signed without reading. He checked her signature and looked up. "I'm supposed to watch, even with the closed fucking cases. But screw it. You want something in there? Hey, have at it."

The clerk stomped away, his belligerence and frustration intact and as mysterious to Detective Barren as it was when she first entered the warehouse. She stared down at the box of evidence. Taped to the top was a disposition sheet listing the items inside and stating the fact of Sadegh Rhotzbadegh's guilty plea and life sentence. There was a large red stamped sign at the top of the sheet of paper: CLOSED/CLEARED.

We'll see, she thought.

She used the penknife from her purse to slit open the tape that held the box together, and, gingerly, as if trying to not disturb the dust collected there, opened the top. She refused to allow herself any excitement, thinking: This is just the first step.

She reached in swiftly and retrieved the yellow tag. It was encased in a plastic cover. As she slid it into her pocketbook, she noted the residue of dust on its surface from fingerprint work. Picking at straws, she thought: Fingerprints rarely come up on paper. She glanced at the box, wondering if there was something else she should steal, then shaking her head and shutting the cardboard flaps.

She breezed past the surly clerk. "Thanks for your help. If I need anything else I'll be back."

"Sure," he said in a voice that implied the opposite.

The late-morning sun caught her as she exited the warehouse. She was not allowing herself to think, to imagine, to process information. One step, two, she said to herself. For a single moment, she felt as if she were winning. She did not think of her niece, then, did not associate the dusty box or the plasticene-covered yellow paper with the memory of the crime scene. Instead her eyes picked out the distant flow of traffic on the expressway. The sunlight glinted off the steel bodies, making it seem like each glowing car was somehow blessed. The movement of the vehicles darting in and out caught her, and she was wrapped in thoughts about commerce and life and progress. Her eyes traveled upward and she fixed on a large, solitary blackbird, flapping purposefully against the morning breeze. She watched the bird's determination outlined against the perfect blue of the tropical sky. The bird brayed raucously once, then seemed to put its beak into the wind and steadily, surely, beat its way across the sky. Detective Barren had smiled and then she walked swiftly to her car to join the flow of people and head downtown.

At the Miami Dolphins team offices on Biscayne Boulevard a secretary made Detective Barren wait. "You're really lucky that Mr. Stark can make time for you," the secretary said. She was a young woman, equipped with the essential prettiness that all receptionists seem required to have: a breezy smile, a soft voice, and slightly teasing look.

"Why is that?"

"Didn't you read the papers?" the young woman asked.

"Not this morning."

"Oh. You didn't hear about the new contract?"

As Detective Barren shook her head, she overheard a loud blare of laughter from one of the offices.

"That's the press conference," the receptionist said.

"Can I see?" she asked.

The secretary hesitated. She looked around quickly. No one else was in sight. "Are you a fan?"

Detective Barren smiled. "Never miss a game."

The woman grinned. "Come on, then. We'll just poke our heads in the back."

Detective Barren followed the swishing skirt of the receptionist inside. The young woman gingerly opened an office door and the two women slipped through the crack. Detective Barren recognized the scene instantly, from a hundred sportscasts watched late at night when sleep was elusive. A half-dozen television cameras, mounted on tripods, dominated the center of the room. They had been placed in front of a table, which was raised up on a small dais. Newspaper and television reporters were scattered about; some in chairs, some lounging against the wall, scribbling in notebooks. Sound men and still photographers crept beneath the level of the television cameras. At the table, talking into a stalk of microphones, were the famous jut-jawed coach, the owner, and the tall, curly-headed quarterback. They were all smiling. Occasionally they all shook hands together, and this would prompt a flurry of pictures, all the camera motordrivers whirring at once. Detective Barren was instantly mesmerized. She felt like a child who captures Santa Claus in the act of placing presents around the tree. "He's bigger than I thought," she whispered in girlish, awestruck tones to the receptionist. "And better-looking."

"Yeah," she replied. "And richer, too. He's going to get more than a million a year."

The young woman was quiet a moment. Then she glumly added, "And wouldn't you know he had to go and marry his college sweetheart, too."

This was said with such undisguised jealously and sudden pout that Detective Barren almost burst out laughing. She turned back and watched the figures on the dais. Someone had made a joke and the three men were laughing. This caused another photographic explosion. The motordrives whirred again. In that instant the sound seemed to invade her heart. My God! she thought, looking about her wildly. He might be here. For a panicked instant she reached for her purse to seize the gun installed there. She stopped herself, just as her fingers wrapped around the cold handle. But who?

Her eyes cast desperately about.

She saw a muscular, bearded man fiddling with a wide lens. She stared at his large hands, seeing them suddenly wrapped about her niece's neck; she turned away, fixing on a thickset, balding fellow who was making wisecracks between shots. There was a special hardness about the corners of his mouth that chilled her. Another man, thin, blond, young, almost ascetic-looking, hovered into her line of sight. He seemed almost delicate, then craven, and she saw him mingling freely with the crowds at the student union, his beady eyes picking out her niece's blond hair.

She closed her eyes tightly, trying to dispel the vision. The noise of the press conference seemed to gain in volume about her; the laughter and gibes filling her head, as if mocking her feelings, her pursuit. She felt dizzy and wondered if she would be sick.

There was a whisper, then, at her side.

"Detective Barren?"

She opened her eyes. A short man in a seersucker sportscoat hung next to her. She nodded.

"Mike Stark here. I'm the guy in charge of this zoo . . ."

He laughed and she gathered herself with a great internal effort and joined him. He looked back at the crowd, then past to the figures washed by the spotlights from the cameras. "So what d'you think?"

She took a deep breath and forced her nightmare thoughts back into oblivion. She constructed a smile.

"I think a million bucks per year is a lot of money."

"He's a helluva ballplayer."

"He sure is . . ."

Stark hesitated. Then he clasped his hands before him as if in supplication.

"You're right. A helluva lot of money for a guy with two bum knees. I hope that whatever God there is that looks after football players is paying close attention." He rolled his eyes skyward. "Hey, are you listening up there?"

Detective Barren's smile was genuine.

"He doesn't pass with his knees," she said.

"For what we're paying him, he ought to be able to," Stark replied.

Their laughter mingled with the general sounds of the room.

The little man looked around. "I'll wrap this up. Thank God we signed this guy in August, before the season really got under way. I hate to think what he'd be worth if he had another season like the last. Why don't you wait in my office?"

Detective Barren nodded.

She was staring out the large glass window, watching power-boats beat white-plumed wakes on the bay, when Stark entered.

157

He took his seat behind his desk and she sat in an armchair across from him. "So?" he asked.

She fished out the tag from her pocketbook. For an instant she held it out of his sight, wondering whether she was taking the right approach. Then, wordlessly, she dropped it on the desk in front of him. She saw his brows furrow quizzically for a moment as he picked up the bag and turned it over slowly.

He put it back down.

"I'm sorry. . ." he said, then stopped.

She thought: The silence hurts. It was like being twisted by some great invisible machine.

He picked up the plasticene bag again and her heart seemed to jump within her.

"Well, maybe," he said. He put it down and wheeled about to rummage in a file cabinet. After a moment he came out with a folder. He opened the folder on his desk and Detective Barren saw a small pile of yellow field-passes. "Last year's model," Stark said. "This year we've printed them in aqua and orange, the team colors, for the home opener." He held one of the tags against the sample in the plasticene.

"Could be," he said. "A definite maybe."

Detective Barren looked at the two slips of paper. They were the same width.

"Right color," Stark continued. He felt through the plastic. "Feels like the right thickness, too. Can't say for sure," he said. "But a real possibility."

He hesitated, then looked at Detective Barren.

"Why?"

She hesitated. Why not? she thought.

"Murder," she replied.

He let out some breath in a long whistle. He looked back down at the two papers.

"I guess it was bound to happen," he said.

"I beg your pardon?"

"Well we live in Miami, right? This is murder USA, right? I guess everybody rubs against a murder in Miami at some time or another, huh?"

"Maybe."

"Well," he said, "that sure could be what's left from one of our field-pass tags. It could be almost anything else, too, for that matter. I mean, what do I know?"

"Do you know who prints those for you?"

"Sure. That's easy. Biscayne Printing up at Sixty-eighth Street. They can tell you in a minute whether that's theirs."

So can forensics, she thought quickly.

"And have you got a list of people that they were issued to?"

"Yep. Which game?"

"Last September eighth."

"Got it right here." He swiveled to the file cabinet, dug about again, and emerged with another file. She wanted to snatch it out of his hands, but held back. "Actually, the game was on the ninth. The eighth was the Saturday before."

An idea struck her. She felt her throat quiver. It was very dry and she had to cough before asking the next question. She felt dizzy again.

"Did anyone request two passes? I mean, did anyone call and ask for an extra because they lost one?"

Stark looked surprised, then nodded. "I get you," he said. He looked down at the folder. "The NFL requires us to keep strict lists of who's shooting the games. Security reasons, partly. But mostly they like to control the photographers, control the publicity. Sometimes I think I'm working for Big Brother." He picked out a typewritten sheet. "There were a lot of passes for that game," he said. "Everybody wanted pictures of the stud who just got the big contract today. He was a rookie, and nobody had good art."

"Good art?"

"That's what they call it. God knows why. A good picture is good art. Rembrandt would turn over in his grave if he ever heard one of those animals say that."

He looked at the list. "Three guys," he said. "Three guys lost their passes. Whoops, sorry. Two guys and a girl. Woman, I mean. The local AP gal, a guy from the Miami *News,* and a guy shooting for SI. He's a contract guy with Black Star. Usually *Sports Illustrated* uses their own guys, but I guess this time they were strung out too thin. Baseball, college football, the pros— you know." He flipped the paper across the desk. "Is a copy all right?" he asked. "I need to keep the original."

She nodded. Her head spun, but she thought of another question:

"Did they give any reason for needing another pass?"

"Yeah," Stark said. "The NFL is real careful about who gets these things. They don't want the sidelines cluttered with everybody's cousin." He looked at another piece of paper. "Let's see, ah, yeah. The AP gal had hers in her bag. She was flying Eastern and they lost the bag. That had to be the truth. The guy from the *News* had his eaten by his ten-month-old, and the guy from out of town, let's see, lost his in a fight . . ."

159

Stark leaned back in his chair. "You know, I seem to remember when he came in that morning for a new one, he had a pretty good welt above his eye. Everybody was kidding him about it. He was pretty good-natured about the whole thing, though."

Detective Barren felt her stomach plummet. I knew it, she thought. I knew she fought hard. Susan would never let anyone steal her life so easily.

She picked up the list from the desktop, looking down at the names printed on the page.

She tried to steady herself, thinking that she couldn't be sure until she went to the printer. Then she would need to have forensics run tests to make doubly certain. The process could take some time, she cautioned herself. Move slowly. Move carefully. Be certain. Inwardly, she doubted her ability to take her own advice.

She stared again at the names printed on the page, but the letters seemed to jump about, as if teasing her. There he is, she thought. There he is.

The old Cuban gentleman who came out from behind the counter at Biscayne Printing to assist her was gracious and deferential.

She produced her badge, which caused him to look up in some astonishment, obviously, Detective Barren thought, slightly disturbed by the idea of a female policeman. Still, he took the torn yellow tag gently from its plasticene cover and turned it over, rubbing the paper texture between his fingers.

"This," he said with a tinged accent, "is certainly similar to the passes that we print for the Dolphins. But this year, of course, the color has changed."

"Could it be . . ." she started, but he held up his hand.

"Last year," he said. "If I can take this, I could show you the bulk lot we purchased, perhaps make a perfect match for you?"

This was a statement presented as a question. Detective Barren knew that the forensics department of the county police could make the same match easily.

She shook her head. "No, thank you. I just wanted . . ."

He held up his hand. "Anything for the beautiful detective." He smiled with an old man's benign lasciviousness.

She retrieved the paper sample and wondered when the next flight to New York took off.

The droning of the jet engines failed to disturb her preoccupation with a single dominating thought, an inability to focus on anything save the name, which she repeated over and over to herself terrified, in a way, at the ordinariness of it. She gave the taxi driver the address almost unconsciously. When she pulled up in front, the huge office building barely registered. Like an automaton, she punched in the seventeenth floor on the elevator, squeezing into the back with a dozen office workers, riding in swooshing silence to the photo agency.

She waited a few minutes in a lobby while a receptionist went to get an editor. She spotted a series of framed photographs, all of disasters or wars, and she wandered over, staring at the first out of curiosity, then with a frightening interest. It was seeing the name that drove her out of the half-light of consciousness she'd fallen into. There, she said to herself. There he is. It steeled her. Several photos displayed on the wall were Douglas Jeffers', including a shot of a grime-streaked fireman, eyes captured by defeat, as a city block burned in the background. It was Philadelphia.

She turned away as the editor came out to talk to her. Her first thought was to lie. Lie cleverly, lie completely, lie blatantly. Do nothing alarming. Create a diversion, she thought. She did not want the photo agency contacting Jeffers and telling him a policewoman was looking for him. She hesitated only briefly before uttering the first lie. She shook a sense of guilt from her mind and sauntered ahead. She recognized the expediency of her falsehoods, but still considered them a momentary weakness when the forces driving her, she thought, were powered by righteousness and honesty. They had to be.

The assistant dispatch editor was friendly but reluctant. "I mean, he's not here. I really don't know how to say any more. Sorry, but . . ."

Detective Barren nodded, shaking her head in mock disappointment. "Boy, you know the old gang is going to be so sorry. Everybody wanted to see old Doug."

"What do you mean?" The assistant editor asked. He was a middle-aged man, wearing a bow tie. He had an understated lecherous air, the sort of slightly disheveled man constantly on the make, and more often than not able to use his rumpled teddy bear approach successfully. She thought she could use this. Detective Barren smiled generously at him.

"Oh, really, it's nothing. It's just a bunch of us who covered the Move bombing in Philly together and got to know each other have this reunion planned . . . no big deal, really. You know how we all met? Hunkered down a little ways back from where the firemen and cops were getting ready to blow the place up. Old Doug was like a racehorse. He couldn't stand waiting. He just had to get his shot, you know, no matter how much shooting was going on. Isn't that just like old Doug . . ."

"Sounds like the crazy kind of thing he'd do . . ."

"Well, no big deal. It just would have been nice to get Doug involved. Everybody loves hearing war stories, you know. That's why I came up here . . ."

"Gee, sounds like fun . . ."

"Yeah, well, last year it got a bit rowdy . . ." She half-winked and added a coy little blush for the editor's benefit. She hoped he wouldn't ask her anything about the incident in Philadelphia. She busily searched her mind for the few news stories she'd read. "But it's okay, really."

"I'm sorry," the editor said.

"No big deal. It's just, well, you know Doug. He keeps to himself so much. We were kind of hoping to draw him out a bit, you know?"

"You're not kidding. Photographers are an odd bunch . . ."

"Well, old Doug, he's one of the best . . ."

"He sure is."

"You know, you'd really be surprised how many people he's made into friends, out there in the boonies, on assignment."

"I always figured he did. Lord knows he keeps to himself around here. But I mean," the editor said, "you can't go into some of those places without learning to risk a bit with other people. Flying bullets make for fast friends."

"Isn't that the truth?" Detective Barren said.

"Where'd you say you were from?" he asked.

"The *Herald*. Just in town for a day or two . . ."

"Well," he said, "all I can say is that he's on vacation and he didn't leave any itinerary with us. He's due back at work in three weeks, if that's any help. You can always leave a message here . . ."

She thought of the wait. Impossible.

". . . Or why don't you try his brother?"

"Doug never mentioned a brother."

"He's a doctor at a state hospital in New Jersey. In Trenton. Doug always lists him as next of kin before heading into some war zone. Why don't you try him? Maybe he can get a message to Doug. I'd hate to see him miss a good party . . ."

"Tell you what," Detective Barren said. "I'll give the brother a shot. If it doesn't work out, I'll leave a message here, okay?"

"Sure."

"Boy," she said in an almost girlish voice, "you've really been a help. You know, we get this together, maybe you'd want to come for a drink?"

"Love to," he said.

"I'll call you," she replied. She smiled. "I can reach you here pretty easily?"

He smiled the vague smile of the hopeful. "Anytime."

But her mind had already closed on the information she'd received, and her heart was tugging her fast toward New Jersey.

CHAPTER
=SIX
AN EASY PERSON TO KILL

11. DOUGLAS Jeffers watched the expanse of inky black highway flow beneath the front wheels of his car and hummed meaningless rhythms to himself. Behind him, morning was sliding up onto the horizon. Light began to filter gently through the car, creeping into the corners and filling the interior. Jeffers glanced over at the sleeping figure next to him. Anne Hampton's mouth was slightly ajar, her breathing even and controlled. The morning light seemed to rest on her features, making them sharp and distinct. He tried to study her dark eyebrows, long, aquiline nose, high cheekbones, and wide lips, stealing glances from his concentration on the roadway. He watched the way the clean early light blended with her straw-colored hair; it seemed momentarily to be glowing. He wondered again whether she was beautiful or not. As far as he could tell, she was, in a clear, simple fashion.

He wanted to run his finger down the side of her face, where the light was marking the edge of her cheek, to wake her with a small stroke of tenderness. He saw that she had a small bruise there and for a moment felt sad. He'd been extremely lucky that he had not had to kill her.

Jeffers turned away and saw the last wan outline of the moon in the sky, before it became absorbed by the sweeping expanse of blue that was building swiftly into daytime. He liked the mornings, though the light was difficult, sometimes nearly impossible to shoot in. But, when captured, it touched the picture with a magic that was undeniable. He thought of a morning in Vietnam when he'd done the foolhardy thing of going out with a South Vietnamese Ranger battalion. He had been young and so had the soldiers. The other cameramen he'd been with—a crew from ABC News, another freelance shooting for Magnum, and a guy from the *Australian*—had declined the offer of a chance to see some combat and quietly tried to dissuade him from going. But he had been caught up in the laughter, shouting, and easygoing camaraderie of the men. They had been all posturing and bravado, waving weapons and grinning with confidence as they climbed in the deuce-and-one-half green trucks that would carry them into the field. He had jumped up with them, smiling, snapping off shots, taking names, and enjoying the relaxed mood so intoxicatingly unfamiliar to men at war.

There had been an easy day of tromping through the rice paddies and fields beneath a friendly and familiar sky. They had bivouacked shortly before dark on a small rise, surrounded by trees and high brush. Jeffers remembered that the men had continued their relaxed laughter into the night, but that he'd stared out into the enveloping darkness with apprehension. He'd crawled into this foxhole early after lifting an M-16 and a half-dozen clips from an ammunition pile and putting it next to his sleeping roll. He made a small stack of hand grenades on one side of the bed, and put his Nikon, loaded with fast film, on the other. He tightened his flak jacket around him, ignoring the discomfort. His last thoughts before sleep had been angry, angry with himself mainly, hoping he would survive the night. The goddamn officer in charge had put only a skeleton platoon out on the perimeter and no one deeper in the bush in listening posts and he had wondered idly, without panic, without fear, but with a sense of frustrated foolishness, whether they were all going to die that night. Or just most of them.

Then he had staggered into a light sleep. The encampment had been hit a couple of hours after midnight, and the firefight had lasted through the remaining darkness, until the daylight chased away the enemy, who retreated in victory, fading into the jungles of their success. Jeffers had crawled from his hole, moving slowly and painfully, streaked with dirt and blood, like some primeval beast from its lair. His grenades were gone, his ammunition expended in the frenzy of night. But, he remembered, he still had rolls of film, and he'd stood, as the darkness slid away, loading his cameras, waiting for the light to reveal the night's toll. The first insinuations of morning had landed on the dead, freezing them in grotesque poses. He remembered staring for a single moment, as the mist curled away, a light breeze blowing away the cold and the smell of cordite, revealing the twisted, savaged figures littering the battlescape. Then he'd seized the

Nikon and started shooting, moving crablike through the wreck-age of men and materiel, trying to pluck both grace and horror simultaneously from the dead, fighting his own battle after the real battle had passed.

Newsweek had used one of those shots in a prescient story on the questionable capabilities of the South Vietnamese Army. He remembered the picture: a small soldier, probably no older than fourteen, flung backward over a bent ammunition canister, eyes stuck open in death, as if surveying the remainder of the life he would not have. It ran some six months before Saigon fell. That was more than a decade ago, he thought.

I was so much younger then.

He smiled to himself.

Athletes like to talk about young legs, legs that can run all day, then run some more, but photographers need them, too. He remembered just a few months past hiking through scrub hills in Nicaragua with a detachment of Guard when the rebels started to walk mortar fire toward them. He'd stayed in position, listening for the high-pitched whine and thump of the mortar shells as the explosions moved inexorably toward where he and the men had clambered down, seeking shelter. He remembered how he'd heard the sound of his motordrive whirring above the noise of the shells, and thinking then how strange that was and how battle made all one's senses acute.

The men surrounding him had broken, of course, and run. It was infectious, the need to run from fear, and though he couldn't remember actually tasting fright on his own tongue, he'd found his feet just as readily. He'd fled with the young men, a dozen years or more his juniors, but outdistancing them easily, confi-dently, so that he was able to turn and catch a picture, one of his favorites, F-1.6 shot at 1000. Violent death had not changed much, he thought. In the background there was a spiral of smoke and a violent upheaval of dirt, while in the foreground three men, tossing weapons and web belts aside, were rushing toward the camera. A fourth man was spinning down, caught at the heels by death, pinned by shrapnel. *Life* had used the picture in their World News section. He thought: Fifteen hundred dollars for a millisecond of time, stolen out of weeks of deprivation, some fear, and much boredom. The essence of news photography.

He looked back down at Anne Hampton.

She stirred and he caught her eyes opening to the sunlight.

"Ah, Boswell arises!" he said.

She started and sat up quickly, rubbing her face hard.

"I'm sorry," she said. "I didn't mean to doze off."

"It's all right," he replied. "You need your rest. Your beauty sleep."

She turned and stared out the windows. "Where are we?" she asked, then she turned back toward him in near-panic. "I mean, only if you want to tell me, it's not important really, I was just curious, and you don't have to say anything if you don't want to. I'm sorry. I'm sorry."

"It's not a secret," he said. "First stop is the Louisiana coast."

She nodded and opened the glove compartment, taking out one of the notepads. "Should I take that down?" she asked.

"Boswell," he said. "Be Boswell."

She nodded and made a notation in the pad.

Then she looked back up at him, pencil poised. She saw that he was watching her as carefully as he could while still eyeing the highway ahead.

"You reminded me of someone," he said. "A woman I saw in Guatemala a couple of years back."

She didn't say anything, but continued to scribble in the book. She wrote: "Memory of Guatemala, several years old . . ."

"The real story," Jeffers continued, "was up on the border, where the military was trying to root out a couple of guerrilla factions. It was one of those little wars that Americans weren't supposed to be involved in, but were, all over. I mean, Army advisers, high-tech weaponry, CIA guys running around in bush jackets and mirror shades on their eyes, and US Navy destroyers on maneuvers off the coast . . ." He laughed a little and continued. "Remind me to talk about delusions. It's what we're best at . . ."

She underlined the word delusions three times.

"Anyway, lost in all this bang-bang guerrilla-hunting was this little peculiarity about the Guatemalan situation. For years, hell, I suppose centuries, the indigenous Indian population has taken the brunt of the bad times. Both sides, Marxist guerrillas, rightist militarists, shit, even the liberals, what there were of them left after being murdered equally frequently by both sides, uniformly slaughtered the Indians from time to time. I mean, they were just not considered people, follow? Like, if an Indian village lay between the two sides, it was ignored . . ."

"How do you mean 'ignored'?" she asked tentatively.

He smiled. "Good. Very good, Boswell. Questions that help clarify matters are always welcome . . ."

He paused, thinking.

"If the sides were in position for a fight, but the intervening land was some large important estancia, well, things would just

167

be moved. It was as if both sides realized certain places were off limits. Like kids playing touch football. Out of bounds was a state delineated less by boundaries than by a mutually agreed-upon state of mind . . ."

He continued: "Anyway, not so with an Indian village. They'd just blast away. Anyone who got in the way, well, tough. That was what I was thinking of. We walked through one of those villages after a fight. I think maybe the government troops had killed a couple of guerrillas and the guerrillas managed to kill a couple of government troops. That's it. No big deal. But they sure as hell had torn the shit out of the village."

He hesitated.

"Baby blood. There's nothing like it. It's almost useless to take pictures of baby blood because no one will run them. Editors look at them, tell you how powerful they are, what a statement they make, but damn, they won't run them. Americans don't want to know about baby blood . . ."

He looked over at her.

"There was one Indian woman, sitting, holding her child. She looked up as I took the picture. Her eyes were like yours. That's what I remembered . . ."

Again he paused.

"I was standing next to this CIA guy named, named, Christ, Jones or Smith or some other lie he told us. He looked down and saw the woman and the child, same as me, and he said to me, 'Probably got hit when those rebel rounds fell short.' And he looked hard at me and said, 'The damn Russians are always short-loading the shit they sell these backwater revolutions. Too bad, huh?'"

Jeffers thought before continuing. "I remember his words perfectly. He was one of those guys that wasn't there, you know."

Jeffers was momentarily silent and drove on steadily.

"Do you understand what he was saying?"

"Not exactly," she replied.

Without hesitation, Jeffers took one hand off the wheel and slapped her hard. "Wake up! Dammit! Pay attention! Use your mind!"

She cowered back in the seat, fighting the tears that formed instantly in the corners of her eyes. It was not so much the pain of the blow, which on the scale he'd established was relatively low, it was the suddenness of it.

She took a deep breath, struggling for control. She could hear the quaver in her voice as she spoke: "He was saying we didn't do it . . ."

"Right! Now what else?"

"He was fixing the blame for murder on everyone but . . ."

"Right again!" Jeffers smiled.

"Now," he said, "isn't it easier to use your head?"

She nodded.

"Gratuitous cruelty. Delusion. If we had not been there, there would have been no battle and the child would have lived, at least a few more days, weeks, who knows. But we were there. But we didn't cause the death?"

He laughed, but not at a joke or anything humorous.

"Delusions, delusions, delusions."

She wrote this down.

Anne Hampton thought of a dozen questions and bit back each one.

After a moment he said, "Death is the easiest thing in the world. People think killing is hard. That's only what they want to believe. In reality it is the simplest thing around. Pick up the newspaper some morning, what do you see? Husbands kill wives. Wives kill husbands. Parents kill children. Children kill each other. Blacks kill whites. Whites kill blacks. We kill in secrecy, we kill in stealth, we kill publicly, we kill with purpose, we kill by accident. We kill with guns, knives, bombs, rifles— the obvious things. But what happens when we cut a federally subsidized grain shipment to Ethiopia? We kill, just as surely as we would had we taken a handgun and put it to the temple of some little kid with a swollen belly. Hell, if you think about it for a moment, our entire national approach to the world, to life itself, is based on the question of who we may or may not kill on any given day. And what weapons we might or might not use. Foreign policy? Hah! We should call it our death policy. Then a spokesman could get up at a nice Washington press briefing and say, 'Well, the President and the cabinet and the Congress have decided today that Guatemalan Indian peasants, South African demonstrators, certain elements of the issue in Northern Ireland, both sides, mind you, and a few other sundry peoples about the world are doomed. Once again, just as I said yesterday, and the day before, and the day before that, the Russians are okay. No need for dying there.'" He stared down the highway and laughed.

"I really sound crazy."

He glanced over at her. "Do I scare you?"

Her heart sped as she tried to decide what the right answer would be. She shut her eyes and spoke the truth: "Yes."

"Well," he said, "I suppose that's reasonable."

He was quiet before continuing. "Well, politics wasn't how I wanted to start this. I mean, we can talk with more sophistication after you come to know me a little better. That's why we're heading this way."

"Can I ask a question?" she tried timidly.

"Look," he answered with a slight tone of irritation. "You can always ask. I've told you that before. Please don't make me repeat things. Whether you get an answer or"—he balled one fist, then released it—"some other response really depends on my mood." He reached down and suddenly grabbed the muscle above her knee, pinching it painfully. She gasped. "Remember, there are no rules. The game simply progresses, stage by stage, until it ends."

He released her leg. It continued to burn. She wanted to rub it to try to reduce the pain, but dared not. "Ask!" he said.

"Are we going someplace where you'll help me know you better?"

He smiled. "Smart Boswell," he said. "Excellent Boswell."

Jeffers hesitated, just to give his words a bit of impact: "That should be obvious. That's the whole point of this little trip." He smiled and aimed the car down the highway.

They drove on in silence.

Anne Hampton daydreamed as they swept past Mobile on the interstate. It was still early and she thought of the pleasant sensation that rising at dawn in the summer brings; a feeling of synchronization with the day. She recalled when she was a child how she enjoyed padding about the house by herself. It was time she spent in special quiet, alone with her things. Sometimes, she remembered, she would crack the door to her parents' room and watch them lie in their bed. When she was sure they wouldn't stir, she would creep across the hallway to her brother's room. He would be flung across the bedclothes, a jumble of sleep, absolutely oblivious to the world. Her brother slept late. Always. Without fail. A bomb blast wouldn't wake the little terror. It was as if her brother's body knew how important it was to store energy for the nonstop way he threw himself into life. Inwardly she smiled. When Tommy died, she thought, the entire world probably slowed, even if just a small amount, an infinitesimal measurement, readable only by the oldest, wisest scientists at the greatest universities with the newest, most exacting instruments. When I die I'll be lucky if there's a ripple on some tiny pond somewhere, or a little gust of breeze in the trees.

She blinked hard several times swiftly, to clear the thoughts from her head. My mind is filled with death, she said to herself.

And why shouldn't it be? She glanced over at Jeffers, who was whistling something she couldn't recognize as he steered the car.

"Are you only going to talk about death?" she asked.

He turned toward her momentarily before shifting his gaze down the road. He smiled. "Good Boswell," he said. "Be a reporter." He paused, then continued. "No. I'll try to talk about some other things. You raise a valid point. The trouble is"—he laughed before going on—"a certain preoccupation with morbidity. Fatalism. Ends rather than beginnings."

He paused again, considering. Anne Hampton scribbled down as many of his words as she could manage, then stared in despair at her handwriting. She didn't trust its legibility, and wondered suddenly, in a moment of fright, whether he would check.

Jeffers broke into a grin and laughed out loud.

"Here's a story for you. The best life-affirming story I can think of off the top of my head. I'll try to come up with some more from time to time, but this one, well, it was when I was with the Dallas paper, the *Times-Herald*, back in the mid-seventies. People used to call it the *Crimes-Herald*, but that's another story...

"Anyway, I was working day general-assignment, which usually meant anything from flower shows and business-page shots of captains of industry—what a silly phrase that is—to accidents and cops, and anything else that might come through the window. And we got this call, I mean, it was one of those sublime moments on a newspaper, which of course, no one ever realizes, but happens nonetheless. Guy calls in and says the damnedest thing just happened. What's that? replies the city-desk man, who's bored out of his skull. Well, the guy says, it seems like this couple was having a fight, you know, a domestic. They were getting a divorce and they were arguing over child custody and grabbing at the baby right and left and screaming at each other, and the dude tries to snatch the baby out of his old lady's hands and whoops! Out the baby goes, right out the fourth-floor window...

"Well, the city-desk editor finally wakes up, because this is a helluva story and he starts yelling for me and a reporter to get going, because there's a baby been tossed out of a window and suddenly the editor realizes that the guy on the phone is trying to interrupt. Yeah, yeah, the editor says, just give me the address. You don't understand, the guy on the phone says, starting to get exasperated. What don't I understand? says the editor. The story, says the guy. Well? says the editor. The story, the guy says, after getting his breath back, is that someone caught the baby. What!

171

says the editor. That's right, says the guy, there was this dude walking right underneath, who looks up and sees this baby come out the window . . . and damn if he didn't catch it right on the fly."

Jeffers looked at Anne Hampton. She smiled.

"Really? I mean, he caught the baby? I can't believe . . ."

"No, no, he did. I promise . . ." Jeffers laughed. "Fourth story. Just like a football player making a fair catch."

"What's a fair catch?"

"That's where the guy receiving the ball can raise his arm and signal the other team that he's going to catch the ball without trying to advance it. Then they're not supposed to tackle him. It's the ultimate act of self-preservation."

"But how . . ."

"I wish I knew." Jeffers laughed again. "I mean, the guy must have had incredible presence of mind. . . . I'd guess that most people would look up and see this shape coming out the window and scurry out of the way as fast as possible. Not this guy."

"Did you talk to him? I mean, what did he say?"

"He just said he looked up and somehow knew right away, split second, really, that it was a baby, and he circled right under the child. He'd been a center fielder on his high-school baseball team, too, which was really funny, because when he said that, everyone nodded and thought, Sure, that explains it, but of course it didn't explain anything, because baseball players don't usually get much baby-catching practice."

"But maybe that's where he learned to catch?"

"I guess so. Football, baseball. It was a story that lent itself to sports metaphors."

Jeffers looked over at Anne Hampton. She caught his eye and shook her head. Then she smiled and the smile widened into a grin. The two of them laughed out loud.

"That's incredible. A bit wonderful, as well . . ."

"In a way, that's what photographers do. They periodically go from one incredible to the next . . ." Jeffers hesitated. "Better get that down," he said, then paused while Anne Hampton scrawled some more notes on her pad. When she looked up again, Jeffers continued. "Anyway, I can tell you that that particular assignment absolutely made my day. Hell, it made everyone's day. Made my week. Made my month, probably. I shot the guy, he had the most, I don't know, delightful, I guess, sheepish grin on his face. We were all of us laughing and giggling, reporters, photographers, television crews, passersby, neighbors, the cop on the beat, everyone. Even the kid's father, standing there in handcuffs, because the cops felt they sure as hell had to arrest *somebody* when a baby gets tossed out of a window. Funny thing was, he didn't seem to mind. Then I got a picture of the mother, too. Have you ever seen a person whose life changes so abruptly, so quickly, so many times? From terror to despair to agony to hope to incredible happiness in a couple of seconds. It was all wrapped in her eyes. An easy picture to take. Just put the baby in her arms, sit her down next to the guy who caught the child, and press the shutter button. Bingo. Instant pathos. Instant joy."

"Unbelievable," she said.

"Incredible," he said.

"You're not kidding me, just trying to make me feel better?"

"No. Not a chance. That's not something I do."

"What?"

"Try to make people feel better. It's not in the job description at all."

"I didn't mean . . ."

He interrupted. "I know what you meant."

He glanced over at her and smiled. "But it should make you feel better anyway."

She felt an odd warmth.

"It's nice," she said. "It's a really nice story. It does."

"Make sure you get it down," he said.

She scribbled quickly in the notepad.

". . . And the baby lived," she wrote.

She stared at the word for a moment: lived. For a moment she wanted to cry, but she was able to stifle it.

They continued down the highway in the first benign silence she'd known for what she sensed was only hours but suddenly seemed to her to be weeks.

Gulfport slid past them as the morning sun took root. Occasionally the roadway would dip toward the Gulf of Mexico and Anne Hampton watched for the insouciant blue of the baywaters. These glimpses comforted her, as did the infrequent sight of a flight of gulls as they floated on the wind currents, just above the waves. She thought they seemed like gray and white sailboats, the way they moved with ease in conjunction with the desires and demands of nature.

It was midmorning when Jeffers said, "Time to tank up."

He pulled off the interstate, heading down a narrow ramp toward the first gasoline station he spotted. To Anne Hampton it seemed to be a ramshackle place; the small white clapboard attendant's building seemed to sway in the morning breeze, leaning against the solid square brick garage for assistance. Two lines of red, blue, green, and yellow pennants snapped in the wind above the pumps. They were the old-fashioned kind that gave off a ring as each gallon was pumped, not the newer, computer-driven style that was more familiar to her. It was called Ted's Dixie Gas and was empty save for three cars parked on the side by the garage. Two of the cars seemed to be derelicts, stripped and rusted, barely recognizable. The third was a cherry-red street racer, its tail end jacked up, oversized tires and chromed wheels. Someone's fantasy, she thought. Someone's time and effort and money wrapped up in small-town heroics. She stared at the car as Jeffers crunched up to the pumps, knowing that a slick-haired teenager would emerge momentarily to take their order.

"Hit the head," Jeffers demanded.

His voice had a sudden roughness in it. She shivered.

"You know the rules, don't you?"

She nodded.

"I don't have to explain anything to you, do I?"

She shook her head. She noticed that he had the short-barreled pistol in his hand and that he was sticking it in his belt, beneath his shirt. She stared, then turned away.

"Good," he said. "Makes things much easier. Now sit still while I come around to open your door."

She waited.

"Hurry up," he said as he swung wide the door. She looked up and saw a gangly teenager with straight dark hair sticking haphazardly out from beneath a battered, faded baseball cap, walking across the dusty station toward them.

"Fill'er up?" he drawled. It took him almost as much time to speak the words as it had for him to lope across the space between the garage and the pumps.

"To the top," said Jeffers. "Where's the ladies' room?"

"Wouldn't y'all want the men's room?" the boy replied, grinning. Anne Hampton thought suddenly that Jeffers would shoot the teenager right there and then. But instead Jeffers laughed. He made his finger into a gun and pointed it at the boy. "Bang," he said. "You got me on that one. No, I meant for the lady, here." The attendant turned his huge grin on Anne Hampton and she smiled faintly in return.

The boy pointed to the side of the building. "Key's on the inside of the door there. The old man will show ya." He waved at the gas station office.

Anne Hampton looked at Jeffers and he nodded.

She felt hot as she crossed the twenty feet to the station. It was as if the wind had suddenly died down, just in the space around her. She stared up at the pennants, which still flapped and twisted above her, and wondered why she could not feel the breeze. She felt dizzy and her stomach churned in quick fashion. She stepped out of the sunlight into the doorway. There was an older man, unshaven, with a greasy striped shirt on, sitting by the register, drinking a can of soda. Her eyes fastened on a sewn name above his shirt pocket. It said Leroy. "The bathroom key?" she asked.

"Right next to you," the man replied. "You okay, miss? You look like yesterday's bacon left in the skillet overnight. Can I get you a cold one?"

"A what?"

"A soda." He nodded toward a cooler.

"Uh, no. No. Yes, actually. Why, thank you, Leroy."

"Hell, it's my brother's shirt. That good-for-nothing never did a solid day's work. I put all the grease there. I'm George. Coke?"

"That'd be fine."

He handed her the cold can of soda and she pressed it against her forehead. He smiled. "I like to do that, too, when the heat gets to me. Seems to get right inside your head, that way. Better with a bottle of beer, though."

She smiled. "How much do I owe you?" Then, suddenly, she almost choked. She had no money. She turned quickly, searching for Jeffers.

"Hell, it's on me. Don't get to buy nothing for no pretty gals too much no more. Make the boy jealous, too." He laughed and she joined him, her breath bursting from inside her in relief.

"I appreciate it." She put the can in her purse.

"No matter. Where you heading?"

She choked again. Where? she asked herself. What does he want me to say?

"Louisiana," she said. "Just taking a little holiday."

"Right time of year," the attendant said. "Even if a tad bit warm. We get a lot of folks traveling through. People ought to stay, though. Got a right fine beach and there's fine fishing. Not so famous though, as some other spots. That's the problem. It all boils down to publicity nowadays. You got to get the word out. No two ways about it."

"Get the word out," she said. "That's right."

"Got to be the right word, though."

"True enough."

"Like take this place," he said. "The boy's a right fine mechanic. Better'n his old man, for sure, though I don't let on noways. Give him a swelled head and all. But got no way to let folks know. They end up taking their cars to those fancy big places near the shopping malls, when, hell, we'd do a better job for half the price."

"I bet you would."

He laughed. "Feeling better?"

"Yes," she said.

"Got to get the word out. Don't make no matter what you're doing in life, fixing cars or selling burgers or fixing to fly to the moon. Publicity is what makes this nation work. Yes, ma'am. You got to tell folks what it is you got and what it is they're gonna get. You just gotta get the word out."

He handed her the bathroom key.

"Just cleaned up this morning. Fresh soap and towels on the back of the door. You need something else, just holler."

She nodded and started out the door. She turned and pointed in a quizzical way and he nodded to her and waved her around the corner.

It was cool inside the rest room, but close, and the air seemed old and tired. She quickly used the toilet, then went to the sink and splashed water on her face. She looked up in the mirror and saw herself pale and drawn. I've seen this scene a hundred times, she thought, picking up the soap bar. It's in every movie on television. She remembered Jimmy Cagney and Edmund O'Brien. *"White Heat,"* she said out loud. He writes on the mirror in the gas station. She thought of Jeffers and pictured him speaking: I'm on top of the world, Ma! She wrote the word HELP on the mirror. Then she wrote, I'VE BEEN . . . what? She rubbed that out. She felt hot and her hand was shaking. Got to get the word out, she thought, mimicking in her mind the slow Southern accent of the old man. CALL POLICE she scrawled, then rubbed that out when she realized she'd written it too swiftly and it was illegible. And tell them what? She felt nauseated and gripped the sink to control herself. She looked down at her hands and pleaded with them, as if they weren't attached to her body. Be still, she prayed. Be steady.

She looked back up. This is where the heroine gets saved, she thought. The attendant comes in and calls the handsome young policeman, who saves her. It always worked that way. Every time. She rubbed the mirror clean, using quick, panicked strokes. What if it doesn't work that way? she thought. She suddenly felt angry and impatient, and she smeared soap across the mirror. The soap bar had gotten wet, and streaks of white ran down the surface. Like tears, she thought. It never happens like in, what? Fairy tales. The movies. The stories her father used to tell her when she was a child. She looked at her reflection between the soap streaks. She could see redness rimming her eyes. She shook her head in dismay and impotence and clenched her fists in anger and helplessness. No handsome prince through that door. It'll be him. He'll come in. He'll see it. He'll kill me. And George. And the boy who fixes the cars. He'll kill all of us. One right after the other.

And then maybe the word will get out.

She heard a scraping noise outside.

Bile rose in her throat. Oh, God, she thought. He's there.

The door rattled.

It's the wind, she said to herself. But she frantically wiped at the soapy residue on the mirror.

What am I doing? she asked herself. Do you want to die?

Do nothing. Go along. He hasn't hurt you yet.

That was a lie and she knew it. She argued with herself quickly. He will. He has. He's going to use you and kill you, he said it himself.

The door rattled again.

He's everywhere, she thought suddenly. The room was windowless, and she spun about, looking at the whitewashed walls. He can see! she said. He knows. He knows. He knows.

Just walk out calmly and apologize, she thought.

She checked herself in the now-clean mirror as if she would see signs of betrayal on her face that he would notice. Then she turned and walked slowly back outside, thinking: I am blank inside. She returned the key to the hook by the door and turned to the gas pumps and froze in sudden and complete terror.

Jeffers was standing next to the car, talking with a state trooper. Both men were wearing large sunglasses and she couldn't see their eyes. She stopped, as if suddenly rooted.

She saw Jeffers look up and smile at her. He gave her a wave.

She couldn't move.

Jeffers waved again.

She screamed commands to her body: Walk! But she was still frozen. She forced herself to push and pull at every muscle and managed to take a step, then another. The walk across the sunlit macadam surface seemed interminable. The heat seemed to build around her, and she had the odd thought that it was burning her. We're all going to die, she thought. She saw Jeffers reach under his shirt and the black revolver jump into his hand. She heard the gun's report. She saw the trooper falling back, dying, but in his own hand was his weapon and it was spitting bullets and fire. She saw the teenager and George the attendant diving for cover as the pumps suddenly exploded into flame.

She took another step and realized none of it was happening.

Jeffers waved again. "Jump in, Annie, I just want to get these directions straight." He turned toward the trooper. "Now, as I get into New Orleans, the road splits and six-ten takes me downtown and four-ten heads to the coastal parks?"

"You got it," said the trooper. He smiled at Anne Hampton and touched his hat brim. The little motion of politeness seared her insides.

"Great," said Jeffers. "Always like to double-check. You've been a big help."

"My pleasure," said the trooper. "Have a nice day."

He turned toward his own car and Jeffers slid down behind the wheel. At first he was quiet as he slowly accelerated out of the station past the trooper's cruiser. Then he asked in a flat, harsh voice, "What were you and the old man jawing about?"

"I'm going to be sick," Anne Hampton said.

"If you're sick," Jeffers replied, his glance narrowing, but his voice taking on a flat tone better suited to a discussion of the weather or rising prices, "everyone dies."

She clenched her teeth and squeezed her eyes shut.

She gulped in air.

"We were talking about publicity," she said. "About telling the world when you've got something to sell. Like his boy's mechanical ability."

"Publicity fuels the world," Jeffers said. "Just as much as Arab oil." He looked quickly at her. She turned away and saw the roadway stretch in front of them. He was steering the car up the ramp, back toward the interstate.

"I'm okay," she said, and she thought: I must be.

She looked over at Jeffers and saw that he seemed to have relaxed. He was smiling faintly.

"Good Boswell," he said. "When you feel good enough, write it all down in the notebook. Exciting, no? Especially the bit with the trooper, huh? Gets the adrenaline flowing."

Jeffers hummed and gunned the engine. Again, she did not recognize the tune, but she hated it nonetheless.

As Douglas Jeffers drove, he daydreamed halfheartedly. Anne Hampton had grown silent beside him, staring out the window with what he thought was a desirable vacancy. He did not want her imagination moving too swiftly. She was still vulnerable to the strengths she had inside her. That she was unaware of them

178

was typical, he thought. She could still break the spell and make some move for freedom, or perform some act that would jeopardize the trip, but her ability to do this would diminish, he knew. It already had been halved, perhaps quartered. Within a day or so, he considered, it will have evaporated save for a dangerous residue which he must always be aware of. Even the most domesticated, cowed, and docile beast will sometimes, when least expected, slash back at the threat of extinction. He resolved to be on his guard for signs of this. Whether they would ever surface he knew was problematical. For a moment he wondered whether she was aware of any of the literature of possession. Certainly, he thought, she's read John Fowles. Did she remember Rubashov and his interrogators? Should he tell her about the Stockholm Syndrome? He thought he would, perhaps a little later. Knowledge, when wielded properly and dangerously, he considered, can be used to further confuse and obfuscate the truth. It would increasingly underscore her helplessness if he told her that psychologically she was caught in a web from which she was not equipped to free herself. Deepen her despair. He looked over at her, examining her profile as she steadily searched the horizon from the car seat. He tried to see a glow of independence, smell a whiff of resolve. No, he thought, not her.

I've taken it. As I knew I would.

She has given in.

I can do with her what I please.

He almost laughed out loud, stifling the sound before it erupted, like some schoolboy who had been passed a dirty picture behind the teacher's back.

She is like clay now. I can form whatever I want. He wondered idly whether she had any inkling that her life had changed completely, that she would never be the same, nor ever be able to return to what she had once envisioned for herself.

To himself he said: No one's going home again.

He thought of the stricken look on her face when she'd spotted the trooper. It had terrified her, he thought. By tomorrow she will be so wrapped up that she will be more frightened of the police than I am. And I'm not frightened at all.

He smiled, inwardly, but with just a trace on his lips.

She's mine.

Or at least she will be within twenty-four hours.

His mind danced with possibilities. What an education she's about to get, he thought.

No harder than my own.

A memory picture crept quickly into his mind, aggressively,

uninvited. He saw himself at age six, being led through the night by the druggist and his wife. He remembered how surprised he'd been at the sight of the house. It seemed to his child's eyes to be huge, imposing, and dominating. He'd been afraid, and remembered how important it had been not to let Marty see how scared he was. It was not at all like the hotel rooms and trailer parks that his mother had dragged them through. His first mother, he thought. For a moment he thought he could smell the battling odors of perfume and alcohol that came back to him whenever she entered his memory. He reached down and cracked the window, letting some air into the car, fearing that he would sicken with all the hatred that churned in his stomach.

The air cleared the memory smell away and he thought of the first look up the flight of stairs to their room. He recalled how tightly Marty had gripped his hand. It had been dark and the few lights the druggist had switched on threw odd shapes on the walls. He could not actually recall climbing the stairs, though they had. But what he remembered next was being half-led, half-pushed into the tiny room. The walls were whitewashed and there were two army cots unfolded. There was a single lamp, which had no shade. There was a single window which was open, letting cold air pour into the room.

It had been bleak and sterile, he thought.

He forced himself a smile. It was not a response to pleasure, but an allowance of irony. That had been the first battleground, he thought. Marty had been exhausted and fallen instantly into sleep. But I stared at the walls. In his memory he saw the morning confrontation:

Can we put something on the walls?

No.

Why not?

You'll make a mess.

We won't. We'll be careful.

No.

Please.

Stop whining! I said no! That's it. No!

It's not like a room. It's like a prison.

I will teach you now that you're not to talk to me that way.

It had been his first beating. First of many. He thought it odd that he felt an absence of emotion when he remembered the flailing fists and staggering blows that this new father poured down on him. His mind filled with hatred, though, when he thought of how this new mother sat by so quietly. Damn her eyes! he thought abruptly. She did nothing! She sat and watched. She always sat and watched. She said nothing, did nothing.

He hesitated, as if catching a mental breath.

Damn her eyes to hell!

His memory filled again, like holding a cup beneath a spigot. He'd been shunted off to a new, strange school for the remainder of the day. That had been a horror in itself. But what he remembered best was the morning art class, where he'd seized the biggest sheet of white paper they'd had and quickly, deliberately, smeared great bands of blue and orange, red, yellow, and green across it, swiftly making a great glowing rainbow. Then he'd grabbed another paper and fashioned a steamship tossing on a wild gray sea. Then a third, and a pirate captain, with a red sash, black beard, and Jolly Roger in his hands. He'd left the paintings drying and returned that afternoon to ask the teacher if he might take them. When she approved, he took them and ran to the bathroom. Locking himself in a stall, he dropped his pants and carefully wrapped the paintings around his leg.

He remembered the stiff walk home. Why are you limping, asked his new mother. I fell at school, he said. It's nothing. Feels better already. He'd hopped up the stairs to their room, where he found Marty trying to play on the floor with an empty shoe box. He remembered his brother's smile when he'd pulled out the paintings and stuck them, with stolen school tacks, on the druggist's careful white walls. He remembered Marty's sudden wide smile and it made him grin in pleasure: A boat, his brother had cried, to take us back to Mommy!

That's been a long voyage, Jeffers thought.

One that we're still on.

He eased the car past a large truck with an engine that roared deafeningly, penetrating the silence of the car's cockpit. He saw Anne Hampton flinch at the sudden assault of sound. He swung the car back into the right lane easily as the truck disappeared behind them and continued down the roadway, forcing his mind back to an easy nothingness, as if, he thought, he could make his own mind as blank and horrible as those damned white walls, vacant, forgetting that which he'd seen, that which he'd done, and that which he still planned to do.

They swept past the outskirts of New Orleans as the early-afternoon sky started to darken and Anne Hampton saw great gray storm clouds fill the horizon. She noticed that Jeffers seemed to accelerate as the weather worsened, and when the first large raindrops splattered against the windshield, he reached for the wipers switch with a muffled curse of irritation.

She said nothing, having learned that he would speak when he wanted to. After a moment he broke the silence, proving her prudence justified.

"Damn," he said. "This fucking rain's going to make things difficult."

"Why?"

"Harder to find landmarks in the rain. It's been a long time since I was here."

"Can you tell me where we're going?"

"Yes."

He was silent.

"Will you? But only if you want . . ."

"No," he said, "I'll tell you. We're heading toward a place called Terrebonne, which is a coastal parish. A little ways past a little town called Ashland. I haven't been here, since, well, since August eight, nineteen seventy-four. This is why anything, like the weather changing, or a new road, and God knows all the roads seem damn new, can screw me up."

Anne Hampton looked out the car windows at the swampy marshland interspersed with pine stands and an occasional willow tree. It seemed to be a place of prehistoric terrors, and she shivered.

"It looks really wild."

"It is. It's a fantastic place. Like another planet. Lonely. Forgotten. Isolated. I really liked it when I was here."

For a moment then she thought that her heart stopped. Her throat closed as if someone had wrapped his hands around her neck. Her mouth went completely dry.

It's where he means to kill me, she thought.

She tried to open her lips to speak but could not.

She knew she had to fill the sudden silence, and she raced through her mind, trying to think of something to say that would fill the cockpit when all she wanted was to scream. Finally she spoke, instantly regretting the weakness and the vapidity of her words.

"Do we have to go there?" she asked.

She thought she sounded like a whining child.

"Why not?" he replied.

"I don't know, it just seems, I don't know, out of the way."

"That's why I selected it."

She saw him glance over at her.

"You're not taking this down," he said irritatedly.

She reached for the pen and notebook, but her hands were

shaking again and the words on the pages were blurred and un-readable.

He hit her then, swiftly, the flat of his hand hardly seeming to move from the rim of the wheel. She gasped, dropped the pen, and using every ounce of presence of mind, instantly reached down and seized the pen again. The pain barely registered.

"I'm ready now," she said.

"You've got to stop being so stupid," he said.

"I'm trying."

"Try harder."

"I promise. I promise I will."

"Good. There's still hope for you."

"Thank you. It's just, just . . ."

She couldn't form the words and she gave in to the quiet that took over. She listened to the engine sounds mingling with the slap, slap of the wipers and wondered what it would feel like when it happened.

"Dumb Boswell," Jeffers said after a few moments had passed by. He thought idly of reassuring her, letting her know that he still had plans for her. But then he thought better of it. Better to have the occasional tears than to have her gain any confidence. "You should think less on the longevity of life and more on the quality."

She nodded.

"Get that down," he said. "Aphorisms. The world according to Jeffers. Poor Douglas Jeffers' Almanac. The sayings of Douglas Jeffers. That's your job."

"Of course," she said.

They drove on and she felt inundated by the rain, the darkness and fear.

"You know where we're going, Boswell?" Jeffers asked. Then he answered his own question. "We're going to visit an old friend. Don't you think sometimes that memories are like old friends? You can summon them up much as you would reach for a telephone. They come into your consciousness and comfort you."

"What if they're bad memories?" Anne Hampton asked.

"Good question," he replied. "But I think, in their own way, bad memories are as helpful as the good. You measure these things on an internal scale, your own set of weights and balances. The nice thing about bad memories is that, well, they're memo-ries, aren't they? You're past them. On to something new . . .

"In a way, I suppose, I don't rate memories. I see them all as part of an overall picture. Like taking a long time-exposure, like one of those fancy *National Geographic* shots, you know, where the camera records the blooming of a flower or the hatching of an egg."

She wrote that down.

Jeffers laughed coldly.

"We're heading toward where the new Douglas Jeffers hatched." He craned forward in his seat, peering up into the enveloping gray sky. "One of the dark places on earth," he said. He glanced over at Anne Hampton. "You know who wrote that?"

She shook her head.

"Actually someone wrote it, but a character said it. Who?"

He snorted, almost with humor.

"You're an English lit major, c'mon. Can't let some battered old newshound outquote you. Think!"

She raced through her memory.

"Shakespeare?"

He laughed. "Too obvious. Modern."

"Melville?"

"Good guess. Closer."

"Faulkner? No, too short . . . uh, Hemingway?"

"Think of the sea."

"Conrad!"

Jeffers laughed and she joined him.

After a minute she asked, "Why are we going to one of the dark places on earth?"

"Because," Jeffers said, matter-of-factly, "that's where I discovered my heart."

They drove on in quiet. Anne Hampton saw Jeffers' eyes glint when he spotted an exit sign for a rural route. "I'll be damned," he said. "That's the road." He swung the car from the highway and suddenly she realized they were on a narrow secondary road, lined with large trees that seemed to block the sky and that parted in the wind to let sheets of rain spatter down. They swooped around one twist in the highway and she felt the car slide slightly, the back tires spinning momentarily, squealing for purchase on the rain-slicked highway, an unsettling feeling, reminding her that they were careening down the roadway, just barely under control.

"Love is pain," Jeffers said.

He waited a moment.

"When I was little, I used to hear my mother's men. They would stumble and clomp about making more noise trying to be careful than they would have if they'd just acted normally. It would be late at night and she would assume I was asleep. I

184

would keep my eyes closed tight. There was a little red light in the room, so I could just crack my lids apart and see. I remember how she would groan and complain and finally cry out in pain. I never forgot . . ."

"It seems very simple, doesn't it? The more love. The more hurt. Sounds like some doo-wop song from the fifties, huh?" He crooned, "You always love the one you hurt . . ."

He looked over at Anne Hampton.

Then he sang again: "You always kill the one you love . . ."

Then he turned away and concentrated on the road.

"We're getting closer," he said.

But she could hardly hear him, she was suddenly so wrapped in fear.

They continued cutting between the stands of trees, heading farther into the swampy darkness. She could see no signs of life save the occasional modest roadside home standing white against the increasing gray of the day. As they drove, she could see more of the sky, filling with even darker clouds, and she knew they were approaching the coast. Jeffers remained silent, concentrating, she hoped, on the highway, staring ahead in a sullen, fixed fashion. She could see great strikes of lightning in the distance, flashes that were flung across the sky, followed by cannon rumbles of thunder that penetrated the car. The rain had increased in volume, pelting the car, flooding the windshield between swipes of the wipers. She prayed they would not have to get out of the car, but knew they would. And then she thought it would probably make no difference, getting wet. Still, she had the odd idea that she didn't want to shiver from the rain onslaught, to seem wet, bedraggled, and pathetic when it happened.

Jeffers turned the car again, and they were on an even smaller road, even more deserted.

She stayed silent, trying to think of home, of her mother, her father, her friends, of the sun and the summer that seemed to have disappeared in the gray flood of rain and wind.

Jeffers turned again, and the road became bumpy. It was unpaved. He swore. "We'll get stuck if we go down there. Hell, it's only a half mile or so . . ."

He pulled to a grassy spot and stopped the car.

She hated the sudden disappearance of the engine noise. The silence seemed to envelop her.

"Douglas Jeffers thinks of everything," he said. He reached into the back seat and pulled out a small duffle bag. He unzipped it swiftly, then shoved a bright yellow poncho at her. Then he pulled out a dark-green set of rain pants and coat. "The best from L. L. Bean," he said. "A big part of photography is anticipating future discomfort. I hope that fits. Use the hood."

He helped her pull the poncho on. Then he slid into the rain-suit. "All right," he said. "Let's go."

There was a clap of thunder and a new sheet of rain hit the car. Jeffers smiled and flung himself through the door. In a second Anne Hampton's door was pulled open. She knew better than to hesitate.

The force of the rain seemed to snatch her breath, and for an instant she stood, disoriented, stunned by the strength of the wind. She felt Jeffers' hand grip her arm with familiar strength, and she let herself be pulled along. The road was sandy and infirm, and she slid in her sneakers, half-pushed by Jeffers. For an instant she wished that she could at least die somewhere dry and familiar, that this was especially unfair. She could not see him, it seemed to her that one instant he stood behind her, the next he was at her side, the next pulling her along from in front. She tried to formulate theorems and conclusions in her mind: Why would he give me a poncho and then kill me? she thought. But what frightened her most was the rain-drenched realization that assigning logic to anything that was happening to her was a mistake. She closed her eyes against the lightning and rain and started to mumble snatches of prayers to herself, as each foot hit the ground, trying to find some comfort in long-forgotten rhythms: "Our Father, who art in heaven, Hallowed be thy Name . . ." Then: "Forgive us our trespasses, As we forgive those who trespass against us . . ." Jeffers pushed her a bit harder and she gasped. "Yea, though I walk through the shadow of the valley of death I shall fear no evil . . ."

"Come on!" Jeffers said. "Should be right ahead."

"Hail Mary, full of grace, blessed be the fruit of your womb. Hail Mary, full of grace, Hail Mary, full of grace, Hail Mary, full of grace . . ."

"Come on, dammit! Let's go!"

"Hail Mary, hail Mary, hail Mary, fullofgrace, fullofgrace, fullofgrace, Hail Mary . . ." She shut her eyes as she walked forward, trying to think about anything other than the rain, the wind, and the pressure of Douglas Jeffers' grip on her arm. She wondered if he would give her a blindfold and a cigarette like some military execution. Her tears mingled freely with the rain striking her face.

Then, suddenly, she put her right foot down and the sandy soil beneath it gave way, and she slipped forward, falling. She let out

186

an involuntary "Ouch!" as she fell, more a sound of some odd indignation than any pain. Then she turned back toward Jeffers, who was standing, shading his eyes as if against the sun, peering about him.

"Damn!" he said.

He kicked the sandy dirt.

"Shit! Shit! Shit!"

He stomped about in a small circle, peering into the distance. He punched the air angrily. "Damn! Damn! Damn!"

She dared not say anything.

Then he turned and looked at her.

She thought she could not breathe.

Then he laughed. His laughter grew, rising up in the wind currents and seeming to mix with the wind and thunder.

He stood above her, laughing for several moments.

"Well," he said finally, after rubbing his eyes. "Well, what a screw-up. We're in the wrong place. I told you it's been years . . . There ought to be a big, I mean really big, willow down there and there isn't. I must have taken the wrong road."

He helped her to her feet.

"Back to the car," he said.

"That's all?" she asked. She regretted it instantly.

But Jeffers seemed not to notice. "That's it," he said. He threw an arm around her shoulders and helped walk her back to the vehicle.

The closeness of the car cockpit seemed comforting to her. Jeffers gave her a small towel and both of them tried to dry themselves as best as possible. Jeffers continued laughing, mildly, as if terribly amused. He started the car and they headed back to the highway.

"You wouldn't think a person like me would screw up, would you?"

"No," she replied.

"I mean," he said, grinning, "I pride myself on thinking of just about every damn thing. Don't leave anything to chance. Just goes to show, the best-laid plans . . ."

He smiled. "What's funny is that this place is really important to me. At least the memory of it is."

He smiled and drove the car slowly.

"Well, too many years, I guess. Too many other roads."

"I still don't know what we were looking for," she said.

He hesitated, then shrugged. "My first date," he said. "My first real love."

"A girl?"

187

"Of course."

He paused again.

"Down one of these damn dirt roads that all look the same," he said, "there's a shady willow tree, set back aways in some scrub brush . . ."

She nodded.

"And that's where I buried her."

He spoke these words with a sudden, unexpected, total harshness. They plunged into Anne Hampton's heart.

She felt a torrent of nausea overcome her and she clenched her teeth and waved wildly at Jeffers. He stopped the car, understanding instantly, threw open his door, and suddenly dragged her across the center console, across his lap, holding her head in the rain, where she was completely, violently sick.

Night closed around them as they drove back toward New Orleans. They had spent the remainder of the afternoon in damp silence, but Jeffers' mind had filled with memories. He was trying to remember the girl's name. He knew it was Southern, like Billie Jo or Bobbi Jo, and he remembered her silver-spangled dress, cut too short and too tight, and which left little doubt as to what her profession was. He'd picked her up, trying to contain himself, knowing what he was going to do, acting nonchalant and flashing a wad of cash. She had complained, at first, when he started driving toward the outskirts of the city, but he remembered taking the extra twenty-dollar bill and tucking it into her cleavage and telling her he'd make it worth her effort. She had babbled on, the singsong accent and vapidity of her words disrupting the essence of his thoughts, and so, at the first available deserted location, he'd stopped the car, turned to her, and, as she lay back, closing her eyes, cold-cocked her. And then he had headed toward the location picked from a map, with its bastardized French name: the good earth. It had been easy to drive into the swampy darkness alone with his thoughts. It made no difference to him whether she was awake or not. It was the act that intrigued him.

"She was a prostitute," he said.

Anne Hampton nodded glumly.

"What life had she that she needed so badly?" he asked angrily.

She didn't respond.

"You're filled with silly antiquated ideas about right and wrong and morality," he said.

"You don't understand," he continued after a momentary silence. "She was born to die. I was born to kill. It was simply a matter of finding one another."

She turned toward him and started to say something but stopped.

He spoke for her: "You want to say it's wrong to take a life, right?"

She nodded.

"So maybe it is. What difference does it make?"

She couldn't reply.

"I'll tell you: it makes none."

He looked at her again.

"Governments kill for policy. I kill for pleasure. We're not all that goddamn different."

"It's not that easy," she said. "It can't be."

"No? You think it's hard to kill? You think it's so damn hard? Okay," he said. "Okay, goddammit. Okay."

The rain had lessened to a drizzle, but it made the headlights from the car streak through the night blackness. New Orleans glowed in front of them, and Jeffers accelerated the car toward the lights. He said nothing as they slid into the city, letting the late-night shadows from the high-intensity vapor lamps crease the darkness. She felt no comfort in the city, no more than she felt in the swamps, and she suddenly realized that to a person like Jeffers they were the same. She looked at Jeffers, at the set to his face and jaw, and felt her stomach churn.

They meandered up and down the city streets. Jeffers peered through the windows, apparently looking for something, but she was unaware what. Suddenly he punched the brakes and steered to the sidewalk.

"You think it's so damn hard," he said angrily. "It isn't."

He searched up and down the street, then reached down into his weapon bag and came up with the short-barreled revolver. He pushed it under her nose. "Hard? Watch. Roll down your window." She complied and the car immediately filled with damp, sticky humidity. She shivered. She did not know what was happening. Jeffers exited the car and walked around to her side. He bent down to the window. "Watch carefully," he said. She nodded.

He stepped away from the curb and she looked and saw a shape huddled in a dark building entranceway. She saw Jeffers look up and down the street again, then stride across the sidewalk.

Jeffers poked at the derelict with his foot.

"Wake up, old-timer," he said.

The man raised a grizzled head, still stuporous.

Jeffers turned and looked back at Anne Hampton. She saw that the man was bearded, with a benign hoary curiosity, not angry at being awakened, only surprised. Her eyes met Jeffers' and he looked hard at her. She felt as if she was caught in an inexplicable downdraft, and that she was tumbling wildly through the air, driven down by some great invisible force. She saw Jeffers turn back to the derelict, who seemed to be trying to find some words from his lost past to form into a question.

"Good night, old fellow. Sorry it had to be like this," Jeffers said.

He leaned down abruptly and in a single fluid motion stuck the gun barrel into the man's slightly gaping mouth. Jeffers raised his left hand to shield himself from any blowback.

Then he pulled the trigger.

There was a single muffled crack and the man seemed to jump, just once, then slump back as if returning to sleep.

Anne Hampton opened her mouth to scream, but could not.

Jeffers stepped away, glanced down the street again, and returned swiftly to the car. They pulled away from the curb slowly, turning at the corner, then again, and again, and again, weaving their way through the darkness in complete solitude.

"Roll up your window," Jeffers said.

Her hand shook on the handle. Her breath came in short spasmodic bursts. She let small whimpering noises emerge instead of words.

"You see how easy it is," Jeffers said.

He looked over at her.

"It's your fault," he said.

He paused.

"If you hadn't challenged me, then I wouldn't have had to do such a despicable thing."

He fixed her with a quick, sharp glance.

"It was your fault. Your fault completely. It was just as if you had taken the gun yourself and pulled the trigger. It was just like you murdered that man. Snuffed out a life. See? Now you're just like me. Do you understand that? Do you understand, killer?"

Anne Hampton nodded behind tears.

"How does it feel, killer?"

She could not find words and he did not press her.

They drove into the expanse of night.

CHAPTER
SEVEN
DISBELIEF

12. MARTIN JEFFERS hurried through C ward, white coattails flapping behind him. He barely acknowledged the patients who shuffled awkwardly out of his path, parting like innocent animals meandering about a barnyard, making way for one with purpose. He managed to nod at the patients he knew, who greeted him with the usual assortment of stares, smiles, snarls, averted looks, and the occasional curse that was the day-to-day standard of the locked wards. He knew that his swift pace would cause some conversation behind his back; it was unavoidable. In a world reflecting the constancy of routine, any behavior that spoke of some external need or force was cause for discussion, debate, and unwavering curiosity.

His own sense of intrigue ran equally unchecked. As he hurried along, he speculated shamelessly about the arrival of the homicide detective; considering as he reviewed the membership of the Lost Boys, trying to think which one might have mentioned being in Miami within the past few years, which member of the group might have been oddly reluctant to talk about some recent event. In a gathering that devoted much of its energies to concealment, Jeffers had become expert at recognizing the hidden or the taboo. He swiftly searched his memory but was unable to come up with an instant answer. He recognized the sense of sudden excitement in himself; there was something compelling about the phrase "homicide detective" that carried with it a weight of mystery and fascination. He tried to form a mental picture of a woman investigating a murder, and thought she must be someone frumpy, hard-edged, and purposeful. He wondered why he thought the idea of investigating death to be a masculine

191

province; as if the nature of bloodied and shattered bodies was somehow inherently male, a violation belonging, in an odd way, to the arena of poker parties or locker rooms.

His mind filled with images of sudden, violent death. He was struck with the quick portrait of his brother, picturing him in bush jacket and khakis, ready for one of his frequent travels to some war, disaster, or other representation of man's folly.

He thought of his brother's photographs from Saigon, Beirut, and Central America. A photo of his brother's leaped out at him, a shot he'd seen in one of the national newsweeklies. It had been of another photographer, standing in the midst of a group of bodies at Jonestown, Guyana. The jungle greens and rich browns had formed a curtainlike backdrop for the man, who stood out in odd incongruity to the creeping dense growth behind him. The photographer had a red bandanna over his nose and mouth. It took just a moment to stare at the picture and realize that it was protection against the stench from the bodies swollen by sun and death. The photographer looked almost like some child's idea of an old Western desperado, in jeans, boots, and denim shirt. In the photographer's hand, though, instead of a six-gun had been a camera. And in the man's eyes had been confusion and a kind of world-weary sorrow. Douglas Jeffers' shot had caught his competitor at a moment of indecision, as if overwhelmed by the litter of suicide, not quite knowing what horrific image to plunder next. It was a perfect vision, Martin Jeffers had thought when he'd first seen it and now when he recalled it: that of a civilized man, standing in a prehistoric world, trying to comprehend behavior belonging to the world of animals, seeking to capture it for the consumption and fascination of a society that is perhaps less safe from aberration than it likes to think.

Jeffers hurried on, thinking of how many of his brother's pictures were of death. He realized they were all individually fascinating, in their own way. We are forever searching, he thought, to understand people's behavior and the act that frightens all of us the most is murder.

But what is more common? he wondered.

And are we not all capable?

Now he sounded like his brother talking, Jeffers thought. He shook his head and listened to the squeaking sound his shoes made on the corridor's polished linoleum floor. Well, some of us are a hell of a lot more capable than others. The faces of the Lost Boys flashed into his head.

That a detective would come to visit was not unusual. He recalled a number of occasions in the past few years when he'd received a similar summons and been brought face-to-face with some dark-eyed, monosyllabic man who'd asked increasingly pointed questions about one or another of the members of the therapy group. Of course, his ability to assist had been severely limited by medical ethics and the concept of patient confidentiality. He remembered one detective, particularly persistent, who, after a frustrating conversation with Jeffers, had stared at him angrily for a long minute, then asked: Does the man have a roommate? No, Jeffers had replied. Does he hang out with anyone in particular? Well, yes, Jeffers remembered saying, he has one friend. Well, said the detective, let me talk to that man.

Jeffers recalled the way the detective had sat across from the compatriot of this one suspect in some forgotten crime. The detective had been direct, forceful, but never overly aggressive. Jeffers remembered thinking he should study the detective's approach, that there were some moments in the therapeutic process when it might be effective. He was impressed that within an hour the detective had had all the information he needed from the man, who was all too ready to sell his friend's life for the promise of a reduction in his own term. Jeffers did not resent it. Ultimately, it was the way things worked in the world occupied by the Lost Boys, a place of trade-offs, deals, and lies.

Treachery as a way of life. Commonplace. Routine. He was struck with the idea that life is no more than a constant series of small betrayals, picayune lies, a constancy of compromise and rationalization.

He wondered again about the woman detective. She complicates things. So much of the work he did with the Lost Boys was to restore some vision of females as individuals, to re-create for them a picture of the opposite sex not dependent on the hatred they all felt. The idea that one of their potential victims would come now to stalk one of their number, that was both explosive and terrifying, as if one of their deepest and most inarticulate fears had risen from some nightmare and knocked on the door to the day room.

It will give us plenty to talk about, he thought. This was part of the challenge of the work: to create some therapeutic value out of the conjunction of memory and day-to-day life.

Maybe I'll ask her to come along to a session, he thought.

That'd scare her. She'd want to arrest all of them.

And it would scare the bejesus out of the Lost Boys. They've been all too complacent lately, anyway. She could provide a necessary infusion of reality. It would shake things up, help focus the sessions, help get things back on track.

He grinned at the idea and knocked loudly on the C ward door for the attendant to let him pass. The door creaked as it opened, and Jeffers thought for a moment that everything inside the old hospital creaked and complained at use. He thanked the attendant, who stood sullenly as he swept through. Jeffers hurried down the corridor and was instantly in the administration wing of the hospital. The offices were nicer, the paint fresher, the sunlight unscarred by dirty crosshatched wire bars on the windows.

He opened the door to the administrator's office. Dr. Harrison's secretary looked up and pointed at the inner office in the suite, jerking her thumb like a hitchhiker. "They're in there, waiting for you," she said. "Which one do you think she wants?"

"In a way, probably all of them," Jeffers replied. It was a small joke, and the secretary laughed as she waved him toward the door.

Jeffers entered the inner office. First he saw Dr. Harrison, who stood up slowly from his seat behind a great brown desk. He was an older man, gray-haired, too sensitive for the peremptory work of a state mental hospital, too old and tired to try to strike out on his own. Jeffers liked him immensely, despite his shortcomings as an administrator. Dr. Harrison nodded at Jeffers, then, with his eyes, motioned toward the other person, who was rising out of a chair.

Jeffers barely had time to assess the woman. That she was close to his own age, he perceived immediately. Then he caught a glimpse of dark-brown hair, a conservative but stylish silk dress and slender figure, before he was fixed by the detective's eyes. They seemed to him to be black and staring rigidly at him. The usual male assessment of whether she was attractive or not was obliterated by the singular force of her glare. He had the disquieting sensation that he was being measured by an executioner, who with expert eye was calculating just how hard a blow with the ax would fell his head. He was immediately uncomfortable and stammered:

"I'm Doctor Jeffers. How can I help you, detective . . ."

The words simply froze in the air.

His own hand, extended in greeting, hung momentarily before she raised her own in reluctant acknowledgment. Her grip was firm, perhaps too much so. She released his hand and he let it drop and the room was filled with a solid silence that Jeffers thought was like a fog bank rolling across the ocean. A cold, dampened moment passed, then another, as her eyes held to his, unblinking.

194

Then she spoke in a voice all the more terrifying for the control he thought she wrapped around every word:

"Where is your brother?"

She damned herself instantly when she saw the mixture of shock and confusion race across his face. It had been unavoidable, she knew. As she had driven toward the hospital earlier that day, she had considered hundreds of approaches, dozens of different opening gambits, knowing all along, however, that when she confronted Susan's murderer's brother that there would be only one question that meant anything to her, and that she would be powerless to contain it. In Detective Mercedes Barren's mind, the question was radioactive, glowing, permanent. She did not doubt that she would get the right reply; when you are willing to spend forever searching for one answer, eventually, inevitably, it arrives.

And when it arrives, she had thought, I will be ready.

A part of her, blissfully optimistic, had hoped it would be obtained easily. She did not trust this optimism, but she knew that a frontal assault often produces a quick, unplanned response, a blurted-out "Why, he's in..." and the name of some city or town, before the forces of caution took over, with the invarible follow: "Why do you want to know?" She saw the brother's mouth open, and his lips start to form a response, and she leaned forward slightly, expectedly, knowing immediately that she showed too much eagerness. Then, just as quickly, he slapped his mouth shut tight, and her own hard stare was met by an equally cool eye.

Damn, she thought again. It won't be easy.

Damn, damn, damn.

In that moment she hated him almost as much as she hated the man she hunted. Flesh and blood, she thought. He's the smallest step away.

She saw the brother swallow hard and glance over at the hospital director as if to buy a few moments of precious time to sort out what she knew must be a torrent of emotions. She sensed in that brief half-light of time that he used the seconds to order himself, coolly, professionally. She thought: He must be used to the unexpected. It must be part of his daily existence. He knows how to handle it. In a moment he returned his eyes to hers and met her silence with his own. Then, without taking his glance from her, he slowly pulled up a chair, and, carefully, as if unwilling to break the electrical connection formed in the small room, sat down. He deliberately crossed his legs, and with a delicate, easy gesture, as if he had not a care or concern in the entire world, motioned her back to her chair, like a teacher to an overanxious, overeager student.

Damn, she thought again. I almost had him.

And now he's almost got me, she thought.

She sat down across from the murderer's brother.

Martin Jeffers worked hard to affect an air of interested nonchalance, much as he would show when a patient blurted out some confession to one horror or another. Inwardly, however, he felt his throat constrict tightly, as if clutched by another's hands, and the little hairs on the back of his neck rose. He could feel the wretched sudden stickiness of sweat beneath his arms and on his palms, but he dared not rub them on his pants.

He was awash in nightmare.

He would not put image to question in his mind; he focused solely on her request, refusing to engage in any dangerous extrapolation. She wants Doug! he thought. Then: I knew it! Then: But why do you know it? He fought against all the ideas that slid unbidden into his imagination: childhood fears, adult concerns.

He wanted desperately to grab hold of something, as if something solid could help steady the rocking sensation within his mind. But he knew, too, that the detective would notice, and he quickly forced everything, from his terror to his curiosity, aside, thinking: Find out. Give up nothing, but find out.

He took a deep breath. It helped.

He crossed his legs, shifting in the chair to a relaxed, comfortable position.

He reached down and adjusted one of his socks.

He put his hand to his breast pocket and removed a pen and a small notepad. He tapped the pen point against the paper several times in slow succession. Then he looked up, and, mustering all the falseness and lies he could, smiled at the detective.

"I'm sorry, detective, I didn't catch your name . . . "

"Mercedes Barren."

He wrote that down, feeling the act of scratching word to a page steady him.

"And what organization . . ."

"City of Miami police."

"Ahh, right," he continued writing. "I've never been to Miami. Always wanted to go, though. Palm trees, you know, sunshine and beaches. Warm all the time. It sounds nice. But I've never made it down there."

"Your brother has."

"Really? I don't think so, but then, he's hard to keep up with.

And of course there's always a lot of news down in Miami. Riots, boatlifts, refugees, all that sort of thing. So, I guess, maybe. And he's been, well, sometimes it seems like he's been everywhere. Globe-trotter is what they call it."

"He was there last year. In September for a football game."

"For a football game? You know, I don't think he cares that much for sports . . ."

"He was assigned to get a picture of a quarterback."

"Oh, you mean on business? Well, that sounds possible . . ."

Jeffers hesitated. He let his eyes wander about the office for a moment, gathering himself. He thought for a moment that his performance was probably not fooling the detective at all. He looked over at her and saw that she had not moved, not even a muscle. She's wrapped tight, he thought. Very tight. Instantly he wondered why. Most detectives want to schmooze, regardless of how tense the situation is. Concentrate on the question, he thought. He felt better; still wary, still in some undefined and vaporish danger, but better nonetheless.

"But what has a football game got to do with . . ."

"The homicide of a young woman. Susan Lewis."

"Oh, I see," Martin Jeffers said, but of course he knew he saw nothing. He wrote down the name and month on his pad. Then he continued:

"You know, detective, you're really getting way ahead of me. What could you possibly want with my brother?"

Revenge! screamed Mercedes Barren's head, but she kept the word to herself. She took her own deep breath, sitting back in her chair and, before replying, she took out her own notebook and her pen. I can play, she thought. And I will win.

"You're quite right, doctor. I'm getting way ahead of myself." She spoke in a carefully modulated tone, affecting some boredom, trying to rein in her intensity. She even managed a smallish smile and an offhand nod of the head. "I'm investigating a homicide that occurred last fall. September eighth, to be exact. We have reason to believe your brother may be a material witness. He might even have photographs of the crime which could help us."

She thought the use of the royal plural particularly effective. She was pleased with the way she'd phrased her response, especially the guess about photos. It would give the impression that Douglas Jeffers could help the police. Perhaps it would appeal to the brother's sense of civic duty. If he had any. She watched the doctor's face for any sign of knowledge or suspicion. He seemed to be weighing every word carefully, she realized. She cursed inwardly again. Try to hit his emotions, she thought. That will open him up. But before she had a chance to continue, he asked a question.

"Well, I still don't understand. Doug never mentioned anything like that to me. Perhaps you could explain a bit more?"

She didn't.

"You're close to your brother?"

"Well, all brothers are close to one degree or another, detective. You must have family and know that."

A nonanswer, she thought.

"When was the last time you saw him?"

"Well, it's been years since we had what I would call a real visit..."

Dr. Harrison interrupted: "Marty, didn't he come to visit just the other week?"

Jeffers wished he could glare at his friend to shut him up, but realized how dangerous that would be. He was trying as hard as possible to understand what the detective was driving at. He trusted nothing she said, not the crocodile smile and sudden easy manner, knowing only with the certitude that comes of a lifetime of fears that his brother was in some kind of trouble and he would be damned if he would add to it.

"Why, that's right, Jim, but he only stopped by for a quick lunch before heading off. It wasn't much of a visit, and it was the first time in years that I'd seen him. Hardly seems to me that that's what the detective is interested in."

"But he said where he was going?" Detective Barren asked.

Martin Jeffers was filled with machine-gun memories of his brother's cryptic description of his vacation plans. He hesitated, thinking: What did he say? What did he mean? Jeffers looked up and saw that the intensity had returned to the detective's eyes.

"Not that I recall," Jeffers replied quickly. He was instantly angry with himself for rushing the words out.

The room was briefly silent.

Mercedes Barren smiled. She didn't believe this denial for a second.

There was another pause, then Jeffers added his own question: "Certainly, detective, you've been to his photo agency? Didn't they provide you with the information you need? I know they try to keep close tabs on the whereabouts of all their staffers. Even when they're tromping about in some jungle somewhere with some guerrilla army..."

"They didn't know..." Detective Barren started, then stopped in mid-sentence. Idiot! she thought. Give out nothing! She bristled as she saw the murderer's brother absorb the words. She tried to recoup: "They couldn't be exact. But they suggested I contact you, which is why I'm here."

She's fishing, thought Martin Jeffers. But how much?

"You know, detective, this is very confusing for me. You come in here asking to see my brother, whom I haven't really had much contact with for years, to question him about some unspecified crime. You don't describe at all what the crime is, of what you think his knowledge about it might be. You imply that it's important that you contact him right away, but without making an explanation why. I just don't know, detective. I don't think we've gotten this off on the right foot at all. Not at all. I mean, I want to cooperate with the authorities as much as possible, but I just don't understand."

"I'm sorry, doctor. I can't give out confidential information."

That was lame and she knew it. She knew what his answer would be.

"No? Well, I'm sorry, too."

Stonewall me, stonewall you, he thought.

They stared at each other, once again in silence.

Detective Barren suddenly wanted to scream. She was filled with pain. I've blown it, she thought. I'm close, and I've blown it. He's got a passport and money and a brother that's going to protect him without knowing what he's done and is going to tell him that someone's looking for him and he'll be gone, just like that.

Martin Jeffers wanted to get out of the room as quickly as possible. Something is terribly wrong, he thought. He needed to sort it out, and yet realized instantly that he didn't know enough even to begin a process of understanding. He realized then that he would need to talk to the detective and he wondered how to get into a dominant position, receiving information without imparting any. He thought of his friends, the psycoanalysts. They'd know, he thought. Get her on the couch and sit down behind her head. He almost laughed.

"Is something amusing?" asked Detective Barren.

"No, no, just an odd thought," replied Jeffers.

"I could use a joke," she said bitterly. "Why not share it?"

"I'm sorry," Jeffers replied. "I didn't mean to make light of . . ."

She interrupted. "Of course not."

He could tell she didn't believe him. At that moment Jeffers looked directly at her eyes and realized that there was something more at stake. He could not precisely say why he knew this. Perhaps it was the angle of her body, the tilt to her head, the intensity of her eyes. He was almost taken aback by the forcefulness she emanated.

This, he thought, is a dangerous woman.

She was filled with loathing at that moment. He knows something, she thought, something greater than simply where his brother is. He knows something about his brother that he won't put words to. So he hides behind cleverness and all that phony psychiatric technique.

It will do him no good, she thought. None at all.

She saw Jeffers look down at his watch, then up at Dr. Harrison. She knew right away what was coming.

"Jim, I've got patients scheduled all afternoon . . ."

She spoke before the hospital administrator could.

"When do you finish?"

"I'm off at five," he said.

"Shall I meet you in your office or would you prefer to go to your home? Or a restaurant somewhere?"

She presented no other options.

"Do you think it will take long?" he asked.

She smiled, but felt no humor. He's damn clever, she thought.

"Well, that kind of depends on you."

He smiled. Fencing, he thought. Thrust and parry.

"I still don't see how I can help, but why don't you meet me in my office a little after five and we'll see if we can't straighten all this out quickly."

"I'll be there."

They both stood and shook hands.

"Don't be late," he said.

"I never am," she replied.

Martin Jeffers closed the thick door tightly behind him and looked about his office, as if expecting to see something that would explain the tangle of feelings in which he was trapped. He felt as if he were on the edge of some moment of panic, about to do something irrational, flooded with visions of his brother. He thought: He has a streak of meanness, that I know. He remembered a neighborhood boy once, filled with taunting and obscenities, who always seemed to get under Doug's skin. It would be a fair fight—they were both about the same size—all the children on the block agreed about that. But it hadn't been. Doug had tripped the boy in a moment, flipping his suddenly helpless adversary onto his back like an upside-down turtle, and proceeded

200

to whale away with his fists at the screaming boy. Jeffers had never seen rage like that, so potent, so unbridled. A killer's anger, he thought. Then he frowned: Don't be ridiculous. He'd rarely seen Doug lose control again. Of course the druggist father had slapped Doug hard, but that was to be expected. A beating for a beating.

He looked about him and thought: Don't be a damn idiot. Don't hypothesize. Don't judge. Don't guess.

Perhaps she was telling the truth: a material witness, that's what she said.

He swiftly pictured the detective's eyes. Not a chance, he thought.

He sat down heavily in his desk chair and swiveled it toward the window. He could see fragments of sunlight as they probed the stands of tall trees that marked the hospital grounds, throwing shadows and light on the well-kept lawns. It was supposed to look more like a campus, as if that would somehow hide the reality of the hospital. He watched as a man in the distance rode across a grassy area on a tractor-mower. For a moment he imagined he could smell the sweetness of new-mown grass. The nice thing about state mental hospitals, Jeffers said to himself, is that externally they are well maintained. It's only inside that one sees the paint peeling, as if steamed away from the walls by unhappy madness. It is the same with people.

He turned away from the window and asked himself: Why are you so quick to believe the worst about your brother? Then he answered the question unscientifically. Because he scares me. He has always scared me. He has always been wonderful and terrifying at the same time.

What has he done?

Jeffers shook the idea from his head. "All right," he said out loud. "All right. Let's see what we can learn."

He picked up the telephone and dialed the nurse attendants on three different floors. With each, he canceled the afternoon appointments of three patients, directing them to go to each man and tell them that he was called away on urgent personal business. He wished he could come up with some better euphemism at short notice, realizing that rumors and suspicions would fly unchecked about the ward. He shrugged. Then he slipped out of his white hospital coat and seized his tan sportsjacket from a hook on the back of the door.

Martin Jeffers locked the door to his office and quickly headed down a back flight of stairs toward the physician's parking lot.

Detective Mercedes Barren switched the air conditioner in the rental car up to full blast and glanced at her watch. This is not a real surveillance, she thought with irritation. She eyed the front door of the hospital. And even if he did come out, what good would following him do? She answered her own question: You never know until you try. She waited, shifting uncomfortably, trying to get out of the sunlight that poured through the windshield of the car. She shifted her glance to the cars lined up in the physicians' parking lot, which was clearly marked with a large sign. There wasn't a Cadillac among the bunch, she realized, which said something about the difference between the private sector and public health.

She was not totally displeased with the way the initial meeting had gone. What she was mainly concerned about was that the murderer's brother would panic and try to reach Douglas Jeffers immediately. But she guessed he would not. He would certainly wait until after the meeting they'd arranged. He would be coy and evasive, trying to probe her for information. He is the younger brother, she thought to herself. He'll need to be more sure of himself before calling.

She closed her eyes and felt sweat form on her lips. The moist salty taste reminded her of easy summer days. She wondered how many times she and John Barren had driven within a few miles of Trenton Psychiatric Hospital. Often, she thought. It was odd to be so close to home. She remembered driving alongside the Delaware River as the hot sun picked its way through the leafy overhanging branches, heading toward some game or party, lighthearted, surrounded by friends, curled under the expansive right wing of her boyfriend.

The pleasurable memory evaporated in the midday sun.

I'm alone now, she thought.

If you need comforting, she said to herself, then do it yourself. She hardened her heart and set her face, staring out through the glare of the sun against the car windshield.

Suddenly she stiffened.

She saw the murderer's brother moving quickly through her line of sight, toward his car. She thought: I'll be damned. He's making a move.

She waited while he crawled behind the wheel, started the engine, and pulled out of the lot. She stifled the desire to hurry, to latch on to him instantly, leechlike. Instead she bided her time, pulling out well after he'd exited, following him carefully, keeping him just at the edge of her vision.

Martin Jeffers figured that the detective was somewhere behind him, but paid it no heed. If she wants to waste her time he thought, she's welcome. He knew he could lose her at any point in the labyrinthine downtown Trenton streets. It was something he planned to do at some moment when it would not seem so obvious.

He paralleled the Delaware River, glancing over at it every so often. It seemed dark and dangerous to him; there were rapids that swept white water over rock points. He turned away, and in the distance caught a glimpse of the shining golden dome of the statehouse. He maneuvered his car through traffic, winding away from the river, cutting between the steady gray block office buildings that housed various branches of state government. He turned onto State Street, which was lined with trees and brownstone buildings on one side, across from the grassy lawns and marble entrance to the statehouse. There was a free meter just down the street from where he wanted to go, and he parked the car quickly. He checked the rearview mirror for some sight of the detective. He did not see her, but again he figured she was back there. He shrugged to himself, locked the car, and headed into the main entrance of the statehouse.

Inside there was a huge state seal inlaid on the floor. It was cool, slightly dark, with a touch of echo gathered about the footsteps of the visitors and office workers who paced through the building. He saw a summer-school class collected in one corner, listening to a teacher recite New Jersey facts. Across the forum he could see the pale-blue-jacketed New Jersey state trooper who guarded the entrance to the governor's suite of offices. The trooper was reading a magazine. Jeffers strode quickly across the center of the entrance forum and ducked down a flight of stairs. There was an underground passageway leading to the New Jersey State Museum. It was empty and quiet and his heels made a snapping sound as he walked swiftly down the corridor. He found the flight of stairs leading up and mounted them rapidly.

There was a librarian at the front. He showed her his state identification card and she whispered, "How can I help you, doctor?"

"I'd like to check whatever newspapers you have on file for last September," he whispered back. She was a young woman with dark hair that slid around her shoulders. She nodded.

"We have the Trenton *Times*, the New York *Times*, and *The Trentonian* on microfilm."

"Can I try them all?"

She smiled, a little wider perhaps than necessary. Jeffers felt a twinge of attraction, then immediately dismissed it. "Of course. Let me set you up at a machine."

There was a bank of blue microfilm machines adjacent to the card catalog. The young woman led Jeffers to a seat, then left him momentarily. When she returned, she carried three small boxes. She removed the first roll and showed Jeffers how to load the machine. Their hands touched briefly. He thanked her, nodding, but thinking instead of what he was looking for.

In the New York *Times* he found a three-paragraph Associated Press story in a corner of an inside page:

CAMPUS KILLER IN MIAMI
CLAIMS FIFTH VICTIM

MIAMI, Sept. 9 (AP)—An 18-year-old coed at the University of Miami was discovered murdered here Saturday, the apparent fifth victim of a killer police have dubbed "The Campus Killer."

Susan Lewis, daughter of an Ardmore, Pa., accountant, a sophomore majoring in oceanographic studies, was found at Matheson-Hammock Park several hours after disappearing from a party at the University's Student Union. She had been beaten, strangled and assaulted, police said.

Police said she was possibly the fifth victim of a killer who has struck at a number of colleges in the South Florida area.

That was all. Space must be at a premium at the *Times*, Jeffers thought. He read the story twice. Then he took out the roll of microfilm and began searching in the Trenton *Times*. It did not take him long to find an obituary in the Bucks County edition of the newspaper.

He read: ". . . She is survived by her parents, a younger brother, Michael, an aunt, Mercedes Barren of Miami Beach, and numerous cousins. The family requests that in lieu of flowers, donations be made to the Cousteau Society."

He read that again.

It explains a great deal, he thought.

He had one other idea. He went back to the librarian at the desk and returned the microfilm. "Is it possible," he asked, smiling, "to find out if there were any follow-up stories on a subject? I mean, is there any way I can give you a name and you could check to see if there were any recent stories?"

She shook her head. "If this was a newspaper library, sure. That's how they file things. It would be easy. But we don't have that kind of computer capacity. The *Times* puts out a yearly index to stories, but this year's isn't out yet. What is it you're interested in?"

He shrugged, suddenly resolved to drive over to one of the local newspapers and see if he could talk his way into their library system. "Oh, it's not that important," he said. "Just a crime down in Florida."

"Which one?" the librarian asked.

"Someone called the Campus Killer."

"Oh," she said, smiling. "They caught that guy. I remember seeing it on the news." She made a face. "A real creep. Almost as bad as that guy Bundy."

"Caught?"

"Yeah, last fall. I remember because my sister was gonna go to the University of South Florida and then she changed her mind, and then changed her mind back again because the guy was arrested. He went to prison, too."

It took Martin Jeffers another half hour to find the short story documenting the arrest of Sadegh Rhotzbadegh in the New York *Times,* and slightly expanded versions in both Trenton papers. He read them carefully, printing the information in his mind. Then he made photostats of the stories.

He thanked the librarian profusely. She seemed disappointed he didn't ask for her telephone number. He managed a wan smile, trying, in a look, to say that he never asked anyone for her phone number, which he knew was the truth. Then he let his mind wander elsewhere, instantly forgetting the look of disappointment on the young woman's face. Instead, he was organizing his thoughts, trying to plan his next step, trying to process what he'd learned, trying to create some reasonable picture in his mind that would result in an explanation for why the aunt of a murder victim in a solved crime would suddenly want to talk to him about his brother.

He knew that outrage would be a traditional response. He could scream: Why are you bothering me? What are you doing? What have I got to do with this crime? Who's in charge?

He knew he would not challenge her.

He looked down at the photostats. CAMPUS KILLER ARRESTED IN MIAMI: CHARGED IN SERIES OF MURDERS. They caught the man, he thought. So what does Doug have to do with this?

He refused to answer his own question. Instead his heart filled with fear, an awkward, disquieting sensation. He thought he should be pleased by what he'd discovered in the newspapers, but he wasn't. His nervousness simply grew. He felt encapsulated by danger, as if every step, every action, every movement were riven with chance.

He hurried back to his car, thinking: Time to lose the detective. He knew there was no particular insistence for this feeling other than the massive need to know he was alone with his fears. He did not think he could handle the added pressure of knowing she was watching him. He needed to be completely, utterly, confidently, alone.

He took a quick turn over to Broad Street, then a fast left, and another right, heading down Perry Street, past the Trenton *Times* offices. He accelerated up a rampway onto Route 1, then, just as quickly, took the Olden Avenue exit. At the bottom of the exit ramp he made an illegal U-turn, and headed back the way he'd just come. He thought he saw the detective then, trapped by the traffic, and he quickened his pace.

Martin Jeffers tried to dissect his feelings. In a way, he thought, it is childish to insist on losing the detective. He realized that, but he wanted to digest what he'd learned, and he wanted to do it in a solitude of his own construction. He headed back to the hospital, slowing, trying to compartmentalize his knowledge.

He knew he was no longer being followed. The downtown area of Trenton is an unlikely maze of streets and construction, daunting enough for the regulars, hopeless for the uninitiated. Miami, he thought, is probably all thruways and boulevards, wide, tree-lined streets, not the tangled confusion of an old Northeastern city clinging to life and livelihood. He envisioned the detective, her cool, silken presence melting in the twisted melee of cars, buses, and work crews. He wondered why it did not seem more amusing to him.

And, at the same time, he was still unable to shake the sense of foreboding that followed him even more doggedly than the police detective.

She, of course, was about a hundred yards behind him, her eyes set dead ahead, her mind a blackness of anger.

At five minutes past five P.M. Detective Mercedes Barren knocked on Dr. Martin Jeffers' office door. He let her in immediately, motioning her to a chair in the cramped office. She sat down, placing her pocketbook on the floor and a small leather briefcase in her lap. She quickly glanced about herself, eyes scanning the rows of books, the stacks of papers, the weak attempt at decoration with a pair of framed posters. She thought to herself: Don't let the clutter fool you; he is likely to be as organized as his brother.

Jeffers chewed on the end of a pencil before speaking.

"So, detective, you've come all the way from Miami, and I'm still confused as to why you need to see my brother with such dispatch."

She hesitated briefly before replying.

"As I said earlier, he is a material witness in a murder investigation."

"Could you explain exactly how?"

"Have you been in touch with him today?"

"You didn't answer my question."

"Answer mine first. Doctor, your evasiveness about this is irritating. I am a police detective investigating a homicide. I do not have to explain myself in order to obtain your cooperation. If need be I can go to your superiors."

That was a bluff. She knew he knew it.

"Suppose I said, go ahead."

"I would."

He nodded. "Well, that I can believe."

She thrust forward: "Did you talk with him today?"

"No."

They hesitated.

"There's an honest answer for you," he continued. "I have not been in touch with him today. Here's another honest answer: I don't know how to get in touch with him."

"I don't believe that."

He shrugged. "Believe what you like."

Again they were silent.

"All right," she said after a moment. "I think your brother has information about a murder. I said that earlier. I do not know the extent of his involvement. That is why I want to speak with him."

"Is he a suspect?"

"Why do you ask?"

"Detective Barren, if you want me to answer any of your questions, then you damn well better answer a couple of mine."

Her mind raced, trying to sort out small lies from big ones, trying to chart a course that spoke some truth, enough to gain the brother's assistance.

"I cannot say whether he is or isn't. A piece of evidence that we have traced to him was discovered adjacent to the crime scene. For all I know he may have a perfectly good explanation for this. He may not. That's what I'm here trying to find out."

Martin Jeffers nodded. He was trying to deduce whether she

was at least in part truthful. Sex offenders are easier, he thought wryly.

"What kind of evidence?"

She shook her head.

"All right," he said. "The crime is . . ."

"Murder."

"And your involvement . . ."

"I'm a police detective . . ."

He pulled out one of the photostats of Susan's obituary and slid it across the desk to her. His voice was rigid with distaste. "I hate lies, detective. My whole business, my whole being, is dedicated to the pursuits of certain kinds of fundamental truths. It is an insult for you to come in here and lie to me."

He thought he sounded properly pompous and angered. He was unprepared for her response. He had expected her to adopt a polar position, either chastened or outraged. She was neither.

"I insult you?" she asked in a frightening, low voice. She did not wait for an answer before plowing ahead. "And now you have the audacity to make a speech about truth? And all the time you're sitting there smugly, playing a little head-game and hiding your brother from—from—from questioning. All right. First you tell me that you think your brother is incapable of this."

She fished about briefly in her briefcase, finally bringing forth one of the crime-scene photographs and tossing it onto his desk.

He pushed it away without looking at it.

"Don't try to shock me," he said.

"I'm not."

He realized then that her words had the force of screams, but that she'd not once raised her voice. He picked up the picture and stared at it.

"I'm sorry for you," he said.

But his imagination was swept into a slippery vortex of fright. The picture seemed like an etching by Goya, each shadow hiding some terror, each line a sense of horror. He saw the young woman stretched in death, savaged. He thought of a moment in medical school when he'd confronted his first corpse. He had expected someone, something, old, tired, misshapen with age and disease. But his first cadaver had been that of a sixteen-year-old prostitute who'd overdosed one unfortunate night. He had looked down into the dead eyes of the girl and been unable to touch her. His hands had shaken, his voice quavered. For an instant he'd thought he was going to faint. He'd turned away, heaving air into his lungs, gasping. It had taken him every fiber of strength to go to the anatomy professor and request an exchange. He remembered switching with another student—a loathsome man who'd remarked, "Nice tits," as he wielded his scalpel. Jeffers could still see the corpse of the elderly wino he'd been assigned, wanting in some strange way, before plunging his own knife into the man's hairless chest, to embrace this skeletonlike shape and thank him for ridding him of some of his terror.

He stared at the picture again and thought of the girl on the slab.

"I could never do it," he said softly.

For a moment he did not realize what he'd said.

She did. It seared her. She summoned more control from her heart.

Detective Barren let the silence mount around them before she cracked it ever so gently with a simple question: "But what about your brother?"

Jeffers felt his insides churn. With difficulty he gathered himself together and retreated into his best clinical tones.

"I don't believe my brother is capable of such a thing, detective. I can't believe it. I won't believe it. I don't believe it. You're talking about savagery, uh, despicable, reprehensible, I don't know. I'm insulted that you'd even ask."

Detective Barren stared at him.

"Are you really?" she asked gently.

He managed an ineffectual snort and an impotent wave of the hand in response.

"Assume, for the sake of this conversation, that . . ."

He interrupted.

"Assume nothing, detective. I don't want to play with hypotheticals. My brother is a prize-winning photographer. He is one of the most sought-after freelancers in journalism today. He travels the world. His work appears in every major publication. He is honored and respected. He is an artist. In every sense of the word, detective. An artist."

"I didn't ask you about his professional qualifications."

"No, that's correct. You didn't."

He hesitated before adding:

"But it's important to realize we're not dealing with some, some . . ."

She cut in: "Ordinary man?"

He nodded. "All right."

Her voice re-formed on the edge of rage: "You think an ordinary man could do this?"

He reeled.

"You misunderstand me."

"No, I don't. I don't at all."

She stared at him and he used the moment to try to regain some distance. Jeffers decided to go on the offensive.

"And this, I suppose, is a routine investigation?"

"Yes. No . . ."

"Well, which?"

"It is not routine."

"It couldn't be, could it, detective? Not when the victim is your niece."

"Correct."

"Then explain to me, detective, if you will, why you are here trying to connect my brother to a crime that has already been solved?"

He reached down and thrust another photostat of a news story across at her. She glanced at it rapidly, then pushed it aside.

"The murder of Susan Lewis was not solved. It was only attributed to that man. I have evidence that indicates he did not commit the crime."

"Will you share that with me?"

"No."

"I didn't think so."

"The evidence is circumstantial."

"I would imagine so. Because if it were more than mere guesswork, detective, then you would have tried to browbeat me with it already."

That was true. She nodded.

"You're correct, doctor."

He paused before continuing. He felt stronger, more aggressive. He returned to his best clinical approach.

"Please, detective, enlighten me. The aunt of a murder victim arrives here seeking to connect my brother to a crime that's been solved. Now why shouldn't I find that confusing and unusual?"

He looked across the desk at the detective and realized that there was something new in her eyes. They seemed to glow. He realized, too, that all of his pedanticism was useless. There was silence before she replied in a singularly deep, even voice.

"You should," she said. She paused again before continuing.

"But if it was so goddamned surprising to hear that your brother was sought in connection with a murder, why didn't you toss me out then?"

She looked directly at him, her eyes harsh and unforgiving.

"Why weren't you shocked? Speechless? Astounded?"

She breathed in and out evenly.

"I know why," she continued quietly, terrifyingly. "Because you weren't surprised to hear it. Not at all, goddammit."

She hesitated again while she registered the effect her words had on him.

"Because you've been waiting to hear exactly that for some time, haven't you?"

Her words were like bullets probing for Jeffers' heart. He forced his mind to go blank, not accepting the questions she'd thrust at him, denying his own imagination simultaneously.

He stood and walked to the window.

She sat watching.

The summer evening was closing in. The dusk seemed gray. He thought it was the hour of the day most like the first few moments after a nightmare, when people are not certain whether they are safe, awake in their bed, or still asleep, trapped by their dream.

He took an immense breath. He released it slowly, then took another. To himself he screamed: Get control! Show nothing!

But he knew these were impossible commands.

"Detective, what you say is provocative. I think we had best continue this conversation tomorrow..."

It was weak and ineffectual, but he knew he needed time. Insist on it! he said to himself.

She started to speak, but he wheeled away from the window and held up his hand.

"Tomorrow! Tomorrow, goddammit! Tomorrow!"

She nodded.

"After my group session, around noontime."

"Okay."

She paused before asking, "You're not going to cancel that like you did today's appointments?"

He glared at her. He didn't reply.

"All right," she said. "I'll take that as a negative."

She stood and looked at him.

"You won't call him?"

"I told you, detective, I can't." Jeffers, she saw, was struggling for composure. What a fragile man he was, she thought suddenly. She wondered how she could use this to her advantage.

"Suppose he calls you? Suppose that happens—what're you going to say?"

"He won't."

"He might."

"I said he won't."

"But if he does?"

"He's my brother. I'll talk to him."

"What will you say?"

Jeffers shook his head angrily. "He's my brother."

CHAPTER
════════════════════════════EIGHT
OTHER DARK PLACES

13. THEY drove north, paralleling the Mississippi River.

Douglas Jeffers called it "The mighty Miss-sah-sip" and gave Anne Hampton a short course on Mark Twain. He was clearly disappointed to learn that she'd read only *Tom Sawyer*, and that when she had been a senior in high school. She was uneducated, he told her bitterly. If she did not know about Huck, he said, she knew nothing. She certainly would find it more difficult to understand him. "Huck is America," Jeffers insisted. "I am America." She did not reply, but scribbled down his words in her notepad.

He spoke this in a low voice. Then he adopted a pedantic, lecturing tone and told her that the river had once been the most important route for commerce in the nation, that it had been the signaling point for the jump across the West, that it slid through the heart of America, carrying politics, culture, civilization, and sustenance on the backs of its waters. To understand the river, he said, was to know how America formed. He told her that the same was true of people; one merely had to determine what river coursed through a man, or woman, then follow it to the basin of comprehension. She looked bewildered and he suddenly screamed at her, "I'm talking about myself, goddammit! Can't you see what I'm saying? I'm trying to teach you things that no one, no one in the world knows! Don't sit there like a slug!" She cowered, waiting for the blow, but he held off, though she saw his hand clench into a fist. Then, after a momentary pause, he continued musing about the river.

Occasionally they would swing close enough in the car for her to see the gleaming wide surface reflecting the daylight, the waters flowing ceaselessly, steadily onward toward the gulf that lay behind them. He insisted she take down all of his rambling speech, almost word for word, saying that someday she would recognize the value inherent in the phrases and fragments, and she would be thankful that she had managed to copy them down properly.

She did not understand that, but during the past days she had found it comforting when he would talk about the future, no matter how vaguely, as if there were some world extending beyond the windows of the car hurtling through the countryside, a life past Douglas Jeffers' long reach. She obeyed, scratching letters, shaping words as quickly as she could.

When he asked her to reread it to him, she obeyed.

He asked her to make a small correction, then a small addendum. She obeyed.

She obeyed everything. To refuse him anything was utterly alien to her.

Several nights had passed—she had trouble saying to herself precisely how many—since he had shot the derelict. Since I shot the derelict, she thought. Then: No, since *we* shot the derelict. They stayed each night in some forgettable motel near the edge of the highway, the kind of places with neon red vacancy signs blinking in the darkness, where the water-glasses are wrapped in paper and the management puts signs on the toilets to say that they have been properly sanitized.

As they were entering their room in one of the motels she saw a man standing next to a soft-drink machine a short distance away. He wore a cheap brown suit and a tie loosened by the day's heat. She thought of Willy Loman and realized that he was a traveling salesman. He was leering at her as he fed quarters into the machine. She watched as he purchased three cans of orange soda and saw that he had a bottle of vodka in his pocket. She cringed at the man's look, shrinking in fear from the design in his eyes. Jeffers snarled at the man like an animal surprised at the door to its den, and the man shuffled away, protecting his soft drinks and liquor and the evening's oblivion that they held out in promise. Jeffers had said, "Why kill him unless you're a punk looking for a fifty-buck score? What he's drinking will kill him just as sure as a bullet. Just not quite as quick."

In bed each night she slept fitfully, if at all, tossing about as much as she dared, but more often lying rigid, listening to his even breathing but not believing that he slept. He never sleeps, she thought. He's always awake and ready. Even when he emitted a snore, she refused to believe that it signaled sleep. When she listened to him, she tried to remain absolutely quiet, as if even the slight whisper of her own breath would rouse him. She thought at those times that she could no longer hear or feel her own body functioning. She would surreptitiously put her hand to her breast and try to sense the heartbeat beneath. It seemed distant, weak; it was as if she were close to death, mortally fragile.

At night he did not try to touch her, though she expected it each minute. She had given up on any idea of privacy, dressing and undressing in front of him, not shutting the bathroom door when she went to the toilet. She accepted these things as part of the arrangement which left her alive. She would have accepted sex as well, but so far it had failed to materialize. She did not expect this hiatus to last.

In the time since the derelict's killing, she had come to realize that she was scared of everything: of strangers, of Jeffers, of herself, of each passing minute of daytime, of each moment of night; of what might happen to her when she was awake or when she slept. When she did manage to fall asleep, her dreams were more often nightmares; she had quickly become accustomed to awakening in terrified flight from some sleep image, only to settle into the constancy of fear that was her waking world. Sometimes she had great difficulty separating the two. She would lie in darkness, remembering the vision of the derelict on the New Orleans street. She saw his mouth circling, puckering in acceptance of the bottle, a safe, familiar act, that gave him a kind of easy joy. Only this time it wasn't the accustomed touch of the wet bottle neck that he felt, but the hard, dry, awful taste of the gun barrel. She could see a glimmer of confusion in his eyes as they looked up in surprise, meeting hers. His eyes were like those of a dog who hears an unusual sound and cocks his head in curiosity. It was a terrible sight; her vision fixing on the derelict's open, accepting mouth, expectant eyes, waiting for all the world as if he were going to be kissed.

And sometimes it would be worse, it would be reversed. She would see the derelict, see him lift a bottle to his open lips. And when her own mouth dropped wide in surprise, wondering where the gun had gone, it would be there, in front of her. She would try to snap her mouth shut, but the gun moved too quickly and she could taste the metallic death on her own tongue.

She would see all this, and then scream.

At least she thought she screamed, and more often than not she felt as if she had screamed. But she realized that in reality she had made no sound. Her own mouth had opened, demanding noise, but none had emerged.

That too frightened her.

Outside of Vicksburg, Mississippi, Jeffers slowed the car and pulled to the side of the road. He pointed past her and said, "See there?" Anne Hampton turned and looked out upon a wide green field with a grassy knoll in the center. At the top of the knoll was a weathered, gray-brown oak tree, an ancient tree with gnarled leafy branches that reached out over the field, throwing shade about with the determination and duty that comes with old age.

"I see a tree," she replied.

"That's wrong," he said. "What you see is the past."

He took the car out of gear and turned off the engine. "Come on," he said. "History lesson."

He helped her over a ramshackle wooden fence, and together they walked up to the knoll. Jeffers looked hard at the ground the entire time, as if measuring something. "It's grown back," he said. "I didn't know if it would, but it's been eight years." He looked pensive. "I always thought that when gasoline burned the ground, it was scorched, it would take decades to grow back. Do you remember those pictures the German war photographers took in World War Two? From the Ukraine? They were very powerful shots. There would be these immense fields of wheat waving about in the distance, surrounding a huge pillar of black smoke. You always sensed the impotence through the picture, that's what made the pictures so damned good; you knew they couldn't do a fucking thing to stop those fires once the retreating Russians set them. Gasoline and wheat burning. Scorched earth. Damning the future to save the present." Then he stopped and pointed. "Look carefully—there! Can you see the way the grass changes color?"

"It seems like a shape," she said.

"Damn straight. A cross."

"You were here before?" she asked. Her voice quivered slightly; she saw the tree and remembered the tree lost in the rain and wind along the Louisiana coastline that they'd been unable to find.

"Standing right there." He pointed down the hill slightly. "It was a great shot," he said. "The fire from the cross framed all the men in their silly little white pointed hats and robes. But that wasn't what made it so good," he continued, "it was the way this huge crowd of blacks—spectators, I guess, I don't exactly know why they came out—anyway, they watched in utter silence. All their faces, every eye, was turned up toward this hill. The firelight drifted across them, as well, and I was able to get it all. A fantastic picture. You know why they chose this tree? Because fifty years ago the old Klan hung three men from that single wide branch, the low one.

"Symmetry is important," he said. "History. We are a nation of memories. The old Klan hung three men from a tree, and so the new Klan wants to evoke the same terror.

"And so out they march, all bedecked in their robes, all their kleagles and klaxxons and grand dragons in silks and some not so grand dragons waving the stars and bars, to have a rally. Not too many of them, really, but I understand that now their numbers are growing. Anyway, this time there were almost as many reporters and photographers as there were Klansmen. And twice as many blacks.

"That surprised me, you know. I mean, I would have thought that those people would have stayed far away. Ignoring the rally. After all, who wants to go listen to a lot of silly, insulting rhetoric? But they didn't. They showed up in droves. And you know what was really curious about it? These weren't educated people. And they weren't organized. They were farmers and sharecroppers and their wives and children. They came in old trucks and cars and I saw some arrive by cart and mule, too.

"I couldn't get over how quiet they were. The more inflammatory the speeches got, the more outrageous the insulting, the more they stood in silence. It was the strangest thing: you'd think that silence is an absolute, I mean, if someone's not making any noise, they can't get quieter, right? Not that night. Those people stood and never made a sound and the longer they stood there, the more profound their quiet was."

He shook his head.

"Now, that was strength. They showed that their memories were just as long and heartfelt. A singularity of purpose."

He looked at Anne Hampton.

"Complete dignity," he said. He paused.

"You have to understand how much I admire true strength. Because to do what I do requires an absolute dedication. A solidarity with your soul." He smiled and broke into a grin. "I like that," he said. "Solidarity." He made a clenched fist.

He looked at her. "To do what I do," he said.

He laughed. She saw that he had a camera in his hand. He lifted it, twisted the lens quickly, and clicked her picture. He bent down, changing the angle, and took another. "What I do, of course, is take pictures."

He laughed again, and she stood stiffly in front of him, awaiting a command with a kind of military attention.

"Come on," he said. "I will explain more."

She scrambled after him as he stalked down the hillside.

In the car he said, "What's the most important thing about America?"

She hesitated, but her mind moved swiftly: She pictured in grainy grays and dark shadows the pictures that Douglas Jeffers had taken the night of that rally, hooded rowdy Klansmen and silent, reproachful farmers. She responded, "Free speech. The First Amendment, right?"

He glanced away from the highway at her, smiling. "Boswell learns!" he said. "Correct."

She nodded and took out the notebook, oddly pleased with herself for answering one of his cryptic questions properly.

"But can you think of a freedom more frequently abused?"

She recognized it really wasn't a question for her as much as it was the start to some speech he was about to make. "Think of the evil generated on that hilltop. Think of the wrongs it represented. And protected by what? Our most important freedom. The Nazis want to march in Skokie and who stands up to defend them? The ACLU. A bunch of Jewish lawyers. It's the principle, they say. And they're right. The principle is more important than any individual act. That's what's so silly. We are a nation of hypocrites because we adhere so strongly to rigid concepts. Right. Wrong. Free Speech. Manifest Destiny. What did Superman defend? Truth, Justice, and the American Way. A scout is trustworthy, loyal, helpful, friendly, courteous, kind, obedient, cheerful, thrifty, brave, clean, and reverent. No one ever wants to mention the scoutmaster who likes dressing up in short pants, telling ghost stories around the fire, and diddling the boys beneath the sleeping bags . . ."

He took a deep breath, paused, then added, "Do you want to truly understand this country? It's simple, really. You just have to understand that on occasion we use our greatest strengths to create the biggest evils. Not always. Just sometimes. Just enough to make it interesting, of course."

He was speaking in a rush. Not angry, just wired. She was writing as fast as she could.

He stopped.

He giggled.

"From the First Amendment to faggot scoutmasters . . ." He threw back his head and shook it wildly, laughing hard.

He looked at Anne Hampton.

218

"I must be crazy," he said, grinning.

"No, no, I mean, I think I understand . . ."

"You're wrong," he said. His voice abruptly changed back to hard and harsh and the smile on his face evaporated. "I am crazy. I'm completely, terribly, totally, mad. We all are, in our own way. It's our national pastime, really. My way just happens to be worse than some . . ." He looked at her. "Worse than most."

He turned back, staring down the highway.

"Tell me," Douglas Jeffers asked, "what you know about death."

She remembered a time when she was young and visiting her grandparents on their farm. It was before Tommy had died: it had been summer and they had wanted to swim in the pond. But when they got to the edge they had found a mess of gray and black goose feathers strewn about wildly. Her grandfather had nodded and said, "Snapping turtle. Big one, too, I'll wager, if he took apart that whole bird." The swim had been canceled and her grandfather had gone back and taken a shotgun from a locked cabinet. He'd let her stick with him, though Tommy had been relegated to the house. Her grandfather set out some leftover chicken by the side of the pond, walked a short ways downwind with her, and then waited.

It had been over twenty pounds. She remembered the explosion of the shotgun, the sound crashing into her ears, deadening them. Her grandfather spread the bloody jaws apart with a stick, saying, "Turtle that big'd break your leg no problem." The turtle died, and then Tommy died and two summers after, her grandfather as well. She thought of the neighbor across the street who died of heart failure one humid summer morning, trying to catch up for too many years of indulgence by taking up jogging. Ambulance lights seemed dull, somehow less urgent, in the bright sunshine. She remembered seeing the man stretched out on the lawn, pasty white, rigid. His shoe had been untied and she'd had the strange thought that it had been fortunate that something had stopped him before he tripped and fell. She'd noticed, too, that his socks didn't match. One had a green stripe, the other blue. She'd thought that terrible. To die was bad enough, but to be embarrassed as well seemed doubly horrible.

She remembered her parents being handed a small white urn containing Tommy's ashes, seeing her mother's hands quake as they reached out. She could still hear the disembodied voices of the guests, mumbling, exhorting under their breath: Be brave. But why? she wondered. What was the point in bravery? Why not simply sob uncontrollably? That made a lot more sense. But

219

she'd seen her mother compose herself, dropping a veil across sorrow. A moment later the urn had been taken away and she had not seen it again. She wondered whether they had burned Tommy's clothes as well. He would probably have preferred seeing the tight blue suit that they'd bought him for church go up in smoke, she thought. All little boys both loved and hated their good clothes. There was a wonderful moment, when they were first dressed, that they looked so grown-up and solemn, handsome and sophisticated. Then, inevitably, they dissolved into the usual melange of dirt, grass stains, flying shirttails, and ripped knees. The turtle had been female, and she had helped her grandfather find the babies. He'd collected them in a sack, but would not tell her what he was going to do with them.

That's death, she thought. When you're not told. But you know.

"I don't know much," she answered. "My grandfather died. A neighbor, too, jogging. I was there. I saw him." She hesitated before mentioning her brother.

No, she thought, that's enough.

But she could not make herself stop.

"My brother died, too. A skating accident. He drowned."

She was silent, then she added, "He was just a little boy."

Jeffers paused before replying.

"My brother is drowning, as well. He just doesn't know it."

She did not know what to say, but she stored the information away: He's got a brother.

"He just doesn't know it yet," Jeffers continued. "But he will, soon enough."

He drove in silence for at least a quarter hour before he spoke again. She had turned, looking out at the other cars that they passed, looking in on families, young men, young women, trying to imagine who they were, where they were going, what they were like. Occasionally her eyes would meet another pair, if only for a second, and she would think how surprised the person would be if they knew of the trip she was on.

Douglas Jeffers only half-concentrated on the task of driving, instead allowing his mind to swing to problems of expression. The countryside that swept around him seemed nondescript, farms and vegetable fields and small towns blending into a constancy of rolling, simple green and brown backdrop. He steered the car back up onto the interstate, still heading north, barely registering speed, distance, destination, traffic. He thought for a while about his brother, then about Anne Hampton, and then about his brother again.

Marty had no passion, he thought. He would never act. He absorbed everything quietly, like those blacks on the hill.

It was odd that they'd never fought. All brothers fight, if not constantly, at least frequently. They struggle over everything, trying to carve out their own fiefdom in the family. It was that tension, he believed, that created the bond between brothers. After enough blood and anger, all that remained was a mutual dedication.

In all the battles with their father, the phony father, he'd maintained a distance. Jeffers grimaced and bit his lip, filling suddenly with a multifaceted anger: rage at the man, rage at the boy, rage at himself.

"I hate neutrality," he said out loud. "I despise it." He saw peripherally that Anne Hampton had been startled.

Well, Jeffers thought to himself, he's not going to be able to remain so damn detached much longer.

He spun a quick glance at Anne Hampton, then turned back to the highway. He pictured her limbs, her body. But his mind wandered quickly back into the past, and instead of his traveling companion, he saw the druggist's wife. When she dressed in the mornings, after her husband left for work, before the boys left for school, she would leave the door ajar. It was a slow, lingering process. She knew he watched her. He knew she knew. When he tried to get Marty to watch as well, his brother had turned away and walked out wordlessly.

"Did you love your brother?" he asked Anne Hampton.

"Yes," she replied. "Even though I thought he was, well, I don't know, strange, I guess. Mysterious."

"What do you mean?"

"Well, I was only three years older than he. And we didn't, I don't know, have much in common. Does that make sense? He was a boy and he did little-boy things and I was a girl and so I did little-girl things. But I loved him."

"It does make sense. In actuality, I think you share little with your brothers or sisters. A certain shared commonality of memory, because your pasts are the same. But they aren't really. Everyone remembers the same things differently. So they mean different things to different people."

"I think I know what you mean," she said.

He nodded.

They were quiet.

"There," he said. "We had an almost normal conversation. Wasn't so terrible, was it?"

She shook her head.

After a moment she asked, "What about your brother?"

"He's a doctor," Jeffers replied. "A head doctor. And he's just as unhappy as the folks he treats. He lives alone and doesn't know why. I live alone but at least I know why."

She nodded. He noticed that she was taking notes.

"Good," he said. She didn't reply.

But her unsaid question was the same as the one he'd directed to her, and he answered it: "No, I don't think I love him," he said. "No more than I love anyone. Or anything."

He shook his head. "I gave up on love a long time ago. Happiness, too."

He laughed bitterly. "I sound like a character in some daytime soap opera. Did you watch them?"

"No," she replied. "A lot of the kids at school were devoted to them. It was like a fad, I guess. But I never bothered."

"I didn't think so."

She hesitated, then asked, "But you love your work?"

He smiled.

"I love my work."

The grin on his face was one that reflected a sudden internal humor, and she felt a rush of panic. What does he think his work is? she said to herself. The thought seemed to punch her insides.

"I mean," she continued, "you talk about these pictures with such respect. Both the ones you took and the ones you've seen."

"I've taken a lot of pictures. A lot of different things."

She nodded and they sped on in silence.

Douglas Jeffers thought of his pictures.

"Always death," he said. "Well, not always. But lately more and more. I shoot death. I did a series, an essay for *Life*, not too long ago. On a twenty-four-hour shift in a big-city emergency room . . ."

"Oh," Anne Hampton interrupted, "I saw those. They were good."

"They were about death. Even the shots of the doctors and nurses and ambulance drivers—the task, you see, was to capture how all that violence and smashed and torn bodies diminished them. Day after day. Night after night. You see, you rub up against something awful for too long and it becomes a part of you. Sticks to your skin."

He paused before saying, "That's what's happened to me."

She nodded, and for a moment felt an awkward sympathy.

Then she remembered the rain and wind, the wrong road and the Gulf waters, and she had a sudden horrible vision of what it would be like, lying beneath the earth. She felt instantly suffocated and gulped her next breath of air.

"I've lost track," said Jeffers matter-of-factly.

She felt her chest contract and air wheezed in and out. She felt asthmatic, feeble.

"Of what?" she moaned her question.

"Of how many deaths I've seen. I used to know, you know. I could count them. But not any longer. They all blend together. When I was in that emergency room, they brought a kid in, a teenager, just a couple of years younger than you. He'd been the passenger in a car driven by a drunk. The other kid, the driver, wouldn't you know it, had a couple of bruises and a fractured forearm. But this kid was going to buy it and the terrible thing was, he wasn't unconscious. He knew it. He knew all the people around him and all the devices and the needles and the machines were all going to be useless. I got a shot of his eyes, right before he went. They didn't use it, though. Not enough clarity in the shot, some sonuvabitch shoved me right as I tripped the shutter..."

He shrugged.

"It happens. It's part of the business."

He paused, then continued.

"I went home that night and wondered just what number that kid was. Was he the thousandth? Or the ten thousandth? I once knew a police reporter who kept a running count, and so I did, too. But the number got out of hand. In Vietnam? Beirut? I was there a couple of times. Talk about cheap life... When that charter flight went down outside of New Orleans, it split apart and people were scattered everywhere. The rescue squads were plucking parts of bodies from the trees, just like culling so much rotten fruit..."

"It just happened," Anne Hampton said. "Things just happen."

"No, they don't," Jeffers replied angrily. "The kid dies because his buddy drinks too much. The flight crashes because the pilot decides to let the copilot try a takeoff and ignores the tower's warning about wind shear. The little kids in Beirut die because they play outside and rocket grenades launched at random have this uncanny way of finding kids in a street...

"There are actions and reactions. Death is just the most common."

He looked at her.

"You see, when I kill someone it's because I want to. It's the only way I have of reminding myself that I'm still alive."

Her hand shook as she took down his words.

He waited.

Silence surrounded them. She knew, though, that he would fill it.

"More than . . ." But he stopped before adding a number.

She closed her eyes and tried to breathe slowly. When she opened them, she saw he was grinning.

She did not ask him for specificity.

He drove steadily, wordlessly, for two hours. When they needed gasoline he pulled into a station along the interstate, telling the attendant sullenly to fill the tank, paying cash, and accelerating out of the station quickly but nonchalantly, giving to all the world the appearance of a normal couple, not pressed by time, but pushing with routine dispatch toward a known destination and some distinct result.

Finally he spoke:

"Boswell, aren't you filled with wonder? Don't you have hundreds of questions?"

Anne Hampton thought that she was filled with nothing save fear.

"I didn't think I should ask," she said. "I figured you'd tell me what you wanted."

He nodded. "That seems sensible."

After a moment he continued.

"Boswell, don't you wonder why we're doing this?"

She nodded.

"I know you've got some plan . . ."

"Yes," he said. "Quite a specific one at that."

He did not volunteer information. Instead he said:

"Do I look old, Boswell? Can you see lines in my face? Do I look tired and frustrated and bilious and cantankerous with age? I feel very old, Boswell. Ancient."

His voice changed suddenly and he demanded harshly:

"What day did we first meet?"

Her throat closed and she choked.

She could not remember. A part of her wanted to say that she'd been in the car forever, that she'd always been with him. Another part, deeper, as if being awakened from sleep, forced itself into her consciousness, with pictures of her apartment, dried flowers in a vase on the windowsill, bookcases, desk, small bed and table. There were some pictures of her parents and a watercolor on the wall of boats in a harbor that she'd seen on a trip east a few years back. It had been too expensive, but there was something in the picture that captured her, perhaps the peace, the order, the calm of boats at mooring in the late day's sunshine. She remembered her classes, the way the summer heat would wake her in the morning, the sticky sensation of sweat as she walked across the campus. Then, just as swiftly, she saw her parents back home in Colorado, sitting about the house, quietly proceeding with their lives. If they knew, she thought, they would be panicked, crying. In agony. She wondered then whether they were people in a dream.

"I don't know," she said.

"You understand, no one knows."

She nodded.

"No one is looking for you."

She nodded again.

"Even if someone were curious, they wouldn't know where to look. They wouldn't know what direction to start searching. Do you understand? You've left no trail."

She nodded a third time.

"People walk away from life all the time. Poof! They vanish. Disappear. One minute they're there, the next, well, gone."

She dipped her head in acquiescent sorrow.

"That's what has happened to you."

He looked at her harshly.

"I am your past now. I am your future." She wanted to cry but dared not. She thought of those funeral voices: Be brave. The memory made her angry.

Jeffers continued.

"It's like those damn milk cartons with the pictures and identifying data of lost children on their sides. Depressing. The children are gone. Stolen away forever. We are a nation of Pied Pipers, you see. Constantly playing a tune to lead others astray. That's what happened to you. Swallowed up."

He paused.

"That's what happened to all of them."

How many more? she suddenly wondered.

Oh, God, she said to herself. I'm next. I'm still next. I've always been next. But she didn't have time to let this fear formulate into some panic-stricken scream. And, after a moment she realized that it was the same fear that had dogged her from the start, and when she assigned this degree of familiarity to it, it suddenly seemed less terrifying. She wondered for an instant whether this was some sort of death recognition, whether she was like the people on an airplane that starts to fall precipitously from the sky. She had read of the momentary screams fading into a calmed acceptance, a peaceful, prayerful time. Like the instants before the firing squad. Do you want a cigarette? A blindfold? asks the captain. No, just a momentary look out at the morning.

She stared out the window, shading her eyes from the brightness of the summer sun. She did not know why, but she felt an odd, unfamiliar ease.

Jeffers hummed a tune. "I wonder what piece the Pied Piper played on his flute. Was it the same for the rats as it was for the children?"

He seemed to consider things briefly.

"I always wondered, even when I was a child, why the parents of Hamelin didn't do anything. You know, they just stood there like a bunch of idiots. I would have . . ."

His voice trailed off for an instant.

"Look," Jeffers asked. "What do you know about murder?"

She thought of the derelict and replied, "Just what I learned the other night."

Jeffers smiled.

"Good answer," he said. "That shows some moxie, huh? Boswell isn't quite as timid as she acts sometimes."

He punched the accelerator and the car jumped forward. Then, just as swiftly, he eased off and they returned to the same droning modest speed.

"Murder is, as you saw, blissfully easy. It's only in Hollywood that people stare down the barrel of a gun, hesitating, filled with moral conflict and guilt. In reality it happens simply and quickly. An argument and bang! Not that much difference, really, between your standard night-the-welfare-checks-come-out argument in the ghetto and some military operation that requires weeks or months of planning. There's always some fundamentally stupid dispute at the bottom. Even in my case, you know, if I was truly introspective, I could probably find the base, shall I say cause, for what I do. Some unresolved anger. Some out-of-control hatred. That's the kind of phrase my brother would use. But what is an unresolved anger? Just an argument between all the different parts of yourself. Life is always a debate between your good side and your bad side, anyway. The bad side wants you to take that extra dessert, right? Just like those Saturday-morning cartoons they show for kids, where a little devil pops up urging Foghorn Leghorn or Donald Duck or Goofy or whatever cute and furry little animal they use nowadays to do something wrong and then a little angel pops up, insisting they take the true and proper path . . ."

Jeffers laughed shortly, sharply, before going on.

"Anyway, do you know why we committed that crime with impunity? Because it was committed at random. Look at us. Are we the type of people who appear like they would go around blowing out the brains of drunken derelicts? Thrill-seekers? Leopold and Loeb? What? Not a professional photographer. Award-winning, no less. Not an honors college student. You see, we had no connection with that event at all. No one saw us. No one suspects us. It was just a simple, single, random happening, or at least that's what the authorities will think.

"In fact it barely happened at all. Just how much time do you think some overworked and underpaid homicide detective is going to want to spend on a dead derelict who probably has no identification anyway? Ten minutes? An hour? A day? No more. Enough time so that he can fill out some form and file it with his superior and move on to the next case. Something a bit sexier maybe. Something with headlines. Something that our society places some value on. A society killing or a love-triangle murder. And who can blame him? You see, it was really so inconsequential. Unknown drifter dies mysteriously. Put out a memo. Check to see if they have any other unsolved derelict-murder cases that seem similar. End of story. At least that's what the official version will be. The political version . . .

"But of course we know differently, don't we? Too bad, in a way, isn't it? Some poor cop could make his career if only he knew, had some inkling what had really happened. Because it wasn't unimportant, was it? Not to us."

After a moment she managed a reply.

"But it can't always be so, I don't know, easy . . ."

She hated that word. For him, she realized, it was an absolute truth. For her, she thought, a total lie. I won't, she said suddenly to herself. I won't be him.

She surprised herself with her determination.

"Of course not. Otherwise there would be no challenge. No adventure. Did you ever read *The Most Dangerous Game?*"

"I don't think so."

He snorted. "Come on, Boswell, where's your education?"

"I've read a lot," she replied defensively. "I've read books you probably don't know about! What do you know about *Middle-march?*" She heard her own voice speaking and she wanted to clap a hand over her mouth. She shut her eyes, expecting a blow.

Instead he laughed.

"Touché," he said. "But on to my question: What is the most dangerous game?"

"Murder isn't a game."

"Isn't it?"

They were silent.

"All right," he said after a second had passed, "I'll be less frivolous. Of course murder isn't a game. But it's not a hobby either. It's a mode of life. My mode of life."

"I just don't understand how..." she started, but he interrupted her.

He was laughing.

"Well, finally. She asks why! She asks how! It's about time."

His voice darkened.

"And now I'll tell you."

She felt then as if she had stumbled foolishly into something she was forbidden to see. She remembered once peering through the crack in her parents' bedroom door one restless night and seeing them wrapped together in subdued but noisy love. Her face flushed with the same mixture of fear and embarrassment. She dropped her pencil and had to lean down to pick it up. She was struck with the realization that knowledge was dangerous, that the more she knew the more entwined she was and the more she could never escape. Her mind filled with black sorrow and she wanted to cry like a child, alone, just as she had after that dark and primal vision, some innocence forever abandoned, smothering her tears into her pillow, cut off from any world save that defined by her own personal and exclusive agony.

He waited, filled with confidence and a kind of runaway excitement, until he knew she was riven with the foreboding that the questions were bound to create. He thought: Finally. His words exploded from him in a torrent of enthusiasm.

"I realized after the first that I'd been incredibly lucky. Picking up a prostitute on the street in a rental car easily traceable to me. Striking her in the car, so that there was her blood type staining the upholstery. Abandoning her in an area that I was unfamiliar with. Why, at any point someone could have seen me. Someone could have latched on to the situation. A passerby. Her pimp. A trucker peering down from twelve feet up in his cab. I left footprints and fingerprints and God knows what else that some forensics lab could trace back to me. Fiber samples, dirt samples, hair samples. Hell, I even used a credit card to buy the shovel I used to bury her. I did everything wrong. Awfully goddamn stupid, you know..."

He looked at her briefly but didn't expect her to answer.

"Do you know what I experienced afterwards? The most seductive fear. The sensation that you get when you realize after the fact that you've been in great jeopardy. The kind of fear that takes shape and re-forms in nightmares. I walked around in a kind of twilight, thinking I was becoming paranoid, imagining every minute that any one of these schoolboy errors was going to manifest itself in a detective carrying an arrest warrant. It never happened, of course, but the feeling was like being electrified, constantly.

"My pictures, too. Sharper. Better. Filled with passion. Odd, huh? From fear came art. I was driven to succeed. I remember being unable to sleep one night a couple of days afterwards. I was so filled with excitement. It had just taken me over, you see. I decided I would drive about, just watching the nighttime city glow. Maybe that could help me contain my feelings. I was listening to the police scanner. All photographers keep lots of radios about, this wasn't unusual. You always listen, because you never know. And this was one of those nights.

"I heard this voice come on, a clear channel, excited, near panic: Help, help, officer down, officer down . . . and then they gave the address. It was only a couple of blocks away. A state trooper, you see, made a routine traffic stop on a car driving with a taillight out. And for his trouble he'd taken a thirty-eight round in the chest. It had been four guys who'd just done a liquor store. And I got there before anyone. Before any other cops, before rescue. Just me, my camera, and the kid who'd witnessed the shooting from across the highway where he'd been changing a flat and had called in for help. He had the trooper's head in his lap. Click! Click! Help me, the kid said. Click! Help us! he said. What are you doing? Click! Please. . . . Click! Thirty seconds, maybe. Then I helped him. I took the trooper's hand and felt for a pulse. At first it was there, but then, just like dusk, it faded and disappeared. And then everywhere, lights and sirens. God! Those were fantastic pictures!"

Jeffers paused. His voice became slower, more cautious.

"So I became a student of murder."

Silence.

"I had to."

She poised her pencil above the notebook, trying to shed anxiety from her mind and simply concentrate on what he was saying. She told herself to think like she was back in a classroom and that this was just another lecture. She realized that was foolish.

Douglas Jeffers' head filled with images and he wondered idly whether he should start anecdotally. He stole a look at Anne

Hampton and saw that she was waiting, pale, shaken, on some rim of terror, but waiting nonetheless. He felt a momentary gratification, thinking: She's mine now.

Then he launched ahead.

"I had been terribly lucky, and I'm not fond of relying on luck. I started spending my spare time in libraries, reading. I read works of literature and works of science. I read legal case histories and medical tracts. I read murderers' confessions and prison reports. I read the memoirs of detectives, pathologists, criminal-defense attorneys, prosecutors, and professional hit men. I purchased books on weaponry. I studied physiology. I put on a white lab coat and went to anatomy lectures at Columbia Medical School. I needed to know, you see, how exactly, precisely, people died.

"I read newspapers and magazines. I subscribed to *True Detective* and *Police*. I spent hours studying the writings of a number of prominent forensic psychiatrists. I learned about sex murderers, mass murderers, professional murderers, military murderers. I studied massacres and murder conspiracies. I became intimate with de Sade, Bluebeard, Albert DeSalvo and Charles Whitman and My Lai Four or the Shatilla refugee camps. I knew Raskolnikov and Mengele and Kurtz and Idi Amin and William Bonney, whom you probably know as Billy the Kid. I know about the PLO and the Red Brigades. I could tell you about Charles Manson, or Elmer Wayne Henley, or Wayne Gacy or Richard Speck or Jack Abbott or Lucky Luciano and Al Capone. From Saint Valentine's Day to the Freeway Murders. From the Salem Witch Trials to Miami's drug wars to San Francisco's unsolved Zodiac. I know about 007 from fiction and MI-5 in reality. I could explain why Bruno Richard Hauptmann probably wasn't a murderer, although they executed him, or why Gary Gilmore was really just a loser who happened to kill, but he got executed, too. In fact, I studied just about every execution I could. I read everything from Camus' essay on the death penalty to McLendon's novel *Deathwork*, and then I read the Warren Commission Report and congressional testimony exposing the workings of the Phoenix Program in Vietnam . . .

"Did you know," Douglas Jeffers continued, "that in some states, court records and police reports become part of the public record? For example: I went down to North Florida not so long ago and read up on the case of one Gerald Stano. Interesting guy. Intelligent. Friendly. Outgoing. Not your reclusive loner by any means. Held a steady job as a mechanic. Did well. Everyone

230

liked him, even the homicide detectives. He had only one small flaw..."

Jeffers paused for effect.

"... When he went on a date with a woman, he wouldn't settle for a chaste handshake or peck on the cheek to say goodnight."

Jeffers laughed.

"No, Mr. Stano preferred to kill his dates."

He glanced at Anne Hampton, assessing the pained look on her face.

"Slicing and dicing them . . ."

Another pause.

"Could have been as many as forty."

Jeffers waited again before continuing.

"You've got to admire him his consistency, if for no other reason. He treated everyone the same. Every woman, that is . . ."

Anne Hampton remained quiet, waiting for Jeffers to speak. She saw him take a deep breath.

"So you see what I became," Jeffers said, his voice fairly ringing. "I became an expert."

"And then," he said, after taking a deep breath, "I was ready to be a killer. Not some lucky jerk who got away with a random murder of a prostitute. But a complete, calculating, professional homicidal machine. But not a hit man, taking orders from some lowlife mobster or Colombian drug dealer. But a murderer completely in business for myself.

"And that's what I am."

He drove in silence for hours.

Jeffers did not elaborate further. He thought to himself: Well, that's enough for her to absorb for a bit. And what he had in mind next he believed would elevate her to yet another level.

Anne Hampton was grateful for the quiet. She tried to force herself to think of simple things, like the smell of an apple pie baking, or the sensation of slipping on a silk shirt, but they were elusive.

They crossed the river in Memphis in the dead of night. She saw the lights reflecting off the steady black water and Jeffers told her about the time the Cuyahoga River burned in Cleveland. The toxic wastes dumped into the water had caught fire, he said. How do you put out a body of water that's on fire? He described shooting pictures of firemen at night, outlined by the soaring flames. They passed a sign as they crossed, which said, in a cheeriness that contradicted the hour: YOU'RE LEAVING MEMPHIS —COME BACK SOON!

Jeffers sang, "Ohhhh, momma, can this really be the end? To be stuck inside of Mobile with the Memphis Blues again . . ."

He looked over at her and saw she did not recognize the tune. He shrugged. "My generation," he said. He laughed. "Don't make me feel so old."

She did not know what to say.

They stayed on the interstate in Arkansas. It was well after midnight when they stopped at a Howard Johnson's. She thought the clash of orange and aqua disturbing late at night, as if the color scheme should be changed as night fell, to something more somber and less jarring.

In the morning they were on the road early, and drove for two hours before stopping for breakfast. Jeffers was ravenous, and he forced her to eat substantially, as well: eggs, pancakes, toast, sausages, several cups of coffee and juice.

"Why so much?" she asked.

"Big day," he replied between bites. "Big night. Ball game in St. Louis. Game time, eight. Surprises to follow. Eat up."

She obliged him.

After breakfast, though, he did not drive immediately back to the interstate. Instead he pulled into the parking lot of a large suburban shopping mall. Anne Hampton looked at him.

"Why are we stopping?"

He reached over quickly and grabbed her face, with his thumb and forefinger digging into her cheeks.

"Just stay close, say nothing, and be educated!" he hissed.

She nodded and he released her.

"Watch, listen, and learn," he said.

He walked quickly through the deepening crowd of people arriving at the mall. She had to hurry to keep pace. Stores flashed about her, and she saw her reflection in the plate glass of one boutique. She heard voices all around, mostly kids yelling and running away from their parents, so she was surrounded by cries: Jennifer or Joseph or Joshua, stop that this minute! Which they never did. She heard couples talking over purchases and teenagers talking over boys, girls, records. These snatches of life around her seemed strangely distant, as if taking place in some other part of history. She quickened her pace at Douglas Jeffers' side. He seemed oblivious to the crowd, striding purposefully ahead.

He escorted her into a sporting goods store, where he plucked out a pair of red St. Louis Cardinals baseball hats. He pointed at a plastic snoutlike hat device and laughed mockingly. "They wear those pig hats to University of Arkansas games. Razorbacks. All

I can say is, you damn well better win if your fans are going to wear those."

He paid cash for the two hats, then headed back through the mall. "One more stop," he said.

Inside the large Sears department store, he headed to the office products section. At the counter he purchased a small ream of typewriter paper and a package of business-sized envelopes. Then he walked over to a line of demonstration typewriters. He turned to her and said, "Watch carefully. Stick very close."

In a swift motion he produced from a pocket a set of skin-tight surgical gloves. He slid them on and quickly tore open the typewriter paper box. Moving without hesitation, he handed Anne Hampton the box and quickly spun a single sheet into one of the demonstration typewriters. He hesitated for an instant, searching quickly about to ascertain if anyone was close or if anyone was paying attention to them. Certain they were not noticed, he bent down to the typewriter.

Then he typed:

Yu guyz ar so dum, yu shud bag it,
Cuz I just naled another faggit

luv an kissies,
Yu no who

He spun the page out of the typewriter, folded it in three, and placed it inside an envelope. Still wearing the gloves, he put the envelope into his pocket. Then he removed the gloves, glanced about to make certain again that they hadn't been noticed, and without a word to Anne Hampton paced off.

Her mind a jumble, she rushed to his side, breathing hard to keep even with his stride.

He said nothing when they returned to the car, but gestured toward the seat belt. She strapped herself in and kept quiet.

He drove steadily throughout the day and into the evening, doggedly keeping to the speed limit, or driving the prevailing speed, so they were passed by as many cars as they passed themselves. She wondered why it always seemed that Jeffers knew precisely where they were going, and how long it would take. He said to her, "We should make it by the bottom of the second inning," but they had to park a little farther from the stadium than he'd anticipated, so that by the time they got to the gate it was the top of the third. They both wore the red caps he'd purchased earlier in the day. Jeffers produced two tickets at the turnstile, whipping them from his wallet with a flourish.

She was taken aback by the gesture, and more by the realization that he'd purchased the tickets far in advance.

"Should be a good one," he said to the gatetender.

"Yeah, except they're up a couple already and ain't no one figured out how to hit that kid yet." He was an old man with white hair growing in his earlobes. One ear had a hearing aid attached to it. She saw he'd plugged in a cheap portable radio earphone in the other ear. He ignored them and reached for the tickets of the next set of late arrivals.

They rapidly made their way through the aisles, bumping into people, stepping around vendors.

The huge crowd and constant throb of noise unsettled her. She felt as if she were afloat in space, weightless, and that the swells of sound would sweep her away. She pressed close to Jeffers; at one point, when a rowdy group of teenagers tried to push between them, she reached out for his hand.

In the home half of the fifth, Jeffers announced he was hungry again. "Listen," he said to her, "just run over to the concession stand and get us some hot dogs."

She stared at him in disbelief.

Around them was a tidal flood of sound: the stately right-hander for the Mets had been throwing in his usual overpowering fashion, and the Cardinals had nothing to show for their efforts but the short end of a 2-0 score. But as Jeffers had made his request, the leadoff man had walked and the next batter promptly lined a base hit to right. The crowd surged in anticipation, and a steady rhythmic clapping of encouragement filled the stadium. She had to yell for him to hear.

"I can't," she said.

"Why not?"

She felt his hand suddenly on her leg, the fingers biting into the muscle, squeezing it painfully.

"I just can't," she said, tears forming in her eyes.

He stared at her. He thought: Perfect.

"What's wrong?"

She shook her head. She didn't know. She knew only that she was terrified of the noise, of the people, and of the world that he'd suddenly let into their lives.

"Please," she said.

He could not hear her; the next batter had singled and the runner had scored from second, avoiding the catcher's lunging tag in a cloud of dust. But he saw her mouth the word and that was enough for him.

"All right," he said. "Just this once."

He released her leg.

She nodded thanks.

"That's what they call a bang-bang play," he said.

"Bang-bang?"

"Yes. It happens bang! Bang! Bang! Bang! Bang! The runner slides, bang! The catcher tags, bang! He's safe! Bang! Or he's out, bang! I always liked that cliché."

He spotted a peanut vendor and waved wildly to attract the man's attention. He gave her a bag and after she started cracking the shells and eating, he reached down and from his ever-present camera bag, plucked his Nikon. "Smile," he said, pivoting in his chair toward her.

He clicked off a series of pictures.

She felt embarrassed. "My hair," she said. "This silly hat . . ."

But he just gestured toward the playing field. "Pay attention to the game," he said. "You may need to remember some details later."

This frightened her, and she tried to concentrate on the action in front of her. I understand baseball, she said to herself. I know about squeeze plays and pitchouts and hitting behind the runner. I was the shortstop on my high-school softball team and I learned the rules.

But the figures on the artificial green of the playing surface seemed mysterious to her, no matter how hard she tried to analyze what was happening before her.

She dared to watch Jeffers. He seemed intent on the game and on the action on the field, but she knew that this devotion obscured some other purpose. Her mind would not form concrete possibilities.

She shivered in the sticky humidity.

Her head felt dizzy and she swallowed with difficulty. Once, when she saw him bend toward the bag at his feet, she almost choked in sudden confusion.

Finally, as the teams were changing sides, she asked in a voice that seemed to her hollow, "Why are we here, please?"

Jeffers turned to her and stared. Then he burst out in a huge laugh. "We're here because this is America, this is the national pastime, this is the Mets and the Cards and the pennant is on the line. But mostly we're here because I'm a baseball fan."

He laughed again and looked at her.

235

"So you see," he continued, "right now we're killing nothing. Except time."

He hesitated. "Later," he said.

She did not ask any more questions.

They stayed until the top of the eighth. Jeffers waited until the Mets scored four to blow open the tight game. Then he grabbed her by the hand and led her, along with the other early and easily disgruntled fans, out of the stadium. As they walked away, a great shout went up from the stadium behind them. He heard a young couple walking a few feet away, listening to a radio, announce to no one and everyone at the same time: "Jack Clark home run with two on!" And he nodded. "They should know," he said softly to Anne Hampton, "that it's never over until it's over. A great American said that once."

"Who?" she asked.

"Caryl Chessman," Jeffers replied.

Jeffers made certain that Anne Hampton was strapped in her seat, then he went to the rear of the car and opened the trunk. He rummaged about for an instant in what he called his miscellany bag, finally coming up with a set of Missouri license plates. To these he'd previously attached metal clips, so he was able to bend down and place them firmly, directly over the car's actual plates. He took a cheap tag frame that he'd acquired in an auto goods store and locked it over the top, so there was no way the telltale yellow of his New York plates would show, but so he would swiftly be able to remove the set from Missouri, stolen sometime before. Then he opened the bag containing the weapons and pulled out a cheap .25-caliber automatic. Taped on the inside of the bag was a specially prepared clip of bullets. He made certain that the soft points were notched, then slid the clip into his camera bag. He searched around for another second before putting his hand on a simple leather briefcase. This he took out before locking the trunk.

Inside the car he switched on the interior light.

She watched as he pulled a small yellow file from the briefcase and opened it on his lap.

The file contained a set of newspaper and magazine clippings beneath a typed checklist. She saw the words: Gun/Typewriter/ Access/Egress/Emergency Backup/Lawyer/ID. Each word-category had several lesser categories listed beneath it, but she was not quick enough and the light was too shallow for her to see what they said. A number of items had been crossed off, and others had received large check marks next to them. A few had handwritten notes next to them. She saw that the file contained two maps, one hand-drawn, the other a grid map of the city. As she watched, Jeffers seemed to be reviewing the lists and the maps. She glanced at the newspaper clips and saw a half-page article from *Time* Magazine. It was from their Nation section and the headline read: RANDOM MURDER OF GAYS CREATES FUROR IN ST. LOUIS. She saw that the other stories were from the St. Louis *Post-Dispatch*.

"All right," Jeffers said with a slightly excited tinge to his voice. "All right. We're set."

He looked over at her. "Ready?"

She did not know how to respond.

"Ready?" he demanded harshly.

She nodded.

"Right," he said. "The hunt begins." He drove into the city darkness.

She was turned around and lost within moments. One second they were up on a thruway, cutting amidst skyscrapers that seemed to leap up into the nighttime next to her, then they were circling through shabby, ill-lit streets that glistened with reflected headlights. After what she thought was at least thirty minutes, Jeffers slowed. Anne Hampton stared from the window and saw occasional knots of men standing outside of bars in the warm summer evening air, talking, gesturing. Jeffers was taking it all in wordlessly.

But, she thought, he still seems to know where he's heading. She forced her mind into a benign blank. After circling through a ten-block area for another half hour, Jeffers steered the car down a darkened side street, finally pulling to the curb near the end of the block. It seemed a residential neighborhood, not houses, but apartments carved from older buildings, with trees planted in sections cut from the sidewalk. But she saw that they were only a few blocks from the brighter lights of the main thoroughfare. She watched Jeffers slide around the front of the car and open the door for her. She thought his movements spidery, predatory. In an instant she found herself virtually lifted from the vehicle and, arm in arm, walking down the sidewalk. As always, she was taken aback by the taut strength of his hands and arms. She could feel his bunched muscles rigid with excitement.

"Say nothing," Jeffers said in a low, awful voice. "Avoid eye contact until I make my choice. But smile and look happy."

She tried but knew she looked merely pathetic.

She concentrated instead on walking steadily.

She knew what was happening, or, at least, she suddenly

knew that she was about to add another nightmare to that possessed by the derelict, but she felt helpless to do anything. Not that anything occurred to her to do, save cooperate.

Look out at the sky, she said to herself. Stare up into the few lights around. She saw the moon hanging above the branches of a tree and suddenly remembered a tune from childhood: The fox went out on a chilly night . . . And he prayed to the moon to give him light . . . For he'd many a mile to go that night . . . Before he reached the town-o, town-o, town-o. The music flowed through her mind like a comforting wave.

They walked around the block three times, each time passing a pair or a threesome of men hurrying through the blackness of the secondary street. On their fourth turn around the block, as they were approaching their car, she felt Jeffers stiffen next to her. She could sense his muscles tightening, and she realized he'd put his hand into his camera bag.

"This could be it," Jeffers said.

They continued to walk toward the solitary man, who was hurrying in their direction.

"Slow a little," Jeffers said. "I want to pass this guy in the shadow of that tree."

She saw that equidistant between them and the man was a large tree that added shadow to the night.

"Keep smiling," Jeffers said.

She had a sudden vision of herself being swept out to sea by a violent undertow. She clung to his arm, suddenly afraid that she would stumble or faint.

Jeffers arranged all his sensations. His eyes darted about the area, taking in all the emptiness. His ears were tuned to noises, searching for some telltale, out-of-the-ordinary sound. He even sniffed the air. He thought he was on fire, or that he was in love, and that every nerve end in his body was on edge, throbbing. Beneath his hand the metal of the pistol seemed glowing hot. He forced himself to measure his pace, slow, so that he would come abreast with the man at the precise moment, the darkest moment. A death march, he thought abruptly.

They moved together.

Jeffers estimated the distance: fifty feet. Then, suddenly, twenty feet. Then ten, and he nodded at the man and smiled.

The man was young, probably no more than twenty-five. Who are you? Jeffers wondered in an instant. Have you loved your life? The man's blond hair was cropped close over his ears and neck. Jeffers noticed that the man had a small gold stud in one ear. He wore a simple open sportshirt and slacks, with a sweater tossed over his shoulders in studied casual appearance.

Jeffers nodded again at the man, and the man returned the look with a small, wan, slightly nervous smile. Jeffers squeezed hard on Anne Hampton's arm and he saw her smile as well.

The man walked abreast, then past.

As the man stepped through Jeffers' peripheral vision, Jeffers slipped the gun from his bag, his finger resting on the trigger.

Jeffers had time only to say to himself: Be calm.

Then he spun around, directly behind the man, dropping Anne Hampton's arm so that he could raise both hands to the pistol grip. When the barrel reached out level with the man's head, Jeffers fired twice.

The cracking sound echoed down the street.

The man pitched forward, slamming to the sidewalk.

Anne Hampton stood frozen. She tried to lift her hands to her eyes to cover them, then stopped, staring out in terror.

Jeffers leaped over the man, who lay facedown in a growing pool of blood. He was careful not to touch the man or the blood. The man did not move. Jeffers bent down, fired one more shot into the man's back, searching for the heart. Then, in the same fluid, continuous movement, he put the gun back into his bag and came out with the Nikon. He raised it to his eye and she heard the motordrive whir as the film advanced. Just as swiftly, he finished, returning the camera to the bag.

He grabbed Anne Hampton's arm and half-dragged her down toward their car.

He pulled open the door and thrust her swiftly into the seat. In an instant he'd jumped around to the driver's side. He did not squeal the tires, but started the car simply and efficiently, rolling slowly past the body on the sidewalk, down the empty street.

She turned and stared at the inert body as they slid past.

Within a few seconds they were away.

She saw that Jeffers was driving a preset route. She could feel the force of his concentration, as if he were creating a palpable sense out of his intelligence. After fifteen minutes she saw they had reached a deserted spot in a downtown warehouse area. Jeffers stopped the car and exited wordlessly. She waited for him to let her out, but he did not.

At the back of the car, Jeffers removed the Missouri license plate, wiped it with a rag, and threw it into a dark plastic bag. He then tossed the bag into a dumpster, climbing up to make sure that the bag with the plate was well situated amidst other garbage.

He got back into the car and they drove through the city into a suburban area. Jeffers stopped at a convenience store and used the light from the front of the building to see what he was doing. First he replaced his surgical gloves on his hands. Then he took out the envelope with the letter he'd written earlier in the day. Then he opened his file folder and pulled out a small brown manila envelope. He shook it open and Anne Hampton saw that there were several words cut from a newspaper. Jeffers produced a small plastic squeeze container of commonly used glue and fastened the words to the envelope. He used the glue to close the envelope.

Then he spoke.

"Can't be too careful. Now, I know they can't raise fingerprints from paper unless I put ink all over my fingers. But the FBI has all this new spectrographic equipment which I'm just getting familiar with and it can break down enzymes and Lord knows what. That's why no saliva. If I licked that envelope shut, they could come up with my blood type, for example. Hell, for all I know, they could come up with my Social Security number. So, caution is the word."

He looked at her. His words had spun out in an excited, almost littleboy delight.

"Look," he said. "Don't worry. We're finished. We got away. Just a few odds and ends and we're home free."

He finished with the envelope and put the car back in gear. In a moment he pulled up to the front of a large postal building. He jumped out of the car and put the envelope in one of the mail boxes.

Back in the car he said, "Now just the gun and bullets, and everything's set. But we won't do those until tomorrow. At our leisure."

His adrenaline still flowing freely, he maneuvered the car back onto the interstate. Anne Hampton pivoted once in her seat, looking out the rear window toward the fading lights of the city.

He saw her shiver.

"Cold?"

She nodded.

He did nothing.

"Tired?"

She realized she was drained. She nodded again.

"Hungry?"

She thought she would be sick.

"I'm famished," he said. "I could eat the proverbial horse."

She thought: It's endless. It's forever.

After a moment he spoke again. "It's the strangest thing," he

240

began evenly. "The homophobe who has killed all those gays in St. Louis, I think seven before tonight, always writes in rhyme. At least according to the *Post-Dispatch*."

Jeffers shook his head.

"The newspapers haven't given him a nickname, which I think is kinda strange. I mean, usually when you have a series of killings like that, they slap some sobriquet on the poor guy. Like Gay Killer or Homo Homicides or something equally dumb and borderline-offensive."

He looked at her and saw the weariness in her eyes.

"Do you know what just happened?" he asked.

"Yes," she said dully.

He reached across the car and slapped her, but not too vigorously, thinking: She's probably pretty tired.

The crack against her cheek aroused Anne Hampton from the sense of lassitude and apathy that had overtaken her since the shots on the street.

"Do you know what really happened?" he asked again.

She shook her head.

"Well, we went in and did a pretty good imitation of a number of other crimes that have taken place in that fair city over the past eighteen or so months. What we performed was what the police call a copycat killing. You see, they always withhold some detail or another from the press so that they are able to tell who's doing what. Copycat killings frustrate the hell out of the police. You have to see it the way they do: While they're all damn busy trying to find some maniac, along comes some other freak to mess up the works. It takes them time, we're talking man-hours here, to sort the killings out. So, by the time whatever task force is assigned to this killer figures out what seems to have happened, we will have disappeared. No evidence. No leads . . ."

She saw that he was smiling, Cheshire Cat-like.

"Oh, not completely without jeopardy, mind you. Someone could have seen us from one of the apartments in the area. Perhaps I dropped something, or you did, that we don't know about. Something that some sullen, dogged detective can latch on to. You see, that's half the excitement. The state of waiting for that knock on the door."

He rapped the steering wheel with his fingers and the drumming sound startled her.

"You see, that's what I figured out with all my studies. Usually police find killers because murderers and victims have some relationship which predates the murder. The police merely have to ascertain which relationship led to homicide. This is the

241

vast majority of cases. Then there are the serial-type murders, where the crimes adopt a distinct pattern. Those are very difficult to solve, of course, because the killers meander about. Once you get into different jurisdictions, the police hamstring themselves. But I have great respect for the police. They've solved many more of these than you'd think. Often because the poor idiot screws something else up and the cops are on to him like sharks. Never underestimate the intuitive powers of a cop, I say. But, still, the hardest for them to figure out, obviously, are random, patternless killings.

"I thought for a while that that was the type I should engage in. Simply go to a city, pick some poor folk out at random, blow them away. But I realized that that in itself would be a pattern, and eventually, somewhere, some cop would see it. It's the million monkeys, million typewriters theory. Eventually one will type out Shakespeare's complete works.

"So what was I left with?"

She did not really expect that he wanted her to answer.

"I needed to combine this random quality with a pattern. I thought hard. I calculated. I figured. And do you know what I came up with?"

Again she was quiet. His voice was mesmerizing.

"A design with great simplicity, and thus great beauty."

He smiled.

"I copy things. I continue studying. I find out everything there is to know about a Freeway Killer or a Campus Killer or a Green Mountain Killer. The press is so helpful with these titles. Then I just go out and organize a reasonable facsimile. So the police, who are looking for someone else entirely, have this aberrational killing on their hands in the midst of something bigger and, they think, more important. It gets ignored. Shunted aside. Put in the out basket. Filed."

He took a deep breath. "Most killers are caught because, in their arrogance and need, they put some signature on a crime. I am more humble. The act is what is important to me. Not signing it at the bottom. So, in order to murder, I become someone else. I put my mind inside that other person's. I use details I know, and those I can surmise, and I create my own little perfection.

"I arrive. I murder. I leave. And no one, save myself, is anything the wiser."

He waited an instant before continuing.

"But I've grown so accomplished, too careful. Too clever, too perfect." He shook his head.

"A knock on the door? A warrant? Never happen. That's not

bravado speaking. Just efficiency and confidence."

She thought she heard sadness in his voice.

"Actually, not much in the way of thrill much more." He looked over at her. "It has, to be blunt, become just too damn easy."

"That's why you're here," he said matter-of-factly. "You're here to help me bring all this to a proper, suitable, sufficiently volcanic conclusion."

He turned away.

"You can go to sleep now," he said. "I'm a bit wired. I think I'd rather drive." He felt, suddenly, a great pleasurable release. He thought to himself: There. I've told somebody. Now the world will know.

"Now we're going home," Jeffers said. "The slow route, granted. But home. Good night, Boswell."

She heard his voice and the word hit her consciousness: home. Try as she might, she couldn't summon up a solid picture of her house and her parents. Instead, what jumped into her mind seemed vaporous and distant, as if hidden behind film, and she had difficulty telling what it was, though she knew it scared her.

She felt the car surge forward and she closed her eyes and welcomed her new nightmare.

CHAPTER

NINE

ANOTHER REGULAR SESSION
OF THE LOST BOYS

14. MARTIN Jeffers sat awake and alone.

But his solitude was busy, peopled by memory. Once when they were young and vacationing on Cape Cod, his brother had found a young hawk with a damaged wing. The hawk summer, he thought. The drowning summer. He wondered for a moment why he thought of the bird, when it was the later events that August that had been so much more important. But his mind filled with the images of reflection. Doug had found the bird on a dirt road, hopping about in misery, wing dragging. For two weeks, Jeffers recalled, his brother spent every minute rooting about in the woods, turning over rotten logs, lifting up moss-covered rocks, in a constant search for bugs, beetles, small snakes, and snails, which he dutifully brought home to the bird, which gobbled them down and squawked for more. Martin Jeffers smiled. That's what they named the bird: Squawk. In the little free time they'd had, they'd haunted the local lending library, taking home dozens of books on birds, tracts on falconry, and texts on veterinary medicine. After two weeks the hawk would perch on Doug's shoulder to eat, and Martin Jeffers remembered the triumphant look on his brother's face when he set the bird on the handlebars of his old bicycle and rode the bike and bird to town and back.

Martin Jeffers put his hand to his forehead and shuddered.

The old bastard, he thought. Doug was right to despise him.

Their father had told him to get rid of the bird.

Doug wouldn't put the hawk in a cage and so it defecated all over the storeroom where he kept it. That had infuriated the druggist and he'd presented the two boys with a simple, terrible

244

ultimatum: Cage it, free it, or else. It was the *else* part that was so ominous. If its wing won't work, his brother had complained, it will die when we free it. He remembered his brother's face reddening with anger. And you can't put a wild thing in a cage! Douglas Jeffers had shouted. It will die. It will die surely and stupidly, gnawing desperately at the bars without comprehension. Doug was resolute. He always was. Martin Jeffers remembered trailing after his brother, running hard with his shorter legs, trying to keep up with the pace Douglas Jeffers set out of anger. My brother always moved quickly when enraged, Jeffers thought. Always in control, but fast.

The bird had remained tenaciously on his brother's shoulder, digging his claws into the shirt and muscle, turning his proud hawk face into the wind, while Douglas Jeffers rowed across the pond that separated their house from the path to the ocean. He'd pulled the rowboat onto the shore and set off down a worn route. They'd come to a wide field of sandy dirt, waist high in green seagrass and tangled beach-plum bushes. The ocean was a quarter mile away, just past a ridge of tall sand dunes, and Martin Jeffers remembered the sound of the waves echoing deeply in his memory. The breeze tossed the grass about them, and it seemed as if his brother were swimming through strong currents. The afternoon sun was bright, spiraling down with summer intensity onto their heads. Martin Jeffers saw his brother lift his arm, holding the hawk aloft, like he'd seen in picture books of medieval falconry. Then he tried to toss the bird skyward. Martin Jeffers saw the wings beating in a flurry, trying to lift up into the sky, then failing, falling back onto his brother's arm. "It's no good," the older boy had said. "That wing just won't make it."

Then he had added, "I knew it wouldn't."

He said nothing else. They trudged back to their boat in silence. He'd rowed swiftly, pushing his back into the effort, as if he could make things different by force of strength.

Martin Jeffers' memory skipped ahead to the following morning. Doug had been up before him and had suddenly appeared at the side of his bed, hair tousled, face set, gray, and filled with rage. "Squawk's dead," his brother had said.

The old bastard had killed the bird while they'd slept. He'd gone into the storeroom and grabbed the poor trusting brute and wrung its neck.

Martin Jeffers was filled with a rage of his own. His heart swelled with the uncontroverted grief of childhood remembered.

He was just a cruel and heartless man and I was damn glad that he got what was coming to him. I only wish it had hurt him more! He remembered shouting those words out at his own therapist, who had asked in an infuriatingly calm voice whether that was true or not. Of course it was true! He killed the bird! He'd hated us! He'd always hated us. It was the only thing he was ever consistent about. That and getting his own damn way. He would just as quickly have crept into our rooms at night and strangled us the same way! He wanted to!

Martin Jeffers remembered staring at the dead bird in his brother's hands.

No wonder he hated him so much. You can't be born with a hatred like that. You have to construct it carefully out of cruelty and neglect, first removing any love or affection. That's what he'd told the therapist. He'd asked the woman poised behind his head where he couldn't see her, If you'd had a father like that, wouldn't you want to become someone who cared about people? Someone who tried to help people? Why the hell do you think I'm here?

And, of course, the therapist said nothing.

The layered memories boiled about in Martin Jeffers' mind.

Sonuvabitch, sonuvabitch, sonuvabitch.

No one said a word that night. No one ever said a thing. We all sat at the dinner table and acted like nothing had happened. He remembered his mother looking over at Doug and him and saying, I'm sorry the bird flew away. Both boys had adopted the same disbelieving stare, and she'd finally averted her eyes and nothing more was said. She never knew a damn thing, he'd told the therapist. She just primped and preened and was forever touching them, especially with wet, nerve-racking kisses, and she never knew a damn thing about anything and if you tried to tell her, she just turned away.

Their father just thrust food into his mouth.

Sonuvabitch.

Martin Jeffers rocked back in his seat. He saw himself again that morning as he fell from sleep's pinnacle at the sound of his brother's voice, awakening to the sight of the dead bird in his brother's hands. The bird was stiff and broken.

Then, in his memory, he just saw his brother's hands.

Then he thought: Ohmigod!

He said it out loud though there was no one near to hear him: "Ohmigod! No!"

He felt the force of memory crushed by his thought, like an exceptionally heavy weight loaded onto his shoulders.

"Oh no. Oh no, oh no," he said to himself.

In an instant his mind filled with black sadness and horror.

And he realized suddenly, right at that moment, who'd killed the bird.

I am timid, thought Martin Jeffers.

Somehow all these things happened to the two of us and I became quiet and introverted and lonely and passive and he became . . . Jeffers stopped himself before putting a word to it.

He pictured his brother in his mind's eye and saw his loose, flushed, grinning face. He forced himself to see his brother at moments of anger and he remembered the force of Douglas Jeffers' silences. Those had always scared him. He recalled pleading with his brother to speak to him, to talk to him. He thought of the detective and the crime-scene photographs of her niece and he tried to reconcile the two visions.

He shook his head.

Not Doug, he thought.

Then he had a worse thought: Why not?

He could not answer the question.

Martin Jeffers stood up and walked about his apartment. He lived on the ground floor of an old house in Pennington, New Jersey, a tiny town tucked between Hopewell and Trenton's suburbs. Hopewell was just to the west of Princeton, and Martin Jeffers recalled with displeasure that whenever anyone mentioned Hopewell, even when they had been growing up, his brother had always reminded whoever was listening that the little, sleepy town was famous for one thing: It was the place where Lindbergh's baby had been stolen.

The crime of the century, Martin Jeffers thought.

He felt cold and stepped to his window. He put his hand against the screen and felt the late-summer warmth. Still, he shivered, and pushed the window down sharply, leaving only a crack open.

They found the baby in the woods, he thought. Decomposed.

He wondered for an instant whether every state marked its history with crimes. He was taken aback when he realized how much his brother knew. He remembered Doug talking about the Camden Killer, who had walked out on a warm early September day in 1949 and calmly shot and killed thirteen people with a war souvenir Luger. A few years back, Doug had been fascinated to learn that his brother frequently saw this person the papers once described as a mad dog as he peacefully roamed the halls of Trenton Psychiatric Hospital, a model patient for more than twenty-five years, never arguing when the orderlies came about with the daily dosage of Thorazine, Mellaril, or Haldol. Vitamin

H, the patients called it. The Camden Killer always took his without complaint. Not even a whimper of protest.

Doug was always interested in that sort of thing.

Martin Jeffers shook his head.

Yeah, but so was that police reporter from the Philadelphia paper who came up to do a story about the hospital. And you tell it at every stupid seminar or convention you go to. A lot of people remember that crime.

That was the problem, he thought. People are always fascinated by crimes. And it was natural for his brother to be intrigued by them. Hell, he'd spent so much time chasing cops and robbers with his camera, it was natural he was interested.

He paused.

But how interested?

He shook his head again. Denial, he thought.

Ridiculous.

You know your brother, he told himself.

He put his head in his hands.

He could not cry. He could not feel anything save a disjointed confusion.

Do you really? he asked himself.

He thought of the men in his therapy group. He suddenly envisioned his brother sitting among them. Then, just as quickly, he saw himself there as well.

He turned away from the window, as if by walking across the room he could change the view in his mind.

"Dammit!" he said out loud. "Goddammit to hell!"

He thought of his father and his mother.

"How could you love them?" he said.

He thought of his woman therapist. There had been an abstract painting on one wall of her office, a Kandinsky reproduction, all brightly colored angles and shapes with dots floating about a snow-white background. Across from it had been a Wyeth print, a muted picture of a barn caught in grays and browns in the wan early evening light. American Realism. He had always been struck by the juxtaposition of the two pictures, but never had managed to ask the woman why she had selected them and placed them where they were. "Well," she had asked, "do you think you loved your real mother and father?"

"They worked in a circus! A drunk and a whore!" he had blurted out in angry response. "They abandoned each other and then they abandoned us! I was only three or four . . . I did not know them. How can you love something or someone that you don't know?"

She didn't answer that, of course.

And he knew the answer anyway.

It's easy. The mind creates something to love out of the slightest memory of a touch, a sound, a sensation.

He thought then of the corollary.

The mind can also create something to hate.

He stepped over to a small desk in a corner of what passed for his living room, really a room filled with papers, clutter, paperback novels, classic novels, medical texts and reports, magazines, a couple of chairs and a sofa, a television and telephone. He looked around at his things. They are cheap. The meager belongings of someone living a meager life. He looked down at the desktop and saw an envelope stuck in the corner of the desk blotter. On it was written in his own handwriting, *Doug's apartment key.*

He remembered his brother tossing the key to him so casually. A sentimental journey, he said.

Nothing is an accident.

Everything is part of some scheme. Conscious or unconscious. He picked up the key in the envelope and held it. He shook his head. Not yet, he said. I'm not convinced. I'm not persuaded. I'm not intruding. Not yet.

He recognized this feeling for the lie it was.

Then he dropped the envelope back on his desk and returned to an easy chair. He glanced at a clock. It was well past midnight. Sleep, he said to himself. He dropped into the chair, knowing that he would not.

He thought of the detective.

Martin Jeffers tried to imagine the forces that drove her. He thought, for an instant, that she was somehow pure; that the only true motivation was justice. If this took the form of war or revenge or anger, it was still honest. Even murder? he wondered to himself. He did not formulate an answer, but he knew: I would not trust anyone who turned the other cheek. Modern psychiatry does not recognize such selfless altruism. Again the detective elbowed her way into his consciousness. He saw her face set, unsmiling, filled with terrifying determination, her hair thrust back severely. What is so frightening, he thought, is that she does not carry herself like a man. A woman detective. She ought to be edged in granite, some middle-aged, bureaucratic type, with farm woman's hands and monocular vision of the world. Detective Barren wears silks and not very sensible shoes and she frightens me all the more. Women do not, as a rule, pursue their quarry all across the United States. They are not motivated by the senseless and stupid egos of insult and outrage like men. They are more worldly, more understanding.

He smiled and thought how silly he was being.

Lesson One, Day One, Medical School: Don't generalize. Don't characterize.

The words obsession and compulsion thrust themselves into his mind, but he was momentarily confused. He considered his brother, the detective, then himself.

It was no wonder, he thought then, that the ancient Greeks invented the Furies and that they were women. His memory tumbled through myth and fantasy. Even if I were to blind myself, I would still see.

Martin Jeffers stared across the room, watching the clock, scared of the night, waiting for the morning, desperately wanting to return to the routine of his life: the morning shower, the quick cup of coffee, the drive to the hospital, the first series of daily rounds and the regular sessions of his group and then his patients, knocking in their tentative way at his office door. He wanted everything to return suddenly to normal. The way it was, the way it was before today happened. He realized how childish the wish was and smiled to himself: I wish I were back in Kansas, back in Kansas, Kansas . . . He closed his eyes and laughed halfheartedly at the memory joke, but knew nothing would change when he opened them. There are no magic slippers, he thought. No heels to click together three times. He suddenly remembered his brother's description of his work: on the heels of evil.

He got up, went to a closet, and pulled a winter comforter from a shelf. He wrapped it around his shoulders and sat back down in the chair. He switched off the bright light on a coffee table next to him and sat quietly in the darkness, wanting to be awake, wanting to be asleep, caught between the two, each an equally terrifying prospect.

Outside, in her car, Detective Mercedes Barren saw the light extinguished. She waited fifteen minutes, to be certain that Martin Jeffers did not leave the apartment. Then she put the seat back as far as it would go and tugged a thin blanket appropriated from her hotel room over her. She double-checked to make sure the doors were locked, but the window cracked to the cool night air. Pennington, she thought, is a place of absolute safety, of families and neighbors and backyard barbecues. She remembered visiting the tree-lined streets on high-school football weekends. He doesn't know, she thought. He doesn't know that I am home, too. She loosened the belt to her jeans, and, glancing eagerly once

250

more at the darkened apartment, relaxed, letting her fingers play against the grip of the 9 millimeter that rested on her stomach, beneath the blanket. Its heft, as always, reassured her. She was confident. She dismissed the thought that had troubled her much of the evening. She knew that she was a policewoman and that there was something terribly wrong about her becoming a criminal.

But only briefly, she said to herself. Expediency.

She cleared the thought from her mind.

Then she closed her eyes to the night.

Her dreams, though, were unsettling, flooded with disjointed combinations of people: her husband and Sadegh Rhotzbadegh, the Jeffers brothers and her bosses and her father. When the headlights of a car passing by awakened her, just before dawn, she was relieved. She glanced at the taillights of the car as it slipped through the gray darkness. She could just make out the red and blue light bar on the roof, and for an instant she wondered what sort of sleepy cop could miss someone alone in a car parked on a residential street. What's the purpose in patrolling if you can't see the unusual? But she was glad that she hadn't been spotted, though she knew that her own badge and brusque manner would have been sufficient explanation.

She watched the red lights disappear around a distant corner. They glowed brightly for an instant as the patrolman touched his brakes, then slid from her sight. She stretched and looked about her. She bent the mirror toward herself and straightened her appearance as best she could. Then she bent down and hunted about for the thermos of coffee and half-eaten Danish that she'd brought along. The coffee was lukewarm, but better than nothing, and she sipped it slowly, trying to pretend it was steaming hot.

She saw the branches on the trees around her slowly etch themselves against the morning light. First one bird chirped loudly, then another. The shapes of the houses seemed to stand out stark and bare as morning took hold.

She reached down and felt her stomach where the thick round welt of the bullet scar hid beneath her shirt. The patrol car passing, the pre-dawn quiet, all triggered her own memory. She thought of the experience of being shot; it had still been dark, but close to the end of the graveyard shift. There were aspects of the entire act that remained a mystery to her. The whole event had happened in some other time frame: some parts were speeded up, played out with dizzying quickness; others seemed slowed to a foggy crawl.

She had spotted the two kids.

They had been walking briskly down the opposite street with a hasty purposefulness that was electric to any police officer with more than a few minutes of experience.

"Now that couple has got to be wrong," she had said to her partner. The teenagers were wearing high-top sneakers. "They've got their second-story shoes on," she had added, "and unless there's some roundball game going on at five A.M. that we don't know about . . ." He had looked over at the two boys for a few seconds and nodded his head.

"Can't you just smell the B and E?" he had laughed. "C'mon. Let's bust them quick and head in."

She had called it in: "Dispatch, this is unit fourteen-oh-one, we're fifty-six at the corner of Flagler and Northwest Twenty-first. We have two suspects in a two-thirteen in view. Request backup."

She always liked the authority that slipped into her voice speaking the particular codes of the patrol officer. There had been static, momentarily, on the radio, as her partner had steered the car into a U-turn and cruised up behind the two boys. Then the dispatcher had acknowledged their call, telling them that backup was en route.

They were only a few feet behind the teenagers, who hadn't turned to notice them, when her partner had hit the flashing lights. "This'll wake them up," he had said.

It did. They both had jumped and froze. She had seen that they were both in their early teens.

"Kids," her partner had said. "Christ."

They had stepped from the car and started to approach the pair.

"I wonder what they stole?" her partner had asked idly.

She thought of those words often: your life.

She had not seen the gun until it was leveled at them. They were only a few feet distant. She remembered struggling, trying to reach her service revolver, while her partner threw his hands out in front of him as if he could ward off the shot. The gun barrel had flashed and his arm had knocked into her as he was thrown back. She remembered seeing the weapon turn, as if it were unattached to anything, and face her. She sometimes believed that she could see the bullet as it was fired and as it had traveled the space between her and the gun.

Then she remembered lying on the ground and looking up and realizing that it would be morning soon and her shift would be ending and she would be able to go home and read the paper over a leisurely breakfast. She had planned to do some shopping that day; perhaps it had been a change in temperature, but she had decided to buy herself something slinky and sexy, even if she never wore it. The names of the stores had flashed into her head. All the time she had thought these things, her hands had been searching for her stomach, and she was able to feel sticky hot blood pumping from her.

Her eyes had focused on the slowly lightening sky, and her breathing had become shallow and she remembered seeing the two teenagers hover into her line of sight. They had stared down at her, meeting her eyes. She had seen one lift the gun and she thought then of her family and friends. But instead of firing, the teenager had dropped the weapon, cursing, and run away. She always remembered the sound of their sneakers slapping away, growing fainter in the distance as the cacophony of sirens had enveloped her, promising her a chance at life.

In the car, she turned away from the memory and watched a paperboy weave his way, first right, then left, up the street on his bicycle, tossing newspapers onto front porches with practiced familiarity and confidence. He spotted Detective Barren and after a momentary look of surprise, smiled and gave her a wave. She rolled down the window and asked, "Got any extras?"

He stopped the bike. "Actually, yeah, just today, I've got one. Old Mr. Macy down the street's on vacation and I forgot. You wanna buy his?"

She fished a dollar bill from her pocketbook.

"Here," she said. "Keep the change."

"Thanks, lady. Here you go."

He pedaled off, waving.

The lead headline was more trouble in the Middle East. There was a picture of rescue workers pulling bodies from a wrecked building, victims of a suicide-car bomb. Below that was the national lead, a tax bill in Congress story. There were two crime stories on the front page, opening day in the trial of a reputed mob boss, story and photo of the man walking up courtroom steps, and a local crime story. She read this one first: A homeowner had surprised a burglar breaking into his house and had shot the unarmed man dead with an unregistered and hence illegal weapon. Prosecutors were still undecided whether to indict the homeowner or give him a medal.

She turned to the sports pages. The pennant races were just heating up and football training camps were heading to the last cuts. She turned to an inside page to read the agate and see whether the Dolphins had cut any of her favorite players, but they had not. She saw, though, that the Patriots had released one of their old linemen. He was a steady block of a man from some solid Midwestern state, who'd always played infuriatingly well against the Dolphins and she had come, over the years, to admire him for the constancy of his effort, carried out in anonymity and pain. She knew he would play hurt, and she respected that, perhaps more than the other fans. She was saddened suddenly by the news, a reminder both of sudden mortality and the changeable nature of life. She thought she would root hard for his replacement to fail.

Everything changes eventually. Everyone passes on to something new, she thought.

She looked back up at Jeffers' apartment and stiffened when she realized that the light had been switched on. She saw a shape move in front of the window and she shrank down in the car seat involuntarily, not really worrying about being spotted, but strongly feeling the need for concealment.

Come on, she said to herself. Come on, doctor. Get the day started.

She was flush with excitement and she rolled the window down, breathing in the damp morning air as if she were scared that her thoughts would suffocate her.

Martin Jeffers moved about the apartment in the weak morning half-light. He had slept, of that he was sure, but he did not know for how long. He felt no sense of refreshment, remaining as exhausted by emotion as he had at the start of the night. He moved into the bathroom and dropped his clothes on the floor. He forced himself into the shower, making certain that it was colder than comfortable. He wanted to shock his system into movement. He wanted alertness and quick wit. He held his face under the cascading cold water, shivering, but feeling vitality creep into his bones and blood.

He stepped from the shower and rubbed himself red with a threadbare towel. Still naked, he shaved with cold water.

He padded into his bedroom and put fresh underwear, shirt, tie, and suit onto the bed. Do twenty, he said to himself. He dropped to the floor and managed a fast ten pushups. He laughed out loud. That's good enough. He turned over and did twenty-five sit-ups, with his knees bent, faithfully holding his hands behind his head. He remembered his brother explaining that that was the only way they were effective. Doug never had to worry about exercise. He was always strong, always in shape. He could eat everything in the house and not gain a pound. Martin Jeffers stood and looked at himself in the mirror over the dressing table. Not bad, he thought. Especially considering all the sedentary work you do. Take up running again or find some tennis partners. Back in shape in no time.

He dressed quickly, glancing at the clock.

He thought of Detective Barren. He had not told her when to come to the hospital, but he knew she would be there early. He shook his head.

No, he thought, nothing's been proven. Nothing at all.

It is in the nature of brothers always to exaggerate, both goods and evils. It comes from childhood, from the constancy of love, jealousy, and unrestrained emotion that is inherent in the relationship. So Doug killed a bird when you always thought—no, assumed—that it was your father. You were mistaken. Still, that doesn't make your brother a killer. Not at all.

Martin Jeffers' hands stopped in midair as he was finishing the knot to his tie. He was almost overcome, suddenly, by the force of the self-lie. He closed his eyes, then opened them, as if he could clear the agony of his thoughts from his mind. He said out loud, firmly addressing himself in the third person:

"Well, whatever Doug is, and you damn well don't have any proof, any real proof of one thing or another despite what that goddamn detective says, he's still your goddamn brother and that ought to count for something."

His words sounding strong in the empty room comforted him momentarily. But he also thought angrily that he'd been a doctor long enough to recognize clinical denial. Even in himself.

Still stretched between the poles of disbelief and realization, not trusting his memory, his feelings, or the knowledge that had grown over the years within him, Martin Jeffers headed off to the hospital. He did not see the detective waiting and watching from her vantage point across the street.

She waited another ten minutes just to be certain.

But she knew from the brisk pace he'd set and the fixed glance he'd worn that he was heading directly to the hospital and to the meeting with her that she assumed he'd spent the night worrying about.

He'll get that meeting, she thought, just not quite as early as he probably expects it. Again, she was mildly troubled about what she was about to do. Part of her argued: You know enough. He will come around and offer to help. But the pessimist within her doubted that the doctor would ever help her to find his brother until she could overwhelm him with necessity. You still need an edge, she told herself, and that apartment is as good a place as any to start looking for something. She was also uncertain about Martin Jeffers. If he's known, she thought, perhaps he's been hiding this knowledge for years. She recalled the look of surprise that Martin Jeffers had so quickly concealed when she'd first blurted out her need. Perhaps he's a killer as well. Perhaps, perhaps. She felt armored by knowledge, weakened by supposition, and realized that she still needed to know more. Facts, she thought. Hard truths. Evidence.

She shut down the mental debate and slid from her car. After glancing about momentarily, she sauntered across the street toward the apartment. But instead of walking up the front steps, she quickened her pace and trotted around the side of the building. Within a minute she spotted the window, cracked to let in fresh air.

Don't hesitate, she said to herself. Just do it.

She grabbed a metal trash can and thrust it against the side of the house. Then she jumped up on top, throwing the window up in the same moment. She punched in the flimsy screen and jackknifed into the apartment in the same motion, landing like some clumsy waterfowl in a heap on the living room floor.

She scrambled to her feet and quickly closed the window behind her.

She had the odd, slightly humorous thought that she'd accomplished a pretty efficient break-in, for a first time. She pictured several dozen assorted burglars and robbers that she'd arrested in her career, and saw them lined up, a rogues' gallery applauding her. Just one of the guys now, she thought.

She stared around her and felt a momentary distaste at the haphazard arrangement of clothes and furniture. But the sensation passed quickly.

She was reminded of visiting John Barren in his freshman year, before they started sharing quarters. She smiled, remembering the socks festering in the corner, the underwear filed in a gray metal filing cabinet along with reading lists and course outlines. At the very least, she'd told him, you could put it in the drawer marked with a U. He'd lived in clutter as well, as if for him it was important to leave the mind unfettered and the surroundings messy. Then she thought that was her memory just being overly kind: that in reality he was just another man who'd become too accustomed to a mother who picked up after him; as if, even though he was away at college, his mother would mysteriously appear and pluck the socks from the corner, delivering them at a later point freshly laundered and rolled. And—she smiled again

—he'd been right: It was almost the first damn thing you did. His damn laundry. You gave him a kiss, then there was a quick roll in the sack while his roommates were out, and then you picked up all his dirty clothes and set out for the local laundromat. Women never learn, she thought. She wanted to laught out loud.

Then she heard a noise in the hallway and froze in fear.

Her mind swiftly sorted through perceptions: Was it a voice? The sound of a door being opened? Footsteps? She swallowed hard and concentrated her listening, trying to hear above the sudden throbbing within her.

He can't be back! she thought.

She pulled the 9 millimeter from her belt and waited stiffly, thinking: I'm crazy. Put the damn gun away. If it's him, just talk fast. He'll be angry, but he'll know why you're here.

Instead she leveled the gun at the door and waited.

She thought suddenly, terrifyingly: It's the brother!

She felt overcome by an immense, uncontrollable evil, as if its stench had instantly filled the room like smoke from a fire. Oh, God! He was hiding him here! They're in it together! It's him!

She crouched, trying to still her noisy heart and quaking hand. She demanded toughness of herself, summoning it from within. Her hands steadied. Her breathing became even and patient. She sighted down the barrel of the gun, just as she had toward hundreds of firing-range targets.

Get him with the first shot, she snarled to herself.

Go for the chest. That will stop him. Then finish him off with a second shot to the head.

She closed one eye and took a deep breath. She held it in.

Then she waited for another noise.

But there was none.

She remained in her shooter's stance. She thought she might be unable to move and that her muscles would never relax. Thirty seconds passed. Then it stretched into a minute. Time seemed elongated by tension.

But the world was precipitously filled with silence.

She would not allow herself to breathe, until finally she could hold it in no longer and she released her pent-up breath in a long, low hiss.

She lowered the gun slowly.

"There's no one there," she whispered out loud. It was reassuring to hear her own voice.

"You have lost your mind completely," she continued under her voice. "Now, stop screwing around and find something and get the hell out of here."

She gave the bathroom a perfunctory look, then swiftly searched the bedroom. She was not being particularly systematic, she realized, but she also knew that anything Martin Jeffers had that might help her find his brother was not necessarily going to be hidden. Underneath the bed she found two cardboard file boxes filled with personal records. She pulled these out and sat on the floor, reading through them as swiftly as possible. They were mostly income tax forms, loan applications, records from college. She saw that his grades at medical school had been mid-range, while in college they had been outstanding. It was as if once he'd arrived at his future, he'd stopped applying himself with the same intensity. That might explain why he was at a state mental hospital, she thought, instead of a Main Street private practice. But that only posed a series of new questions and she threw the papers back into the box, rifling through some more. She came across a certified letter from the state Catholic Charities organization that was a half-dozen years old. Idly, she opened it and read:

> . . . We are unable to provide any information about your natural mother. Although the adoption was between family members, we **did** handle the paperwork. Unfortunately, when St. Stephen's Parish burned in 1972, many of the old records that had not been transcribed on microfilm were irretrievably ruined.

Detective Barren stared down at the letter, thinking how interesting a piece of information it was but not knowing precisely why. She thrust it back and flipped through the remaining papers. There was one letter in an unmistakably feminine handwriting. "Dear Marty," she read. "I'm sorry, but it's just not going to work between us . . ." And the rest was maudlin self-recriminations by a woman named Joanne. Detective Barren recognized the style: Say you're to blame when you know the opposite is the truth. She'd helped a dozen friends write that letter during her teenage years. Her heart jumped and she remembered her niece at age sixteen once calling her with the same request for help.

She dropped the letter into the box and pulled out a yellowed, brittle copy of a newspaper. It was the *Vineyard Gazette* from Martha's Vineyard and it carried an August date from nearly twenty years before. She scanned the front page rapidly; the main headline was: STEAMSHIP AUTHORITY REACHES AGREEMENT ON NEW FERRY DOCK. On the other side, above the fold, there was a picture and story: SWORDFISHING FLEET SETS ONE-DAY RECORD

WITH 21 FISH. Next to that, in smaller type, was: *Swimming Accident Claims Life of Summer Visitor.*

She glanced at the lead paragraph: "Summer visitor Robert Allen lost his life Tuesday when he was caught in a sudden undertow while swimming off South Beach in the early evening. Police and Coast Guard officials surmised that the businessman from New Jersey struggled against the flood, exhausting himself, and was unable to reach shore after being swept a half mile from the beach." She was struck by the fact that the man in the story was from New Jersey, but his name was different, and she went on to the next. Butting against that story was: TISBURY SELECTMAN REJECT BLUE LAW MODIFICATION PROPOSAL.

She stared at the page for a moment and thought: Maybe there's something on the inside, and she started to flip through the pages rapidly. Nothing jumped out at her. It was the usual run of summer stories; she was familiar with the style of small-town resort newspapers. Some marriages, agricultural reports, who's visiting whom, cautious assessments on how many ticks there were in the woods. Warnings about shellfish contamination. Story and pictures of the prizewinning apple pie at the Tisbury Fair. The usual mixture of everyday things. She turned back to the front page and looked at the picture accompanying the swordfish-capture story. It had no credit line. She stared at the composition of the photograph and wondered: Is that his? The eyes of the fishermen seemed to burn on the page, while the dead eye of one of their catch looked out in eerie contrast. It's his style, she thought. But she was impatient, which she recognized was an awful quality for someone conducting a nonspecific search. She ignored this recognition and dropped the newspaper back into the box. She pushed both cases back under the bed to the locations they'd previously occupied.

So far, nothing.

She went into the living room and saw the comforter tossed onto an easy chair. That's where he slept last night, she thought. If he slept at all.

She noticed that there was a bunch of magazines littering the floor around the chair. So he tried to get his mind off things. Well, I'm sure it didn't work. She started to cross the rooms when something struck her about the pile of magazines. She turned and looked back at them.

"What's wrong?" she whispered. "What is it?"

She focused on the one magazine dropped in her direction.

She stared, then chided herself: Out of date. Pay attention, dammit!

259

She stepped across and knelt by the pile. She picked up a six-month-old *Life*. It seemed hot in her hands. She knew what would be inside. She let the magazine waft open and she saw instantly what it was—the by-line leaped out at her: PHOTOGRAPHS BY DOUGLAS JEFFERS. She looked at the page and saw the grainy gray of a picture. It was of an emergency-room physician staring out through the camera in exhaustion. The palpable sense of closeness between the camera and the subject struck her sharply and she had to push the page back.

I know what he was looking for, she thought. She could see the doctor brother sitting in the chair, looking into the pages, trying to see what the pictures could tell him.

She quickly spread the magazines about her, searching each for the pictures inside. People and shapes jumped out of the pages, exploding about her.

But none told her anything she did not know already.

He's good, she thought. But we already knew that. We knew he was one of the best.

But what else is there to see?

For a moment she felt the same frustration she knew the brother had felt hours earlier. There is so much to see, she thought, but it shows so little.

She closed the magazines and arranged them in a close approximation of the positions in which she'd found them.

She complained to herself: Find something!

She crossed to the desk and looked down on it and saw the words: *Doug's apartment key.* It was so obvious that for an instant she did not realize what she was staring at. Then her hand shot out, as if bidden by something other than her conscious mind, and she seized the envelope. She felt the key inside, and put back her head and barely managed to stifle the cheer welling up inside her. She stuffed the envelope into her pocket, then raised her hands above her head, balling them into fists like an athlete at the moment of victory. The exultation dissipated swiftly in the face of a quick demand for discipline: Get ahold of yourself, she thought angrily. Then, with near panic, she started to look about her: Address, address, I need the address. She looked across the room and spotted a small black book next to the telephone. She jumped to it and flipped it open. The Upper West Side of Manhattan address of the brother stared out in black ink. She looked about for a pen and scrap paper and saw none. She ripped the page from the book.

Then, feeling flush with heat, she walked to the front door, opened it, and, after looking back briefly, exited the building.

She could think of nothing save the electric feeling that the stolen key in her pocket gave off.

On the street outside the apartment, she passed an elderly lady walking a small dog, carrying an old-fashioned parasol as protection against the rising sun. "Good morning," the woman said cheerfully.

"Beautiful day," replied Detective Barren.

"But hot," said the lady. She looked down at the Sheltie panting at the end of the leash. "Dog days," she said. "Too hot in the summer. Too cold in the winter. Isn't that the nature of life?"

This was a joke and both women smiled. Detective Barren nodded in farewell and crossed the street. For a moment she was overcome by the bright late summer morning sun and the routine conversation with the woman. Everything is normal, she thought. Everything is simple and ordinary and in its place. Birds singing. Children playing. Light breeze blowing. Temperature soaring. Woman walking her dog. Norman Rockwell America. Simple steady rhythms and melodies.

She shook her head and thought of the dissonance in her pocket. I'm getting closer, she thought.

Pennington faded around her and she envisioned the hard city streets of her destination.

She slid back into her car, and within seconds was heading toward New York.

The tidal flow of argument ebbed around Martin Jeffers.

He had started the session by asking the Lost Boys a simple question: All of you have relations, he'd queried. What do you think they think of your behavior? Do they have any connection with your crimes? There had been a momentary uncomfortable silence, and Jeffers knew he'd struck a nerve within them. He knew, too, that his question, not so innocently posed, came from within his own heart. He had instantly pictured his brother, then forced the image from his mind while he listened to the men's memories unfold. There had been a rush of denial, almost en masse, which he had, as always, taken as representing an opposite reality. It was a simple formula: that which the Lost Boys most vigorously denied was closest to the truth.

Now he waited for the voices to subside so he could interject some comment that they would pick up and argue more about. But his attention wandered in and out, and he had trouble concentrating on the progress of the group. Luckily, the Lost Boys were in active form; they needed little input of his. He found himself nervously eyeing his watch, hoping for the end of the session. Where is she? he wondered.

"You know what was funny?" It was Meriwether speaking in his small, reedy voice. "When I got busted and sent away to this country club, my wife was more upset than I was. I mean"—he breathed through his nostrils with a wheezy laughter—"I would have thought that she'd divorce me. Shit, I thought she would shoot me herself. Christ, she's twice my size anyway, she coulda just walloped me a couple . . ."

All the men laughed at this.

Jeffers thought: What does she want? Arrest him? He remembered the ice in her eyes.

". . . But she didn't. She was crying and wringing her hands. And even while I was copping out, she was, you know, denying it. It was like she thought that neighbor's kid I did somehow, you know, seduced me! She had to believe that."

Meriwether hesitated.

"Hell, the kid was only eleven . . ."

In the momentary pause, Jeffers' mind worked quickly: He has always involved me! I've always been a part of everything he did. Always on the edge, just barely included, but connected nonetheless. He's always wanted it that way. And he's always gotten it the way he wanted. That's the older brother's prerogative. What younger brother ever refuses the older?

"Fucking weird woman. Now she visits twice a week and bothers the parole board."

He looked out at the group.

"Somebody here explain it to me."

Jeffers could think only of the words: A sentimental journey. He was suddenly suffused with a complete frustrating anger. What the hell did he mean by that? he asked himself furiously. Where has he gone? What sentiment is there in our lives? Did he visit the old family house? It's right down the fucking road in Princeton. He could have gone and seen the old man's drugstore. A chain owns it now. He didn't have to take off to do that! So where's he gone? What's he visiting? He would never tell me anything!

A thousand dark thoughts flooded Jeffers' mind.

Wasserman spoke quickly in reply to Meriwether's question:

"My mom was the same. I get a package from her every week. She wouldn't believe anything. I coulda fucking killed some gal right under her nose and she would have looked down and said, 'Well, honey, it seems you fucked her too hard 'cause now she's had a heart attack and gone to heaven . . .'"

Jeffers noted that Wasserman's usual stutter had deserted him momentarily. My brother, he thought, was always direct and cryptic. He told me only what he thought I needed to know. What he thought! And now when I need to know something, he's left me a void. Empty! Nothing!

But then he said to himself: You do know.

He shook his head. What do you know?

Around him the men were snorting and hooting.

"S-s-s-sometimes I thought M-m-m-Mom was crazier than I am."

The men nodded in agreement. Jeffers heard the stutter return.

Pope spoke in his solid con-wise tone. "They never want to believe. They don't want to believe you could do it when you lift a candy bar from a store shelf. When things get worse, they just refuse harder, you know. And when you get busted for fucking, like all of us here, they won't accept it at all. It's easier for them to believe something else. Simpler."

"Not always," interjected Miller.

The men turned to the hard-edged professional criminal.

Miller looked about the room as if assessing a stolen jewel. "Think about it. There's someone for all of us, probably a father, maybe a mother, who knew what we were and hated us for it. Someone you couldn't con. Someone who beat you, maybe, or left you, maybe, because they couldn't beat you. Someone who got out while the going was good. . . ."

This comment made him laugh, but the other men had grown silent with their thoughts.

"Maybe someone you wanted to get rid of. Maybe someone you did get rid of, only the good doc there and the proper authorities"—he said this sneering—"don't have such a good idea about."

He paused, and Jeffers saw that he was delighting in his opinion and the dampening effect it had on the other men.

"There's always someone who can see just exactly what we all are inside. It's no big deal, really. You just got to handle that person a bit differently, huh? But they're out there. We all know it."

The room filled with murmuring, then subsided into silence.

Jeffers tried to prevent himself at that moment of quiet from asking the question that seared across his imagination, but was unable. His words were like his thoughts: runaway, out of control, embodied by a purpose of their own. They frightened him terribly. But he was powerless at that moment. So he asked:

"Well, turn it around for a moment. What would you do if you learned that someone you loved, a family member, was committing crimes? How would you act?"

There was a short hesitation, as if all the Lost Boys had inhaled at the same time. Then he was quickly enveloped in a cacophony of opinions.

Detective Mercedes Barren drove north, passing up the exit on the New Jersey Turnpike for the Holland Tunnel, which would have been a more direct route. She headed toward the George Washington Bridge, with its great gray bulk stretching across the Hudson. She made her decision to avoid the tunnel consciously, despite the press of excitement and the furious sensation that time was growing shorter, compressing around her; she always avoided tunnels as much as possible. Ever since she was a child, she worried about the weight of the water pressing down on the tiles and cement just above her head. She could still see it, with that same child's imaginative vision, cracking and buckling and the dark water suddenly pouring in on top of her. The confinement of the tunnel caused her breath to grow short and her palms to dampen unpleasantly. It's like a kind of little claustrophobia, she thought. It's not that terrible. Indulge it.

As she accelerated across the bridge, she looked back quickly over her shoulder, glancing up at the Palisades. She saw the cliff faces tumbling precipitously into the water. Sunlight glinted on the surface of the river and she caught a glimpse of white sails plying back and forth. She had always understood, especially on bright clear days, why old Henry Hudson was convinced when first he steered up the great river that he had discovered the Northwest Passage. It seemed reasonable to her, when you removed the buildings and boats and saw the river and the cliffs without progress littering them, that anyone would believe that around the first or second bend would be China.

She stared at the city, with its massive phalanx of skyscrapers standing stiffly, like a great army at attention. She clutched the address paper in her hand and wove aggressively in and out of traffic. She stared dead ahead as she entered Manhattan, refusing even to look in the rearview mirror, pointing singularly for her destination.

To her surprise she discovered a legal parking place on the street barely a block from the apartment. But before approaching the apartment, she stopped in a local delicatessen and purchased a haphazard bag of groceries. Carrying the bag and holding the key, she headed toward Douglas Jeffers' home.

He lived in a midsized, older brick building on West End

Avenue. There was an ancient doorman who held the door open for her as she breezed through.

"You're going to see?" he asked in a cigarette rasp.

"Just staying at my cousin's while I take in the sights. He's out of town," she said cheerfully. "Doug Jeffers. He's the best photographer..."

The doorman smiled.

"Four-F," he said.

"I know," she replied, tossing him a smile. "See you."

She boarded an old elevator, closing the door firmly and punching up four. She saw the doorman had already turned back to his vigil. The elevator creaked as it carried her up slowly. It seemed to bounce into place and she stepped out carefully.

To her great relief, the hallway was empty.

She swiftly found 4-F and set the grocery bag down. She put the key in her left hand and pulled the 9 millimeter from her pocketbook. For an instant she listened, but she could hear no sounds through the thick black door.

She took a deep breath and said: Go!

She thrust the key into the lock and turned it. She heard the deadbolt release and she pushed hard.

The door fell open and she crouched and jumped in.

She swung the pistol up, still bent over, aiming, letting the pistol barrel guide her sight. She swung right, left, center, and saw no one. She waited. No sound. She straightened up and lowered the gun. Then she retrieved the bag of groceries and set them on the floor inside the apartment. She closed and locked the door behind her, putting the chain on as well.

Then she turned and, still holding the gun, truly looked at Douglas Jeffers' apartment.

"I can feel it," she said out loud. She was flooded suddenly with visions from a hundred crime scenes and bloodied, decomposing corpses that she'd visited over the years. They came back to her as if in some parade from the Grand Guignol. The ghoulish sights and sticky, awful smells filled her imagination and for an instant she thought that there was a body there, in the apartment.

She shook her head as if to clear it and said, "Well, let's look around."

She moved from room to room gingerly, still holding the pistol. When she was finally convinced that she was alone, she began to assess what surrounded her. The first thought that struck her was that it was clean and orderly. Everything seemed in its place. Not so organized as to be oppressive, but straightened up and shipshape. The contrast with Martin Jeffers' apartment was striking.

It was not a large apartment. There was a single bedroom and bathroom, a small kitchen and dining alcove, and a wide, rectangular living room. A half-bath off the living room had been transformed into a darkroom. The furniture was comfortable and stylish, but not to the extent that a designer had created a distinctive look. More that it reflected someone who understood quality and purchased an occasional piece. There were a few antiques, and in each room there were knickknacks on shelves and bureau tops. Detective Barren picked up a shell casing from what she took to be a mortar round. There were small artifacts, a statuette from Central America, a fertility statue from Africa. She saw a large shark's tooth encased in plastic and an old rock also encased. It bore a legend: OLDUVAI GORGE, 1977. TWO MILLION YEARS OLD.

She saw that Jeffers had a worktable—a draftsman's bench, situated near the bank of windows which let the room fill with light. She saw the paraphernalia of a photographer: negatives, enlargers, paper, piled neatly about the table.

There was one large bookcase, which covered an entire wall in the living room.

The walls were white. There were two posters, framed: The Art of Photography, an exhibition at the Museum of Modern Art, and a Horn Gallery Exhibit of Ansel Adams.

Everything else was by Douglas Jeffers.

Or, at least, that is what she took them to be.

There were dozens of pictures covering all the walls. They were in all shapes and sizes, framed in different styles. She glanced in their direction, thinking: They are what I saw in the magazines. They'll tell you everything and nothing at the same time.

But her eye was caught by one small frame, in a corner. She walked to it and stared. It was of a man on the near edge of middle age, but with a clearly contradictory youthful vitality. He was dressed in olive fatigues and blue workshirt, draped with cameras and lenses. The background was of some anonymous jungle. She could see tendrils and vines flowing from the twisted branches of a thousand interwoven trees. He was sitting on a stack of boxes marked with ammunition numbers. He was grinning widely out from the picture, his hand cocked in a mock pistol, making a shooting motion toward the camera. In a corner of the frame typed on a small white piece of paper, were the words SELF-PORTRAIT 1984, NICARAGUA.

"Hello, Mr. Jeffers," she said.

She took the picture from the wall and held it up.

"I am your undoing," she said.

She replaced the picture and told herself to get started. She cautioned herself to be careful and systematic with this brother's apartment. She turned toward the desk and saw, neatly placed in the center, a large white envelope. On it was written in strong block type: FOR MARTY.

Her hand shot out for it.

There had been much disagreement among the Lost Boys.

Opinions had ranged from Weingarten's whining "Jeez, what could you do? I mean, ask 'em to stop? But people do what they want anyway. You can't just force them to do anything. I mean, I never could, and nobody could ever get me to stop . . ." to Pope's stolid "If I knew somebody in my family was doing what I do, I'd shoot the fucker, real fast. Put 'em out of their misery," to which Steele had interjected, "Are you in such misery? Dear, dear, you don't act like it . . ." And Pope had replied, "Watch out, faggot, before I fucking well do you." This, despite the integrity of the threat, had caused everyone to laugh. Killing a man such as Steele struck most of them as a great waste of time. This opinion was shared among the members of the group with great enthusiasm.

It seemed that they, who should have been experts, did not know what to do any more than anyone would.

Any more than I know what to do, Martin Jeffers spoke to himself.

He despaired inwardly.

He sat alone in his darkened office. Outside, the night had swept up and taken over the hospital grounds, throwing shadows across the stately lawns. He could hear an occasional shout, an infrequent cry, which were the sleeping norms of the hospital. The night awakens our fears, he thought, just as the day calms them.

He thought of all the things the Lost Boys had said. "You see," Parker had sputtered in the midst of the argument, "you got to do the right thing. But what is the right thing? What's right for some cops maybe isn't what's right for your family: You go to the cops and they're gonna want to know everything and they sure as hell aren't gonna be your friend. All they're looking to do is bust somebody. And, man, you're gonna give them your mother or brother or father or sister or anybody. Shit, even your cousin, man? Blood is thicker, you know . . ."

To which Knight had interrupted: "So you make yourself into an accomplice? You do. By being quiet, don't you become as bad as the person doing the crimes?"

The room had filled with both agreement and disavowal.

He remembered someone saying, "If you know, and you stay quiet, you're just as guilty. There ought to be a special prison for people like that!"

There is, he thought ruefully.

Acquiescing to the knowledge of crime is almost as bad as the crime itself. He thought of the Holocaust and remembered the particular problems at Nuremberg, dealing with the people who'd merely remained quiet in the face of depravity. It was easy to single out the performers and punish them. But those people who'd turned their backs? Politicians, lawyers, doctors, business-men . . .

He wondered: What happened to them?

Jeffers considered the enthusiasm with which the group had greeted the issue. He wondered why he'd never posed the question before. What struck him was the idea that virtually everyone in the group seemed to have considered the problem that they themselves posed to their own families. How would they deal with themselves? They didn't know.

He remembered the shouting back and forth through the sunlit day room. They'd run some twenty minutes over the regular end of the session. Finally he'd held up his hand.

"We'll continue this tomorrow. Everyone think over your re-sponses and we'll talk it over some more."

The men had stood, starting to exit in their usual small knots, when Miller, the man Jeffers thought perhaps the least percep-tive, turned and asked, "Why'd ya ask us? You got some rea-son?"

The men had stopped, looking back at Jeffers.

He'd shaken his head in negative, swiftly adopting his usual exterior countenance of mildly amused intellectual curiosity, and the Lost Boys filed out in silence, without further comment. He thought: No one believed that denial. Not for an instant.

He looked out the window into the darkness.

I will not believe, he said to himself angrily, that my brother is a murderer! They arrested a man for the crime this detective hounds me on! Why is she here?

She isn't, he said to himself.

Where is she?

When Detective Barren failed to call by noontime, he'd tele-phoned her hotel. There had been no answer in the room. He'd rung the desk clerk back and ascertained that she had not checked out.

He tried to toughen himself inwardly. Just wait, he told himself. Wait for the next development. She has a lot of explaining to do. Wait to hear what she has to say.

Then he thought: She's not the only one who owes me an explanation.

He crumpled a paper from his desktop and threw it on the floor. He picked up a pencil and broke it in half. He looked around for something to punch, but saw nothing suitable. He turned to the wall and slapped his open palm against the whitewashed surface until he felt it redden, and he welcomed the pain, a sensation that replaced, if only for a moment, his frustration. He thought of the detective and felt a great, uncontrollable anger. He wanted to scream at her: I want to know!

Where the hell is she? he asked furiously.

And then his anger fled him and he had the awful thought: Where the hell is he?

Detective Mercedes Barren sat cross-legged on the floor of the living room in Douglas Jeffers' apartment, surrounded by the mass of her search. She had turned on every light in the apartment, as if scared to allow any of night's darkness to crawl in beside her. It was late and she was tired. She had systematically searched the entire place; from the toilet in the bathroom to the files of negatives in the darkroom. She had taken apart the couch and the bedding, hunting for weapons, without success. She had pulled everything out of the shelves in the kitchen. Every closet had been emptied. Clothes had been rifled, drawers dumped out, papers read and discarded. There was not even a ticket receipt from the Miami trip. Not even a picture postcard. The detritus of her search lay in piles about her.

Useless, she thought.

She could feel tears of rage and despair in her eyes.

"Nothing. Nothing. Nothing," she said out loud.

She knew that he must have a safety deposit box, or a locker or a room somewhere else. Some place that collected the residue of crime. Something somewhere that connected him to her niece.

She could barely stand the tension she felt in the room. That she was close to murder, she knew. She could sense it, smell it; it entered her body through every pore and orifice, covering her, absorbed within her. She recognized the sensation from a hundred crime scenes that she'd visited.

That he was the killer was obvious. A glance at the bookcase had told her that. Virtually every book on the shelves was about some aspect of crime. Novels, textbooks, nonfiction accounts — all lined up in row after row. She was familiar with many, but not all, of the titles. That had impressed her deeply. He is a man who knows his business, she thought.

But a literary interest in crime was not evidence.

It was something she could show the brother, and he would just deny that it was anything other than a slightly morbid preoccupation, and certainly nothing out of the norm for someone who'd photographed so much upheaval and death. She looked up from her seat on the floor at the pictures that covered the walls and she wondered angrily how anyone could stand to be surrounded by so many violent and disturbing images.

She had nothing. She pounded her fists on the floor.

Then she picked up the letter from one brother to another and read it for the hundredth time:

Dear Marty:

If you get this note, one of a number of possible scenarios has come to pass. I suppose you will be expecting some kind of explanation.

You don't need one.

You know it already.

Still, I'm sorry for the trouble I've caused you.

But it was unavoidable.

Or maybe inevitable.

See you in hell.

Your loving brother,
Doug

P.S. What do you think of the pictures? Intense, no?

Detective Barren dropped the note to her lap. It told her nothing. She was overcome by a massive, enraged hatred. Her heart seemed to burn in her chest. Her throat filled with vile-tasting bile. She wanted to spit in the face of the murderer. She wanted to get her own hands around his neck, just as he'd done to her niece.

She wanted to say something out loud, but all that emerged from her throat was a growl, animal-like and savage.

Finally words formed: "It's not over," she said. "I'm never finished with you. I will get you. I will get you."

She thought of her niece. "Oh, Susan," she moaned. But it was a sound less of sadness than of fury.

Her anger stiffened her and she rose to her knees in the center of the room. Her eyes suddenly fixed on the self-portrait that hung on the wall in the corner. All she could see was the mocking smile, as if it were laughing at the futility of her efforts. Her hand shot out and siezed the plastic-encased stone from the Olduvai Gorge, and, without thinking, without realizing anything save the rage that enveloped her, still kneeling on the floor, she wildly threw the artifact at the photograph.

The sound of the shattering glass instantly composed her.

She shut her eyes, took several deep breaths, and looked at the wall. She saw that the ancient rock had missed the picture of Douglas Jeffers, which still grinned in infuriating elusiveness out at her. Instead it had crashed into one of the other framed photographs, splintering the glass and knocking the picture from the wall to the floor.

She sighed deeply and got to her feet.

Feel better? she asked herself mockingly.

She stepped over to the shattered picture frame.

"Well, just add this to the tab," she said. She had no intention of cleaning anything up. She poked at it with her foot. It was a full-color shot of a riot on a city street. In the deep background was a pillar of smoke and fire, and in the foreground a melee of policemen, firemen, and their vehicles. The lights seemed to blend hypnotically. She kicked at it. "A good shot," she said. "Not one of your best, but pretty damn good." As she started to turn away, she noticed that a corner of the picture had peeled back when the frame had buckled and come loose after falling.

She stopped then and looked down.

She did not know exactly what it was that caught her attention. Perhaps it was the odd contrast between the vivid colors of the picture and the muted gray of the paper behind. She still was unsure what she was looking at, but she thought that something was unusual. She tried to remember whether she'd ever heard of someone mounting a photograph on top of another picture, the way some artists paint over earlier images on their canvases. She could not recall hearing of such a thing.

Not allowing herself to hope for anything, she bent down and picked up the broken frame and photograph. She moved over to the desk and put it under the light. She examined the corner that had peeled. She touched the paper and saw that there seemed to be a double thickness. She grasped the top photo and tugged it gently.

It slid back another inch, revealing a black-gray background beneath.

She touched this underneath paper and felt the glossy exterior of a photograph.

She breathed deeply.

Move cautiously, she said to herself.

She pulled at the photo again and it slowly peeled off, like an apple skin.

One inch, then another. The two sheets of photo paper had not been glued solidly together. She worked the paper carefully, making certain that she did not rip the two. When it stuck, she moistened a finger with saliva and gently worked the top loose.

It was only when the entire photograph came free that she dared to look beneath. She thought in that instant of the sensation a child feels when picking off the top of a scab, that it is painful, but there is a great release when it comes off.

She looked down and saw that there was a picture beneath the picture.

She dropped the riot scene to the floor and looked at the other. It was black and white.

The breath rushed out of her suddenly as the image took shape in her eyes.

It was a nearly naked body.

It was a young woman.

Detective Barren's hands shook. She could feel an instant clammy sweat moistening her forehead.

"Susan," she said.

But then she looked again.

The young woman's legs were chunkier. Her hair was shorter. She was lying in a different position than that her niece had been found in. And the underbrush, illuminated by the flash which cut away the darkness, was different; no Florida fronds and palms. The photograph's subject seemed to be lying amidst Northern forest leaves. Detective Barren's head spun and she felt flushed with a dizziness created by reining in sharply on her imagination. What she could make out of the young woman's features seemed to be all wrong.

"It's not Susan," she said.

For the briefest of moments she felt defeated. It's just another one of his damn pictures, she thought.

Then she realized: It's a snapshot. She saw none of the composition, the care, the attentiveness and thought that went into Douglas Jeffers' work. It was a picture taken hastily, under duress. Under fire.

272

She held it up.

"You're not Susan," she said to the picture.

"Who are you?" she asked.

She looked again and saw a large dark splotch on the young woman's chest. Blood, she thought.

She scanned the picture quickly for the signs of search, of police presence, of official investigation.

There were none.

And then, creeping unbidden into her imagination, came a thought that she would not contemplate. She dropped the picture to the table and looked up wildly. Around her were dozens of pictures, Jeffers' home gallery. She jumped from the chair and tore from the wall a large photograph of two Far Eastern farmers and their brace of water buffalo, outlined against the changing sky of evening. She threw the picture frame violently to the floor.

From the shattered glass, she picked up the picture. She felt the double thickness of paper. She tried to peel this photo back, but this time it seemed stuck. She bent it and creased it and worried at it swiftly, finally seizing a small X-acto knife from the desk and scraping away a part of the top picture.

Beneath was another black and white image.

She could see a naked leg. Then a naked arm. It was streaked with dark. She had seen too much blood in too many crime-scene photographs not to know what this was.

She stopped and looked in panic at the walls.

"Susan," she said again, her voice a mirror reflecting agony. "Susan, oh, my God, Susan. You're here somewhere."

Again her gaze swept the photo gallery. Suddenly she felt stupid, embarrassingly so.

"Oh, my God, Susan, you're not here alone."

It was so obvious that it terrified her more.

"Oh, God, you're all here," she said to all the eyes in all the pictures that stared out at her. "All of you."

She felt nauseated. She pictured Douglas Jeffers, sitting casually in his living room, glancing up at the picture in her hands, of the men and the water buffalo. Only he wouldn't see this image, he would see the one concealed beneath.

She sat back hard on the floor, overcome by the faces that looked down from the walls at her. She slid past despair into a realm of utter agony. She thought: I am a reasonable person. I use logic, precision, science. My life is ordered, routine. I deal in facts that lead to logical deductions. I do my job with effectiveness and devotion. Things are in place.

She shook her head.

I lie poorly, she realized. Especially to myself.

She spoke then, out loud, hoping that the sound of her own voice might chase her sudden runaway fear and comfort her.

It didn't.

"Oh, my God, you're all here. I don't know who you are, or how many of you there are, but I know you're all here. All of you. All of you. Oh, my God. All of you. My God, my God, my God. You're all here. Oh, oh, oh no."

And then a thought she realized was worse:

It's up to me.

CHAPTER

TEN

MANY ROADSIDE ATTRACTIONS

15. ANNE HAMPTON sat alone in the car, half-watching Douglas Jeffers as he fiddled under the hood, checking the oil and water. It was early morning and they were outside the Sweet Dreams Motel in Youngstown, Ohio, a short drive from Interstate. Jeffers had made a joke shortly after they had first set eyes on it, calling it The Bates Motel. She turned away and her eyes rested on the stack of notepads that she kept near her seat. She lifted up the pile and counted: eleven. She picked one out from the center of the stack and flipped open to the middle. She saw the words from one of Jeffers' frequent history lessons: January 1958. Charles Starkweather and Caril Ann Fugate. Lincoln, Nebraska, and environs: "Murders without plan, without much rhyme, without thought or care, random pretty much, except for her family. A true American nightmare, when our children turn on us. Charlie styled himself a rebel after James Dean and killed ten people, including her baby sister. He went to the chair in '59." Below that entry she'd scrawled her synopsis of Jeffers' terse commentary: "They were in love, but in the end she turned on him. She was fourteen years old."

When she had to hurry, her handwriting grew large and childlike, she thought, not like the careful, precise note-taking that she remembered from her courses at school. That was a vague and distant memory, as if her time at the university had been years beforehand, not merely weeks.

Anne Hampton considered: ". . . In the end she turned on him."

Jeffers had said this bitterly, "as if this were what was shocking, not the events that preceded it. She spoke the words out loud, under her voice, so that he could not hear her: "In the end she turned on him."

She must have wanted to live, thought Anne Hampton.

She must have believed that life was dear and precious and that she could make something special of herself or maybe even just ordinary of herself despite all the blackness and blood and death, and that living was not ruined by what had happened to her. She was only fourteen and she knew there could be more. She must have felt something magical and wonderful and strong and decided to live.

At any cost.

Anne Hampton wondered where she could find this something, too.

She gazed back down at the words on the white, blue-lined pages. Jeffers had once watched her as she wrote furiously and told her that she reminded him of many of the reporters that he'd worked with, men who'd had their own systems of shorthand that resulted in hieroglyphics that not even an expert cryptographer could read, but which to the author were as clear as a printed page.

She shivered and remembered the dizzying sensation she'd felt two nights earlier when he'd announced that he needed to check her notes.

The moment had been terrifying.

He made the demand late, after they'd checked into another forgettable motel, dragging from too many hours on the highway, depleted by noise and speed and headlights that cut through the dark right into them. Jeffers had grabbed their bags and grunted, "Bring the notebooks." She had carried them gingerly, agonizingly, as if she were not strong enough to hold anything else. He had opened the door and tossed their bags onto one of the twin beds. "Let me see," he'd said. He had sat at a small vanity, poring over the pages. She had shrunk into a chair in the corner, trying to blank her mind. But one thought had flooded her imagination: He won't be able to understand the words and he will realize how useless and ineffectual I've been and, oh God, I'm lost. She'd shut her eyes, trying to shut out fear, but the scratchy sound of the pages turning had seemed deafening. After a few minutes he'd tossed the notebooks aside after quickly flipping through the final entries. He then stretched and said, "Christ, I'm tired. Look, these are okay. Good, actually. I can read them fine. Oh, there's a rough spot occasionally, like when you were trying to write on that road up in Michigan with the frost heaves from last winter. Felt like a roller coaster and the writing kinda goes up and down, up and down, on the page." He'd smiled. "But all in

276

all I'd say you were doing a good job. Just fine. Like I knew you would."

She wished she'd felt less pleased by his praise.

He had handed her back the notepads and then touched the top of her head, almost like patting an animal or bestowing a benediction. The sensation was relaxing to her at first. She'd remained seated, watching him exit into the bathroom.

Then another fear returned.

You are alone, she'd told herself. Don't forget it.

Don't confuse the pleasure of praise with the pain of a blow. She'd tried to toughen her heart, lying awake in the darkness until sleep had captured all her mingled confusion and resolve.

In the morning he'd told her how to use her memory as well as her notes; to take just a word or phrase down and then, through concentration, to recall word for word what was said. To her surprise she had discovered that by using his techniques it seemed her memory had gained a novel precision, which had pleased her, like receiving a gift. He also told her to note situations and times, that it would help her reconstruct the notebooks when he needed her to. She wondered, though, whether that was possible. It seemed to her that everything was disjointed, each location they visited was distinct and apart; the only linkage between the spots was Jeffers' memory. Each stop, like his mood swings, was unexpected and equally frightening and dependent solely on his own rationale and his design.

They'd driven as far north as Hibbing, Minnesota, as far west as Omaha, Nebraska, almost close enough for her to envision the Rockies rising up above the plains, stirring memories of her home and family that seemed as elusive as the sight of the mountains. Kansas City, Iowa City, Chicago, Fort Wayne, Ann Arbor, Cleveland, and Akron. The locations had blended together in her mind in a melange of rural areas and urban streets. Oddly, she thought that she was fortunate that Jeffers had insisted on such careful note-taking, because even with her newfound precision, her memory still jumbled together the details of the trip.

Outside the car she heard Jeffers humming. He did this, she now recognized, when he was pleased as he performed simple tasks.

She closed the notebook and her eyes and tried to remember. She knew that Chicago had been a lecture on Richard Speck and the nurses and the defective-gene theory of murderers. Thin, bony men with acne and arrested sexual development, he'd said. This had been funny to him, and he'd scoffed with laughter. Then they'd driven to the suburbs and a look at Wayne Gacy's house, where the one-time kiddie clown buried the thirty-three boys in the basement. Jeffers had made her get out of the car and stand in front of the unpretentious white clapboard home. Then he'd quickly taken her picture. It had been raining and he'd said "Smile" and "Say cheese" as she huddled nervously, miserably, against a tree. But northern Minnesota had been dry and hot and she remembered light-brown wheatfields that seemed to wave in invitation like the sea as they drove past. That had been a trip to . . . she hesitated, unable to remember the name. But Jeffers had told her that the crazed farmer who'd eviscerated and stuffed his victims had served as the spiritual basis for the film *The Texas Chainsaw Massacre*, which he'd disliked, although he'd said he'd admired the director's sense of expressing fear through visual imagery. She had been unable to understand this, but had not asked him to explain. When Jeffers pontificated, which he frequently did, she knew it wise to let him ramble. It was when he entered more personal areas, that, contradictorily, he allowed her to ask questions.

He told her that he'd wanted to drive past the Clutter farm in Kansas, but that it was too far out of the way, though that seemed odd to her, as the trip to Minnesota was farther. But near Madison, Wisconsin, he showed her the shopping mall where he had picked up a young woman named Irene, and said her death had been attributed to a rapist-murderer who had plagued the malls and campuses of Minnesota and Wisconsin for nearly a year in the late seventies. In Ann Arbor, he showed her the road outside the university where a half-dozen hitchhiking young women had, in his portentous words, taken their last ride. He claimed one of those as well, saying it had been particularly easy. He drove some five miles down a secondary road, through some wooded areas, slowing and pointing into the forest at one moment, telling her that he'd left the victim two hundred yards in. "Campus Killer, they called him. He was in 1982. The papers made up the same name as they did for that guy in Miami."

When they had headed to South Bend, she thought that it would be another campus murder, but he'd stopped beside a brace of nondescript middle-class houses on a quiet, tree-lined street. She saw for sale signs on each lawn. She did not need to look at her notes to remember the words of his long description: "Now, this was interesting," Jeffers had told her. "I wanted to see this for myself. Just six months ago. Seems like the family on the right was pretty normal. Mother. Father. Five kids and a Saint Bernard. One of the teenagers apparently was pretty heavy into the local drug scene, which screwed the police up for quite a bit.

That's the kind of interesting bit of information that someday I figure to use. Anyway, on one side the All-American-apple pie-Boy Scouts-and-let's-run-up-the-flag-on-Memorial-Day family. On the other, well. . . . Well, let's just say not quite the same. One child. Abusive parents. Kid grows to be a teenager harboring some pretty legitimate feelings of persecution. Always hated the neighbors. Thought, you know, that they had everything and he had nothing. Do you know much about psychology? Anyway, my brother would tell you that the situation was ripe for a paranoid personality with a psychotic break. This is pretty much what happened.

"All-Americans head out to work and school one day, lunch pails, kiss one the cheek and see-you-laters all said. Twisted neighbor breaks into the house with his old man's forty-five and a couple of clips of bullets. First thing he does is nail the Saint Bernard and drags her body into the basement. Buffy was the dog's name. Then he pops the family one by one as they come home, putting all the bodies into the basement. Then he exits, walks home, puts his dad's gun away, and acts like nothing's happened. You know what really got people upset, I mean, besides the idea that there was some crazy killer in the neighborhood? The dog. The local paper ran three pictures out front, but the biggest, widest, deepest was a shot of the ambulance crew carrying out that dog. The readers went berserk. They wanted to lynch the guy who killed that dog. What kind of monster would shoot a big, lovable, defenseless—you know what I mean . . . that's what all the letters to the editor said. It took the cops weeks to guess that the weirdo living next door did the crime. Finally, when they hauled him in, he told them everything. He was pretty proud of himself. Which is, more or less, what you'd expect. I mean, after all, he had this hatred and this problem and he'd solved it. Why not be satisfied? Didn't like dogs much, either."

Anne Hampton picked up the notebook numbered 10. Near the back she found her notes on this crime, including much of Jeffers' long soliloquy. She checked her memory against the rapid scrawl which covered a half-dozen pages and found they fairly closely matched. Sitting in the car, she remembered a phrase or two that weren't in the notes, and she wrote these into the margins. She saw that she had taken down verbatim the joke with which he'd ended his speech: "The paper should have called it the Canine Caper."

She looked up sharply as Jeffers slammed down the hood.

The car was still quivering when he jumped into the driver's seat and said, "Time to go. Many a mile before we sleep and all that."

Then he asked, "Do you like the races?"

"What kind of races?"

"Cars."

"I don't know. I've never been to one."

"They're loud. Engines roaring, tires squealing. Lots of smells, gasoline, oil, suntan lotion, beer and popcorn in the stands. You'll like it."

She nodded. He glanced at his watch. "We've got to go now if we want to catch the first heats. Don't you remember driving around in some boy's convertible in the summertime listening to the radio and all of a sudden this mad, frantic advertisement would come on . . ."

He changed his voice into the tinny wild radio sound:

"Sunday! Sunday! At Fabulous Aquasco Speedway! Dragsters! Fuel-injected Funny Cars! Sunday! See the Big Daddy take on the Okie from Fenokee in a three-race eliminator! Sunday! See the Bad Mama with its two-thousand-horsepower jet engine! Sunday! Tickets still available! Sunday!"

She smiled. "I remember," she said. "But the name of the racetrack was different."

"Aquasco is outside of New York, on Long Island, I believe. In New Jersey we used to hear the same ad for Freehold Raceway. And, in the summers, the family would drive up to Cape Cod and we'd hear it for Seekonk Speedway, just past Providence. My brother and I used to do a fair imitation of the ad together, shouting back and forth, 'See Fabulous Funny Cars! Fuel-injected dragsters! Sunday! Sunday! Sunday!'"

She paused.

"I'd forgotten what day it was."

"Day of leisure for most. But not us. Much work."

He steered the car onto the interstate.

It was noontime before they approached the exit for the raceway. The interstate was nearly empty through the morning hours, and Jeffers kept up a steady pace, just a little below the average of the eighteen-wheelers that rushed past, the immense diesel noises seeming to threaten to crush everything they found in their path, buffeting the car with wind velocity. Truckers driving Sunday mornings are invariably late, Jeffers thought. They've rammed a broom handle down on the accelerator and popped a couple of black beauties with coffee and they'd just as soon run over you as past you.

He passed a pair of Pennsylvania state troopers with radar who were scanning the road and decided that the next time he took a road trip he would get a fancy radar-detector, the kind that reads several bands of police radar. He also thought that by investing in a portable police scanner he could monitor police radio traffic. He considered flying down to Miami and visiting a store that he'd heard about from a journalist returning from a trip to Colombia on a drug-connection story. The store, the man had told him, was a favorite of the folks in the trade. It specialized in surveillance gear and the latest in high-tech electronics. Devices that let you know if a wiretap was listening to your phone. Devices that turned on your car from fifty yards away. Perfect for those people who might be worried what else would happen when they switched on their car engine. Night-vision binoculars and portable secure-channel radios. Jeffers wasn't exactly certain what the store held that would help him precisely. But, he thought, we're entering a more technical age and it is important to stay abreast. He knew that the police would. Then he realized that in effect this was defeatist thinking. His whole approach, he told himself, was predicated on the supposition that the police would not ever be searching for him.

I am invisible, he thought.

Anonymous. Deadly.

And that is what makes me completely safe.

He glanced over at Anne Hampton and saw that she seemed to be dozing. "Boswell?" he whispered, but she didn't reply. He decided to let her sleep.

She'll need her strength, he thought. But not for too much longer. He reflected on the road ahead and thought there was something inherently comforting about America's highways. They stretched out in endless lines, looping back and forth, hundreds of thousands of small connections forming a great grid of the country, like the arteries through a body. There is no beginning and no end, he thought.

Anne Hampton stirred beside him.

No end to anything.

He spotted a billboard for the racetrack and felt a rush of excitement. A lesson in acquisition, he thought. To help round off her understanding.

Anne Hampton awoke when Jeffers pulled into the toll booth. She stretched her arms as wide as the confined space inside the car would allow. She pushed her legs against the firewall, trying to reinvigorate the muscles. "Are we there?" she asked.

"Almost. Couple of miles down the road. Just follow the signs and the hot rods."

A ten-year-old fire-engine-red Chevrolet with its tail end jacked up blasted past them. She knew it was a Chevrolet because each window in the vehicle was adorned with huge white CHEVY decals.

"How can that guy see out?" she blurted.

Jeffers laughed.

"He can't. But you got to understand that's not the most important consideration. Appearances are crucial; they take precedence over such mundane considerations as safety, any day."

"But wouldn't a policeman stop him every time for having obscured windows? And no muffler, either."

"First off, he does have a muffler. Probably a set of glass packs. At least that's what everybody talked about twenty years ago, when I was in high school. Gotta have glass packs and a hemi engine, whatever that is. Or maybe was. And the reason most cops won't stop a kid driving one of those is that it wasn't so long ago that they were that same kid. And they remember how much *they* hassled the local fuzz just a couple of years back, so now that they've got the gun and badge, they're smart enough to leave things alone. The kid would have to be doing eighty to get hauled over. Or the cop would have had to have had an argument with his wife this morning, kids late for school and screaming in the background and the coffee burned and his whole mood just one big jangle of nerves and bad attitude, to flag the kid. It would be like giving a ticket to your entire history."

Jeffers looked over at Anne Hampton, who grinned and nodded.

"You see," he said, "everything comes around."

They had to wait in a line of almost a score of cars at the entranceway to the racetrack. Anne Hampton rolled down the window and absorbed the sounds coming from the stadium. The whining and roaring of the engines seemed to her at first to be like the sounds of animals searching for partners. Then she realized that each engine made a different noise, uniquely its own, and that all together they blended into a wall of different-pitched loudness. It was like an aural quilt of many different patches of fabric.

The parking lot was a dusty field, filled with rows of brightly colored cars and trucks that stood out against the brown dirt of the ground. Jeffers parked close to a telephone pole that was marked with a handwritten sign that designated the area 12A.

"Wait a minute," he said.

She sat quietly, watching as he exited the car. She saw him jog down the aisle of cars a short ways. She saw him pause behind a pair of sports cars. He wrote something down and then loped back. Before opening her door he paused at the trunk and took out some items which she couldn't see.

She thought: It's part of a plan.

Her heart plummeted and she glanced around at some of the couples and knots of people straggling through the lot toward the racetrack. The flow of people was steady and she imagined there would be a significant crowd.

She felt hot, then cold, and if she could have made herself be sick, she would have. She thought of the derelict and the man on the street in St. Louis.

We're going to do it again.

She shook her head, shivering slightly. Somehow the act of visiting Jeffers' memories and his landmarks, regardless of how macabre, was at least safe, separate from action.

Jeffers opened the door and she got out.

But her knees buckled as she stood and Jeffers had to catch her.

He stared hard at her for a moment.

"Ahh," he said finally, slightly amused, but with a horrible calculating flatness to his voice that she had not heard since St. Louis. "You've guessed that we're here not just because we're racing fans. . . ."

He didn't complete the sentence. Instead he took her by the arm and directed her to the back of the car.

First he took two khaki photographer's vests from a bag. He slid one onto her, one onto himself. "Good fit," he said. He took half a dozen boxes of film from a case and fitted the canisters into the loopholes on her chest. Then he hung a camera bag around her neck. "This," he said, picking up a long black lens, "is obviously the long lens." He replaced it in the bag. "This shorter one is the wide-angle. When I ask for one or the other, or for the camera, you just hand them over as if you were an expert." He hung a pair of cameras around his neck. One rode in a chest harness, just beneath his chin, the other swung loosely.

"All right," he said. From his bag he produced a stack of small white business cards. He opened the breast pocket on her vest and stuck them inside. "Hand these out to anyone who asks for one." He plucked one out and showed her. It read:

JOHN CORONA
PROFESSIONAL PHOTOGRAPHER
Representing *Playboy, Penthouse* and

"The name is an in-joke," Douglas Jeffers said, "especially for Californians. Obviously you call me Mr. Corona. Or John if it seems appropriate. You are my assistant. I'll introduce you. Listen carefully and you will get the story quickly enough. Ready?"

She nodded.

"Let me hear your voice," he demanded harshly.

"Ready," she replied quickly.

"Remove the little-girl scaredy-cat tone and try again."

She swallowed hard. "I'm ready," she said firmly.

"Right." He looked hard at her. "I shouldn't have to remind you of these things."

"I'll be good," she said.

"Make me believe that."

This was more a threat than a request. She nodded.

Douglas Jeffers turned swiftly and she hurried after him.

Halfway across the parking field, Jeffers started talking again, but his voice seemed distracted.

"One thing I've always wondered about was why we are so mystified by certain types of animal behavior. We can't understand why lemmings dash into the ocean. Scientists spend years studying why pilot whales suddenly beach themselves and broil to death, which, if you think about it, must be a horrible way to go. Ecologists haul the whales back out to sea, and the silly beasts nine times out of ten just head for the beach again. And these are intelligent animals. Healthy, too. I went and shot a bunch of them once, on a North Carolina coast, for *Geo*, which paid great and promptly went out of business. But the whales were beautiful. They are jet black and wonderfully powerful, with bodies that seem like great blunt bullets. They can communicate across great expanses of ocean with hearing-and-sound capabilities that we mere humans can only emulate electronically. They are an ancient and proud race, related to the greatest beasts. Why, then, would they upon occasion commit mysterious mass suicide? What reason do they have? Sickness? Delusion? Confusion? Mass hysteria? Madness? Boredom? How do they become tired of life? It makes little sense.

"Yet they do it. Often, or at least often enough to cause interest and dismay. It is the same with people."

He seemed lost in thought.

"Have you any idea how frequently people beach themselves? I'm not talking about the solitary, despondent type, clinically depressed and naturally suicidal. There are enough of them around. But people who acquiesce in their own deaths. How they contribute to the worst things happening to them.

"They marched in orderly fashion into the gas chambers. No one ever seemed to say, 'Screw you! I'm not going in there!' and grasp for a moment at their own humanity. Did you know that on the first day of the Battle of the Somme, the British lost sixty thousand men? And, knowing this, on the next day, when the whistles blew, the men still went over the top into a wall of machine guns and fortified positions. This was 1916. The modern world! Impossible!

"On death row in just about every state, prisoners scheduled for execution are watched carefully throughout their last night. The fear is that they will somehow find a way to kill themselves. The state," he said bitterly, "doesn't like to be cheated, you see. But what would be the difference, really? Ultimately, I think, suicide is the greatest act of freedom. That's what we can't seem to learn from the goddamn whales. They're sick, with what, we just don't know. AIDS for whales, hell, or something. So they abbreviate the processing of their own deaths. They take charge of their lives, take control, and make their choice. And we wonder why. Inexplicable, the scientists say. They act baffled. What is inexplicable is that we can't understand why they do it when it seems so damn obvious."

Jeffers picked up the pace. He was shaking his head back and forth.

"Boswell," he said in a tone that rang of solitude, "I'm confusing two different issues. It will be up to you to sort things out."

After hesitating a moment he added:

"Today's lesson is really on acquiescence. Lemmings. Watch carefully how people will embrace the means of their demise. Remarkable. I remember reading about this photographer from Florida. Do you remember? It was only a couple of years ago. His name was Wilder, which I suppose created a good bit of punning in news rooms around the nation. Anyway, the guy snatches a gal from a grand prix race in Miami. Then up in Daytona, I think. Off he goes on a cross-country tour, killing as he goes. Always uses the exact same technique: heads to a sporting event or a shopping mall, pulls out his camera, and starts taking pictures of girls. Before long he has one following after him and the next thing you know they're in his car and . . ."

He looked down at Anne Hampton.

"Fill in the rest yourself."

"I remember," she said.

"But you know what was truly fascinating," Jeffers continued, "was that everyone knew! The FBI, the local police, the newspapers, the television stations, everybody! Wilder's picture was on every station, every front page, every station house. His modus operandi was described, discussed, dissected, you name it. It was everywhere! You could hardly be a part of popular culture and miss it. There wasn't a dinner-table conversation or bull session in a high-school bathroom with the girls having a smoke between classes where it wasn't said: If a guy with a beard wants to take your picture, don't get in the car with him! But you know what happened?"

"He died."

"But not before another half-dozen women got into his car and got themselves killed. Remarkable. You know something? He never even bothered to shave off his beard, which was the dominating aspect of every description in every paper. Now that's a phenomenon that deserves study."

"He died in the Northeast, I think."

"Yeah. New Hampshire. We're going there shortly."

"He got shot by a trooper and the last girl lived," she insisted.

"He was stupid and careless," Jeffers said brusquely.

But the last girl lived, she thought.

They approached the raceway grandstand. "Stick close," Jeffers said. "And watch the magic work."

It did work.

Inside the grandstand area, a blurred melee of people, machines, bright colors, and constant sound, Jeffers worked the sidelines expertly. He maneuvered amidst the crowd of spectators and the car crews, picking out young women, singly or in pairs, starting by taking their picture from afar, then moving closer until he not only had their attention, but they were posing for him. Anne Hampton was almost overcome by the rush of raised shoulders, sucked-in cheeks, turned profiles, and perfect smiles that greeted Douglas Jeffers' camera lens. She heard him give the same story over and over again, and she dished out business cards with a blind enthusiasm that mocked her sickened heart. He told the young women that he was on assignment for *Playboy* and they were going to do a feature called "Racetrack Girls." He was doing some of the preliminary photography, he explained. He and a couple of other photographers were shooting young women at tracks in various locations. Then the editors back in Chicago would look at the pictures and decide where to head for their photo spread.

He had Anne Hampton take the names and numbers of some of the young women; she did this hesitantly, ill, knowing that it was merely a part of the general playacting. In the background the crowd cheered the cars and drivers, but often the noise from the track was so great that it drowned out the sounds from the stands. She looked up as one particularly immense black dragster filled the air with mechanical tumult, to see the crowd rising to its feet in appreciation. But she was unable to hear their response and she thought suddenly of the appearance of a row of fish in a market, lined up on the white shaved ice, eyes and mouths open, as if with animation, their deaths masked by the lights and sounds.

"Boswell," she heard his voice fade in as the car noise flew away down the track, "another roll, please. Ladies, this is my assistant, Anne Boswell. Say hello, Annie . . ."

She nodded her head at a pair of young women, probably close to her own age. One was blonde, the other brunette, and both wore tightly fitting tank tops and cut-off blue jeans. She did not think them particularly pretty, the blonde's teeth seemed to bump about in her mouth haphazardly so that her smile came forth slightly skewed, while the brunette's nose was too pert for real beauty, rising ski-jump from her face. Anne Hampton thought that the young woman probably had a mother who always told her that she was cute, and thus she aspired only toward cuteness, not realizing that it would translate from high-school cheerleader into a simple marriage and family and small home in rural Pennsylvania or Ohio, with the television on every night and a weekly trip to the beauty parlor to keep her looks in check after suffering the ravages of childbearing. She tried to remember her own mother talking to her about beauty. She could hear in her head her mother, speaking calmly but enthusiastically, brushing her hair with long strokes, telling her how pretty she would be when she grew up, which, at age twelve, had seemed such an impossibility. She recalled her mother's look of dismay when she returned home from her first college semester with her hair cropped to her shoulders. *I always did so much to distance myself,* Anne Hampton thought. Even when it grew out long again, something was different. A loss of trust. A voice intruded on her memory.

". . . Must be exciting, huh?"

It was one of the young women. The blonde.

"I'm sorry," Anne Hampton said. "I didn't catch what you said."

"Oh," said the young woman, waving her hands about, "I just said that I thought being a photographer's assistant must be exciting. A really special job. I mean, I just work in a bank and that's nothing special at all. How did you get the job?"

Douglas Jeffers interjected: "Oh, I picked her from hundreds of possibilities. And she's worked out pretty good so far, right, Annie?"

She nodded.

"Well," said the young woman, "I bet it's real exciting."

"It's different," Anne Hampton replied.

The brunette was examining one of Jeffers' cameras. Anne Hampton saw that she'd stuck the business card in her front pocket.

"Well," she said, "I think being in *Playboy* would be just too wild. I mean, I'd just love to have *my* picture in that magazine. And so would Vicki." She gestured at the blonde. "And my boyfriend would think it was neat! But I bet my folks would just die!"

Anne Hampton saw Jeffers smile.

"Well," he said, "like I explained, these are just preliminary shots. But sometimes the really pretty girls like you two get called back for the spread . . ."

"Isn't there any way we could, I don't know, help make sure they choose us?" asked Vicki, the blonde. "I mean, take some extra pictures of me and Sandi, maybe."

Jeffers looked at the pair of young women intently.

"Well," he said, "I can't guarantee anything. Here, stand together for an instant . . ."

He held his arms wide, then narrowed them, directing the two young women. He raised the camera and Anne Hampton heard the motordrive speed forward as he clicked off a series of pictures, moving about the two young women, dipping up and down, framing them rapidly.

". . . You certainly have the look," he said. "But, you know, they're searching for more than just a look, if you know what I mean . . ."

Anne Hampton saw the two young women put their heads together and giggle. She thought suddenly: I'm not here. This isn't happening. It can't be happening.

Then she heard Jeffers' voice again.

"Look, the best I could do, and I don't want you to count on anything, would be to take a few, uh, slightly more revealing shots. That might impress the editors. It's worked before, but, of course, no guarantees."

She heard the two women laugh together again, nodding their heads.

"Well," Jeffers was continuing in his most upbeat and harmless voice, "if you're really interested, why don't you meet me at my car, section 13A, in half an hour. Please don't tell anyone what you're doing, because I've told all these other women that I wouldn't do anything special for them and I'd hate to have it get around that I was doing you two a favor..."

Both women shook their heads rapidly.

"So if you can keep a secret, sneak out and meet me and we'll see what we can do. Boswell, give me the long lens, please."

Jeffers looked at the women. "Just got to take a couple of action shots to give the editors the right flavor, if you know what I mean. After all, I want them to come back here for the spread."

Again the girls nodded. Jeffers gave them a little wave and started to wade away through the crowd. Anne Hampton turned and looked back once, seeing the two girls talking animatedly together. For an instant she was confused: she'd heard Jeffers give them the wrong location number for the car.

"How will they find the car?" she asked.

"They won't. They will go to a spot fifty yards away."

"But..."

"Come on, Boswell, use your head. If they mention it to someone else, or if someone tags along with them, then I, from the position I have the car in, have the capability of exiting without fuss. And without being seen. But," he added, "it won't make any difference. This is really an unnecessary precaution if ever I've seen one. Those two are in for the ride. They won't tell anyone, and they'll sneak out just like I asked them. They'll be there, ready, willing and able, don't you think?"

Anne Hampton nodded her head.

"Lemmings," said Jeffers.

He thought a moment as he plowed through the mass of people.

"Boswell," he said, "does it ever seem to strike you as contradictory the way we in America can tolerate the most fundamental, righteous, religious prudery on the one hand, and yet the easiest thing in the world is to talk someone out of their clothes? Watch."

She followed after Jeffers as he made a simple loop of the field, actually pausing occasionally to take a few shots, then heading back out to the parking lot. She thought of a night in her junior year of high school. She and her date had parked on an empty street. She could still feel the sensation of his fumbling hands exploring her body; his lack of guile and barely contained excitement were what forced her to give in—at least in part. He was not someone that she particularly liked. But he was there, and he was a nice fellow, and she had so wanted to experience some of the things that were forever being talked about at school, and so she let his hands wander, discovering that the benefits were pleasing.

When he tried to pull off her underwear was when she realized the necessity of stopping, a moral necessity, to be certain, one that upon later reflection seemed silly. She remembered a frightening moment when she resisted, and he resisted her and she recognized then how much stronger he was. She could still feel in her memory the sudden sensation of force that gripped her and the awful helplessness that penetrated her at that moment. She shivered at the thought. This had made a great impression, the instantaneous fear and terror that she was weak and that she could be forced. But when she gasped out a panicked "No!" he'd honored that request, his muscles slackening suddenly. Her gratitude had been boundless. Six weeks later, prepared in her mind, she'd let him continue. It had been alternately painful and exhilarating, and she found that memory oddly comforting. She wondered where he was now. She hoped he was happy.

Jeffers reached the car and opened her door. "We'll put them in the back," he said.

Her memory fled and she handed him the equipment bag and her vest, which he stowed in the trunk.

"Get in and wait," he said. She noted that the iron edge had returned to his voice.

She did as he said. Her mind raced about her, envisioning the two young women and what was about to happen. She shut it down, forcing thoughts from her head. I can think of nothing, she said to herself. Nothing surrounds me. She sat in the car and closed her eyes, trying to concentrate completely on the distant noises from the racetrack, letting the sounds fill her and exclude all else.

"Hi!"

"Hi!"

She looked up, opening her eyes quickly, and the sunlight blinded her.

"Shall we jump in the back?"

"If you don't mind," she heard Jeffers' voice. "It's a bit cramped. Sorry."

"Oh, no problem. My boyfriend has a Firebird, which is pretty much the same, and I've spent a lot of time in the back seat . . ." Both Vicki and Sandi laughed. "I didn't mean it quite that way," said Vicki. "Anyway, boy, is he gonna be surprised!"

The two women squeezed in the back. They were flushed and excited, giggling and laughing, at the limit of control.

Jeffers swung into his seat. "I know a little park, almost a forest really, not too far from here. We'll drive over, take a few shots in a nice, idyllic location, then Boswell and I will drop you back here, okay?"

"Sounds great," said Vicki.

"Okay by me, just as long as we're back by six."

"No problem," said Jeffers.

The women laughed again.

Jeffers steered the car out of the raceway area.

Anne Hampton's mind screamed at the two women: Why don't you ask! Ask how he just happens to know of a deserted park! How does he just happen to know exactly where he's going? He's mapped it out before!

She said nothing.

Jeffers broke her silence. "Keep your notepad handy," he said softly to her. Her hand shot out instantly for a pad and pen. Then he raised his voice into a gregarious singsong. "Now I don't want you gals to be nervous, this will be pretty tame stuff, really. But I got to ask—you're both over eighteen, right?"

"I'm nineteen," said Sandi, "and Vicki's twenty."

"Not till next week!"

"Hey," said Jeffers. "Well, happy birthday a week early, then. Let's see if we can't make the birthday something special to celebrate, okay?"

"You bet!"

"Mr. Corona," Sandi asked tentatively, "I don't want to intrude or, I don't know . . ."

"Go ahead," said Jeffers in as good-natured a voice as possible. "What's on your mind?"

"Does *Playboy* pay for the pictures they use?"

Jeffers laughed.

"Of course! You don't think we'd put you through the drudgery of a photo session without paying, do you? A photo session is hard work. There's makeup and posing, and high-intensity lights, and, you know, something always goes wrong. To get one picture suitable for the magazine can sometimes take hours. The usual rate, I think, at least the last time I did this, was a thousand dollars a session . . ."

"Wow! What I could do with that!"

"But this is kinda informal," Jeffers continued. "I don't think the magazine will pay more than a couple of hundred bucks for your work this afternoon."

"We're gonna get paid! Fantastic!"

The two women started talking excitedly between themselves. Anne Hampton sat blindly in front. Jeffers spoke to her quietly: "Boswell, please make an effort to get this down." His voice was like blackness crawling over her.

Then, with fake cheer, he said briskly, "Almost there!"

He was driving into a park.

"I know just the right spot," he said.

"Boy!" gushed Vicki or Sandi from the back seat, Anne Hampton wasn't certain which, but she got the words down anyway. "I can't believe this is happening to me."

Think of nothing, she told herself. Do exactly what you're told. Just stay alive.

"Here we are," said Jeffers. "Now, I know this little spot . . ."

Anne Hampton saw they were entering a wooded area, staying on a small roadway that cut between the shadows thrown by the leafy overhanging branches. There was a brown National Parks Service sign which said the park was open only from dawn to dusk. She saw that they passed up a large gravel parking area, continuing on into the center of the forest. They drove what she guessed was another half mile, then turned onto a dirt secondary road which they followed for several bumpy minutes until they reached a bend where the trees dropped back sharply so that a brief space was plunged into bright sunlight. There was a single chain stretched loosely from one side of the dusty brown trail to the other and another small sign that read, AUTHORIZED PERSONS ONLY BEYOND THIS POINT.

"Luckily," Jeffers said brightly, "I've got park service authorization. Most professional photographers do. Hang on, ladies, while I deal with this chain."

Jeffers jumped from the car, leaving the two women laughing in the back seat and Anne Hampton staring out blankly at the forest colors from the front. He felt a twinge of concern. *She seems to be lost, he thought.* Though his back was to the car, his mind pictured her sitting there, fastened to her seat by the layered fears of knowing what was happening and being unable to say or do anything, caught by the event just as surely as if he'd tied her with rope. He wondered for an instant whether she would be able to control herself. *I want her to make it to the end. I don't want to have to leave her here with the others.* He considered whether she recognized the danger she was in and thought that she must, for she seemed to have entered a detached state, like a mannequin in a store window or a marionette dancing on the end of a set of strings.

This, he realized, was exactly as it should be.

My strings, he thought. Dance, Boswell, dance. When I jerk the strands holding you, jump.

He smiled.

Keep things in order, he told himself. Boswell represents time and effort and investment.

He heard more laughter from the car.

They don't.

The chain was just as it had been when he visited the park a month earlier. He reached down and grasped the links a few inches above the spot where it was fastened to a small brown post. With his free hand he flaked wood chips off the post. It had rotted with age. He gave the chain a sharp tug and it came free. Then he walked the chain across the road, clearing it out of the way.

He shuffled his feet in the dusty road surface as he walked back to the car. No sense in leaving an impression of his shoe.

"All set," he said to the three in the car. "Just up the road."

He goosed the car ahead gingerly and they bumped for some two hundred yards until they pulled around a corner. Anne Hampton recognized then that they could not be seen from the main roadway.

"All right, pile out," Jeffers said with a brisk enthusiasm. "We don't want to take up too much time, and everybody wants to get back to see that last race, so let's do it."

Anne Hampton saw that he had thrown his brown photographer's bag over his shoulder. She hesitated for an instant, watching the two young women follow Jeffers into the forest. They are blind, she thought. How can they rush after him so? Then she felt her own feet hurrying her forward, and she ran to keep up with him.

"Boy," said Vicki or Sandi—she had gotten them confused—"this sure is exciting."

"It always is," replied Douglas Jeffers. "In more ways than one." The two women giggled again.

Anne Hampton thought she would be sick if she stopped. Her breath came in short bursts and she felt her head spin. The heat rested on her body like a wool blanket, prickly, uncomfortable, and she felt dizzy. Vicki or Sandi heard her laboring and turned to her.

"Do you smoke? No? Good. But you sound out of shape. A little walk in the woods shouldn't get to you . . ."

"I've been a little sick," Anne Hampton replied. She heard the words quiver weakly.

"Oh, I'm sorry to hear that. You should take vitamins like I do. Every day. And regular exercise. Have you ever tried aerobic dancing? That's what I like to do. Or maybe do some running to build up that wind. I'd like to quit my job at the bank and get a job teaching dancing at the health club. I think that would be neat. Are you okay?"

Anne Hampton nodded. She didn't trust her voice any further.

"Try doing some running," the young woman continued. "Start out slowly, maybe just a mile or so a day. And then gradually build up. It'll make the world of difference."

Douglas Jeffers suddenly stopped.

"So how do you like it? Pretty, huh?"

He stood under a pine tree at the edge of a small open clearing. Even Anne Hampton, in the midst of her growing terror, thought it a pretty spot. That made her feel worse.

There was a large boulder cropped up in the midst of the clearing. Sunlight spread around it, making the small patch of green grass glow. The entire area was encircled by forbidding pine trees that seemed to stand against the blue sky like so many silent sentinels. When she stepped into the clearing, Anne Hampton had the sensation of striding into a quiet room, the door closing shut behind her.

"All right, ladies, over to the rock if you please. Boswell, next to me."

She walked over to Jeffers' side and they both watched the two young women take up positions on the boulder. Each was affecting what she thought was the freshest come-hither appearance possible. Jeffers stepped out into the sunlight and glanced up at the high sky. "Bright," he said. "Harmless, bright sunshiny day." He quickly approached the two young women and held up a light meter beside them. Anne Hampton saw him adjust his camera, then start clicking off shots. He kept up a steady, hypnotic stream of encouragement: "That's it, now smile, now pout a little, now throw that head back, good, good, great. Now twist about a bit, keep moving, good again, good . . ."

She watched the performance before her, wondering: Where does he have the gun? Or will it be a knife? It must be in the photo bag. How is it going to happen? Quickly? Is he going to drag it out? What is he going to do to them? He will take his time. We are alone and it is quiet and he will not be hurried. The heat from the sun caused her to grow dizzy and she feared she would faint. She closed her eyes, squeezing them tightly shut. I remain me, she said to herself. I am alone and apart and I am myself and I will be strong and I will make it. Make it. Make it. Make it. She repeated this over and over, mantralike.

She looked up and saw that Vicki and Sandi were trying to look seductive. "That's good," she heard Jeffers say. "But I think it's a little, I don't know, restrained, maybe . . ."

She saw the two women look at each other and she heard their mingled laughter. They were having a good time. She hated this. It filled her with guilt. She closed her eyes again.

"Now, that's better!" she heard Jeffers exclaim. "Wait until those editors get a load of this!"

She opened her eyes and saw that both women had stepped out of their clothes. They seemed sleek, animal-like. They were both deeply tanned and she stared at the white skin that brought their breasts and crotches into relief. She watched as they stretched, and, within seconds, lost whatever residual modesty they might have had. They offered their breasts to the camera; they spread their legs when the lens pivoted toward them. Jeffers bounced about before them, bending and twisting, caressing them with the camera. She could hear the motordrive whirring.

She thought it seemed like some hideous ballet.

Jeffers maneuvered around the two women, bringing them closer, until finally they were slapped together, entwined, all legs, arms, buttocks, and breasts on the rock before him. Anne Hampton stared at their bodies, which seemed to her to be strong and full and terribly, horribly, filled with life. She could not continue to look and turned away.

"Hey, Boswell, come here!"

She hesitated one instant, then trotted to his side. She could see that both women were flush and excited.

"Stand there so I can get a shot of the three of you."

She stepped between the two naked women.

"Boy! I've never felt so free," said Vicki or Sandi. "It makes me feel beautiful."

"It's got me hot," said the other, a little under her breath. "I wish my boyfriend were here."

"I bet," whispered her friend, "that Mr. Corona gets a lot of extra surprises when he takes pictures."

Anne Hampton felt an elbow nudging her. She understood suddenly that this last statement was a question.

"He does okay," she said. "He likes taking pictures."

"Fine, Boswell. Step out. Now, Vicki, just put your hand on

Sandi's breast, good, good, continue stroking it, right, and now reach down toward her thigh, good, good, that's right, put your hand right there, perfect! Great, great. Exciting, huh?"

Anne Hampton heard both women exclaim in agreement. She stood next to Jeffers and saw that they continued to stroke each other despite the pause in the sound from the motordrive. She could see sweat glisten on their bodies and she knew they were aroused.

"Well," he said, "it'll be more exciting in just a second. Let me change film . . ."

She saw his hand reach down into the photo bag.

It's now, she thought. Oh, God, it's now.

She wanted to race away, to somehow jump high into the sky and flee like a startled bird.

She was frozen in her spot. Rigid under the sun.

Oh, God, she thought. I'm sorry. I'm so sorry. I wish I were someplace else, suddenly, magically, anywhere, just not here right now, at this moment. Oh, God, I'm sorry, sorry, sorry.

She saw that Jeffers had put his camera into the bag and she could see his hand on the butt of a pistol.

I wish I could do something, she thought. I'm sorry, Vicki and Sandi, whoever you are. I'm so sorry.

She shut her eyes.

She could hear the two women giggling and the sound of their bodies slapping together. She could hear a pair of birds calling out in the darkness of the forest, raucous and harsh. She could hear Douglas Jeffers' breathing beside her. It was even, rapid, but she thought it ice cold, and she believed behind her closed eyes that she would be able to see the vapors of his breath. Then every sound seemed to fade from her and she was enveloped by silence. She awaited the first noise of confusion and panic from the two women. She wondered: Will they gasp? Scream? Cry? Time seemed empty and she waited for the first moment of recognition and terror. But it did not come.

Instead she heard a distant blare.

The sound seemed foreign, unconnected to the clearing. Alien. She could not at first place it. It sounded again.

She opened her eyes.

Jeffers stood beside her. He was listening.

A moment passed.

"Everybody stay right here," he said. Command had taken over his voice. Anne Hampton saw the two women look up, surprised. "It's probably nothing," he said. "But I need to check." He looked at Anne Hampton. He spoke quietly to her.

"Get them into their clothes. Act as if nothing is happening. Wait right here for me. Say nothing. Do nothing."

Jeffers lifted the photo bag and, after giving the two women a smile and a wave, stepped into the pine forest. Anne Hampton thought it was as if he had suddenly been swallowed by the shadows.

She turned to the women. They were looking into the hole in the woods that Jeffers had disappeared into. They were still wrapped together, their arms in casual connection, draped across each other.

Run! thought Anne Hampton. Get away! Can't you see what is happening?

But instead she said, "Why don't you two get dressed? I think we're just about finished."

"Oh," said one, frowning, "I could do this all day."

Anne Hampton could say nothing. She sat, enveloped by fear, waiting for Douglas Jeffers to return. She glanced down at her hands and told herself: Make them do something.

But she was unable.

Douglas Jeffers felt the coolness of the forest dry the sweat on the back of his neck as he stepped away from the clearing. He walked slowly for ten feet. When he knew that he couldn't be seen by any of the three women behind him, he picked up his pace. He jogged first, then ran, cutting between the shadows, leaping like a hurdler over the occasional rock or limb in his path. He kept one hand on the bag, to prevent it from bouncing about wildly, the other clearing branches from his eyes. His footsteps made a crunching sound against the pine needles of the forest. He raced the last few yards and emerged from the mottled forest light into the brightness of the road where he'd parked.

A dark-green park service jeep was pulled up next to the car.

A ranger wearing a Smokey the Bear hat sat on the hood.

He's unarmed and alone, Jeffers thought.

Jeffers commanded himself: Be quick. He swiftly searched the scene. There was no one else around. His eyes scanned the jeep. He saw no shortwave radio antenna on the car, no telltale shotgun fastened to a holder on the dashboard. He glanced at the ranger and saw that the man did not have a hand-held radio strapped to his waist. He's isolated and unsuspecting, Jeffers thought. He took a few steps closer and saw that the man was really a boy. A college student, working for the summer. His hand went into the bag and he felt the solid metal barrel of the automatic. You could do it. You could do it and no one would be the wiser.

Inwardly, then, he screamed at himself: Control! What are you? Some punk killer in a convenience store?

He slid his hand from the bag, bringing out his Nikon.

He waved and the ranger waved at him.

"Hi," Jeffers said. "I heard your horn. You screwed up my shot good."

"Oh, sorry," said the ranger. Jeffers saw that he was an unprepossessing type, wearing wire-rimmed glasses. He was slightly built and Jeffers knew the young man would be no match for him. Not physically or mentally. "But this is supposed to be a restricted area. You're not allowed to bring a car up here. Didn't you see the sign?"

"Yes, but Ranger Wilkerson told me it was okay after I found the owl's nest."

"I'm sorry?"

"Ranger Wilkerson. He's at central headquarters in the state capital. He's the guy all the nature photographers talk to when they want to get into the restricted areas. It's no big deal, really. Did you know I found an eagle's nest last year?"

"In here?"

"Yeah, well, not exactly here, but over that way." Jeffers gestured widely with his arm, pointing off into nowhere. "Took me by surprise, too. I got the pictures into *Wildlife* Magazine, too, and the Audubon Society came out en masse, almost a little parade through the woods, you know. It was a pretty big show, you know. Weren't you here then?"

"No, this is my first year."

"Well," said Jeffers, "I'm surprised you didn't hear about it. I think they put up one of the pictures at your headquarters."

"Did, uh, you get some kind of pass or something?"

"Sure," said Jeffers. "It should be in your photography file back at your office. Probably right under the picture of the eagle."

"I'll have to check," said the ranger. "I didn't know we had a file."

"No problem. Check under my name: that's Jeff Douglas."

"Are you a professional?"

"No," replied Jeffers. "I wish. I mean, I've sold some shots. Even sold one to *National Geographic*, but they never used it. But it's just a hobby, really. I sell insurance."

"Well," said the ranger, "I'll still have to check."

"Sure. And what's your name, so I can call Ranger Wilkerson if there's some mixup?"

"Oh, I'm Ted Andrews. Ranger Ted Andrews." He smiled.

"By the time I get used to saying that, it will be time to head back to school."

Jeffers smiled. "Look, I was just about finished for the day, anyway. I want to just go back and make sure I didn't leave any film boxes or anything laying around. I don't like to make a mess."

"We appreciate that. You wouldn't believe what some folks just toss away. And I end up cleaning it up."

"Low man on the totem pole?"

The ranger laughed. "Right."

"You don't have to wait for me," Jeffers said. "Go check your file, and next time I'll stop by the office and you'll see it's all arranged."

"That'd be okay," said the young man. He started back to his jeep and Jeffers looked hard at the man's back. I could do it now, and it would be easy. He measured the distance. A single shot, no one would hear a thing. No one would know. His hand closed on the pistol butt, but then he dropped it back into the bag. He waved instead, watching the jeep pull out past his car, bouncing up the secondary road.

"Damn," said Jeffers coldly to himself. "Dammit to hell."

For a moment he felt flushed with fury and he had an overwhelming urge to crush something with his hands. He took a deep breath. Then another. He spat on the ground, clearing his mouth of a bilious, evil taste. Someone's going to pay for this, he thought.

Out loud, though, he said to no one: "They get to live."

CHAPTER
ELEVEN

ONE TRIP TO NEW
HAMPSHIRE

16. DETECTIVE Mercedes Barren drove hard through the glowing vapors of gray-green highway lights that beat back the early-morning darkness. It was nearly three A.M. and she was almost alone on the turnpike. An occasional tractor-trailer careened past in the distance, wailing like some great heartbroken beast into the edge of roadway lights and night blackness. She pushed the accelerator down, as if she could transform the engine's surge into energy for her own body. She was exhausted, yet powerless to seek sleep. She knew the burning images she carried vividly in her head and sloppily thrust into a paper bag on the seat next to her would preclude sleep for some time.

The car droned around her and she tried to force the sound to fill her and take away the terrors of the past hours. She refused to think of Douglas Jeffers' apartment, though a final vision was imposed on her memory: She could see shattered glass and dozens of broken or twisted picture frames littering the floor. In her panic and horror, she had finally simply torn the pictures apart, seeking the hidden images. The detritus of Jeffers' art lay in piles strewn haphazardly about the apartment's living room, ripped faces and severed moments, staring out at her in violation. She'd taken the bag of groceries that had been part of her ruse dedicated to the inquisitive doorman and dumped them out on the floor. Then she'd refilled the paper sack, stuffing it with the hidden pictures, creased, folded, mangled by her impatience and anxiety. When she closed and locked the door to the apartment, leaving it behind, it had been like pitching from a nightmare into a waking fear; like arising from an uneasy dream at the midnight

300

sound of an entering burglar breaking glass, or the tiny crackle of fire from another room.

She drove up a rise on the turnpike. To her right, a huge cargo jet whined and powered in takeoff from Newark Airport, while to her left the massive white oil storage tanks of the port of Newark glistened in flood-lights. She felt an incongruity, surrounded by technology, in pursuit of something prehistoric. When the highway swept away from the coast and into darker countryside, she felt comforted. She bent down and peered up into the black sky, catching a glimpse of the moon, hanging low over some trees and buildings.

"Good night moon," she said out loud, the words bursting out from long-held memory, unchecked. "Good night room and the red balloon and the three little bears sitting on chairs, good night house and good night mouse, good night to the old lady whispering 'hush,' good night nobody, good night mush . . ."

She tried to remember the other good nights from the book, but she was unsure after so many years. Mittens? Kittens? She saw herself, her niece perched on her lap, head lolled down and eyes closed, bottle drooping from her mouth, welcoming the deep sleep of childhood. She remembered how the words of the book always worked, but she never cut the rhythms short; if Susan fell asleep before the end, I would still read on.

"Good night moon," she said again.

She had found her niece's picture behind a large full-color portrait profile of three starving African children, whose wide eyes and distended bellies shouted out in agony. It was perhaps the fifteenth or twentieth photograph that she had torn apart in frenzied search. She had reached the limit of self-control when she ripped into the frame, breaking it with her hands. A piece of glass had cracked off, cutting her thumb, not deeply, but enough to streak the picture with fresh blood.

At first she had not recognized her niece. She had seen too many savaged bodies in Jeffers' apartment to instantly draw a distinction. But then the shape of the limbs had suddenly plucked her memory, and the shock of straw-blond hair, clearly visible even in the black and white picture, had touched her familiarity. The features were in some repose, too; the portrait had been taken from a lower angle and from the side, removing some of the horror that was so clear in the crime-scene pictures that she had gazed at so many times. She could see an immediate difference between the caressing portrait that Jeffers, even in his hurry, had taken and the clinical, bright, horrible photos taken by the medical examiner's office and her fellow crime-scene specialists a few short hours after Jeffers had slipped away into the night. In the photo she had held in her hands, Susan seemed merely asleep, and she was thankful for that small touch.

She had stared deeply at the photograph. She did not know for how long. She had not cried, but it seemed to her to drain her soul. Then she had carefully, almost tenderly, put it aside before going on with the terrible task of checking the other frames.

She had thought herself calm and in control, but her hands had shaken wildly when finally she had put her niece's photo in the growing pile along with all the murdered others and had readied herself to leave.

Driving through the darkness, she said to herself: I don't know who you all are, but I'm here for you now.

I'm here. I'm here. I know. Now I know everything.

And I will make things right.

She gripped the steering wheel tightly with her fingers and continued fast toward the morning.

Martin Jeffers could not sleep. Nor did he want to.

He sat in the center of his apartment, the only light coming from a small desktop lamp off in the corner. He debated with himself the single question whether it was better or not to know. He questioned whether, if the detective disappeared, as he supposed she had, and his brother returned, as he knew he would, his usual cryptic, smart-guy self, whether he could simply return to the status quo, the usual uneasy peace between brothers.

He did not know whether he had the strength to reimpose this normality on his life.

He tried to envision facing his brother. In his imagination he saw himself stern, prosecutorial, strong, suddenly invested with the powers that accompanied being firstborn, easily dismissing his brother's weak jests and jousts until Douglas Jeffers finally succumbed to his relentlessness and told the truth.

And then what?

Martin Jeffers plunged his face into his hands, trying to hide himself from the fantasy he'd created. What would he say? He could not envision his brother tearfully confessing to the crime that had brought the detective into their lives. What would he say? I'm sorry, Marty, but I picked up this girl and everything was going great until she said no, and then I got a little carried away, you know, and maybe I used a little too much force. I'm strong, Marty, and sometimes I forget and suddenly she wasn't breathing, and it really wasn't my fault, but hers, and anyway, someone else took the rap for the crime, so why do anything? It's gone, it's past, it really, when you think about it, never happened.

He stood up and paced about the dark room.

I knew it, I knew it, I knew it, he said to himself. He was always wild, he always thought he could do whatever he wanted. He wasn't like me, he wasn't organized, patient, I can't stand it. He never, never, never listened to me.

He killed that girl, dammit!

He should pay.

Martin Jeffers sat back down.

Why?

What good would it do?

Again he stood up, then, just as swiftly, slumped back into his chair.

Why do you jump to these conclusions? He addressed himself in the third person, like a debater.

The detective has disappeared. She was crazy anyway. Why are you so swift to believe the worst about Doug? You've been too long with the men in the therapy group. You've heard too many lies, too many evasions, too many phony reconstructions. You've heard blame shifted about from one person to the next, never assumed by the guilty. You've heard horror after horror year after year and nothing has ever changed and it has finally skewered your thinking about completely so that now you're willing to leap to the most ridiculous conclusions.

Go to bed. Get some sleep. Things will sort out.

He smiled to himself. That is hardly the kind of attitude that four years of medical school and four more years of internship and residency at the mental hospital should prompt. Where did Freud write: Things will work out? What neo-Jungian approach is that? Did you pick that up from some journal or some scholarly lecture? Perhaps from Dear Abby or Ann Landers? When have you ever known things just to work out? He heard himself laugh, briefly, and the sound echoed emptily in the apartment. Still, it was a tenet of his profession to await events rather than prompt them, and there was nothing wrong with that.

We shall see, he said to himself.

We shall see what Detective Barren has to say—if she ever shows up again.

We shall see what Doug has to say.

And then we shall figure out what to do.

This seemed to him to be like a plan of action, the decision to wait for something to happen. It pleased him and he felt suddenly tired. Christ, he said to himself, how do you expect to ever reach any conclusions about this mess without getting some rest?

He rose again and looked over at a small digital clock that blinked its numerals in red. It was four A.M. He stretched and yawned. He ordered himself: Go to bed. His mind answered with a military snap: Yes, sir!

He took three steps toward the bedroom.

Things will sort themselves out.

And the doorbell rang.

It was a high-pitched, irritating sound that struck his heart. It startled him deeply and he jumped involuntarily.

He took a great breath.

Who? he wondered.

My God, he thought.

He took another breath. What the hell? It's four A.M.

It rang again, buzzing swiftly and insistently.

His mind twirled in confusion and he walked to the door. There was a small, circular peephole, and he peered through it.

Standing outside was the detective.

His heart plunged and he felt suddenly dizzy and nauseated and he wanted to be sick. He fought off the sensation and he reached for the doorknob.

As soon as she heard a hand start to open the door, Detective Mercedes Barren reached behind her, to where she had stuck her 9-millimeter pistol beneath her shirt, tucked into the belt of her jeans. She freed the weapon and swung it forward, just behind the paper sack she carried in her other arm.

She raised the gun to eye level as the door swung open.

She thrust the barrel forward so that it hovered an inch from Martin Jeffers' nose.

She saw him pale quickly and take a sudden step back in surprise.

"Don't move," she said, her voice deadly cold and even. "Is he here? If you lie I will kill you."

Martin Jeffers shook his head.

Using the gun to gesture, she slipped into the apartment. She glanced around quickly. She could sense they were alone, but she was not willing to put trust in her sensation.

"Please, detective, put the gun away. He's not here and I still don't know where he is."

"I'll believe you after I take a look around." She maneuvered so she could see into the other rooms. After a quick inspection, never moving the gun too much, so that it could not instantly be brought to bear on Martin Jeffers, she returned to the living room and gestured for the doctor to sit down.

"I can't believe that..." Martin Jeffers started, but she cut him off sharply.

"I don't care what you can or can't believe."

They were both silent. After an instant he spoke.

"You were supposed to meet me yesterday morning. Not here. Not now. What's going on? And please put that cannon away. It scares the bejesus out of me."

"It should. And I'll put it away when I want."

They continued to stare at each other.

"Where is he?" she asked.

"I told you I don't know."

"Can you find him?"

"I don't know. No. Maybe. I don't know. But certainly not..."

"I haven't got too much time. No one does."

Martin Jeffers managed to compose himself. He ignored her mysterious statement.

"Look, detective, what are you doing here in the middle of the night? We had an agreed-upon appointment and you never show and then suddenly you're at my apartment at four in the morning threatening me with a gun. What the hell is going on?"

Detective Barren sat in a chair across from him. The gun still waved in the air between them. She pulled the envelope containing Douglas Jeffers' apartment key from her pocket and tossed it to the brother.

He looked at it. "Where the hell did you get this?"

"From your desk."

"You broke in here? Christ, what kind of cop are you?"

"Would you have given it to me?"

"Not on your life."

Jeffers started to stand, filled with violation and anger.

She raised the gun.

He stared at it and sat back down.

"Threats are childish," he said.

"I went to your brother's apartment," she said.

"So?"

She had placed the paper sack at her feet. She reached in and pulled out the photograph of Susan. She tossed it to Martin Jeffers, who looked at it for several seconds.

"That is my niece," she said bitterly.

"Yes, but..."

"I found it at your brother's apartment."

Martin Jeffers' head spun suddenly. He breathed harshly. He blurted out: "Well, there must be some explanation . . ."

Her voice was like a frozen morning: "There is."

"I mean, he must have . . ."

She interrupted:

"Don't make some fucking stupid excuse."

"I mean, he could have obtained this picture in any number of ways . . . I mean, after all, he's a professional."

She did not reply. She simply reached into the paper bag and pulled out another photo. She dropped this in front of Martin Jeffers. Again, he looked deeply at the two photographs.

"But this isn't the same person," he said finally.

She threw another photo in front of him.

He spread the three out, looking carefully at the pictures.

"But I don't get it, neither is . . ."

She slammed another picture in front of him.

He glanced at this, then he sat back in his chair.

She was breathing hard, as if near the end of a long run.

She slapped yet another picture down. Then another and another and another, until finally she dumped the entire stack on the brother's lap.

"You don't get it? You don't get it? You don't get it?" she repeated as each flopped in front of him.

Martin Jeffers looked around wildly, as if searching for something to grasp hold of and steady himself.

"Now," she said with all the pent-up rage barely leashed, "where is he? Where is your brother? Where? Where? Where?"

Martin Jeffers put his head into his hands.

She leaped across to his side, pulling him back sharply by the shoulder.

"If you cry I will kill you," she said viciously. She did not know whether or not she meant this; it was that she suddenly couldn't stand the idea of the murderer's brother shedding a tear for himself, for Douglas Jeffers, for anyone other than those people spread about him.

"I don't know!" he said, his voice cracking with stress.

"You know!"

"No!"

She stared at him. He looked at the pictures.

Her voice was filled with controlled fury: "Will you find him?"

Jeffers hesitated, two answers screaming inside his head.

"Yes," he said finally. "Maybe. I can try."

She slumped into a chair. She wanted to cry, then, herself.

But instead they just sat across from each other, staring into the gap between them.

The dawn light caught the two sitting amidst the pile of photographs, silent. It was Martin Jeffers, his own mind a disaster of crushed emotions, who spoke first:

"I suppose the first step, now, is for you to contact your superiors, tell them what you think you're up against . . ."

"No," replied Detective Barren.

"Well, maybe we should talk to the FBI," Jeffers went on, oblivious to her refusal. "They have a branch office down in Trenton, and I know a couple of the agents. They're equipped to help, I guess . . ."

"No," she said again.

Jeffers looked over at her. He swiftly filled with rage. He tried to bite back his words, but his tongue was loosened by exhaustion and sorrow.

"Look, detective, if you think I'm going to help you hunt my brother down to satisfy some personal vendetta, you're mistaken! Worse, you're crazy! Forget it and get the hell out of here!"

Detective Mercedes Barren looked at Martin Jeffers.

"You don't understand," she said quietly.

"Well, detective, it seems to me that you're awfully good at making threats with that big fucking gun . . ." He surprised himself by using an obscenity. "But you're not too damn forthcoming with details. If my brother has committed crimes, well, then, there's an established procedure for investigating him . . ."

He had the unsettling feeling that he'd said those words before and they had been equally useless then.

"It won't work," she said. Defeat mocked her.

"Why the hell not?"

"Because of me."

She sighed deeply and felt fatigue insinuate itself throughout her body and mind. Martin Jeffers watched her, aware suddenly that something was bent, twisted, wrong; he slid effortlessly into his professional posture, waiting, quiet, patient, knowing the explanation would eventually arrive.

The silence filled with weak morning light.

"Because of me," the detective said again.

She took a deep breath.

"I am the best, you know? I was always the best. I made one mistake, once, and I've got the scar to show for it. But that was all. I lived. I recovered. I made no more mistakes. It didn't matter what kind of case it was, I was always the best. The information I got, the evidence I procured, the arrests I made, everything! It was always right. It was always true. It was always accurate. When I got onto a case, there was only one conclusion: the bad guys got busted. Then they went to prison. It didn't matter to me what kind of lawyer they got, what kind of defense they had. Alibi? Forget it. I put them away. All of them . . .

"I was together, you know? I had to be. All my life people stole from me and I was powerless to do anything about it. But not when I became a cop. I was right. Always. I was always right."

She slung her head back and looked to the heavens. After a moment she looked at Martin Jeffers.

"You have to understand: there is no evidence."

Martin Jeffers shook his head.

"What do you mean? Look at the pictures."

"They don't exist."

"What the hell are you talking about?" He picked up a handful of photographs and shook them at her. "You come in here and tell me my own brother has committed these, these . . ." He stumbled over the word and finally just raced on. ". . . And now you say they don't exist! What the hell?"

"They don't exist."

Jeffers sat back and folded his arms in front of his chest angrily. "I'll listen to your explanation."

"I always did it right, you see. Until this time. Finally, when I handle something that means something, everything, to me, I screw it up. Ruined."

She reached out and picked up some of the pictures.

"I broke in here. I stole the key. I broke in there. This goes far beyond the definition of an illegal search . . ."

"A technicality!"

"No!" she screamed. "It's the rules. Worse: it's the reality!"

"So," he said, trying hard to remain calm and analytical, "why don't we go to the FBI? At least show them the pictures."

"You don't see," she said. "We walk into the FBI and I say, look, Mr. Agent, I want to show you pictures of homicides which I've obtained in the course of an investigation. The first thing they'll ask is what investigation. And I'll say, no, actually I'm on medical leave from my department. That'll ring their bell and then they'll call my boss and he'll say she was distraught and obsessed and, Jesus, I hope she's okay. But he won't say, Believe her, because he doesn't believe that himself. And then they'll call the county homicide people, who'll say, yeah, she hasn't been the same since her niece got killed and sure, we cleared that case and busted the guy, he's doing a trillion years in solitary. And Mr. Agent will learn that I have access to hundreds of photographs, just like these, well, not quite, but close enough, and he'll just conclude I'm crazy. End of story..."

"Suppose I say..."

"Say what? She's convinced me about my brother? Mr. Agent will just figure we're both out of our minds. But even if he does think maybe, just maybe, I better cover my ass, then what he'll do is some sort of computer check on your brother and he'll come up with zero. Well, not zero. He'll find out that your brother has a security clearance into the White House, for starters, approved by the Secret Service, because that's what I found when I did the same damn check. And then you know what he'll do? I'll tell you. He'll write one short little memo and file it under distraught-head cases. In other words: nothing."

"Well, can't you persuade your own people?"

"They think I'm crazy and distraught."

Her eyes narrowed.

"They're right of course."

Martin Jeffers looked about himself, wondering what next.

"So what do you want to do?" he asked.

"Find him."

"So you can kill him?"

Detective Barren hesitated.

"Yes," she said.

"Forget it."

"I could have lied and said no," she said.

"Right. You could have. One point for your honesty."

He stared bitterly at her and she returned the look with equal intensity.

"All right," she said. "You take a look at those pictures again. A real good look, and think about them for a minute and then you suggest a compromise."

He answered quickly.

"We find him and arrest him and confront him and he'll confess."

"Like hell he will."

"Detective, I have a great deal of experience with people who commit multiple crimes. They almost invariably want to take credit for what they've done..."

He stopped suddenly. My God! he thought. I'm talking about Doug!

He stood up and lurched around the room as if drunk on memory.

309

"This is crazy, you know . . ."

"I think I admitted that," she said.

"I mean, this is my brother! He's one of the top people in his profession! He's a journalist. He's an artist. He couldn't have done these things! It's just not in him! He's never been violent . . ."

"No?"

They looked across at each other. Both knew the room was filled with denials, disbelief, anxiety, and confusion. Detective Mercedes Barren thought suddenly: This is my only chance. He will never return to that apartment. He will disappear. He will be swallowed up somewhere in the country and be lost forever. If the brother won't provide the link, then there will be no link at all.

She swallowed and forced her face to hide the despair and dismay she felt pumping through her body like blood.

Martin Jeffers looked over at Detective Barren, trying to make his own face a mask of his emotions. He thought: I cannot lose sight of this woman. If I do, she will head off on some murderous tangent of her own.

And then a harder thought crept into his imagination: I must find out for myself what Doug has done.

He felt an almost palpable bond fixing him and the detective, in an equal but vastly different pursuit. He said brusquely:

"If I help to find him, so that we can clear this up intelligently, I must have your promise."

"Promise what?"

Martin Jeffers stopped short. He wasn't sure. He took a deep breath.

"Promise you won't start shooting. Promise you'll listen. Just goddamn promise you won't kill him! He's my brother, for chrissakes! Otherwise, forget it."

She did not rush into a hasty agreement. Let him think that you're giving this careful consideration, she said to herself.

"Well, I'll promise this: I'll give you a chance first. After that, well, whatever happens, happens."

She said this solidly, confidently.

It was, she knew, a complete lie.

"All right," he said, measured gratitude in his voice. "That's fair."

He did not trust her for an instant.

They did not do anything as foolish as shake hands over the deadly business they were about to embark upon. Instead they both settled into their seats and stared ahead, waiting for the next moment to arrive with whatever novel revelations it contained.

The bright morning light enveloped them, imposing some reason, some clarity on their thoughts. Detective Barren finally broke the silence they'd maintained with an orderly question:

"So," she said directly, "where do we start? What did he tell you about what he was going to do?"

"He didn't tell me much. He said he was going on a sentimental journey. Those were his exact words. I pointed out that we didn't have much to be sentimental about."

"He must have said more."

Martin Jeffers shut his eyes briefly, picturing his brother in the hospital cafeteria, grinning, as always.

"He said he was going to visit some memories. He didn't specify what kind."

"Well, what do you think?"

"I'm not sure."

"You don't have to be sure."

Jeffers paused, considering.

"Well, it would seem to me that, assuming all this is true"—he waved a hand in the direction of the photographs—"that he could have been talking about two kinds of memories. The first, obviously, are those memories he has from our childhood. The second group, of course, are the memories of these"—he stumbled—"events."

Jeffers thought his voice sounded reasonable and calm. He hated it.

"Or, most likely, a combination of the two."

Detective Barren suddenly felt invigorated, as if all the exhaustion slid away abruptly. Her mind raced ahead. She stood up and strode about the room, punching her fist into her palm, thinking.

"Usually," she said, "the process of deduction for policemen is to figure out why something happened and how. The two are generally linked . . ." She realized then that she had adopted almost the same lecturing tone that Martin Jeffers had. She ignored this, and continued. "It is rare that we are asked to anticipate . . ."

"My profession is no different," Martin Jeffers said.

She nodded.

"But now we have to."

She could see agreement in his eyes.

"So assume for a moment that it would take us months to

311

figure out which picture belonged in which locale . . ."

"Which is true. Nor do we know what sort of priorities he places on each, which would affect his itinerary," Jeffers interjected.

"So we look at the other type of memory: personal."

"Well, the problem there is almost the same. We have no way of telling what priorities he puts on things. Nor do we know the order he might be traveling in."

"But at least you can make some guesses."

"But that's all they would be. Guesses."

"That's enough! At least it's doing something!"

Jeffers nodded.

"Well, for starters, we were abandoned in New Hampshire. That's probably on his list of places to visit."

"How do you mean, abandoned?"

Martin Jeffers snapped his reply: "Given up! Kicked out! Let loose! Shown the door! What the hell do you think?"

"I'm sorry," she said, surprised by his sudden anger. "I didn't know what you meant."

"Look," he said firmly, "it's nothing that unusual, really. Our mother was the black sheep of the family. She ran away from home with a guy who'd just been discharged from the service. They worked in a carny show—you know, one of those fairs that travel around the country. She never married the guy, as best as we can tell. Anyway, Doug arrived. Then me. I don't think either of them cared too much for children. First he left, then she arranged to have us adopted by some cousins. She was supposed to bring us here to New Jersey, but I guess she got impatient, because she left us in New Hampshire. Manchester, to be exact."

He hesitated.

"I can still remember everything about that damn police station where we waited. It was dim and the walls were scraped with drawings and grafitti, none of which I could decipher, but which I knew was somehow wrong. And everyone seemed so huge. You know that sense you get when you're little that the entire world is built for big people . . ."

"Your brother?"

"He got me through it. He took care of me."

"What was his reaction?"

Jeffers took a deep breath.

"He hated her for leaving us. He hated her for not loving us. He hated our new parents just as much. Phony parents, he would say."

"And you?"

"I hated. But not to the same degree."

He wondered then if he was lying.

"Where did you end up?"

"Here."

"No, I mean . . ."

"I know what you mean. Here is correct. The cousins who adopted us lived in Rocky Hill, just on the other side of Princeton. He was a druggist. Actually, though, he was a businessman. A damn good one. He owned a drugstore on Nassau Street which he finally sold to a chain for a helluva lot of money. He invested wisely. He was solid. Middle-class."

"You don't sound . . ."

"I didn't. Doug hated him worse. The bastard wouldn't even give us his name after the adoption went through. Jeffers is our natural mother's name. Do you know how hard that is, growing up? You feel like you've got to explain things every time you register for school. Or make a new friend. Or anything. If he gave us anything, we worked for it."

"You did okay."

"You think so?"

She did not know what to say. Jeffers' voice had grown in bitterness and anger. She wondered how he dealt with all the rage he had. She knew how his brother did.

"Why don't we try Manchester?" she said.

"What good will it do?" Jeffers fairly spat out the words.

"I don't know," she said evenly, but her own temper rising through the words. "But at least it will be doing something other than waiting around for him to telephone you. Which he hasn't done."

"Not yet."

"Do you think he will?"

Jeffers paused.

"Yes."

"Why?"

"Because if he's pursuing shared memories, he's bound to remember something that he will want to say to me. Or he'll visit somewhere that prompts some need in him to express something, and I'm the only logical place to express it . . . other than that . . ." He gestured toward the photographs. "That's how the mind works. It's not a guarantee, but a good guess. An educated guess."

She thought for a moment.

"I don't want to wait around."

He nodded.

"It's Saturday," he said. "I don't have to be back at the hospital until Monday."

She stood.

"New Hampshire," she said. "We can show his picture around, make some inquiries." She thought for an instant, then asked:

"Where are your folks now?"

She saw Martin Jeffers take a deep breath, as if marshaling his anger into some military row. When he did speak, it was in low, barely controlled tones. His voice surprised Detective Barren, chilling her. She sat down in her chair and watched as Jeffers struggled with his emotions and his memory, and for a moment she reminded herself instantly: Remember who he is. Remember they are brothers.

"Adoptive parents, both dead," said Martin Jeffers coldly. "Natural father? Who knows. Probably dead or in some state home somewhere. Natural mother? The same, unless . . ."

He paused.

". . . Unless Doug managed to kill her."

He first drove her past the drugstore, rolling slowly down Nassau Street in Princeton. The university, with its ivy-covered buildings, rested across the street, quiet, as if patiently awaiting the fall with its excitement and bustle from behind a great black iron fence and wide grassy lawns. Martin Jeffers pointed out that it was a few weeks before the semester start, which transformed the entire town. This she knew. She did not tell him how familiar she was with the entire area. She did not want him to know any more than was barely necessary.

She saw the stone classroom buildings and dormitories and thought of her husband. She smiled, remembering how comfortable he'd been at college and how strange it was for him to leave it for the Army. He had loved the internal world of school, she thought. He had been swept up in the false society that placed value on books and ideas and measured achievement through scholarly papers and skilled presentations. On what? On literature, on mathematics, on political theory, on science.

My father's world, too, she thought.

Not mine.

She had showered at her hotel while Martin Jeffers waited in his car outside. She had changed her underclothes and slipped into her jeans, dragged a comb through her hair, and was ready, oblivious to the lack of sleep, wide awake, excited, thinking only that she was getting closer, that she was narrowing down the world of Douglas Jeffers and that she would keep winnowing away at it until his world contained only her and her pistol. This thought had forced a bitter smile to her face.

She had looked in the room's mirror, but instead of checking her appearance, she lifted up her weapon, pointed it at the reflection. She had said, alone, out loud, "This is what it will look like."

She froze in the position and absorbed it silently.

Then she had seized a small duffle bag packed with overnight gear and put the 9 millimeter inside. In the top of the bag she had also placed the self-portrait Douglas Jeffers had taken of himself in the jungle, along with two extra clips of bullets.

Martin Jeffers had insisted on using his car, which was fine with her. She thought that he wanted the elusive sense of control that driving his own vehicle gave him, as if in some way he were in charge of the expedition. She acquiesced quickly, thinking that it would allow her to relax, store up energy, even sleep, while he would be burdened with the added fatigue of driving.

After seeing the pharmacy, Martin Jeffers drove out of town and within a few moments was winding through narrow, tree-shaded country roads. After a moment they came to a quiet, small subdivision of houses, plunked incongruously down amidst some farms. He stopped and pointed.

"Third one in. The family homestead. I haven't been here in ten years."

She saw a modest, trim, three-story, gray and white frame house, with a green, well-kept lawn and a garage and a foreign car parked out in front.

"When we lived there," Martin Jeffers continued, "it was painted brown. A dull, ugly, dark brown. The inside reflected the outside; it lacked imagination. It was never friendly, outgoing, open, the way kids' houses ought to be. It was always dark and uncomfortable."

"But it was a home. You weren't abandoned like some street kids."

He shrugged. "People sometimes overestimate the exterior factors. But the interior factors are what are critical for children."

"What do you mean?"

"Love. Contact. Affection. Pride. Support. With them you can survive, and actually flourish, amidst the most horrendous circumstances. Without them, money and family and education and hired care, whatever, are all relatively useless. The ghetto child who works his way through school and becomes a lawyer.

The younger-generation Kennedy kid who dies from a drug overdose. See what I mean?"

"Yes," she replied. She thought of her niece, and her heart tightened for a single instant. She shook off the sensation by asking a question:

"You said both your adoptive parents are dead?"

"That's right," Martin Jeffers answered. "Our adoptive father died in an accident when we were teenagers and our adoptive mother died three years ago of what pathologists like to call natural causes, but which was really the result of too much drinking, too many tranquilizers, fast food, smoking, no exercise, and a heart that was too burdened by all this crap to go on any longer. In reality, totally unnatural causes."

"Where are they buried?"

"They were both cremated. One doesn't erect monuments to people like them. Not unless one is totally out of..." He stopped, thinking that his brother was, in an unusually oblique, psychiatric way, doing precisely that.

Detective Barren gathered in the information, mentally filing it, and looked up at the house. There's a monument, she thought, and an idea struck her.

"Wait here for a moment."

"Not a chance," he said.

They both exited the car and walked up to the house.

Detective Barren rang the doorbell. After a few seconds she heard footsteps running inside and a young voice crying, "I'll get it! I'll get it! It's probably Jimmy!" The door was flung open and she looked down at a towheaded child of five or six. He looked at Detective Barren and Martin Jeffers, seemed disappointed, and turned and yelled back into the house, "Mom! It's adults!" Betrayal tinged his voice. Then he turned and said, "Hi!"

"Is your mom or dad at home?" she asked.

Before the child answered, Detective Barren heard the quick pace of embarrassment, and a woman about her own age, dressed in jeans and carrying a gardening spade, hove into view.

"I'm sorry," she said, wiping her forehead. "I was out back and we're expecting a playmate. What can I do for you?"

"Hello," said Detective Barren. She held up her gold detective shield. "My name is Mercedes Barren and I'm a police detective. We're investigating the disappearance of this man..." She held out the photograph of Douglas Jeffers. "We wondered whether you might have seen him?"

The woman looked at the picture, clearly taken aback by the

thought that she was talking to a detective in the middle of a hot Saturday morning.

"No," she said. "Why? Why would I see him? Is something wrong?"

"It's nothing to be alarmed at," Detective Barren lied. "The gentleman, who is related to my partner here, used to live in this neighborhood. We just thought, since he was missing, that he might have come looking at where he grew up, that's all. Nothing to be alarmed at. And this was a real long shot, as well."

"Oh," said the woman, as if Detective Barren's mingling of lies and truths answered questions as opposed to raising a thousand new ones. "Oh," she said again. She looked at the picture. "I'm sorry, we haven't seen the man."

"Let me see," said the child.

"No," said the mother. "Billy, leave us alone."

"I want to see!" he insisted.

She looked at Detective Barren.

"He needs his playmate," she said.

The detective bent down and showed the child the picture.

"Ever see him?" she asked.

The child regarded the picture at length.

"Yes. Maybe he was here."

Detective Barren stiffened inwardly and she felt Martin Jeffers take a quick step forward.

"Billy!" said the mother. "This is serious! It's not a game."

"Maybe I saw him," said the child. "Maybe he came here, too."

"Billy," said Detective Barren evenly, friendly. "Where did you see him?"

The child half-waved, half-pointed out toward the road.

"Did he say anything? What did he do?"

The child was instantly shy.

"No. Nothing."

"Did you see a car? Or anyone else?"

"Nope."

"When was this?"

"A while ago."

"So what happened?"

"Nothing. Maybe I saw him, that's all."

Detective Barren heard a car crunch down the gravel of the driveway behind her. She saw the child's eyes brighten.

"There they are!" he said to his mother. "There they are! Can I go out, please?"

The mother looked at Detective Barren, who straightened up

and nodded. "Sure," said the woman. The child burst out of the house, past the detective and Martin Jeffers. His mother stepped out beside them, watching the child and his friend start to play. She waved at the other mother, behind the wheel of the typical large station wagon. "I'm not sure I'd place too much credence . . ." she started.

"Don't worry," Detective Barren interrupted. "I don't. And I don't think he saw anyone."

"I don't think so either," she said.

"Thanks for your help," Detective Barren said. She and Martin Jeffers walked back to his car. She paused and waved at the boy, but he was swept away in excited play and did not see her.

In the car Martin Jeffers asked, "What do you really think?"

She hesitated for a moment.

"I don't think he was here," she said.

"Neither do I," he added.

They both paused.

"Maybe, though," he said.

"Maybe."

Another pause.

"I think he was here," he said.

"So do I," said Detective Barren.

Martin Jeffers nodded and put the car in gear. It was not lost on him how easily and simply she'd lied to the mother. Then he gently turned the car and drove away from the house and the elusive, hallucinatory vision of their quarry and all their combined, unspoken memories.

Much of the drive to New Hampshire was done in silence, with only the roadway sounds intruding on their individual thoughts. They made a few efforts at small talk. Just past New Haven, Martin Jeffers asked:

"Are you married, detective?"

She thought of lying, of obfuscating, then inwardly shrugged, thinking the effort would be too great.

"No. Widowed."

"Oh," he said. "I'm sorry." This was convention.

"It was many years ago. I married young and he died in the war."

"The war seemed to affect everyone one way or another."

"Did you go?"

"No, they instituted the draft lottery when my time came up and I pulled three hundred and forty-seven. I'm not usually a lucky person, but this time I was. They never came knocking."

"What about your brother?"

"It's odd, really. He was over there a couple of times, but always on assignment from some magazine or newspaper. And he dropped out of college, too. He should have been a prime target for the draft, but he never was nailed. I don't know why."

He paused, then asked:

"You seem young. But you never remarried?"

She smiled despite herself.

"High school sweetheart. Hard to find someone who can compete with all those runaway teenage emotions and the way they translate into adult memories."

Martin Jeffers had laughed a little.

"Quite true," he said. He continued, asking, "Why police work?"

"It was an accident, I guess. They had had an equal-opportunity suit down in Miami right about the time I got there. I saw an ad in the paper because they were under a court order to hire more women and minorities, and thought I'd give it a shot..." She laughed again. "Isn't that the American way? Well, I answered the ad, almost on a lark, really. Then I discovered it was something that I did well. Finally, it was something I did best. How about yourself?"

"Psychiatry? Well, two reasons, actually. One, I didn't really like blood, and you've got to be pretty familiar with the stuff to be a successful physician; and two, I couldn't stand the idea of losing patients. That steered me away from a lot of branches of the profession. I guess there's a three, too. It's always interesting. People create infinite variations on several common themes..."

"That's true," she said.

"See," he replied, "we sound alike again."

She nodded. She thought of the Dear John letter she'd read in his files. "No one to share all this with?"

She saw him order his thoughts before speaking.

"No... not really. I'm not sure why, but I have developed a pretty closed life, what with the work at the hospital demanding so much time. And then, in psychiatry as well as any branch of medicine, there's a great deal of self-education and keeping up that requires a lot of time. So, no—no one really."

She nodded and thought: And you're terrified, too. Terrified of yourself.

The conversation evaporated in the rhythmic thump of tires on macadam and the steady drone of the engine. Detective Barren thought they jousted well. She conceded a significant degree of impressiveness to the doctor; he has been put under a great deal

319

of stress, she thought, yet he still controls his tongue. She had dealt with many sophisticated men, criminals mainly, who, when put under less stress than he'd confronted would open up like flowers in bloom.

She wondered if he was correct about his brother: Confronted with evidence and the truth, perhaps he would confess. She considered this as a problem. A confession, even an egotistical, boasting one, could be sufficient to make him on the crimes. She pictured her niece's body lying beneath the ferns and dark palm shadows. Perhaps not all, but certainly some. Police literature is filled with the confessions of men who, when picked up for jaywalking, suddenly start admitting to serial murders. She remembered the man in Texas, with his claims exceeding two or three hundred. He was a drifter with a peculiarly homicidal bent. Lucas, she recalled. She recollected seeing a picture of him in a news magazine, standing with a detective who wore a ten-gallon hat, in front of a map of the southeastern United States. The hat was white, which she supposed was the way things were done in Texas. Maybe the bad guys were required to wear black. The map on the wall behind the two men was dotted, littered with small colored push-pins, and it had taken her a moment to realize the connection between the map, the pins, and the man grinning obscenely for the camera.

All artists are egotists, she thought. So are all murderers.

She envisioned Douglas Jeffers. Perhaps his brother is correct. Perhaps he will lay claim to his crimes, gaining a degree of satisfaction from the publicity.

She visualized him smiling, posing, accepting that extraordinary and perverse American celebrity that accompanies sensational crimes. He would revel in the attention.

She was flooded with images: Charlie Manson in a courtroom, suddenly holding up the Los Angeles *Times* for the jurors hearing the Tate-LaBianca cases to see, with its massive, screaming headline: MANSON GUILTY, NIXON SAYS; David Berkowitz slipping into his own sentencing hearing, chanting "Stacy was a whore, Stacy was a whore," drawing out the *o* sound like some crazed mantra and the poor victim's family frantic and struggling, trying to reach their tormentor. The New York *Times* had carried a remarkable pen-and-ink drawing the following day. She and the other detectives in her unit had stared at it in sad disbelief; Dr. Jeffrey McDonald telling an interviewer from *60 Minutes* that he did not kill his wife and two small children at all, certainly not in some near-psychotic fit of rage, and that his murder conviction was all some mistake, or worse, some conspiracy.

She envisioned others made into instant celebrities by crime and accusation: She pictured the aristocratic Claus von Bülow, wearing a contented, wry smile, posing for a celebrity photographer from *Vanity Fair* in black leather alongside his lover in the days after he was acquitted of the crime of injecting his wife with insulin and plunging her into an irreversible coma. She could see Bernhard Goetz pausing before a bank of microphones, peering benignly over the rims of his glasses and telling the mass of notepads and flashbulbs and the six o'clock news that he didn't do anything wrong when he shot the four teenagers who accosted him on the subway.

She saw Douglas Jeffers joining the same parade and the thought sickened her.

She rolled down her window and breathed in deeply.

"You all right?" asked Martin Jeffers.

"Yes," she replied. "I just needed a little fresh air."

"Do you want to stop?"

"No," she said firmly. "Not until we get there."

They drove on.

It was well after dark when they reached the outskirts of Manchester. They had stopped once for gasoline and Detective Barren had run into the cafeteria-style restaurant at the thruway rest stop while Martin Jeffers filled up the tank and checked the oil. She had purchased some coffee, a couple of sodas and two sandwiches, tuna fish and ham and cheese. The sandwiches were on soggy white bread and came sealed in see-through plastic containers. When she got back into the car, she had offered them to Jeffers. "Take your pick," she said.

"More like pick your poison," he had replied, eyeing the sandwiches. He had seized the ham and cheese and bitten into it quickly. "I love tuna fish," he had said.

She had joined his laughter.

He thought then how long it had been since he'd heard a woman laugh unfettered. He did not think he would hear her laughter again. He reminded himself why she was with him and what she would do if she had the opportunity.

So he cautioned himself to be apprehensive. Not outwardly, he told himself. But question everything inwardly.

Do not mistake some laughter for trust, he said to himself. Or a smile for actual affection.

Trust nothing. Stay alert. He steeled himself against the fatigue of the road and of emotion and drove on into the increasing darkness.

On the outskirts of Manchester he spotted a Holiday Inn sign standing sharply against the blackness of the New Hampshire night. He gestured and asked:

"How's that? We're not going to get anything done tonight anyway. And we've both been up for hours . . ."

She nodded, part of her refusing to accept her exhaustion, another part of her demanding that she acquiesce to it. "Fine." Each filled out registration papers and used their own credit cards, which seemed to take the night clerk by surprise. When he handed them their keys, Detective Barren suddenly produced the picture of Douglas Jeffers and thrust it at the man.

"Seen him?" she demanded. "Has he been here anytime in the past few weeks?"

The man looked at the picture.

"Can't say that I remember the face," he said.

"Check your register," said Martin Jeffers. "Look for Douglas Jeffers. He's my brother."

"I can't do that . . ." said the clerk.

Detective Barren produced her gold shield.

"Yes, you can," she said.

He looked at the badge.

"We don't have a register," he said. "It's all computer. It cleans out the names every week . . ."

"Try it anyway," Martin Jeffers said.

The clerk nodded. He punched some letters in on a computer keyboard.

"Nope," he said.

"Does that tie in with other Holiday Inn computers?" Detective Barren asked.

"Yeah, actually, it does," said the clerk. "Just for the three that are in this area."

"Try them," she demanded again.

"Well," he said, "I'm not sure I know how to do that, but let me try." He fiddled with the keyboard, making a rapid clicking noise as he tried combinations of letters and numbers. "Hey!" he said suddenly.

"The name!" said Martin Jeffers.

"No, no, no, sorry," said the clerk. "It's just I figured it out. Now let me check names." Again he punched letters. Then he shook his head. "Not in the last seven days," he told them.

"Thanks for trying," said Detective Barren.

"Is the guy in trouble?" asked the clerk.

"You might say that," said Detective Barren. "But at the moment he's just one of the missing."

The clerk nodded.

Martin Jeffers carried her duffel bag to her room. She let him do this to give it an air of innocence. She knew that if she had insisted on carrying it, he would recognize that was where she kept the gun. She knew he would probably figure it out anyway if he thought about it. But perhaps he wouldn't, and she was always searching for whatever edge she could find.

At the door to their rooms, they looked at each other.

"Do you want to try to find something to eat?" Martin Jeffers asked.

She shook her head.

"Good," he said.

They stood in silence.

"I need your word," he said.

"What?"

"Promise that when I go in here, you won't head off without me."

She almost smiled. That was what she had feared from him.

"If you'll make the same promise."

He nodded. "We're agreed then?"

She nodded as well.

"Why don't we start at nine," he said. "Leave a wake-up call at the desk."

"Eight," she said firmly. "See you then."

Moving at the same speed, each opened the door to their room and stepped inside. It seemed an odd ballet, out of sight, but not, thanks to thin motel walls, necessarily out of hearing. They both paused, straining to hear some noise from the other's room. Then each moved into the center of the room and, realizing that the other was next door, and probably listening with the same lack of trust, each bustled about for a moment before falling into bed.

Manchester was once a busy industrial town, and it still retained a sense of blue-collar grime and hard work, with stolid brick buildings and factories that were only partially concealed by the richness of New Hampshire's late-summer green. Detective Mercedes Barren and Martin Jeffers ate a quiet, brief breakfast, then set out amidst the early churchgoers and bright sunshine. They spoke little, nor did they have some established plan; they merely cruised the streets, stopping at fast-food restaurants, gas stations, other motels, and hotels—anyplace that Douglas Jeffers might have settled briefly and made just enough of a connection for someone to recall his picture.

She doubted, even if someone remembered him, whether they

would have any knowledge that was worthwhile. But, as Martin Jeffers pointed out, if they were to locate him, just once, then they would have some sort of idea what direction he was heading in.

She was skeptical. He was skeptical. But both conceded inwardly that they felt much better doing something—even if it was only creating the illusion of doing something—than it would have been sitting around.

And both longed for the same thing: some slight contact that would bring them within reach of Douglas Jeffers. It was as if by arriving at the same location that their quarry had been, they would gain a scent.

Still, Detective Barren felt slightly foolish. She knew the probabilities of any kind for success were very small. But, she thought to herself, you've never disliked this part of police work. Some detectives hated the drudgery of asking the same questions over and over, trying to sort through the entire haystack, much preferring leaping ahead somehow. She, on the other hand, realized that much of her success was due to her doggedness, and she could be perfectly happy, indeed contented, asking question after question. He felt much the same; much of his work was devoted to going over and over, repetitively, the same memories, the same circumstances, the same facts, until by dint of persistence they were defused.

It was late afternoon when Jeffers asked, "Why don't we try the police station? Just see if he's gone in there."

"I was saving it for last," she replied.

"We're at the end," he said. "If he's been here, he certainly hasn't made much of a fuss about it."

"I don't think he's been here," she said. "Which only means that he may show up, anytime."

Jeffers nodded.

"But I've still got a job, and appointments waiting for me after an eight-hour drive back to New Jersey. If you want to hang around . . ."

"No," she said. She thought: We're in this together. "No, we're going to stick together until . . ."

He interrupted. "Until we get this sorted out."

"Right."

"Okay, the police station."

Martin Jeffers looked up the address of the Central Police Headquarters while Detective Barren showed the picture to one more gas station attendant, unsuccessfully. He got directions from the attendant and they drove through a depressing series of city streets, each seemingly more rundown than the next. The police headquarters was in the grimiest portion of the city. Detective Barren noticed the number of squad cars rolling through the neighborhood and thought they must be close. She spied, to their left, a large red-brick building.

"There," she said, pointing.

Martin Jeffers hesitated.

"That's not it," he said. "That's new. I mean, it's relatively new. The building I remember was old."

He pulled the car up next to the building. "Look at the cornerstone," he said.

She turned and followed his glance and read ERECTED 1973 on a gray slab set on the corner of the building. Martin Jeffers parked the car and said, "Let's go ask."

Inside the building was all fluorescent lights and modern design, but slightly scarred with use. They approached a desk sergeant and Detective Barren produced her shield. The sergeant was a corpulent man, probably happy to man the desk, equally as adept at avoiding controversy as he was at dodging a street assignment.

"Miami," the man said, pleasantly enough. "My brother-in-law runs a bar in Fort Lauderdale. Once went to visit, but too many kids, if you know what I mean. Whew. And hot! So what can I do for you, detective from Miami? What's in Manchester that you need?"

He pronounced the city's name with a broad *a* that made Detective Barren smile.

"Two things," she said, smiling. "Have you seen this man? And wasn't there once an old police station in central Manchester?"

The sergeant looked at the picture.

"No, can't say that I've seen him. You want me to make some copies and have them distributed at roll call? If this guy's wanted, we ought to know about it. What d'you think?"

Detective Barren thought hard and fast about the offer. No, she thought. He's mine.

"No," she said, "at the moment he's just wanted for questioning and I don't really have enough for you to pull him in on. I'm just making a few inquiries, you know."

The sergeant nodded. "Have it your way," he said. "Just wanted to offer."

"And it's appreciated," she replied.

He smiled.

"Now," the sergeant added, "about that old station. There

were a couple, actually. Up until the mid-sixties we were like a lot of little cities. We had station houses all over. Then they were consolidated into this new and beautiful spot you see here..." He waved his hands about before continuing. "Most were torn down. One got made into a bunch of lawyers' offices. That's the one that was closest to the courthouse. I think one was made into a condominium. That's in the other part of town, the nice side..." He laughed. "Sometimes I think that's what's gonna happen to all of us when we pass on. We're gonna be made into a condo. Right up in heaven, I guess." He laughed again and both Jeffers and Detective Barren smiled with him, each recognizing a certain truth to his plaint.

"Which would have been the Central Station? The biggest?" Jeffers asked.

"That'd be the one across from the courthouse."

"How do we get there?"

"Break the law."

"I beg your pardon?"

"Just having a little joke. How do you get to the courthouse? Break the law... Oh, well, I said it was a little joke. Go straight down this street for six blocks and turn right on Washington Boulevard. That'll take you there."

They thanked the sergeant and left.

"Let's roll past," Detective Barren said.

Jeffers nodded in assent. "Lawyers' offices. Seems appropriate. Kind of like recycling trash."

She smiled.

"Another little joke," he said.

They found the building without any trouble. Jeffers was silent for a moment, looking up at it.

"The façade seems the same," Jeffers said then. She thought his voice had taken on a sudden false determination, as if by sounding strong, he would be. He parked the car in front and stared through the car window. "It was windy and dark and raining," he said. "I remember that night it looked evil and hopeless, like it should have had a sign over the door: Abandon Hope All Ye Who Enter Here..."

Not waiting for Detective Barren, he abruptly jumped from the car and then marched up a broad flight of stairs to the front door. He seized the handle and pulled.

"Locked. It's Sunday and the offices are locked."

She looked at him.

"Thank God," he said. She saw him shudder slightly. "Do you know the sensation of being a child and being alone? Children

326

can adapt wonderfully to specific fears, like a pain, a sickness, or a death. It is the unknown which is truly terrifying for them. They have no fund of knowledge in how the world operates, and so they feel completely vulnerable. Do you know what I remember from that night? Oh, everything is vivid and terrible, but I can also remember that my shoes were too tight and I needed a new pair and I thought I would never be able to get them, and how was I going to grow up with no shoes, ever? I remember sitting, having to go to the bathroom so much it hurt but too scared to say anything to anybody. I just knew I wasn't supposed to get off that bench, where they put us to wait. Doug took care of me. He knew, somehow. You know, it always seemed to me, when I was young, that he knew what I was thinking before I even thought it. I suppose all younger brothers ascribe such magical properties to their elder brother. Probably I was squirming around so much. Anyway, he took me to the bathroom. And he told me he would take care of me and not to worry, that he would always be close by. I don't know how much he meant it, but it made me feel safe and wonderful hearing those words. I think I thought I was going to die that night, until he held my hand . . ."

The sun was starting to fade and Martin Jeffers' voice slid into the shadows.

She thought: That's what childhood is, seeking refuge from one fear after another until you become strong enough and old enough and wise enough to battle the fears away. Only some fears can never be defeated.

She looked at Martin Jeffers. He was staring up at the building.

"He's my brother," he said. "Now we're grown up and he's doing these terrible things and I have to stop him. But he saved my life that night. I know it."

Martin Jeffers turned away from the building.

"Let's leave now," he said. "Let's just get the hell out of here."

He grabbed her by the arm and half-pulled her down the flight of steps. She did not resist.

"Let's just go. Go, go back to New Jersey. Now," he said.

She did not say anything in reply, but nodded. She could see the conflict and agony returning to his face. For an instant she felt a kind of dual sadness, one for the memory of the abandoned child who continued to seek his lost parent throughout his life, one for the adult torn by terrible knowledge. She thought then, oddly, that it was unfortunate that she had met Martin Jeffers in this awful way, that under different circumstances she probably would have come to like him. And this made her feel sad for herself. But she shook the feeling away rapidly and moved to her side of the car. I'm sorry, Martin Jeffers, she said to herself. I'm terribly sorry, but lead on. Lead me to your brother. This, she knew he would do. But she knew too, right at that moment, as Jeffers turned away from the building, holding his head in such a way that he thought she would be unable to see his tears and threw himself behind the wheel of the car, that he would never betray his brother.

It was close to midnight, near the end of another wordless journey, when they crossed the George Washington Bridge, passing New York City with its constancy of light on their left and rapidly leaving it behind. Detective Barren's eyes were closed, and Martin Jeffers assumed she slept in the passenger seat. He maneuvered through the still-thick nighttime traffic. His eyes caught the series of huge green roadway signs directing travelers in a dozen different directions, and he considered the great convergence of people and machines and highways that came together at the bridge: routes 4 and 46 and 9W and the Palisades Parkway and the great ribbon that is Interstate 95 heading north-south and the equally great black rope that is Interstate 80, heading east and west. The lights from oncoming cars blinded him as they sliced through the darkness, a quick rush of brightness, then disappearing. When he looked at the lanes in the opposite roads, he could just barely make out the shapes of the other cars, and the odd thought struck him that his brother was out there. He could be anywhere, he said to himself. He could be anywhere, but I know he's here. He could be any one of the sets of lights passing. That one, or that one or that one, but he's one of them. He wanted to call out to him, but was unable. You're there, he thought. I know it. Please.

Then he shook his head to clear away the idea, and realized he was silly and exhausted and probably hallucinating as well, and drove on, not knowing that he was also right.

CHAPTER
TWELVE

ANOTHER TRIP TO NEW HAMPSHIRE

17.   HE had tied the ropes too tight and the nylon strands cut into her wrists agonizingly. She had given up struggling against the pain, realizing that when she pulled or twisted, the cord rebelled, chafing away her flesh. She tried to shut away the throbbing in her arms and find sleep, but when she closed her eyes she saw only the redness of hurt, which was impossible to avoid. So, despite having passed some undefined limit of physical and mental exhaustion, she remained wide awake. The gag around her mouth was giving her problems, as well. She could only breathe through her nose, which he'd bloodied, each breath drawn past clogged blood and mucus with immense difficulty. When he'd gagged her, he had pulled her head back sharply, tightening the knot on the kerchief behind her neck, not paying care to what he was doing. Then he'd slapped a piece of gray gaffer's tape over her mouth. The tape stank of glue and she was afraid she would gag. This might kill her, she knew; if she vomited now out of pain and fear and confusion, she might drown. She surprised herself by realizing the danger and despite the cloud created by her restraints was struck by how far she had traveled, how much more she seemed to know. This thought reshaped itself into a fear; she felt a unique vulnerability, having lived so far. She shut her eyes to the idea that he would kill her now.

Anne Hampton did not know why Douglas Jeffers had beaten and tied her this night, but it did not surprise her.

She assumed it had something to do with the failed murder of the two young women earlier in the day. But he had not been his usual specific self. He had reverted to rage alone.

In a way, she had known it was coming.

He had driven fast from the racetrack, sullen, speechless, his silence scaring her more than his usual speechifying. Darkness had crushed them, still he had not stopped until past New York, at midnight, near Bridgeport, Connecticut. He'd found their usual misbegotten accommodations, checking in with a sleepy, unshaven night clerk with hardly a word, paying for the room, as he always did, in cash. Almost as soon as he'd closed the motel door he was on her, pummeling her with open hands, knocking her about the room. She had held up her hands to ward off the first blows, but then had resigned herself and received what he had wanted to dish out. Her passivity may have disappointed him, but the idea had struck her almost as swiftly as his fists that if she were to fight back, she might take the place of the two women. They had lived and she didn't want to pay for their good fortune right then and there.

So she slunk down, barely covering herself and let him flail away.

The beating had been like a spasm, brief, terrifying, yet over quickly. Then he'd shoved her disdainfully into a corner, wedged down past the sagging twin beds of the motel room. She had not seen him grab the rope; suddenly he'd thrown her down and she'd felt the bonds looped tightly around her, constricting her like some horrid snake. The rope was followed with the violence of the gag around her mouth. She had looked up, trying to catch his eyes, trying to discern what was happening, but she'd been unable. He'd pushed her away with a final, irritated thrust, and left the motel without explanation other than a cryptic promise: "I'll be back."

She was, by far, most frightened of the rope. He had not used it since the first day and she feared that it signaled some terrible change in their relationship. She was back to being his possession, as opposed to, in some unusual way that she could not quite discern, his partner. She had lost identity, lost importance. If she lost relevance, she knew, he would abandon her. Her mind used the word "abandon," but she knew that it was a euphemism for something else. She recognized her position as precarious and intensely dangerous. She did not think he would kill Boswell. But he could easily murder some nameless, faceless, bound-and-gagged woman who bothered him with her presence and who reminded him of a failure. She searched about the motel room as best she could. She saw an old dresser and a mirror and two beds with brown corduroy covers that were faded and cheap, and she thought it was a horrid and squalid place to have to die.

She pictured Vicki and Sandi, who'd seemed so reluctant to put on their clothes. She had been confused; Jeffers had emerged from the woods smiling, joking, playful—as if nothing were wrong—yet she knew something had disrupted the plan, which had frightened her even more. He had teased the two about their good looks and promised that they would get a real shot at the mythical photo spread.

She remembered hearing all that as if from a great distance. She had remained rigid with expectation; looking up and seeing the gun in his hands a dozen times, only to blink and realize that it was the camera.

After a few more shots he'd hustled them all back through the woods and into the car. He'd driven to the racetrack, still bantering away with the two giggling women, who had kept saying, "I can't believe how lucky we are."

She would have laughed, had she not been so terrified.

She thought that the absence of murder was twice as frightening as the act itself. She did not know what had happened, what accident or stroke of luck had saved the two women's lives. She knew only that he'd dropped them back at the grandstand, given the pair a gay little wave and laugh, then accelerated hard, back to the highway. That false laugh had been the last sign of anything from Douglas Jeffers save building rage.

Anne Hampton relaxed against the rope's pain and considered what had happened.

She determined that when he returned, she would make him free her. She focused on this, saying to herself: Nothing else matters. Nothing else is important. You must make him acknowledge who you are. And he will not do that until he removes the bonds.

She swallowed hard and felt her stomach pitch like a boat in a storm.

She bit back the nausea of fear.

I am closer now to death than anytime since the first minutes.

Make him need you.

Make him.

Make him.

Force him.

She waited for him to return, repeating the words over and over to herself, like some nightmarish lullaby.

Douglas Jeffers drove aimlessly through the dark streets, searching for an outlet for his frustration. For a moment he considered the idea of driving into the inner city and simply assassinating some hard-luck person on the street. He thought of finding a prostitute; they were the easiest of targets, almost accommodating in the creation of their death. The idea of driving into an all-night gas station and simply blowing away the attendant appealed to him as well. That was the occupational hazard associated with taking money for gasoline at night. Every so often, somebody else wanted the money and was quite willing to kill for it. Douglas Jeffers thought all the possibilities had a certain common charm; they were the stuff of everynight police blotters. They would get no more than a couple of paragraphs in the morning paper. They were the urban blighted norm, moments of diminished importance, almost routine. That a life ended was of little consequence, an afterthought of night that faded in the light of morning.

They were not the types of crimes that an expert like himself needed to study for more than a couple of seconds.

He shook his head. Another time, he thought, I'd simply do it. Perhaps a liquor store that stayed open a bit too late. Get a ski mask and a big handgun. A truly American moment.

He let out his breath in a long, slow whistle.

Not now. Not this close to the end.

Don't screw up.

He alternately wished he'd killed the young ranger, then the two women, but mostly he was angry with himself for not having anticipated all the problems that were associated with the crime. He went back over the details in his head, bitterly castigating himself: I have always properly prepared for every eventuality; I have always foreseen every dilemma. I should have discovered a better hiding place. He berated himself for choosing the glen in the woods. I liked the damn light and background. I thought like a damn photographer. Not like a killer. So all that work was worthless, worthless, damn, damn, damn!

He tried to defuse his anger with the thought that the ranger's arrival had been random, unexpected. But this seemed to him to be the stuff of excuse, which was distasteful. I always get the shot, he said to himself. I always get it.

He pounded his hands against the steering wheel and thrashed about sharply in his seat, barely maintaining control over the car, even at a slow speed. He wanted to scream, but was unable. Then he remembered Anne Hampton tied in the motel room. Let her wait, he told himself angrily. Let her worry. Let her suffer.

Let her die.

He inhaled sharply and held his breath for a moment.

He was surprised that these harsh thoughts left him slightly uncomfortable.

He pulled the car to the side of a deserted street in a warehouse district. He put his head back and suddenly felt tired.

It wasn't her damn fault. It was yours. She did what you asked of her.

He closed his eyes.

Damn. The plan was faulty.

He sighed. Well, it just goes to show: nobody's perfect.

His anger fled him suddenly and he rolled down the window, letting the stale air of the car mingle with the dark cool of the night.

He laughed out loud. The laughter turned to a childish giggle. Nobody's perfect, he thought. Right.

But you're pretty damn close.

He thought of the two women cavorting about in the nude. You didn't have to kill them, he realized. They will probably die quickly from boredom and stupidity and routine lives that promise nothing and deliver less. What was truly hilarious, he imagined at that second, was that they had just experienced the most unique, exciting, and dangerous moment that they would ever have, regardless of how long they lived. For one sublime afternoon they had come into contact with genius and managed to live through it. And the sows didn't know it.

He laughed again. Exhaustion crept inside him and he realized that it was important to get some sleep. Well, he thought, everything is still on track. A nice easy drive to New Hampshire in the morning. He thought of taking her to Mount Monadnock or Lake Winnipesaukee or some other nice spot before settling in for the evening. Something quiet and relaxing. He considered a town he knew in Vermont. Out of the way, but beautiful—and still a quick drive to the appointment in New Hampshire. Then a little bit of business before the drive down to the Cape.

His mind filled suddenly with rolling, thick, swelling electronically synthesized music and a picture of the grinning actor wearing the white jumpsuit, black bowler, parachute boots, and fake proboscis. A little bit of the old ultraviolence, he said to himself. Real horror show.

And then freedom.

He thought of Anne Hampton again. Boswell is probably scared out of her wits. He shrugged. That wasn't terrible; it was wise to keep her off-balance.

But he still felt a twinge of guilt.

Let her up to breathe, he thought. She remains necessary.

That gave him a sense of purpose, and he searched about himself briefly, getting his bearings, ready to head directly back to the motel. He started to consider how he would apologize to her. As he was about to put the car in gear and leave, he spotted the van parked two hundred yards down the street. He knew instantly what it was: Warehouse. Outside of regular police patrol areas. After midnight. Van. It was a simple equation, the sum of which added into breaking and entering. An idea struck him and he smiled.

No, he said to himself.

Then: Why not?

He wanted to burst out laughing, but he cautioned himself: Be careful.

He did not turn the lights on, rolling the car as quietly as possible down toward the van. It was light-colored and suitably battered and nondescript. He could see no movement from the truck, but he kept his pistol in his hand just in case. When he was next to the van, a distant streetlight threw just enough illumination so he was able to make out the license plate number. He paused, noting the doorjamb on the warehouse door that seemed sprung, though it was difficult for him to tell without getting out of the car. This he was wise enough not to do. Not that he feared the man or men inside, but then he would lose the element of surprise. He rolled past, not turning on his headlights until he reached a spot a couple of blocks away.

He stopped at the first gas station with a pay phone and dialed 911.

"Bridgeport police, fire and rescue," came the flat voice with its studied indifference to emergency.

"I want to report a break-in in progress," replied Douglas Jeffers.

"Is it happening right now?"

"That's what I said," Jeffers insisted, with just the right amount of indignation. "Right now." He gave the policeman the address and a description of the van and license plate number.

"Thank you. We're rolling. Can I have your name for our files?"

"No," said Douglas Jeffers. "Just consider me a concerned citizen." He hung up the phone. A concerned citizen: he liked that a lot. If they only knew, he thought. He envisioned a pair of robbers, dressed in dark clothes, surprised suddenly by the lights from a police cruiser. He imagined them cursing their luck, rattling their handcuffs in frustration as the police officers passed on those small moments of congratulation and success that accompany a good arrest. If they had any idea who it was that tipped them. Either the good guys or the bad guys. Imagine the looks on their faces.

Then he laughed wildly at the sheer outrage of it all.

Anne Hampton heard the key in the door lock and she stiffened against the ropes. From where she lay, she could not see the door, but she heard it creak as it opened. She made a muffled sound through the gag and tape as the door closed and footsteps approached her. She lifted her head so that her eyes could meet Douglas Jeffers'. She had concentrated hard to remove the weak animal fear that she felt within and replace it with an obstinate, defiant, demanding look. Their eyes met, and Jeffers seemed surprised.

"Well," he said, "Boswell seems angry."

He reached down and tore the tape from her mouth. The ripping sound made her think that her lips and cheeks were cut. She held herself motionless while he loosened the gag.

"Better?" he asked.

"Much. Thank you." She kept her voice even and slightly irate. Douglas Jeffers laughed.

"Boswell is angry."

"No," she said. "Just uncomfortable."

"That's to be expected. Are you hurt?"

She shook her head.

"Just stiff."

"Well, let's do something about that."

Douglas Jeffers produced a knife. She could see the blade reflecting the light from the bedside lamp. She breathed in hard, thinking, Boswell, Boswell, he called you Boswell, you have nothing to fear. Not yet, not yet.

He placed the blade flat against her cheek.

"Have you ever noticed how hard it is to tell whether a knife is hot or cold? It depends on what kind of fear you're experiencing. The touch can seem red-hot or ice-cold, just like the feeling in your stomach and around your heart."

She didn't move. She stared ahead.

After a moment he pulled the blade away.

He started to cut the rope and her hands came free.

"I shouldn't have struck you," he said matter-of-factly. "It wasn't your fault."

She didn't reply.

"Just call it a moment of weakness." He paused. "A rare moment."

He helped her to her feet.

"There you go. A little unsteady, but not so bad. Use the bathroom to clean up."

She took a few uncertain steps, using the wall to help her maintain her balance. Inside the bathroom she saw that blood had clotted around her lips and nose, but that it washed away with some vigorous scrubbing. She felt all her exhaustion rush back, then, and she had to grip the edges of the sink to keep from collapsing.

When she came out, she saw that Douglas Jeffers had turned down the bed for her. She dropped her jeans to the floor and crawled in gratefully. He disappeared into the bathroom and she heard the water run, then the toilet flush. He came out and hopped into the other bed. He switched off the light and she felt the darkness wash over her like a wave at the beach.

He was silent for a moment, then he spoke:

"Boswell, have you ever thought how fragile life is?"

She didn't reply.

"It's not just the living that's so delicate, but the entirety of, I don't know, life's balance. Think of the mother who turns her back for an instant and whose child wanders into the roadway. Or the father who just doesn't bother, this one time, to fasten his seat belt on the way to work in the family car. Accidents. Disease. Bad luck. Death ends life for some, certainly. But worse, it unsettles. It throws the living off balance, out of whack. It disrupts their centers. Think of all the people you've known and who've loved you. Imagine for an instant what your death will mean to them . . ."

She closed her eyes and suddenly all her brave intentions vanished and she wanted to sob.

". . . Or what their death would mean to you. Emptiness. A certain vacuum space inside. Some memories that persist. Maybe a photo album, somewhere. A gravestone. Perhaps a once-a-year visit. We are all linked in so many ways, so dependent on the others to maintain our equilibrium. Sons and fathers. Daughters and mothers. Brothers. Sisters. Everything a tenuous relationship. Too many connections. Everything completely, delicately, chinalike fragile."

He paused, then repeated the word.

"Fragile. Fragile. Fragile."

Again he hesitated.

"I hate that more than anything," he said. His voice was filled with the barest of controls, defined by bitterness. "I hate that you don't choose who you are. I hate that you have no choices. I hate it, I hate it, I hate it, hate, hate, hate . . ."

In the darkness, Anne Hampton could see that Douglas Jeffers was lying on his back, but that both his fists were clenched in the air in front of him.

He exhaled sharply into the night.

"Everyone's a victim," he said. "Except me."

Then she heard him roll over and devote himself to sleep.

In the morning they drove north, finding Route 91 in New Haven, heading past Hartford into Massachusetts. She thought that Jeffers seemed to be acting with control again; he was watching his watch, measuring the distances, careful with his timing. That reassured her, and she relaxed, waiting for something new to happen.

They reached southern Vermont in the early afternoon, continuing north at a steady pace. Anne Hampton wondered, almost idly, whether they were going to Canada. She tried to recall any crimes from that nation, thinking, What could there be up there that he wants to show me? She was unable to remember any, but she was certain that people killed each other there. It's cold, she thought, it's frozen and dark and long winters must mean some horror or another emerges.

Before any other thought took root, Douglas Jeffers said, "There's a little town up here that you should see . . ."

He did not describe Woodstock further, preferring to drive a few hours in quiet. She will see for herself, he thought. He mentally reviewed the elements of the plan that remained. He wanted to check in his briefcase for the letter from the New Hampshire bank, but he knew that was unnecessary. They are expecting you in the morning, he said to himself. It will be quick and precise and the way things should be.

When he turned off the thruway toward the small town, he said, "Have you ever noticed that almost every one of these old New England states has a Woodstock? Vermont, New Hampshire, Massachusetts. Probably even Rhode Island, if they can squeeze it in. Rhode Island. They say: Rowdilan. Or NeHampsha. Of course the important Woodstock was New York's Woodstock and the festival that actually was held elsewhere. Do you remember it?"

"I was only a kid," she said. "I didn't know."

"I was there," Jeffers said.

"Really? Was it as big as the books say?"

He laughed.

"Actually, I wasn't there . . ."

She looked confused.

337

"There are certain common events that become common memories through popular culture. Woodstock was one of them. I knew a guy, once, in the newspaper business, who was the guy who created the Woodstock myth. He was just starting out, the college stringer for the New York *Daily News*. It was summertime, and so they asked him to go up to the festival, just in case something unusual happened. They had no idea that the crowds were going to be, well, like they were.

"Anyway, he went up the day before, to check on the festival preparations, which was real lucky, because by midmorning the next day, cars had backed up for ten or twenty miles. People were streaming in. Longhairs. Hippies. Bikers. College kids. You probably saw the movie. Anyway, as you know, it became this massive jam of music and people and suddenly a front-page story. So there was my buddy, sitting behind the stage, on the phone to the city desk at the *News* and there was some editor yelling at him, 'How many people are there? How many people?' and of course he had no fucking idea whatsoever. I mean, everywhere he turned there were people and trucks and helicopters buzzing the place and bands turning up the volume and you name it. And the editor yells, 'We need an official police estimate of the crowd!' so he runs over to some cop and asks what they're estimating in terms of crowd size, and of course the cop looks at him like he's totally berserk, and how the hell should they know. He goes back to the phone and the editor realizes suddenly it's his ass on the line because here's the biggest story to come down the pike in some time and he was stupid enough to send some college stringer up to cover it and he can't get a real reporter in because the roads are jammed and there aren't any more helicopters for rent because the damn television stations have grabbed them all.

"And my buddy has this inspiration. He decides to lie. He yells into the phone, 'Police are estimating more than a half-million people have descended upon this sleepy burg. Suddenly Woodstock is the third-largest city in New York State!' And this the editor loves. Just loves. Because it's the front-page screamer for the next morning. After the *News* put the figure on the front page, the *Times* picked it up and then the AP, and that meant the world. And suddenly my buddy's lie becomes historical fact . . ."

He snapped his fingers.

"Just like that. And everybody got happy and everybody always assumes that's how many people were there. Just because my buddy had the good sense to lie to someone who desperately wanted to hear a lie."

Douglas Jeffers paused. His voice, as so many times before,

seemed to ratchet between a schoolboyish storytelling delight and some ominous hatred.

"So now I lie as well."

He grinned, then grimaced.

"I just say I was there. I mean, who's to check?"

Douglas Jeffers paused, and Anne Hampton saw that he'd diluted the lightheartedness of this story with some darker thought. She plucked out a notebook and scraped down a quick series of notes about Woodstock and a half-million people and some fellow her age plucking a figure from midair.

"You see, in a way, that's what we do in the news business. We create a commonality of experience. Who can say they weren't in Vietnam? The pictures invaded us. How about the Watts riot? Or get more current: Beirut. The Mexico City quake. The TWA hijacking. They held a press conference, if you can believe it. The final answer in absurdity. Criminals in the midst of a crime seeking publicity and receiving it. And we were all there, right there, right with them. It depends, it depends."

He hesitated again.

"The news business is like the old saw about the tree falling in the forest. If no one's around to hear it, did it make a sound? If a thousand Indians die in the rain forest, but we don't report it, did it happen?"

Jeffers laughed out loud. His first burst was one of anger, then followed one of release.

"I am sometimes so boring I'm surprised you haven't killed me."

He laughed again.

She knew she wore a stricken look.

"Lighten up, Boswell, we're near the end. That was a joke."

He smiled.

"Or was it? Poor Boswell. Sometimes she doesn't think my jokes are at all humorous. And I can't say that I blame her. But indulge me with a smile, a little bit of laughter, please."

This last was a demand.

She complied instantly. She thought the sound sickening.

"Not much of an effort, Boswell, but appreciated nonetheless."

He paused.

"Work on it, Boswell. Work on all those little things we do in life that remind us of who we are. Concentrate, Boswell. I think, therefore, I am. I laugh, therefore I am . . ."

". . . If I laugh, I breathe. If I smile, I feel. If I think, I exist."

He fixed his eyes on the road.

"Boswell lives on," he said.

She felt her heart tighten with despair.

"But so does Douglas Jeffers."

He looked down the highway, turning onto a small two-lane road. Evening was sliding up on them; the rich greens and browns of the Vermont hills flowed about the car, the shadowed darkness broken by the occasional wan shaft of late daylight. They passed by the Quechee Gorge, which is on the road to Woodstock, and he saw Anne Hampton crane her head to see the precipitous drop from the car.

He cruised through the quiet streets. Anne Hampton saw trim white clapboard houses behind wide lawns with gazebos that had clinging vines next to small flower gardens.

"You see," he said, pointing toward a stark white church that rose up against the green darkness of the Vermont night. "You see how relaxing it all is? Who would think that such terror was abroad at night in such a little safe town?"

He parked the car.

"Well," he said, "even terror gets hungry."

He looked at Anne Hampton.

"Another joke," he said.

She forced a smile.

"But the best humor is always based on reality."

He took her hand and led her into a restaurant. It was candlelit and lovely, glowing with a golden warmth. She could smell food cooking, the mingled sensations pouring over her palate. It all made her nauseated.

What is happening? she wondered.

What is going on?

Why are we here?

Why is everything in the world so normal when it isn't?

What is happening to me!

This last thought screamed through her head. She could barely keep from collapsing. I'm standing, waiting to be seated in an elegant restaurant in a beautiful town. Everything is backwards. Everything is wrong. What's going on?

Again she felt sick to her stomach.

"I could eat a horse," said Douglas Jeffers.

They ate quietly, efficiently, joylessly. Jeffers ordered wine, and he sipped from the goblet, staring over the edge at Anne Hampton. She could see the light reflected in the glass.

After he'd paid, Douglas Jeffers took Anne Hampton's arm and led her through the darkness around the town common. He felt her shiver. The warmth had fled the day, replacing the air with Vermont's promise of autumn.

"Quiet," he said. "Peaceful."

She felt no sense of relaxation. It was all she could do to keep her arm loosely on his. She wanted to grab him and scream: What next?

But she didn't.

He led her back to the car. Within a few moments they were enmeshed by darkness on the backroads of the state, heading toward the interstate. Douglas Jeffers was driving slowly, obviously thinking, his concentration diminished by the wine, a full stomach, and his plans.

He started to say, "I know a couple of nice inns, down the road a little ways . . ."

A sudden car horn shattered his words and bright lights filled their car.

He pulled abruptly to the gravel shoulder, the car swerving sickeningly as another car roared past. She thought that the other car was somehow inside theirs and she shouted out some sound of half-fear and warning.

She caught her breath sharply and cried, "Watch out! Oh, my gosh!"

She was aware of the terrifying closeness of the other car. Then she heard a pair of voices yelling in the night and saw the taillights of a jeep roar past. It was a hopped-up model, with fat tires and bright paint, a roll bar, and two kids hanging out the side, gesturing wildly.

Jeffers was cursing uncontrollably.

"Teenagers!" Douglas Jeffers said angrily, his voice a runaway cacophony of rage and relief. "Must be a week or so before school starts and they're blowing off steam. Christ, I almost dumped the car . . ." He gestured toward the side of the road. "I know this road. Damn! It drops off sharply over there. Down an embankment and into a little river. Christ, we'd have been killed. The little bastards. Christ. Out joyriding on a Monday night, for crying out loud. They could have killed us."

He continued driving at his slow pace.

"Are you okay?" he asked.

"Oh, sure," she replied. "But they scared the daylights out of me."

"It was my fault," he said apologetically. "I should have seen them coming up behind us so fast. Sorry."

He smiled. "They scared me, too."

He held out his hand, holding it palm down, horizontally.

"Look at that. A little shake. Nerves, I guess."

He smiled again.

"I suppose it means that regardless of who you are, an auto accident that just barely doesn't happen still gets to you. A moment of complete fear, then life goes back to its own petty pace."

After a moment he added, "There is nothing, nothing, as obnoxious as a teenage boy with a car and confidence and a little bit of booze. Christ, they act like they own the world. Immortal. Boy, did that piss me off."

Then he laughed. "And it makes me feel old."

The darkness ahead on the road was interrupted by the luminous presence of a gas station. As they drove past, both Anne Hampton and Douglas Jeffers saw the jeep parked at the pumps.

"Look," she said, almost inadvertently. "There they are." She could see two boys, backs to them, standing by the soft-drink machine. Both were tall and thin and wore baseball caps and slouched with a natural insouciance and rebellion.

Jeffers drove deliberately past the station. After a quarter mile he accelerated sharply, throwing her back in her seat. She reached out to steady herself.

"I have an idea," he said. "The classic highway fantasy."

His voice was suddenly suffused with excitement.

"There's an interesting spot up ahead," he said. "Where the road forks and one side heads down a small ravine, next to the interstate."

In seconds they'd reached the fork. He took the upper half, and, after a hundred yards, slowed. He found a dark turnout and parked the car.

"Now," he said. "We'll see if luck's with us. You don't move."

Again command entered his voice. She didn't even twitch.

Douglas Jeffers raced to the back of the car and flung open the trunk. His hand reached out and seized the polished steel of the Ruger semiautomatic rifle. He rummaged about amidst the other weapons until he found the clip of nine long shells. He slid the clip into the gun, feeling the satisfying click as it locked into place.

Jeffers left the rifle on top in the open trunk and searched for a moment until he found a long, cylindrical leather case. He grabbed this and turned, jogging back down the road. As he ran, he sharpened his eyes, trying to pluck shapes from the black of the night. He surveyed the area, looking for any sign of life. He peered into the darkness, looking for the telltale sweep of headlights in the distance. He concentrated his hearing, trying to find some sound that might indicate the presence of another person or of a vehicle heading in his direction. All was silent save for a slight rustle of wind in a nearby stand of pine trees. He looked off into the distance, toward the ravine, and tried to hear the sound of the water rushing through the bottom. He suddenly remembered the childhood adage: If you want to be able to see at night, eat lots of carrots. I ate lots of carrots. All the time. And my night vision is fine. But it is a lot finer when I use a night starlight scope.

He opened the leather case and held the cylinder up to his eye. It made the landscape a dirty green, and he swept it about to satisfy himself that his senses had not lied. He was alone. He thought that he must have appeared for all the world to be like some ancient and abandoned mariner, desperately searching for land. He peered down the roadway, into the distance.

"Aha," he said out loud. "Company comes calling."

He saw the fancy jeep moving erratically through the night.

"Well, well, well, will wonders never cease."

The vista remained deserted save for him and the approaching vehicle. He envisioned the two teenagers in the jeep, laughing, heads thrown back in the rush of wind through the open sides and convertible top. The stereo would be thumping, he thought, and their attention will be stripped by a couple of beers. He turned and rushed back to his own car. He saw Anne Hampton's face through the window, watching him. He could see her shrink into the seat, beaten down by the force of action. He moved quickly, but deliberately, grabbing the rifle and feeling its heft in his hands. Nothing is as comforting in one's arms as a rifle, he thought. He hurried back through the pitch-black night toward his vantage point, slightly hunched over, but assured, like a veteran soldier evading small-arms fire.

He glanced about himself quickly one last time to be certain of his solitude. He thought of Anne Hampton in the car, then shut her away. He lifted the rifle to his cheek and brought the sight to bear between the front headlights of the jeep, tracking it carefully.

"Take the bottom trail," he commanded.

They did.

He was impressed with the almost electrical connection that linked him, his finger on the trigger, and the target in his sights. He snugged the gun up against his cheek, caressing the trigger with his finger.

"Good night, boys," he said.

He fired seven shots. The cracking sound seemed to him

oddly heavenly, as if the rifle were being held up in the dark sky, sighting down some minuscule shaft of light from a star.

As he lowered the weapon, he saw the jeep start to swerve, battling for purchase on the roadway. He could hear nothing, though, save the echoing of the gunshots. The sound was like the music one hears in one's head from an oft-recalled song. He suddenly remembered a moment in Nicaragua—or was it Vietnam?—when he'd turned at the stolid sound of a rocket-propelled grenade bouncing into a jeep. There had been an explosion and he'd lifted his camera swiftly, firing the shutter as he focused, trying to catch the great ball of fire and shattered bodies pitching through the air. He remembered how little he'd heard then. No screams, no explosions, no cries for help, just the brother noises of the shutter and the autodrive. He started to lift his rifle, then realized that it wasn't a camera and let it rest.

The jeep flipped onto its side. He knew that it was screeching with the sound of twisting metal and complaining tires. He saw it thud toward the edge of the ravine, like some dying dinosaur seeking the refuge of dark waters. He thought of the millisecond of time after touching the first domino before it leans up against the next in line.

Then the jeep rolled over, disappearing into the black.

He could no longer envision the teenagers inside.

He turned away, knowing that it had slammed into the bottom. He felt a complete satisfaction. He did not turn around when he felt the shock wave from the explosion. He saw Anne Hampton's face in the car, horrified, her eyes catching the glow of flames from behind him. He walked toward the car with the steady discipline of Lot.

He dropped the rifle in the trunk and slammed it shut.

Jeffers moved behind the wheel and deliberately put the car in gear and accelerated away gently. Within a few moments they swept around first one dark turn in the road, then another.

Anne Hampton swiveled in her seat and shivered.

"I told you," Douglas Jeffers said. "The ultimate highway fantasy."

She threw one more quick glance back and thought she could see the glow from the wreck. She turned away and saw the signs for the interstate. Hurry, she thought. Get us away from here. Please.

Jeffers maneuvered the car through the ramps and accelerated on the thruway. "We are," he said, "a nation of assassins and snipers. John Wilkes Booth and Lee Harvey Oswald. Charles

Whitman and the Texas Tower. We have a great and storied tradition of ambush."

"They didn't have a . . ."

"Not really. That's what's important in an assassination. An X-ambush. An L-ambush. Think of it. Bushwacked. Drygulched. Nowhere to run. Nowhere to turn. Nowhere to hide. That's the point of the entire exercise."

She did not reply. Nowhere, she thought. She watched the headlights peel away a sliver of light from the darkness. Sixty miles per hour. A mile a minute. Every second takes us farther.

"Where are we going?" she asked.

She knew the answer: All the way to the end.

"The Granite State," Jeffers replied. "Luckily, our little adventure took place in Vermont. And by the time anybody figures out what happened, which they won't, by the way, we'll be history. What a shot," he said. He seemed suffused with excitement. "What a shot. Damn! And you know what the cops will think? Nothing. They'll find some beer cans in the jeep and that's that. An accident, until someone thinks twice. Out of sight, out of mind. And who would suspect a nice-looking pair of tourists, anyway?"

He sang: "We'll be gone, gone, gone . . ."

"Why Vermont?" she asked hesitantly. "Can't you kill anyone in New Hampshire?"

"Well," he laughed, "the Devil had a bit of unpleasantness in Marshfield a few centuries back. And since then he keeps his works in the neighboring states. As per agreement, of course. And so I follow suit."

He smiled.

"But that doesn't mean we can't pay a little visit."

He drove on.

The morning sun was strong and Anne Hampton shielded her eyes. For an instant it reminded her of Florida, and she looked about her for a palm tree clattering in the light breeze. She stared down the main street of Jaffrey, New Hampshire, and wondered whether she had dreamed everything. She tried to pick out specifics from her memory; there was the fear, when they'd almost been driven off the road; there was the darkness on the bend; Jeffers walking with the rifle into the deep black; the cracking sound followed by the nauseating muffled roar of the car exploding. She examined each facet of her recollection like a jeweler assessing a precious stone. Surely, she thought, there was some flaw that would show her that it hadn't happened, something to show that this was a dream, a fake, a piece of cut glass refracting light.

She shook her head and forced order on her memory.

Of course it wasn't a dream, she said to herself. She thought of her night, tossing on sweat-soaked sheets. The dreams are much worse.

She turned and peered through the plate-glass window of the delicatessen. She could see Jeffers at the cash register, paying for coffee and doughnuts. She watched as he pocketed his change and sauntered from the store. As always, she felt amazement. He was whistling, unencumbered by anything so mundane as fear or guilt.

"I got you the jelly kind," he said as he slipped into the car. "And coffee and juice."

He gestured toward the town. "Pretty, huh? Filled with antiques and outlet stores. *Yankee* magazine always has pictures of Jaffrey. Happy white women standing in front of tables heaped high with freshly baked goods. Calico. This is a calico town. Calico and ragg wool in the winter. Not the kind of place where anyone would notice a visiting couple driving a car with out-of-state plates."

He rolled down the window.

"It's going to be a scorcher," he said. "Late summer up here is completely unpredictable. A little Canadian air tumbles in one day and it'll snow. Then the cross-country currents bring something humid up from the South on the next, and it hits a hundred." He took sunglasses from his pocket and cleaned them on his shirttail. She felt the heat entering the car, penetrating her, almost sensual. She sipped the coffee as Jeffers opened a newspaper. He scanned the pages rapidly.

"No, no, no, see, I told you so, aha! Here's something."

He paused, reading. Then he read out loud:

"Two killed in Vermont crash. A pair of Lebanon teenagers were killed Monday night when their four-wheel-drive car failed to negotiate a curve on a back road four miles from Woodstock, Vermont. Police suspect that the youths, Daniel Wilson, seventeen, and Randy Mitchell, eighteen, had been drinking prior to the nine-forty-five crash at the juncture of State Road eighty-two and Ravine Drive . . ."

He looked over at Anne Hampton.

"I could go on. There's a couple more paragraphs."

She didn't reply. She drank her coffee and savored the bitter taste.

"No? I didn't think so."

He dropped the paper on her lap. "Read it for yourself."

She sat up sharply when she heard the edge in his voice.

"Now, I have business. I want you to wait in the car."

She nodded rapidly.

"Good. It's almost ten. I should be about an hour."

Jeffers seized his briefcase and left. She watched him walk across the street and into the New Hampshire National Bank. She felt a momentary panic, looking about wildly, thinking: He's going to rob a bank! Then she recognized that she was being foolish. She settled back in the seat and waited. The idea of escape did not occur to her, even when a police car rolled past. That she could rise up and flag down a patrolman and end it for herself seemed simplistic and impossible. She had no confidence in some obvious and easy dénouement. She knew that she was still powerless; that Douglas Jeffers pulled all the strings for the two of them. So, instead, she thought only of the moment, letting the building heat around her take over her imagination. She wondered what would happen next, and she closed her eyes to the outside world, looking inwardly, thinking: Find some strength. She inspected her heart for bravery, wondering whether there was any there. She knew she would need it to survive.

The bank was cool and dark inside, and Douglas Jeffers removed his sunglasses slowly. It was an old-fashioned building, with high ceilings and polished floors that made shoe heels click. Jeffers walked over to a section of desks where the bank officers worked. A secretary looked up at him, smiling.

"Miss Mansour, please. Douglas Allen. I have an appointment."

The young woman nodded and picked up her telephone. Jeffers saw a middle-aged, open-faced woman at the rear desk pick up her receiver and listen. In a moment he had shaken hands with the woman and was seated at a chair next to her desk. She pulled out a folder with the name written on the top.

"Now, Mr. Allen, we hate to see a longtime customer depart. How many years has it been . . ."

"Ten."

"Is there any way we can help you? Perhaps at establishing a new account at your. . ." She hesitated.

"Atlanta," he said. "Company transfer."

"I mean, I'd be happy to call someone . . ."

He shook his head. "So kind of you," he said. "But the relocation service with the firm handles most of those things. But I will take your card, and if there's any problem I could have someone call you?"

"That would be fine." She checked out the forms. "Now, in your letter you said you wanted the account closed and the funds in traveler's checks. I have those waiting for you. So all you have to do is sign them and then sign this closure statement and then clear out the safety deposit box, hand me the key, and you're all set."

She handed him a stack of traveler's checks and he started signing. He looked down at the name and mentally rolled it about. For ten years, he thought, here in New Hampshire I've been Douglas Allen. No more limitations. No more pretenses. We shall expand our horizons.

"Please count them," Miss Mansour said. "It's over twenty thousand dollars."

Spare funds from a decade, he thought. Compounded daily.

He followed her into the safety deposit area, and she handed him his key. "Just bring both keys back after you're finished," she said. "I'll be at my desk."

He nodded thanks and went into a cubicle. A secretary brought him the locked box and then closed the door behind her. He hesitated, reveling inwardly in the ease of the plan.

He opened the box.

"Goodbye, Douglas Jeffers," he said.

On top was the old copy of the defunct *New Times* magazine that had been the germ of the idea. He flipped the worn pages open to the article. He thought it ironic that the piece had been prompted by the activism of the sixties and seventies. It had seemed such a simple premise: How easy was it to go underground? How hard was it to establish another identity? The answer was: Not very. Particularly in a state such as New Hampshire, with its dogged emphasis on individual freedoms and privacy. He'd followed the article's path religiously, from obtaining a Social Security number, to opening a post office box, to giving himself an address. Then the bank account and a pair of credit cards, used only enough to keep them active. At the same time that he'd established credit, he'd obtained his driver's license under his new name and Social Security number. His greatest triumph, however, had occurred after he'd doctored his own birth certificate into his new name. The wonders of modern copying machines, he thought. When he'd presented the battered copy, along with all his other documents, at the local post office, no one had raised a word in protest. Six weeks later, in the mail, arrived his most prized possession. He lifted it from the box. A brand new US passport in the name of Douglas Allen. No fake, no forgery.

He stuck it in his briefcase along with the driver's license, credit cards, and Social Security card.

I'm free, he thought.

He laughed to himself. Well, not completely. I can't go to Albania or North Vietnam.

He stuffed his emergency cash reserve, several thousand dollars in twenties and hundreds, into his pants. He checked his ticket, which lay in the bottom of the box. It was a first-class airplane ticket, open date, one-way, New York to Tokyo. He knew that from Tokyo he could easily backtrack to wherever he wanted, instantly losing himself in the Far East. Sydney, he thought. Perth. Melbourne. The names seemed exotic yet oddly familiar. It'll be like going home. The last item in the safety deposit box was a clean, blue-steel .357 Magnum revolver, which also went into his briefcase. He had purchased it in Florida several years beforehand, just weeks prior to the time the state legislature passed a new, slightly restrictive gun law. Then, conveniently, he had reported it stolen. Thank God, he thought, for the NRA. For an instant he stared at the empty safety deposit box and thought how comforting it had been to know everything was there, just in case he'd ever needed it. My emergency outlet.

He sat back in the chair. Australia, he said to himself. A wonderful place to start over. Tie me kangaroo down, sport.

He hummed "Waltzing Matilda" to himself as he walked back to Miss Mansour's desk.

"All set?" she asked cheerfully.

"All in order," he replied.

He signed some papers. He looked down at his signature and felt comfortable with it. Hello, he said to himself. Glad to meet you. And what was it you said you did for a living? Anything you liked. Anything at all.

The sunlight hit him as he exited the darkness of the bank, and it took a moment for his eyes to readjust. He picked out the sight of Anne Hampton sitting in the car, waiting. Not much longer, Boswell.

Humming pleasantly to himself, he crossed the street. He nodded to an elderly lady who walked past him, and said good morning to a pair of young boys, probably no older than six or seven, savoring their final days before school started with a set of chocolate ice cream cones.

Anne Hampton looked up at him as he returned to the car.

"Let's go to the beach," he said.

Much of the day she dozed as Douglas Jeffers drove across Massachusetts toward Cape Cod. He seemed preoccupied, but in a carefree fashion. He turned on the radio and found a station that played sixties rock and roll, which he told her was the only music worth listening to on the radio. He insisted in a lighthearted way that the only musician he would pay any attention to whatsoever was the guy from New Jersey, and that was because he behaved like a refugee from two decades back. He told her about the one time he'd been assigned to get some pictures at a rock concert. "Only time I was ever really afraid for my life. They had us down in front of the stage and when these four guys in leotard pants, glitter makeup, and feather boas, for Christ's sake, strutted out, everyone behind the barricades in back of us pushed forward. I thought I was going to be crushed by a phalanx of teary-eyed adolescents. All the cameramen were fighting for air and space and I looked up and saw this one guy with blond hair down to his ass and beady eyes waving his arms, whooping it up, encouraging the crowd. Death by rock and roll..." Douglas Jeffers laughed. "There I was, getting pushed back against the stage, no room to move, screaming kids everywhere, and all I could think about was it was what our parents warned us against. A commie plot. At least it seemed so at the time."

He drove leisurely, letting the other cars slide past. She thought he seemed in no rush, yet he was clearly keeping to a schedule.

The afternoon was fading when they reached the turnoff for Route 6, which meanders up Cape Cod. She had never seen the Cape before, and looked carefully at the rows of battered antique stores, saltwater-taffy shops, and tee-shirt emporiums that mixed with fast-food restaurants and gas stations by the side of the road.

"I don't understand," she said. "I thought Cape Cod was supposed to be beautiful."

"It is," Jeffers replied. "At least where we're headed it is. But no one ever said the road there was beautiful. And it isn't. In fact, it sets some kind of world record for ugliness."

They passed over the Bourne Bridge in the day's last light. Anne Hampton could see barges far beneath them, moving steadily down the canal. There was a rotary ahead, and Jeffers made jokes about the free-for-all, survival-of-the-fittest element to driving in the state of Massachusetts. They ate a quick dinner at a diner in Falmouth, then proceeded down the road to the Woods Hole Ferry dock. She could see a Coast Guard cutter's bright white paint gleaming in the darkness. The ferry itself was bathed in light from mingled streetlamps and car headlights. There was a row of cars lined up on the street and a teenager in a baseball cap carrying a walkie-talkie. Jeffers rolled down the window.

"I have a reservation on the eight-thirty boat," he said.

"Great," said the teenager. Anne Hampton thought he probably looked exactly like the young men they'd seen the night before. "Just pull in behind the station wagon."

Jeffers drove down. Another teenager came up and he produced tickets.

"You know what I've always loved about this ferry?" he asked. He didn't wait for her acknowledgement. "It has this perfectly functional design. The boat has no front, no back. That's to say, the front is like the back. You drive on in Woods Hole, drive off in Vineyard Haven. It has the same big old opening on either end. The boat just yo-yos between the two docks."

She looked over and watched people stream in and out of the squat ferry office adjacent to the dock. She saw a line of bicyclists with backpacks move to the front of the line of cars. She could see boat handlers waving vehicles into an opening on the ferry, which loomed up stark white and black against the evening sky. She could not see the open water from where she sat, but she sensed the sea in the air that tumbled through Jeffers' window.

"Where . . ."

"The island of Martha's Vineyard," he said. "Summer home to the upscale. Old money, new money, all dressed down in jeans and work shirts. It's where they filmed *Jaws* . . ." He started to mimic the ominously familiar music. "All sorts of Kennedys, too. You remember when Teddy swam from Chappaquiddick to Edgartown? At least he said he did. Jackie O has a place and so does Walter Cronkite, half the staff of the New York *Times*, and more poets and novelists per square foot than you can count. John Belushi owned a house in Chilmark for about five minutes before he managed to get himself killed in L.A. and now he's buried there. A striking place called Abel's Hill. Kids go to the graveyard all the time. It's a very benign island," Jeffers said. "Filled with East Coast elite sophistication. It's quiet, pleasant, beautiful, and relaxed. The islander's idea of controversy would be a shortage of swordfish steaks or too many mopeds on the roads. It's friendly, and filled with appreciation of the nicer things available to anyone with scads of money, wrapped up in this faded-blue-demin approach to day-to-day life. Lots of beautiful people living in intellectual harmony. From June first through Labor Day."

He hesitated.

"The perfect place for something unspeakably unsettling."

Jeffers drove the car in a haphazard course around the island, slicing through the narrow, unlit roads. The headlights tore bizarre shapes from the light fog and overhanging trees. Around one corner they came up upon a Great Horned Owl feeding on some muskrat or rabbit that had failed to maneuver the road successfully. The bird's huge white wings spread out abruptly, and it cried in irritation at the unruly interruption. It seemed to rise ghostlike in front of them right over the hood of the car, and for an instant she thought they would collide and she gasped in a sudden fear that penetrated her exhaustion.

She did not know what time it was, but she knew it was past midnight, crawling into morning. Jeffers seemed indefatiguable, his adrenaline coursing, his voice alert, bantering.

He drove back and forth across the island several times, thoroughly confusing Anne Hampton, despite the fact that he kept up a running travelogue throughout. He would point at different locations and link them with memories, like any person visiting a favored spot after many years. She tried taking some notes, but found that his attention ricocheted from one mundane recollection to another. None had anything to do with death or dying. Instead, he talked about the best place to find wild blueberries, or the secret paths down to the nicest beaches on the island. He drove her out to the Gay Head cliffs and let her stand up by the edge, looking out toward the ocean. She could see white foam where the waves pounded up onto the beach, and even in the darkness could make out the steady movement of big rollers on the black sea. There was a steady breeze that pushed against her face and she felt it restoring her. But the height made her dizzy and for an instant she fantasized tumbling down over the great red and gray cliffs, spinning into oblivion. She felt his hand on her arm, and she saw he was pointing out into the deep ocean night.

"Out there," he said, "is an island called No Man's Land, where the Navy tests weapons. You can see it on a clear day, and if the wind is right occasionally you can hear the thump thump of high explosives. I've always wanted to go there, ever since I was a kid. Not because of the practice runs the Navy makes, which are interesting, sometimes you can see the jet vapors, but to see what it looks like after being bombed so steadily for so many years. Like some vision of the future, I think . . .

"Never went, though. Got pretty close once, when I was a kid and we went out fishing for blues. We were in some pretty good action, when all of a sudden there was this Coast Guard helicopter hovering overhead, telling us to get the hell out of there."

He laughed.

"We obeyed."

"Did you come here often?" she asked.

"A bunch of summers when I was a kid. We stopped after, well, when I was a teenager."

He looked about.

"It's changed. It's the same, yet different. Some new things. Lots of old things. There's steadiness, continuity. But growth, too."

He laughed again.

"Everything changes. Everything stays the same. Like life."

He thought of the passport, air ticket, and money waiting in his briefcase. Like me.

They got back into the car and he slowly headed back into the center of the island. She did not dare ask about plans or accommodations.

Jeffers wondered why, instead of his usual rigid delight, he felt a sort of leisurely pleasure, almost a lassitude. He felt a headiness, like having drunk too much of some excellent wine, not stumbling drunk, but giddy. After adhering so strictly to ideas and concepts, having planned right down to the ferry tickets on and off, now he was in no rush. He thought he wanted to savor this last act, draw it out. He felt a rush of blood through his veins, warm, exciting. He listened to his own heart, and thought that it was going to prove to be hard to say goodbye to his old identity. But—he smiled inwardly—think of the creation of the new.

They passed through the tiny town of West Tisbury and Jeffers summoned himself to attention. Not far now, he thought. He tightened himself mentally, concentrating on the problems at hand.

Anne Hampton looked over at Jeffers and saw that he was suddenly paying close attention. He had hunched forward in the seat slightly, and she knew that this meant something was going to happen. It caused her body to stiffen and she moved to the edge of her seat. He had said so much about an ending, and, she thought, now it is starting. She could feel her own sleepiness flee her, and she marshaled her emotions like a military reserve being held in check for that critical moment in any battle when victory and defeat are held in balance.

Jeffers turned down a sandy secondary road and immediately they were bumping along a washboard dirt single-line trail. The scrub bushes and gnarled trees of the island seemed to envelop them in a tunnel, and she felt immediately as if they had stepped from civilization into some wilder, prehistoric place. The car pitched and yawned as he steered it slowly down the road. Occasionally the tires spun briefly in sand, and the cockpit was filled with the scratching, screeching noise of bushes rubbing against the car sides. After traveling what she guessed was more than a bumpy mile, deeper into the beech forest, they arrived at a juncture of four tiny roads. There were a few small arrows in various colors pointing down the alternate routes. The dirt roads seemed ever smaller, tighter, and darker.

"The arrows are for the different homes," Jeffers explained. "It's precious. You have to know the right color to get the right house. Otherwise you end up on the wrong side of the pond."

He steered down the left-hand fork.

The yawning and bumping of the car started to make her nauseated. She tried to see through the overhanding branches and she caught a glimpse of the moon, high in the sky.

They traveled another ten minutes. At least a mile, she thought. Perhaps farther.

Then, as if by some stroke of a knife, they passed out of the forest into an open area. Jeffers doused the car lights as they emerged from the trees, steering the car slowly by the moonlight.

She could see off to her right a wide expanse of water.

"That's the pond," Jeffers said. "Pond isn't a good word. It's actually as big as a lake and as deep as one." He stopped the car and rolled down the window. "Listen," he said.

She could hear the surf pounding on the shoreline in the distance.

"The pond separates the houses from the beach," he said. "We used to have to take a little motorboat or a rowboat over. A lot of people used little sailboats. Canoes, kayaks, windsurfers, too, I guess. Now, look carefully. See across there?"

He pointed over the pond.

"It's all wild land. The only person who lives out there is an old sheep farmer named Johnson. He's crazy. Literally. Steals motorboat engines from the summer people whose boats he doesn't like. He shoots his shotgun at folks who drive their cars on the sand dunes. Once he made a homemade land mine and tank trap for the kids and tourists who tried to use his road to get to the beach. The old bastard once chased me off his property at gunpoint. That was twenty years ago, but he hasn't changed a bit. He was discharged from the Army with a mental disability and it hasn't gotten any better. He's certifiable, but an old islander, so they let him get away with things. The summer people, of course, think he's quaint."

Jeffers paused. When he spoke again, it was with complete fury.

"They're going to blame him at first for what we do."

Then he pointed down the road.

"This land ends in a point that projects into the pond. Finger Point. A half mile down this road is a house. If you look carefully, you can just see the roof line. It's the only place out here. People pay great sums of money for the right kinds of isolation. Anyway, that's where we're going."

Jeffers abruptly rolled the window up and thrust the car into reverse. The car bumped wildly while he backed it into the forest. He spun the wheel sharply, sliding the car into a small turnoff that she hadn't noticed. Then he shut off the engine.

"All right," he said. "We're here. Wait."

Jeffers walked to the back of the car and seized the duffle bag where he kept the weapons. He opened the zipper and pulled out a pair of black workmen's coveralls and several other items. He slipped one of the set on, then put a pistol in the belt. He reloaded the rifle and chambered a round. Then he slung the duffel over his back.

"All right," he said. "Out of the car."

She complied instantly.

"Put this on."

She slid on the black coveralls and thought: I am part of the night.

He appraised her.

"Good. Good. You almost look the part. You just need this."

He handed her a small knit hat. She looked at it quizzically.

"Like this!" he said, his voice suddenly at the edge of rage. He stepped to her and grabbing the hat, thrust it on her head. Then, in a single, violent motion, he pulled the rolled brim down. It was a ski mask. She thought she might suffocate beneath the tight-fitting wool. She saw he'd pulled his down as well.

"Real horror show," he said. He turned and trotted down the road and she hurried to keep pace.

CHAPTER
THIRTEEN
AN IRREGULAR SESSION OF
THE LOST BOYS

18. DETECTIVE Mercedes Barren waited impatiently in Martin Jeffers' office, agonizing over lost time. She had trouble sitting; whenever she rested in a chair, she felt as if an angry impulse surged through her, reminding her that the killer wasn't waiting for her somewhere with his feet up on some desk. He's out there, she told herself, just past my reach. He's doing something. Her head flooded with the images she'd stolen from his apartment. She grimaced and thought: I'll never lose them. Those pictures will be with me forever.

She slowly rubbed her hands across her eyes and remembered a lecture from her first days at the police academy, when an FBI agent had come in, arms and pockets and head filled with crime statistics. He had used clock models and a steadily droning voice to demonstrate how often each armed robbery, each burglary, each murder took place in the United States. She thought: ten P.M., a ghetto crap game turns to knives; eleven P.M., a suburban couple's argument results in gunplay; midnight, Douglas Jeffers sweet-talks another woman into his car. She wanted to grab hold of something and shake it violently. She wanted to see something shatter and break. She wanted crashing noise. But all that surrounded her was a steady, infuriating silence, and she had to console herself by pacing around the room, fiddling with her papers, envisioning moments past and moments to come, trying to prepare herself mentally for confrontation.

It will happen, she told herself.

And I will be ready.

She thought of herself as a warrior preparing for battle.

Mercedes Barren remembered how Achilles had oiled his

body before his fight with Hector. He'd known he would win, because that was preordained, but known as well that his own demise was fast approaching, signaled by his victory that day. Then she dismissed the image: He won, but lost. That isn't what you intend. Knights in the Middle Ages would pray before a fight, imploring divine guidance, but you know what you have to do. No one, not even the heavens, needs to tell you. Of course, Roland was obstinate; he would not sound his horn, and it cost him his friend's life and his own, but he gained immortality. She smiled to herself: Bad idea. Then she asked herself: Are you any different? She refused herself an answer. She considered the rituals of the samurai and the ghost-dancing of the Plains Indians. The spirit filled them and they believed that the horse soldiers' bullets would pass right through them. Unfortunately they were right. The only problem was that the bullets took their lives, as well, which wasn't what had been advertised. Sitting Bull was old and wise, and knew this, but fought anyway.

She considered whether John Barren had done anything special before a fight. Had he dressed with any special care, like some superstitious athlete who wears the same socks every game so as not to upset the god that guides victories and prevents injuries? She imagined that he had; he was a romantic, filled with foolish ideas about chivalry and myth that probably penetrated even the muck and swamps of Vietnam. She smiled, recalling that when they had sent home his possessions, weeks after they'd sent back what remained of him, what made her eyes redden and tears flow freely was a dog-eared copy of *The Once and Future King*.

She wondered what he'd failed to do on the day he died. Was there some special charm or amulet that he'd neglected? Did he violate the order of dress in some small yet deadly way? What did he do to upset the delicate equilibrium of life?

She wondered too, whether he knew it, walking along beneath the sun, eyes wide, senses on edge, but aware in the recess of his mind that something was not right on this day that looked and smelled and sounded like every other day.

He would have shaken it off and marched on, she thought.

March on.

He would say to me: Do what you must. Do what is right.

She thrust her hands out in front of her.

They were steady.

She turned them over, looking at the palms. Dry.

It is time to get ready, she thought.

Then she clenched the hands into two solid, balled fists.

Choose the battle ground, she said, directing her mental energies at the ethereal Douglas Jeffers. Do something. Contact your brother.

She envisioned Martin Jeffers. She glanced at the wall clock. He's on his way to that damn group, she thought. I'm stuck here, waiting for him to remember something, or his brother to call, or the mail to arrive with a postcard that says: Hi! Having wonderful time! Wish you were here!

Fury filled her and she struggled around the office for the hundredth time, realizing how tenuous was her grasp on the brother, how dependent she was upon him and thus incapable of doing anything save the hardest, most impossible work of all, which is waiting.

Martin Jeffers stared out at the assembled men and saw that he had always been wrong, pitying them the weakness of their perversions when his acquiescence and unseeing impotence were infinitely more depraved.

Oedipus, at least, looked upon the horror and tore his eyes from his face. His blindness was just. Martin Jeffers forced a smile, reflecting the inward thought that the Oedipal myth was sacred to his profession. But we don't acknowledge what happened after. We don't remember that after the desire and the act, the one-time king was forced by guilt to wander blindly through life in rags, his feet driven step upon step by the depth of his despair.

He wondered if the same emotions were so clear on his own face. He tried to force his usual semidetached professional gaze out into the center of the room, but he knew he was unsuccessful. He looked across at the men, warily.

The membership of the Lost Boys was restless. They shifted about in their seats, making small, uncomfortable noises. He knew they had noted his fatigue in the previous day's session, knew, as well, that he had spent another sleepless night, and he wore that exhaustion equally obviously. He had sleepwalked through Monday, after returning late from New Hampshire, barely listening to the usual mix of mundane complaints and ills that made up his routine day. He had thought he would embrace a day of regularity, that it would somehow postpone all the difficult feelings, but he discovered that they were too powerful. His mind remained filled only with images of his brother.

He was overcome with a sudden rush of anger.

He saw his brother in a familiar pose, insouciant, grinning. Without a care in the world.

Then the vision grew darker and he pictured his brother with eyes set, deadly: the stalker, all business and bitterness.

A killer.

Why have you done these things? he asked the man in his mind's eye. Why have you become what you are? How can you do it, over and over, and not show it every waking instant?

But the brother in his mind faded, refusing to answer, and Martin Jeffers realized how foolish his questions were. Even if it is ridiculous to ask, he thought, I still must.

He felt his hands tighten on the arms of the chair and his anger redoubled, bursting forth, flowering, and he wanted to scream at the brother in his mind: Why have you done these things? Why? Why?

And then a greater anger still:

Why have you done these things to me?

He took a deep breath and looked out again at the waiting therapy group. He knew he had to say something, to get the group started, and then he would be able to lose himself in the steadiness of their conversation. But instead of tossing out a subject or idea for the men to worry and chew, he thought instead of New Hampshire and tried to remember the last moment he'd seen his real mother. She was fixed in a memory, a pale face, framed in a car window, turning back just once before rolling steadily out of his life. He could see it as clearly as on the night it had happened. He had never described the sight to anyone, least of all his own therapist. He knew that violated a fundamental trust, one that he hypocritically demanded of his own patients. I am not free, he thought. I don't expect to be. I never will be. He thought again of his real mother. What had we done wrong? He knew the answer: nothing. The ancients had it completely backward, he thought. Psychiatry has proven that it is the sins of the parents that are visited upon the children. We were abandoned, then we were treated cruelly, lovelessly. The twin pillars of despair. Is it any surprise that Doug has risen up, as an adult, to exact a measure of revenge on a world that hated him so?

But why him and not me?

Where is he?

"So, doc, what's bugging you? You look like you've got one foot in the grave."

"Yeah. You gonna take us with you?"

This prompted nervous laughter from the room.

Martin Jeffers looked up and saw that it was Bryan and Senderling asking the questions. But all the men's faces wore the same impatient inquisitiveness.

His first reaction was to ignore the questions and try to launch the group into another direction. That would have been the proper technique. After all, the group's focus should be on themselves, not on the group leader. But at the same time he was filled with an insistent anger that told him to throw away all the precious tenets of his profession and rely, for a moment, on the street smarts of the men.

"Do I look that bad?" he asked the assembly.

There was a momentary silence. The direct question surprised them. After a moment Miller growled from the back of the room:

"Yeah, you look bad. Like something's on your mind . . ."

He laughed cruelly.

". . . which sure is a change."

Again quiet dominated the room until Wasserman sputtered:

"If you d-d-d-don't f-f-f-feel so hot, we c-c-c-can come back tomorrow . . ."

Jeffers shook his head. "I feel fine. Physically."

"So what is it, doc? You got some kind of emotional flu?" This was Senderling, and Bryan laughed with him. That was a good image: emotional flu. I'll use that, someday, Jeffers thought.

"I'm concerned about a friend," he said.

There was a pause before Miller jumped back in. "You're a hell of a lot more than concerned," he said. "You're worried sick. Hell, I ain't a doctor, but I can see that. Something a lot more, huh? More than just concern?"

Jeffers didn't answer. He searched the eyes, glowing about him, and thought the twelve men were like some damned jury waiting for him to slip and convict himself from his own words. He fixed his eyes on Miller.

"Tell me," he said, filling his voice with insistence. "Tell me how you got started."

"What do you mean?" Miller replied, shifting in his seat.

Like all sex offenders, he hated a direct question, preferring to be queried in some oblique fashion so that he could control the route of the conversation. Jeffers thought they were all probably taken aback by bluntness.

"I want to know how you got started doing what you do."

"You mean, the, uh . . ."

"That's right. What you do to women. Tell me."

The room had gone completely quiet. The forcefulness of Jeffers' demand had stopped all of them. He knew that he was violating established procedures. But suddenly he was tired of rules, tired of waiting, tired of passivity.

"Tell me!" His voice was raised louder than it had ever been within the confines of the day room.

"Hell, I don't know..."

"Yes, you do!" Jeffers eyed all the men. "You all know. Think back! The first time. What went through your mind? What started you?"

He waited.

Pope broke the silence. Jeffers looked at the older man, who stared back with obvious hatred for anyone who probed at his memory. "Opportunity," he said.

"Please explain," Jeffers replied.

"We all knew who we were. Maybe we hadn't quite said it to ourselves yet. Maybe the words hadn't formed in the head, the way they do, but still, we knew, you know. And so it became a matter of waiting for the right opportunity. The demand was there, doc. You know you're gonna do something, you know. It's gonna happen. It just needs the right—I don't know what do you call it—circumstances..."

He saw heads start to nod in agreement.

"Sometimes"—it was Knight, interrupting—"once you make the decision to be what you are, it like takes over. You just start looking. Looking and looking and looking. Nothing's gonna come along and change anything, because it's already all set. You're looking. And when you find what you're looking for..."

"I s-s-s-still hated it," Wasserman interrupted jerkily.

"So did I," said Weingarten. "But that didn't mean a thing."

"Right." It was Pope again. "It didn't mean nothing..."

Parker: "'Cause once you're started, it's happening, man."

Meriwether: "Whether you hate it, or you hate yourself, or hate the person you're going to do it to, it makes little difference."

Martin Jeffers absorbed the men's words.

"But the first time..." he started, only to have Pope jump in.

"You don't understand! The first time is only the first time it happens physically! In your head, man, in your head, you've already done it a hundred times! A million!"

"To whom?" Jeffers asked.

"To everyone!"

Jeffers thought hard.

He saw the men sitting forward, on the edges of their chairs, anticipating his questions. They were alert, interested, excited, more engaged than he'd seen them before. He saw the predatory ridge in their eyes, and thought of all the people who'd seen the same hard look before being smothered, or choked and beaten and then violated.

"But there had to be something," he asked slowly. "There had to be some moment, or some word, or something had to happen that allowed you to become what you are . . ."

He stared hard at the men.

"Something allowed you. What?"

Again silence. The men were considering the question.

Wasserman stuttered: "I r-r-r-remember my m-m-m-mom telling me I'd n-n-n-never be the m-m-m-man my d-d-d-daddy was. I never f-f-f-forgot that, and when I d-d-d-did it the f-f-f-first time, it was all I could t-t-t-think about."

He looked about the room and his stutter evaporated for an instant:

"And I damn well was!"

"Well, it wasn't anything like that for me," Senderling said. "It was just I got tired of waiting, you know. I mean there was this one gal in the office, a real tease, you know, and, man, I guess everybody had a piece of her action, so I just took mine."

Bryan snorted. "You mean she wouldn't go out with you."

"No, no, it wasn't like that."

The men started to hoot.

Bryan kept at it. "She turned you down and so you waited for her in her apartment building's garage. You told me about it yourself."

"She was a bitch," Senderling said. "She deserved it."

"Just because she said no?" Jeffers asked.

"Right!"

"But why did you decide to do it this time? Other women had told you no, certainly," Jeffers asked.

"Because, because, because . . . well . . ."

He waited.

"Because I was alone. My sister and brother-in-law, that jerk, had finally moved out, and I didn't have to support his lazy ass anymore, or hers, 'cause all they did was lie around fucking like a pair of fucking rabbits while I was doing all the work and bringing home the fucking paycheck so we could at least eat. And so I kicked 'em out. And then the bitch wouldn't go out with me! Christ, she deserved it."

"So you were free?"

"Yeah! Right. Free. Free to do what I fucking well wanted."

Jeffers looked around the room again.

"Something freed all you men?"

He saw heads slowly nod in agreement.

362

"Talk about it."

He saw hesitation.

Knight said: "It's different for everyone."

Weingarten added: "It can be a big thing, or a little one, but . . ."

Knight repeated: "It's different for everyone."

Martin Jeffers took a deep breath. All is lost, he thought. Then he asked:

"Suppose it was more. More than just what you've done, suppose you went a step further."

The men seemed to rock under the suggestion.

"There's only one more step," said Pope. "You know what that is."

"Why didn't you?"

"Maybe some of us have," said Meriwether. "Not me, you know, I'm not admitting anything. But maybe some of us have."

"What would allow you to do it?"

The men didn't reply.

Jeffers waited. He, too, said nothing.

"Why do you need to know?" Meriwether asked.

He hesitated, trying to choose his words carefully.

"I need to find someone."

"Someone like us?" Bryan questioned.

"Someone like you."

"Someone worse?" It was Senderling.

Jeffers shrugged.

"Someone you know well?" Senderling tried again.

"Yes. Someone I know well."

"And you think he's gone someplace and you can figure it out, is that it?" Parker asked.

"More or less."

"Someone real close?" Senderling asked again.

Jeffers fixed him with a stare and didn't reply.

"You figure we can help you?" Weingarten said.

"Yes," Jeffers replied.

Weingarten laughed. "Well, damned if I don't think you're right."

"This someone," Parker questioned, "he's at it right now?"

"Yes."

"And you need to get to him to make him stop?"

"Yes."

"Or something . . ."

"Right," Jeffers said. "Stop or something."

"It's r-r-r-real important?" Wasserman jumped in.

"Yes."

Miller started to laugh hard. "Well, fuck you, doc. This puts things in a whole new light."

"Yes, it does," Jeffers said. He stared hard at Miller, who instantly stopped laughing.

"Well, tell us some more."

Jeffers hesitated.

"I think," he said slowly, "that he's visiting the scenes of some crimes."

Miller laughed again, but less maliciously. "The criminal returns to the scene of the crime?"

"I suppose."

Miller grinned. "Maybe it's a cliché, but it's not so stupid. Crimes become memories, you know. And everybody likes to visit their pleasant memories."

"Pleasant?" Jeffers questioned.

The men in the group laughed and snorted.

"Haven't you learned anything here?" Miller asked. The rapist's voice was rife with sarcasm. Jeffers ignored the question and Miller continued: "Everything's turned around for men like us! We love what we hate. We hate what we love. Pain is pleasure. Love is hurt. Everything's skewed about and upside down and backwards. Can't you see that? Christ!"

And suddenly he could.

"So," Miller said, and the men around him joined their heads in nodding agreement, "look for a memory that's filled with all the worst. And that will be the best."

Jeffers took a deep breath, scared of the thoughts that started to gather and form, like great storm clouds in his imagination. He looked up as Pope, grizzled, tattooed, filled to completion with anger and hatred and irrevocable in his antipathy to the world, spoke in a low, awful voice:

"Look for a death or departure. They're the same. That's what cuts you loose. Someone dies and you're free to be yourself. It's simple. It's fucking simple. Look for a death."

The first image that flitted into his head was of the darkness trapped in the trees on the night they were abandoned in New Hampshire. I went there, he told himself. I went back to that memory and he was nowhere to be found! That's where he was supposed to be and he wasn't.

But another image forced itself into his mind.

Another night.

And not a departure, but a death.

He slid his head into his hands, ignoring the way the men grew silent in the room around him.

I know, he told himself.

I know where my brother is going.

Jeffers looked up at the ceiling, and the white paint seemed to spin about, dizzyingly, for just an instant. How could you not have seen it? he said to himself. It's clear. It's obvious. How could you be stumbling about so blindly? Anger, sadness, hope, and despair all rushed through his body. He knew he had to get there, he knew he had to leave right away. Time suddenly bore its great weight down on top of him and he felt trapped in its vise grip. He exhaled slowly, gathering himself together. He looked out at the men, whose eyes were alive, expectant.

"Thank you," he said.

He stood up.

"There will be no more sessions. Not for a few days. Check the ward announcements for their resumption. Thank you again."

He saw a great surge of angry disappointment in the men. They are curious, he thought. They like to gossip and be in the know as much as anyone. He would not apologize, and, instead, he ignored the murmuring, excited sounds from the group, pitching headlong into the darkest nights of his own memory. I know, he said to himself again. I know.

He thought of the detective waiting for him in his office.

She will be watching. She will be alert for any change.

For an instant he felt a terrible sadness.

Then he turned from the men and walked steadily out. As he closed the door, he heard their excited voices join together. He shut them from his mind, concentrating on the importance of the next hours. He toughened himself inwardly. Be careful. Show nothing, he told himself. Show nothing at all.

Martin Jeffers stepped quickly away from the door, and the voices faded. He picked up his pace as he headed through the wards. His walk became a quick march, and, finally, a jog, his shoes making a slapping sound as they hit the linoleum floor. He ignored the surprised eyes of patients and staff as he broke into a run, his breath coming hard, oblivious to everything save the knowledge that vibrated in his head. I know, he repeated, over and over. I know.

He slowed as he entered the corridor where his office was located. He waited, catching his breath, thinking of the detective again. Then, composed, he slowly walked the last hundred feet, devising his escape.

Detective Mercedes Barren was standing, staring through the window, when Martin Jeffers entered the room. He beat her to the punch:

"Anything happen? Any news?"

She hesitated. "That was my question for you."

He shook his head, avoiding her glance momentarily. He stiffened himself. Meet her eyes, he insisted inwardly. So he raised his head as he took a seat behind his desk.

"No," he told her. "I've heard nothing. I told the switchboard operator that I was to be paged for any call, regardless of whether I was in a session or not. So far, nothing."

Detective Barren dropped into a seat across from him.

"What about at your home?"

"I left the answering machine on." He picked up his telephone and opened the desk drawer, producing a small black device. "It's got one of those playback thingamijigs," he said. "We can check." He dialed his home phone number and put the electronic instrument to the receiver. There was a series of squeaks and beeps before the tape started to play.

They listened to a message from a plumber and a tape-recorded sales pitch for a local candidate. Then the tape hissed emptily.

"There was nothing in the mail here," Jeffers said. "But it doesn't get delivered at home until about four."

"Screw the mails," Detective Barren said blankly. "He's not sending any postcards."

"He has before."

"And so we get one. Then we're only four or five days behind him."

"But it would tell us, maybe, what direction he was heading."

She knew this might be true. Still, her frustration gripped her. "Screw the mails," she said again. She sighed. "What about your memory? I have more confidence in that."

"I thought he would be there," Martin Jeffers replied. "I was sure that he'd be there in New Hampshire. It seemed the most logical place to start."

"So think again."

He rolled his head back. "Aren't you exhausted, too?" he asked. "Christ, we've been pushing. It's getting hard to figure. Don't you want to take a break?"

"I'll rest when it's over."

Martin Jeffers nodded. He knew she would not stop until his brother was—and then he paused. He would not fill in the remainder with a word, though he realized what she was saying.

"You're right," he said. "I'll keep at it."

He saw her relax, if only slightly.

After a moment she said:

"It's not a difficult proposition, really."

"What?"

"The idea that at any given time one ought to know where one's brother is. Or sister, for that matter."

He thought the question provocative. But he droned his answer.

"Maybe as children. When we were growing up I always knew. Even through school I always could have told you where he was. But when we became adults, well, adults head off on their own ways. We become independent. We have our own lives. We become more ourselves, less someone's brother or sister."

She shook her head irritatedly.

"Don't lecture me. That's not true. Your own profession tells us that the adult only masks with age and responsibility and morality and ethics all the desires of the child. So force yourself back! Think like you used to, not like you do today!"

She glared at him with eyes rimmed with equal parts of exhaustion and tension.

She was completely correct, he realized.

So, instead, he rose from his chair and circled around her nervously. "I'm trying, I'm trying. My mind is filled with possibilities. But there are a hundred shared moments between brothers growing up. A thousand. Which is the one that triggers him now?"

"You know," she said. "You just block it."

He smiled. "You sound like me."

Detective Mercedes Barren lifted her hands to her face and tried to rub away her fatigue. She smiled faintly. "You're right," she said. "I'm sorry. I push too hard sometimes."

Her confession surprised her.

"But you're right, too," he continued. "I'm probably blocking it."

His own bare smile joined hers.

Martin Jeffers looked over at the detective. His stomach clenched as he thought how deep her despair must be. For an instant he thought they should embrace and shed tears together, onto each other's shoulders, tears for the living, tears for the dead, tears for all the memories. He wanted to touch her in that moment, both angry and sad at the reason they had been thrust together into this small room, in the ever-changing world created and defined by his brother. He felt his hand start forward to touch her arm, but just as swiftly he ordered the muscles to stop, and he jammed his hand into the white pocket of his laboratory coat. Instead, he spoke:

"Detective, what are you going to do when this is over?" He held up his hand to make her pause before replying. "Regardless of how it comes out."

She laughed, but without humor.

"I haven't really thought of it," she said. She shook her head. "I suppose I'll go back to work, as before. I enjoyed what I was doing. I liked the people I worked with. No reason to change."

That was surely a lie, she thought. She expected nothing ever to be the same again.

She looked at him.

"And what about you, doctor?"

He nodded.

"The same."

We lie well together, she thought wryly to herself.

"Most lives," she said, "don't present that many options, do they?"

"No," he said sadly, "they don't."

But both were struck then with the same vision: each knew of one man's life that seemed filled with options.

Detective Mercedes Barren looked over at Martin Jeffers and for an instant tried to envision herself in his position. Then, as the first empathetic feelings crowded her heart, she hardened herself. Concentrate! she shouted to herself. Remember! She saw the lines that ridged the doctor's eyes, the gray pallor to his skin, and thought he was indeed filled with remorse. What has happened to me has happened, she told herself. What remains for me is justice, which is not an emotion but a need. He's still living his grief.

She wanted to say something, then, but could not think of anything even vaguely appropriate.

Martin Jeffers was aware of the silence between them, and the suddenly lessened degree of tension. He recognized the moment for what it was, knowing its duration would be short. He leaned back in his chair, stretching. But if he appeared relaxed on the outside, inwardly he was rigid:

Spring the trap, now!

"Look," he said slowly. "You're absolutely right. We've got to keep at this until I figure out where he's gone. Someone's life may be at stake—we don't know. Let's just do it, okay?"

Detective Barren nodded in agreement.

"Here's what I think," he said. He glanced up at the wall clock. "It's getting late in the afternoon. I'll drop you at your hotel for an hour or so. Just give me long enough to take a shower and get a second wind. Then meet me at my house. We can have a couple of drinks and I'll pull out every old picture and letter I've got, and we'll try to free-associate an answer to all this. We can set up some sort of chronology. You'll have to listen to my life story, but maybe if I start to talk it out something will strike true. And anyway, if the phone rings, we'll both be right there. He's far more likely to call me at home than here."

Detective Barren considered the plan. The thought of hot water flooding her body was seductive. For an instant a voice within her shouted caution and she forced her eyes to set on Martin Jeffers. She watched as he rocked slightly in his seat. She searched for anxiety, for nervous motion, for anything other than the discouragement and fatigue that she felt insistently within herself. She saw nothing. He's already had a hundred opportunities to run, she thought. He won't. Not until he hears from his brother.

"Start with a clearer head," he said blandly. "See what jumps in."

"All right," she replied. "I'll be there at, say, six thirty."

"Six would be fine," he said. "And we'll keep at it until we've got at least a good idea where to head. And then we'll just go. The hospital can cut me some time."

"Good," she said. She felt a sense of body-slackening release at the idea that they would be acting instead of waiting. She felt a hot flood inside her, thinking hard of Douglas Jeffers, feeling once again that she was embarking on his trail. That comforted her, and blinded her to the fact that the murderer's brother had turned his eyes away suddenly, averting his glance.

Martin Jeffers pulled to the curb in front of Detective Barren's hotel in Trenton. He took the car out of gear and turned to her.

"Look, what kind of sandwiches do you like? I'll stop at the deli on the way to my place so we can eat later."

She opened the car door and put one foot to the sidewalk.

"Anything's okay," she said. "Roast beef, ham and cheese, tuna fish." She smiled. "Protestant sandwiches. No corned beef or brisket. No mustard, plenty of mayonnaise."

He laughed.

"And some sort of salad if they've got anything."

"No problem."

He glanced at his watch.

"Look," he said, "be there by six. Let's get this thing moving."

She nodded. "Don't worry. See you then."

"All right," he replied.

He watched as she strode across the hotel entranceway and disappeared into the lobby. He thought that the banality of his plan had been its strongest element. She was so focused on her quarry and the evil he represented in her mind that she neglected the more mundane possibility that Martin Jeffers might abandon her. Mingle obsession with exhaustion and one is ripe for the unexpected. For an instant he regretted his betrayal. She's going to kill me, he thought. Then he realized that the colloquialism that had formed in his head was probably not impossible. She might actually kill me.

He argued to himself: Be realistic.

He pulled the car out into the street. Don't stop. Don't go home. Do without a change of clothes, or a toothbrush, or anything. Just go. Now. He exhaled sharply and thought of his destination. If I hurry, he told himself, perhaps I can make the last ferry. His mind started to picture the detective at the moment his disappearance became clear to her. He rationalized: This is about saving lives. My brother's. The detective's. My own.

Still, he thought again, she's going to be angry enough to shoot me when she sees me again. It did not occur to him that his brother might feel the same.

Martin Jeffers cleared his head and drove hard, struggling with the late-afternoon traffic.

Detective Mercedes Barren stepped naked from the shower, toweling herself off slowly. After she had rubbed her body into a gleaming redness, she wrapped the white bath towel around her hair and flopped onto the bed, refreshed in part by the water, but equally by a moment of solitude. She stretched her body, feeling the muscles tense, then slowly relax. She lay back and ran her hands over her figure. She felt sore, as if she'd been in an accident, or in a fight, and her injuries were all concealed beneath the surface of her skin, internal. She closed her eyes and recognized the drowning pull of sleep. She fought against it, opening first one eye, then the other, blinking away the demands of her body. She argued with herself, pleading with all the currents in her body that demanded rest, first cajoling, then negotiating, and finally promising nerves, muscles, and brain that she would rest, surely, soon, and deeply as well.

But not yet.

She summoned some strength from within her and sat up on the bed. She shouted orders, Prussian-like, to her arms and hands, a drill sergeant for the body: Get the clothes. Put them on. Get going.

Still battling against the rebellious demands of her body, she dressed herself in jeans and sportshirt. She took time to fix her hair and apply some makeup. She had a need to look less bedraggled by events than she actually felt. She refused to let frustration defeat her. After a few moments she looked at herself in the mirror. Well, she insisted, if not refreshed, at least you look ready.

She glanced over at the red digital alarm clock that rested on the bedstand table. So I'll be a little early, she thought. We can just get started sooner.

She drove slowly through the lengthening shadows, leaving the small city behind and maneuvering through the suburban traffic toward the doctor's apartment in Pennington. She was reminded of John Barren's opinion of the state of New Jersey. He had always loved the state, she remembered, because no other place combined so many varieties of life: abject Newark poverty, incredible Princeton wealth, funky Asbury Park, Flemington farmland. It was a state capable of extraordinary beauty in some regions and exceptional ugliness in others. Her eyes roamed about, fixing on the tree-lined road which cut through rolling green hills. This, she thought, is the nice part.

She turned off the primary highway and drove into Pennington. She could see the usual suburban-evening theater: fathers arriving home in business suits, kids playing on the sidewalks or in side yards, mothers fixing dinners. It grated on her somehow. It seemed too normal, too ideal. Detective Barren spotted a pair of teenage girls, giggling on a street corner, heads together in typical teenage conspiracy. But you're not safe! she thought suddenly. Her heart tightened and her breathing constricted. She had an overwhelming urge to stop and shout at all the assembled; happy people: But you don't know! You don't understand! None of you are safe!

She exhaled slowly and turned the car onto Martin Jeffers' street. She halted across the street, barely looking around. She did not want to see any more portraits of unfettered happiness. No more Norman Rockwell, she told herself. Back to Salvador Dali.

She stepped from the car and stopped dead.

Her skin suddenly seemed to crawl.

371

Something is wrong, she thought. Something is out of place and mistaken. Her head reeled suddenly.

He's here!

She looked wildly about, but saw nothing that wasn't in its proper location. She informed herself that she was being exceptionally paranoid, but she still scoured the windows of the houses on the street, trying to detect a pair of eyes burning into her.

She could see none.

Moving very slowly, she maneuvered her purse around to her right side. Trying to be as unobtrusive as possible, she lowered her hand beneath its brown leather flap. The 9 millimeter took up almost all the pocketbook. She gripped the handle.

She felt a momentary panic: Is a round chambered?

She could not remember. She clicked off the safety and told herself to assume there was no bullet in the firing chamber. Cock the gun first, she told herself. You're being crazy, because there's nothing wrong, but chamber a round anyway. She kept hold of the grip and slid her left hand in on top, slamming the gun's action back, loading it, ready to fire. She could feel the short hairs on her arms standing on edge, she thought of herself as a dog, filled with unusual smells, hackles rising without really understanding what the danger was, but accepting the demands of instinct born of centuries.

She looked at Martin Jeffers' apartment. She felt her mouth go dry.

Where's his car? her brain screamed.

She took a step sideways, then another, peering into the small driveway. No car. She walked out into the street to give herself a better look up and down.

No car.

She told herself: He probably went to the deli. That's it.

But every nerve in her body told her reassurance was wrong. She made certain that the pistol would slip free from her purse when she demanded it.

She walked to the front door and stepped inside.

What she saw made her heart plummet.

Martin Jeffers' mail lay uncollected on the floor in front of his apartment.

No, she said. No!

She stepped to the door and removed the pistol. With her free hand she pounded on the wood frame.

There was no response.

She waited, then pounded again.

Again nothing.

She made no effort to conceal the gun as she walked outdoors and around the side of the building. She stared in the windows, pausing at the one where she'd broken into the apartment what suddenly seemed a very long time before.

She saw no movement. The interior remained dark.

She walked back to the front door and pounded again.

Silence continued to greet her.

She stepped back, staring at the bolted door. She thought it oddly symbolic. I'm locked out. I should have known, I did know, I just refused to acknowledge it, that he would close me out. They are brothers, she thought. Then she slumped down, sitting on the steps that rose to the upper floors of the building.

He's gone, she said to herself matter-of-factly.

He knows and he's gone.

She felt one momentary rush of rage that evaporated as swiftly as it arrived. She remained sitting, feeling nothing save a great, gray, utterly absorbing cloud of defeat that rained despair on her heart.

A tractor-trailer had jackknifed on Route 95, nor far from Mystic, Connecticut, backing up traffic for a half-dozen miles. Martin Jeffers shifted impatiently in his seat, his face bathed by the blue and yellow strobes of a rescue crew and the state police cruisers. Every few seconds the red taillights of the car in front of him would flash and he would have to brake hard himself. He hated the jam-up; it intruded on the frantic press of memories which called to him from the recesses of his imagination. He tried to think of good moments they'd shared, instants in time that create the relationship between brothers: a night spent camping, the construction of a tree house, a halting, embarrassed discussion about girls that disintegrated into a conversation about masturbation. That made him smile. Doug never admitted to anything, but was always filled with the advice of a frequent practitioner, regardless of the subject. He remembered a moment when he was six or seven and had been set upon by other neighborhood boys armed to the teeth with snowballs. He'd been unable to outrun the missiles or the gibes of the others. It was a benign challenge, one that stemmed not from competition or animosity but from six new inches of snow falling steadily and the cancellation of classes that day. Doug had listened to his story of ambush and attack, then carefully decked himself in scarf and winter coat and galoshes and led the way out the rear door. His brother had led him around the deck, around the block, and finally up from behind, crawling the last fifty yards on their stomachs behind a white-decked hedgerow. Their assault was commandolike and marvelously successful. Two shots crashed in snowy explosion into the faces of a pair of his tormentors before they had any idea where the grenades were coming from.

Even then, Martin Jeffers thought abruptly, Doug knew how to stalk his prey.

He looked ahead and saw a row of flares burning orange into the roadway. A state trooper with a yellow-lensed flashlight was waving the cars through frantically. Still, people slowed to peer at the wreck.

We are always fascinated by disaster, Martin Jeffers knew.

We crane our heads to see nightmare. We slow to investigate misery.

He wished, suddenly, that he were above curiosity, but realized he wasn't. He, too, slowed in passing, catching a glimpse of a single shrouded figure deathly still on the road.

In ancient times, he told himself, a traveler spotting such an inopportune omen would turn back, grateful that the heavens had shown him a sign foretelling the tragedy that awaited him. But I am modern. I am not superstitious.

He drove on. He glanced at his wristwatch and knew that he would miss the last ferry at Woods Hole. Damn, he said to himself. I'll have to catch the first boat in the morning. He hoped the ferry company still scheduled a six A.M. boat. He remembered a good motel within walking distance of the dock. For a moment he toyed with the idea of calling the detective once he'd checked in; not to tell her where he was, but to apologize and try to explain that he was doing what he must, what was dictated by flesh and blood. He wanted her to forgive him. He wanted her to forgive herself. She will blame herself for leaving me alone, even if just for a few minutes. She should realize there were a dozen moments that I could have abandoned her. He knew it was the sort of rationalization that would infuriate her. Well, he said to himself, you were wrong about New Hampshire. Maybe you're wrong about Finger Point as well. The head plays a confidence game with the heart.

"Maybe he won't be there," Martin Jeffers said aloud. "Maybe I'll just embarrass myself by knocking on the door of some vacationing family who'll think I'm crazy and that will be it."

Detective Barren slipped from his mind's eye, replaced by his brother. He felt a great swirl within him. He was caught in a perfect pull of emotions: equal parts demanding he confront his brother and equal parts hoping he wouldn't have to.

The night had moved into position and he felt more alone than he ever had since the evening in New Hampshire more than three decades earlier.

Detective Mercedes Barren remained rooted on the hallway steps outside Martin Jeffers' apartment, letting the darkness sweep over her.

She was filled with memories of her own; of her husband, of her niece. A portrait of Susan filled her, but it wasn't the Susan that she'd seen strangled and molested and discarded beneath a few scrub ferns in the park, but the Susan who would come to dinner and play loud music and dance about Detective Barren's home, suffused with sounds, barely able to contain all the life she had. Then this image faded, and Detective Barren saw the little girl, dressed in pinks and bows, running to greet her, making the detective feel, if only for an instant, completely whole, completely loved. She thought of John Barren, rolling over in the middle of the night with demands of affection, and the friendly, familiar sensation of welcoming him to her body. She thought: If only I'd known. If only someone had told me: Make every moment special, for your time is short.

She saw herself as a child, gripping her father's hand.

She looked over at the dark door to Martin Jeffers' apartment. Well, she said to herself, use some of your father's logic. It was the only thing he had to will to you. It's helped you before. What would he do?

Examine the facts. Investigate each element.

All right, she said to herself. Let's take it simply.

He said: Meet you here.

A lie.

She thought what a wondrous lie it was. Simple, benign, especially the touch about the sandwiches. Use the familiarity of the past days against her.

But when did the lying start?

She reviewed their last meeting, in his office. He didn't indicate anything had changed. But something obviously had. He didn't receive any phone calls. There was no mail. He clearly didn't return to his apartment and then decide to leave. The decision had to have been made by the time they were in his office. She reviewed the situation again. No, she thought quickly, there was nothing from Douglas Jeffers.

So it must have been something he remembered.

She sat back in the darkness and thought deeply.

He went to individual sessions and then to that damn group of perverts. Then he came back to the office and then he began lying and then he disappeared. She sat up and then stood up. She began to pace about the entraceway, concentrating hard. Her exhaustion slid away in the fury of her mind at work. She felt a wealth of adrenaline pumping through her. Back on the case, she thought. You're back on the case. Act like a damn detective. Now, though, you've got two quarries.

"All right," she said out loud. "Start at the hospital. Start with the patients he saw. Get the list from his secretary. If she won't give it to you, steal it."

These last words echoed in the small area.

She breathed in hard. She saw again her niece, her husband, her father. She smiled and dismissed the images from her head. Work, she thought. She replaced the vision with twin portraits of Martin and Douglas Jeffers.

I'm coming, she said to herself. I'm still after you.

Weak dawn light flowed over the ferry bow, and Martin Jeffers felt the chill of morning air surround him. He pulled the lapels of his lab coat tighter and let the breeze wash over him. He could see miles of rolling gray-green ocean glistening in the first light. He turned his back to the wind and watched the island loom up in the distance. He could see the shoreline trimmed with proper summer homes, then, a short ways farther in the distance, the white glow of Vineyard Haven, where the ferry would dock. Sunlight hit upon a row of a half-dozen fuel tanks next to the docks. In the harbor, dozens of sailboats bobbed at moorings. He thought of the small slapping sound that wavelets make against the hull of a sailboat.

The ferry moved fast through the morning seas. As it approached the slip, it blared out a single raucous blast on the air horn. Martin Jeffers saw some of the other passengers jump, startled by the sound.

The ferry bumped to a stop, its huge diesel engines grinding the bow into the dock. There was a momentary pause while gangways were lowered and people started to exit. Martin Jeffers pushed through the early crowd of people. The lines of cars waiting to get on the ferry were already stretched up the street. It reminded Jeffers how close they were to the end of the summer; the boat over had been almost empty. Returning to the mainland, it would be filled.

He looked about briefly as he exited the ferry and walked across the loading area, past the ticket office. He thought: It's all the same, but different. More buildings. New shops. A new parking lot. But it's all the same, still.

I thought I would never come back here.

He started to count the years, then stopped. He knew the house would be there, just the same, next to the pond, across from the ocean. His eyes scanned the crowds of people and cars. It will still be isolated and wild, he said to himself. It will have stayed the same.

He did not base this conclusion on any fact, more an overwhelming sensation of familiarity.

It was, he thought, the best worst place.

He remembered what the Lost Boys had said. And he'd come to that place where they'd told him to look.

Look for a death.

Well, he said to himself, I'm here.

And this is the place for both.

He hurried across the street to Island Rent-A-Car, washing his mind of everything save the insistent fear that he would be right.

The clerk was eating a doughnut and sipping coffee.

"How can I help you?"

"Martin Jeffers. I made a reservation last night with the late guy."

"Yup. Saw his note this morning. On the early ferry, right? Said you wanted a car for a couple of days, right? A little vacation?"

"A little business. Could be short. Could drag out a bit."

"Just so's we have the car back Friday. Labor Day weekend, you know. All booked up. Everything is."

"No problem," Jeffers lied.

"You got an island address for the form?"

He hesitated. "Yeah. Chilmark. Out on Quansoo. Sorry, there's no phone."

"Best beach, though."

"Right you are."

"Of course," the clerk said as he filled out the forms, "I don't go down there too much. I ain't much of a swimmer and those waves and the undertow and all that stuff scares the daylights out of me. But the surfers, they love it. You ain't a surfer, are you?"

"No."

"Good. Those kids are always renting the cars and trying to drive them out on the beach and getting them stuck and tearing up the transmissions and all."

The man picked up a set of keys hanging on the wall behind him. "You need a map?" he asked.

"No, unless things have changed much in the past couple of years."

"Things always change. That's the nature of life. But the roads ain't, if that's what you mean." The clerk shoved a form at Martin Jeffers for his signature. "All set. It's the white Chevy just outside the door. Return with a tank of gas, okay? Before Friday."

"See you then."

Martin Jeffers started up the car and fought his way through the building morning traffic. He realized he had no plan other than simply barging in on the people who were there. What are you going to say? he asked himself. What are you going to tell them? Excuse me, sir or madam, but you wouldn't happen to have seen a man bearing a family resemblance to yours truly dripping blood in the neighborhood?

What can you say other than the truth?

He realized that was impossible. This particular truth was too far removed from reality to absorb at eight A.M. on a late-summer morning, when eating a leisurely breakfast before heading to the beach.

So, he thought, just tell them he's lost and you're trying to find him. Tell him he's in a fugue state, wandering between poles of memory, disengaged from life, like everyone's crazy Aunt Sadie, who one day simply walked off and took a train to St. Louis. Tell them he's harmless. Tell them you're concerned. Tell them anything.

Every construction he tried sounded equally far-fetched.

Just tell them you're looking for your brother and once you lived in this house and you thought he might have come visiting.

Tell them what they want to hear.

This, he admitted to himself, is going to be impossible.

But he realized that embarrassment was by far the least terrible thing that could happen.

He drove through the rising morning, darting between the shadows the green trees tossed so casually across the road. He was driving unconsciously, letting his memory take over and steer the car. Distances seemed strangely different, first longer, then shorter. He saw the houses that he remembered, and new buildings that he didn't. He was pleased, in an odd way, to see that the general store in the tiny town of West Tisbury had not changed. He cruised past, heading toward the turnoff.

He continued following the path of his past. He thought: The hospital is that way. But we didn't have to drive fast, because there was no hope.

He saw the great sand-pit entrance to the road off to his right and slowed. He was surprised that he'd found it, and equally surprised that it looked the same. He hesitated only momentarily before heading down the road. The washboard dirt surface pitched the rental car about, and he heard the paint being scratched on the sides where the bramble bushes bent toward the road. He recalled why the road had never been improved: the people who lived down it wanted to discourage anyone from coming sightseeing. He hit a bump and heard the bottom of the car scrape violently against the rocks and dirt. They were always successful, he thought.

He had driven several miles when he came to the trees with the colored arrows. He didn't bother to check; he knew which fork to take, even after so many years. He could feel his pulse quickening as he steered through the overhanging trees.

I never thought I would return, he said to himself for the thousandth time.

He emerged from the trees and caught his first sight of the pond off to the side of the road. In the far distance he could see, just barely, the glint of the sun as it hit the ocean. There were a half-dozen bright triangular sails from small boats already cutting across the pond toward the beach. His eyes focused on a farmhouse several hundred yards across the water. Old man Johnson, he thought, smiling. The old bastard. I wonder if he's still shooting at kids who drive on the sand dunes? He stopped and rolled down the window. He could hear the surf in the distance, and he wondered why such a constant and violent sound was also so soothing.

He looked down the road and caught sight of the house.

The best worst place.

He closed his eyes and tried to think of what he would say and realized that he would simply have to rely on whatever words came to him. The important thing, he thought, is to seem open and friendly and nonthreatening. Just get in the door, he thought, and then see what happens.

He drove the last quarter mile and pulled into a small driveway. He got out of the car and stared up at the house. He could see that it had received some new gray shingles and some of the windows appeared new. It was a low, single-story, old Cape design, with a front door that looked back at the road and a back side of the house that looked out over the pond toward the ocean.

Finger Point, he thought. The spit of land reaches out into the pond, pointing at the ocean. Not a particularly interesting method of naming a piece of property, but accurate. He looked out at sea

379

grass waving in the breeze across the water on the Johnson property and remembered running through the grass, the blades slicing at him, oblivious to the sharpness of the pain, trying to keep up with his brother. He shut his eyes and felt the sun striking his head and shoulders. For a moment he felt completely foolish, then completely terrified. He wanted to get back in the car and drive away. He's not here, he thought. He's somewhere, lost in America, doing terrible things. He's gone forever. Just turn and leave and never think of him again.

He knew that was impossible and he opened his eyes.

You made it this far without turning back. Might as well make a complete ass of yourself.

He walked up to the front door and knocked loudly.

Sorry, he said to himself. I hope I'm not getting anyone out of bed. He heard footsteps from inside and then the front door opened.

It was a young woman, pretty, in her early twenties, Jeffers guessed, with blond hair that was set off by her black mechanic's outfit.

"Excuse me," Martin Jeffers started. He thought she was dressed unusually for a summer morning, but he did not have time to assess this idea. "I know it's early and I'm terribly sorry to be bothering you, but . . ."

And then he stopped.

The young woman was staring wide-eyed at him, as if shocked by his appearance. He saw her eyes absorb the details of his features.

"I'm sorry . . ." he started in again.

"But why?" came the terrible, mocking, but totally familiar voice behind him.

The membership of the Lost Boys filed slowly into the sunlit day room and took their customary seats. This they did out of habit and the demands of hospital scheduling, which told them that in this time period they were to be in this room, doing this therapy. Deviations from the normal routine were discouraged. So they went, knowing that the normal routine had already been shattered. But they were all well versed enough in the ways of bureaucracies to understand that, even if there were to be no session, they surely were required to be there until told explicitly to the contrary. They knew that Martin Jeffers would not be there, for he'd told them that himself. They knew that their session would consist of sitting about while some other doctor, thrust by his precipitous departure, filled in. They also knew they'd tell the new doctor nothing.

They waited, smoking, talking quietly amongst themselves, idly curious as to what would happen.

They were, to a man, shocked when Detective Mercedes Barren walked through the door.

In the silence that accompanied her entry, Detective Barren fixed the room with a rock-hard glare. These, she thought, are my natural enemies. She could feel goosebumps on her skin.

The room was empty of sound.

She waited for an instant, then walked to the front of the group. She could feel their eyes on her. They did not know who she was, of course, but she knew they hated her, instantly, profoundly.

As she did them.

She turned and faced the group.

Slowly, exaggerating her movements, she reached into her bag and brought out her gold shield. She held it high, so they could all see it clearly. It reflected the sunlight, glowing in her hand.

"My name is Mercedes Barren," she said firmly. "Detective. City of Miami Police Department."

She paused.

"If it had been me on your case, you'd be doing hard time."

This was stated as a blunt fact.

The room remained quiet. She had little doubt that the men absorbed her words carefully. Now, she thought, throw them the curve.

"Your regular group leader is Doctor Martin Jeffers. He left the hospital suddenly yesterday afternoon, not long after meeting with you men . . ."

She paused.

"Where is he?"

The room exploded into a cacophony of conversation; the men had their heads together, everyone talking at once.

She held up her hand, and the twelve pairs of eyes rested back on her.

"Where did he go?"

There was another flurry of talk that faded swiftly into a belligerent silence. Finally one man, a pockmarked, heavyset man with a ready sneer, said, "Fuck you, lady."

"What's your name?"

"Miller."

"You facing a little prison time after this holiday is over, Miller? Maybe you'd like to do it in maximum security?"

"I can do the time," Miller replied.

"I hope so."

Again silence took over until a smallish round man waved his hand at Detective Barren. She nodded in his direction and he spoke in a sarcastic, effeminate voice:

"Why, detective, should we bother to help you?"

"What's your name?"

"I'm Steele," he said. "But my friends call me Petey."

"If you had any," said another voice. She couldn't tell who and she had to force herself not to smile. There was a smattering of laughter in the room.

"All right, Steele, I'll tell you why you should help me. Because you are all criminals. And just who the hell do you think helps the police? That's the way things work, you know. Bad guys know where other bad guys are."

"You saying the doc's a bad guy?" This was Bryan speaking.

"No. I'm not. But he went after somebody real bad."

"Who?" It was Senderling and Knight together.

She hesitated. Well, why not?

"You all help me, I'll tell you. I just want an agreement first."

She looked around the room. She saw the men leaning their heads together. "All right," said Knight and Senderling, both. "We'll help." They laughed. "Got nothing to lose."

"Except maybe the d-d-d-doc's trust," stuttered Wasserman.

That made the men pause.

"What's in it for us?" Miller asked.

"Nothing solid. You just get to know a little bit. Information is always valuable."

Miller snorted. "You're just like every cop, even if you ain't got the right equipment. You want to get something for nothing."

She didn't reply.

"Look," said Parker, "if we help you a little, can you promise that the doc won't get hurt? I mean, legally, too, not just physically."

"Doctor Jeffers is not the subject of my investigation," Detective Barren replied. "But he knows the person who is. I want to keep him from getting himself into more trouble. How's that?"

"I don't trust no cops," said Miller.

"Well, is the doctor in danger?" asked Bryan.

Maybe. Maybe not. She didn't know. So she lied.

"Yes. Absolutely. But he doesn't know it."

This made the men start murmuring again.

"Tell you what," Knight said. "You tell us what the deal is, who this bad dude is, and we'll see if we can help."

Detective Barren shrugged. She knew that if she were to get any information out of the group, she would have to keep the conversation flowing. If she stonewalled, so would they.

She took a deep breath and answered:

"His brother."

There was an instant's silence, then Steele began to whoop and clap his hands. He jumped from his seat and danced about the day room. "I knew it, I knew it. Pay up! Pay up! You, Bryan, two packs of cigarettes. You, Miller, three packs. All you dumb fuckers who bet against me—I told you it was a relative! It had to be! Pay up! Pay up!"

She saw the men grumbling.

"So," she demanded, "where did he go?"

"He d-d-d-didn't say," Wasserman replied.

"He wasn't specific," Weingarten jumped in. "He just said this guy, he didn't say who, was worse than us. He said the guy was visiting memories. I didn't think we said all that much to help him."

"Yeah, except all of a sudden he jumps up and takes off." This was Parker.

"He had it all fucking backwards anyway," Miller grunted. "He wasn't sure what sort of memory he was looking for. We had to straighten him out. We told him to look for the worst memory, because that would be the best for someone like us."

"What did you say exactly?" Detective Barren leaned forward.

"Shit, who knows? We said a lot of things."

"Yes, but one thing you said made him think of something."

The men all started talking together again.

"We said a lot of things," Miller insisted.

"Come on, dammit! What was said?"

"He wanted to know what happened so that we became free, you know, free to do what we do."

"What?"

"He asked us what started us. You know. What got us going."

She took a deep breath and it made perfect sense to her. He had demanded the key. And they'd given it to him.

"So what was said? What was it?"

The men in the room stared at her angrily. She could sense the strength of hatred that they had for her, not merely as a policeman, but as a woman. She met their eyes, filling her own gaze with all the power she could find within her.

The silence was like oil, spread over everything.

She wanted to scream.

Tell me, she shouted in her mind. Tell me!

"I know," came a deep voice from the back. It was Pope. She leaned forward and met his eyes. Here, she thought to herself, is a truly terrifying man. She had a sudden horrifying image of the man, grabbing her, ripping at her clothes. She wondered how many women had had that nightmare in reality.

"I know what I said. And it made him think of something."

"What?"

Pope hesitated. Then he shrugged.

"I hope everyone dies," he said under his voice.

He looked at Detective Barren. "I said, 'Look for a death or a departure.' It always starts with one or the other. Sometimes they're the same."

She leaned back in a chair. A departure, she thought. We went there. New Hampshire.

"That's it?" she asked. She hid the defeat from her voice.

"That was it. He stood up and took a hike."

"S-s-s-sorry, d-d-d-detective . . ."

She stared at the men. She wondered how many deaths were spread about the room. How many ruined lives. She shivered inwardly.

Then she thought: A death. A ruined life.

The idea formed slowly, like a cyclone deep in the distance, but gaining power and strength with each passing second. She felt flushed, as if the heat in the room had suddenly spiked, and she thought of something Martin Jeffers had said in passing a few days beforehand: The bastard didn't even give us his name. And he died, in an accident.

She put her hand to her forehead, as if feeling her temperature. She looked out at the glowing eyes of the men around her. She stood up, unaware that she was mimicking Martin Jeffers.

"Thank you," she said. "You've been extremely helpful."

I know, she thought. I know.

Maybe, maybe, maybe. At least it's a place to start.

She pictured the aged newspaper in the box beneath Martin Jeffers' bed. Go! The voice deep within her screamed. Go! It will tell you where he's gone! She had only a moment to berate herself for missing the obvious the first time she broke into Martin Jeffers' apartment. This time, she thought, you know what you're looking for. Go! Go! Go!

She turned abruptly and left the men muttering behind her.

Her heels echoed a staccato, machine-gun sound, as she rushed from the hospital.

CHAPTER
══════════FOURTEEN
NO MAN'S LAND

19. HOLT OVERHOLSER, sixty-three years old, the chief of the West Tisbury police force, and its only year-round member, fiddled with the paperwork on his desk, inwardly complaining about the influx of summer people who paid his salary every year, but who also neglected to obey the posted speed limits and were forever trying to toss out their garbage at the town dump on days it was officially closed. He had spent much of the afternoon with his radar detector, ticketing cars. The selectmen had put up a SPEED LIMIT 15 sign a half mile from the center of town, knowing that no one would slow that much until they at least got past the Presbyterian Church. This was where Holt parked, waving every other car over and handing the driver a $25 speeding ticket, which he'd had the sense to fill out in advance.

This had become a major source of revenue for the town; the selectmen were pleased and Holt was pleased. Last year they'd made enough to get him a new Ford Bronco with four-wheel drive and the special police package. This year, he thought, they'd get those new walkie-talkies that clip onto the belt, with the microphone up on the shoulder, like the ones they wore on *Hill Street Blues* sometimes. That was Holt's favorite show, and much of his police training had been acquired from a religious watching of it and other shows, dating all the way back to *Dragnet*. Every time he signed off the radio, he said, "Ten-four," in the same gruff manner that Broderick Crawford had made famous. He wondered whether there would be any good police shows in the upcoming television season. He doubted it; cops seemed to have swung out of favor again and it would probably be a couple of years before television tried something new. He didn't count *Miami Vice* as a police show.

Holt leafed through the ticket book, making certain everything was legible before sending it over to the town clerk's office. He'd written forty-seven tickets in four hot hours. That was three shy of his record, he thought ruefully. But Labor Day was fast approaching, and he was confident that he would not only break his record but shatter it.

He stretched and stared out the window of the small office. Darkness had insinuated itself onto the warm late-summer night. All that remained of the day was a fast-fading red glow off to the West. Holt had never traveled farther in that direction than his sister's home in Albany at Thanksgiving, but he read avidly, mostly novels and travel books, and he longed to go. He liked to think of himself as a throwback to some earlier era, in the Old West. He saw himself as the peacekeeper in the small town, tough yet likable, fair, yet the wrong man to cross, a good man to side with in a fight.

Of course he had never had a fight in thirty-three years of police work on Martha's Vineyard. The occasional belligerent drunk had been the worst he'd ever faced.

He closed his **eyes** and rocked back in his desk chair. There would be fresh bluefish casserole for dinner, cooked with vegetables from his own **garden**. Holt congratulated himself on eating well, which was actually more the result of his wife's dedication. He thumped his heart: Sixty-three and still going strong, he thought. The selectmen had tried to retire him three years earlier, but Holt had passed the state police physical examination ahead of a half-dozen men a third his age, and that had persuaded the selectmen to keep him on. They were amused, too, the way Holt always relieved a good deal of money from the summer kids whom he hired as temporary police help. Holt could out–arm wrestle all of them with his left hand; forty years earlier he'd worked on a lobster boat out of Menemsha, and hauling crates hand over hand from the bottom had left him with a considerable upper body strength. He'd also learned poker as a young man, which now supplemented his income handsomely. College kids always think they can play the game, he thought. They learn.

He examined the stack of tickets and decided: It can wait until morning. Most things could, even in the summer season. He yawned and lazily picked up the police radio on the corner of his desk.

"Dispatch, this is One Adam One, West Tisbury, I'm ten-thirty-six from HQ. Please put us on emergency link, ten-four."

"Hello, Holt, how are you tonight?"

"Uh, fine, dispatch."

"Did Sylvia get the recipe I sent her?"

"Uh, dispatch, that's a roger."

He hated it when Lizzie Barry was doing the late shift on the 911 network for the island. She was older than him and half-senile. She never followed the proper terminology.

"One Adam One, roger, ten-four."

"Nighty-night."

He hung up the microphone and started to collect his things, when he saw the woman walk through the door. He smiled.

"Just getting ready to close up, ma'am. What can I do for you?"

"I need some directions," said Mercedes Barren.

"Well, sure," replied Holt, sizing the woman up. Despite the blue jeans and sportshirt, she did not seem like a vacationer. She had a big-city air about her, and Holt could smell business. Probably another damn real-estate developer, he said to himself.

"I'm looking for a place where an accident took place about twenty years ago."

"An accident?" Holt sat down and gestured at the chair opposite him. His curiosity was pricked.

"Some twenty years ago a businessman from New Jersey, guy owned a drugstore, drowned off South Beach. I need to know where that accident took place."

"Well, hell, South Beach is seventeen miles long, and twenty years is awhile ago. You're gonna have to give me a bit more information."

"Do you remember the incident?"

"Ma'am, begging your pardon, but we have one or two drownings every summer. After a while they pretty much seem the same. Coast Guard handles 'em, anyway. I just push some paperwork about."

"I have the newspaper account. Would that help?"

"Can't hurt."

Holt leaned forward while Mercedes Barren fished the old copy of the *Vineyard Gazette* from her bag. Holt caught just the barest glimpse of the automatic pistol barrel, and without thinking of some clever response he simply blurted out: "You carrying a weapon, ma'am?"

"Yes," she said. She reached down into her bag and produced her gold shield. "I should have introduced myself. I'm Detective Mercedes Barren, City of Miami police."

Holt was instantly delighted.

"We don't get many big-city police, uh, people, up here. You here on a case?"

"No, no, just visiting friends."

"Oh," he said, disappointed. "Then why the gun?"

"Just habit, sorry."

"Unh, hunh. You maybe want to leave it with me?"

"Chief, if you don't mind, I've got to leave early and it would be more convenient to keep it. Can't you bend some rule for a fellow cop?"

He gave her a smile and little wave, signifying that she could keep the weapon. "Don't like handguns on the island much. They never do anybody no good no how."

"Chief, that's true in the big city, too."

She shoved the newspaper copy over at him. He scanned the page quickly. "Yeah, I remember, but vaguely. Guy got caught in a riptide, I think. Didn't have a chance." He looked over at Mercedes Barren. "You don't get riptides on Miami Beach, I bet."

"No, chief."

"Well, a rip is caused when the wave motion disturbs a bit of the bottom sand, like opening a new hole. The water pours in, and suddenly it has to go back out. It peters out a couple of hundred yards from shore. Trouble is, most people just fight like crazy when they feel that current pulling them out. They don't know that all you got to do is ride it out, then swim back in. Or, if you got to do something, you swim parallel to the beach. Rip's probably only twenty, thirty yards wide. Nope, people don't keep their heads. They fight hard, get exhausted, and bingo! More paperwork for me, and a body search for the Coast Guard boys. Happens once or twice a year on South Beach."

"The paper just says South Beach."

Holt kept reading. "It says the family was staying in West Tisbury, but it don't say where."

"I know. I thought you might remember."

He shook his head. He looked at the newspaper again.

"Say, what's this got to do with visiting friends?"

Mercedes Barren laughed. "Well, chief, it's a long story, but I'll try to make it quick. My friends are renting the house and they came across this old paper. They knew I was coming up to visit and they thought it would be interesting to me, so they sent it down to Miami, along with directions on how to find the place. Well, wouldn't you know it, I lose the paper with the directions and phone number, but kept the silly old newspaper. So now I'm trying to find them."

"Unh-hunh."

"I bet you get a lot of weird ones in here during the summer."

"Unh-hunh."

"Well, just file me under your silly-summer-people file and help me figure out where to go."

Holt broke into a smile.

"That'd be a helluva long file, if I kept one."

They both laughed.

He looked at the story again. "I suppose we could call around to some of the realty people, see if they handled the rental. But that might take some time. Lot of realtors up here on the island nowadays. Did you try calling the *Gazette?*"

"Yes, but they had gone home for the night."

Holt thought for an instant.

"Well, I got one idea, might as well give it a shot."

He picked up the police band microphone and said:

"Dispatch, this is One Adam One, come back."

"Hello, Holt," said Lizzie Barry. "You should be home. That dinner's probably getting cold on the table."

"Dispatch, I've got a woman here, looking for her friends. It's a long story, but they're staying down at the same place where a guy named Allen was staying the summer he drowned. Twenty years ago. Do you remember that case? Over."

The radio crackled momentarily.

"Sure, Holt. I remember. He was taking an evening swim. It was that summer we had the hot spell, remember, when it went up to a hundred and five that one time. I remember because the same day my old dog died. Heatstroke. He was a good old dog, Holt, you remember him?"

Holt didn't. "Sure. Sure. A setter?"

"No, a Golden Retriever."

"Oh." Holt waited for the voice to continue, but she didn't. "So, dispatch . . . Lizzie, do you remember where the guy was living? Over."

"Think so. Not certain, but seems to me that he was staying on Tisbury Great Pond. On Finger Point. Could be wrong, though."

"Thanks, Lizzie. Ten-four."

"Anytime, Holt. Over and out."

Holt Overholser hung up the microphone. "How about that," he said. "Old Lizzie's like an encyclopedia. She remembers damn well near everything that ever happens up here. Anything exciting, at least. Look, though, it's gonna be real tricky to find your way down there at night. You ought to find a hotel room and stay the night, go down in the morning."

"Sounds like a good idea. Could you just show me, though, on the map?"

Holt shrugged. He walked over to the wall. He showed her the sand pit entrance and where the washboard dirt road curved about. He showed her the fork in the road and which path led down to Finger Point. He couldn't remember the last time he'd been down that road. Probably not in the twenty years since the drowning. He shook his head. "Got to remember," he said. "No lights down there at all. All looks the same. You could get real lost down there. Wait until morning."

"That's good advice, chief. I appreciate it. I think I'll just head into Vineyard Haven and find a hotel room. But I appreciate your taking the effort."

"No problem."

Holt Overholser walked Mercedes Barren outside into the night. "It's right warm tonight," he said. "Dropped down to forty-five three nights ago, so these old bones still say we're gonna have an early fall, and a tough winter. Course, you get to be my age, all the winters are tough."

Mercedes Barren laughed. "Chief, you look like you could handle anything that winter sends your way."

"Well, I guess you don't worry about the cold too much down there in Miami."

"That's right." She smiled. "You want to recommend a hotel?"

"They're all pretty good."

"Thanks again."

"Anytime. Drop by and we'll talk police work."

"Maybe I'll just do that," Mercedes Barren said.

He watched as she got back into her car. He did not see the instant disappearance of her friendly, outgoing demeanor, replaced immediately by a rigid, hard-eyed concentration. She pulled out of the driveway to the small police station. Holt then started to anticipate his waiting bluefish, although he noticed that Detective Barren had taken the road which led not to town, but into the island's dark core, which made him pause briefly, filled with vague concern, before heading home.

Detective Mercedes Barren drove carefully through the thickness of the night, thinking: The darkness will make finding the house more difficult, but it will allow me to approach Douglas Jeffers under concealment, which would give me an advantage. She had no real plan other than to not give him a chance. I will shoot him in the back if I have to, if I can. I will take the shot

390

that's open. Don't hesitate. Don't wait. Just seize the shot when it is there. One shot, make it count. That's all I'll get. It's all I'll need. She watched the road, peering ahead of the weak light thrown by the car headlights, looking for the turnoff that would lead her down toward Finger Point.

Images from the day seemed distant, yet intrusive on her concentration: She could see the Lost Boys, circled around her, poised on the edge of their perversion, watching her. She thought that she'd handled them well. She was struck, momentarily, by the power of suggestion, how the right words spoken in the right context can trigger almost any conclusion. She'd walked away from that session completely convinced that Martin Jeffers had gone to find his brother at the location where their adoptive father had died. That persuasion had remained firm, unshakable, as she'd taken a tire iron to the doctor's window, jackknifing into the apartment as she'd done before, only this time she was oblivious to any noise she made and she made no pretense toward stealth.

She had gone directly into the bedroom for what she needed: the faded old newspaper. She had been filled with a momentary anger when she scanned the story for details, only to learn that it was less specific than she needed.

But, she thought, that old country cop was perfect.

She remembered how she'd driven hard out of New Jersey, battling the afternoon traffic around Manhattan, screaming with frustrations at the delays on the road.

She had had to wait what seemed an interminable time in Woods Hole, pacing about the ferry office, clenching her hands together. The ferry ride itself had been tedious, the picture-postcard images of the setting sun and sailboats cutting through the green waters had been lost on her.

But she'd had singular success when she'd gone to the rental-car location closest to the ferry landing. She thought of the smallish man who'd taken her credit card and handed her the keys, and who had also informed her that she was absolutely correct, a Martin Jeffers had come in on the morning ferry.

"Said he had business down island. Friend of yours?"

"Well, competitors, really."

"Must be real estate. All you guys are always hustling about, trying to beat out the next guy. Or gal."

She had not corrected him. "Well, it's a tough buck."

"Not here. Everybody's making out like bandits."

He had looked at her license. "Don't get too many from Florida here. Mainly New York, Washington, Boston. Not Miami."

"I work for a large firm," she had lied. "Lots of offices."

"Well," the clerk had continued, "I think there's too much damn development up here, anyway."

She had sensed a touch of anger in his voice.

"Really?" she had replied. "I work for a company that specializes in antique-property restoration. Not like my buddy Jeffers. He does motels and condo complexes."

"Damn," the clerk had said. "Wish I hadn't given him the car."

"What sort of car was that?"

"A white Chevy Celebrity. Tag number eight-one-seven triple J. Keep your eyes open for it."

"Thanks," she had replied. "I will. Did he say where he was going exactly?"

"Nope."

"Well, I'll run him to ground."

"Good luck. Bring that car back by eight P.M. tomorrow to avoid the extra charge."

She clicked on the high beams and went down a small dip in the highway. Every hundred yards she saw another dirt road leading off to her right, and she swore angrily to herself, thinking each one looked the same. Keep going. Keep going. Look for the sand pit, like the chief said. Another car came toward her, lights blinking, signaling her to lower hers. She finally complied, and the other car slid by on the narrow roadway with a whooshing sound. It seemed to Detective Barren to have passed only inches from her and she felt a momentary panic. She watched the red taillights disappear and was suddenly surrounded by blackness again.

She stared into the night.

"It's here," she said out loud, the sound of her voice in the car comforting. "I know it is."

She drove on, slowing the car to a crawl.

"Come on, come on, where are you?"

She was alone and adrift, the island's dark like the ocean. She stared up at the skyline, barely able to distinguish where the trees ended and the heavens started. She felt unsettled, as if she were dangling above the water, holding on to the slimmest strand of rope. She could feel tension racing unchecked through her body. I'm close, she thought. I'm close. She felt a smothering sensation, as though there were no air inside the car whatsoever. He's here, I know it. Where? Where? She gritted her teeth together, grinding them. She squeezed her hands on the steering wheel until her knuckles were white. She raised her voice to herself, almost shouting against the solitude of the car and the night: "Come on, come on!"

And then she saw the turnoff.

Anne Hampton sat at the table, staring at the open notebook in front of her. She saw the words: I do what I do because I have to, because I want to. Because something within all of us tells us what to do, and if we ignore it, it will crush us with desire.

She had scribbled the younger brother's reply beneath: You can get help. It doesn't have to be.

She shook her head. That was the completely wrong tack to take with Douglas Jeffers. She looked at the notes again. This part of the conversation was several hours old. Perhaps he's figured out another approach. But she doubted it. She thought the brother seemed lost, unable to comprehend, driven to confrontation, then barely able to articulate a sentence, much less persuade the older brother to set down his gun. She closed her eyes. I could have told him that, she said to herself. I could have told him that it was all set, now, there was no way out, no end to the script other than the one Douglas Jeffers had invented sometime earlier, in some other era, deep in the past, when I was still just a student and someone's daughter and eons before I became the murderer's biographer.

Anne Hampton wondered idly what would happen to them all now. She felt detached, almost as if she were someone else, standing outside her body, invisible to all the others, watching the events unfold on a stage. She remembered that she had felt this way before, during some of the murders, during the first moments in the motel. How long ago was that? She could not tell. She thought that was always what memory was like; it seems like so many snapshots in the mind, film clips with ragged edges and blinking, jerky motions. I can see myself running through the snow, she thought. I can see the hurt and cold in my face, but I cannot recall how the sensation felt anymore. I couldn't save him, she thought. She saw the derelict and the lone man on the street and the two lucky women—what were their names?—then the teenagers in the car. I can't save anybody. I can't, I can't. I wasn't allowed. I wanted to, oh God, I wanted to save him, he was my brother, but I couldn't, I couldn't. I can't.

She wanted to weep, but knew it would not be permitted.

"Boswell!"

She looked up sharply at the sound of Douglas Jeffers' voice. She jumped from her chair.

"Take some water in to our guests."

She nodded and ran to the kitchen. She found a pitcher in the cabinet above the stove and filled it with water. Walking quickly, but careful not to spill any, she maneuvered past the living room, where the two brothers sat opposite each other, now wordless, after a day of talk. She opened the door to the downstairs bedroom and entered softly. She thought they might be asleep and didn't want to wake anyone. But at the scraping of her feet on the wood floor, she saw four sets of eyebrows soar in panicked anticipation.

She felt wretched.

"It's all right, it's all right," she said. She knew how silly her words sounded, how foolish it was to try to comfort them. She knew they would die, and soon. That had been the plan all along.

That they were nobodies didn't matter to him, this she knew. What was important was that they were there, in this location, which she knew was important to him. She remembered his words, spoken under his breath, seconds before breaking in through a sliding porch door, left benignly unlocked, open to summer breezes:

"I need to fill this house with ghosts."

She put her hand on the woman's arm gently, reassuringly. "I've brought you some water," she said. "Just nod if you want a drink. You first, Mrs. Simmons?"

The woman nodded, and Anne Hampton loosened the gag from the woman's mouth. She held the jug up to the woman's lips. "Don't take too much," she said. "I don't know if he'll let me take you to the bathroom." The woman stopped in midgulp and nodded again.

"I'm scared," the woman said, taking advantage of the loosened gag. "Can't you help us? You seem like such a nice girl. You're not much older than the twins, please, please . . ."

Anne Hampton was about to respond when she heard a voice from the living room. "No talking. Just one drink. Don't make me enforce the rules."

"Please," the woman whispered.

"I'm sorry," Anne Hampton whispered back. She replaced the gag, but not so tightly. The woman nodded gratefully.

Anne Hampton moved first to one of the twins, then the other. "Don't talk," she whispered to each. When she reached the father she hesitated. "Please," she said, "don't try anything. Don't force him." The man nodded and she loosened the gag. He drank and then she replaced the handkerchief. For a moment he strained against the rope that bound all of them together. She heard the man say, despite the gag in his mouth, "Help us, please," but she could not respond.

"I'm sorry," she said.

She closed the door on the family and went back into the main room. "How're they doing?" Douglas Jeffers asked.

"They're scared."

"They should be."

"Doug, please," Martin Jeffers said. "At least let them go. What have they done . . ."

The older brother cut the younger one off abruptly.

"Haven't you learned anything all day? Christ, Marty, I've explained and explained. It is important that they haven't done anything. That's crucial. Can't you see? The guilty never get punished, only the innocent. That's the way the world works. The innocent and the powerless. They make up the victim class."

Douglas Jeffers shook his head.

"It can't be that hard for you to understand."

"I'm trying, Doug, believe me, I'm trying."

Douglas Jeffers looked harshly at his brother.

"Try harder."

They lapsed into silence. Douglas Jeffers toyed with his automatic pistol while Martin Jeffers sat quietly. Anne Hampton moved across the room and took up her seat, opening a new notepad.

"Get it all down, Boswell."

She nodded and waited. She thought: It is all madness. Everywhere. There is no normalcy left in the world, only hurt and death and insanity. And I'm part of it. Completely.

She took the pen and wrote: No one gets out alive.

She surprised herself. It was the first time she'd written any thought of her own in the notebooks. She stared down at the phrase. It terrified her.

The words on the pages shimmered and wavered like heat above one of the black highways they'd traveled. She fought off the exhaustion and the deadly thought and reconstructed the day in her head, blocking fear with memory.

She did not know why Douglas Jeffers had postponed killing the Simmons family, only that they had herded them all from their beds, tied, blindfolded, and gagged, into the side room. He'd left them there while he'd relaxed, feet up on the couch, savoring the rising sun. He'd then fixed a leisurely breakfast. He had only said that keeping them caged for a day heightened the game. She had been surprised; it had seemed almost as if he did not want to hurry himself, that he was luxuriating in the situation, not wanting to rush on to the next. The jeopardy of their circumstances seemed not to affect him. She did not know what it was that was causing him to pause and greet things with such studied delay, but it scared her.

We're at the end, she had thought.

It's the last scene, and he wants to play it for what it's worth. Two thoughts had intruded in the maze of her fears:

What will he do to them?

What will he do to me?

Douglas Jeffers had made eggs and bacon, but she had been unable to swallow anything. They were just finishing when the car came down the driveway. She had been horrified at the thought of somebody stumbling in on Douglas Jeffers. Then her terror had redoubled at the sight of the brother. She had instantly assumed he would be the same. When he wasn't, it had confused and disturbed her more.

She looked at the two men again.

They were only a few feet apart, but she wondered how distant they really were. She had the vague understanding that it was important to her, but she could not guess why.

She wanted to scream at them: I want to live!

But, instead, she sat patiently, quietly, awaiting instructions.

So far they had spent the day just as one would expect any pair of brothers. They'd talked of old things, of memories. They had laughed a bit. But by the early afternoon the conversation had disintegrated, wilting under the inexorable pressure of the situation, and now they sat apart, waiting.

She looked back a half-dozen pages in her notebook and saw some of what she had written down. Martin Jeffers had said, "Doug, I can't believe why we're here. Can we talk about it?"

And Douglas Jeffers' reply: "Believe it."

She looked up at the pair and saw Martin Jeffers shift in his seat. She did not know what to think of him. Will he save me? She wondered suddenly.

"Doug, why are you doing this?"

"Asked and answered. That's what the attorneys say in a court case when they're trying to protect their witness from cross-examination. Asked and answered. Go on to the next question."

"There is only one question."

"Not true, Marty, not true. Certainly there's why, I'll grant you that. But there's also how and when, and what are you going to do now. That seems most relevant."

"All right," Martin Jeffers agreed, "What are you going to do now?"

"Don't ask."

Douglas Jeffers burst out laughing. The sound seemed alien, impossible, in the small room. Anne Hampton recognized the laugh from all the worst moments. She hoped the younger brother would have the sense to back down.

He did. He sat quietly. After a few moments the older brother waved his hand in the air as if clearing the space between them.

"Tell me," said Douglas Jeffers. "How much do you know?"

"I know everything."

The older brother paused.

"Well, that's not good. Not good at all."

He hesitated before continuing.

"So that means you went to my place. I thought you would wait until it was over. You were supposed to wait."

"No, actually, someone else did."

"Who?"

Martin Jeffers stopped. He suddenly had no idea what to say. He thought of all the times he'd been in intense conversation with one criminal or another. He'd always known what gestures to make, how to act. This time he drew a complete blank. He stared across at his brother, and at the gun waving about in his hands. But he saw the child behind the man and realized: I am one, too. The younger brother. A massive, burning resentment started to grow within him. Always last to know. Always the last to get anything. He always did exactly what he wanted, regardless of what I thought. He never listened to me. He always treated me like some unwanted appendage. He was always in charge. He was always important. I was always nothing. The afterthought. Always, always. He suddenly hated everything and wanted to hurt his brother.

"A detective."

The word was out of his mouth swiftly. He regretted it immediately.

"He knows, too?"

Martin Jeffers saw his brother stiffen, struggling but maintaining composure. But in the same moment whatever lilt and relaxation emptied from his voice, replaced with an instant harsh noise. It was a tone Martin Jeffers had never heard before, but which he knew with a familiarity born of years. He thought: Killing tones.

"Yes," he said. "Actually, it's a she."

Douglas Jeffers waited, then said:

"Well, that brings dying time a bit closer."

*   *   *

Detective Mercedes Barren had trouble controlling the large American car, with its mushy suspension that bounced and yawed back and forth, trying to take the bumps in the dirt road. A high-pitched scratching sound filled the interior as a tree branch scraped paint from the side of the automobile. She heard the tailpipe slap the ground, but she continued on, doggedly, ignoring the difficulty.

She would not acknowledge that she was lost. But the enveloping black of the night and the forest created a sense of despair within her, as if reason and responsibility had been abandoned back on the main highway, and she was descending into some netherworld where the rules were created by death. The shadows seemed to leap from the headlights, each one a bansheelike wraith with the face of Douglas Jeffers. She gasped in fear and drove on, her heavy gun now clutched in her right hand, balanced on top of the steering wheel.

When she arrived at the multiple fork in the road, her headlights picking out the four different-colored arrows, she stopped the car and got out.

She stood, looking at the four different paths.

Her heart was filled with frustration. She remembered the police chief's description, and she formed a mental picture of the map that hung in his office. But it had no correlation to the dark choices that faced her now. She thought of the lady and the tiger, but knew that she wanted to open the door that contained the beast.

"It must be that one," she said, pointing down one black path. "I'm certain," she added in defiance of the fear of her actual uncertainty. The disjointed idea that she would arrive, gun in hand, at some other summer vacationer's house, floated about for an instant in the back of her mind. Then she dismissed it.

"Let's go," she said, the sound of her own voice seeming small and puny against the forest. She got back behind the wheel of the car and drove ahead.

Two hundred yards down the road, it forked again and she followed her instincts to the left. She knew that she was searching for the pond, and that the point of land where she would find her quarry waiting was long and narrow. She rolled down the window, trying to get a sense of where the water was, but only the night penetrated into the car. She kept driving, rolling through an open wooden fence and a large KEEP OUT THIS MEANS YOU sign. She ignored it, pushing deeper and deeper into the scrub brush and pines, until the forest seemed to envelop her. She was afraid of being smothered and she sucked in air, hyperventilating.

She would not allow herself even to think for an instant that she might be heading in some completely wrong direction.

"Keep going," she said.

She saw a break in the trees ahead and she punched down on the accelerator gratefully. The car jumped forward, then crunched down, seeming to fall, like an athlete tripped just short of the finish line. She shouted out in sudden fear. She heard a snapping sound, followed by a grinding noise.

She stopped the car and stepped out.

Both front wheels were driven into a small yet unfortunately effective pit. The car's front axle was ground into the sand.

She sighed and closed her eyes. Keep going, she told herself again. She opened her eyes and got back into the car. The rear wheels spun furiously when she tried to back out of the pit. She pounded the wheel in momentary frustration, then swallowed hard and looked about her. She shut off the engine and switched off the lights. All right, she told herself. You can go the rest of the way on foot. This isn't terrible; you planned on abandoning the car soon anyway. Just keep going, keep going.

She headed toward the break in the trees, her eyes adjusting rapidly to the night light. She kept her pistol in her hand and started to jog, just gently, afraid that she would do to her ankle what the pit had done to the rental car. But the hurried movement encouraged her, and she pressed farther, listening to the thudding sound her feet made as they hit the sandy road surface.

The road seemed like a tunnel to her, and she could see the end. She picked up her pace and suddenly shot out of the overhanging trees into a wide grassy field awash with moonlight. She dizzily stared up into the skies, overwhelmed by the thousands of star lights that blinked and shone in the endless expanse. She felt minuscule and alone, but comforted by being out from under the trees. For an instant she thought she would be blinded by the moonlight, and she stopped, breathing hard, to get her bearings.

She saw a great glistening reflection off to her left and she stared out at the pond. She could clearly see the strip of sand that stood between the edge of the field and the start of the pond water. She held her breath for a moment and realized that she could hear the steady rhythmic pounding of surf against the shore. She looked toward the sound and could easily make out the black line of South Beach a half mile distant.

I found it, she thought.

I'm there.

She looked ahead, expecting to see the house, but could not.

She turned and looked to her right, expecting to see the pond, also, but all she could see was the dark forest stretching back into the island.

"That's not right," she said out loud, hesitant, suddenly worried. "That's not right at all. Finger Point is supposed to be narrow, with water on both sides."

She moved forward ten feet, as if by looking at it from a slightly different angle the topography would change.

"This isn't right at all," she said.

Dozens of conflicting emotions reverberated like so much dissonance within her.

"Please," she said. "It must be."

She walked down to the edge of the water and stared out across the pond. The moonlight shimmered on the light, choppy waves. She stared into the night, across the water.

Then she sank down to her knees in the sand.

"No," she said softly. "Please, no. No, no, no."

In front of her was the pond water, stretching out in one direction across to the rolling sandy dunes of South Beach. But back, just across from where she knelt, she could see a single long, black spit of land that pointed out into the center of the pond.

"No," she said, under her voice. "It's not fair."

She could see the house on the end of the point and knew then that she was looking at the place where the Jeffers brothers waited. She concentrated her eyes in the darkness and saw the moonlight catch what she guessed was the white shape of the rental car checked out to Martin Jeffers.

She pitched forward at the waist and pounded her fists on the sand. "No, no, no, no, no," she moaned. Still kneeling, she turned and looked back at the forest. The wrong road, she thought, the wrong damn road. I've come down the wrong edge of the pond. All this way, just to take the wrong damn turn. Dismay filled her precipitously. She battled within herself against herself.

Finally, breathing hard, as if she'd just run a race, not was about to start one, she gained control.

She stood.

"I will not be defeated," she said out loud. She raised her fist at the house. "I'm coming. I'm coming."

Holt Overholser pushed himself back from the table, staring at the few remains of his second helping of bluefish casserole that were left on his plate, and said, "Damn, damn."

"What is it, dear?" his wife asked. "Something wrong with the fish?"

He shook his head. "Just something happened that's kinda bugging me," he said.

"Well, don't keep it to yourself," his wife replied, clearing the dinner dishes. "What's on your mind? Worries just get in the way of digestion, you know."

He thought for an instant that his wife had the world figured out pretty squarely: everything was digestion. If the Arabs and the Jews ate more grains, they wouldn't always be fighting. If the Russians were more balanced in their diet and cut their caloric intake, they wouldn't forever be thumping their chests and threatening world peace. If terrorists would stop eating red meat and partake of more fish, they wouldn't need to seize airliners. Republicans ate too many fatty foods, which gave them bad hearts and conservative outlooks, so she always voted the Democratic ticket. He'd once tried to ask her about some of the more substantial members of the Massachusetts congressional delegation, like Tip and Teddy, but she wouldn't listen to him.

"Well, right before closing shop, I had this visit from a detective. She came all the way from Miami."

"Was she on a case, dear? It must have been exciting."

"She said she wasn't."

"Why didn't you bring her home for dinner?"

"But she was armed. And she had a funny story that makes less and less sense the more I think about it."

"Well, dear, what are you going to do?"

Holt Overholser thought hard for a moment. Maybe he wasn't any Sherlock Holmes, but he sure could match Mike Hammer.

"I think I'm gonna take a little ride," he said. "Don't worry none. I'll be back in time for *Magnum P.I.*"

He slung his Sam Browne belt over his shoulder and headed out to the big four-wheel-drive police truck.

Martin Jeffers remained frozen in his seat, watching his brother pace angrily about the room. He tried once to catch Anne Hampton's eyes, but she was rigid, at the table, pen poised. He wondered for an instant what she must have been through; he could not guess, but knew that it must have been severe to bring about the state of near-catatonia she seemed trapped within.

His observation surprised him. It was the first reflection he'd had since arriving at Finger Point that at least displayed some rudimentary psychological knowledge. He tried to give himself commands: Use what you know!

Then he shook his head slightly, just the barest of acknowledgements, signaling to himself that it was hopeless. At this moment, he thought, I am nothing except the younger brother.

He looked up at Douglas Jeffers and thought: With him, it is all I will ever be.

He fixed his eyes on his brother, who seemed filled with excitement. He seemed to be assessing the situation with every step about the room.

"Isn't it funny," said Douglas Jeffers in a voice devoid of any semblance of humor, "how one enters into a situation so emotionally complex it cries out, yet there is little, if anything, actually to say to one another? What are you going to do? Tell me I can't be the way I am?"

The comment brought forth a short explosive laugh.

"So," said the older brother, "tell me something relevant, something important. Tell me about this lady cop."

"What do you want to know?"

His brother stopped and pointed the gun at him.

"Do you think that I would hesitate for an instant? Do you think that your status as my brother gives you some special dispensation? You came here! You knew! So you knew the risks as well . . ."

He paused.

"So don't screw around with me."

Martin Jeffers nodded.

"She comes from Miami. She believes you killed her niece . . ." He couldn't state what he knew, and what his mind insisted: You did kill her niece! You killed all of them! ". . . She was the one that broke into your apartment and found the pictures."

"Where is she now?"

"I left her in New Jersey."

"Why?"

"Because she means to kill you."

Douglas Jeffers laughed.

"Well, that seems sensible from her point of view."

"Doug, please, can't we . . ."

"Can't we what? Marty, you were always such a dreamer. Don't you remember? All those books I used to read to you when you were little. Always fantasies, adventures, filled with heroes and battling for just causes against insurmountable odds. You always liked reading about soldiers who fought desperate fights, about knights that charged dragons. You always liked the ones where goodness triumphs . . .

"You know what? It doesn't. It never does. Because even when goodness wins, it lowers itself and has to beat evil at its own game. And that, dear brother, is a far worse defeat."

"That's not true."

Douglas Jeffers shrugged. "Believe what you want, Marty. It makes no difference." He paused, then continued. "Tell me more. Is she a good detective? What's her name?"

"Mercedes Barren. I suppose she is. She found me . . ."

Douglas Jeffers snarled: "You think she'll find me, too?"

Martin Jeffers nodded.

His brother laughed, raucously, angrily.

"No fucking chance. Not unless you told her where to come. You didn't, did you, brother?"

Martin Jeffers shook his head.

Douglas Jeffers scowled. "I don't fucking believe you." He paused. "Oh, you probably didn't know you were telling her, but you did. I know you, Marty. I know you as well as I know myself. That's part of what being older means: the older brother is burdened with understanding, the younger brother is filled only with equal parts awe and jealousy. So, even if you think you left her behind, you probably didn't. You said something, probably didn't even know what it was. But you said it and now she's on her way. Especially if she was smart enough to get to you in the first place. But how close is she? There, dear brother, that's the real question. Is she outside the door?"

Martin Jeffers' eyes involuntarily flicked to the sliding glass doors. His brother laughed again, menacingly.

". . . Or is she a little ways behind? Maybe a few hours."

He smiled, not with any enjoyment that belonged on the earth.

"You see," Douglas Jeffers continued, "after tonight I will be long gone. I thought coming to Finger Point an excellent place to be born again. And not in some silly fundamentalist religious sense. We've got a lot of memories, shall I say, floating about around here. That's a joke. Anyway, here is where it all begins again for me. Starting over. Back to square one, free as the proverbial bird."

"How?"

Douglas Jeffers gestured towards his photo satchel. "Details, details. Suffice it to say, inside the bag is the new me."

"I still don't understand," Martin Jeffers said.

"There's only one thing you need to know," Douglas Jeffers said abruptly. "The new me doesn't have a brother."

The words punched Martin Jeffers in the core. He thought he

would be nauseated and he tried to steady himself by grasping the arms of the chair.

"You won't," he said. "I don't believe you could."

"Don't be ridiculous," Douglas Jeffers said irritatedly. "Boswell can reassure you: I've never had any qualms about killing anybody, have I, Boswell?"

They both turned and looked at Anne Hampton. She shook her head.

"... So why should I hesitate to kill my brother? Come on! Cain slew Abel, didn't he? Isn't that the deepest secret all brothers harbor? We all want to murder each other. You should know that, you're the shrink. Anyway, what better route to complete and total freedom could there be? With you alive, I would always know you were out there, one solid, unshakable link to the past. Suppose we bumped together on the street one day? Or maybe you saw my picture somewhere. I could never be certain, you know, never be really sure. You know what the silly thing is? I was willing to take that chance. Right up to the moment you showed up here. Then, as soon as I saw you, I realized how wrong that was. If I wanted to live, well ... you see, don't you? With you gone, well ..." He shrugged. "Seems reasonable to me."

"Doug, you're not, don't be, what do you ..." His voice trailed off. He was confused and astonished. Martin Jeffers kept thinking: But I came here to save him!

In a single terrifying leap, Douglas Jeffers crossed the room, thrusting the barrel of the automatic up under his brother's throat. "Can you feel death? Can you smell it? Can you taste it on your lips? They all could, all of them, if only for an instant, but they could."

"Doug, please, please ..."

Douglas Jeffers stepped back. "Weakness is disgusting." He looked at his brother. "I should have let you go, then you would have died, too."

Martin Jeffers shook his head. He knew immediately what his brother was talking about. "I was a strong swimmer. As good as you. Much better than he was. I would have saved him."

"He didn't deserve to be saved."

Their eyes locked and both men's minds filled with the same memory.

"It was just like tonight," Martin Jeffers said.

"I remember," his brother joined in, some of his menace sliding away in recollection.

"It was hot and he wanted to swim. He took us to the beach,

but you said not to go in. You could see the water tossing about. I remember."

"There'd been a storm a few days earlier, remember? Storms always knock the hell out of the beach. That's why. I thought there might be a rip and you couldn't see it coming at night . . ."

"That's why you wouldn't let me go in."

Douglas Jeffers nodded. "But that old bastard called us chicken. He got what he deserved."

Martin Jeffers hesitated.

"We could have saved him, Doug. It wasn't a bad rip, but he fought it. We were much stronger than he was. Much. We could have saved him, but you wouldn't. You held me on the beach and said let him swim in his own shit, I remember. You held me and I heard him call for help. You kept holding me until he stopped calling."

Douglas Jeffers smiled.

"I guess it was my first killing. God, it was so easy."

He looked at his brother.

"In their own way they've all been easy."

Martin Jeffers asked, "Is that what started you?"

Douglas Jeffers shrugged. "Ask Boswell. It's all in the notes."

"You tell me!"

"Why?"

"I need to know."

"No, you don't."

Martin Jeffers paused. That was true.

After a moment he asked, "So what are you going to do?"

Douglas Jeffers stepped back, rising. "I told you, Marty, I should have let you go that night. Then you both would have drowned. That was what should have happened. Do you know that was the last time I ever showed anyone pity? No, I don't suppose you know that. I took care of you that night. It didn't matter how hard you fought or how hard he screamed. I wasn't letting you go into the water to save that bastard. I saved your life that night. I gave you all these good, bad, sad years. Now I'm calling in my marker. Time's up. Game's over. All-y-all-y-in-come-free. Don't you see? All I'm really going to do is what has been delayed all these years: I'm going to let you rush to your own death."

He paused. "Maybe you would have saved him. He didn't deserve it. But maybe you would have. It would have been nice for you to do something brave . . ."

"But you didn't get the chance."

Douglas Jeffers took a deep breath.

"You'll never get the chance."

He raised the gun, pointing at his brother.

"You probably have some romantic idea that this is difficult," Douglas Jeffers said blankly.

"Well, it isn't."

He fired the gun.

The echo of the gunshot fled across the black waters and rushed up into the starry sky. Detective Mercedes Barren raced back to the edge of the water, peering into the ink-dark night, knowing that the shot came from the house directly across from where she stood. She could feel the gentle pond wavelets slapping at the toes of her sneakers. Her insides were churning and her head was screaming: No time! No time! It's happening now! I know it!

She stared at the water, filled with impotent rage. I can't swim! Oh, God, I can't, I can't.

Maybe it's shallow, she tried to persuade herself.

She knew that was a lie.

She took a single tentative step into the water. It chilled her heart and she could feel the suffocating darkness start to close on her. She felt dizzy and stepped back. She turned and peered behind her, at the long road back through the woods.

No time.

She thought: I am a hundred yards from success. It might as well be a million miles.

Her half-determination, half-panic swirled within her, filling her with despair and devotion. I will get there, she said to herself, gritting her teeth. I will. I will.

But she did not know how.

She turned and looked up the beach. The moonlight caught the water, spinning wan light about into odd figures and shadows. She saw a dark, oblong shape perhaps fifty yards away at the lip of the water. She took one hesitant step toward it, then another. Her mind would not form the word: boat. But her heart shouted orders and she found herself suddenly running, racing across the sandy beach, toward the shape. With each step it took greater and greater form, until, finally, she could see that it was a small skiff.

I'm coming, she thought. Thank you, thank you. She rushed to the side of the boat and grasped it.

Then she stopped dead.

There was no engine. No oars. Just a single mast, without sail.

Not allowing disappointment to move within her, she slid to

the front of the boat. It was chained to a post sunk into the sand. The chain had been padlocked.

She slipped to the sand, frustration and dismay unleashed within her. She breathed out hard, fighting tears. She thought she could not deal with the capriciousness of life anymore. It's all wrong, she told herself. Everything's been all wrong. All along.

I'm sorry. I'm sorry. Oh, God, I tried. I tried so hard.

She stared back at the lights across the water.

He'll get away, she said to herself. I was never any closer than I am now. There was always something that would keep me from him.

I've lost.

She put her head down on her arms, leaning against the gunnel of the boat.

I'm sorry, she said again.

The moonlight seemed to make the boat glow in the darkness. It caught the ridge of something white, stuck in the corner of the hull.

She sat up, instantly curious, a vague sense of reprieve filling her. She reached out her hand and seized a plastic-coated cushion. It had two looped handles on either end. Her hands twitched: a floatation cushion.

She looked across to the house, where she knew Douglas Jeffers was getting ready to leave, to disappear forever from her grasp. This is it, she told herself. This is your only chance. Then she stared at the water, curling black and bottomless in front of her. She thought of her niece and she remembered the effortless way Susan slipped through the opaque blue pool, graceful, at ease, fearless. "Oh, God," she said again. She remembered the crushing green fury that boiled around her and slammed her down, tearing her breath away, trying to rip the life from her little-girl lungs. She thought of the promise she'd made as a child and kept as an adult. Her mind filled then with the sum of every nightmare she'd ever had and her entire body revolted, shaking.

"I can't," she said.

She remembered her father coming padding through the dark house to the side of her bed, comforting her when a nightmare awakened her. He would take his big hands and gently rub her temples, saying to her that he was going to coax the bad dream out of her head. After a moment he would hold his palm up, as if he held the frightening thought in the air before her. She remembered he would say: Goodbye, bad dreams; begone, nightmare. And then he would take a deep breath and blow the unsettling thoughts into some childhood oblivion. She remembered stroking her niece's forehead the same way so that Susan could settle back into the easy sleep of youth. She took a deep breath and exhaled slowly. She said to herself, Begone, nightmare!

She took a step toward the water.

"I can't," she repeated.

But she slipped the loops on the cushion over her arms. She dug her pistol into her belt.

"I can't swim."

She felt the water curl around her ankles. It seemed to be grasping for her, trying to pull her into its dark void.

"I can't," she said a last time.

Then she pushed herself gently into the water.

For the first twenty yards her toes bounced against the bottom and she felt confident. It was in the twenty-first yard, when her legs bounced down, expecting to touch the mushy bottom and found nothing save more fluid, that panic started to grip her. She shouted to herself: Keep going, keep moving.

She paddled gently with her arms and kicked steadily with her feet.

You can make it, she told herself with false bravado.

A wavelet rose up and slapped her in the face.

It caused her to lose her equilibrium, and she teetered as if on some pinnacle. She twitched, then thrashed, trying to regain control. Another wavelet punched her and she spun about, feeling herself slipping. Black panic started to explode within her, and she struggled to regain her balance. But each movement, no matter how little, only pitched her back and forth harder. She squeezed the cushion, but it bucked and fought her.

She wanted to scream but could not.

A small wave broke against her, and she could feel everything sliding away from her.

No! No! No! she screamed inwardly.

Then she rolled, turtlelike, the black water suddenly slamming over her head like a closet door shut around her.

Oh, God! I'm dying!

It was as if the water were tugging her down. She battled against the flood pulling her to the bottom.

The water held her, embracing her like some demon lover, squeezing the breath from her, twisting her into its darkness. She could no longer tell which was up and which was down. The night had been ripped away, replaced by the thick grasp of the pond.

Where is the air!

Help, me! Help, me! Oh, God! Please! Don't let me drown!

She thrashed and fought like a tigress alone in the blackness against death.

I won't, I won't, I won't let it happen like this! Susan! God! Help me! Susan, no!

She suddenly thought that it was all wrong to die so close to victory. And in some microsecond of reason that penetrated the fear that gripped her, she thought: Do not give in.

And so she didn't.

Within the vacuum of panic, she knew to clutch the floatation cushion. She seized it with a fury, screaming to herself her desire to live. She wrestled it around, so that it was suddenly riding beneath her chest. She could feel, abruptly, the cushion pushing her up, and in a second her head broke the surface of the water.

She did not understand exactly how it had happened, but she gratefully gulped in great gasps of air, resting.

Her eyes remained on the house. It was closer.

"I'm still coming," she said between gritted teeth.

As she started to work herself forward, she saw an extraordinary sight: a flight of six ghost-white swans soaring three feet above the pond surface flew directly over her as if pointing the way. She watched as the birds, their wings glowing in the moonlight, pivoted above the house and then disappeared into the night sky. "Susan," she said out loud in near delirium. "I'm coming."

She realized then that she had lost her mind.

Perhaps I did die, she thought. Perhaps I'm dreaming this.

I'm really dead, beneath the water, and this is all the last fantasy before entering the void.

She paddled on, stretching with every fiber for the mixed safety and danger of the waiting shore.

"Well," Douglas Jeffers said rigidly, "that proves something."

Martin Jeffers stared wide-eyed, on the promontory of panic. He could smell cordite and powder, and the gunshot still rang in his ears, deafening him. He did not dare to turn and inspect the wall where the bullet had slammed in, a foot, perhaps two, above his head.

"Now you know," said Douglas Jeffers. "Now you know."

Know what? Martin Jeffers thought. He did not speak.

Douglas Jeffers turned and stepped to the sliding glass doors, standing, looking out over the water. He paused, seeming to absorb all the night sensations.

Martin Jeffers blinked his eyes and took a deep breath, as if double-checking to be certain he remained alive. He watched his brother. He's right. He has no choice.

"I would never tell," Martin Jeffers said.

"Yes, you would." Douglas Jeffers snorted, a small laugh. "You'd have to, Marty. They'd make you. Hell, you'd make you."

"I keep confidences—in my profession . . ."

The older brother interrupted. "This isn't part of your profession."

"Well, there are lots of families with great dark secrets that they never tell anyone. It's in all the literature. It's in dozens of novels and plays. Why not . . ."

Douglas Jeffers interrupted, a weak smile flitting across his troubled face. "Awww, come on, Marty."

He paused before continuing.

"And, anyway, it would ruin your life. Think about it. No one could carry that kind of knowledge about their brother forever. It would eat away at you, gnawing like some determined rat at your guts. No, you'd tell. And then she'd find me."

"How?"

"She just would. Never underestimate what madness and revenge can drive someone to."

Martin Jeffers said nothing. He knew his brother was right.

A silence filled the room.

"So?" said Martin Jeffers. He was filled with confusion. He heard his own voice speaking in the room, but it was as if it were someone else giving the commands to talk. What are you saying? he said to himself. What are you doing? Stop, for Christ's sake! But his voice continued, unchecked: "I guess you're just going to have to kill me."

Douglas Jeffers continued to look out the door. His silence was his answer.

"What about Boswell?" Martin Jeffers asked.

Again Douglas Jeffers didn't reply.

Anne Hampton stared at the two brothers and thought: This is the end. He does not need anyone. He has the notebooks. He has a new life.

She tried to will her body to move. Run, she thought. Escape! she was unable to. I know I can, she said to herself. I know I can. She gritted her teeth together and squeezed her hands. She looked down and saw that her knuckles were white around the edge of the pen and started to push it against her other hand. Pain filled her. You're still alive! she screamed to herself. It hurts and you're alive. She looked at the two brothers and, slowly, she said to herself: My name is Anne Hampton. Anne with an *e*. I am twenty years old and I attend Florida State University. I have a home in

Colorado and I am a literature major because I love books. I am me.

She repeated this over and over to herself.

I am me. You are you. We are we. I am me.

Martin Jeffers watched his brother, filling with dread at what he might do, despair at what he was.

"Doug, why did you become you? Why not me, too?"

Douglas Jeffers shrugged.

"Now who the hell knows? Maybe it was the difference in years. A few months can mean you see things differently, feel things differently. It's like asking ten people to recall the same event that they witnessed. They'll all come up with slightly skewed versions of the same thing. Why is it any different with people?" He laughed. "I'm just a slightly skewed version."

"I'm sorry," Martin Jeffers said.

"Fuck you, little brother," Douglas Jeffers responded. "Do you think I don't want to be the way I am?"

He turned and eyed his brother.

"I am one of the greats of all time."

He gestured at Anne Hampton. "She can tell you."

Douglas Jeffers looked back at his brother.

"You will be forgotten. Me? Never."

Douglas Jeffers warred within himself. He refused to let his brother see the raging factions of his heart, masking the internal battle with all the savage words he could muster. It's all gotten screwed up, he thought. And it was all moving so perfectly before he showed up. He was supposed to learn after I disappeared. Damn! Damn that damn detective! He kept his back to his brother for fear that the younger would see the indecision that had crept into his eyes. Hundreds of images from their childhood swept him. He remembered the night in New Hampshire. He remembered all the nights that he'd crept to his younger brother's side, to comfort as best he could the little boy's tears. Does he remember? Douglas Jeffers wondered. Does he recall all the lullabies and stories, all the times I rocked him to sleep? Does he remember how I pinned him to the sand so that he wouldn't rush out into the water to his death? That man would have killed us both if he could. But I protected him. I always protected him. Even when I teased him or mocked him. Even when I knew what I was becoming. I always took care of him because he was always the good part of me. He laughed inwardly: They're wrong, he thought. Even psychopaths have some emotions if you dig deep enough.

Then he thought: Maybe we don't.

He measured, on the balance scale within him, his life against his brother's.

One of us starts over tonight.

One of us dies.

He could see no other options.

He turned away, staring back out across the night waters. "You know, all those summers we were here, I always loved it," he said. "It was always so damn wild and beautiful at the same time."

His eyes caught a flashing shape of white, and he watched a flight of swans skim the surface of the pond.

"Have you noticed?" he said. "Everything is the same. Even the swan family that lives on the pond."

"Nothing is the same," said Martin Jeffers.

But his brother didn't hear him, his attention suddenly riveted elsewhere.

It was as if someone had sent a red-hot stake through his core. Douglas Jeffers stiffened, his eyes burning into the darkness, directly at the shape he saw struggling in the water. For an instant he was confused. What the hell is that? he asked himself. Then, immediately, he knew.

She's here!

He pivoted and abruptly brought the automatic to bear on his brother.

"Boswell! The rope and the tape!"

Anne Hampton was incapable of refusing the summons. She grabbed the satchel with the equipment in it and rushed it to Douglas Jeffers.

"Marty, don't screw around. Don't try anything. Just reach out your hands and let me tie them."

Martin Jeffers, suddenly filled with apprehension, complied unwittingly, as any younger brother would do. He felt the loops of rope encase his wrists tightly. He wanted to complain, but before he had a chance, his brother had slapped a piece of tape across his lips. He looked up, trying to say, I don't want to die tied like some animal, but his brother was moving too quickly to stop and meet his glance.

"Boswell! Stand there. Don't move. Regardless of what happens, don't move."

Anne Hampton froze in position and waited.

Douglas Jeffers took one quick look about and slid through the open porch door, disappearing into the blackness that pressed against the weak light of the living room.

For a moment he stood on the porch, peering down toward the

water where he'd seen the shape. Then he cast about quickly. An idea struck him and he moved into position.

Relief flooded her as her toes and knees scraped against the bottom.

Detective Mercedes Barren pushed forward, suddenly realizing that the water had grown shallow. She stood, liquid dripping from her like great tears, her eyes lifted upward as if in gratitude. She strode through the water, trying to make as little noise as possible, then threw herself on the beach. She dug her hands in, feeling the dry solid sand slip like wealth through her fingers. She allowed herself one totally unbridled moment of relief and joy.

Then she breathed in and whispered to herself, "That was the easy part."

She climbed to her knees and retrieved her bearings.

She got up, crouching over, and moved to the edge of the sand, hiding behind gnarled and tangled beach scrub brush. She could see the lights of the house, but she couldn't see anyone inside from her position. She removed her weapon from her belt and started to maneuver forward.

She crawled through the brush.

It seemed as if the night were alive about her. She could hear the scurrying sound of a small animal, perhaps a skunk or muskrat, that dashed away. The steady hum of cicadas filled her, almost deafening, though she knew that it would not mask the sound of her movements.

She remained in a half-crouch, half-crawl, as she approached the house. She stopped once to make certain her weapon was ready, safety off, round chambered. Don't hesitate, she told herself for the millionth time. Take the shot when it is there.

She longed for some sound from the house, but it remained quiet. She kept moving, steadily, patiently. Death never hurries, she thought. It moves at its own pace.

She reached the edge of a wooden deck and slowly raised her eyes above it. She could see past a set of lounge chairs to the living room. She saw that the sliding glass door was wide open, as if in invitation. Well, she said to herself, here we go.

She crawled up onto the deck, thinking that every squeaking sound she made was like a bell pealing in the night. She got to her feet gingerly, maintaining her crouch. But now she put both hands on her pistol and steadied herself. She was surprised that she didn't feel more anxiety. I am calm. I am deadly.

She slid to the edge of the doorway.

She took a deep breath.

Then, slowly, she peered around the edge.

Confusion struck her. She saw Martin Jeffers, tied and trussed, sitting directly across from the door. She saw a young woman standing stock-still, a few feet away from him. She could not see the brother anywhere. She took a tentative step toward the opening.

And then she heard the voice.

"Behind you, detective."

She didn't even have the time to fill with panic.

I'm dead, she thought.

But she pivoted, bringing her weapon up, trying to get it into position to fire at the sound of the voice. She caught one small glimpse of a shape, stretched out on one of the outdoor lounges, and then everything exploded before her, as Douglas Jeffers fired his gun.

Pain impacted on her entire being.

The force of the shot ripping into her right knee spun her like a child's top, throwing her back into the living room, where she sprawled desperately on the floor, writhing in agony. Her own weapon had slipped from her fingers, flung violently across the room as she spun in helpless agony.

She squeezed her eyes shut and thought: I failed.

She opened them when she heard the voice above her.

"Is that her, Marty? Boswell, rip that tape off my dear brother's mouth so he can respond."

Douglas Jeffers stood over Mercedes Barren.

"My hat's off to you, detective. At least it would be if I had one."

Holt Overholser swore as the big Ford bucked and scraped its way down the dirt road. He had paused, almost giving up, when he reached the multiple fork in the path. Damn, he said to himself. Which damn road is it? Got to be the blue arrow. He made a mental note to contact all the homeowners on Tisbury Great Pond and inform them that for security reasons all roads had to be clearly marked with names and addresses and all sorts of identifying material. Damn! he thought again.

Every ten yards he changed his mind.

"What the hell are you doing, Holt?" he swore.

"Have you really got some damn good reason for being out here in rich people's heaven in the middle of the night? Jesus H. Christ, I hope the selectmen don't hear about this little escapade.

You ought to turn around now and get out of here before you make more of an ass out of yourself."

His speech made him feel better. He kept on driving.

When he broke out of the forest into the clear, he felt better still.

"Well, it ain't all that late, and if nothing's up, why, she'll probably appreciate your concern. Hell, she's a cop, she'll understand."

He laughed. "Well, maybe."

He stopped the truck, switching off the engine and stepping outside into the starry night.

"This better be the right place, Holt, old boy, or you're gonna look pretty damn stupid."

He was about to get back into the truck when he heard the shot.

"Now what was that?" he asked himself.

"Just what the hell was that?"

He answered his own questions out loud:

"That sounded to me like a handgun. Damn. Damn. What the hell's going on?"

He got back into his truck and quickly drove ahead.

Martin Jeffers did not ask how she'd found them. He simply said what jumped into his mind: "I'm sorry, Merce." He realized it was the first time he'd used her first name. "I'm sorry you found us . . ."

"But clever, very clever. Tell me, quickly, what was it? How did you guess?" Douglas Jeffers interjected.

"It was something one of them said," she moaned.

"One of who?"

Martin Jeffers answered. "She must have talked to my group. They were the ones who gave me the idea of coming here."

Douglas Jeffers looked at his brother. "We are all Lost Boys," he said. He stared at the detective. "Clever. Very clever."

She twisted in pain on the floor. She wished that she could look defiantly at him, but the pain surging like some runaway electrical impulse within her prevented any brave looks. She realized that her eyes were filled with tears, and she thought again: I tried. I'm sorry. I did my best.

Douglas Jeffers aimed his automatic at her head.

"This is like shooting a horse with a broken leg."

He hesitated.

"I'll give you a few seconds, detective. Welcome death."

She closed her eyes and thought of Susan, of her father, of

John Barren. I'm sorry, she said. I'm terribly sorry. I would like to say goodbye to all of you but I haven't the time. She hoped there was a heaven, suddenly, and that she would be pitched by pain into their waiting arms. She squeezed her arms tight and said to herself: I'm ready.

The explosion filled her.

Her head spun in red and black, dizzy, out of control. I'm dying, she thought.

And then she realized she wasn't.

She opened her eyes and saw Douglas Jeffers standing over her, pistol still poised but unfired.

As she watched, he seemed to step back in slow motion.

Her eyes searched about madly and she saw the young woman standing a few feet away. In her outstretched hands was Detective Barren's large handgun.

"Boswell," Douglas Jeffers said, genuine surprise covering his voice. "I'll be damned."

He looked down and saw a streak of red on his shirt.

The shot had torn through his side, ripping the flesh of the waist, then spinning off into the night. He knew instantly that it was not a killing wound, that it would be painful, but he could live.

And in the same thought he knew it had killed him.

He was rapidly flooded with emotions. I can't go to a hospital, he thought. Walk into an emergency room and say, here, fix this gunshot wound without asking any questions. He was struck with a simple, almost silly realization: It's over. Ended by an unlucky shot from a confused child.

"Boswell," he said gently, "you've killed me."

He raised his own weapon, bringing it to bear on Anne Hampton.

She gasped and her fingers let slide Detective Barren's gun. It crashed to the floor. She stood rigid, expecting her own death to storm from the pistol. I tried, she thought. I tried.

Detective Barren saw the young woman drop her hands to her sides, giving in to stunned acquiescence. She saw Douglas Jeffers sight down his weapon, ready to fire. It was as if everything that had happened to her coalesced in that second, and memory and strength combined to defeat pain. She dragged herself toward the murderer, screaming, "No! No! No! Susan! Run! I'll save you!" and knowing that this time she could, she could, she could. She thrashed across the floor with every fiber of residual strength she could find. She reached out for the murderer's leg, to pull him off-balance, to bring him down on her. "Run!"

she cried again, her mind now oblivious to anything except all the agonies that had dogged her for so many months. "Susan," she moaned, as she flung her hands forward, nails scratching, in a desperate effort to seize the man she had chased for so long.

Martin Jeffers threw himself out of the chair, still bound by the rope. He was screaming "No! No! No!" as he stumbled, falling to one knee, then rising, pushing himself forward as his brother paused so curiously in the deadly business at hand. Martin Jeffers thrust himself in front of the young woman.

Then he turned to his brother.

"No, Doug," he said. "No more."

The two brothers' eyes met. Martin Jeffers saw his brother's leap first with flame, then suddenly subside.

"Please," he said.

Douglas Jeffers stepped back, still aiming at Anne Hampton, and now at Martin Jeffers as well. He glanced down at the detective writhing on the floor.

"Please." He heard the voice and thought of his brother in all the lost moments of childhood, when Marty called out and needed him at his side.

Douglas Jeffers hesitated again. He put his hand to his waist and it came up bloody. He heard the word "Please" one more time.

Then he turned and disappeared through the door.

Holt Overholser came sailing down the driveway to the house on Finger Point and spotted the man rushing from the front porch. He flipped on the switch that turned on the red and blue strobes on the truck's roof. As Holt braked the truck violently, he saw the man turn and carefully assume a shooter's stance.

"Sweet Jesus!" Holt shouted, ducking as the windshield exploded. "Holy Mother of Christ!"

He scrambled for his own service revolver, the terrible thought jumping unbidden into his mind that he just might have forgotten to load the damn thing this year.

He didn't bother to check. Brandishing the pistol, he slid from the car and fired four shots in the direction of the fleeing man. The first shot struck the hood of the Ford, making a sound like a cat in heat. The second shot exploded into the ground about ten feet in front of the truck. The third crashed into the house filled with the people he was unwittingly trying to save, and the fourth sped off into night's oblivion.

"Jesus H. Christ," Holt said. He tried to force himself to remember what he'd been taught, and he finally assumed a proper ance, feet spread, both hands on the weapon, slightly crouched, ready for action.

But there was none to be had.

The night opened endlessly before him.

"Holy Christ," Holt said. He rushed toward the house. If the West Tisbury police department had any procedure for events such as these, Holt surely would have written it. But he hadn't, and they didn't, so he just barged ahead blithely into the house, gun held ready.

What he saw simply confused him more.

Anne Hampton had loosened Martin Jeffers' hands, and the two of them were helping Detective Barren onto a couch.

"Jesus Crutch on a Christ," Holt said loudly.

Anne Hampton gestured toward the back room.

"The Simmons family is in there," she said. "Help them."

Holt raced to the door and saw the family tied and gagged. He bent down and tore the bonds off Mr. Simmons. "Get your family free," he said. Then he ran back out into the main room. Anne Hampton and Martin Jeffers were trying to treat Detective Barren's bleeding leg.

Holt saw the telephone and picked it up. He dialed 911 and waited until he heard Lizzie Barry's voice. She seemed infuriatingly calm to him.

"Police, Fire, Emergency," she said.

"Jesus, Lizzie, it's Holt. I've got some kinda situation here, I don't know, Jesus, I mean, he was shooting at me!"

"Holt," replied Lizzie Barry with utter control, "what is your location exactly?"

"Jesus, I mean, gunshots! I coulda been killed. I'm down at Finger Point, Jesus!"

"All right, Holt, stay calm. Is this an emergency?"

"Jesus Crutch on a Christ," Holt misspoke again. "You bet it is!"

"All right," she said. "State police will be moving within minutes. Do you need an ambulance?"

"Jesus, we need an ambulance, we need everybody! The Coast Guard, the state cops, Christ! We need the Marines!"

"All right, Holt, help is on the way."

Lizzie Barry began making the proper calls and sirens started up throughout the night.

Martin Jeffers and Anne Hampton sat on either side of Detective Barren. Anne Hampton asked, "Can you take it? Help is coming."

Detective Mercedes Barren leaned her head on the young

woman's shoulder. She nodded. Martin Jeffers looked confused for an instant. "Did you get that, Boswell?" he asked. "Did you hear what he said? He said, "'Jesus Crutch . . .'" Anne Hampton smiled. "I got it," she said. Martin Jeffers laughed and put his arm around both women.

The three of them looked at each other. "It's over, I guess," Anne Hampton said. The others nodded, and they all bent their heads together. Tears started to run down Martin Jeffers' face, and he was joined then by Detective Barren and Anne Hampton, neither of whom cried from pain, but from some great, unfathomable release that moved within all of them.

Holt Overholser looked upon the three people sitting on the couch and thought first they must be crazy and then that the detective would be crippled forever with a wound like that. He did not realize that the same was equally true for all three.

Douglas Jeffers ignored the shots fired by the policeman who'd blocked his route to the car and raced across the sandy spit of land to the spot where he knew whoever lived at Finger Point would leave their boats. He saw two Sailfish pulled up on the beach and a dark inflatable dinghy with a small outboard engine next to them. He grabbed the anchor rope to the inflatable and within seconds had the boat pointed toward the crashing surf sounds of South Beach. He pumped the small bulb on the gas line twice, then pulled the starter cord. The little engine coughed once, then caught, and he thrust it into gear.

He was aware of the engine noise interrupting the night solitude. He thought: It cannot be helped.

He steered the boat out of the absolute confidence of memory, for the spot where the pond came closest to the ocean and where he knew the rolling surf was only fifty yards of flat sand away from the calm pond waters.

I could have killed them all.

He smiled. They know it.

As he drove, he checked the clip in his pistol. There were seven shots remaining in the 9 millimeter. She was using the same weapon, he thought idly. Probably says something.

He saw the beach looming ahead, a strip of vague blond light drawn across the endlessness of night. The sound of the waves on the ocean side seemed redoubled. He pointed the dinghy into the beach and felt the sand grab at the underside, scraping at the thick rubber.

He cut off the engine and pivoted it up so to not lose the prop

419

in the sand. He stood and stepped from the inflatable onto the beach.

It's just the way it always was.

He stayed motionless, almost entranced by the steady explosion of waves against the sandy beach. It is so constant, so powerful, he thought. It makes us small.

He bent and grasped the inflatable by the bow, pulling it from the water. The effort made his side ache and he was suddenly aware of the pain created by Anne Hampton's shot.

He shrugged it off.

Struggling, he pulled the boat ten feet across the sand.

I never would have thought she had it in her. I never would have thought she could do it. He was oddly proud of her. I always knew she had strength. She just didn't know where to look for it.

He forced the boat across the beach. It made a swishing sound as he tugged at it.

Images surrounded him, from all the places he'd been and all the photos he'd taken. No one could touch me, he thought.

He leaned against the weight of the sand, moving the inflatable inexorably toward the surf.

My pictures were always the best. Color, black and white. Made no difference. I always caught the moment just right. They spoke. They cried out. They told stories.

He sank to his knees in the water wash, grasping his side, his head spinning.

It hurts, Marty, it hurts.

He shook himself upright. Keep going.

He started to sing then: "Row, row, row your boat, gently down the stream . . ."

He lunged forward with each word, pulling the inflatable into the shallow water that ran away from him, back to the ocean. He dropped his grip on the bow and moved to the side as the rubber boat started to bob in the thin water. He could see a steady, thick roller heading toward the beach and he pushed forward to meet it.

White-green water crashed about him, swirling, as he thrust the boat into the waves.

He grabbed the side and flung one leg over as the inflatable spun about. With his one leg, he straightened the dinghy and shoved hard against the mushy sand, meeting the next wave bow-first.

He rode up, dizzyingly, catching a glimpse of the moon hanging just above the waters, so close he thought he could grab it. Then he was swept down the back side of the wave, into the trough. The surf exploded around him, and in the bottom of the dinghy he was awash. He spun about and jammed down the motor, pulling the starter cord simultaneously. The engine started right up, and he goosed it, just catching the next wave as it rose up in front of him, threatening to dash him back on the beach. The dinghy shot forward, riding past the crash of boiling white water.

He jammed the accelerator handle, and the inflatable surged again.

In a second, as if touched by some mystery, he was out of the surf action, riding on the deep black water, bobbing about, the engine noise steadily driving him from shore.

No Man's Land, he said to himself.

I've always wanted to go to No Man's Land.

He steered away from the beach, leaving the dark mass of the island behind, heading toward the open sea. He guessed at the direction of the target range and pointed the dinghy that way.

He saw the moon again, and it comforted him.

He whispered to himself: "Oh, the Owl and the Pussycat went to sea in a beautiful pea-green boat . . ."

He smiled to himself and skipped ahead. He sang out blissfully: "So hand in hand, they danced on the sand by the light of the moon, the moon, the moon . . ."

He thought of his brother. Marty always liked rhymes. He pictured his mother and wondered what had become of her. He realized that she had looked out upon the night when she left them, just as he did this. And it swallowed her up forever, he told himself.

His adoptive father jumped into his imagination. He scowled but understood. "I'm coming, you bastard!" he shouted. "I'm coming!" The words raced across the swells, devoured by the night. He thought of the end of the fight against the rip that pulled so terrifyingly. He must have been exhausted and defeated. It must have been like falling into a deep and painless sleep.

He felt the blood again, and torn flesh.

"It hurts," he said.

Then he comforted himself. "It'll be all right."

The land had dropped far away by now, and he shut his eyes. The engine lulled him, and the steady, gentle pushing of the waves was like rocking a baby, beckoning, urging him to sleep. I'm tired, he said to himself. So tired.

It was wondrously peaceful and he remembered the snatch of another rhyme. He whispered: "Weary wee flipperling, curl at thy ease . . ." He rolled his head back and felt a great and final exhaustion within him. He sang low to himself: ". . . asleep in the arms of the slow-swinging seas."

The idea filled him with a satisfied defiance.

"They never caught me," he said. "They couldn't."

It seemed terribly right to him.

He shut off the engine and sat listening to the ocean flowing about him. Then he took his pistol and aimed it down between his feet. He fired all seven shots.

The dinghy shuddered.

Black water boiled up around him.

It's warm, he thought with childish pleasure. It's warm.

He reached out and embraced the coal-dark sea.

About the Author

John Katzenbach has been the criminal court reporter for *The Miami Herald* and a featured writer for the *The Miami Herald's Tropic Magazine*. Previously, he was the criminal court reporter for the *Miami News*, and his work has appeared in many other newspapers, including *The New York Times*, *The Washington Post*, *Chicago Daily News*, and *The Philadelphia Inquirer*. His novel IN THE HEAT OF THE SUMMER was a final nominee for the Mystery Writers of America's Edgar Award for the best first novel and was made into the movie THE MEAN SEASON. He is also the author of the highly praised true crime story FIRST BORN.

Mr. Katzenbach, born in Princeton, New Jersey, is the son of former Attorney General of the United States Nicholas Katzenbach. He lives in South Florida with his wife, Pulitzer Prize–winning journalist Madeleine Blais.

"And in chute number four, we have Sam McPhee," said the announcer over the PA system.

⌒

The world stopped turning.

Applause erupted from the bleachers. Michelle stood at the rail and gripped the rungs hard. She knew she hadn't heard wrong. Oh, God. *Sam.*

Michelle looked at the chute at the end of the arena, and there he was. From a distance, he resembled any cowboy on a quarter horse. Yet she knew him. Knew the tilt of his head, the set of his shoulders, the fringe of sandy hair touching his collar. Sam appeared leaner, stronger, and quicker than ever. He retained that unique grace of movement she recalled so well. The years had hardly left a mark on him.

Michelle stared, spellbound, unable to move. He still had that slightly crooked grin that had once made her heart melt. . . .

The You I Never Knew

SUSAN WIGGS

WARNER BOOKS

A Time Warner Company

WARNER BOOKS EDITION

Cover design by Diane Luger
Hand lettering by David Gatti
Book design by H & H Roberts Design

Warner Books, Inc.
1271 Avenue of the Americas
New York, NY 10020

Visit our Web site at
www.twbookmark.com

Ⓦ A Time Warner Company

Printed in the United States of America

First Printing: January 2001

10 9 8 7 6 5 4 3 2 1

To the women of my tribe:

my grandmother Marie
my mother Lou
my sister Lori
my daughter Elizabeth
who understand the necessary labors of loving

"Most of us become parents long before
we have stopped being children."

—MIGNON MCLAUGHLIN,
The Second Neurotic's Notebook (1966)

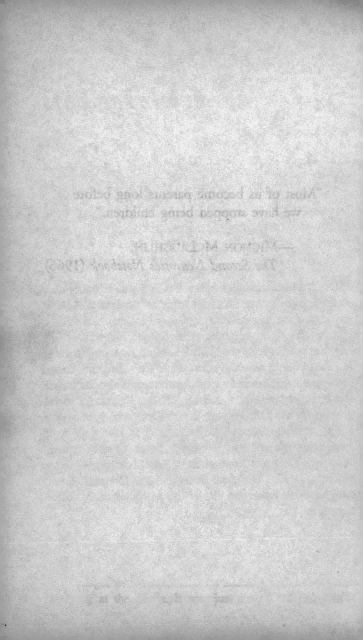

Acknowledgments

Writing a book is a joyous act, but it's also a lonely one. The support, advice, and fellowship of professional advisors and friends anchor, motivate, and inform me, and for this I'm deeply grateful. In particular, to Robert Gottlieb and Marcy Posner of the William Morris Agency for pushing me off in a new direction, to Joyce, Christina, Betty, Barb, and Alice for reading the manuscript with open minds and blood-red pencils, to Kristin, Jill, and Debbie for moral support, to my gifted editor, Claire Zion, who held up the mirror that transformed this work, and to Sara Schwager for careful copyediting, to Sandra Brashen, M.D., Leslie Townsend, Peggy Moreland and Curtiss Ann Matlock for technical advice, and most particularly to Donna Roberts, who gave her father the gift of life and generously shared her story.

Saturday

Saturday

Chapter 1

After seventeen years, Michelle Turner was going back. Back to a past she didn't want to remember, to the father she barely knew, to the town where she grew up too fast, fell in love too hard, and wound up pregnant and alone.

During the long drive from Seattle to Montana, she rehearsed—under her breath so Cody wouldn't hear—what she would say when she got there.

"Hello, Daddy." Funny how she still thought of him as Daddy, even though he'd never been much more than a picture on the wall or sometimes a face on the TV screen late at night when his old movies played. "Sorry I didn't come sooner..." Sorry...sorry...sorry. All those regrets. So many of them.

Sorry wouldn't do. Gavin Slade—her father had kept

his professional name after retiring—knew damned well what had kept her away so long.

She flexed her hands on the steering wheel of the Range Rover and glanced over her shoulder at her son in the backseat. Cody was lost in the space between the headphones of his Discman. Maybe I'm the one who's lost, she thought. Here she was, thirty-five years old and the mother of a teenager, and the thought of facing her father made her feel like a kid again. Defensive. Powerless. Inadequate.

The Washington landscape roared by as she drove eastward, heading toward a place where she'd find no welcome. She and Cody had left their waterfront town house before dawn. The lights had still been shining in the steel skeleton of Seattle's Space Needle. By sunup, the Cascade Range had given way to rounded hills and scrubby flatland, then finally to high plateaus, a bare and colorless midwinter moonscape, a neutral zone.

She saw nothing out her window to interest the eye, nor to offend it.

Long ago, she used to be an artist, painting in savage color with emotions that spilled unrestrained over the canvas, dripping off the sides, because her feelings could not be confined to a finite space. But somewhere along the way she had reined in those mad and glorious impulses, as if a thief had come in the night and stolen the dreams inside her and she hadn't noticed they were gone until too late.

All that remained of the wild soul of her younger days was a cold, mechanical talent and a photographic eye. Airbrush and mousepad had replaced paint and canvas.

Her subjects had changed, too. She used to create art with passion and purity, whether it be a horse on her father's ranch or an abstract scramble of feelings. Inspiration used to govern her hand, and something far more powerful ignited her spirit. Once seen or imagined, the work rushed from her, generated by a force as strong as the need to breathe.

Now subjects came assigned to her by memo from the ad agency where she was up for full partner. She used a computer to design and animate dancing toilet brushes, talking dentures, or an army of weed-killer bags marching toward a forest of weeds.

Tugging her mind away from thoughts of work, she clicked on the wipers to bat away a few stray snow flurries. The day wore on. Spokane passed in a whisk of warehouses and industrial smokestacks. The interstate arrowed cleanly across the panhandle of Idaho. Between empty stretches of highway lay glaring commercial strip centers, tractor barns and silos, wood-frame houses huddled shoulder to shoulder against the elements. Deeper accumulations of snow formed crusty heaps on the side of the road. East of Coeur d'Alene, the landscape yielded to endless stretches of nothingness.

The monotony of the drive, and her purpose for racing across three states, caused an almost painful tectonic shift in her thoughts. Memories drifted toward dangerous places. Against her will, images from the past turned the barren snowscape to brilliant summer.

She saw herself as she was at eighteen. A little breathless at everything life had to offer. A little scared, but mostly happy and secure in her world. She finished high school with honors she didn't care about, a raw talent she didn't appreciate yet, and no sense of impending disaster. Her mother's cosmetic surgery was supposed to be routine. No one even considered the possibility that Sharon Turner would die from the complications.

In a shockingly short span of time, Michelle had found

herself alone and motherless—suddenly in need of the father she barely knew. She had expected him to hustle her off to college and breathe a sigh of relief when she was gone, but instead he'd surprised her. He had invited her to take a year off before college and spend the time with him in Montana. A year to grieve for her mother and to learn who her father was.

In that one brief season she experienced the events that were to shape her life: She learned what it was to be a motherless daughter. She fell in love. She became a painter. Not necessarily in that order. Everything sort of happened simultaneously. Even now, the years-old bittersweet ache rose as fresh as yesterday. It shouldn't still hurt, but it did, even though he was gone, long gone, from her life.

Except for the daily reminder he had left her.

She glanced into the rearview mirror again. Cody, who was sixteen and impossible, hadn't moved from his long-bodied position in the backseat. A tinny beat of heavy-metal music escaped from his headphones. He stared out at the endless swags of electrical lines strung along poles that bordered the highway. When a green-and-white sign welcomed them to Montana, his only reaction was to blink and shift position.

A billboard with a nauseating cartoon cowboy invited them to "Stop N Eat" in one mile.

"You hungry?" She raised her voice so he would hear.

He stuffed a wad of Fritos into his mouth. "Nope," he said around a mouthful of food. The roadside café, lit up by neon wagon wheels, disappeared in a smear of artificial light.

Just for a flash, she saw him as a toddler, cramming Cheerios into his cheeks like a baby squirrel. It seemed like only yesterday that he was her Cody-boy in Oshkosh overalls, with milk dribbling from his chin. That child was gone from her life now, she realized with a lurch of regret in her chest. He had slipped away when she wasn't looking. He'd vanished as swiftly and irretrievably as if he had wandered off at an airport, never to be found. In his place was this cynical, smart, exasperating stranger who seemed determined to push every button she had.

His sheer physical beauty then, as now, took her breath away. Only back then, she could tell him how adorable he was to her.

Now she could tell him nothing.

Cody had begged to stay in Seattle while she made this trip alone. He claimed he'd be fine, staying by himself at the town house. As if Michelle would consent to that.

Cody had even suggested that Brad could look after him.

Right. Brad couldn't handle Cody. Or wouldn't. And she was in no position to expect that level of support from Brad, their relationship notwithstanding. Her entire life was on hold until she dealt with her father.

A semi swung out and passed her, blasting its air horn. No speed limit in Montana, she recalled, and here she'd been dutifully doing sixty-five.

Life had trained her well for duty.

Defiantly, she pressed the accelerator. Sixty-five, seventy, seventy-five. She reveled in the speed, in the hum of the Rover's tires on cold bare pavement. Everything passed in a wavy smudge—streaks of cottonwood groves, shale rock ridges, coulees and brushy creeks, the blur of avalanche fence traversing the high meadows. The wind blew a dusting of snow along the highway. The snakelike motion and the subtle flickers of muted color were oddly exhilarating, and for a while she simply emptied her mind and drove.

The landscape lifted, a subtle change at first, but before long they would reach the high country of serrated crags, endless valleys, hanging alpine lakes. A chill of anticipation prickled her skin. Before long they would be at Blue Rock Ranch.

At Missoula, they turned northward, passing a giant statue of a Hereford bull at a combination tourist shop, café, and gas station.

"We're not in Kansas anymore," she murmured to Cody, but he didn't hear.

The Wild West kitsch was a sign that they had entered a different zone entirely, a land where the cowboy myth revolved around the solemn rites of rope and leather, where a sense of place and tall, endless skies surrounded and seduced her. Some said Montana was an empty land, but that wasn't quite right. It was just that the space was so vast it expanded the soul. She felt herself being drawn toward an encounter she had resisted for years. She tensed, unable to enjoy the beauty because this landscape held too many reminders of her past.

Highway 83 took them along the final leg of the journey. Against the brooding afternoon sky rose the peaks of the Swan and Mission Mountains. Shadows flickered in and out of coulees and valleys, creating a palette of sage and ocher and mysterious, restful earth tones that had no name.

"Cody, look!" She pointed out the side window. A huge herd of elk, winter migrants from the high country, grazed on the scrub-covered hills.

He stared at the milling herd, then yawned.

Well, what did she expect? "Gee whiz, Mommy" from a sixteen-year-old?

But oh, she wanted to share this with him, this sense of wonder inspired by the wild animals, the deep conifer forests and staggering snow-clad mountain peaks. A jewel-like chain of lakes bordered the highway. She wanted to tell him the lakes were formed as flood depressions in glacial moraines, filled when giant chunks of ice melted in each depression.

She wondered if that was what happened to people: When loss created a void that stayed empty too long, did the space fill up with ice?

They reached the turnoff for Crystal City, and the road began to climb in a series of sharp twists up into the mountains. Glacial violence made this harsh, craggy landscape as resistant to invasion as any man-made fortress. It took a special skill to breach it.

She hadn't driven in snow in ages, and the Range Rover fishtailed a little.

"Nice move, Mom," Cody observed from the backseat.

She gave silent thanks for the Rover's four-wheel drive. The tires gripped the sand-sprinkled snow. Forced to a Sunday-drive crawl, she saw everything with crystalline clarity. Open rangeland and broad meadows flowing past. A ring of mountains surrounding the valley like the walls of a mythical stronghold. Every tortuous inch of this road was familiar to her, so familiar that it made her eyes ache.

The valley slumbered in midwinter splendor, as if the entire landscape was holding its breath, waiting for the far-distant springtime.

She read the names on every rural mailbox they passed—Smith, Dodd, Gyenes, Bell, Jacobs. Most people who settled in the area seemed to stay forever. Each farm lay in perfect repose, a picture waiting to be painted: a white house with dark green shutters, a wisp of smoke twisting from the chimney, windowpanes glowing at the first touch of twilight.

There was a time when this sight had pierced her in a tender spot. She had painted this very scene long ago. Her brush had given life to the hillocks of untouched snow, to the luminous pink of the sunset, and to the fading sky behind alpine firs with their shoulders draped in white and icicles dripping from their branches. On a poorly prepared canvas with second-rate paints, she managed to convey a sense of soaring wonder at the world around her. It was a good painting. Better than good. But young. Impossibly, naively young as she had never been since the day she left this town in anguish and disgrace.

She wondered what had become of that painting. A part of her insisted that it was important to know. Creating that picture had been a defining act for her. It had opened a window into her future and sent her dreams off in a direction that would bring her joy and heartbreak for the rest of her life.

She peeked at Cody to see his reaction to their arrival. He stared out the window, his hands playing the air drums in his lap. His narrowed eyes were filled with nothing but indifference. She shouldn't be surprised. Indifference and contempt were the only emotions he exhibited these days.

A fading Rotary Club sign marked the city limits.

I'm back now, really and truly back. She knew it was just her imagination, but she heard a rush of wind as she felt herself going forward . . . into the past.

Across the Lions Club sign stretched a banner announcing the WINTER ROUNDUP—MARCH 2–3.

Great. That meant she wouldn't find her father at home. As the leading rodeo stock contractor in the state, he was bound to be at the arena. She punched his number into her cell phone—Lord, did *any*one but her father keep the same number for twenty-five years?

"Blue Rock." A young voice, not her father's, answered. One of his personal assistants, she supposed.

"Is Gavin in? This is . . . his daughter, Michelle Turner."

A pause. "I'm sorry, he's out for the evening. He was expecting you tomorrow, ma'am."

"Is he at the arena?" she asked.

"Yes, ma'am."

She supposed she could go to his place, sit, and wait for him, but she was too edgy to put the meeting off any longer. The entire town would witness their reunion. Would anyone remember her, and what had happened that year? Would heads shake and tongues wag? Would they look at her son and exchange knowing glances?

The next road sign posted a greeting from the Calvary Lutheran Church: YOU'RE ENTERING GOD'S COUNTRY.

"I'll find him there, then." She hung up the phone.

Main Street stretched before her, cold and straight as the barrel of a rifle. She passed the saddlery with its false log façade, Ray's Quik Chek, the Northern Lights Feed Store and Café, the Christian Science Reading Room, LaNelle's Quilt and Fabric Shoppe, a bank, and a picket-fronted bar that hadn't been there seventeen years ago. Blue-and-white signs pointed out the turns to the county hospital and the library.

On the other side of town was a flat-roofed restaurant hunched atop a knoll and surrounded by eighteen-wheelers with their running lights on—the Truxtop Café. She winced, recalling the last time she had set foot in that place.

Crystal City was a part of Michelle Turner, no matter how hard she tried to forget that fact.

Every once in a while she used to fantasize about coming back, but in her mind it was always a triumphant return. Not like this. Not with her heart frozen, her world in disarray, and her purpose to save the life of the father she hadn't seen in seventeen years.

Chapter 2

Sam McPhee stared out the window at the ripples of snow on the hills behind his house. Though it was a familiar sight, he lingered there, watching as the last light of day rode the broken-backed mountains. The sight was a restful thing for a man to hold in his chest. In his youth, he'd carried the image with him no matter where he went, from Calgary to Cozumel, and when the time came to figure out where home was, he didn't need to look any farther than these hills.

He adjusted his hat and flexed his fingers into a pair of gloves. He straightened up and hitched back his hip, stomping his foot down into the boot, a characteristic gesture caught dozens of times by rodeo photographers.

Sam was a hard-bitten man, a loner who depended on no one, but sometimes the loneliness howled through him. Sometimes he wished he had someone to share these moments with, someone he could take by the hand, and say, "Look up at the hills tonight. Look at all those colors." After such a long time on his own, it shouldn't matter. But every once in a while, in the empty hover of time between evening and twilight, it did.

He flicked off most of the lights in the house, leaving one burning on the porch.

His boots crunching on the frozen drive, he went out to finish loading his trailer: saddle, tack, rope, blankets, Yellow Arrow liniment, an extra pair of gloves. These things were sacred to him and he handled them with the reverence and care of a priest performing the rites of consecration. They were the trappings of something so much a part of him that he couldn't even really think of it as a sport. Rodeo. His second love.

The sharp cold air needled his lungs as he crossed the yard to the bunkhouse, a squat log dwelling the former owners had remodeled into a guesthouse. Sam's partner in the horse ranch lived there now. He pounded on the door, then opened it. "Hey, Edward, you about ready?"

"Coming, coming. Hold your horses."

"My horses are already trailered, no thanks to you, pal."

"Yeah, well, I was busy," Edward called from the back bedroom.

"Did Diego get those stables done?" Sam closed the door behind him to keep in the heat from the woodstove.

"Diego took off. Got a job in a restaurant up at Big Mountain."

"Damn. That's the second stable hand we've lost this month."

"What you need is a slave," Edward called.

"Last time I checked, it was against the law to keep slaves."

"In this society," Edward said, "we call them kids."

"Yeah, well, I don't happen to have any handy." Sam didn't let himself dwell on it. "I guess I'll call Earl Meecham, see if one of his boys'll work after school each day."

Edward Bliss came out into the timber-ceilinged hall, a stack of folded blankets in his arms. Sam's partner was five-foot-two, half Salish Indian, and one hundred percent hell-raiser.

"What's with the blankets?" Sam asked.

"Ruby Lightning wove them. Asked me to put them out at the bake sale table tonight."

They climbed into the old Dodge truck, shivering against the chilled vinyl seats. The engine coughed in protest, then turned over with a flatulent blast of exhaust. Sam put it in gear and eased down the gravel drive. A thread of fiery orange sunset stitched across the peaks of the Mission Range. Foothills shadowed the lower pastures in shades of purple. The landscape looked bleak and cold, beautiful in a way few could admire.

He followed the dark rein of the road, glancing in the side mirrors to check the trailer. Rio and Zeus were probably dozing. The big quarter horses were used to the routine of loading up, driving, then waiting in the holding pen for a lightning ride that, in the old days, used to determine whether or not Sam got to eat that week.

"So what's Ruby up to lately?" he asked.

Edward took out a stick of Juicy Fruit, offering Sam the pack. "You ought to call her up and ask her."

Sam folded the gum in half twice and put it in his mouth. "Maybe I will. She doing all right?"

"You could ask her that, too."

An English teacher at the local high school, Ruby Lightning was also a single mom and an activist in the

Kootenai tribal government. She was scrubbed, earthy, and available, living in a frame house just a quarter mile down the road. They'd had some good times in the past, shared a few laughs, and could have shared more if he'd been so inclined.

Sam had simply stopped calling her. He wasn't proud of the way he drifted in and out of relationships. He'd tried marriage once and discovered it was a bad fit—like boots that were too tight. He didn't need a shrink to explain the parallels between his failed romances and his lousy childhood.

"How's that daughter of hers?" Sam wondered aloud.

"Molly's in the barrel-racing competition for sixteen-and-under."

"No kidding." It seemed only yesterday that he'd met little Molly Lightning, a dark-eyed waif, completely devoted to an old Welsh pony Ruby had bartered from Sam. Now Molly was nearly grown, slim and lithe as a bull-hide whip, probably leaving the halls of Crystal City High littered with broken hearts. Christ, where did the years go?

Like the best horses Sam had known, the girl had fire and heart. She also had, he recalled, a great mom.

Yeah, maybe he would give Ruby a call.

"How much does she want for those blankets?" he asked. Ruby was an expert weaver, using Montana-grown wool and traditional patterns and totems in her designs.

"Fifty bucks apiece," Edward said. "You want one?"

Sam grinned as he turned into the arena parking lot. "If I win the purse tonight, I'll buy them all."

"So you think you and old Rio'll win, eh, cowboy?" A gold tooth flashed in Edward's grin.

"Hey, we *always* win." It was a lie, and both he and Edward knew it. But there had been a time when Sam truly did rule the roping competitions. One winning ride used to net him $22,000, sometimes more. Most cowboys spent their winnings on silver-studded saddles and fancy rigs. Sam had used his for a different purpose altogether, a purpose that set him apart from other rodeo stars and made him something of an oddity in the circuit.

After he became a national champion, the trade sheets had a field day with him, focusing on the unorthodox choices he'd made. They'd documented his dazzling style, his natural grace in the sport. They'd published his hefty earnings. Plastered his face on calendars. For several seasons he'd been the golden boy of the circuit, the cowboy with a career plan.

What the reporters hadn't documented was the god-awful loneliness. The grinding tedium. The aches and bruises so deep they made him feel older than rock itself. It was a solitary life, traveling from show to show in a beat-up truck hauling a horse trailer, chasing down trashy, roped-out steers. But the prospect of another ride, another purse, had sustained him through the roughest times of his life.

"Nice rig," Edward said, as Sam drove past a white Ford 350 dually with a pristine white Cattleman trailer at least thirty-six feet long. Gleaming in the floodlights, the thing looked like a giant suppository.

On its side, in perfect custom commercial script, was a familiar logo in indigo paint: BLUE ROCK RANCH.

"Gavin Slade must've bought himself another new toy," Sam said. He used to resent everything Slade had and everything he was. But that was a long time ago.

Lately the whole town had been gossiping about Gavin in concerned undertones. Throwing his money away on expensive rigs wouldn't fix what was wrong. But it sure as hell wasn't Sam's place to tell Gavin that.

Edward spotted a cluster of women at the doorway

of the concession hall. "So hurry up and park already. I got people to see."

Despite his bantam-rooster stature, Edward Bliss was a ladies' man. He wrenched the rearview mirror toward himself, took off his Stetson, and checked his hair. He worked at flirting as seriously as he worked the ranch.

Sam yanked the mirror back and angled the truck toward his usual parking spot at the north end of the arena. "Damn," he said, cranking down the window and spitting out his gum.

"What is it?" asked Edward.

Sam glared at a late-model silver Range Rover with Washington plates. "Some idiot's parked in my spot."

Chapter 3

T his is totally bogus, Mom," Cody said through chattering teeth as they walked toward the main building of the arena. "I can't believe you're making me come to a Wild West show."

"It's not a Wild West show. It's a rodeo."

"I can't believe you're making me come anywhere near—shit!" Cody stopped walking and looked down.

"Horseshit, to be precise. Wipe your foot in the snow."

He got the worst of it off, grumbling the whole time. Somehow, it was impossible for Cody to be cool when he was scraping manure off his hundred-dollar Doc Martens.

"Can't we just go to his place and wait for him?" Cody demanded. "You said he had a guesthouse."

"Guesthouses—plural. My father never does anything part way." Blue Rock Ranch was the epitome of contemporary Western living: several thousand pristine acres complete with streams, ponds, and a compound of houses and barns that resembled a small, elegant village in a storybook setting. Some years back, *Architectural Digest* did a spread on the main house. And Michelle's father—never one to shun the public that validated his existence—made the most of it.

She had come across the article by accident. She'd been sitting at her drafting table at work one day, paging through magazines and looking at the ads to see what the competition was cooking up. Unsuspecting, she turned a page and found herself staring at a perfect shot of Blue Rock Ranch in high summer when avalanche lilies blanketed the hills and the grass was so green it hurt the eyes. The ensuing pages displayed room after perfect room. She recognized the window seat where she used to read and sketch, the rustic porch where she'd sat in the Stickley glider, spinning dreams she was absolutely certain would come true.

"So what say we go hang out in one of his 'plural' guesthouses?" Cody inspected the bottom of his shoe.

"No. We're here, and we're going to find my father."

"What's he doing out anyway? I thought he was sick."

"He's sick, all right, but not bedridden. His condition—"

"Jeez, it's cold." Cody stamped his feet on the straw-covered snow. "I guess if we're going in, let's go." He hunched his shoulders and headed for the main entrance. He never wanted to talk about her father's illness, never wanted to hear the details of what had to be done. He had a teenager's abiding horror of things medical and refused to consider his own mortality or that of anyone he knew.

Michelle bought tickets from a smiling girl with crooked teeth and loftily teased hair. "Right through there, ma'am." The girl gestured, displaying a lavishly fringed polyester sleeve.

"Don't say a word," Michelle warned Cody as they pushed through the turnstile. But the sarcastic look on his face said it all.

They found themselves amid a crowd of men in sheepskin-lined denim jackets and women in tight jeans with the creases ironed in blade-sharp. Michelle took a moment to inspect her son. Out of place would be putting it mildly. Torn black jeans with thick chains inexplicably draped from the pockets. A leather jacket studded with rivets along every seam. His hair was oddly colored—white sidewalls around his ears to show off a row of stainless-steel earrings, a long ponytail over the top and hanging down his back. The ends were still slightly green from when he'd dyed it for a Phish concert last summer.

Ah, but that face. Sullen, yes, but still so beautiful. *What happened to you, my precious boy?*

She resisted the urge to tell him to straighten his shoulders. Part of his determined coolness involved a studied slouch that gave his body the shape of a question mark. *Stand tall, like your father did.*

Her stomach constricted nervously as they walked along the front of the bleachers in search of Gavin Slade. She'd see him soon. Good grief, what would they say to each other?

Their last face-to-face conversation had not been pleasant.

"I'm pregnant, Daddy."

Gavin had gone all stony-eyed. Then he'd said: "I'm not surprised. Your mother was careless, too."

"My *father* was careless," she'd shot back.

That same day, she'd left Blue Rock Ranch, vowing

never to return. But here she was, years later, her nerves strung taut with anticipation.

Heat blew into the arena through long tubes connected to generators. The smells of horse and leather and popcorn filled the air with poignant reminders of the past. Michelle couldn't help but notice the spot where she used to sit in the bleachers and watch the cowboys putting quarter horses through their paces. And there, in the middle of the arena, was the place where she'd lost her heart to a horse called Dooley.

She remembered the feel of the spirited animal beneath her as she learned the heart-tightening, dangerous joys of barrel racing. An experienced dressage rider, Michelle thought she knew how to handle a horse. But Dooley wasn't just any horse. He was a quarter horse bred for athletic ability, agility, and quickness, with Thoroughbred blood for extra speed and an explosive disposition. He took the turns around the barrels, expertly pivoting on one back leg. She still remembered the exhilaration of the flat-out run, the check at full speed, the turn 180 degrees around the barrel in a dizzying cloverleaf pattern. Across the years, she still could hear a voice calling encouragement, calling to the Michelle she used to be.

You're doing great for a city girl. Let him have his head. I think he likes you. . . .

Willing away the reminiscence, she watched a slim girl in black and turquoise ride into the ring on a piebald mare. Horse and rider flowed like water as they chased the cans. The girl, her shining black braid slapping as rhythmically as her quirt, wore a look of intense, exultant concentration on her face as she exited the course and the crowd applauded. The PA system blared an impressive time—17.5 seconds.

Ah, that smile, Michelle thought, studying the girl. Had she ever been that young? That happy?

Cody was watching the girl, too, and for once the expression on his face wasn't so snide. Even her urban animal of a son couldn't resist an event that featured beautifully dressed girls, powerful and good-looking horses, and fast action. Then he caught his mother studying him, and his rapt expression faded. "Well?" he asked. "You going to go find him or what?"

They passed the Chamber of Commerce table. She spotted a familiar face, and it gave her a start. Earl Meecham, owner of the Truxtop Café, was handing out flyers or coupons of some sort. He hadn't changed much— a little more paunch, maybe, a little more jowl. Shadowed by a ten-gallon Resistol hat, his grin reached from ear to ear.

Briefly, Meecham's eyes met Michelle's, but she could tell he didn't recognize her. She was a lot different from the girl with the long blond ponytail and the stars in her eyes.

Turning up the collar of her jacket, she moved toward the bleachers near the judges' booth. There, standing with one Lucchese boot propped on a hitch rail, a printed program clutched in his fist, was her father.

Instant panic set in. She had the urge to flee, to hide. *I can't do this.* Not here, not now. Yet at the heart of the panic lay something far more powerful. Love or hate or maybe a wrenching combination of the two. Resolve. *Duty.* She shoved the panic away.

Cody must have sensed her tension, because he stopped walking and followed the direction of her gaze. "That's him, isn't it?" His voice was bland, bored.

"Yes, that's him." The noise of the crowd and the

milling calves and horses fell away as she studied her father.

Gavin Slade. Thirty years ago he had been the hottest ticket in Hollywood, building a career on a body of tense, gritty Westerns and hard-edged police dramas. His rugged good looks had graced fan magazines and tabloids from *Life* to the *National Enquirer*. He was still good-looking, his face chiseled and lean, his air of command still evident, his magnetic charm still powerful.

At the height of his fame he had left Hollywood, migrating to Montana before it became fashionable to do so. He had discovered Crystal City during a location shoot and spent years building Blue Rock Ranch, becoming a rodeo stock contractor with an international reputation. Some of his bucking stock was better known than the champions who rode them. The people in the town lionized him. They considered him one of their own because he predated all the other California transplants. She'd never really known why he'd moved or what he hoped to find in Montana. Was he running away from the Hollywood rat race or was he running away from Michelle and her mother?

"He doesn't look sick," Cody observed, trying to appear casual but sounding relieved instead.

Gavin was a little too thin, perhaps, and maybe a yellowish cast haunted his complexion and the whites of his eyes, but Michelle allowed that the coloring might be from the arena lights. She took off her Gore-Tex gloves and stuck them in her pockets. Despite the midwinter cold, sweat dampened her palms. She wiped them on her jeans. "Let's go tell him we're here."

A short, bandy-legged cowboy carrying a stack of woven blankets jostled her as he passed, but she barely noticed. When she was a few feet away from her father, he glanced up. She didn't know this man well enough to read his expression. After all, she'd only spent half a year of her life with him. He'd always been a stranger to her. A stranger she called "Daddy."

"Michelle, honey." His trademark thousand-watt smile lit up his face, showing off his perfect teeth. "Come and give your old man a hug."

His arms went around her. She closed her eyes and inhaled. Clean laundry, breath mints, expensive aftershave. A strong embrace that enclosed her entirely. She told herself that it shouldn't feel this good. It shouldn't feel this right. He was a stranger. But when she drew back and looked up, tears swam across her eyes.

"Hi, Daddy."

"I didn't think you'd show up until tomorrow."

"We got an early start. The roads weren't bad, so we drove straight on through." She stepped back, blinking fast, refusing to shed the tears. "This is Cody."

Gavin's smile froze. She held her breath, hoping he'd look past the leather and chains, praying he'd see through the rebellious attitude. But Gavin had missed the wonder years with Cody, just as he had missed them with Michelle. He never knew the radiant joy of a toddler's face on Christmas morning, the triumphant exuberance of a nine-year-old who had just caught his first fish, the perfect tenderness of a boy holding a newly hatched duckling in his cupped hands, or his shy pride as he delivered breakfast in bed on Mother's Day.

Gavin saw only what stood before him now. His mouth took on the brittle edges of a false grin as he said, "Well, now. How do, youngster?" He stuck out his hand.

Cody took it briefly, then let go. "Okay."

Michelle found herself wishing she'd coached him for

this moment. Not that he would have listened, but shouldn't she have instructed him to be a little less sullen?

Awkwardness hung like a bad smell in the air. A dogie bawled in the pen outside. Michelle tried to will away her disappointment. What did she expect, that they'd fall into each other's arms just because one was her father, the other her son? That was something that might have happened in one of Gavin's old movies, not in real life.

She cleared her throat. "I knew we'd find you here."

"Wouldn't miss it, honey. Wouldn't miss it." He was the reason a town this size even had a rodeo. He needed a place to work his stock, and the arena had been built with civic funds—but with Gavin Slade in mind. He focused on the refreshment stand. "Can I get you two something to drink?"

"I think I'll go look around some." Cody jammed his hands into his pockets. His already sagging jeans lowered a notch. Michelle hoped her father didn't notice the *South Park* boxers that showed above the waistband.

"All right." She had promised herself she wouldn't try to force her father and son to get along. "Be back here in a half hour." As a reflex, she almost told him to stay out of trouble. She bit back the words. He generally took her warnings as invitations to step out of line. Watching him saunter away, she said, "I think he's a little tired and cranky from the long drive."

"How about you?" Gavin asked. "Can I get you something—coffee? A beer?"

"I'm fine."

He touched her shoulder. "Michelle. I feel stupid saying thank you for coming. How the hell can I thank you?"

She felt the color rise in her face. "Don't even try. I'm here. I'm going to help." She was filled with an impulse to milk this occasion, to bask in his gratitude. She was clearly the martyr here. She could use this to stitch together their tattered relationship.

But the impulse faded. That wasn't her purpose here.

"Help? Is that what you call it?"

"What would you call it, Daddy?"

"Hell, I don't know." He took off his hat and scratched his head. His hair was as thick and abundant as ever—but it had turned snow-white.

She hadn't pictured him white-haired. When she had reached him by phone, hearing his voice for the first time in seventeen years, she had envisioned the young, vital man he'd been during her eighteenth summer.

"I never meant for you to find out about my condition, Michelle," he said. The gravelly waver in his voice worried her. "And I sure as hell never meant for you to come riding to the rescue."

"This is one time you don't get to call all the shots, Dad." Out of the blue, a trust agreement had arrived in November. She'd been at work, fiddling on the computer with some coffee-bean graphics when a courier delivered a thick envelope bearing the logo of Blue Rock Ranch. She had nearly dropped the package in her surprise. Then she'd shuttered the blinds of her office, sat down at her desk, and opened the package. There was no cover letter, just little Post-it arrows indicating where to sign.

It had taken Michelle a few stunned moments to figure out what was going on. After nearly seventeen years of silence, her father was putting a staggering fortune in trust for her son.

She had broken a nail pecking in the phone number given on the trust agreement. The law firm in Missoula would tell her nothing, so she refused to sign the agreement.

That was when her father had called. He'd caught her

at home, loading the dishwasher and wondering why Brad hadn't phoned to tell her he'd miss dinner. The sound of her father's voice had banished her annoyance at Brad.

"Michelle, I've been sick."

She had closed her eyes and let out her breath. "What's the matter?"

"Damnedest thing. They call it end-stage renal failure."

"Kidney failure?"

"Yep. I had a spell of strep and ignored it, let it go on too long. There's a rare complication called glomerulonephritis—that's what developed. So far the tabloids haven't picked up on it, but the buzzards are circling."

The hated tabloids. They had made her childhood, as the daughter of a matinee idol, a nightmare. "So what's going to happen?"

Long hesitation. "I've started dialysis."

"Is there a cure?"

"Well, sort of."

"What's that supposed to mean, sort of?"

"My specialist in Missoula says I need a transplant."

"A kidney transplant." Comprehension burst over Michelle in a blaze so bright that she flinched. "From a living donor, right?"

"No. I'm on a waiting list for a cadaver."

Hearing the words, Michelle had the distinct sensation of stepping off a cliff. The knowledge of what she had to do came swiftly, pushing up through her like a geyser—unstoppable, filled with its own energy. She backed herself against the kitchen wall, sliding down it while the phone cord pulled to its limit. She knew she could stretch this strange moment out, make him talk to her, force him to ask, to beg, maybe. But instead, she shut her eyes and plunged right in.

"You don't have to wait for someone to die. I'll do it, Daddy," she practically whispered. "I'll give you a—"

Oh, Jesus. "—a kidney."

"Michelle?" Gavin Slade's movie-idol voice beckoned her back to the present. "If you're tired from the drive, we can leave right now."

"No, let's stay. I'm too wired to relax just yet." She had gone through nine weeks of multiple preliminary screening exams at Swedish Hospital in Seattle: blood tests, chest X rays, detailed urinalysis, sonograms and MRIs. Against enormous odds, five out of six antigens matched. Physiologically, she was a near perfect donor for Gavin. Because her father's health was otherwise excellent, he made the ideal recipient.

He sent her a look she couldn't read. "We've got a lot to talk about."

At least he acknowledged it. At least he acknowledged that he'd broken seventeen years of silence only because he needed one of her kidneys.

Michelle stared at the arena ring where the barrels were being removed. She was determined to keep her face neutral. *I will not be angry at him,* she told herself, as she had told herself ever since learning of his condition. Anger had no place in this matter.

"So you remember how to get up to Blue Rock?" he asked.

"I could do that in my sleep, Dad. I might even let Cody drive. He got his license last summer, and he's been bugging me all day."

Gavin nodded to a passing couple, but they didn't stop to chat. The barrel racing had ended, and it was time for team roping. People took rodeo seriously in Crystal City, and there wasn't a lot of socializing going on. That would come after, when winners and losers alike headed out to the Grizzly Bar, a local honky-tonk, for drinking and dancing.

"So your boyfriend decided not to come?" Gavin asked.

"He's snowed under at work." She tucked her chin into the collar of her jacket. "His name's Brad, and he's more than a boyfriend. We've been together three years."

"Getting married?"

Her cheeks filled with color yet again. *Marriage.* That would force her and Brad to define their relationship. "We're in no hurry."

"Well, I'd like to meet him. So he's a pharmacist?"

"He's part owner in a big pharmacy franchise. He's helped me a lot—understanding your illness and what's going on with this transplant. At one time he was thinking of becoming a doctor—a surgeon—but pharmacy suits him better."

At least, that was what he always said. Michelle realized, with a start, that she really didn't understand what lay in Brad's heart. Odd. She usually thought of the two of them as knowing each other so well.

An announcement crackled over the PA system, and Gavin perked up. "Michelle, I have to go over to the chutes. I've got some new saddle broncs I'm testing. You want to come?"

"No, thanks. I was just going to see what Cody's up to."

"You do that." Gavin started to walk away, then turned back. "Michelle?"

"Yeah?"

"It feels good to have you home."

"Ditto, Dad." She forced the words out. Everything felt strange, dreamlike, with the shadows of a nightmare hovering at the edges. It was just nerves, Michelle told herself. If all went well, she'd be back in Seattle in a few weeks. "See you up at the house later."

Michelle had no trouble spotting Cody in the bleachers at the far end of the arena. Having never been to a rodeo before, he probably didn't realize it wasn't the best place to view the action.

She opened her mouth to call out, then stopped herself. She saw exactly why Cody had parked himself there. The barrel racer—the one in black and turquoise—sat a few rows over, sipping a Dr Pepper and talking to the girl with the teased hair and fringed shirt. They appeared completely unaware of Cody, but then, he appeared completely unaware of them. And Michelle knew damned well he was burning up with awareness.

Good, she thought. Maybe he'd finally get over his obsession with Claudia Teller, his girlfriend since the start of the school year. Claudia was a beautiful pale predator who never met Michelle's eyes and who answered her admittedly chirpy questions with monosyllables. Claudia had introduced Cody to cigarettes and Zima, and probably to things Michelle hadn't found out about yet. There was no creature quite so intoxicating as a provocative teenage girl. And no creature quite so malleable as a teenage boy on hormone overload. A girl like Claudia could make Eagle Scouts steal from their grandmothers. She wore makeup with the brand name Urban Decay. She had bottle red hair and kohl-deepened eyes, and she was as seductive as Spanish fly on Cody's defenseless adolescent libido. The most popular girl in the school, she wielded her power over him with casual ruthlessness.

Since Cody had taken up with Claudia, Michelle felt herself losing her maternal hold on him. Her son was a stranger. When he lied to her, she didn't know what to do.

Maybe the sojourn in Montana was a test period, Michelle thought. Could she win her son back, or was he already lost to her?

The barrel racer didn't look quite so predatory. Perhaps he'd see her in school. Against his will, Cody was going to have to attend Crystal City High during their stay in Montana because his grades had been terrible lately. He despised the idea, but his grade-level advisor had laid down the law. Attend school in Montana or repeat the term.

Michelle wandered off, pausing at the baked goods table to admire a plush wool Salish blanket. Handwoven in rich earth tones, the design touched a chord in her. She thought of Joseph Rain, the master painter she had once studied with. His work had held echoes of these ancient motifs. On impulse, she went out to the car to get her checkbook. There was no cold quite so piercing as the cold of a Montana winter night. The new snow was powdery and light beneath her boots. The Swan River was almost frozen over. Only a miserly trickle down the middle remained, though in spring it would transform itself into a roaring gush of white water.

When she returned to the arena, Cody had moved down one bench closer to the girls. The calf roping had started, bawling dogies and lightning-quick horses kicking up dirt as the cowboys flew at them. The chase lasted no more than a few seconds, but there was a peculiar drama in the frantic flight of the calf, the moment the rope drew taut, the cowboy vaulting from his saddle to bind the feet, the flagger's arm streaking up to mark the moment.

". . . and in chute number four, we have Sam McPhee," said the announcer over the PA system.

The world stopped turning.

"Ladies and gentlemen, please put your hands together for Sam McPhee. . . ."

Time, breath, heartbeat, everything seemed to stop.

Applause erupted from the bleachers. She stood at the rail and gripped the rungs hard.

Sam McPhee. Sam is here.

Michelle prayed she'd heard wrong. But she knew she hadn't. Oh, God. *Sam.*

"Six-time national champion Sam McPhee retired from the circuit in 1992, but we're lucky to have his local talent here in Crystal City. . . ." The announcer droned on, enumerating accomplishments that didn't surprise Michelle one bit. The only thing Sam McPhee hadn't done right was stick around.

After a few moments, she remembered to breathe again. She looked at the chute at the end of the arena, and there he was. From a distance he resembled any cowboy about to rope a calf. Battered hat jammed on his head, the brim angled down, piggin string clamped between his teeth, coiled rope clenched in his fist.

Yet she knew him. Knew the tilt of his head, the set of his shoulders, the fringe of sandy hair touching his collar. She couldn't help herself. She moved along the rail to get a closer look.

Sam nodded briefly, almost imperceptibly, at the guy in charge of the chutes. The calf lunged out. Sam followed on a glossy-hided, athletic quarter horse. He roped and dispatched the calf with a speed that drew gasps of admiration from the crowd. Admiration for a six-time national champion.

Michelle stared, spellbound, unable to move, a fly caught in a pool of honey. Sam appeared leaner, stronger, and quicker than ever. He retained that unique grace of movement she recalled so well. More than brute strength, it was an aura of raw ability coupled with arrogant confidence. He waved to the crowd. Everyone knew he'd made the winning time. Everyone knew he was the champion.

Sam had it in spades—the star power and magnetism of a true pro. She got a good look at him as he led his horse, showman-style, along the rail. The years had hardly left a mark on him. He still filled a pair of jeans like a Levi's poster boy. He still had that slightly crooked grin that had once made her heart melt. Accepting the accolades, he still had that funny, enchanting "aw-shucks" manner about him.

And he was still caught up in the shallow thrills of the rodeo, she reminded herself with a superior sniff as a leggy brunette handed him a trophy, accompanying it with a kiss.

Was it the rodeo that had seduced him away from her? That had made him disappear overnight? She had never seen him again. Until now.

"That was kind of cool, wasn't it?" Cody came up behind her.

"What, the calf roping?" Good God, thought Michelle. Panic beat so hard in her chest it felt like a heart attack. Cody didn't know. She never thought she would have to tell him. *Good God.*

"Yeah, the calf roping, whatever." He watched the handlers, done up like clowns, shooing dogies into pens. "It was pretty cool."

Was it genetic? Michelle wondered. "I thought you were into wholesome pursuits like slam dancing and body piercing."

"How about driving, Mom? Can I drive from here to your father's place?"

Michelle nodded, thinking irrationally that if she gave in, she wouldn't have to deal with the other. "All right. You can drive."

For a few moments longer, he watched Sam with interest. And why not? The tall cowboy, with his easy smile and smooth way with the ladies, was sure to appeal to a boy's imagination.

Her heart chilled, aching in her chest. Sam was here. Sam and Cody were both here. And they didn't know about each other.

Chapter 4

It felt damned good to win. Winning always gave Sam a rush. Cheap thrills. They never lasted long, but they were easier to come by than the real thing.

"Nice ride." Edward Bliss fell in step with Sam while he walked Rio to cool out the big horse. "You done good, pardner." Beyond the paddock, some of the rigs were getting ready to leave, diesel engines idling.

"I guess I'll be buying all of Ruby's blankets." Sam led Rio in a wide circle. Steam rose from the quarter horse's body and plumed from his nostrils.

"You're too late. I just sold the last one. To a pretty blond lady I didn't recognize." Edward handed him a bottle of water.

"I assume you introduced yourself." Sam took a swig from the bottle.

"Nope. She was in a hurry. Had some whiny long-haired kid with her who kept saying it was his turn to drive."

"When you're a kid, it's *always* your turn to drive." Sam finished the water. Out in the parking lot, the sound of gunning engines roared. "So, you got a hot date?"

"Does a coyote have fleas?" Edward gestured at a plump, dark-haired woman in denims and a chinook jacket. She waved to him. "Pearl, from the bank. We're going up to Polson to have a few beers. Want to come?"

Sam grinned, thinking about the suggestion Loretta Sweeney had whispered in his ear when she'd given him the winner's trophy and check. "I've had a better offer."

Edward read his mind. "Loretta's a slut."

"That's what I like about her."

Edward took off. Sam bent to put on Rio's boots— he always put boots on the horses so they wouldn't damage their hooves in the trailer—when the whir of a spinning tire made the horse shy.

"Damn it." Sam dodged an iron-shod hoof.

A second later, he heard the unmistakable metal-on-metal crunch of two vehicles meeting. Rio grunted and flattened his ears. Looping the horse's lead around a rail, Sam went to see what the problem was.

"Shit," he said. "Shit, shit, shit."

The yuppie Range Rover from Washington had backed into his trailer. Its bumper was hooked into the rear, brake lights casting an eerie red glow over the dirty, churned-up snow. As Sam stalked across the parking lot, the yuppie gunned it again. With a wrenching sound of metal, the bumper unhooked. The Rover lurched forward.

Sam put two fingers to his lips and pierced the air with a loud whistle. "Hold on there!" he yelled, breaking into a run.

A few people stopped, shaking their heads when they

saw the damage. The driver's side door of the Rover opened and out jumped a slender teenage boy.

Great, thought Sam, eyeing the studded jacket and sleek ponytail. An underage driver to boot. He could see someone in the passenger seat of the Range Rover. The kid's date, maybe?

"Guess you had a little trouble backing up there," he said, keeping calm with an effort.

The kid tossed him an insolent glance. Light glinted off a small silver nose hoop. "Guess so. Sorry about your trailer. Insurance'll cover it."

The boy's nonchalance grated on Sam. Hell, he looked too young to have a license. A learner's permit—possibly.

When Sam thought of the time and expense repairs would take, he got more pissed. From the corner of his eye, he could see the boy's passenger rooting around in the glove compartment.

"Yeah, insurance'll cover it," Sam said, "but only after I fight with them for about six months. Tell you what— this looks like a few hundred dollars' worth of damage. You could come out to my place and work it off."

"Work it—"

"You know, work. Like with a shovel and a ton of horseshit." Sam dug in his pocket for a card with the ranch name and address on it. He held it out. "You show up to- morrow, and you can get started on the stables."

The kid didn't take the card. "Hey, I'm not from around here—"

"I never would have guessed," Sam snapped. "Look, you be there or—"

"He'll be there," said a soft voice behind Sam.

He froze, feeling a jab of premonition. *That voice*. He knew that voice. It was something the heart remembered long after the mind forgot.

He made himself turn slowly to face her. Awareness exploded over him, but there was only silence, and the smell of snow and exhaust, and a vague notion of folks walking to their cars in the parking lot. Each moment seemed endless, drawn out, excruciating. Denial reared in his chest, but he couldn't refute what his eyes were seeing.

"Michelle?"

"Hey, Sam." She had that same low, sweet voice and wide, fragile eyes, the same soft blond hair, cropped short now but curling in the same breezy way around a face he'd never forgotten.

The boy blew on his hands to warm them. "You guys know each other?"

"Reckon we do," said Sam, his gaze never leaving Michelle. Holy Christ, *Michelle Turner*. When he had first met her, she was the prettiest thing he'd ever seen in his life—long yellow ponytail, big blue eyes, a smile he liked better than air. Now she wasn't pretty anymore. She was beautiful, the way a goddess is beautiful, the way the moon is beautiful. Perfectly formed, luminous, chilly, and . . . distant. That was the word for it. Distant.

Where've you been, Michelle?

The unexpected quake of emotion pissed him off. He didn't need this, didn't want the memories she stirred up. Turning away from her, he tucked the card back in his pocket. "Look, kid, forget about the trailer."

The boy let out an explosive breath of relief. "Hey, thanks. That's pretty cool of you—"

"He'll be at your place tomorrow." Michelle's voice was flat, neutral. Sam had no idea what he was seeing in her eyes, her face. A stranger. Michelle had become a stranger. The person who had once been the sole keeper of every hope and dream he'd ever had was now a complete mystery to him.

"You don't have to—" he began.

"Yes, he does, and he will."

"*Mo-om,*" the kid said.

What an annoying little shit. Sam got prickly hearing some kid call Michelle "Mom." He felt even more weird thinking that somewhere in the world there was a guy the kid called "Dad." So where was he? Sam wondered. He knew he wouldn't ask.

"Now," she said, "where's your 'place'?"

He reluctantly held out the card. Their hands touched as she took it and stuck it in her pocket. A cold, impersonal brush of the fingers. A stranger's touch. What was he expecting? Fireworks? Electricity? Christ, violin music?

She wore a thick, artsy-looking ring that was more sculpture than jewelry. A wedding band? He couldn't tell. He wouldn't ask.

"I'll have Cody there in the morning," she said. "Is nine o'clock all right?"

"Yeah, okay. Nine o'clock."

"Mom," the kid said. "Do I really have to—"

"Get in the Rover, Cody," she said brusquely. "And *I'll* drive."

Chapter 5

Chapter 5

Michelle shivered against the cold as she walked across the guest compound to the main house at Blue Rock Ranch. The moon was out, dazzling above the peaks of the Swan Range. She could see all the lunar craters as if through the lens of a telescope. Icy silver light poured invasively across the snow-covered meadows.

She experienced a gut reaction she hadn't felt in a very long time. It was a strange, impossible-to-forget combination of pain and ecstasy that always preceded inspiration. Artist's inspiration. Joseph Rain, who had been her teacher that long-ago summer, called it the touch of the damned, because it hurt, it burned, it was beautiful.

When was the last time she'd felt this desire, this ache? This sharp need to create an image, to speak in color and shape when there were no words?

She couldn't remember, because she had learned to squash the feeling as quickly as it came over her. She didn't have time. She was too busy at work, too busy with Cody and Brad.

But here? Would she be too busy here? The thought of actually having time on her hands frightened her, it really did. Back in Seattle she took a certain comfort in having so much to do that she never found time to think.

At the moment she couldn't do anything *but* think. Sam McPhee was here. He had a ranch called, according to the business card he'd given her, Lonepine. It was located up the old logging road between two hanging lakes. A guy who wasn't supposed to amount to anything had a place of his own. And first thing in the morning, she had to take his son to see him.

She hugged herself, staring up at the white winter moon, wondering if he'd guessed yet. Wondering if he would stay up late tonight, thinking about the past.

The garden gazebo rose like an ice sculpture in the middle of the front yard. She had been sitting on the steps of that gazebo, drawing, the first time she met Sam. She remembered the quiet of that afternoon, the scratch of her pencil on the Firebrand tablet she held in her lap. Joseph Rain had called Montana a "place of great breathing," his apt phrase for the expansiveness of the landscape.

"Nice picture," said a voice behind her.

She froze, charcoal pencil in hand, at the sound of that voice. It was nice, a baritone, but youthful, too.

"You think so?" she asked, getting up. And it was him, just as she had suspected—hoped, prayed—it would be. The boy from the training arena. She'd spotted him the day she arrived. Her first glimpse of him had been from a distance.

He'd been working in a round pen with a mare on a

lunge rope. She had been watching from the porch. He wore scuffed boots and blue jeans, a plaid shirt and battered cap with the Big Sky Feed Company logo on it. He was tall and rangy, like Gavin's favorite trail horse. She knew, to the very depths of her eighteen-year-old soul, that no one in the entire universe had ever looked so good in a pair of Levi's.

Up close, she noticed that he had sandy brown hair, a lean, suntanned face, and eyes the color of her birthstone.

"Yeah, I think so," he replied. "Haven't had much call to look at art, but that's a fine picture."

She stuck her pencil behind her ear, suddenly self-conscious in her cutoffs and cropped T-shirt. "I'm Michelle."

"I know. I've seen you around with your sketchbook."
He noticed. Hallelujah, he noticed.

Michelle had been drawing ever since she was old enough to hold a crayon. It was all she ever wanted to do, and she excelled at it, blazing like a comet through high school classes and special courses she took outside of school. Her inspiration and talent had served her well when she went to Montana to spend that precollege year with her father. Montana seemed so huge and limitless that she got into the habit of drawing constantly just to feel a measure of control over something so overwhelmingly vast and wild. She drew everything: the placid bovine face of a cow; a line of trees along the creek with the stars coming out behind them; the silhouette of a mare and her foal on the slope behind the paddock; a common loon nesting in a marsh.

"I never go anywhere without my sketchbook," she said.

"I'm Sam. Sam McPhee. I work for your dad." He

grinned, and her heart began to melt. If she looked down, she figured she'd see it in a puddle like hot fudge at her feet.

"I know." She grinned back, hoping her neck didn't go all splotchy the way it usually did when she blushed.

"So you're an artist?" he asked. Not with the hefty skepticism a lot of people exhibited when she told them her ambition, but with genuine interest.

"I want to be." She gestured at the sketch. "This is practice. I want to paint for real."

"You mean like on an easel with brushes and a palette and a beret and stuff?"

She laughed. "Exactly. Well, maybe not the beret."

"So do it."

"Do what?"

"Paint for real. Don't just say you're going to. You can't be an artist if you don't paint, right?"

"Guess not." She scuffed her foot against the gazebo steps. "You ever heard of Joseph Rain?"

"Sure," Sam said. "He eats at the café where my mom works. I heard he lives out on the Flathead reservation, but he's a recluse."

"Well, he's just about the most famous painter in the West," she explained. "I came here to study with him." Her father had arranged it all. Though the artist rarely accepted students, Gavin had sent him a box of her sketches and attached a very large check. Mr. Rain had kept the sketches, returned the check, and agreed to work with her—for a fee, not a bribe.

"Yeah? I'd heard he was an artist or something."

"He did a series of paintings for the National Trust." In her mind's eye she could picture them—deep burning emotional scenes that haunted her long after she had walked away from them. "I'm lucky he agreed to be my teacher."

"Is that the best offer you've had all summer?"

"So far." She dropped her sketchbook. Klutz, she thought.

Both she and Sam reached for it, their hands touching. He gave an easy laugh, keeping her hand in his.

The sound of Sam McPhee, laughing. The feel of his hand, touching her. These were the first things about him that she had loved. In the years that ensued, they were the things she remembered more vividly and more frequently than she wanted to.

She wished she had never come back. How would she bear the beauty of this place with its pure light, its slashing cold, and now Sam McPhee? Gritting her teeth, she let herself into the main house. When she stepped inside, she remembered her first visit here, how grand and solid everything had looked. Back then, she'd had her own room upstairs. Now she and Cody occupied a guesthouse. Gavin thought Cody would feel more comfortable in his own space.

"I'll be right out," Gavin called from somewhere upstairs. "Make yourself a drink."

She crossed the living room—a Ralph Lauren ad in 3-D—and stepped behind the wet bar. On a polished shelf, she found a heavy crystal highball glass and shook some ice from the undersized freezer. As she perused the bottles of exotic, expensive whiskey and liqueur, she tried to get her thoughts in some sort of order.

She tended to put things into compartments. Here, in this box—worries about Cody. She spent a lot of time sifting through them, never getting to the bottom, because every day he came up with a new challenge, from asking to get his eyebrow pierced to wanting permission to go to an overnight rock concert.

In another box—work. The agency liked her because she did good work and kept her clients happy. This spring, she would make partner and would earn more money than she ever dreamed of. The other partners lived in fear that she would leave them for a bigger, more lucrative firm, taking her clients with her. But why go elsewhere? To draw bigger, more lucrative ads for fertilizer and tampons?

Another box—Brad. After three years together, they hovered in the same spot where they had begun. They'd bought side-by-side units in a tony Seattle town-house complex, their outdoor decks divided by a wall of cedar planks. They were socially compatible. Sexually compatible. Financially compatible. Rough when it came to Cody, because he and Brad didn't get along.

Now she had a couple of other boxes under construction. Her father, whose life depended on her giving him one of her kidneys, took up a lot of space in her thoughts. For most of her life, he had ignored her, and only when his survival hung in the balance did he acknowledge her existence. A psychiatrist would have a field day with the two of them, she reflected wryly. Sharing their flesh, an organ, the mysterious life force—so damned symbolic. And—she kept telling herself not to think this but she couldn't help it—it was *icky*. There, thought Michelle. I'm a terrible person. Acting like Mother Teresa on the outside, while the coward inside trembled in horror at the ordeal to come.

And now Sam. Good God, Sam McPhee.

"I don't need a drink," she muttered under her breath, regarding the array of bottles. "I need a twelve-step program."

"Try the Booker's. Used to be my favorite."

She whirled around, startled. "Daddy. I didn't hear you come down."

He winked, looking spruce in a thick terry-cloth robe and leather slippers. "Light on my feet."

Obediently, she poured a splash of Booker's over some crushed ice. The first sip brought tears to her eyes. "That's lighter fluid, Dad."

"Good, huh?"

She coughed a little, feeling the rich amber liquid burn her throat. "You want something?"

He held up a tumbler. "My trusty cranberry juice. I've been on restriction for a long time."

A long time. When had he first fallen sick? How long had he suffered with no one to talk to about what was happening to him? Michelle didn't know him well enough to ask.

They sat together in the sunken living room. Rustic millionaire, she mentally classified it. Muted evergreen-and-burgundy plaid, peeled lodgepole pine, a massive field-stone fireplace. She stared intently at the flames lapping at a big log and sipped her single-barrel bourbon.

"So here I am," she said, hopelessly inane.

"Here you are. My angel of mercy."

She blinked fast, taken aback by the bitterness in his voice. "You're mad at me?"

"Hell no, honey, I'm mad at the world. Have been ever since the frigging diagnosis. I failed the medical standard for renewing my pilot's license."

"Daddy, I'm sorry." Everyone knew how much flying meant to him. A week seldom went by that he didn't take off, even for a little while, in his beloved airplane. He had brought her to Blue Rock for the first time in his vintage

P-51 Mustang, modified to accommodate two seats, and she used to love flying with him.

"Do you still have your plane?"

"Yep. I keep the Mustang out at the Meridian County Air Park. And a biplane for stunts." He held up his glass. "Can't even have a drink with my long-lost daughter. The kidney specialist has some diet Nazi monitoring me almost twenty-four hours a day."

"Does it help?"

"Yeah, kept me off dialysis longer than it should have. The biggest culprit is protein—damned hard to stay away from. Cheating isn't an option, either. If the kidneys have to work extra hard, it just hastens the breakdown. I guess that's why I'm resentful. And because I wish I was brave enough to just shoot myself rather than take a goddamned *organ* from my own child."

"Stop it." Michelle was starting to worry, trying not to show it. "We already agreed it's the right thing to do."

He fell silent, staring at the fire in the grate. His famous profile was illuminated by kindly soft light. He still had the charisma that made him a beloved icon in the world of film and a stranger to his family. After a while he let out a heavy sigh. "Anyway—" he clinked his glass against hers "—welcome home, long-lost daughter."

"I was never lost, Daddy."

"You stayed away a long time."

"You should have invited me back."

"Didn't think you'd want to come." He rubbed his cheeks, looking no less handsome than ever. Lord, the man was an android. Dorian Gray with bigger shoulders. He never seemed to age. Even sick and white-haired, he appeared tanned and fit, mature yet ageless.

"Dad, you should have asked me to come back. Before it was too late, got too awkward."

"What would you have said?"

She laughed humorlessly into the crystal highball glass. "I'd have told you to piss off."

"That's what I figured."

They finished their drinks, and somewhere in the house a case clock struck eleven. All the things they weren't saying to each other—about Cody, about the transplant, and now about the surprise cameo appearance of Sam McPhee—hung like cobwebs in the air between them. Why hadn't Gavin told her the father of her child was in Crystal City?

The prospect of an explosive, accusatory conversation held no appeal at this late hour. Without even speaking a word, they made a tacit agreement to avoid touchy subjects—for now.

Gavin looked tired. Frighteningly tired. And she could see, hidden in the folds of his robe . . . *something.*

"It's a sac of dialysis fluid," he said.

Her cheeks heated. "I didn't mean to stare."

"Not to worry. I don't have much dignity left since I got sick." He smiled, but there was a hardness in his face that gave away his fury and frustration. "The stuff in the sac flows through an abdominal shunt. Want to see?"

"Dad, please."

"Okay, I apologize. I stare at it too, sometimes, like it belongs to someone else. Can't believe my own body's turned traitor on me."

They sat for long moments, sipping their drinks and watching the fire, not speaking. The silence swelled. Only in the mountains in winter, Michelle reflected, did the quiet have this all-pervasive quality.

Suddenly she realized what she and Gavin were doing. Another battle of wills. Who would admit to being tired first? Who would make the first move?

No more games. She yawned elaborately, stretching her arms behind her head. "The Booker's did the trick."

"Guess I'll hit the hay, too." Gavin got to his feet. He was too good an actor to look relieved, but she figured he was. "You sleep in, now, Michelle. Since I didn't expect you until tomorrow, I didn't make any plans."

"Plans?"

He cleared his throat. "You know . . . appointments."

"Oh." The impending procedure was becoming more grimly real to her with each passing moment. "We can talk about that tomorrow."

"You got everything you need in the guesthouse?"

"It's fine." She stood, feeling awkward. "Thanks for stocking the fridge." She wondered if she should kiss him good night. Self-consciously, she lifted up on tiptoe, gave him a peck on the cheek, and let herself out the front door.

As she crossed the silent, starlit compound, she knew she wouldn't be sleeping in tomorrow. She had to take Cody to work at Sam's place. She had to figure out how to tell her son who Sam was without destroying him, without destroying them all.

Sunday

Sunday

Chapter 6

A t 8:45, Sam heard the growl of a motor and the grind of tires over snow. Out in the yard, Scout, the Border collie who ruled the ranch, launched into a barking frenzy.

Sam had taken Loretta Sweeney home early last night. He'd been up since six, and felt all jumpy in his gut; didn't even want his morning coffee. Damn it, he was a grown man. The last thing in the world he should be doing was getting nervous over seeing an old girlfriend.

Except that the words "old" and "girlfriend" didn't seem to apply to Michelle. Though their love affair had burned like a forest fire half a lifetime ago, she didn't seem old at all. Just . . . different. He remembered a girl with yellow hair and a quicksilver smile. Now she seemed far away and sort of fragile. But still so damned beautiful. And as for the girlfriend part—you didn't call your first grand passion a "girlfriend." The term was too inadequate to cover the delirium, the ecstasy, the sweaty palms and fevered dreams of that lost, intense season.

The sound of car doors slamming made him wince. Shit. He *was* nervous.

Going to the window, he expected to see Michelle's Range Rover. Instead, he spied Ruby and Molly Lightning getting out of their old Apache pickup. Scout's "who-the-hell-are-you" barking changed to "I'm-all-yours" whimpers of ecstatic greeting.

Sam gritted his teeth and tried to smile. Ordinarily he'd be glad to see Ruby and her daughter. But it wasn't an ordinary day. He was expecting Michelle, and he didn't look forward to entertaining her, the kid, and now these two.

He went out onto the porch. Sunlight glinted off the snow in the yard and driveway. A row of icicles dripped from the eaves. The Border collie nuzzled Molly's hand.

"Hey, ladies," he said. "You're out bright and early this morning."

Ruby propped an elbow on the battered hood of the pickup. She had a broad, pleasant face, one gold tooth, and an ease around people that made her a popular teacher at the high school. "Hey, Sam," she said.

"Hiya, Sam." Molly scratched the dog behind the ears. "Nice ride last night."

"You, too," he said.

Ruby opened the door of the truck and started rummaging around. "I heard you wanted to buy a blanket."

"Ma'am, I wanted to buy them all."

Molly rolled her eyes.

"I did," Sam said. "It gets mighty cold up here in the winter."

"Well, I brought you one." She held out a folded blanket.

At that moment, another car turned off the highway and started up the drive. The Range Rover. Scout launched into her watchdog routine.

Sam took the blanket from Ruby. The thick wool felt warm against his hands. Plenty warm. "Hey, thanks." He reached into his back pocket for his wallet.

Ruby reached around behind him and grabbed his wrist, holding it firmly. "Sam McPhee, don't you dare. It's a gift because you never let me pay you for delivering Glenda's babies."

He laughed. "Glenda's an Irish setter. She didn't need much help."

"Whatever. The blanket's to say thanks."

Michelle parked and got out of her car. And there stood Sam with Ruby's arm halfway around him, her hand pressed against his hip pocket.

He stepped back. "Morning, Michelle."

She inclined her head politely. Distantly. "Hello, Sam." The collie hung back, head tilted to one side, waiting to see how friendly this one would turn out to be.

"This here's Ruby Lightning and that's her daughter Molly over there."

"Pleased to meet you." Although Michelle smiled readily, the temperature seemed to drop a few degrees. "Look, if this is a bad time—"

"Not at all. You ladies want to come in for coffee?"

Ruby shook her head, winking at him. "I better get going. We've got church this morning."

Molly walked over from the paddock adjacent to the barn. A few of the horses, their coats thick with inch-long hair, stood at the fence waiting for their morning feed. "I could stay and help out with the horses," she called out.

Then Michelle's son got out of the Range Rover, looking as sulky and undernourished as a Calvin Klein ad. Interest sparked in his eyes when he spotted Molly, but he was quick to hide it with a squint that reminded Sam eerily of Gavin Slade. The kid would probably love having her around all day.

"Not today, Molly, but thanks for the offer," Sam said. He didn't want her to have to put up with the little hoodlum.

"My son's name is Cody," Michelle said, motioning him over.

It occurred to Sam that he didn't know the boy's last name, or if Michelle had a married name now. The kid shook his hair back. Stuck his thumb in the top of his belt. "Hiya."

"Hi," Molly said, transparent in her interest. She regarded the kid with the same fascination Red Riding Hood had for the Big Bad Wolf.

Ruby climbed into her truck. "See you around. Nice meeting you both."

Molly took her time getting in. "'Bye, Sam. 'Bye, Michelle and . . . Cody." The smile she sent him was way more than the kid deserved.

As the truck pulled away, a sense of amazement crept over Sam. Michelle had been dead to him. For seventeen years she had been gone, as permanently and irrevocably as if she had been buried six feet under. Now here she was, back again in all her beauty and all her strangeness, and he found himself vacillating between elation and rage. He found himself with a hard-on that made him glad his jacket was zipped.

"Cody's ready to get to work," Michelle said.

"Is that right?" Sam asked Cody.

The kid shrugged, slouching in the time-honored fashion of teens with attitude. "Guess so."

Sam flicked his gaze over him from head to toe. Shining light-colored hair cut too long in some places, too short in others. A leather jacket that would get him knifed in certain neighborhoods. Black jeans and designer combat boots.

The humane thing to do would be to give the kid one of the Filson coveralls from the stable lockers, but Sam wasn't feeling too humane about this guy.

"Let's go to the barn," he said, putting on his John Deere cap. "I'll introduce you to Edward and he can get you started."

"Started on what?"

Sam thought of the heap of manure Diego had left unshoveled. "Oh, I've got a real treat for you, Cody."

He turned to Michelle, flashing her a grin. She blinked at him as if his smile startled her. "Go on inside, Michelle. Make yourself comfortable. There's coffee in the kitchen."

She opened her mouth to say something, then seemed to think better of it and went toward the house. He stopped for a second and looked at her on his porch, and their gazes caught and held.

Though he made no move, a part of him stepped back, and he caught his breath. Michelle, here at his house. Looking as pure and brittle as the sun-shot icicles that lined the eaves above her, a dripping frame of cold and light. Sam felt as if he was in the middle of a dream. This wasn't real. *She* wasn't real.

Just then, the sun won its battle with the ice, and the row of icicles crackled and fell, coming away in slow motion and then falling all at once, stabbing into the snow-covered hedge in front of the porch. The sudden, glittering tumult seemed to startle her into action. She gave a brief, taut smile and disappeared into the house.

Sam started toward the horse barn, the collie leaping at his side. He didn't look back to see if the kid was following.

Situated inside the barn door was an office with papers, certificates, and permits plastered all over the wall, a cluttered kitchenette and coffee bar, and a refrigerator with a keg tap on the door. A pellet stove heated the room.

Edward Bliss sat with his feet up on a battered metal desk, a phone cradled between his shoulder and his ear, and a beatific smile on his face.

"Morning, Romeo," Sam said.

"I'll call you later, darlin'," Edward crooned into the receiver. He hesitated, listening, and his grin widened as he hung up. "You took the purse last night, boss, but I was the one who celebrated."

"So what else is new?"

"That biff on the back of your trailer. Did you see that? Looks like some idiot nailed you last night."

"As a matter of fact . . ." Sam stepped out of the doorway and motioned the kid into the office. "This is Cody. He's going to be helping out around the place. Cody, this is my partner, Edward Bliss."

Edward glanced up distractedly. Then he did a double take, looking from Sam to Cody and back again, his eyes wide. "Jesus H. Geronimo Christ—"

"Something wrong?" Sam knew Edward didn't care for punks, but he'd never known his partner to make such a snap judgment. So the kid had hit the trailer, so he'd made a mistake. It wasn't the end of the world.

Edward stood up, gathering the papers on the desk into a stack. "Nope, not at all. Cody's going to take Diego's place, then?"

"That's what I figure. For a while, at least." Sam hadn't even had time to ask Michelle how long she'd be visiting.

Scout lost interest in the entire situation and trotted out to the yard. Edward kept staring at the kid as if to drill a hole through him. Cody stared back, eyes narrowed.

"All right." Edward snapped his suspenders and reached for his battered plaid coat, flecked with hayseed and oat grains. "Let's get started."

Most of the stalls were empty, the horses turned out for the day since it promised to be sunny. The barn had the feel of a cathedral. Daylight streamed through high windows under the eaves, and the echo of footsteps sounded loud in the hush.

"So what do I do?" Cody asked, dubiously eyeing the area. Mild suspicion tinged his voice.

Edward opened the door to one of the stalls. "Simple. You move the manure out and the cedar shavings in."

The kid swallowed, staring at the floor of the stall. "Just this one?"

"Nope." Sam gestured down the length of the barn. "What've we got here, twenty jugs?" Sam told himself not to enjoy this, but he couldn't help it.

"Great," said Cody.

"Don't go into this one without Edward or me present." Sam showed him a roomy stall in the middle. "That's Sylvia. She's expecting, and she's getting kind of cranky."

Cody peered over the top of the half door. The roan mare flared her nostrils at him and laid her ears back in warning. Her sides fanned in and out like a set of bellows.

"Yeah?" Cody asked with the first spark of interest he'd exhibited since seeing Molly.

"The foal could come tonight," Sam said. "Sylvia's

showing signs of her labor. We'll be bathing her today and getting the birthing stall ready."

The mare glared white-eyed at the stranger. The boy glared back. Sam added, "Just relax, act a little friendly, and she'll warm up to you." He made a clucking sound in his throat. The mare's ears eased up, and she stuck her head out of the stall. Cody hung back a moment, then put out his hand. The mare sniffed his shoulder. He rubbed her nose and cheek, hesitantly at first and then with more force.

"Don't put any cedar shavings in Sylvia's stall," Sam said. "Sawdust and chips are bad for the foal. Straw only. Edward'll show you, and you can help hose her down, too. But remember—she's cranky."

"Just wait till we give her that phosphate enema," Edward said.

Cody winced. "I can wait."

Edward held out a pair of leather gloves and rubber pac boots. "Put these on and let's get started."

Cody looked askance at the boots, but took them and sat on a plastic milk crate to unlace his faux-biker shoes.

"I'll leave you guys to get after it." Sam started walking back toward the house, then turned.

"Glad you showed up," he called.

"Yeah, right." Cody tossed his hair out of his eyes and rammed his foot into one of the boots.

When Sam reached the doorway, he turned back one more time, intending to tell Cody to help himself to a drink from the barn fridge if he needed one. But the words froze in his throat.

The light from outside slanted down just so, and in the uneven yellow glow, Cody stood out sharply in profile. He straightened up and hitched back his hip, stomping his foot down into the boot, a motion so familiar to Sam it was like looking in a mirror.

He leaned back against the door of a stall, feeling as if he'd just been sucker-punched. He couldn't seem to grab a breath of air.

Slow down, McPhee, he told himself. Take it easy and think for a minute. Think think think. Think of the kid, and of Michelle's cold manner, her nervousness. Think of the look of amazement on Edward's face when he'd seen Sam and Cody standing side by side.

Think of the calendar, the years that had passed. Do the math.

Count the years.

Piece by piece, he put it together. The kid looked younger than sixteen, but Sam's first impression had been wrong. Cody *was* sixteen.

"Holy shit," Sam said under his breath. "Holy goddamned shit." An icy wind blew over him from outside, but he barely felt it. He stood motionless in the doorway of the barn and watched Cody wield the shovel. His slim form bent and straightened; the light from the cracks in the eaves streamed down over him, down over the shining sandy hair and the clean profile and the unsmiling mouth and the eyes that were not quite blue.

"Holy shit," Sam said again. Then he turned on his heel and strode away from the barn.

am McPhee's kitchen appeared lived-in but not fussed over. Stainless-steel appliances, tile countertops, a garden window with a few tired-looking potted herbs struggling along. A coffeemaker hissed beneath a set of wall hooks with an array of mismatched mugs bearing imprints of various feed brands and drug names. Drug names? Atarax. Was that a veterinary drug?

Brad would know, thought Michelle. Brad the pharmacy franchise owner. Her "boyfriend," Gavin called him.

Feeling like an intruder, she helped herself to coffee. She had a devilish urge to poke around the rest of the house, but she resisted and sat down at the table. A tabby cat leaped onto the seat of the chair next to her, peering solemnly through crystal eyes.

"Hi there." She offered a finger for the cat to sniff, then rubbed its fur. It turned its head nearly upside down beneath her scratching finger. "I bet you wonder what I'm doing here," she said, and sipped her coffee. "I'm wondering the same thing myself."

Outside, the wind kicked up whirlpools in the snow. The Border collie pounced on the snow dervishes, making a joyous game of it. In her wildest imaginings, Michelle had never dreamed she would find herself sitting in Sam McPhee's kitchen, drinking his coffee and petting his cat. He wasn't the sort she even thought of as *having* a kitchen, much less a cat.

It took all her self-control to stay seated, to keep from running outside, grabbing Cody, and driving away, not stopping until Seattle. She dreaded telling Cody the truth. She wasn't stupid; she knew her kid. Sam represented the sort of dad—the fantasy dad, the Disneyland dad—Cody had been secretly wishing for all his life. The swift ride, the cheap thrill.

What Cody was too young to realize was that the minute he gave himself to a guy like Sam, he was a goner. Sam would break the boy's heart the way he broke Michelle's so long ago.

But she was going to stay in Crystal City no matter what her instincts urged her to do. Because when it came to self-control, Michelle Turner was an expert.

On some level, she might even savor the visit, she told herself, watching the cat curl into a ball on the braided seat cover of the chair next to her. This morning she had awakened early to sunshine and new snow that had come silently in the night, covering every flaw of age and softening all the sharp edges of the world. The landscape looked as clean and stark as an unpainted canvas. The miles of white meadows and the mountains rearing against a tall cerulean sky had a calming effect on her; they always had. Here, she felt a sense of drama and richness she had been missing ever since her adolescence had given way to the brutal chaos of instant adulthood.

Though her mother had raised her in the hushed elegance of Bel Air, Sharon Turner had lived way beyond her means. Her unexpected death had left Michelle a legacy of unpaid taxes and debts. By the time all accounts had been settled, there was nothing left but grief.

Michelle could have prevailed on her father for help even after she'd left Crystal City. Writing checks was what Gavin Slade did best. But she had never asked. All the money in the world couldn't provide what she needed far more than monthly rent—love, support, stability. Money was the least of her problems, and it was the first one she solved.

On her own she built a life she could be proud of— a kid who, until recently, had been great; a waterfront town house filled with furniture from Roche-Bobois, a Lexus, a ski condo in Whistler.

Hers had been a life that hadn't slowed down since she'd fled Montana all those years ago. And now she was back, and she had no idea what to make of it, what to think, how to feel. Slowing down and giving herself time to think was dangerous. Seeing Sam again was even more dangerous. He had broken her heart once. She wanted to believe he had no power to do it again. But when she saw him at the arena last night, she knew a secret, fragile part of her still belonged to him.

All her instincts had rebelled against bringing Cody here this morning. But honor demanded it. Cody had trashed Sam's trailer, and he had to make amends.

Truth to tell, Michelle had been incredibly curious. She had always assumed Sam had never amounted to anything more than a rodeo bum, rambling from show to show until the inevitable injuries of his sport retired him. She used to picture him battered and stiff at age thirty, tending bar in some little Western town. He'd wear his champion's belt buckle, and behind the bar amid the array of beer nuts and whiskey bottles, there would be a few dusty trophies and photographs of him looking like a young Paul Newman.

There wasn't a single photo in sight in this kitchen, not even one taped to the refrigerator. Odd.

She finished her coffee and rinsed the mug, taking a long drink of icy tap water. The window over the sink framed the distant mountain peaks rearing against the sky. As she gazed out across the empty, perfect meadows, a wave of nostalgia had swept over her. She'd spent so little time in Montana, yet it seemed like the place where her soul had always dwelt. What a magnificent sight to greet Sam when he got up in the morning. How different it was from the soulless cocoon of her office at the agency in downtown Seattle.

Sam had managed to confound her expectations. He didn't seem to suffer any permanent injuries from the rodeo. He had a horse ranch with a comfortable house, sturdy outbuildings, covered and open-air arenas and pens. But in a way the place seemed as empty as her own town house.

Had he surrendered his dreams? Had it hurt? Had he simply awakened one morning to discover that the life he'd envisioned for himself didn't match the one he actually had? Did she dare to ask him?

"Of course not." Michelle stroked the cat. "It's none of my business."

As she watched out the window, a stocky dark-haired man on a tractor came out of the barn, towing a load of manure on a stone boat. The Border collie cavorted like a clown through the drifts of snow. Cody followed, wearing oversize boots and hefting a shovel over one shoulder. Amazing. He was actually working. It had been forever since Michelle had been able to make him do anything.

She took another drink, savoring the sweetness of mountain well water. Footsteps thudded on the back porch and a door slammed. She turned to see Sam standing in the kitchen doorway. Faded jeans, fleece-lined denim jacket, battered John Deere cap, gloves protruding from a hip pocket. The Marlboro man without the cigarette.

"I helped myself to coffee," she said uncertainly. "Want some?"

He ignored the question. He flexed his jaw, shifted his weight to one side. Though he barely moved, a subtle threat seemed to emanate from him. It was hard to explain, but Michelle sensed a dangerous turbulence in the air between them. Old intimacy mingled with fresh suspicion.

He took a step toward her. "So when were you planning on telling me I have a son?"

His blunt words pounded at Michelle, but she felt no shock. In the back of her mind she had known since last night that he would figure out the truth based on Cody's age. She folded her arms protectively across her middle. "God, if you said something to Cody—"

"What the hell do you take me for? Of course I didn't say anything. Thanks to you, I don't even know the kid." His gaze flicked over her, measuring her contemptuously from head to toe and back again. "So I guess that means you've never told him, either."

She returned his glare. "I didn't see the point. I didn't think he'd ever meet you."

He grabbed the back of his neck in a distracted gesture. "Jesus Christ. You had my kid, and you never told me."

"And this surprises you?" Too many years had passed for Michelle to feel bitter, but she did. The regrets, the resentment, the frustration, all came bubbling to the surface. "I was eighteen years old and pregnant. You'd run off to be a rodeo champ. Do you think I had the slightest idea how to track you down? And what makes you think I didn't try?"

"Did you?"

"Of course I did, Sam. I was in l—" She broke off, unwilling to continue down that path. "Are you telling me it should have been easy to find you? Did you and your mother leave a forwarding address? Did you stay anywhere long enough to have one?"

"Permanent addresses were never my mother's strong suit." His voice was low and hoarse. "We weren't all brought up in gated communities in Bel Air."

She flinched at the implication. She and Sam came from different worlds, though at eighteen they had sworn it didn't matter.

"I didn't have a whole lot of time to spend trying to figure out where you'd gone. I had a baby to raise. Beyond the twenty-four hours a day that took, I couldn't seem to squeeze in a missing-persons search."

"I deserved to know, damn it."

"Oh, right. So you could do what? Marry me?"

"So I could have a say in what you did with my kid. You never even gave me a chance."

"Tell me an eighteen-year-old cowboy wants a *chance* with a baby."

She was dangerously, humiliatingly close to tears. She refused to shed them. She had wept an ocean for Sam McPhee and he'd never come to find her. Crying now would only prove what Michelle had been trying to deny since seeing him last night. Seventeen years ago he had taken possession of her in ways she was too young to understand. She had never given herself so wholly to another person, nor taken so much from someone else. After Sam left, she had dreamed of meeting someone new, but she'd never found that depth, that completion, with any other person. So she learned to do without.

Michelle forced herself to get a grip, to stand up from the table so she didn't feel at a disadvantage. "This is stupid. We shouldn't argue about the past. We can't change what happened."

"Maybe not." Unhurried yet unrelenting, he walked toward her, stopping only inches from her. The smell of snow and wind clung to his clothes, underlying the unique scent of him. She thought she had forgotten it.

"Sam—"

"We've got a lot of talking to do." His low voice caught at her, mesmerized her. "Problem is, now that you're here, I want to do a hell of a lot more than talk."

"You're crazy." She didn't know this man anymore, but she could feel the anger and passion seething from him. She searched his face, wondering about the lines that fanned out from his eyes.

"Crazy? I've been called worse." He took another step toward her. "I couldn't sleep for thinking about you last night."

She inched back. "You came in here wanting to talk about Cody."

He stuck a thumb into his jeans pocket, his hip propped on the edge of the counter. "So talk. I'm listening."

This can't be happening, Michelle thought. "I don't know where to start."

"You had my child and you never told me." He spoke coldly, the words hard as stones. "How about starting there?"

"The day I found out I was pregnant, I went to see you. And you had left without a trace. I don't believe I owed you a thing."

The heat of his glare was a tangible thing; she could feel it blasting away at her. "I won't discuss this with you if you're hostile," she added.

"Excuse me if I'm a little disoriented by all this. It's not every day a woman I used to sleep with shows up with a kid she had sixteen years ago."

"I didn't know I'd find you here."

"Well, here I am, honey." He spread his arms mockingly. "I'm surprised your daddy didn't warn you."

She was surprised, too, but she wouldn't admit it to Sam. She wondered if he knew she and her father were strangers, and that only Gavin's illness had brought her back.

"We should be talking instead of arguing." She sat back down at the table, took a deep breath. "Maybe I was wrong. I should have searched high and low for you. But everyone said I'd get over you. Said I was better off without you, that I'd go off to college and meet someone who—" She broke off and shrugged.

"—wasn't a born drifter with a hopeless lush for a mother," Sam finished for her.

"I never said that."

"You didn't have to."

"I had to think about Cody, too. I spent my childhood ducking the paparazzi. I'm very protective of him in that way."

His eyes narrowed. "Oh, yeah, the tabloids would've had a field day with us. Gavin Slade's only daughter makes it with a ranch hand."

She flinched, knowing he wasn't far off the mark. As a child, she had shown up occasionally in the scandal sheets—a grainy photo taken through a long lens: *Gavin Slade's Love Child*, the caption always read.

A juicy story like an illicit Romeo and Juliet–style affair would have revived the attention she shunned. That was why she worked so hard to maintain her anonymity. Every once in a while a reporter in search of a scoop came sniffing around. One even snapped her photo when she was pregnant. The incident had scared her so much that she moved to Seattle, where no one knew her.

Sam sat down across from her. His hands were big, not as work-scarred as she would have thought. She caught herself staring at those hands, remembering how she used to rub Bag Balm on them to soothe the calluses.

"None of that old stuff can matter now, Michelle. What matters is that we have a son." He clenched his hand into a fist on the table. "A son. I can't believe it."

She was terrified to ask the next question, but she had to. "Sam, what are you going to do?"

"Do?"

"About . . . learning that Cody's your son." She tasted the burn of resentment in her throat. "Your biological son." Yes, that sounded better. More distant.

He studied her hands, and she wondered if he remembered the Bag Balm, too. On her right one, she wore a Cartier onyx ring. On the left forefinger, a large sapphire.

"Did you raise him alone, or are you in a relationship?"

She guessed that meant he wasn't thinking about the Bag Balm. *In a relationship*. It was such a modern thing to say. Like so many modern things, it had no meaning.

"Alone, more or less."

"Explain more or less."

"I've been with someone for the past three years. But

it's not—he's not—" Damn. How could she explain Brad? "He's not raising Cody."

"I see." Sam got up from the table and poured himself a cup of coffee. He seemed hesitant when he turned. "So did Cody ever ask about me?"

"Of course he asked."

"And you told him what? Obviously my name doesn't ring a bell with him."

"I was worried about the tabloids. So I left the father's name blank on his birth certificate."

"Christ—"

"Sam, I was young. Scared. I grew up with cameras shoved in my face every time I sneezed. I didn't want that for Cody, and I didn't want anyone to go snooping through records—"

"—and finding the name of a mongrel cowboy."

"Quit putting words in my mouth. I didn't know what to do."

"Didn't he want to know, just for him? Jesus, a name wouldn't have sent him off the deep end."

"A name's just . . . a name. And maybe I was afraid—" She stopped, wishing she could reel in the words.

"Of what? What were you afraid of?"

"That maybe he'd get mad at me one day and go off looking for you." The confession rushed out like air escaping a balloon. "Since school started this year, he's been . . . in rebellion."

Sam hesitated, took a sip of coffee. In his face she saw more than she wanted to see—interest, understanding. Compassion. "The kid's mad at the world, Michelle."

Ouch. He had seen that so quickly. "We've had rough times before. We've dealt with trouble. This year . . . is more difficult than most." Damn. She knew she should keep her thoughts to herself, but with Sam, it was hard.

Years ago he'd had that effect on her, and it hadn't changed. He still drew truths from deep inside her, made her say things better left unsaid.

"So what's going on?" he asked. "Is he having trouble in school?"

All right, thought Michelle. You asked for it. The good, the bad, and the ugly. "His last grade report was awful. Up until this year, he's been an A and B student. Now it's Cs and Ds. At first I thought it was a normal, predictable rebellion, but I don't see the end of it."

"Is he hanging out with his regular friends?"

"Not as much as he used to. He's got a girlfriend, and they're pretty exclusive."

"So what are you doing about his problems?"

"I'm working on it, Sam! Do you think this is easy? Do you think you could do better?"

"Is it my turn to take over? You had him the first sixteen years, I get the next sixteen?"

"I didn't bring him here because he's a troubled teen. I brought him here . . . to see my dad." She didn't feel like discussing Gavin's health with Sam. "My father's never met Cody." She got up from the table and went to the door. She was afraid. She was angry. And God help her, she felt an old, old yearning unfold in her heart, a burning ache she thought she had buried forever. "What time should I pick him up?"

Outside, Cody and the dark-haired man were loading bales of hay onto a flatbed truck. It was startling to see her son doing physical labor. It had been ages since he exerted himself doing anything more strenuous than lifting the telephone receiver.

"He'll be done around five, I guess," Sam said. "Edward can give him a lift over to your father's place."

"All right." Taking her jacket from a hook outside the kitchen door in the mudroom, she shrugged into it. "Sam?"

"Yeah?"

"You won't . . . say anything to him, will you?"

"Hell, no, I won't say anything. I don't even know the kid." He held open the door for her. He was as tall as she remembered, and broader in the shoulders and chest. His face was more deeply carved with character. His scent, God, why did she remember it so perfectly? Perversely, she had an urge to touch him, just once, but she resisted.

"'Bye, Sam."

"'Bye." He followed her out onto the porch and waited while she got into the Range Rover. "Hey, Michelle?"

She rolled down the window. "What?"

"That doesn't mean we're not telling him."

She leaned back against the headrest, closing her eyes. "Damn. I was hoping for a quick getaway."

"No such luck, Sugar. Tell him. I want him to know exactly who I am."

"But—" She opened her eyes. "All right. I'll tell him."

"When?"

"I'll . . . figure out the right time. Sam, I've got a lot on my mind. My father isn't well, and the next few days might be pretty difficult."

He stared at her for a long time. She couldn't read him. Didn't know him anymore. Yet that stare was as compelling now as it had been the first time she had met him. "All right. But I want him to know, Michelle. Soon."

Chapter 8

Cody felt like a cockroach in his grandfather's house—gross, unwelcome, and out of place. After shoveling horseshit at Lonepine all day, he wanted to shower for about nine hours and then crash facedown in his bed.

Instead, they were having dinner with Legendary Actor Gavin Slade. That was how Gavin was always referred to: Legendary Actor. Elder Statesman of Western Classics. In capital letters, like the guy was a walking headline or something. Lately, instead of showing him with his arm around some bimbo with big tits, the fanzines showed him alone on a horse, his cowboy hat pulled low over his brow. The headlines announced that he'd been in touch with aliens.

Cody liked the bimbo pictures better. It was pretty bizarre, thinking about his grandfather getting laid by women younger than his own mom, but it was even worse thinking about his grandfather dying of kidney failure. Mostly, he tried not to think of Gavin at all. It wasn't like Gavin thought about *him* all the time.

Cody had tried his best to weasel out of dinner, but he hadn't gained much sympathy from his mom. After crunching that cowpoke's trailer last night, he'd used up most of his goodwill points with her. Not that he had many to begin with. Since last summer she'd been driving him nuts, hovering over him, waiting to pounce the second she caught him doing something she disapproved of.

He'd tried a minor whine—*I'm too tired, I worked like a dog today*—but all he'd gained was the Look. That cold jackhammer of a stare still affected him sometimes, although he was getting pretty good at ignoring her lately.

When he was little, he used to be moved by the Look. He used to want to do just about anything to please her. Little by little over the years, he'd figured out that there was no way to please his perfectionist mother. No way to win a smile that wasn't sad at the edges, or to get praise from her that didn't demand things he didn't even know how to give.

So he quit trying, and he wasn't even sure she noticed. She was so lame, she and that loser Brad. All Brad cared about was making the almighty buck and showing off to the world that Cody's mom was his lady, like she was some sort of bowling trophy with boobs.

That was the only good thing about coming here. It gave him a break from Brad the loser.

"Hiya, Cody." Gavin Slade came into the living room. Unlike Cody, he looked exactly right in his surroundings. Jeans and a red corduroy shirt and cowboy boots. Big white hair that made his eyes look bluer than the heated swimming pool on the patio.

"Hi." Cody hadn't decided what to call his grand-father, and it would be too dorky to ask. Jamming his hands into his pockets, he pretended great interest in the objects arranged on a lighted glass shelf by the wet bar. After a couple of seconds, he didn't have to fake it anymore.

Holy shit. He was looking at an Oscar statue.

"That's pretty cool," he said, pointing to it.

"You think?" Gavin hooked a thumb into his back pocket like he was posing for a picture or something. Except he didn't even seem conscious of the pose—it was the natural way he held himself. "I guess so. I liked that movie. *The Face of Battle*. You ever see it?"

Only about a zillion times.

"I think maybe I caught part of it on TV once," he lied.

"It's about a misfit, a real loser. Nobody cared whether he lived or died. After a while, he quit caring, too. And in the end, that's why he was able to save his battalion. He quit looking for guarantees, and he made the sacrifice."

Cody pictured the scene in his head. It was one of those film sequences the experts always showed when they were going over classic movies—the moment Gavin's character stood alone on a tank-destroyer turret, the only volunteer of his battalion, shooting through a deadly hail of sniper fire at a 77mm tank gun. Like the image of Gary Cooper in *High Noon*, Gavin Slade's *Face of Battle* moment had put him on the pages of the film history books. The memorable image showed a close-up of a face filled with nobility, anguish, and the wisdom of a man who knows he is about to die. It had become one of the most famous movie stills ever published.

"How come you stopped making movies?" Cody asked.

"It was always a job to me, to tell you the truth. A job I liked most of the time, and either loved or hated the rest." He had this intent way of speaking, leaning forward and lowering his voice so you had no choice but to listen. "The business is brutal, Cody. You live and die by the box office. Your looks and your image are everything. Sometimes you don't get a minute of privacy, and other times you can't buy attention for yourself. I got sick of the roller coaster. As soon as I could afford to retire, I got out of acting. I still coproduce things here and there, but it's pretty low-key. Haven't seen a film on the big screen in ages."

"Mom said the movie theater in town is closed down."

"That's a fact. They were going to tear the Lynwood down, so I bought it."

A spark of interest flashed in Cody. "Yeah?"

"I'd like to reopen, for old time's sake. One screen, maybe show some independent films."

"That'd be cool." Cody studied the other objects in the case—a baseball autographed by Joe DiMaggio, the stub of a ticket to a Beatles concert, a display of prize rodeo belt buckles, and photos of Gavin posing proudly by his vintage airplane. Pretty radical stuff, he decided.

His perusal drifted to a framed picture of his mom on a horse. "When was that taken?" he asked, to fill the silence.

"First summer after high school," Gavin said. "I invited her to spend a year up here before starting college. She studied painting with a local artist."

"She never finished college," Cody said, hearing contempt in his own voice. He didn't care. All his friends' parents had degrees and stuff. His mom had, well, her job. And him. And lame-ass suspicious Brad who lived in fear that Cody and his friends were going to help themselves to uppers or painkillers from his sample cases.

He looked at the picture, taken in a pasture with the mountains in the background. Slender and suntanned, long legs and bare feet, her head thrown back with laughter, she looked pretty amazing. For the past couple of years, his friends had been giving Cody a hard time about his mom. She was a lot younger than most moms. She looked like a shampoo ad or something. It was kind of cool sometimes, having a mom who was a babe, but mostly it was embarrassing as hell.

"I still have that horse," Gavin said.

"The one in the picture?"

"Yeah, that's Dooley. Your mom learned barrel racing on him."

"He must be pretty old."

"Twenty-something. Do you ride, Cody?"

"Not horses."

Gavin chuckled, showing perfect teeth. And his eyes— they had that crinkly, twinkly look Cody recognized from old movie posters. He didn't trust this guy. How did you know he was being sincere when he was an actor?

"I guess that'll change now that you're here," Gavin said. "Or maybe I'll take you flying once I pass my physical and get my license renewed. You interested?"

"We're only staying until you get through with your recovery period." Even that was too long for Cody. Worse, he had to enroll in the local high school here in Noplace, Montana. He had stormed for weeks in rebellion, but his mom was adamant. He got a minor reprieve this week— it was winter break in Noplace. But pretty soon he was going to have to be the new kid. A fate worse than death. "Mom says a few weeks or so. Then we're out of here."

Gavin's grin stayed fixed in place. But the movie-star

gleam in his eyes dimmed as if Cody's words were a light switch that suddenly turned it off. "Let's go see if supper's ready."

Cody felt kind of shitty as he followed his grandfather into a big dining room with fancy crystal and china laid out. What did the old man expect? Instant bonding, like on those long-distance phone commercials? He and Gavin Slade were complete strangers. After this transplant thing was over, they probably wouldn't ever see each other again.

Grandfathers made friends with grandsons when they were little and cute, not when they were sixteen, wearing a ponytail and combat boots. Not that Cody wanted to cozy up to the old man, anyway. It was gross, thinking about his illness. He had some kind of fluid bag attached to a tube going inside him, doing the work his kidneys were supposed to do. The very idea of it made Cody want to hurl.

His mom joined them in the dining room. She was smiling in a nervous way. Her gaze kept darting from her father to Cody. "Hi, guys," she said.

Gavin held a chair for her. It was corny but kind of nice seeing the old guy do that. Once, Cody had tried holding a chair out for Claudia. "What, like it's going to get away from me?" she'd asked, then cracked up. Cody had laughed, too.

Dinner was about the best thing that had happened since his mom loaded him into the car at the crack of dawn yesterday. Prepared by an Asian nutrition expert named Tadao, it consisted of pasta with fancy sauce, fresh bread, a bunch of grilled veggies, and a big salad of exotic fruit.

After shoveling away about nineteen pounds of food, Cody glanced up to see both his mother and his grandfather watching him. Neither of them had eaten much. Gavin was on some sort of low-protein diet. He couldn't eat things that made his kidneys work hard because they didn't function at all anymore.

"You must've worked up an appetite out at Lonepine today," Gavin commented.

"It's good," he said, and sucked down a whole glass of milk.

"Be sure you tell Tadao you enjoyed it," his mom said.

Shit. She was always doing that. No matter what it was—having a good meal, talking on the phone, whatever, she had to add her own little goody-goody twist on it. Her own little adjustment or correction. This morning he'd expected her to totally humiliate him in front of that girl, Molly. But for once his mom had shown mercy.

She'd seemed kind of flustered around Sam McPhee, like she couldn't quite decide what to make of him. Cody wasn't sure what to make of the guy either. He was okay, but Cody thought it was totally bogus of him to make him pay off the trailer damage with slave labor.

He helped himself to more milk from a cut-glass pitcher, feeling a slight sting from the blisters on his hand. *Blisters*, for chrissakes. He was pretty sure he'd never given himself blisters before. Especially not by shoveling horseshit.

He got the idea from that Bliss guy that Lonepine was some kind of hotshot horse breeding and training ranch. It was cool, working in a barn where a mare was about to give birth any minute. When it was time to go today, Cody had felt a twinge of disappointment. He wouldn't have minded seeing the horse being born. It would have given him a good story to tell Claudia.

Maybe the manure story was funny enough. But honestly, he hadn't felt much like laughing. There had been a moment, when he was alone in the barn, with the smells around him and the light falling between the rafters, that an odd feeling had settled over him. Maybe it was the quiet or the sense that he was totally alone; he didn't know. But it had felt kind of pleasant.

"It's nice to be together with the two of you," Gavin said suddenly, pressing his palms on the table as if he never planned to eat again.

"We let too much time go by," his mom said in a quiet voice.

"I know, Michelle," Gavin said. "I'm sorry. I can't tell you how many times I picked up the phone, but I never knew what I'd say—"

"Let's not do this, Daddy. Let's not drag up all the old regrets. We can't get back the years we lost. We can only go on from here."

Cody did his best not to roll his eyes. This was just what he'd been hoping to avoid—a big emotional scene where they go "I'm sorry I'm sorry" all over each other and then drag him into the middle of everything as The Grandson You Never Knew.

"Can I be excused?" he asked too loudly.

They both looked at him as if he had a booger hanging out of his nose.

"I told Claudia I'd call her."

"Girlfriend?" Gavin asked.

"Yeah." Cody felt about two feet taller just saying it. He loved walking through the halls at school, hearing everybody whisper: *He's going out with Claudia Teller....*

"So can I be excused?" he asked.

His mom nodded. "Go ahead, honey."

"Thanks . . . for dinner," he said, then hurried out into the cold night. When he got to his own room, he collapsed on the bed, clicked on the TV, and realized that working outside in subfreezing temperatures all day had made him more tired than he'd ever been in his life. He was asleep before he even remembered he meant to call Claudia.

Monday

Chapter 9

Y ou're kidding, right?" Cody asked at the breakfast table.

"Don't talk with your mouth full." Cradling a coffee mug between both hands, Michelle regarded her son in the clear light of the mountain morning. His cheeks were stuffed with blueberry muffin. Chewing slowly, he washed it down with a big gulp of black coffee.

When did her son start drinking coffee—black, of all things?

He took a final swallow. "I said, you're kidding, right?"

She'd heard him the first time, but making him repeat himself for the sake of manners was ingrained in her. Funny how he'd never learned that lesson. The second time around, he was supposed to fix his tone of voice, ask his question politely and without food in his mouth. Yet in all his life, he'd never done it.

Maybe he kept thinking she'd get tired of correcting him. He'd worn her down on so many other matters. When he wanted something—ridiculously expensive shoes, a pierced ear, a snowboard—he became like water dripping on a rock: constant, incessant, wearing her away until she caved in.

"No," she said. "I'm not kidding. You're going back to Mr. McPhee's today."

"I'm not going." Cody jutted his chin defiantly and held up his hands, palms facing out. "I have blisters because I spent eight hours shoveling horseshit yesterday. Horseshit, Mom."

Michelle felt her lips twitch. Laughing now would enrage him, so she composed herself. "When Mr. Bliss dropped you off yesterday he said there was lots more work to be done and to be there at nine again."

"That sucks." He shoved back from the table, giving his long two-colored ponytail an insolent toss.

"What sucks is backing the car into a guy's trailer," she reminded him. *What sucks is that the guy's your father, and I have no idea how to explain it to you.*

"So go get ready." She put the mugs in the sink. "I need to phone Brad, and then we'll leave."

"Hey, I was going to call Claudia—"

"Later. When you get home tonight—"

Cody curled his lip. "I'll call her when I damn well please."

Her face felt hot, burning hot, yet the anger was directed at herself. When he spoke to her like this, she had no idea how to make him stop. It was frightening sometimes, knowing how completely out of her control he was.

"Let's not argue, Cody. Gavin and I have an appointment

in Missoula and we need to get going. In case you've forgotten, we're here for Gavin."

Cody tugged on his jacket, yanking out a pack of Camels, flashing them as he jerked open the door. "Yeah, I almost forgot. You're here to offer spare parts to your long-lost father."

The kid had great timing. He knew just when to pick a fight. She had to call Brad, drop off Cody, and accompany her father to Missoula. She didn't have time to deal with the rage and the hurt that had been ricocheting between her and her son since he turned sixteen.

The kid's mad at the world. Sam had seen that instantly.

She snatched up the phone and punched in Brad's number. He sounded groggy when he picked up.

"Oops," she said. "I forgot you're an hour earlier."

"Hey, babe." A sleepy smile softened his voice.

Michelle tried to relax, but she was too jumpy. "I wanted to call and say hi. I miss you."

"Miss you, too. Is everything okay out there? Do you need me to come out?"

What she needed, she realized suddenly, was for him to come without asking. To understand her well enough to know that of course she needed him. She was facing a terrifying ordeal; he was supposed to support her.

Dumb. If he showed up now, he'd be bored and fretful about missing work, and Michelle knew she'd feel guilty and that would make her cranky, and then she'd have a terrible attitude about the surgery. She shook her head, trying to veer away from that line of thinking. It was enough that he'd promised to fly in the day of the surgery.

"No, we're fine," she said. "Did anyone call?"

"Natalie." Distaste rumbled in his voice; he'd never

liked her best friend. An oft-unemployed cellist, Natalie Plum was the original free spirit. She drove a diehard planner like Brad crazy. "She's bringing her stuff over to your house today."

"Good. I was hoping she'd house-sit while I'm away. So how was your weekend?"

"Excellent. Dinner at Canlis with the Albrights. A round of golf at Port Ludlow. Babe, we should really look into getting a place up there. Mike was saying the lot values for the waterfront area have really shot up . . ."

She tuned out the monologue about real-estate investments. She did that a lot lately. He loved to collect things—resort property, sports equipment, luxury cars—displaying them to the world like hunting trophies. She admired his ambition, the way he was so driven to succeed in his career. In addition to the pharmacy, he had made a killing in the stock market, and money was an obsession with him. Sometimes she wished he'd slow down.

". . . he's a vascular surgeon at Swedish, got into the resort development on the ground floor . . ."

Michelle made the appropriate murmurs as her mind wandered further afield. She remembered the day she'd finally figured Brad out. He'd just put money down on a thirty-six-foot Hunter yacht, and she told him he was crazy. The vacation home, the ski lodge, the golf membership at Lakeside, the ski place at Whistler—he was wearing her out.

"Brad," she'd told him last summer while standing on the dock next to the gleaming new sailboat. "Wouldn't it be easier simply to *become* a doctor?"

His reaction had been unexpected and sharp. "No, god-dammit. It wouldn't. What the hell sort of question is that?"

He so rarely spoke in anger that she didn't press. But

she knew she had touched a raw nerve. He used to want to be a doctor the same way she used to want to be an artist. Now he owned a chain of pharmacies and she was a commercial illustrator.

She listened patiently as he finished his recitation. She waited for him to ask how Cody was doing, but he paused in the middle of talking, yawned, and said it was time to get up and into the shower.

"Wish you were here," he said, the suggestion in his voice both sexy and familiar.

"Me too." Out the window she could see Cody puffing away on a cigarette. Dear God. Her kid was smoking, and she had no idea how to stop him. She wanted to tell Brad everything—that her father still had the power to make her cry. That Cody was doing his best to drive her crazy. That she had met Sam McPhee again.

That she couldn't think of anything but Sam—oh, shit. She'd have to tell Brad. How was she going to tell him?

"I'll call you later, Brad."

"Yeah. Take care, babe."

She gathered up her coat and purse, pausing to glance into the mirror over the hall tree. What, exactly, did one wear to meet a transplant team? They sounded so important, so intimidating. Would they think her red wool blazer was too boldly colored? Should she have gone with the black angora instead?

She shoved aside the ridiculous questions. She was nervous about the appointment. She was nervous about being with her father again. She was nervous about Sam. Clothes should be the least of her concerns.

She stepped into boots and went out to find Cody. He tossed his cigarette butt into the snowy yard.

Fixing a glare on him, she groped in her purse for

car keys. "You know, you really should take up bungee-jumping from live power lines. It's a lot less risky than smoking."

"Very funny." He got in the car.

She didn't want to launch into yet another big lecture about smoking, not this morning. She had to be focused on her father.

When she'd first found out about his illness and bullied Gavin into the transplant, she started some of the tests in Seattle. Once she'd qualified as a donor, she had donated some of her own blood for the surgery ahead of time, and it had been shipped from Seattle and stored. She had more blood and X rays taken, did a lung capacity test, and did the twenty-four-hour urine collection study, a delightful routine she hoped she didn't have to repeat.

She felt as if she had been holding her breath for twelve weeks, and she was about to let it all out soon.

At today's appointment, the team wanted to go over more details, schedule a renal angiogram, and make sure she was mentally prepared for this.

She was not doing so hot on that count.

"So," she said, flexing her hands on the steering wheel. "What did you think of Mr. McPhee?"

"He said to call him Sam. And the other guy said to call him Edward."

"So what do you think of Sam?" She tried to keep her voice light, casual.

"He's okay."

"Just okay?"

"You want me to think he's great for making me work in the freezing cold like a farmhand?"

"Ranch hand."

"Whatever."

"I think, given the circumstances, you're lucky to get off with a few days' work. So you like him?"

"Did I say that, Mom? And why do I have to like anyone around here? We're leaving as soon as you finish this thing with your—with Gavin."

"I'm not leaving him until the critical period is over." She shuddered inwardly, horrified by the possibility that the surgery wouldn't work, that her kidney would be rejected. "It wouldn't hurt to make a few friends."

Trying to push that worry aside, she watched the scenery. The morning sun on the majestic landscape brought out the harsh poetry of the high country. The sight of blanketed fields and soaring mountains filled her with a strange yet familiar yearning. The truth was, she needed the mountains, the air, the clarity of light found only in Montana in order to paint. And maybe she needed to be the person she had been all those years ago, too. A person who dared to love, dared to dream.

But she knew of no way to recapture that young, naive self. The disappointment ate at her, a quiet dull pain, the surrendering of hope. Sometimes she believed her gift was only slumbering or maybe frozen inside, waiting. When she was pregnant with Cody, she had enrolled in a small liberal arts college, and for one glorious semester she had painted. She had a rare talent, and she knew it. Her instructors knew it. The gallery owners who approached her knew it. But making a career as a painter would take years of work and study and time.

After Cody was born, reality intruded. She counted herself lucky to land an entry-level position at an ad agency. Late at night, after Cody was asleep, she'd fall into a dream world that was hers and hers alone. Those hours were precious; the work she did was dark, important, and expressive. She produced dozens of paintings, working from pain rather than joy, producing fast as she was wont to do. Perhaps a part of her understood that the creative burst would fade away.

Time crept on, eating secretly away at her soul. Inch by inch, her imagination and energy deteriorated until she simply stopped painting. She dropped her art classes and changed the direction of her dreams. It was easier to collapse on the sofa, take her precious baby boy in her lap, and read stories to him. Those paintings lay stacked against a wall in a spare closet. She rarely looked at them. Once Cody started school, she had more time to pursue her art, but she never did. The prospect terrified her. It was like standing in front of the door to a dark, forbidding room. She'd be nuts to go there.

At the firm she did good work, got promoted through the ranks, achieved some recognition in her field, and quit thinking about painting.

But sometimes she still wanted to. Oh, how she wanted to.

"I used to know Sam," she said carefully to Cody.

"I figured that out when he called you by name after I hit his trailer."

"He worked at my father's place. I met him when I came here after my mother died."

Before her death, Sharon Turner had advised Michelle to start college straight out of high school. Always chilly, self-absorbed, and distant, Michelle's mother had suggested a practical course of study in design or architecture. Her death had left Michelle adrift, vulnerable. Terrified. And then, like the cavalry riding to the rescue, Gavin had made his offer. "Don't go rushing off to college at a time like this, honey," he'd said, his charm and warm sympathy palpable. "You'll never again get a year of your life to do anything you want. I showed your work to a local teacher, and he agreed to meet you. Come to Montana."

And so she had gone, never asking herself what he expected from the relationship, what he hoped it would become. Perhaps she had wanted to believe he acted out of selfless compassion, opening his home to the grieving daughter who hardly knew him. If there was such a thing as the classic absentee Hollywood dad, Gavin was it. He had sent checks, phoned her, and showed up on significant occasions—her first ballet recital, her Bluebird fly-up, a dressage championship—and she'd been thrilled to stand back and let him be the center of attention. She remembered her first communion at All Saints in Beverly Hills, the girls in stiff white dresses and new gloves. She'd felt like a bride that day, and when her father, incandescent as the Holy Ghost and twice as handsome, came striding across the parking lot toward her, she'd squealed and wrenched her hand out of her mother's grip. Racing to greet him, she flung herself into his arms and he picked her up, swinging her round and round as she laughed with joy. She could hear camera shutters clicking and people whispering *Gavin Slade. It's Gavin Slade. He's even better-looking in person. . . .* The days with her father, few and far between, stood out vividly in her memory. When his visits ended she always experienced a gaping emptiness. The world was duller, flatter, when Gavin wasn't around.

She glanced over at Cody, waiting for him to say something else. Waiting for him to ask more about Sam.

But Cody said nothing, and neither did Michelle. It wasn't the right time to bring up all the events that started here so long ago. They'd need hours for that. You always need hours to recover after a bombshell drops into the middle of your life, thought Michelle. She pictured them buried by the rocks and relics heaved up by her confession. Each bit of rubble would have to be removed with care to avoid damaging the fragile, angry victim beneath it. Hours, yes. Maybe days. Maybe a whole lot longer.

When they arrived at Sam's place, Edward greeted them and set Cody to work loading avalanche fencing onto a stone boat on stout wooden runners. Sam was already gone, Edward explained, pointing at a snowmobile trail leading into the low, distant hills. A mountain lion had been lurking around, and Sam went to check it out.

Her eye wandered along the corrugated track while her knees turned to lime Jell-O. A reprieve, she thought weakly. For now, at least.

Chapter 10

Gavin insisted on driving to Missoula. Michelle couldn't discern his state of mind. He seemed quiet, preoccupied. A crimson rash marred the side of his neck. She wanted to ask him about it, but she didn't. Somehow it seemed too personal.

It was going to get worse before it got better, she knew. He'd told her this morning, a little sheepishly, that his last mistress had left him when she found out how sick he was. She'd recently sold her story to a sleazy magazine. Once it hit the stands, it was sure to bring the paparazzi flocking around like carrion birds.

Michelle felt a peculiar violence when she thought about the mistress. Her name was Carolyn and she was about Michelle's age. If I ever run into her, thought Michelle, I'll set her hair on fire. It was one thing to sponge off a guy when you're his mistress, but to sell the story after dumping him was disgusting.

The road to Missoula rolled out in front of the chrome-grilled truck, and the land was deep and stark, lit by a sun that shone brighter than anywhere else in the world.

"It's a boring drive to the city. You might want to get some shut-eye," her father said.

A little hitch of disappointment caught in her chest. Part of her wanted to talk with him, to get to know him. But another part kept its distance, circling warily around the whole bizarre situation. It would be noble indeed to insist she was going through this because of the selfless filial love she felt for him, but how much of that love was a sense of obligation?

And was there any way to tell the difference?

She used to know exactly what love felt like. She closed her eyes against the glaring snowscape and let the years roll away until she was back in the past again, the week before Thanksgiving, 1983. A fresh snowfall had blanketed the farm. Flush with excitement, she'd rushed into the guesthouse Gavin had set up as an art studio for her. There, on a sunny morning not much different from today, she had finished the best painting of her life. After laboring over theory and composition with Joseph, she had produced something of merit and value. She couldn't have known back then that she would never again equal that effort.

She had painted for hours, stopping when Sam came in from work, his cheeks chapped and his lips cool until he warmed them by kissing her. She was covered in paint and all awash with the wonder of creating a work that grew from every level of her heart. He'd peeled oranges for her and brewed steaming cups of tea while she worked. And when she took a break, he'd made love to her.

"It's unbelievable, Michelle," he'd said that chill November day, tackling her on the low sofa in front of the woodstove.

"I bet you'd say that if I was painting Elvis on velvet."

"Maybe." With the frank lust only teenage boys exhibit, he lifted her sweatshirt and unhooked her bra.

Michelle still remembered the way he kissed her neck, her breasts, her stomach. Trusting him, she relaxed and let it happen. Since the very first time they'd made love, he had created a world of sensation for her. Colors glowed brighter. Edges appeared sharper. When they struggled out of their clothes and came together, she saw a million glinting stars behind her squeezed-shut eyelids.

Later as they lay spent in each other's arms, she had listened to the beat of his heart, drifting, dreaming. She'd done a lot of pictures in the summer and autumn—landscapes and wildlife, abstracts with bold splashes of color and subtle shadows hiding in the hollows of space.

"I want to be an artist," she said.

"You already are."

"No, I mean I want my paintings to hang in exhibits where anyone who wants to can see them, even buy them."

"So go for it." His belief in her was unshakable and straightforward.

She had loved that about him, how he never doubted her. But what did he believe about himself? It used to worry her sometimes, how quiet he was about his own life, so she asked, "What about you? What do you want?"

He'd chuckled without a great deal of humor. "For my mother to quit fucking up."

Michelle hadn't known what to say. Tammi Lee Gilmer was holding down a waitressing job at the Truxtop, yet she knew Sam was concerned. If Tammi Lee's pattern held true, she'd go on a binge, miss work, lose her job, then collect unemployment until it ran out and she drifted to another town, dragging Sam along with her.

It was the only life he had ever known, and thinking about it made Michelle's heart ache.

"That's not what I meant, Sam. I meant you. What do you want for you?"

"For me?" He hesitated.

"Come on, you can tell me. What, do you think I'd laugh at you? I'm the one who wants to make a living as an artist."

"At least you know what you want."

"So do you. But you have to tell me." She figured he was headed for the rodeo circuit. Already, he'd placed in a lot of the local shows, riding her father's bucking stock, competing in team-roping and bulldogging. "Come on. Truth or dare."

He wiggled his eyebrows comically. "I'll take the dare."

"I want the truth."

Another hesitation. Finally, without looking at her, he said, "Would you believe medical school?"

Michelle had pulled back, studied him. The shaggy light hair, serious eyes, and a mouth that made her melt inside were all so blissfully familiar. But this was a stranger speaking. It was the first she'd heard of medical school. "Since when?"

"Since forever, I guess." He began getting dressed. The ranch hands were riding fence, and he was an hour behind because of their diversion. "I've never told anyone."

"I'm glad you spilled the beans. You should go for it, Sam."

He shook his head, flashing a self-deprecating smile. "I'm a high school dropout."

"You can get a G.E.D."

"I can't afford college."

"My dad could help with—"

"He wouldn't, and I wouldn't ask him."

"Then *I'll* ask him."

"In case you haven't noticed, I'm your dad's best roper. Why would he want to lose that? And why would I beg some rich guy's help? Believe me, I wouldn't be worth a bucket of spoiled oats if your dad ever found out how I've been spending my lunch hour."

"We're consenting adults."

"Right. You think that would make a difference to your old man?"

"He's been a hound dog for years. He's got no call to talk. I don't know why you insist on keeping this a secret. I *love* you, Sam."

He paused, touched her cheek. "Aw, honey. That's why we can't let him catch on. He'd try his damnedest to keep us apart."

"He can't keep us apart. It's a free country."

Sam had laughed at that. "Is that what they taught you in that fancy-ass girls' school in Cal-if-orny?" His smile was tinged with a weary tolerance that made him seem infinitely older and wiser than Michelle. "That's not the way the real world works. In the real world, the daughter of a rich movie star doesn't go out with a waitress's son. Believe me, your dad wants you to fall for some guy with a golf handicap, not a PRCA rating."

"That's dumb. Besides, I've fallen for you. And that's not going to change. Not ever." As they finished dressing, she had considered telling him that she was alarmingly late with her period. But she'd said nothing. If it was a false alarm, there was no need to worry him.

He took her hand. "Honey, I don't want it to change. That's why we're better off keeping this quiet."

His words made her feel hopelessly naive. There were differences between them, class differences she didn't want to see. Looking back, she realized that had been apparent to Sam right from the start. That was probably why he didn't think anything of simply disappearing one November night.

She had walked outside with him, into the dry cold and sunshine, bringing along the finished winter landscape.

"Damn." He squinted in the direction of the training arena.

"What's wrong?"

"Jake Dollarhide. I think he saw us."

The foreman's son. She saw the gangly young man standing in the distance, and he was staring directly at them. "So what?" she'd said with breezy disregard. "Let Jake Dollarhide stare all he wants." She put the finished painting behind the seat of the truck.

"I can't take that, Michelle—"

"Yes you can. I'll paint a hundred more for you."

"Believe me, honey, this is enough."

She hadn't known back then that those would be his last words to her. That his last kiss would be a quick, furtive brush of his lips over hers. But after that moment, she had never seen him again.

"Ms. Turner, we're ready for you in Dr. Kehr's office."

Goose bumps rose on Michelle's arms as she entered a comfortable office with a generic but good-quality Robyn Bloss serigraph print on the wall behind the desk. Michelle studied it for a moment, remembering that she used to paint freely, in intense colors of her choosing, not in hues to match the burgundy wing chairs in doctors' offices where people waited for the bad news.

The Bloss print was supposed to be pacifying. To some it might have been. But to Michelle it was profoundly disturbing. Seeing that print was like looking into a mirror.

She seated herself in a leather armchair beside her father. A large window behind the desk afforded a view of the city, gray and bleak in midwinter, the river a colorless vein through the middle of town. Dr. Kehr, the nephrologist, sat opposite them, her ultraclean hands folded atop a stack of files and charts. She had a bland but pleasant smile, no discernible personality, and somehow meeting her for the first time made the whole situation starkly real.

They were going to cut out one of her kidneys and sew it into her father.

Sucking in a deep breath, Michelle shifted in her chair and waited for the rest of the team to arrive. They met Donna Roberts, the transplant coordinator, who was a registered nurse specializing in organ transplantation. Donna did a lot of touching and hand-holding, which Michelle didn't particularly need at that moment, but she figured she'd be grateful for later. Then there was Willard T. Temple, the psychologist and social worker. He could scuttle the whole thing if he didn't think her father and she were mentally prepared for it.

They would each have their own surgeons. They showed up in scrubs, alike as Tweedledee and Tweedledum but with firmer handshakes. Neither of them could stay long because, after all, they were surgeons and they spent all day cutting people, not talking to fading movie stars and their neurotic daughters.

To Michelle's surprise, one of the surgeons held the door open. "This way, Mr. Slade."

Gavin got up. Briefly, he rested his hand on her shoulder. "I'll be back shortly, okay?"

"You're not staying?" Panic pounded in her chest.

"I think they need to draw lines on me or something."

After the door closed, she scowled at Dr. Kehr. "He should be here."

Temple, who held a clipboard with a yellow legal pad, said, "Your father's been drilled on this procedure for months. We wanted a private meeting with you."

"Why?" *Oh my God. Are they going to tell me he won't make it?*

"Because if you have any uncertainty whatsoever about the transplant, we need to determine that. Living kidney donation is an emotional decision. It's natural to feel anxiety about the procedure, even though you want to help. You can speak freely to us. If you decide against the surgery, your father will be told you're not a good match. Our hope is to maintain the relationship between patient and donor, regardless of donation decision."

"I've made my decision," Michelle snapped, stung because she knew she and Gavin didn't have any relationship to maintain. "I already passed all the tests."

"We still have to do the renal angiogram," Dr. Kehr reminded her. "Chances are, you'll be a near-perfect donor. But there could be other issues that make you less than an ideal candidate."

"I'm here, aren't I?" she said fiercely.

"Sometimes there are emotional issues," Temple said in his low-key voice. "Your father indicated you've been estranged for many years. This decision—"

"Don't you get it?" Her voice rose. "There was never any decision to be made. You're welcome to explore my feelings all you want, but you're not going to get me to change my mind." She forced herself to glare straight into his eyes. "My father is dying. My kidney can save him. *That's* the issue, Dr. Temple."

He nodded briefly, and annoyingly made a note on his legal pad. "You should be aware that this procedure alone won't mend the estrangement between you and your father. Flesh and blood alone can't accomplish that."

"I just want him well again," Michelle said, painfully close to tears. "The rest . . . we'll deal with."

When Dr. Kehr started speaking, she was thorough, encouragingly so. She explained what everyone's role would be. She talked about recovery periods, follow-up care, side effects of the meds, and long-term prognosis. She took out badly drawn charts—medical illustration was not terribly lucrative—to show what would happen in the procedure.

That's what she called it. The Procedure.

"Unless the renal angiogram indicates otherwise, the surgeon will take the left kidney." The doctor pointed to the chart.

"I had no idea there was a difference." A heaviness weighted the atmosphere. Though he had left the room, her father's need pressed at Michelle, smothering her. Her hands in her lap ripped a Kleenex to shreds. Guiltily, she balled up the evidence and tucked it into her palm. Too late. Temple had seen. He made a note on his clipboard.

"Using the left kidney is standard," the doctor continued. "The connecting vessels are longer, so we've got more material to work with."

Michelle's hand, out of control now, stole back to press against her left side.

"You have a couple of options for entry." The chart was propped up again. "Later, we'll discuss whether it'll be the front or the back." Her finger traced incision lines on the chart. "Generally, we advise against the back entry, because although it's a more direct route, the recovery is quite painful due to the splitting of the rib cage."

Michelle wished she hadn't said anything about splitting her rib cage. It was hard to keep from looking terrified when the doctor talked like this.

"Also, an incision scar on the back might be troublesome," Donna added.

"What do you mean, troublesome?"

"In the fashion sense. If you like wearing dresses cut low in the back, the scar might show."

"That's not important."

"It doesn't seem like it now. But it's a consideration. A team in Seattle pioneered a harvesting technique that only requires a four-inch incision in the donor."

Harvesting. "That's good to know," Michelle said wryly.

"The long-term effects of having only one kidney are minimal. But there *are* long-term effects." Donna smiled pleasantly. She had honest eyes; Michelle liked her.

"You mean I should avoid cliff diving and logrolling?"

"That would be advisable, yes."

"Suppose I were to get pregnant." She had no idea where that came from; it just slipped out.

"You'd be at a higher than normal risk, but pregnancy isn't prohibited."

"Just asking." Quickly, to cover up her embarrassment, Michelle said, "Here's the big one. Will I be able to play the violin after the surgery?"

"Of course," the nurse assured her, though Michelle could tell from the smile in her eyes she knew this joke.

"Great," Michelle said. "I never could before."

"Just use good sense. Protect that one kidney."

By the time the meeting ended, Michelle was feeling both exhilarated and frightened. Her father came back as everyone was filing out. Dr. Kehr shook hands with her, and she held on to her longer than she should have. Her life and that of her father would quite literally be in this woman's hands.

"Any more questions?" Dr. Kehr asked.

Her father stood still and upright, looking heartbreakingly stoic. It was one of the things that distinguished him as an actor. He had a way of touching people's hearts without moving a muscle.

"Not at the moment," Michelle said. "You were really thorough. Dad?"

"No questions either. I've been doing my homework on this for months, so I guess I'm as prepared as I'll ever be." He sent the doctor a grin. Michelle could see her visibly falling for him. "Can we call you if any questions come up?"

"Of course." She held out a pale blue business card. "You have my home, office, pager, and cell phone. Call anytime." She walked them to the door. "Until next Saturday, then? If Michelle's final tests check out, Monday's our day."

Michelle held the stack of brochures and paperwork in front of her like a shield as they walked out of the hospital annex. "You want me to drive home?"

"No. I'm fine." Before long, they were heading back down the highway.

"The psychologist kept making notes on me," she remarked.

"Temple? He's got a bunch of notes on me, too."

"What do you suppose he was writing?"

Gavin stared straight ahead at the road. "I imagine he's wondering if we're up for this."

"That's stupid. You need a kidney, I'm a match, end of story."

He cleared his throat, seeming to draw words from a hiding place deep inside him. "You have every right to resent me, Michelle."

"I don't resent you."

"Sure you do. Christ, I don't blame you. I wish I'd been a father to you when you were growing up."

Before she could stop herself, she thought of her childhood, the older split-level home in Bel Air. Though there were plenty of single-parent families in Southern California, Michelle always focused on the unbroken ones. She couldn't help the sharp envy she felt watching her friends with their two doting parents. The terrible ache that would engulf her when she saw a girl playing Frisbee in the park with her father . . .

"Is it too late to be a father now?" she asked, the words surprising even her.

A long, awkward silence. His hand came across the seat, touched her shoulder. "I'm willing to try, Michelle. But remember, I'm new at this. I've got a lousy track record."

"What's that supposed to mean?"

He took his hand away. From the corner of her eye, she noticed a furtive flash of guilt in his expression. "You know, last time. You took off, and I didn't know what the hell to do. So I did nothing."

Michelle shut her eyes, but the memories rushed in. *"I'm pregnant, Daddy."*

"I'm not surprised. Your mother was careless, too."

"I figured that McPhee boy was up to no good," her father had said on that bitter November night.

She hadn't asked him how she knew it was Sam's. Jake

Dollarhide had probably ratted on them, just as Sam had predicted.

"I shouldn't have told you," she had said, scared and hurt by his reaction. "Sam will help me through this."

"Is that what he promised?"

"He will when I tell him."

Gavin had snorted with disbelief. "He's cowboy scum, and his mother is trash. Even if he says he'll stick by you, Tammi Lee will drag you both down. You'll be living in some trailer park trying to hold off the law from her. Don't look for any promises from him."

And—damn him—Gavin had been right. That evening when Michelle went to tell Sam about the baby, he was gone without a trace, the shotgun house he'd shared with his mother an empty shell.

"Michelle?" Her father's voice brought her back to the present. "You got mighty quiet there."

"I guess that's because there's so much to say."

Chapter 11

Sylvia was in labor. The mare had been restless all night, hadn't eaten. She was fully dilated, her sides bellowing in and out in the peculiar manner of laboring mares. She kept looking back at her own flanks as if they didn't belong to her. As Edward had taken such glee in showing Cody the day before, her udder was full, her nipples waxy, the milk veins distended. Now she was covered in sweat, a sure sign that her water would break soon.

Sam walked across the field where Edward Bliss and Cody were uncoiling snow fence, readying the slope for the avalanches the spring thaw would bring. He had to force himself to walk at an even pace, to keep his expression neutral when what he really wanted to do was rush headlong and gawk at his son. His *son*. His own flesh and blood.

How was it that Cody had been born and Sam hadn't realized it? Shouldn't he have felt some upheaval inside himself, some alteration in the most essential part of his being?

Babies were born all the time without their fathers knowing. Maybe Sam was no different from Calyx, the champion stud quarter horse that had sired Sylvia's foal. But he still couldn't understand how a baby boy with half his chromosomes had been born and he hadn't even felt a ripple in the pond water.

At the time of Cody's birth, he'd been running. After he and his mother had left Crystal City only hours ahead of the law, they hadn't made much of a home anywhere for a while. Hot checks, unpaid bills, and collection-agency notices had trailed behind them like kicked-up dust.

On that long-ago night, when everything had fallen apart, he hadn't even had time to button his shirt. In the months that followed, they stayed in motels with weekly rates, lay low in a couple of run-down trailer courts, even slept at a roadside park or two. Nothing lasted—not their jobs, not their money, not their luck.

Until the Lander rodeo. It had been pure dumb luck that the Valiant had broken down in Wyoming, right under the billboard for the annual summer event. Tammi Lee had scrounged up enough cash for a pint of Ripple, and Sam had walked into town, hoping to earn a few bucks helping out as a gate runner.

Instead, he'd encountered a guy lying on a stretcher, his face floury white and his severed thumb in a Dixie cup with a piece of ice. Sam had looked on with more interest than horror as the paramedics whisked the cowboy off to reattach his thumb.

It was a classic injury for a team roper. If he dallied the rope the wrong way, the tug of the fleeing steer could sever a thumb. The guy's roping partner had cast a worried eye at the pay window. He didn't want to disqualify himself, even though without a heeler, he couldn't compete. With nothing left to lose, Sam had stepped up. Everyone was so ball-squeezed by the accident that there hadn't been much discussion. They pinned a number on Sam and off he went.

By the end of the night he and the header had won the regional title and nine thousand dollars. Fired up by good fortune, he'd launched a new career by buying an old beat-up trailer and pickup. Then he'd gone looking for a horse. It took him four months to find Sherlock and several more good purses to acquire him, but the quarter horse was worth the trouble. He became Sam's business partner and best friend.

Sam went solo, specializing in calf roping. He didn't want to split his earnings with half of a team. Leaving his mother in a motel on the outskirts of Cheyenne, he took off in the pickup, entering rodeos from San Angelo to Calgary. At night he slept in the gooseneck of Sherlock's trailer and ate his meals out of fast-food bags. He often went home with a woman—there was no shortage of rodeo groupies, and they loved a winner—but he always felt hollow after those encounters. Always caught himself thinking too much of a soft-limbed girl with soulful eyes. He'd lie awake listening to the crickets and consider calling her, and once he actually picked up the phone.

"You got a lot of damned nerve, boy, calling here," Gavin Slade had roared at him.

Sam had braced his fist on the window of the phone booth, an ovenlike kiosk in Oklahoma City. "I want to talk to Michelle, Mr. Slade."

"Over my dead body. You stole from me, McPhee—"

"That's a damned lie." Over the months of rambling,

Sam had put the puzzle together. The day Jake Dollarhide had seen him and Michelle come out of the art studio, several hundred dollars had turned up missing from the foreman's cashbox. Sam had been set up, plain and simple. He wasn't certain Gavin was in on it directly, but it sure as hell was convenient timing—Sam being run off the day he'd been caught nailing the boss's daughter.

"Don't call here anymore," Gavin had warned him. He'd slammed down the phone.

Sam didn't try again. There was no point. His mom was in trouble, and he had to stay on the circuit. Michelle had to go to college. The impossibility of a rich girl–poor boy romance was finally real to him. Shame and hurt pride burned away the last of his innocence. Did Michelle believe he was a thief, or would she realize he'd been framed? Shoot, it really didn't matter.

By the end of that season, Sam had won enough purses to lease his mother a little clapboard house near Seguin, Texas. A year later, he'd passed his G.E.D. and saved up for college tuition. Between rodeoing and school and his wet-brained mother, he hadn't had time to come up for air, much less realize the only girl he'd ever loved had given birth to his son.

As he approached Cody, Sam told himself not to wonder about him as a baby, a toddler, a little boy. That child was gone now, and in his place was an angry teen. The hell of it was, Sam didn't know what to think. Did he really want to know this kid, learn his rage and his flaws, excavate his virtues from beneath the layers of resentment?

"Hey, guys," he said, scanning the fence. "How's it coming?"

"Okay." Cody stood back and gestured at the long line

of pickets curving under the brow of a hill where the avalanche danger was the worst. "I guess."

Sam held his breath. *Did she tell you, Cody? Did she tell you I'm your dad?*

Clearly not, judging by the kid's offhand manner. He held his shoulders hunched up, and his nose was bright red from the cold.

"See any sign of that cat?" Sam asked.

"You mean the mountain lion?"

"Yeah, Edward spotted a carcass last week."

"Snowshoe hare," Edward said. "How's Sylvia doing?"

"That's why I came to get you," Sam said. "It's time."

"What?" Cody snapped to attention, forgetting to sulk.

"Sylvia, the mare," Sam explained. "Her water's about to break, and the foal will come pretty fast after that."

"Yeah?" The kid's face brightened a hundred watts. He was a damned good-looking kid even with the ponytail and earrings. "Can we see her?"

As Sam returned to the snowmobiles, he concealed a smile. "You're not squeamish, are you, Cody?"

"Me? No, man. I got a stomach of iron."

The icy wind blasted their faces as they drove back to the barn, dismounting fast and running inside to attend the birth.

A low grunting sound issued from the birthing stall. A foaling kit, with OB sleeves, tape, the foaling record, a stopwatch, instruments, and drugs lay on a crate. Sam hurried in to find the mare bobbing her head up and down, pawing the straw and acting skittish.

"Everything okay?" Edward asked.

"Let's have a listen." Sam took a stethoscope from the foaling kit and pressed it to the mare's abdomen. The vigorous hiss and swish of her pulse reassured him. He could detect the faint racing pulse of the fetus as well.

But it was beating too fast and shallow for comfort. "Might be some fetal distress, possible dystocia."

"Should I call the vet?" Edward asked.

"Go ahead and put in a call, but I have a feeling the foal will arrive before the vet does. Let's see what kind of shape the amniotic sac's in when it emerges." He set his jaw against a curse. He loved this mare. He sure as hell didn't want to lose her.

"What's that mean?" Cody peered over the edge of the stall. "Dystocia. Sounds bad."

"It means a bad presentation and stress on the foal. Not great news. Edward," he called down the breezeway, "see if you can get the heat turned up higher in here. Don't want the baby to catch a chill." He indicated a bucket outside the birthing stall. "Cody, do me a favor and wrap her tail with that white tape. Then you can wash her perineum and teats, okay? If we don't get everything clean, we're risking infection."

"Wash her . . ." Cody gaped at him in disbelief.

"Teats. And perineum."

"What's a—"

"It's exactly what you think it is."

"Oh, man."

"You said you had a stomach of iron."

Cody grumbled, but he picked up the wrapping. Gingerly, he lifted the mare's tail, grimacing as Sam palpated the abdomen.

"Gross," Cody commented.

"A mare in labor urinates and defecates a lot," Sam said unapologetically.

"Great."

But the boy did a good enough job of wrapping the

tail; then he brought out the bucket of water and disinfectant. With all the diligence Sam could have hoped for, he scrubbed away at the teats.

"Hey," he said, "something's, um, dripping from her."

Sam examined the teats. "Colostrum."

"What does that mean?"

"It means you might want to hurry and get that perineum disinfected, because things are going to speed up pretty soon." Sam tried not to seem anxious. He and Edward had yanked foals many times before, usually with good results. But God. Sylvia. She was the best mare he'd ever had.

The kid took a deep breath and dipped a clean cloth. He lifted the wrapped tail and dabbed hesitantly at first. Then he blew out his breath in a show of determination, planted himself right behind her, and finished the job.

"You might want to stand a little to one side," Sam advised as Cody was rinsing. "Because if you're directly behind her when her water breaks—"

Too late. It broke before he could finish speaking.

She spewed like a fire hose, directly at Cody. The projectile of warm fluid, probably a couple of gallons of it, completely drenched the boy.

"Holy shit," he yelled, jumping back.

"Sorry." Sam bit the inside of his cheek to keep from laughing. "I tried to warn you."

"Thanks for nothing, man."

"You want to go find some dry clothes?"

Cody made for the door, then hesitated. "Will I miss anything?"

"The foal will come any minute now."

"I'll stay then." He ripped off his coat—the black leather thing Sam hated—and dropped it on the floor in the corner. And it was odd, but it seemed to Sam that the kid shed some of his cynicism along with the coat. He could look at Cody now and see a boy, eager and bright-eyed, his young face ablaze with interest.

"Holy shit," he said again. His eyes grew round.

The silvery-slick balloon of the amnion started to come through. "Lie down, baby," Sam said to Sylvia. "Lie down, there's a girl."

After a few minutes, she complied, lowering herself with a grunt of effort.

"Stay down, baby." Sam knelt by her head, holding it and murmuring in her ear. "Stay—"

With a defiant clearing of her throat, Sylvia lurched to her feet.

"That's bad, right?" Cody asked, his face paler than it had been a minute earlier. "She shouldn't be standing up, right?"

"It's better if she lies down," Sam admitted. "But it's pretty pointless to argue with a fifteen-hundred-pound horse. She—"

He broke off as the mare's sides began to fan violently in and out. "Here she comes," Edward said, returning from the office with a cordless phone in his hand.

Sam gave Sylvia's neck a pat. "Vet?"

"Up in Big Arm. He can't get here for an hour."

"Then we're on our own," Sam said. "Get down again, baby, there you are . . ." He coaxed gently, stroked her, massaged her. "Down, that's a girl." Eventually she obeyed. Sam hoped she'd stay put as he knelt to see how things were progressing. "Cody, give me a hand here."

The boy hesitated just for a beat. "Yeah, okay."

The foal was trying to present with its legs sticking up toward the croup, a dangerous situation. Sylvia rolled and twisted, driven by instinct to correct the position. When that didn't work, Sam nodded at Edward. "She needs some help turning it." He held the mare's head, murmuring mindless phrases, trying to soothe her. Edward and Cody stripped down to T-shirts to wrestle with the slippery emerging legs, Edward uttering low curses and Cody goggle-eyed with fascination and worry.

"I keep losing hold. Damn, that's narrow," Edward said, his hand caught inside. "Cody, are your hands smaller than mine?"

"I guess. You want me to try?"

Edward hesitated, then eased back when the contraction ended. He passed a tube of lubricant to Cody. "Here's what you do. We want the forelegs first, but turned this way, see?"

"Yeah." Cody smeared on the lubricant and took a deep breath. A few seconds later, his hand disappeared inside the mare. If the situation hadn't been so dire, Sam would have laughed at the expression on the kid's face. Edward coached him, instructing him to bring the legs down and around, working between contractions.

Sylvia grunted and pushed, expelling Cody's hand and then, pulse by pulse, the foal, hooves first. Cody didn't move out of the way in time but caught it against his knees, rearing back when the hindquarters slipped out.

"Easy there." Sam bent to examine the foal, suctioning out its mouth and nose. It gave a jerk of its bony body, then a strange cough, and began breathing on its own. Its pale muzzle took on the color of life. Its umbilical cord, still attached, pulsed in time with the mare's heartbeat. She stood with a lumbering effort, twisting to lick at her baby.

"Wow," said Cody, his eyes bugging out, his entire front covered with birth fluid, his mouth wide in a grin. "Wow."

Sam squirted iodine on the umbilical cord. He should have become a vet. Or a teacher.

Instead, he was a father who didn't know his son.

That, he decided, as he looked at Cody's sweat-streaked face, was about to change. Whether Michelle liked it or not.

The sac still hung from the mare, slapping against her hind legs. Sam saw the reflex coming, but before he could speak, she kicked out. In a flash of movement, the hoof caught Cody, right on the temple.

Chapter 12

As they approached Crystal City, Gavin kept his gaze fixed dead ahead, his jaw perfectly square, his hands relaxed on the steering wheel. Yet Michelle could tell—there was some subtle turbulence in his manner—that the hospital appointment had rattled him. Monday: 6:45 A.M. Perhaps knowing the precise day and time of the transplant was disconcerting.

It sure as hell was for Michelle.

"Are you all right?" she asked.

"I'm in end-stage renal failure," he said. "How all right can I be?"

"I'm sorry. I wish I knew what to say to you."

"You don't have to apologize for anything." He flexed his hands on the steering wheel. "I'm a lousy father, have been from the get-go. Being sick only makes me lousier."

"I don't know." She tried to keep her voice light. "A

true believer would say it's the universe's way of bringing us together."

"Are you a true believer, Michelle?"

She stared out the window. Long gray-white smudges of highway and snow. "I used to be."

He trained his eyes on the road. "When your mother told me she was pregnant, I panicked. I was just getting started in my career. I was in the most cutthroat business in the world, and I didn't think I'd make it on my own, much less with a family to care for. Kept seeing myself as a failure, pumping gas for a living, trying to make ends meet, chasing down bit parts and making everyone miserable. Didn't have a pot to piss in, Michelle. I had a rented room in Studio City and a risky role coming up."

His words sounded like lines recited from a script.

"That must have been *Shelter from the Storm*." The film had made him a star and a household name.

"As excuses go, it's pretty weak, but my career was everything at the time. I thought all a father did was send a monthly check, maybe show up for special occasions. The truth is, I never knew how to be a father, and I was too scared to try. Michelle, I'd give anything to change that, but I can't. It's one of the lessons people never seem to learn—that you can't change the past." He glanced sideways at her. "I just hope it's not too late to fix things."

"Why didn't you even try, Daddy? Didn't you know I needed you?" The anguished question burst from her.

"Michelle—"

The mobile phone chirped, startling them and shattering the tension in the truck. Michelle felt a twinge of annoyance. For once she and her father were actually beginning to talk, and now this. He clicked on the speaker phone. "Gavin here."

"It's Edward Bliss, from over at Lonepine."

"What can I do for you, Edward? You're on the speaker phone."

"Is Michelle with you?"

"I'm here." Like a sudden shadow, a chill swept over her. "Is everything all right?"

"Michelle, I'm at Meridian County Hospital. Your boy, he—"

"Jesus Christ." Gavin's foot pressed to the floor, and the truck shot forward, hurtling down the highway toward town.

"What happened?" Her chest pounded with dread.

"He's going to be okay," Edward said quickly. "He was kicked in the head by a horse."

"Oh my God—"

"It happens sometimes, it—" Static crackled, obliterating Edward's voice. As the peaks of the mountains plunged the road into gloom, the connection died.

"We'll be there in five minutes," Gavin said. "You got your seat belt on?"

Michelle nodded. She couldn't speak, could only hang on as they sped into town. The hardware store, the café, the municipal building and library passed in a blur. She died a thousand deaths, racing to get to her son. She imagined Cody, her beautiful boy, broken and bleeding in some emergency room, his head bashed in. *Please. Please. Please.* She could barely find the words to pray.

The truck screeched to a halt in front of the community hospital. Built of narrow reddish brick and small windows, it had an awning that stretched over the emergency entrance. She jumped out, dragging her purse along. The automatic doors hissed open. Lurching to the admittance desk, she was barely able to catch her breath.

"Cody Turner." The lump of dread in her chest started to hurt. "He's my son. He was kicked in the head—"

"—by Sam McPhee's mare," the attendant said. "Curtain area in the examination room, ma'am." She held up a clipboard. "Now, if we could just get some information—"

"Later." She raced down the hall. Earthtone linoleum, green-tiled walls, extra-wide doors with frosted glass windowpanes—were all hospitals alike? A nurse holding a tray of instruments was in the exam room. "You're the mother?"

The Mother. Spoken that way, it sounded so weighty, so dire. She straightened her shoulders, forced herself to get a grip. "I am."

The nurse, whose name tag read Alice O'Brien, nodded at an aqua-colored half curtain enclosing a wheeled cot. Blue jeans tucked into snowmobile boots showed at the bottom. She could hear a low, masculine voice murmuring something indistinct.

"The doctor's with him right now," Nurse O'Brien said.

Michelle parted the curtain. "Cody?"

"Hey, Mom." His voice was small. A flesh-colored patch covered part of his head. Rusty bloodstains streaked his hair. A bluish cast tinged his complexion. His clothes were wet, smeared with blood and a whitish slime. She wanted to touch him, hold him, scream with relief that he was conscious.

The other person in the cubicle was Sam McPhee. "Sam? Where's the doctor?"

Then she noticed what he was wearing. A green fiber gown and a pair of high-intensity lighted eyeglasses. Surgical gloves.

Michelle blinked fast, confused.

"Mom, Sam *is* the doctor," Cody muttered.

"He's what?" She stared at Sam. "You're what?"

"The doctor." Sam lifted a corner of his mouth. "Why do I feel as if I should apologize for that?"

"My God." She sank to a metal swivel stool beside the gurney. The information was coming at her too fast. "Okay, just tell me about Cody. He's a mess. Is he—"

"It's a head injury, Michelle. And he was lucky—it appears to be mild." Sam's voice was gentle. "The other stuff all over him is from the mare."

The nurse arrived with another tray and set it on a rolling table by Sam. The attending clerk came in, too. "Ma'am, you need to sign this."

"What is it?"

"A consent form."

She took the clipboard and lifted her gaze to Sam. He looked like a stranger in the gown and headgear, tall and slightly mystical, the high priest of some alien nation. "What am I consenting to?"

"Treatment. In this case that means you're authorizing me to debride and stitch this head wound."

"I don't want any stitches, man." Cody's lips were practically blue, stark against the shocked pallor of his face.

"We'll numb the area. Easier than going to the dentist," Sam said.

Michelle scribbled her name across the bottom of the sheet. On the next page, she swiftly answered a series of questions about Cody's health history, allergies, reactions to medication—all negative. The form under that was covered with small print. "What's this one?"

"An admit form," the clerk said.

"I want to keep him overnight," Sam explained. "His GCS scale was fifteen—that means all his neurological responses are fine. The CT scan showed a mild subarachnoid hemorrhage, so observation for a short period is probably the only treatment needed. We'll do a routine follow-up later, but I don't expect any complications."

Her hand trembled wildly as she signed. She heard her father come in. "Hey, Sam," he said.

"Gavin." Sam didn't look up from Cody.

Gavin seated himself in a molded-plastic chair inside the door. For a moment an eerie sense of unreality closed in on her. Here she sat, surrounded by her father, her son, and Cody's father in a situation straight out of a nightmare.

One thing at a time. She needed to force herself to concentrate on one thing at a time. "So tell me what happened."

"Cody was helping with a mare in labor," Sam said. "And doing a damned good job of it. Tweezers," he said to the nurse, and began to pick at the edges of the wound. "He helped Sylvia give birth to a gorgeous little filly. That's the good news. Hold this clamp, will you, Alice?"

"The bad news is," Sam continued, "Sylvia got a little antsy during the afterbirth and started kicking." He teased away the patch, revealing an alarming curved gash. The flesh gaped open, showing blood-drenched tissue. "Breathe through your nose, Michelle. This isn't pretty."

She rolled the stool closer to the bed. Cody's hand crept out from beneath the blue-paper sheeting and she grasped it, holding on hard. His fingers were icy cold.

"It's okay, Cody-boy," she whispered, calm now, although she knew that later she would fall to pieces. "Just hold real still."

He swallowed, his cheeks and his neck pale. For once he didn't sneer with disgust when she called him the old pet name.

Sam and the nurse cleansed the wound. Somehow she maintained a measured stoicism even though the large flap of skin and copious flow of blood terrified her. The wound was an upside-down crescent shape. She sat transfixed by Sam's hands, noting with a strange, horrified awe how deftly and delicately they worked, how sensitive they were.

His intense absorption in his work both reassured and frightened her. Like a rock tumbling in a stream, the revelation turned over and over in her mind. Sam had become a doctor. A *doctor.*

An ugly, sinking sensation spiraled downward through Michelle. She didn't want to feel this, didn't want to think this, but she realized she had convinced herself that Sam would never amount to anything more than a rodeo bum. That was how she had rationalized the past seventeen years. That was the excuse she gave herself for not moving heaven and earth to find him. She had convinced herself that he'd be a tumbleweed, a ne'er-do-well, hardly a fit father to Cody.

Yet now she saw that Sam had held on to his dream, pursuing it long after she'd abandoned her own.

Don't let me be this small, this petty, she thought. *Don't let me resent this.*

In the end, it was Cody who saved her from her own thoughts. The nurse turned on a pair of buzzing clippers. Cody squeezed her hand in sudden surprise and terror, and a powerful wave of love washed over her. Sam had become his dream, but she had become Cody's mother, and there could be no comparison.

"Mom," Cody said breathlessly.

She forced a smile. "I've been nagging you for months to get a decent haircut. I guess now's as good a time as any."

She couldn't be certain, but as Nurse O'Brien clipped away at the hair, Sam's mouth twitched, just a bit shy of a smile.

She shouldn't be surprised that he actually became a doctor. It made sense, after the way his mother raised him. He wanted a way to make people better.

The attending clerk brought Gavin a cup of water. Michelle had forgotten he was there. The glaring overhead light magnified the lines of fatigue around his eyes.

"Dad, you should go on home. It's been a long day."

"I'll stay."

"No, really. The last thing I need is for both of you to be laid up. I'd feel a lot better if you waited at home. I'll call."

"I'm staying," he said in his deep actor's voice.

He had known. He had known all along that the father of her son was a doctor, living here in Crystal City, and he had never bothered to tell her.

"Damn it." The coiled tension in her sprang up. "You make me nervous, sitting around and waiting. *Please*, Dad—"

"I'll give Michelle a ride home when we're done," Sam said, an edge of impatience in his voice. And he was right to be impatient. He had to concentrate, not mediate family squabbles.

Gavin hesitated; then he nodded and got to his feet. He came over to the table and gave Cody's shoulder a squeeze. "Take care now, you hear?"

Other than their first handshake, this was the only time she had seen him touch her son.

"Yeah," Cody said. "See you."

"We're going to numb the area now," Sam said. Nurse O'Brien finished clipping, then disinfected and draped the wound.

Because of the draping, she could no longer see his face. A calculated move, she surmised once she saw the needle Sam was using.

"This'll sting," he warned, being honest but not alarming. "You'll feel a pinch, and it'll probably make your eyes water."

Pretty smooth, thought Michelle. Giving the kid an excuse to cry if he needed to.

Cody squeezed again. She squeezed back. Sam injected Xylocaine in a few spots, then set aside the syringe.

"Okay, we have a few minutes to talk," he said. "Need to give the anesthetic time to work."

Michelle swallowed, the lump in her throat still painful. "So talk."

"It's a big laceration." Without touching Cody, he followed the curve of it with a finger. "Cody and that mare were really up close and personal. It could have been worse, but Edward removed the horse's shoes last night, because we knew the birth was imminent. So the damage is slightly less than it could have been."

She thought about the strange yet familiar smell on Cody's damp clothes. It was musky, faintly sweet, yet with an oceanic tang. The birth smell. Her son was drenched in it.

Sam pointed again. "See how this goes down to his temple?"

She nodded, thinking how delicate the tracery of tiny veins looked. How vulnerable. The terror pushed upward from her chest, but true to form she contained it.

"That means I'll be stitching in the region of his face, just here."

There was about an inch between his brow and hairline. The wound was stark there, the flesh amber in color from the disinfectant. "Now, I'm not a plastic surgeon," he said. "I usually refer cases like this to a specialist."

"But this is unusual?"

"Somewhat. I'm inclined to do this myself, here and

now. I can take a lot of tiny stitches—I had practice during a clinical rotation I did with a cleft palate specialist in the Yucatán."

The Yucatán? It was strange to think of all the places Sam had been, all the things he had done in the years they'd been strangers. He had gone to the Yucatán while she had raised his son.

"You're probably going to see a scar," he concluded.

"So is there an alternative?" she asked.

"I could clamp the wound, and then you could take him to Missoula. There's a great face guy there."

"The plastic surgeon wouldn't come here?"

Sam hesitated. "Not this guy."

"So you want me to decide."

Sam regarded her for a long time. She wondered what was going on in his head, what it was like for him to have his wounded son lying here yet to have no say in his treatment. She thought of all the times she'd had to make a decision about Cody, wishing for someone else to talk it over with. She'd felt so alone on those occasions.

"I've given you the options, Michelle."

"I don't want to know the options. I want to know what to *do*."

"Chances are excellent that a trip to Missoula won't do him a bit of harm—"

"Quit being such a . . . a *doctor*. I want you to tell me the right thing—"

"Just stitch the damn thing up." A small, annoyed voice crept out from under the draping.

Both Sam and she looked down at Cody. "Really?" she asked.

"Yeah. I want to get it over with. A drive to Missoula doesn't exactly sound fun."

"How big a scar?" she asked Sam.

"You can see where it'll be. A thin line. Red at first, and eventually it'll fade to white."

A shiver eddied over her. It was an accident, yes, but Cody was going to be marked by this incident, marked for life. He'd never be the same.

"Go for it," Cody said miserably.

"All right." Her voice was soft. "Go ahead and finish, Sam."

He held himself very still for a few moments. He didn't move, though she sensed an odd calm settling over him. It was invisible, yet she could see it happening, like some new sort of medical Zen.

True to his word, he took tiny stitches, working with a needle and silk so fine she had to squint to see it. During the procedure, she sat holding Cody's hand as he lay silent and still.

Despite what Sam said about not being a specialist, she could tell one thing for certain. He was a good doctor. He worked smoothly with the nurse. The two of them had a comfortable rapport as if they'd known each other a long while. From time to time the attending clerk came in, and he answered her questions without so much as glancing up or breaking his concentration. His hands moved with a precise, mesmeric rhythm.

Through it all, Cody lay motionless and admirably calm, his hand in Michelle's.

As Sam was finally finishing up, she decided to say what was on her mind. "So I guess this means you know about my father."

"I'm a family practitioner."

"But you know about his illness."

"My partner, Karl Schenk, is his primary-care physician. Gavin didn't tell you?"

"It's all I can do to keep up with the nephrologists and surgeons."

Sam tied off a stitch. "He's getting good care in Missoula."

"He's getting one of my kidneys."

He hesitated for a beat, then took another stitch. "That's really something, Michelle. I figured they'd eyeball him for a transplant."

"How did you figure that?"

Without even looking up, he seemed to sense her getting defensive. "Now, don't turn all prickly on me. Gavin's general health is excellent. Nonsmoker, nondiabetic. Physiologically, he couldn't be a better candidate. That's all I meant. No doctor I know would use Gavin's fame to make a transplant poster boy of him."

He removed the draping. Cody looked pale but relaxed, his eyelids heavy.

"Okay, cowboy?" Sam asked.

"I guess." He took his hand away from Michelle's. He seemed embarrassed that he'd been clinging to it the whole time.

Sam beamed a pen-sized light in Cody's eyes, first one, then the other. "You're not going to kick me in the head like your last patient did to you?"

"I'll decide after I see the stitches."

Michelle liked Sam's ease with the boy. He'd only known him two days, yet his manner was open and natural. Sometimes she wished Brad would—

Alice, the nurse, held up a hand mirror.

Sam grinned. "Take a look, Frankenstein."

Cody grimaced. "Nice haircut."

"You can have Hazlett fix it. He's the local barber, does house calls at the hospital. Or you could wait until you're discharged," Sam said.

"Hey," said Cody. "Do I have to stay?"

Sam's gaze was level and direct. "Yep. Just overnight, okay?"

Michelle studied Cody's dubious face, then Sam's. Dear God, she thought, they look alike. The similarity was apparent now that Cody's long hair had been cropped. He looked almost exactly like Sam did, back when Sam had been the beginning and end of her world.

She got up quickly. "I'll stay with him."

"Oh, no you don't, Mom," Cody said. "I can handle spending one night in the hospital."

She patted his leg. Again she felt that dark hollow of loss, as if her little boy had disappeared before her eyes. "Tonight's going to be a lot harder on me than on you."

"Don't worry about me, Mom."

"I'll always worry about you." The lump in her throat swelled. "Thanks for holding my hand through that."

He lifted half his mouth in a crooked grin. Sam's grin. "Right, Mom."

Chapter 13

When Sam left the hospital, he found Michelle sitting in the dark outside, cradling a Styrofoam cup of tea and crying.

The sight of her on the concrete bench, looking so small and alone, stopped him in his tracks. "Hey," he said, easing down next to her. "Have a Kleenex."

Nearby, the door opened and Alice O'Brien came out, a duffel bag slung over her shoulder. She had that weary sort of prettiness common to a lot of nurses, and she regarded him with more kindness than he deserved, given their history together. "'Night, Sam," she said.

"See you tomorrow, Alice."

Michelle's gaze followed her until night cloaked her in darkness. "She doesn't call you doctor."

At some point he'd have to explain about Alice. But not now. There were other things to discuss now. "To these folks I'm just Sam McPhee. One of them. One of the tribe." He turned to her, noticing the silvery track of a tear on her cheek. He wanted to touch it. Taste it. Make it go away. *Christ*. He shoved his hands into his jacket pockets. "You okay?"

She wiped her face with the tissue. "A little over-whelmed, I guess. It's been a long day."

"You held together like a champ in there," he said, and he meant it. If she was like other mothers of injured kids he'd treated, her insides were a train wreck. Yet outwardly, like so many of those steel-spined mothers, she had been calm and efficient while helping Cody get settled into his room. She'd bought him a paperback Anne Rice novel and a kit of toiletries from the gift shop, sat with him for a while, then left after dinner was served and a Bruce Willis movie came on.

"I can always hold together for Cody," she said.

"He's never seen you lose it?"

"No." She scrubbed away the last of her tears. "I told myself right from the start that I'd be the Rock of Gibraltar for him."

His heart heard what she would not say. That she had been all alone. That in two-parent families, one had the luxury of the occasional breakdown while the other took over. That during all her parental crises, no one had ever been there to hand her a Kleenex.

He couldn't help wondering what it would be like to be in that picture with her. Couldn't help wondering what this strange grown-up Michelle was like. Did she still cry when she heard a sad song on the radio, still get the hiccups when she laughed too hard? Did she still make that funny sound in the back of her throat when she came?

He stood up, his head spinning with anger, frustration, loss—and a lingering fascination with this woman who, despite years of separation, had never quite left him. "Let me buy you dinner."

"No." Her refusal came swiftly, automatically.

"Wrong answer, ma'am. Remember, I'm your ride home."

"But—"

"No buts. Stay right there. I need to change out of my scrubs, and then I'm taking you out to Trudy's for a steak." He walked toward the automatic doors. "People from Seattle eat steak, right?"

She lifted her face to him, the parking lot light carving graceful shadows on her cheeks. And finally, fleetingly, she smiled. "I guess people from Montana would be insulted if we refused, right?"

Sam tried not to make too much of her acceptance as he headed inside, but the light warmth in his chest was the most pleasurable thing he'd felt all day. He went to his locker in the lounge, thinking how unreal it had been to treat his own son. To know that the fragile flesh and bone beneath his hands belonged, at least biologically, to him.

He thought about the day he'd decided to become a doctor. He'd been eight or nine years old, riding in a beat-up old car along a straight, flat road. It was a Valiant with a fake Navajo rug covering the torn upholstery. A bag of Cheetos and a bottle of something red lay on the seat beside him. His mother was smoking a cigarette and singing with the radio.

His mother knew the words to all the rockabilly songs, because for one amazing year she had been the vocalist for a Denver band called Road Rage. Sam was too young to remember it, but she claimed it was the best year of her life. They'd traveled all over the country, and their hit single, "Dearly Departed," had rocketed to number one on the *Country Billboard* charts.

Finding success even harder to deal with than failure, the band had broken up, its members scattered. Still, his mom sang along with the radio, her voice harsh with the static of drinking and cigarettes.

Sam had sat silent, watching bugs squishing on the windshield. After a while, he told his mother he had to pee, so she pulled off at a rest stop. By the time he finished in the men's room, Tammi Lee was asleep in the car. So he climbed on top of the hood to wait.

There he was, a towheaded little kid sitting alone on the hood of a beat-up old car, watching people pull off the highway to rest. Whenever he saw families, he felt a funny tugging sensation in his gut. A mom, a dad, two or three kids, a dog. Doing stuff as simple as having a game of catch or sitting at a concrete picnic table, eating sandwiches and pouring Kool-Aid from a plastic jug. These things—these simple, unremarkable rituals—were things he wanted so bad he ached inside.

On that particular day, he twisted around on the hood of the car, stared at his mother, and wished for some magic spell to make her wake up, smile at him, ruffle his hair, ask him if he wanted a glass of milk.

Her eyes flickered open and just for a second, he thought the spell was going to work. Then she wiped the back of her hand across her mouth, dug in her pocket, took out some quarters. She held a trembling fist out the car window and said, "Get me a Tab, will you, hon?" in what he thought of as her tired voice. Later he figured out it was her hungover voice.

And even though she wasn't like the mothers pouring Kool-Aid, he loved her. Kids, he found out later when he became a doctor, loved their monster parents, no matter what.

On the way back from the vending machine—cold can of Tab held in both hands—a boy and his dad ran past, tossing a softball back and forth. The kid almost slammed into him, but sidestepped at the last minute. He never looked at Sam. Just sort of moved on by. They drove a nice car with M.D. plates. Sam was on the road so much he knew about M.D. plates.

His mom was acting funny when he got back to the car. Her face was white and shiny with sweat, her eyes glazed and rolled back in her head. She arched her back against the seat of the car and a thin, terrible noise crawled from her throat. Sam dropped the cold can on the ground and raced for the man with the softball. "Hey, mister," he yelled. "Are you a doctor?" When the man nodded, Sam said, "My mom's sick."

The doctor came over to the car and put his hand on her forehead, lifting her eyelid with his thumb. "Ma'am?" he asked. "Ma'am, can you hear me?" His wife came over with a bag. The doctor asked some questions—what had she been drinking, how long had she been like this—and Sam babbled out the answers. Rummaging in the bag, the doctor went to work. A short time later, Tammi Lee lay groggy but calm, acting sheepish as she spoke with the doctor, assuring him she'd seek help in the next town.

Sam decided right then and there he wanted to be a doctor. He wanted to be the kind of guy who drove a nice car and played catch with his son and when someone got sick, fixed her.

That little kid seemed a distant stranger now, and many years passed before Tammi Lee kept her promise to get help. Sam hurried, getting into his street clothes in record time, worried that Michelle might change her mind, disappear like a bursting bubble from his life.

Sort of like he'd disappeared from hers.

He shoved his feet into his boots, combed his hair, and slammed his locker shut. When he got outside, she was gone. He stood there, a curse forming on his mouth.

She came out of the hospital behind him. "I went to check on Cody one last time."

He exhaled, the curse unspoken. "And?"

"He's sleeping."

"Good. Best thing for him."

She bit her lip uncertainly. Sam took her hand, feeling the shape of it through her winter glove. She pulled away, and he didn't try again. "He's going to be fine. I'm on call all night, and Raymond's on duty."

"Raymond?"

"Raymond Bear, the head nurse. We call him the Shaman. He can sense a patient in distress even before the monitors, I swear it. Damnedest thing you've ever seen."

"Is he the guy reading *Soldier of Fortune* magazine at the nurses' station?"

"That's him. If he's reading a magazine, that means he's not worried." His hand flexed, remembering the shape of hers. "Come on. My truck's over here."

Only four of the eighteen tables at Trudy's were occupied, but that wasn't unusual for a cold Monday night. With its red vinyl tablecloths, gold plastic tumblers, and longhorn salt and pepper shakers, the place resembled a garage sale from the seventies. What it lacked in elegance it more than made up for in good, simple food.

"Just stick with the straightforward stuff, and you can't go wrong." Sam opened his menu.

"I see the wine list is a no-brainer." She cracked a

smile that did funny things to his insides. "Red, white . . . I assume Rosy means rosé?"

"Welcome to Crystal City."

Her smile lingered. "Still pretty provincial around here."

She was a stranger to him. She was a vast, uncharted continent. Mysterious, but something he wanted to explore.

"You can find all the glitz and sophistication you want in Kalispell and Bozeman. Your old man was one of the first to move up here from Hollywood, but he sure wasn't the last. In downtown Whitefish you can buy a Tiffany bracelet and millesime cognac."

"You could have made a lot more money setting up your practice in one of those towns." She closed her menu.

"Why do people always assume doctors are in it for the money?"

"All the doctors I know are."

He thought of Karl, and of Dr. Brower in the Yucatán. "Then you know the wrong doctors," he said. "There used to be three of us in the practice here, but one defected to Kalispell." He didn't say so, but the third partner made a fortune writing prescriptions for Valium and Zoloft.

"So why didn't you follow the money?"

"I belong here. Karl and I work for the tribe up at the Flathead reservation. It's not about money, Michelle. If it was about money, I could make fifty grand roping calves for a week in Vegas."

"You're not only a doctor, but you're noble."

"Is that what you think?"

"I think you came back here just to give everyone an inferiority complex."

He laughed. "Right."

"Why *did* you pick this particular town?"

No one had ever asked him that before. His credentials were good enough; he'd gone through a six-year combined degree program, and his training from UT was first-rate. He could have gone anywhere.

"I started thinking about a small-town practice when I was working in the Yucatán, mainly with Mexican Indians. I learned more than medicine there. A child is born with a cleft palate? You fix it, and the kid has a better life. A man suffers from hepatitis? You treat him, he survives, and you immunize his family. That's the beauty of working in third-world countries."

"So why not stay in a third-world country?"

"Because we have those right here in our own backyard. Small towns, Indian reservations, depressed areas that can't support a lucrative practice." He studied Michelle, noting the understated elegance of her gold watch, the French designer earrings. "I know what it's like to have money—I had that in my rodeo days. Well, some of the time, at least. I know what money can and can't do for a man."

"See? You are too noble."

He thought about the early days when he'd slept in his horse trailer or the back of his pickup truck, and how he'd lie awake nights on fire and in agony from wanting what rich folks like Gavin Slade had. It had been a sickness with Sam, that need to feel he could measure up, and it probably explained why he drove himself so hard, both in the arena and in the clinic. Only time, and the deep self-knowledge that came of healing people, had cured him of the sickness.

"I'm not noble, Michelle," he said. "I'm just a guy."

They ordered steak dinners and a bottle of wine from a waitress who knew Sam by name. When she departed, Michelle watched her from the corner of her eye. "Are we fueling gossip?"

"In a place this size?" he asked. "Are you kidding? You'll probably read about this dinner on the front page of the *Towne Tattler*."

"I didn't know the paparazzi were so vicious here." She smiled with an old mischievous sweetness he remembered well. Too well. He was getting dizzy gawking at her. It should come as no surprise that the daughter of Gavin Slade turned out to be even more of a knockout at thirty-five than she had been at eighteen. But then again, she had always surprised him.

She watched him with an expression that made his gut churn. Dewy eyes and moist lips. Total absorption in what he was saying. "And so you chose Crystal City," she said.

"Yeah. I knew Edward Bliss from the circuit, he needed a partner for Lonepine, the town needed a doctor, so it all worked out." What the hell, Sam thought. He might as well level with her. He wanted to be in the place where he had been with Michelle, where his dreams had been born and where hope had lingered in spite of everything. "And I figured I'd see you again."

She had no reply to that, but contemplated it with a silence he couldn't read.

While they ate, he thought about the night he'd left. The old Valiant had puttered through the quiet streets of Crystal City, passing the Truxtop and the feed store and the Lynwood Theater, the one-screen cinema where he and Michelle had sat holding hands in the dark. He remembered the yellowish beam of the headlights, the cigarette smell of the blanket covering the seat, the tinny sound of the radio playing a cowboy song, the too-quick rasp of his mother's breathing.

She was nervous, even though Sam, full of outrage,

had wanted to stay and fight his accusers. "I didn't steal a thing," he insisted. "Not a damned thing."

"I know that," his mother had said with weary resignation. "Do you think that matters? Gavin Slade doesn't want you hanging around his daughter. This is his way of telling you that."

"Let's not run away, Mama. It's a free country—"

"Gavin Slade owns this town. If he wants us gone, we're gone." She had looked at him sideways, peering through the darkness. "You're not the only one they've decided to pin something on."

He braced himself. "What do you mean?"

"I had a little visit from Deputy O'Shea this evening. Seems he suddenly discovered a couple of hot checks, a couple of parole violations, and at least two outstanding warrants in Colorado. And that *wasn't* a set-up. I'll have to do time, son. Is that what you want?"

"What I want is for us to quit running."

"Well, we sure as hell can't afford a lawyer. And I sure as hell don't want to be a guest of the state for the foreseeable future. So off we go." Tammi Lee had reached out to punch in the cigarette lighter. "I guess it won't help much to tell you I'm sorry," she said. "I screwed up. Again. Just when you were starting to like living around here."

He had a fierce urge to fling himself out of the car. For years he'd been fleeing with her, but now he had someone to fight for. Michelle. And his own innocence. But he knew he had to stick with his mom. Tammi Lee Gilmer would never survive without him.

Michelle would.

"At least let me stop and say good-bye to her," he'd said.

Tammi Lee grabbed his arm. "This is serious, son. It's

the real world. People like us can't take a risk like that. We set foot on that property, and we're toast."

Sam knew what she wanted him to say. *It's okay, Mama. We'll find someplace else. Something will work out for us. . . .* That's what he always said to her, every time they left a town on the lam. Well, not this time. This time, he wasn't going to tell her everything was okay.

The full moon rode high in the cold November night, and he could see Blue Rock Ranch on the way out of town, a snug compound in the distance, lights twinkling from the windows, a twist of smoke coming from the chimney of the main house.

'Bye, Michelle.

Knowing her had taught him something medical school never could—that the human heart could sing. He had vowed that night to come back to her once he and Tammi Lee settled down somewhere. But there was no time to call the next day, or the day after that, and when he finally scrounged up a handful of change to call from that pay phone in Oklahoma City, he was too late.

"I left Blue Rock the day after you disappeared," she said softly, after her long silence. "My father wasn't terribly understanding about my pregnancy."

Now, that didn't surprise him. Gavin Slade was a man devoted to his own image. The perfect acting career, perfect stock to parade at rodeos, perfect daughter . . . until she had turned out to be human and flawed. After that, she couldn't be part of his image. He had excised her swiftly and cleanly from his life.

"I wish I'd known that," he said quietly.

She sipped her water, a droplet gleaming on her lower lip. Sam tried not to stare. "There's probably a gloat factor involved in my coming back, too," he admitted. "Maybe

on some level I wanted to say 'screw you' to guys like—"
He broke off, catching himself.

"Guys like my father."

"Yeah, okay."

"He should have told me you were living here. But I can't seem to get all worked up over old business like that. His illness makes everything else seem so petty." Michelle set down her water glass with a nervous rattle of ice. "So tell me how you did it," she said. "Tell me how you became a doctor."

"Rodeo."

"What do you mean?"

"I used rodeo money to put myself through school."

"You're kidding."

"No, ma'am." He took a bite of his steak. "I passed my G.E.D. and got into a combined degree program, so I could get my bachelor's and M.D. in six years. It was a pain in the butt, living on the road, sleeping in a horse trailer most nights. I lived on autopilot for a lot of years. Didn't look left or right, didn't let myself falter. I stayed focused on that one and only goal—to get through school and residency, and I didn't let up until I made it." He picked up a breadstick, snapped it in half. "Sometimes I wonder what I missed in those years." A shadowy wave washed over him. "The birth of my son, for one thing." He took one look at her face and said, "Aw, shit. I didn't mean to—"

"I want to know the rest. What about your mother?"

"She's okay. On the wagon, living over on Aspen Street." It sounded a hell of a lot simpler than it had been. With Sam pushing, sometimes bullying her into rehab, she'd fought every inch of the way. But each time she stumbled, he picked her up, checked her back in to rehab or sent her to yet another AA meeting. Sometimes he had to be harsh with her, because sometimes that was the only thing that worked. The experience had given him an edge of ruthlessness he didn't particularly like.

Finally, after years of battling Tammi Lee's addiction, sobriety stuck. She had been sober for five years.

"Really? That's great, Sam."

"She works at LaNelle's Quilt Shoppe in town." Ah, Christ, he thought. He was going to have to tell Tammi Lee about Cody. He had no idea how she'd take it. She was sober, but she'd always be fragile. You never knew what might set her off. "So what about you? I'll bet you've got paintings hanging in the Met."

She stared down at her salad plate. "Maybe the *rest room* of the Met. I work for an ad agency."

"Functional art, then." He immediately wished he could reel his words back in.

She laughed, but the sound was brittle and forced. "Oh, yeah. Pictures of scrubbing bubbles and industrial extrusions."

He felt a sinking regret. She had been so vibrant, so damned talented that people caught their breath when they saw her paintings. She had loved art the way most folks loved food or air. "So is painting a hobby for you now, or—"

"I don't paint, Sam." She stabbed her fork at her salad. "I never had the time. I was busy with Cody."

Shit.

"You should have found me," he said, an edge in his voice. "Should have made me help."

"Oh, right. In between roping championships? Clinical rotations? Trips to Mexico?"

"I want those years back," he said brusquely. "All those years I didn't know I had a son."

"You weren't there. I couldn't find you."

"How hard did you look, Michelle? It wasn't like I was in hiding."

"Neither was I," she snapped.

"But I wasn't keeping anything from you, god-dammit."

"If I'd tracked you down, would it have mattered? Would you have given up rodeo and medical school for us?"

"Why would I have to choose? We could have done it all, Michelle."

"You're dreaming. I tried doing it all, and it's too hard."

He thought of the drawings and paintings she'd turned her back on. Was it because her passion was gone, or because she just didn't have time? "Okay, so I missed my son's childhood. We can't get back the years we lost. But maybe we can go on from here."

Even as he spoke, he wondered why he thought he could succeed with Michelle, who was infinitely more complicated, more demanding, more challenging than any woman he'd known.

"I don't understand."

"Damn it, Michelle, I'm not going to apologize for my goddamned life. You got the kid, I got the career. Which one of us should be gloating?"

She winced. "Sam. Please."

He reminded himself that her son had been injured while in his care, and that she'd been in Missoula all day with a transplant team questioning her, poking at her. "What say we change the subject?"

She relaxed against the back of the red Naugahyde booth. "Think we have anything in common after all these years?"

A son. A boy I never knew. He forced himself not to say it. "Keep talking, and we'll see."

The tension eased up a little. Never in a million years did Sam think he'd be here, with her. Watching her pick at her meal, he wondered what she thought about, what she wished for, these days. When he'd first come back to Crystal City he figured he might see her now and again when she visited Gavin. But local gossip had put that expectation to rest. Everyone in town knew Gavin Slade and his daughter were estranged. But no one knew the reason.

"So where do we start?" he murmured.

She set down her fork. "You mean, telling Cody about us?"

He wasn't sure what he meant. But he nodded, because it made sense. "Yeah. Do you want to tell him yourself or together or what?"

"Um, I guess I thought I'd do it myself. I'm not used to consulting with anyone on decisions that have to do with Cody."

"Whose fault is that?"

"Oh, Sam. I'm not trying to hurt you. I'm trying to be realistic here. I raised Cody alone. I made some good choices and some bad ones for him, just like any parent. I never expected to have to deal with *this*."

"You say *this* like it's a case of VD or something."

"That's not what I mean. Damn it, Sam. You jump on everything I say. Just like—" She shook her head in bewilderment. "Just like Cody does."

"How do you think he'll take the news?"

"After today?" There it was again, that soft smile that drove him crazy, reaching across the years to remind him of how well he used to know her. "He'll be amazed."

"Yeah?"

"He's a complicated kid. Used to be a pretty great

kid, actually. You'd never know it to look at him now, but this is a boy who used to bring me the paper in bed every morning. He'd sit in my lap and fiddle with my hair while I read him the funny pages."

Sam closed his eyes. And he saw the picture so clearly it nearly choked him. *Why couldn't I be there? Goddammit, why couldn't I be in the picture?* He felt a jolt of anger—heated, irrational.

"Anyway, he's not so warm and fuzzy anymore," Michelle said.

Sam opened his eyes. "Hell, I noticed."

"Some days I don't even think I know him. But I believe he'll be . . . glad to learn you're his father."

"Glad. What do you mean by glad?"

"Just . . . glad. Wouldn't you, if you finally met *your* father?"

"Assuming my mother knew for sure who he was. But yeah. Maybe I'd be glad." He cleared his throat. "Once we—once you tell him, what do you think about asking him if he'd like to stay with me for a while?"

She reared back in her seat. *"What?"*

"You heard me, Michelle."

Her hand closed into a fist. She seemed to grow in stature, a lioness defending her cub. "Out of the question."

"Why?"

"We didn't come back here for good. We live in Seattle."

"You said yourself he was giving you a rough time—"

"That doesn't mean I'm willing to give him up. He's not a dog you take back to the pound because he turned out to be a pain in the neck. Jesus, Sam, what can you be thinking?"

"That I have a son you never bothered to tell me about. I want to find out what he's like, what his plans are for college." He hesitated. "I intend to contribute to that and everything else."

She pressed her palms on the table. How clean her hands and fingernails were. They used to always be smeared and spattered with paint. He remembered that about her, remembered her paint-smudged hand touching his cheek, his chest, lower . . . *Damn.*

"Child-support payments? I don't expect it, Sam. And I certainly don't need it."

"Too bad. I intend to contribute anyway."

She stared off into space. "That's the kind of father I had. The one with the checkbook."

He glared at her, but the truth echoed through him. He wasn't sure Cody was something he wanted or needed or was ready for right now, but one thing was certain—if he wanted a place in the boy's heart, in his life, he'd have to earn it. And he sure as hell couldn't do that in a few weeks.

Tuesday

Tuesday

Chapter 14

W hen the phone rang, Michelle jerked herself out of the restless half sleep that had tormented her all night. Fumbling for the receiver by the bed, she felt a swift revival of every fear and nightmare that had plagued her since leaving her injured son in the hospital.

She clutched the receiver with both hands. "Yes?"

"Mom?"

"Cody!" Her heart shot straight to her throat. "What's the matter? Are you all right? Did something—"

"Hey, Mom, slow down. I'm okay. Sam said I should call and let you know."

Her chest sagged like a deflating balloon. She felt as if she had been holding her breath, bracing herself, for hours. "Wow, Cody. It's good to hear your voice."

"Sam says I'll be discharged today. No sign of concussion."

She glanced at the clock: 6:45 A.M. For all his teenage bravado, Cody probably hadn't had a great night, either.

"I'll come right away." She sat up against the headboard.

"Okay. Sam wants to talk to you for a minute. See you, Mom."

During the pause while she waited for Sam, she let her mouth form a tremulous smile of relief. Nothing, absolutely nothing in the entire universe matched the terror of a mother's fear for her child. When the fear was alleviated, it left in its wake a powerful euphoria, almost a giddiness.

"Hi, Michelle." Sam's voice raised the giddiness to a windstorm in her chest.

Get a grip, she told herself. This is Cody's doctor. *Doctor*.

"Thanks for letting him call. I earned another four hundred new gray hairs last night."

"So wear a hat."

Not even a smart remark could dim her mood. "As soon as I let my dad know what's going on, I'll be there."

A scant ten minutes later, Michelle had put on wool leggings and an oversize Irish sweater, and she was considering the array of hats on the hall tree. She knew she should take the time to call Brad and fill him in on all the drama, not to mention letting him know how the appointment in Missoula had gone.

But she couldn't phone him yet. It was too early in the morning, and Cody was waiting.

There was another reason she was reluctant to phone Brad, but she refused to ponder it right now. Feeling guilty was just something she had learned to do—must be a mother thing. Or a woman thing.

She snatched a heather wool cap from the hall tree, jammed on her boots, and trudged outside. Faint dawn veined the mountaintops in the east, drawing a stark, fiery line over the highest peaks and sending shadows of pink down the ridges and valleys. Snow had dusted the area in the night, and it was cold enough to squeak beneath her boots as she walked across the compound to the main house. Steam wafted gently from the pool on the patio.

A single light burned in the kitchen, sending a fan of gold across the new-fallen snow in the yard. Before mounting the steps to the front porch, she stopped, spying her father inside.

He stood at the counter with the robe half open as he did something with the dialysis apparatus he'd been so reluctant to discuss. It was a private moment, and she couldn't intrude; she knew she mustn't. She took a step back. Gavin turned his head slightly, and she saw him in profile.

Just for a second or two he fell still, bringing his hand to his forehead and leaning the other hand on the counter.

Her throat constricted as she forced her gaze away. For the first time since learning of his illness, she felt the thudding reality of the disease, and it was strange to feel the truth while standing out in the cold fire of dawn, looking in at a scene so painful and private that she nearly choked on her own breath.

Her father was sick, dying, desperately in need of the operation. Urgency pumped through her like adrenaline. She wanted to have the surgery *now*, not next week. Dear God, if she could pluck out the organ with her own hand and give it to him right this moment, she'd do it.

Hurrying back to the guesthouse, she scribbled a note

of explanation to her father and left it at the front door. On the porch she hesitated. Maybe she should go in, say good morning, ask him if he needed anything. What if he wanted Michelle, her company, the comfort she could offer?

But she couldn't go do it. Couldn't go in there, intrude. Couldn't be the daughter he needed. They were strangers in too many ways.

As she drove into town, she grabbed the cell phone and punched in the renal specialist's number. The doctor's answering service asked if there was an emergency. When she admitted there was not, she was advised to call during regular office hours.

"I need to speak to her now," she said.

"Ma'am, I'd be happy to take your number—"

"My father is sick now, not during office hours."

"The emergency number is—"

"I know the emergency number." She dragged in a long breath. "What about Donna Roberts, the transplant nurse. Is she in?"

"She's on duty at nine o'clock."

"Temple, then. Damn it, is he taking calls?"

"I'll forward the call, ma'am."

Simple as that. Temple, the psychologist, knew people didn't get neurotic on a schedule.

"This is Dr. Temple." He sounded crisp and alert, considering the hour.

"It's Michelle Turner, remember?"

"Of course. What can I do for you?"

The words came out in a rush. "Look, I want the transplant to happen sooner. I'm not willing to work around the surgeon's ski trip or whatever's holding it up. This morning my father—I saw—" She broke off, picturing Willard Temple at a Corian breakfast counter in his suburban tract mansion, drinking coffee and looking out over the golf course that backed up to his yard.

"Anyway, I can't stand seeing him like this. Why can't I do the rest of the tests today and the surgery tomorrow?"

A pause. An ominous, doctorlike pause. "Actually, Ms. Turner, I was going to recommend that your surgery be postponed until you and your father could go through some more counseling about the procedure."

A silent scream echoed through Michelle. Her knuckles whitened as she gripped the receiver. "Um, wait a minute. Run that by me again?"

"I don't have your records in front of me at the moment, but there's some concern that there are issues that need to be explored and resolved before we proceed."

Devastation and rage had a taste, she realized. They tasted rusty and bitter, like blood.

"Just a goddamned minute." She tried not to shout, but it wasn't working. She didn't care if her voice blasted him out of his brick McMansion onto his ass in the snow. "After all these weeks of testing, after meeting all those difficult physical criteria, you're telling me we have 'issues'?"

"Ms. Turner, your relationship with your father is unusual. You've spent very little time together—"

"What the hell do you want from me?" she raged. "Do you want me to have some big confrontation with him? Do you want me to accuse him of never being a daddy to me, for chrissakes? Should I accuse him of not seeing me as a daughter, but a donor? Not wanting anything from me except to harvest a few more years? Are those the sort of fucking 'issues' you're getting at?"

His next silence was so long she started to get embarrassed.

"Very impressive, Ms. Turner."

"I'm trying to impress you," she forced out through her teeth. "I'm trying to impress you with the fact that we've waited too long already. I want the surgery now—"

"There is nothing simple about this surgery. It's not a rare procedure, but it's a serious one."

"You're damned right it is. Because—" She shut her mouth, realizing that she was about to threaten Willard T. Temple with death. Not a wise way to dazzle him with her sanity. "Listen. I'm calm now, Doctor. But I don't want any further delays."

As she turned off the phone, she checked the speedometer. Her speed had climbed way out of control. Easing her tense foot off the accelerator, she tried to force the rest of her to slow down, too. It was hard, though. She felt as if she was running from one crisis to another.

Natalie, her best friend, often told her the benefits of slowing down, of being "in the moment." Easy for Natalie to say. She could live "in the moment" as much as she pleased. She flitted from one day to the next with nary a care in the world. She was Michelle's polar opposite, yet they had been best friends for years.

"Okay, Nat. I'm trying to be in the moment." Her breath fogged the air of the still-cold Range Rover. "I'm going to pick up Cody. I've got nothing else going on today, so I can bring him home and make him soup and mother him all day long. I'll see if Sam can figure out a way to get the transplant done sooner. How does that sound?"

Like she was losing it, talking to herself while driving along the highway. But somehow, taking the day step by step calmed her. By the time she walked into the hospital, she had most of her sanity back.

She stopped at the desk, manned this morning by a

different clerk. "I'm Cody Turner's mother. He's being discharged today."

The clerk tamped a stack of file folders together and set them in a metal tray on the counter. "So he is. I think he's getting dressed now. Here are a few forms for you to sign."

"I'd like to see the bill, please."

The clerk opened a folder and handed her a pen, then clicked at a keyboard. A long sheet drifted out of the printer. She studied the itemized bill and pointed to a line. "Does this mean the doctor waived his fee?"

The clerk nodded. "Appears so."

For some reason, this made her mad. She turned the page, spotting the financial liability sheet. Another unwelcome bit of charity leaped out at her.

"It says here the balance has been paid in full."

"That's right, ma'am."

"By Gavin Slade."

"I understand he's the boy's grandfather." The clerk smiled with the dreamy admiration Michelle remembered from Gavin's fans years ago. "Must be something, having him for a father."

She scrawled her signature beside all the Xs. "Oh, it's something, all right." Be in the moment, she reminded herself. She would confront Gavin about the bill later. And Sam waiving his fee. Damn them both. She had a good job with benefits. She didn't need either of them to come blasting into her life, taking over.

"Morning, Mrs. Turner." Nurse O'Brien looked crisp and pretty in pink slacks and tunic, a cardigan draped over her shoulders. "Your son's looking good."

Michelle summoned a smile. "I didn't have a chance to thank you yesterday. I appreciate everything you and Sam did for Cody."

"You're more than welcome."

She didn't seem to be in a hurry to go anywhere. To make conversation, Michelle asked, "Have you worked with Sam long?"

She hesitated, giving Michelle the strangest look. The desk clerk stopped typing, and from the corner of her eye Michelle saw her lean forward. "Nearly five years, since he came on at County," Alice O'Brien said.

Michelle sensed there was a lot more the nurse could tell her about those five years, but not now. Hiking her handbag strap securely on her shoulder, she hurried down the hallway. The door to Cody's room stood slightly ajar. She knocked. "Cody? It's Mom."

"Yeah, I'm ready."

She was unprepared for the sight of him. The pony-tail was gone. A thick white bandage covered the stitches. There was an actual, recognizable style to his hair. She remembered the way it used to grow when he was tiny, in gorgeous swirly waves as if his head had been licked all over by a friendly golden retriever.

He looked at her and his cheeks colored up, and all she could think was *thank God*. The pallor was gone. He actually had blood flowing to his face. A good sign.

And even though she felt like crying, she forced her mouth into a momlike smile.

"Love the haircut, son."

"Some guy came in at the crack of dawn and said he'd just even it out, and look what he did."

"It's fine, Cody. Really."

"It sucks."

It was creeping back over him, she saw. The attitude. After an injury or a bad sickness, a kid usually had a pe-riod of perfect sweetness. Cody had been that way yes-terday while Sam was stitching him up. He'd been that way on the phone with her. But now things were getting back to normal.

Did he do that on purpose? she wondered.

He held up a white plastic bag with MERIDIAN COUNTY HOSPITAL printed on the side. "Here's all my stuff. Can we go now?"

"I have to see Sam first," she said, her mouth tasting the name, tasting wonder. "I've got some questions for him."

Cody handed her a pink slip. "He already gave me this prescription."

"Watch two hours of MTV and call me in the morning," said a voice from the doorway.

Michelle turned, and there he was, leaning with one shoulder propped against the doorframe. Sam McPhee in scrubs. Yesterday she'd been too worried about Cody to appreciate the sight. It was so different from the way she remembered him, the way she'd always imagined him.

This was the man who wanted to barge his way into Cody's life, she reminded herself.

"Take that prescription for the pain." Sam came into the room. The photo ID tag hanging from his pocket—not to mention the stethoscope and drug-company pocket protector—gave him an air of authority that made her feel strange. "Use as directed, and he should be all right." He propped some films in a lighted display box on the wall. "He checked out fine this morning." With a pencil, he pointed out some areas that reminded her of Rorschach figures, symmetrical paint blobs that shrinks used to see how the mind works.

"This one's from yesterday, and here it is this morning. Head trauma was minimal."

For some reason, she felt like crying. She studied the film. Did it show where the sweetness was hiding? Did it tell you why Cody was so hateful all the time? She bit her tongue against asking.

Sam grinned at Cody. "You've got a thick skull, kid."

"You've got a lame barber," Cody grumbled.

"Hazlett? We're lucky we've got someone who makes house calls."

Cody shuffled toward the door, his jeans dragging at the heels. "I'll be in the car, Mom."

"All right." She waited, biting down on her lower lip, because she knew what she wanted him to do, but she didn't want to tell him to do it, because it wouldn't be the same. *Turn around, you little shit. Turn around and tell Dr. McPhee thank you.*

He didn't. She was not surprised. She didn't think Sam was, either. After only a couple of days, Sam knew good and well that Cody was a surly kid, dancing on the edge, too cool for his oversize jeans.

"Anything else I should know?" she asked.

"The usual. Take it easy for the next couple of days. Stitches come out on Friday or Saturday."

She nodded, looking down at her hands. She was suddenly and unpleasantly conscious that she'd barely slept all night, and here she was unshowered, no makeup, in clothes she threw on in five minutes.

"You waived your fee," she blurted out.

"The kid was in my care when he got kicked in the head. You've got a dandy lawsuit here if you care to pursue it."

Oh, that would be fun, thought Michelle. She could see the tabloids now. *Celeb Mom Sues Dad for Injury to Love Child.* "Don't even think about a lawsuit, Sam."

"I wish everyone had that attitude."

"I have another question."

"Shoot."

"It's about Gavin and the transplant." Her insides twisted into knots. "Um, there might be a glitch."

"A glitch?"

"A postponement."

His face didn't change, but something about the quality of the light in his eyes did.

"Is Gavin having trouble?"

She shifted from foot to foot. The room felt overly warm. "Well, not specifically. It's just that . . . I got up this morning and saw . . . I realized this has gone on too long already, the stuff with the dialysis and all the meds. So I spoke with Dr. Temple, the psychologist from the transplant team. I told him that every single moment of waiting is cruelty." She took a deep breath, feeling tears of exhaustion and frustration pressing to get out. She willed them away. "And the son of a bitch said he's not sure we're ready."

"Ready. You mean they need to order more tests, or—"

"No, the renal angiogram's the only thing left. He's playing head games, Sam. He doesn't think Gavin and I are ready *psychologically*."

"And you think you are?"

"I know I am, goddammit. My life has stopped, and nothing can start again until this is done. And he wants me to determine whether I'm acting out of guilt or loyalty or God-knows-what? How can that matter, Sam?"

He was quiet for a long time. Too long. She was starting to think it was a doctor thing. A conspiracy. Torture the patient until she's over the edge, then collect your fee.

Finally he said, "I'll offer a personal reference."

The bones in her legs turned to water. "Oh, Sam. Would you? Please?"

"I'll do what I can. I've met Maggie Kehr. I could

give her a call." Her business card said "Dr. Margaret Kehr," but Sam called her Maggie. "She's the best," he added.

"That's good to hear." *So what's this about you and Maggie?*

"Anyway, I'm sure she told you how complicated this procedure is. It's got to be orchestrated down to the last second. Everything's got to come together at the right moment. The scheduling can be a nightmare."

"I'm trying to be patient. But it's so damned hard."

"A few more days aren't going to matter, not with Gavin. Like I told you before, he's in great shape. That's not likely to change."

Michelle caught herself putting her hands on her hips. No, not on her hips. At the back of her waist, in the vicinity of the kidneys. She had been doing that a lot lately.

"All right," she said, suddenly self-conscious. "I'll take the reference. Just tell them I'm not a psycho trying to earn cosmic brownie points by giving my dad a kidney."

His eyes twinkled. "I can do that."

"Thanks."

"And Michelle, I meant what I said last night. About Cody."

He couldn't have planned his stealth attack better. He'd waived his fee, offered to intervene on her behalf with the transplant team—and now this. "Are you blackmailing me?" she asked. "A personal reference if I say it's okay for you to steal my son?"

"I don't aim to steal a damned thing from you, Michelle. Do you think it'll damage him to hear the truth? That knowing who I am could harm him?"

She slumped against the doorframe. "I don't know

what I think. I haven't even had my first cup of coffee yet."

Eerily lit by the glow from the light boxes behind the films, he was both strange and painfully familiar to her. The white of the light accentuated his features—the fine nose and high cheekbones and Val Kilmer mouth she remembered from so long ago. Yet she also saw the lost years imprinted on his brow, the maturity put there by Lord-knew-what, and somehow he looked totally alone.

"Sam, I'm going to tell him."

"When?" His response was instantaneous, as if it had been balanced on the tip of his tongue during the entire conversation.

She made herself hide the fear. "I'll do it today."

"How do you think he'll take it?"

Lord, but she wanted to touch him, right now. Take his hand and give it a squeeze. Because for the first time, she finally realized that he was scared, too. Knowing the vulnerability that lay at the heart of this mysterious, familiar man made him so much more to her than a memory.

"I couldn't say, Sam. Really. Cody is ... unpredictable lately. I never know if something's going to please him, annoy him, anger him."

"Doesn't he still ask?"

Michelle felt as if she was balanced on the blade of a knife. Did it matter what she told this man? Sam was not in their lives now. But ... how could she lie? What would it serve?

"He used to every once in a while after he started school." Before that he had no idea a two-parent family was the norm.

"And ... ?" Sam held himself stiffly. She could see the taut cords in his neck and part of her exulted in his suffering, because she had struggled, too, raising her son alone. But another, softer part of her still wanted to touch him.

"I said you were someone I met when I was too young to make good decisions. I told him you were a cowboy, following the PRCA. I explained that I never heard from you again after a brief . . . affair." She almost said love affair.

A muscle tensed in his jaw. "Made me out to be a real prince, did you?"

"There was no point in telling him more. It was dangerous because of the press. Because I'll always be Gavin's daughter. I didn't want them writing things . . . about us, about Cody. If I'd told him your name, given him details, some snoopy reporter would have found out. That's not fair to a kid."

She wished Sam would say something, but he just kept looking at her, and suddenly she was remembering how it used to be between them. His silences, her ramblings. How he'd pretend to be mad at little things, like when she wore his chambray work shirts, but she could tell he was secretly pleased. How those shirts smelled exactly like him.

She had taken one with her the day she'd left Blue Rock Ranch in disgrace. When she was pregnant, she used to take it out and hold it wadded up against her chest, letting the texture of soft faded cotton soothe her skin as she inhaled the scent of him. She had never laundered that shirt, because she was terrified the smell would wear off and it would just be a shirt. When that happened, she told herself, Sam would be gone from her life, finally and irrevocably.

Something very unexpected happened with that old blue shirt. She might tell him about it some time, but not now.

"All Cody knows about the past," she said, "is that I was a statistic, an unwed mother who had to grow up too fast." A shadow crossed his face, and she hurried on. "I didn't tell him in those words. I'd never make Cody feel guilty simply for being born. He is the greatest blessing in my life." There was a little hitch in her throat, because that part was true. "I would lie down and die for that child, and he knows it. I've loved him more than I ever thought possible. I've given him the best life I could. Kept him out of the camera's eye and kept him in school. And . . . that's about it." She was running out of steam, and the thought teased a wry smile from her.

His beeper went off, startling her. He checked the number. "We'll talk later. I'll see Cody later in the week about the stitches."

"All right."

As he walked away, long tails of his surgical coat belling out behind him like a cape, she thought about the task ahead, and she shivered. Not with cold, but with fear. Some small, icebound part of her lived in terror that Cody—her angry, beautiful, troubled boy—would leave her if he had a place to run.

Chapter 15

Sam and his partner, Karl, each spent one day a week at the reservation about twenty miles from Crystal City. They served as medical advisors for the Confederated Salish-Kootenai tribes. There, in a trailer adjacent to the tribal elementary school, he practiced the type of medicine he was best at—direct, hands-on care. The doctoring was frustrating, often sad, sometimes infuriating, and every once in a while, rewarding.

For his troubles, he received a minuscule stipend from the BIA and, if circumstances permitted, an hour of athletic, no-strings-attached sex with a woman named Candy who lived at the north end of the settlement in a Pan-Abode cabin.

Today at the free clinic he'd done a four-month well-baby checkup and booster shots on a perfect baby boy. Moments later he'd seen a diabetic seventy-year-old who wouldn't stop drinking. He had delivered the usual warnings and produced the usual pamphlets and brochures, he'd written a prescription and sent the old guy, who moved with a curious dignity, on his way. If the man lasted the winter, it'd be a miracle.

He treated a shame-faced teenage girl for chlamydia, and extracted a pinto bean from the nostril of an inquisitive three-year-old. He'd seen Linda Wolf, not for the first time and certainly not for the last. She claimed to have a problem with clumsiness. Sam could tell she was too weary and in too much pain to work hard making up a lie. She'd mumbled vaguely that she'd fallen; then she'd wept silently as Sam taped her up and prescribed something for the pain. It was torn elbow cartilage this time, but over the years he had treated the funny, caustic, and ultimately pathetic woman for cracked ribs, lacerations, a detached retina, countless contusions.

When he questioned her, she always gave her usual reply. "I'm a big girl, Dr. McPhee. I know what I'm doing."

And there it ended. Her husband would abuse her until he stepped over the line and committed murder, or until she wised up and left him.

Each time he saw Linda, Sam did everything short of kidnapping the woman to convince her to leave her husband. He talked to Social Services, urged the tribal police to pick up the scumbag on another charge—running a red light, illegal waste disposal, expired tags. But Randy Wolf was, oddly enough, a model citizen, working in the timber industry. His only crimes were against Linda, and she refused to press charges. Once, a few years back, Sam had confronted him. And Randy had gone home and beaten the crap out of his wife.

At the end of the day, Sam parked at the back of a cabin north of the village. Candy opened the door, letting out a herd of cats as Sam stepped inside. She wore a smile and a hand-painted silk kimono. "Hey, Doc," she said. "Long time no see."

He grinned, nodding his thanks as she handed him a cold beer. "Ditto," he said, taking a swig and then setting down the bottle. He kissed her hard, walking her back to the bedroom without lifting his mouth from hers. In a matter of minutes they were naked, straining together, twisting the bedclothes every which way. He liked her softness, the beer-and-perfume taste of her, and the way she used her hands and mouth.

But afterward, he never wanted to stay for long. He got dressed in a hurry, handed Candy her kimono, and went out to his truck. Wrapped in a wool coat, she stood watching him, her face thoughtful. "You're in a hurry today, Doc."

"Uh-huh. I've been busy."

"You want to stay for supper? I got a pot of beans on."

"Not tonight, Sugar-Candy. I'd best be going."

"You take care now," she said, shivering as he got into his truck. Her cats darted in from the woods, swirling around her ankles as she stood watching him.

Sam waved and pulled away, vaguely disgusted with himself for being able to dismiss her so casually, vaguely annoyed at her for letting him. He came away from the encounter with a hollow sense of futility. Sam knew he was deliberately shying away from commitment, even though a part of him ached for it. He snapped on the radio for the drive home. He thought about the four-month-old. Even now he could feel the creamy texture of the baby's skin, the downy fluff of his black hair. He could picture the crooked toothless wet grin when the baby focused on his face.

His gloved hands tightened convulsively on the steering wheel. What had Cody been like as a baby?

Just start where you are, common sense told him.

Start with an angry teen who was probably more at risk than his mother dared to believe. Start with a kid who was well past the age of giving a rat's ass who his father was. Start with a kid Sam knew he'd have to work at liking.

Christ. What sort of father had to work to like his own kid?

Sam stopped his truck in front of the yellow-trimmed bungalow at the edge of town. Late-afternoon sunlight spilled across the ripples of snow in the small yard. He knew she'd be waiting for him inside. She always was on Tuesday afternoons, her half day off. Ever since he'd moved to Crystal City, he'd saved Tuesdays for her.

He sat at the steering wheel, unloading the invisible burdens, mentally leaving all the baggage from the long, trying day inside the truck. Then he slammed the door behind him and walked across the yard to the front porch.

He knocked lightly and let himself in. The familiar smells of vanilla-scented candles and cigarette smoke greeted him.

"Hey, Mama," he said, stomping the snow from his boots onto the doormat.

"Hiya, son." Tammi Lee Gilmer tucked a bookmark into the paperback novel in her lap. Late in life, she had discovered something she enjoyed almost as much as she used to enjoy drinking and partying. She read voraciously: detective novels, romance novels, thrillers, memoirs, and her beloved *National Enquirer* and *Country Billboard*. Sam had no memory of books among their possessions. It was as if Tammi Lee was making up for lost time.

She got up from her lounger and crossed the room,

giving him a brief hug and a kiss on the cheek. Her scent of cigarettes and Charlie perfume clung to the sweater she wore. She was a thin, angular woman whose body had miraculously survived years of self-abuse. Though attractive in an old-fashioned Patsy Cline way, her face bore a delicate webbing of lines and creases, a busy road map of her past.

"You doing all right, Mama?" Sam asked her.

"Sure." She went to the kitchen and poured two cups of coffee, handing him one. "Just made it fresh."

"Thanks." He had a seat at the table as she rummaged in the refrigerator for something to feed him. Though he wasn't hungry, he knew better than to stop her.

This was the woman who had raised him in a beat-up Plymouth Valiant, who had parked him in a playpen while her band laid down the tracks of her one whiskey-voiced hit, who had taught him to buy cigarettes from a machine before he was old enough to count, who had used him to wrest suspended sentences from disapproving judges, who had made him leave the only girl he'd ever loved. She had taken from him any chance of a normal upbringing.

Yet when Sam looked at his mother, he felt only one emotion, a feeling that radiated out from the middle of him and reverberated through his soul. And that emotion was love.

Because in the middle of all the travels, the running, the ducking, the hiding, the arrests, the arraignments, the shouting and the pain when he'd grown old enough to force her into treatment, she had loved him with all that was in her.

Sometimes that wasn't much. Sometimes looking for love from her was like going to the auto-parts store for milk. But during her brighter periods, she'd managed to give him enough to get by on. She used to touch his cheek, tell him she was sorry for missing a parent-teacher conference or forgetting to buy groceries or running out of money when he outgrew his clothes. Without really intending to, she had taught him to dream.

These days, at LaNelle's shop, she listened to the local gossip and snipped fabric for curtains and quilts. It was a quiet life compared to her raucous past, but she didn't complain. She did a lot of serenity work with her AA sponsor, and it seemed to sustain her.

She set down a plate of processed cheese and crackers. "So how are things with you? How's my son the doctor?"

"I'm having an interesting week. Started off by winning a rodeo purse Saturday night."

Tammi Lee wrinkled her nose. "I don't understand why you keep on with that, hon. You're going to hurt yourself."

"Going to? Mama, I've hurt myself in so many places, there's nothing left to hurt." He spread his arms. "Rodeo's my sport."

"Doctors are supposed to be into golf and skiing."

He laughed. "Now, where did you read that?"

"Some magazine I found in your office."

"I reckon I'm not that kind of doctor." With his practice, his service in a public hospital, and the indigent patients he treated, he'd never get rich.

His mind flashed on Cody. The kid's leather jacket alone was probably worth a week of malpractice insurance. Everything he wore was expensive. Was it just his age, or was he the sort of kid to whom status symbols mattered?

Tammi Lee drummed her fingers on the table. He knew she wanted a cigarette, but she tried not to smoke too much around him. As a kid, he'd probably inhaled enough secondhand smoke to choke a moose. He ate a cracker, sipped his coffee. "I ran into someone at the rodeo," he said carefully. He'd learned early to insulate his fragile mother whenever he could, but this wasn't something to hide from her.

Tammi Lee's hands fell still, and she regarded him with a sharp-edged, penetrating look. "Yeah? Who?"

"Michelle Turner, Gavin Slade's daughter."

His mother leaned back in her vinyl-covered chair and let out a low whistle. "Theda Duckworth was in the shop this morning, and she mentioned something about that. She here because Gavin's sick?"

Sam nodded. He didn't want to discuss details with his mother. In a town the size of Crystal City, Gavin's illness could hardly be kept a secret, but it wasn't Sam's place to divulge the progress and treatment of the disease.

"So . . . how'd your old girlfriend turn out?" Tammi Lee asked. She'd known Michelle only vaguely as the blond actor's spoiled daughter Sam had been seeing as a teenager. He suspected his mother knew how far the relationship had gone, but Tammi Lee had never said much. Once, he recalled, she'd tried to warn him about Michelle.

"That girl's going to be nothing but heartache for you, son," Tammi Lee had said.

He remembered the day she'd said it. She'd come home from waitressing all afternoon at the Truxtop Café. In her white polyester uniform, she'd sat in a stained easy chair and unlaced her white leather Reeboks, massaging her aching feet as Sam got ready to meet Michelle at the boathouse. He'd been in a great mood.

"You hear me, son?" Tammi Lee had repeated. "Nothing but heartache."

"Give me a break, Mama," he'd said, toweling his hair after his shower. "We have a great time together."

"You do now. But you can't let yourself forget who she is, and who you are."

Sam's patience had worn thin. "I'll see you later." He'd left her sitting in the rickety rental house, an old wood-frame dwelling on the wrong side of the tracks, with a caved-in garage attached by a shotgun corridor to the main house. It was all they could afford on Tammi Lee's tips and Sam's paycheck from the ranch.

When Sam had first returned to Crystal City to start up his practice, he'd driven past the house, finding it abandoned. The windows had been blown out, probably by kids with BB guns. The roofline sagged like the back of an ancient horse, and the siding had weathered until it was the color of the dusty, sage-choked yard. He'd battled an urge to set fire to the place and watch it burn to the ground.

"Well?" his mother prompted. "How'd she turn out?"

"She's a commercial artist in Seattle."

"I recall she was some kind of artistic prodigy."

"And . . . a single mother."

Her tweezed eyebrows lifted. "Guess she and I have something in common after all."

Sam thought about that for a moment. Like Cody, he too had rarely asked about the man who'd fathered him. "Some old guy," Tammi Lee had always replied, pulling a name out of thin air. "Some old guy, name of . . . McPhee."

Sam had made no attempt to learn more. Because when he'd grown old enough to know how to track someone down, he'd also been old enough to understand just how little it took for a man to father a child. And because, in Sam's mind, no man could equal the fantasy dad he'd created for himself.

He wondered if Cody had done that. Lacking a father in his life, had he fashioned the perfect dad out of wishes and whimsy? Had he imagined someone big and strong, someone who laughed and tossed a football to him and took him fishing? Someone who turned on the hall light at night and checked on him?

The elusive father had been a powerful figure in Sam's life, and he had been wholly imaginary. Sam tried to decide how he'd feel if he had the chance to know the actual guy.

He was bound to be disappointed.

"Michelle's son is sixteen, Mama. She was pregnant with him when she left Crystal City that winter."

Tammi held herself very still, though her pale gray eyes filled with amazement. Finally, she said, "He's your son, then."

"Yes."

"And you never knew about him?"

"No. We left town before Michelle told me."

"She never tried to contact you?"

"No." Sam didn't want to get into it with Tammi Lee. Didn't want her to feel guilty for dragging him along her rocky road. Her sobriety had been hard won. She had gone off a few times before; an emotional upset could push her unmercifully toward that next drink.

"So what do you make of all this?" she asked.

"I'm still getting used to the idea. The kid's name is Cody, he's sixteen, and pissed at the world."

"Sounds like a typical sixteen-year-old."

"When I was sixteen, I don't remember being pissed at the world."

She stared down at her lap. "You were too busy trying to hold down a job and stay in school, son. And you had to give up school when we kept moving. I'm sorry for—"

"Don't be sorry, Mama," he cut in. "You kept me from being a rebellious little shit, so I ought to thank you for it."

"So this guy's a rebellious little shit?"

"Pretty much, yeah."

"What's he think of you?"

"Michelle never told him I fathered him. But she said she'd tell him soon, maybe today. And then . . . we'll see."

"Any boy'd be proud to call you his dad," Tammi Lee said. She credited him for saving her life, dragging her kicking and screaming into rehab again and again. No matter how many times he explained it was her strength, not his, she insisted on giving him credit.

"He might want to meet you," Sam suggested, and he couldn't resist adding, "Grandma."

Tammi Lee froze for a moment. Then she stood up. "I need a cigarette." With quick, jerky movements she grabbed a pack of Virginia Slims from a cupboard and lit one, turning on the exhaust fan over the stove and leaning against the counter.

"He'll hate me." She blew out a stream of smoke.

"If he does, it won't be your fault. I told you, the kid's trouble. Michelle's dealing with it the best she can."

Tammi Lee eyed him through a thin veil of bluish smoke. "Any chance the two of you will start seeing each other again?"

Even though the possibility was as remote as the moon, Sam had been seared by it from the moment he'd seen her in the arena parking lot.

"No way," he said quickly. "She lives in Seattle, and she's . . . involved, I guess. My life is set, Mama. I don't gamble. I tried marriage once, and you know what happened. I'm not about to screw around with an old flame."

Tammi Lee nodded. "Nobody ever ends up with their childhood sweetheart. Or if they do, they wind up dead, like Romeo and Juliet."

Sam laughed. "I guess you're right, Mama."

"So what happens next?"

"I suppose, next time I see Cody, he's going to know I'm his father."

She ground out her cigarette in a fluted aluminum ashtray on the stove. "You scared, son?"

"Hell, yeah, I'm scared, Mama."

Chapter 16

I t was insane, thought Michelle, mooning over Sam
McPhee like a lovestruck schoolgirl. But she couldn't
seem to stop herself from thinking of him, picturing
his big hands, and how delicately they had handled Cody's
stitches. She couldn't keep from remembering the color of
his eyes or the look on his face when he was watching
her from the hospital-room doorway. She had an almost-
grown son, a sick father, a significant other in Seattle. She
had no business speculating, even to herself, what it would
be like to know Sam again.

"So you never did tell me about the foaling," she said
to Cody on the ride home, as much to distract herself as
to get him to talk.

"It was way cool. There was a dys—dyst—um, a difficult presentation, and the vet couldn't make it on time,
so we all pitched in. Sam, me, and Edward. The mare kept

getting up when she wasn't supposed to, so that was kind of bad. I had to get my hand right up inside her to bring the foal around."

"I'm getting this incredible mental picture. So you didn't gross out?"

"Nope. Like I said, it was kind of cool."

Maybe it was the blow to the head. That had to be it, Michelle thought, because no son of hers would think sticking his hand up a mare's birth canal was cool. But on the other hand, horses had once filled her life and made it beautiful. She wondered if a horse could do that for Cody.

Dooley had been four years old the summer she'd moved to Montana. A trim quarter horse with a splash of white on his forehead, he had snagged her interest when she'd seen him kicking up his heels in the paddock. Her father, eager to spoil her during the year she'd given him, had offered the gelding to her.

Everyone at Blue Rock Ranch must have thought she was a snooty city girl, with her tight buff-colored riding pants and tall English-style boots, an array of dressage ribbons and trophies spread out on her bedroom bureau.

Dooley had no patience for a dressage rider who wanted him to skip over little ivy-covered jumps and arch his neck and trot prettily around a ring. It took a lot of spills—and a lot of coaching from Sam—for her to figure that out.

They rolled up to the house and she cut the engine, turning to Cody. That haircut! She tried not to smile, looking at it, but it made her ridiculously happy to see the last of that obnoxious dual-colored ponytail hanging down his back.

"How do you feel?" she asked him. "Can I fix you something to eat?"

"I'm thrashed, Mom. I think I'll zone out for a while."

She resisted helping him out of the car. When he shrugged off his jacket and flopped down on the sofa, flipping on the TV, she resisted grabbing the afghan and tucking it around him. He used to be hers to tuck and touch and mother as much as she pleased. Now when she did it, she felt as if she was trespassing.

Okay, so tell him, she urged herself. Tell him about Sam.

But as soon as she opened her mouth to speak, he picked up the phone on the end table and punched in a long string of numbers. "Is Claudia there?" he asked. "Hey, Claudia. It's me. You won't believe what happened . . ."

Feeling like an intruder, she left the guesthouse with her coat still on, and crossed to the huge barn at the end of the main drive. It resembled the set for a sentimental movie, the sunlight on the snow, the weathered cranberry-colored structure too perfect to be real.

In the barn, she ran into Jake Dollarhide. The sight of him startled her; she never expected that he'd still be around.

"Jake? It's me, Michelle Turner. Gavin's daughter."

"Welcome back, Michelle. Good to see you." He was only a couple of years older than Michelle. His father used to be ranch foreman, an important and lucrative position on a spread the size of Blue Rock. Jake looked a lot like he did seventeen years ago. Thicker, more weather-beaten. He had the big, callused hands of an experienced horseman, the limp of a longtime cowboy, and the reserved manner of a man who felt more at home with animals than with people.

"Is there a gelding called Dooley here?" A long shot, but she had to ask him.

"Oh yeah. The old man's still one of the boss's fa-vorites."

She didn't want Dooley to be an old man. She wanted him to be as young and quick as she remembered.

Jake led her down the middle aisle of the barn. She wondered if he remembered what happened all those years ago and what part he played, but she knew she wouldn't ask him. They stopped at one of the stalls. A long, paint-splashed chestnut head came out over the half door.

Dooley. Her best guy. She didn't ever remember lov-ing a horse the way she had loved Dooley, and now he stood there in front of her, chewing indolently on a mouth-ful of alfalfa, the steam puffing gently from his damp nostrils.

Dooley.

They said horses, like elephants, never forgot. She be-lieved that. She believed it with all her heart, because the minute she said his name aloud and hugged herself up against his long, hard skull, he whickered and blew gen-tly into the quiet of the barn.

And Michelle, for no reason she cared to name, burst into tears. She supposed it was because this moment was the culmination of everything that had been building up inside her. In a world that had gone crazy while her back was turned, Dooley lived his life and chewed his alfalfa and stood patiently in this stall. Now he was old, and he was glad to see her.

Jake stepped back, probably embarrassed by her dis-play. Eventually she looked up, wiped her face on her sleeve. "Sorry, Jake. This is my favorite horse in the world, and it's overwhelming to see him again."

He stared at her intently. He used to do that when they were young. It always gave her the creeps, because there was a quiet hunger in his look. "You ought to take the old man for a ride," he said, making her feel foolish for her suspicions.

Michelle knew she should protest, object, think of a bunch of reasons she shouldn't be out riding Dooley for an hour when there was so much else going on, but when she opened her mouth, the only word that came out was "Yes."

In the tack room they took down reins, a curb chain, a Twickenham bit, and a Flores saddle she remembered from years ago. Her father might be one of the Hollywood upstarts Montana loved to hate, but he was a serious upstart. Blue Rock Ranch gave every attention to the animals. The success of a rodeo stock contractor depended on the quality of his livestock. Each piece of tack and saddle was perfectly scrubbed down and oiled. She thought someone must vacuum the blankets; they were that clean.

Dooley stood patiently—she fancied willingly—in the crossties while they saddled him.

"He's fat," she said, grinning as she pulled up on the girth.

"Doesn't get much exercise. This'll be good for him."

"Is he okay, then? No lameness?"

"He's just slow. Lazy. But he'll do what you ask him to do."

She walked him out into the yard where the snow was deep and feathery light. The sunshine and sharp cold nailed her, and Dooley arched his neck in exactly the way she remembered. He knew the route to the vast, covered arena. Her leg cues were superfluous. She started him off slowly, an easy walk around the arena. As he loosened up, he naturally rolled into an easy canter, a smooth-as-wind gait that matched her own heartbeat.

Out of respect for his age, she didn't ask him to extend into a gallop. She just listened to the thud of his nimble hooves against the soft earth, the rhythmic huff of the horse's breath, and the steady creak of leather.

Like windblown leaves, bits and pieces of the past tumbled through her mind. The first time she ever rode Dooley, she'd put an English-style saddle on him and tried to coax him over jumps. He'd balked mulishly, and in the battle of wills that followed, neither horse nor rider won. Then one day Sam came along. She had been bashful and defensive when he came to the fence, wedged a foot up on the rail, and said, "You ought to try barrel racing that horse. That's what he's been drilled on."

She told him she knew how to ride, thank you very much, but he just laughed and waited her out. When she was about to quit in frustration, he gave the horse a break, then set a Western saddle on him and put him through his paces around the barrels.

From that moment on, she was hooked. To hell with prissy ribbons and plastic bouquets bordering fake fences. She gloried in the speed and agility of barrel racing— never in competition, just for the joy of it. Dooley must have been born with the pattern imprinted on his memory, because he did it perfectly, with all the heart she could wish for. A lightning gallop out of the alley, clockwise around the first barrel, counterclockwise around the second, and then finishing with a gallop so swift she felt as if part of her got left behind each time.

And always, flowing with the bits of memory, Sam was there, his loose and long frame a friendly presence at the edge of the arena.

She had thought, that summer, when Dooley and Sam filled her days and nights, that she had found a perfect happiness.

She had thought it would last forever.

Dooley wasn't stupid, he felt her mood slump, and he

took advantage, slowing his pace to a rocking-horse gait. It soothed her; she wondered if he sensed that. He sweated so much that steam rose from every inch of him, so she slowed him to a walk, letting him cool out.

"You both look great," said Gavin. He was no longer the vulnerable invalid she saw in the kitchen early that morning. Looking deceptively hardy and vigorous, he wore a sheepskin jacket and wide-brimmed hat, the tips of his ears and nose red with the cold.

How long had he been there? She'd been so absorbed in riding that she couldn't say.

"I hope you don't mind." She dismounted and led Dooley in a long oval a couple of times around the ring.

"Hell, no, I don't mind. It's good to see him getting some exercise."

"I think he remembers me."

"Wouldn't surprise me. That's one of the smartest horses I've ever had."

Things were quiet and easy between Michelle and Gavin as she put Dooley up, taking the time to grain him, curry him out, paint a bit of red disinfectant on his hock, where she had noticed a small cut. She cleaned the tack while Gavin looked on approvingly.

They checked on Cody to find that he had fallen fast asleep, so they went for a drive out to the small local air park. Gavin greeted people by name there, and showed her into the hangar where he kept his two planes—the vintage biplane, and the P-51 Mustang, his prized possession. The Mustang still had its original D day invasion stripes. It was one of the few surviving WWII planes. Most were in museums these days.

"As soon as your license is reinstated," she said, "I'm going to expect the ride of my life, Daddy."

"You're on," he promised her.

It was early twilight when they returned and walked over to the guest quarters to see Cody. He was curled up, still asleep on the sofa, the TV on but the volume down. Seizing the opportunity to do what he wouldn't let her do when he was awake, Michelle covered him with a knitted striped afghan and brushed a curl of hair off his forehead.

"He all right?" Gavin whispered as they left.

They started across to the big house. "He's doing fine."

"I can't say I'm sorry to see some of that hair disappear."

They stomped the snow off their boots, leaving them in the mudroom. Inside, they sat staring at the fire. Tadao brought cocktails—Dry Sack for her, watered-down cranberry juice for Gavin, a bowl of salt-free pretzels neither of them touched.

"I had a chat with Dr. Temple this morning." She sipped her sherry. "He said he might advise postponing the surgery."

"Yeah?"

"I told him he was full of shit, that I wanted to go ahead right now."

Gavin shook his head. "I've been living with this for a long time. Another week or so isn't going to kill me."

She stiffened against the back of the leather sofa. "I wish you wouldn't talk like that." When she looked at his face, she wanted to think that she was seeing what all daughters saw when they looked at their fathers. But the memories simply weren't there. Maybe that was what she was seeking now. If not history, then at least something dear, something precious. They didn't have that. Maybe there was still time. Would having the transplant bring a new intimacy?

It seemed a fanciful notion. A kidney was just an organ. A spare part, as Cody liked to call it. There wasn't any sort of mystical power in a kidney. And yet she kept thinking, because of what she gave him, he'd be healed.

He clearly had no inkling of her thoughts, because out of the clear blue he asked, "So what does Sam think of the boy?"

"Of Cody?" she asked stupidly.

"That would be the one." Gavin spoke with exaggerated patience and humor.

"He thinks Cody is angry and rebellious."

"So is this a phase the boy is going through, or is there a problem?"

She gazed at her father incredulously. "You really don't know, do you?"

"About raising a teenager? I don't have any experience at it, Michelle."

And she felt it again—the anger, the resentment. "It's both a phase and a problem."

"Maybe getting him together with Sam wouldn't be such a bad idea," Gavin suggested.

"Um, I haven't told Cody that Sam's his father." She swirled the ice in her tumbler. "Why didn't you ever tell me Sam moved back to Crystal City?"

"I didn't think you were interested in hearing that or anything else from me."

She sensed something more beneath his words, some judgment or evasion. She couldn't quite put her finger on it. "I could have done with a word of warning," she said.

He combed a splayed hand through his white hair. "Hell, honey, I guess I was afraid you wouldn't come if you knew Sam was here."

"I would have come anyway," she insisted. "I'm going to let Cody know about Sam this evening." Helplessly she watched the flames leaping in the grate, reflecting against the iron fireback. "I have no idea what he's going to think when I tell him."

"So how's Sam taking all this?" he asked.

"He says he wants to get to know Cody, but that's what's making me so insane. You can't know a kid in a few weeks. You have to raise a child from birth to truly know him."

"You believe that?"

"Yes."

"Then I don't know you? I can't know you?"

She gulped the rest of her drink. "We're talking about Cody."

"Fine, so talk."

"I just . . . don't understand what Sam expects. What if he wants something I can't give? Like more time with Cody?"

"Are you willing to allow that?"

"Of course not." The refusal flew from her, surprising her with its swiftness. Was she that settled in her ways? Certain that nothing unexpected could ever happen to her? Like a middle-aged matron, was she so inflexible that she couldn't imagine straying from a path she'd mapped out long ago?

"Brad and I have goals." She tried to convince herself as much as her father. "We've made commitments. We're building a life together, and I'm not about to change that just so Sam McPhee can get used to the novelty of having a son."

"Honey, believe me, it's not a novelty."

Something in the tone of his voice tugged at her, and she set down her glass. The mica lamps overhead cast radiant heat down into the gathering shadows of the room, and she couldn't help but think they resembled stage lights, showering over his broad shoulders, his magnificent hair, his face craggy with living and troubles. Was she looking at Gavin Slade the actor, or Gavin Slade the man?

"What do you mean, Daddy?"

"Knowing you've got a child somewhere in the world is like carrying a tube of nitroglycerine around. You're scared stiff all the time, scared you're going to drop it, or someone's going to jostle you and the world's going to explode."

"I'm not sure what this has to do with Sam."

"Maybe you should cut him some slack. Let him spend some time with Cody while you're here and see what happens."

"I was sort of hoping you'd spend time with Cody, too."

He wouldn't look at her. "He's not interested. What do I have in common with a sixteen-year-old kid?"

"You never know. Your airplanes?" She remembered the problem with Gavin's license and quickly changed the subject. "He likes the movies. You ought to give him a tour of the Lynwood."

"Okay, maybe I could screen an old movie or two for him."

The whole idea was, her dad should sit in there with him. But she stopped short of suggesting it.

"Always thought it'd be nice to renovate and reopen the place," he went on, surprising her. "I own the adjacent retail space, too. Seems a shame to let it all just sit there."

"It sounds like quite a project," she said. "But first things first," she said. "We'd better concentrate on getting both you guys well in this next week."

They were silent with their thoughts during dinner, perfectly prepared and served by Tadao. Eyeing the young man as she helped him clear the table, she wondered if he was good company for her dad, if he was more than an employee. As a teenager, Michelle had enjoyed the folksiness of the ranch help. Though it was always clear her father was the boss, there was a casual ease at Blue Rock she'd never known at her mother's house in Bel Air. At the ranch, they were like a big family. Though she had only lived a short time at the ranch, it was the only place she had ever really fit in. Despite being born in Southern California, she had never quite belonged there, never quite lived up to her mother's high style and standards. Once, long ago, she had asked her father why he had moved away from California, and he had said simply, "For the breathing room." One of the few things they had in common, she thought. There might have been more if Gavin hadn't—

She stopped herself. Vowed she would not dredge up all bitterness, old regrets.

After dinner, Tadao gave her a covered tureen of soup and a turkey sandwich for Cody. She thought she had done a pretty good job playing it cool in front of her father, but when she said good night, the last thing he said to her nearly made her drop the soup.

"Don't put it off any longer. Tell the boy tonight, okay?"

Chapter 17

Cody's mouth tasted rank when he woke up to find the evening news flickering in his face. He stared unseeing at the TV for a few minutes, trying to decide if his head hurt. Barely. When he held perfectly still, not stirring except to breathe, he didn't feel any pain at all.

Sam McPhee had given him some pills. The little brown bottle was on the counter. Maybe he'd take a couple tonight.

No, he told himself. Those were for Claudia. When he'd told her about his injury, her first question had been to ask what kind of pain pills the doctor had given him. She liked getting high on pills. Cody had done it with her once or twice, stealing some Darvons from Brad's sample kit. Brad was so lame, with his designer clothes and big plans, he never even noticed. Clueless, too, but that worked in Cody's favor. He could get away with a lot when Brad was around.

Last Friday, right before a school dance, he and Claudia had swallowed a couple of pills with mouthfuls of beer. The world had turned blurry and bright, and everything he said made Claudia laugh. He loved the way she laughed, shaking back her head with all those red curls and her voice going up and up with each syllable. She had a sexy laugh. He'd walked her home after the dance—his mom was a pain in the butt about not letting him drive unaccompanied at night.

On a storage bench in the darkened mudroom of Claudia's house, she had let him go almost all the way. Cody got a hard-on just thinking about those soft curves and soft lips. She had this amazing way of sucking his tongue that made him nuts. Her spicy-smelling perfume and her taste of Zima and Lifesavers got him higher than any pills could.

Inside the house, someone had flicked on a light, interrupting the magic. He knew Claudia would let him go all the way the next time. They just needed a little more privacy.

But he never got the chance. The very next day, Cody's mom had dragged him all the way out here to the middle of nowhere so he could work his butt off on some guy's ranch and get kicked in the head by a horse.

By the time his mom came in from the main house, he'd worked himself into a lousy mood. And she, of course, put on that chirpy smile of hers. "Tadao sent you soup and sandwiches. You hungry?"

He was starving after that nap. "I guess."

"Stay there. I'll bring your dinner on a tray."

"Okay."

"How's your head?"

"Hurts when I move it."

She banged around in the kitchenette for a few minutes, then walked into the den with a tray of soup in a mug, a sandwich, and a glass of milk.

"Thanks." For some reason, it annoyed him that there was a sprig of parsley floating on top of the soup and that she'd cut the sandwich into triangular halves. His mom was always doing stuff like that, trying to make a nice thing nicer.

Maybe it was because she was an artist. Once, when they'd moved to the new town house next door to Brad, Cody had taken a look at some of her old paintings and drawings. Incredible, wild stuff, tons of it, nothing like the ad layouts she did for work. He couldn't believe his own mother used to paint stuff like that. It was almost scary.

While he ate, his mom had the news on, but she didn't seem to be paying much attention. In fact, she seemed jumpy. Scared about the transplant thing, he figured. It was too gross to think about, but from the second she'd heard about her dad's sickness, she'd insisted on going through with it.

"I have to do this. I *want* to," she'd told him and Brad. "The transplant works best from a living, related donor—a blood relative."

Deep inside Cody lay the knowledge that his mom wasn't Gavin Slade's only blood relative. But when he thought about surgeons cutting him open, taking out a whole organ, for chrissakes, he couldn't even speak, much less volunteer as a donor. So he kept his mouth shut and let his mom be the martyr.

"You want seconds?" she asked.

"Nope, I'm full."

"Dessert? There's ice cream in the freezer, and a bag of cookies—"

"No *thanks*." His voice had a rude inflection, and she flinched, but he didn't care. After telling him to save her some of his pain pills, Claudia hadn't found much to talk about, and their long, awkward silence echoed in Cody's ears now.

His mom took the tray away and returned to the living room. Cody reached for the remote to turn the channel to MTV, but she intercepted him, grabbing the device and killing the power.

He glared at her, surprised and affronted. "What gives, Mom?"

"I need to talk to you about something."

"Yeah?" He was starting to feel bored already. Maybe she was feeling nervous about the surgery, and she wanted to say how much she loved him and all that shit in case something went wrong during the transplant. It was the last thing Cody wanted to discuss.

"Yes." She tucked one foot up under her in the chair and picked up a throw pillow, her right index finger fiddling with the tassels. "This is serious, Cody. I need you to pay attention."

He lifted both hands in an exaggerated shrug, even though it hurt his head. "Do I look like I'm going anywhere?"

"I, um, I need to talk to you about the man who fathered you."

Holy crap. Cody felt himself come to full alert. He forced himself to stay still on the sofa, his face expressionless and his voice bland when he said, "Yeah? You said he was just some cowboy, and you'd never seen him again."

"That's true. I mean, I thought it was true. But he's living here, Cody. In Crystal City. I had no idea where he was until I saw him Saturday night."

Oh, man. He didn't know what to do with himself, with his hands, with his eyes, with his mind. So his mouth said a lazy, "No kidding."

But his brain went into overdrive. He tried to picture the crowd at the rodeo arena. All he remembered from Saturday night was the girl named Molly Lightning. And a mass of people who looked like hicks and hillbillies.

"I wouldn't kid about this, Cody."

"So who's the guy?"

Her finger kept twirling the tassel, faster now. "It's . . . Sam. Sam McPhee."

"Whoa." The exclamation escaped him before he could stop it. His heartbeat sped up. A father. He had a father. Sam McPhee was his goddamned father.

It was too weird, knowing now, after all the years of imagining, who he was. Stranger still knowing Sam and his mom had been bonking each other as teenagers.

"Thanks a lot for never telling me, Mom."

"I didn't know how to tell you. It was a shock, seeing him so unexpectedly." She hugged the pillow up against her chest. "And really, we've been so busy, this is the first chance I've had."

Suddenly, in the place in his life where there had been a blank picture frame, a face showed up. A cowboy's face, tan and lean, some guy dressed in a plaid flannel shirt and Levi's. A guy with big hands and a screw-you attitude. A guy who made his voice go all serious while he was sewing Cody up with the same big hands he'd used to heft a wheelbarrow full of manure.

Christ. Sam McPhee. His father. There was an earthquake heaving up inside Cody. The world was rearranging itself, and he had no idea what it would look like when things settled.

"Cody?" His mother's voice was light, quavery. He

hoped like hell she wouldn't start bawling or trying to get him to talk about his feelings. "Is there anything . . . you want to say?" Her voice kept wobbling.

He wanted to say everything, and nothing. He wanted to yell at her for keeping this huge secret from him. He wanted to ask what was so goddamned wrong with him that he didn't deserve to know his father. He wanted to hide behind a wall and wait for the world to return to normal.

But most of all, he wanted to know the answer to one big burning question.

"So does he know . . . who I am?"

"Yes."

"Shit, you told him before you told me? Thanks a l—"

"I didn't tell him. He figured it out based on your age. Or, I guess it was your age. Might have been something else."

"What else?"

"You're alike in . . . subtle ways. The way you hold yourself sometimes, I suppose. Certain movements. It's hard to say." She started picking at the tassel. It was driving him crazy, the way she kept fidgeting. "But I imagine it was your age. He realized you were born just a few months after we . . . after I—"

"After he fucked you," Cody exploded.

He heard his mom draw in a breath, but he didn't look at her. Gripping the arm of the couch, he pushed himself up. Battling a wave of dizziness, he stalked down the hall to his room and slammed the door as hard as he could.

Damn it. Goddamn it to hell. *Now* what was he going to do?

Chapter 18

Oh, *that* went well, thought Michelle. With a savage tug, she jerked the stupid tassel off the stupid pillow. Then she tossed both pillow and tassel aside.

Her cheeks were on fire. Her insides—stomach, heart, throat—were all on fire.

After he fucked you.

Cody's words hung in the room. She couldn't hide from them. She couldn't make them not be true. She couldn't make them not hurt. Sure, he had much worse problems than using foul language, but the moment seemed to crystallize all their issues into a single, sharp hammer blow of a syllable.

She wanted to go to him, sit at the side of his bed, tell him she knew, she understood what a shock this must be, yet it didn't change anything between them—

But it did. It already had. She couldn't put things back the way they were.

Pulling her knees up to her chest, she stared at the blank screen of the TV, then at the wall shelves filled with old novels and knickknacks. She wondered if the knick-knacks had any meaning, or if Martha Stewart had been a guest here, putting dried flowers in rusty horseshoes and making an umbrella stand out of an old cowboy boot.

Cody's furious reaction had thrown the universe out of whack for her. He'd been rebellious lately, but in a strange way it had seemed like a manageable anger, not some out-of-control dark substance that hardened, like coal into diamond, into indestructible hate.

Dry-eyed, she forced herself to assess the situation. Minimize the problem. He was in shock over finding out about Sam, but the shock would fade, and he'd be back to his old self again. She and Cody would be here only a short time. After that, there would be no need to come back.

I just stopped by to drop off a kidney and save my dad's life. Then I'm out of here.

Sam claimed he wanted to know his son, to get involved, but his involvement ended the day he skipped town seventeen years ago. The only reason she had told Cody was that it felt deceptive not to. She didn't owe Sam a thing. He didn't owe her a thing.

And really, she had no business thinking about him.

She picked up the phone and dialed Brad's number. He needed to hear this, too. Would he worry? Feel threatened?

Early on in their relationship, he had asked about Cody's father, and she'd told him exactly what she always told Cody—a youthful mistake, they'd never been in contact, she had no idea where he was.

That had all changed now.

Sam McPhee was real and rock solid. He had a career and a ranch and a business partner and the respect of a town that had once kicked him in the teeth.

He had large gentle hands and a way of watching her that brought warmth to forbidden places inside her.

She hung up the phone when Brad's answering service picked up. He'd always hated answering machines, so he paid strangers to take his messages for him. She couldn't imagine telling a stranger what had just happened. What would she say? "Tell Brad to call me, because I just told my son who his real father is, and now he hates me."

The phone rang, startling her. She grabbed it, praying it would be Brad. He'd never been the sort of guy who popped up just when she needed him, but she kept thinking he would be one day.

"Hello?"

"Michelle, it's Sam."

God. Oh, God. "I don't want to talk to you right now."

"Is this a bad time?"

"The worst." Her heart pounded. Her throat ached with the things she wanted to tell him.

"Cody's all right, isn't he?"

"Of course he's not all right—" She broke off. Sam meant the injury. "His head's fine. He had a nap, and a pretty good dinner, and he's in his room right now."

"Then why did you say he's not all right?"

She swallowed hard, and it hurt, as if something enormous was stuck halfway down. "I told him about us. I told him you're his biological father."

Silence. In the background on his end, a dog barked. The Border collie. The morning she'd gone out there, she had noticed that Sam had an unconscious, affectionate way with the dog, idly stroking her head and ears without even seeming to know he was petting her. He was probably doing that right now.

"How'd he take it?" Sam finally asked, his voice low.

"He's not a happy camper. After he said the word 'fuck' to his mother, he walked out and closed himself in his room."

"I'm coming over."

"No, Sam, you can't—"

His end of the line went dead. She couldn't stop him now. She felt helpless. Should she tell Cody that Sam was coming over? No; then he might barricade the door, or worse, run off somewhere.

She settled for straightening up the bungalow, doing the most mundane of chores. A fresh hand towel in the bathroom. A light on over the front door. Minutes dragged by, and she ran out of things to do. Restless, she took out her sketchbook and favorite pencil—a Primacarb Number One. Accustomed to bringing her work with her from the office, she never went anywhere without a sketchbook. Even though she had given up painting, she still thought in pictures, and she never knew when an idea for an ad design or concept would hit her.

Her pencil swirled and danced over the page, and she felt a tug of sensation, something she hadn't felt in a long time. Nerves, she told herself. That's what it was. And when she saw what had emerged onto the paper, she knew it was nothing more. The image she had outlined was icy cold, a vineyard everyone had seen before on a dozen wine labels. It came from her mind's eye but not from her heart. Perfect for one of their big winery accounts.

She shut the book and put it back on the table. A few minutes later, a knock sounded at the door. She went to Cody's room and said, "Sam's here."

No response. He probably had his Discman on, fitting the headphones over the dressing on his head.

Sam took his boots off at the door. He didn't smile when he greeted her. He just sort of stared, those eyes probing, seeing her in a way she didn't think anyone else ever had. Finally, he said, "You look awful."

"Thanks. I'm having a swell evening." She gestured at the fridge. "Can I get you something to drink?"

"Not right now, thanks. Where's Cody?"

"In his room." She indicated the door.

Sam didn't hesitate; that was the first thing she noticed. She had always hesitated when it came to dealing with Cody. She tended to stop, weigh the options, rehearse the scenario in her head, and proceed with caution. Sam plunged right in. Of course, he had a lot less to lose than Michelle did. Sam couldn't lose what he'd never had.

He knocked on the door and said, "Cody, it's Sam. Your mother and I want to talk to you."

Your mother and I.

Michelle had never thought she'd hear those words, not in the context of her own life. There had never been a unit known as "your mother and I." The phrase conjured up images and yearnings Michelle didn't want—a partnership, a union . . . a dream she once had.

Cody's reply put the sentimental thought into perspective: "I got nothing to say to either of you."

At this point, she generally let him be, let him chill out. But Sam didn't know Cody's implacable moods. He put his hand on the knob. "I don't recall giving you that option. Now, you can either come out here or I'll come in there. Either way, it happens in the next five seconds."

"Or what? You'll spank me?"

Sam twisted the doorknob, and Michelle was surprised it didn't come off in his hand. He looked perfectly calm as he strode into Cody's room. The bedroom was done in muted plaids and stripes, like an upscale resort hotel. Cody lay on the bed, his hands clenched into fists, his eyes full of hate as he watched Sam.

Michelle stood in the doorway and held her breath.

"I'd never hit you." Sam kept his voice soft and low, the way he always did when he was angry. That was one of the things Michelle remembered about him. The madder he got, the quieter he got. "I'd never hit anyone. But I also don't take no for an answer. So why not get up off your butt and get into the living room?"

"Maybe I don't feel like it."

A small, evil part of Michelle took pernicious delight in this exchange. In the past she had been the one on the receiving end of Cody's defiance. Finally, someone else had to hear it. Sam stood like a shield between Cody and Michelle, absorbing the boy's contempt as if it were nothing.

"So you want us to camp out in here?" He moved Cody's suitcase off the luggage bench and had a seat. "Fine with me."

Cody didn't say a word, but levered himself up from the bed, marched out of the room, and plunked himself down in an armchair in the living room. He didn't look at either Sam or Michelle. She was amazed that Sam got him to come out.

"I guess I'll start, then." Sam lowered himself to the sofa, and she did the same, folding her arms, unconsciously protecting herself.

"First of all, you've got to know this, Cody. Finding out about you is the biggest thing that's ever happened to me."

This was a man who had been a six-time national rodeo champion. A man who had saved lives, delivered babies, told people a loved one had died. And yet he could still say this was a bigger deal.

Cody stared straight ahead, stone-faced. And Lord, even now, startlingly good-looking, a fallen angel with a mended head.

"Second thing," Sam continued, "is that if you ever talk to your mother like that again, you'll be sorry you ever found me."

Cody turned to her, contempt written in hard lines around his mouth. "Great, Mom. Already running to him and telling him private stuff."

"I don't blame you for wanting to keep it private. I'd be ashamed, too, if I said stuff like that to the woman who raised me." Though Sam's voice was mild, there was an edge to his words, an edge that was sharp with warning.

Watching Cody, she could see that he sensed the sharpness, too. He was out of his league here. Sam had grown up fighting his way through the rodeo, through school, through seventeen years of battles she could only imagine. Cody's attitude might have the power to hurt her, but to a man like Sam it was nothing.

"So what are you doing here, anyway?" Cody asked.

"Same thing as you are. Trying to figure out what to do next." Sam crossed one foot over his knee. He wore flecked gray thermal socks. Bits of snow still clung to the cuffs of his jeans. "I have figured out what not to do. And that's mouth off to your mother. I won't tolerate it, Cody. Do you understand?"

Their gazes locked. From the very start, there was no question who was going to win. Within a few seconds, Cody shrugged and looked away. "Whatever."

"Your last outburst was just that," Sam said. "Your last. Believe me, I know what you're thinking. You're thinking I'm just some old guy. I have no authority over you."

"You don't," Cody pointed out.

"You know what?" Sam leaned back congenially. "You're absolutely right. I won't take you over my knee. But I can tell you this. Don't be such a little shit to the person who's put in sixteen years and nine months raising you."

Cody did his best to look bored, but she could tell he was fascinated by all this. "Why not?"

Still maintaining a relaxed pose, Sam nailed him with a stare that would wither grass, and he spoke softly, with deadly control. "Don't ask me that again."

Michelle unfolded her arms and studied them both, and in a flash, she saw an uncanny resemblance. They looked so much alike she was surprised the whole town hadn't figured it out by now.

"All right," Cody said at last, keeping his chin up despite his capitulation. "Whatever."

"Well," Michelle said, trying to dissipate the tension. "I suppose we have to decide what's going to happen next."

"You're going to finish this operation thing and then we're going back home," Cody said.

"It could happen that way," she conceded. "Is that what you want?"

"Why would I want anything else?"

"No reason, maybe," Sam said, and she was glad he spoke up, because she couldn't think of anything more to say. "But then again, maybe there is a reason."

Silence. And sadness. Sam's words filled Michelle with a huge ache. Because in her heart she knew they had both made cocoons of themselves. And somehow, it had diminished them. No strings, no connections. *Safe from love, safe from hurt.*

"So what are you talking about? You think I want you to take me to baseball games and buy me stuff and all that crap?" Cody demanded. "I'm a little old for that."

"Good. I can't stand baseball. Hate shopping." Sam drilled him again. That stare was powerful. Where did he learn to do that? Michelle wondered.

"So here's the deal," Sam continued. "If you feel okay in the morning, and it's all right with your mom, you come out to my place. See how that foal's doing. Maybe we'll talk some, maybe we won't. We'll just see."

Cody sat stiff and silent for a while. "What if I don't feel like it?"

"Then you don't come." But Michelle and Sam had both seen it. The spark in the boy's face when Sam mentioned the horse. "You stay here and . . . do whatever it is you do."

More silence. Cody was as still as a stone, but she knew a battle raged inside him. Finally, he said, "Can I go to my room now?"

Sam's face turned hard with a silent demand.

Finally, reluctantly, Cody added, "Um, please?"

Wonders never cease, thought Michelle. He asked permission.

Sam looked at her. "Michelle?"

"See you in the morning, Cody," she said. "You can let me know then if you need a ride to Sam's place."

Chapter **19**

S am watched Cody leave the room, noting the studied slouch, the hands jammed in his pockets. Despite the attitude, he was still a good-looking kid, and Sam had thought so even before he'd figured out who fathered him.

He wanted to ask Michelle what Cody had been like as a baby, a toddler, a little boy, but each time he thought of all those lost years, he nearly choked on rage and frustration. Those years were gone and there was no way to get them back. But that didn't stop the hunger in him to know.

"What's going through his head right now?" he asked softly.

"In a minute, probably Marilyn Manson on his Discman. I hate his music. And I hate it that I hate his music, because I love music."

"Believe it or not, I understand what you're saying."

That coaxed a fleeting, weary smile from her. Sam knew he should go, but he didn't want to. Leaning forward, he picked up a sketchbook off the table. "May I?"

"Sure. It's work, though. I doubt you'll find it very interesting."

He'd always liked looking at her drawings. When they were young, she'd had the sort of talent that made people do a double take. They'd look, then look again, and then the low-voiced comments would start.

But when he opened the sketchbook, he didn't see the wild, emotional abstractions he'd been expecting. These were studies, mostly of inanimate objects—furniture and running shoes and grapes and shower nozzles—and a chilly, anatomical study of a winter merganser in flight. Each was rendered with remarkable control and perfection, as if a computer had done it.

Michelle shifted on the couch, tucking her feet up under her. "I told you, it's work. I'm a graphic designer."

"You're damned good," he said with total honesty. "I can't believe you quit painting. You were so passionate about it."

"Sam, I was eighteen years old. I was passionate about everything—about my art, about horses . . . about you. The trouble was, life outlasted passion. Some people call it growing up."

Her statement thumped into him like a dull blow. The firelight flickered off her cheek, illuminating a haunting sadness in her face. He didn't like seeing this wistful melancholy in her. But he sure as hell didn't know how to make it go away.

"Aw, damn it, Michelle." He moved closer to her on the sofa. "I didn't mean to upset you." And because it was late and he was on autopilot, he did the next thing quite naturally. His arm extended across the back of the seat and went around her.

In the space of a second, she softened against him, and he couldn't believe the rush it gave him to feel her like this, pliant and giving. But only a heartbeat later, she seemed to realize what she'd done and pulled away. He let out his breath in relief. His life was finally on track, and getting involved with Michelle Turner could cause a train wreck. Nobody in his right mind wanted a train wreck.

"I'm all right, really," she said with a quaver in her voice. "Things've been difficult lately."

"That's putting it mildly. But you and your dad are strong. You'll do great with this procedure. I had a talk with Maggie Kehr today, and she accepted my personal reference. The surgery's going forward as scheduled."

She shut her eyes for a long moment. "Thanks, Sam." Then she opened her eyes and looked at him. "And . . . thank you for coming over tonight."

"So is Cody what parents like to call a 'handful'?"

"Oh, yeah. Year Sixteen has been a real picnic."

"I got that idea."

"Let's see. He came home the first week of school with a pierced navel and a cigarette habit. He didn't even try hiding either one from me. I think he liked seeing the effect self-mutilation had on me."

"I imagine he did. What's the point of piercing something if no one notices?"

"And your suggestion would be?"

"I guess I'd ignore it until he injures himself zipping his pants. Then let the wound heal over."

"And the smoking?"

"That's tougher. Maybe the smell will gross out some girl and he'll quit."

"Cigarettes are one of his girlfriend's major food groups."

"He needs a new girlfriend, then."

"Oh, and my telling him so is going to work? Sam, you're not that naive."

He *had* been once, long ago. He'd believed in a love so strong no outside force, certainly no parental disapproval, could interfere. It had taken Gavin Slade precisely one evening to lay waste to that belief.

Sam pushed away the thought and concentrated on Cody. "Does he play any sports?"

"Skateboarding and snowboarding. Even a smoker's lungs can handle both. Here's the deal, Sam. I haven't been the most perfect parent in the universe, but I haven't been awful, either. Something happens to a kid who's growing up, something the Dr. Spock books don't mention. The kid becomes his own person. And sometimes that might be a person who does things that drive you nuts, and nothing you can do will stop him."

"Is it possible he *wants* to be stopped?"

"You mean is he looking for limits? Of course. Do I draw the line? Of course." She stood up, went to the window, stuck her hands in her back pockets. "Does he step over the line, of course."

Clearly this was familiar territory to Michelle. But there were hidden facets she wasn't seeing.

"You know, I reckon it's none of my business, but it appears to me that you're so concerned with making the kid happy, giving him some kind of life that looks good on paper, that you're forgetting something."

She turned to face him, defenses going up like an invisible wall. "And you've figured this out based on knowing us three days?"

He sent her a lopsided grin. "Hey, it's a gift."

She rolled her eyes.

"Seriously, Michelle, it's my job to figure out somebody's problem based on a fifteen-minute office visit. Sometimes that's all I get—it happens a lot around here, where most people don't pay regular visits to the doctor and don't follow up. I have fifteen minutes to work on a patient's trouble. In the past five years I've had a lot of practice."

She folded her arms beneath her breasts and eyed him warily. "All right, you have my attention. Tell me your expert opinion, Doctor."

Shit. Why was he doing this?

He planted his elbows on his knees. "My opinion as a doctor is this—Cody's like a lot of kids I see. The more rope you give him, the more ways he finds to tangle himself up. He needs a shorter rein."

"He didn't come with a how-to manual," she said. "That's the thing about raising a kid, Sam. You have to figure it out as you go along."

He felt himself teetering on a precipice. Common sense told him to pull back. His heart made him dive in. "You know as well as any doctor that kids who have unhappy parents wind up a lot more troubled than kids whose parents are relatively content. It doesn't have anything to do with how much money they earn or the sort of house they live in. It has to do with their perception of their place in the world."

"Oh, you're good, Sam. Let's make it my fault."

"Damn it, Michelle—" He was talking himself into deep shit, so he stopped and studied her, petite and slim, unsmiling and coldly beautiful as she stared at the black squares of the window. Then he glanced at the sketchbook on the table. And finally, he stood, taking a wad of keys from his pocket.

"Michelle, get your coat. I want to show you something."

"But Cody—"

"We won't go far."

She pulled on a jacket and boots while he did the same. The night wind slashed at them as they stepped outside. A high three-quarter moon spread a frozen blue glow over the area, and lights from the main house fanned across the yard. Sam led the way along the darkened drive past the cluster of bunkhouses. At the last one, he turned and waded over the unshoveled walk to the front door.

Angling his wad of keys toward the light, he selected one, old and worn, nearly lost in the mass of other keys. "Wonder if it still fits."

Michelle stood silently by as he inserted the key. It stuck, but that was mainly from the cold. Then it turned, and he opened the door, stepping into a room he hadn't seen in seventeen years.

Ghosts haunted this moonlit place. The presence of sheet-draped furniture heightened the eerie effect. He flicked a switch, and the light came on. "Remember this?"

"What would you do if I said no?"

"Call you a liar." He plucked a sheet off a threadbare chair, and one off a nearby table.

"Sam, I don't see the point—Oh."

He watched her take in the scene, wishing he knew her better, wishing he knew what she was feeling. He'd counted on Gavin Slade having a hidden streak of sentimentality, and he'd been right. The old man had left this place alone, a shrine to the daughter who had walked out of his life.

"It's exactly the way it was when I used to work here." Michelle's words made little frozen puffs in the air.

Gavin had equipped the bungalow especially for her.

It had a drafting table, easels and clipboards, tons of canvas and jars of brushes, tubes of paint. Everything was still there, left to atrophy with time and neglect. Sam removed another sheet to reveal an old-fashioned sofa, covered in flea-bitten velveteen.

The sight of it gave him a flash of memory so hot that he nearly shoved Michelle down on the musty cushions. He remembered the feel of her beneath him, the way her legs went around him, the sound of her breath in his ear. He remembered what it felt like to be buried to the hilt inside her. He remembered what it was like to feel a love so pure and strong that it burned like a flame that would never go out.

Jesus. It was eighteen degrees in here, and he was starting to sweat. He cast a furtive glance at Michelle to see if she noticed.

She was blushing red to the tips of her ears.

"I wonder if it happened there," he said. softly, recklessly. "I wonder if that's where we made Cody."

She caught her breath with a little hiccup. "No. It was the boathouse. It . . . happened at the boathouse."

The place by the river had been their secret retreat, where they could steal away and find privacy together. Suddenly Sam was inundated with memories of that summer. It was the one time in his life when he saw everything with perfect clarity, when he felt absolutely certain he was going in the right direction, absolutely certain he knew what the outcome would be.

Funny thing about life. It had a way of spinning you around, shooting you off in a totally different direction, like a wild ride on a greenbroke horse. You had no idea where you were heading until you landed ass-first in the dirt.

"Sam, why did you bring me here?"

I keep remembering what it was like to be with you. He gritted his teeth to keep from saying it. Instead, he said, "There's a lot of waiting around involved in transplantation and recovery. You could be painting while you're here."

"No." She spoke swiftly, decisively. Almost defensively.

"Why not?"

"I draw and paint for work. As long as I have this enforced sabbatical, why would I do anything that resembles work?"

He wanted to say that the paintings she used to do were so different from the sketches in her book that they didn't resemble work at all, but a gifted mind and eye and hand creating something extraordinary.

He didn't say anything. She was hard to read, this grown-up Michelle. One thing was certain—she was in a skittish state, and he didn't seem to be helping matters.

He could feel himself moving fast toward a conviction that there were things he and Michelle should explore. What would it be like to get to know her again, to look at her through adult eyes? He could see the yearning in her eyes, the shadows of unfulfilled dreams, and he knew he couldn't dismiss her from his life when the transplant was over.

"Besides," she said, picking up a frozen paint tube, "the supplies are spoiled."

"You could replace them easily enough. Next trip to Missoula, you could lay in a bunch of paint and brushes."

"I'm really not interested, Sam."

He let her words sink in. "We'd better get out of here before we freeze to death."

He walked her back to her door and stood there for a moment, studying her in the glow from the porch light.

212 / Susan Wiggs

Suddenly he felt like a trespasser. "I've got to go, Michelle."

"'Night, Sam."

"'Night." His hand, without consulting his head, came up and cupped her cheek.

She didn't move. "Your hand is cold."

"Your cheek is warm." He leaned down and kissed it, soft skin and a subtle fragrance of perfume and snow. "I guess I'll be seeing you around . . . or not," he added. Then he walked to his truck, resisting the urge to whistle.

Chapter 20

When Michelle rushed back inside the house, she pushed aside the kitchen curtain to catch a last glimpse of Sam. The moon, a cold white smile, threw a stream of light over him, and he held up one hand in farewell. Embarrassed to be caught, she dropped the curtain and leaned against the counter. She was shaking all over. Shaking with memories and wanting and, most of all, with fear. Sam McPhee was part of her past, part of a past she had traveled far, far away from, and she shouldn't be having this explosive chemical reaction to him. But he was so bound up in things that were important—Cody and her art and Montana and Gavin—that she felt both wildly attracted to him and terrified of him.

She checked on Cody, finding the door to his room firmly closed. Then she brewed a cup of tea, using two bags to make it stronger, and when she sat down on the sofa, her hand went to the phone.

After two rings, she was tapping her foot with impatience. He picked up on the fourth ring. "Brad Lovell."

"It's me."

"Hiya, babe." He sounded warm and comfortable.

She smiled, her insides watery with relief. "What are you doing? Are you busy?"

"Going over some papers. Looks like we'll be able to afford a condo on Kauai after all—"

"Brad?"

"Yeah, babe?"

"I have to tell you something."

"What, you'd rather find a place on Maui?"

"No, nothing like that." God. When did he get the impression she wanted a condo in Hawaii in the first place?

"What is it, Michelle?"

She blew on her tea, took a sip. "It's about Cody."

"Shit. Is he in trouble already?"

It bugged her no end that Brad's first assumption was that Cody got in trouble. It bugged her even more that, basically, he was right.

"Well, there's trouble . . . and there's trouble."

"So you want to tell me, or are we going to play twenty questions?"

She took another sip, then set her cup down. "It's about his . . . about the man who fathered him."

"The cowboy."

"Yes. Um, he lives in Crystal City now. The other night I . . . ran into him." She made a swift decision not to explain the details.

"So did he recognize you?"

She was a little insulted by the implication. "Yes. And

it didn't take him long to put two and two together and figure out about Cody."

"Silence.

"Brad?"

"I keep waiting to hear you say you're going on *Oprah* with all this."

She smiled in spite of herself. "Right. Anyway, we—I told Cody tonight. He wasn't thrilled, but I think he's still getting used to the idea."

"What about you, Michelle? Are you thrilled?"

She felt a sting of guilt, because she wanted to be able to say that seeing Sam again meant nothing to her. That she felt nothing.

"I was shocked, I guess. Surprised. I never thought I'd see him again. But it turns out he did all right for himself, became a doctor, and he's a partner in a horse ranch about ten miles from here. His name is Sam McPhee."

"Do you think he wants something from you?"

She thought about the way Sam had touched her, the way he'd said good night. A shiver passed over her. "Like . . . what?"

"Like visitation rights or something."

A terrible chill touched the base of her neck. "I have no idea. It all came about so fast. He hasn't asked for a thing." *Yet.* But tonight she had seen the questions in his eyes.

"Well, if he gets some idea that playing the dad is all fun and games, remind him of what college tuition costs these days."

"It's not a matter of finance."

"Sweetheart, everything is a matter of finance."

"Not this. I'm going to let Cody get used to the idea and . . . see what happens. Oh, God, Brad, what if he wants

to be with his father more than he wants to be with me?"
She poured her fears into the receiver.

"Why would he want that?" Brad sounded genuinely
baffled. "Look, don't worry. You're good to Cody. He loves
you. He's just having a tough time right now, like any
kid." Brad changed the subject easily enough, and she let
him, grateful for once to hear him ponder the merits of
Kauai over Maui. After making the appropriate murmurs,
she said good-bye and hung up.

The conversation left her with a vague, ineffable sense
of dissatisfaction. Why can't Brad be as decisive about us
as he is about vacation property? she wondered.

Restless, she finished her tea and made a second cup,
knowing the caffeine would keep her up, but she was past
caring. For a long time, she gazed at the small framed picture of her mother, which she carried in her briefcase
everywhere she went. Sharon Turner stood swathed in a
Dior gown, her hair and makeup perfect as she blew a
kiss to someone behind the camera. "Miss you, Mom,"
Michelle whispered. "I sure as heck would like to hear
your voice right now." She drummed her hands on the
phone. She knew who she was going to call. She knew
she'd probably regret it, but she was going to do it anyway. She punched in the number and waited.

On the third ring, a voice said, "Hello?"

"Natalie, sorry to call so late. It's me."

"Michelle!" she squealed in unfeigned delight.

"Are you busy?" Michelle asked, though she knew
that whatever Natalie was doing would come to a halt, because she was that sort of friend.

"I've been practicing arpeggios on my cello. Very exciting. But I love house-sitting at your place. Awesome
hot tub. Now *you*, sweetie! What's happened? How's it
going?"

Aside from Cody and Brad, Natalie was the only one Michelle had told about the transplant. It wasn't the sort of thing to be discussed with casual work acquaintances. And with Gavin Slade for a father, Michelle had learned to keep quiet lest the media sense a story.

"I'm all set to go into the hospital Saturday for one more procedure. If that checks out, we'll get a thumbs-up for surgery on Monday."

"When's Brad going over? Will he meet you at the hospital in Missoula?"

Soft leather creaked as she shifted position on the sofa. "Brad and I had a long talk about this before I left. I can't decide what I need from him. Maybe I don't even need him to come at all."

"Oh, for Pete's sake. You're taking this I-can-cope-on-my-own crap too far. Of course he needs to come."

"If Brad's around, I'll worry about what he's doing and thinking, pacing the halls of a hospital in a strange city. I'll go nuts wondering if he and Cody are getting along. It might be better to let him stay in Seattle, keep him posted by phone. Anyway, he's on standby. He promised that if I decide I want him with me, he'll drop everything and come."

"Brad's never dropped a thing in his life. Except maybe hints that I should take a hike."

There was a grain of truth in that. Brad and Natalie drove each other insane. "My dad and I are prepared. Everything will be fine."

"You're going to save your father's life. I'm getting a rush thinking about this."

"Don't knock yourself out, Natalie. It's just a surgical procedure."

"Just? *Just?* Not hardly, sweetie. I know you don't believe in this stuff, Michelle, but it's real. You've got to think about the spiritual aspect of it. You're giving life to the father who gave you life."

"I'm giving a kidney to the father who gave me a monthly check."

"No, listen, you have to listen." Michelle could picture Natalie sitting forward in that in-your-face way of hers. She wondered what color her friend's hair was tonight. Natalie had discovered hair mascara and hadn't been the same since. "There is a deeper meaning to this. It's not just plumbing."

"Natalie, it *is*. And thank God that it is, because that means it can be done at all. If it required magic and miracles, we'd be in big trouble."

"Okay, at least think about this. Physiologically, it *is* just plumbing. But you have to stay open to the possibility that something more is going to happen to you. Something amazing. You're going to connect with your father on a *cellular* level."

Michelle laughed, trying not to spray tea. "Yeah, Nat, that's the part I'm really looking forward to."

"You wait and see. How are you and your dad getting along?"

"I hate to disappoint you, but we're like a couple of cordial strangers. He's embarrassed and apologetic about the whole thing. Like he committed a faux pas by getting sick. And now that we're together again, it's . . ." She paused, feeling a sting of regret. "Let's just say there's been no cellular connection."

"There will be. I bet he went bananas over Cody."

This time she almost choked. "Natalie," she gasped into the phone, "you're killing me."

"What? Your dad's never seen Cody. It must be wonderful, bringing them together."

"It's like bringing together Johnny Depp and Charlton Heston. Cody's being horrible, my dad doesn't know what to make of him, and they're both inches from exploding."

"Oh, Michelle. I'm sorry. Let me talk to the Cody-boy." She had known him since the day he was born—literally. As Michelle's birthing coach, Natalie was the one who, sobbing as hard as Michelle was, had cut the umbilical cord. She decided then and there that she loved him, and her love hadn't wavered since.

"He's asleep. He had a little accident."

"*Accident?* You bitch, why didn't you call me?"

"It was minor. He cut his head."

"How?"

"On . . . a horse's hoof."

"Hold the goddamned phone, Michelle. You're telling me he got kicked in the head by one of your father's horses?"

"Actually, he got kicked in the head by one of *his* father's horses."

"Michelle!" She could picture Natalie now, totally agitated, pacing up and down in her designer living room, shrieking into the phone. "Do you mean to tell me the cowboy's there?"

She had never told her any more than she told Brad or Cody. "He lives in the area now."

"*Get out.* Did you know he was there?"

"No, it was a complete surprise. He's actually a physician now."

Silence. Complete and utter stunned silence. It was rare, a totally quiet Natalie, and Michelle grinned, enjoying the novelty of it.

"Holy goddamned horseshit," she said at last. "So let me get this straight. The no-account cowpoke who knocked you up came back to town and is now a respected citizen and doctor?"

"That's about it."

"And your dad never thought to tell you?"

"We never spoke, Natalie."

"Okay, get to the good part. Is the cowboy doctor married?"

"No."

"Involved?"

"I don't know."

"If he was, you'd know. What did he and Cody say when you told them?"

"It's . . . complicated."

"Fine. I'm coming."

"What?"

"Probably take me a day and a half in the Volkswagen."

"Natalie, you can't—"

"I said, I'm *coming*." She slammed down the phone.

Though she knew it was fruitless, Michelle hit redial a couple of times, but she got the expected voice-mail pickup.

"Nat, I've got enough going on without you showing up," she said, knowing her friend was ignoring her as she flew around the town house, flinging mismatched, inappropriate clothes into a woven Costa Rican shoulder bag. "I think," Michelle said, speaking to the tape, "there's such a thing as being *too* good a friend." She went on in this vein, trying to dissuade Natalie, but she knew it was useless.

When she hung up the phone, she felt strange and sort of disoriented. She was happy Natalie was coming. She was dismayed that Natalie was coming. She couldn't make up her mind how she felt. But one thing was certain. Natalie was the sort of person who got everything out in the open. And she knew Michelle better than anyone else in the universe.

Natalie would take one look at Michelle when Sam was around, and she'd *know*. Natalie would know that Michelle couldn't stop thinking about him, and that she had no idea what to do about him.

Michelle kept reminding herself that she had a life. She had Cody and Brad and her career. That was what she needed to focus on. That, and getting through the surgery.

She lay down on the sofa, shut her eyes, and suddenly the ideas started coming. There was a part of her, a wild, out-of-control part, that had some very explicit ideas of what to do about Sam McPhee, and if she knew what was good for her, she'd ignore them.

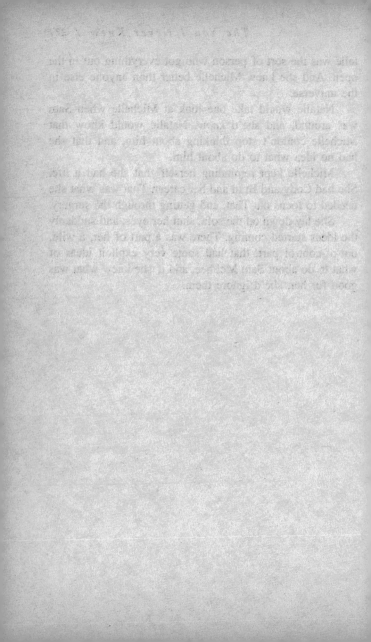

Wednesday

Chapter 21

C ody was glad his mom didn't demand some big explanation when he said he wanted to go to Sam's in the morning. All he had to tell her was that his head felt fine, he'd wear a hat, and he wanted to see the foal he'd helped deliver.

Her face took on that tight, nervous expression she got when she suspected he was up to something, but she drank her coffee in thoughtful silence. He wondered what she was thinking. Then he decided he didn't really want to know.

Cody waited, stiff and apprehensive, while she called Lonepine. But she didn't talk to Sam. She talked to that Indian guy, Edward Bliss. Edward was okay, kind of goofy but not too bad. He said it was fine to come, so by nine o'clock Cody was jumping out of the Range Rover and heading for the barn. The dog—Sprout? No, Scout—came churning across the snow to accompany him.

He heard his mom calling stuff after him—keep his hat on, call if he started to feel bad, all that crap—but he simply waved without turning. It was rude to blow her off, but if he didn't walk away, she'd sit there for an hour telling him be careful of this, watch out for that, and he wasn't up for maternal lectures this morning.

"Hello," he called as he stepped into the barn. Scout trotted around, sniffing loudly, acting important. The central breezeway was dim and a little warmer than outside thanks to some heat lamps hanging from the rafters.

He poked his head into the cluttered office. "Anyone here?"

No one in sight. He figured Sam was probably at work, and Edward was either out on the range somewhere or still in his cabin across the way. The Border collie found a heap of old blankets by the wood-burning stove and curled into a ball for a nap.

"Excellent," Cody said under his breath. It felt good to be alone, away from everybody. He didn't like people hovering over him.

Outside the office, he put on the boots he'd worn the other day. He picked up a set of tan coveralls and stepped into them. Stomping his feet to warm them, he was glad there wasn't a mirror around, because he was sure he looked like a complete dork. As he pulled on a pair of gloves, he quit thinking about how he looked. He wanted to see the mare and her foal.

The birthing stall had its own set of heat lamps in all four corners. The light from them fell at an angle over the mare and the baby, and for a second Cody gawked at them with a hitch in his throat. Sylvia stood calmly in the middle of the stall. She made a noise, like someone clearing her throat, when she spotted Cody. It was a friendly sound. At least, he was pretty sure it was friendly. Then she used her big muzzle to nudge at the foal, which was sleeping curled up like a kitten near her feet. The little one lifted its head, then staggered up, all wobbly. First it splayed out its front legs, then its hind legs, and after a minute it figured out how to get up on all fours. Cody was tempted to help, but Sam had said it was best to let the baby get up on its own.

It lurched against its mother, lips nibbling comically at her belly. She nuzzled it some more, twisting back to guide it to her udder. After a while, the foal stuck its head in the right place. Cody had never expected the sound of nursing to be audible, but it was—sucking, swallowing, gurgling. He'd probably be embarrassed if anyone else was around, but he had the moment all to himself, so he leaned on the stall door and grinned.

The soft morning light, the little drift of steam from the mare's nostrils, the funny sucking sound made by the foal and the way its skinny legs splayed out. Aunt Natalie—she wasn't his real aunt but his mom's best friend—would get all gushy at this point. But hell, Natalie got gushy over Hallmark commercials on TV.

When he'd talked to Claudia last night, he'd tried to describe what it was like seeing a foal being born, but she'd just said "Gross" and started nagging him about the pain pills. He sort of wanted to tell her about finding his father, but he couldn't figure out a way to bring up the topic. Sometimes he wished Claudia was the kind of friend he could tell this stuff to, but the fact was, she never really seemed interested in heavy personal stuff. She was too into having a good time, and when Cody was with her, that's what he wanted, too. But sometimes he wondered what it would be like to have someone he trusted, someone he could really talk to, because some days, like today, he had news burning a hole in him.

Maybe he couldn't unload about Sam, but he'd try to find a camera somewhere, take some pictures of the horses to show Claudia. The filly was so goddamned cute, how could anyone not want to see it?

His mom used to draw awesome pictures of horses. He thought of the paintings stacked in the closet of her study at home. The large, flat folder was filled with old sketches and watercolor and acrylic studies. When he was little, he had asked her about them, paging reverently through the stack and regarding the horse drawings with astonished admiration. "What are these, Mom? Did you do these?"

"Years ago, baby." She always used to called him baby, sometimes even slipped and did so now. "I don't have time for that kind of drawing anymore. I'm too busy drawing for work."

"I like these better than work."

She'd looked at him with big, sad eyes and tousled his hair. "So did I, baby. So did I."

She had never said much more about those pictures, but Cody used to look at them in secret sometimes. Now that he'd seen his grandfather's ranch, he knew where those drawings came from. Horses and mountains and a rushing river. A tall fir tree next to a salt lick. A nest of loons in a marsh, the still water mirroring a snow-peaked mountain. They were all pictures made while she was at Blue Rock Ranch.

Sam's mare and foal would have fit right in with those pictures. His mom could have made a hell of a drawing of those two. But she had given up painting when he was a baby, and he had no memory of her doing anything but agency work. Still, she kept her old pictures.

One Fourth of July when he was about ten, Cody had been awakened by the boom of fireworks over Elliott Bay. He'd gone looking for his mom, and he'd found her in her home office, the drawings spread out on the floor. She was drinking a glass of wine and silently crying. Disconcerted, Cody had crept back to his room.

Now he knew the source of her memories and her sadness. When she had lived at Blue Rock Ranch all those years ago, she'd met Sam McPhee.

His father. His goddamned father.

Cody scowled the thought away. He actually did some work, cleaning the lines and pans of the watering device. The contraption served all the stalls, filling with fresh water when one of the horses pressed its tongue against a bar in the center. He filled the wheelbarrow with manure from empty stalls and hauled it outside. He kept stopping to check on the mare and foal.

After a while, the filly quit nursing. The mare started doing motherly things, like sniffing it all over, giving it a lick here and there. Cody wondered if he'd be welcome in the stall. The kick in the head had been an accident. A reflex. Even with his limited experience, he knew that.

When he lifted the latch of the stall door, his hand trembled a little, surprising him. He didn't think he'd be afraid. That was stupid. He made himself open the half door and step inside, boots sinking into the soft layer of straw. He made a smooching sound with his mouth, the way he'd heard Edward and Sam do.

The filly shied, but the mare looked up, nodding her head in a funny way that made him smile. "Hey, Sylvia," he said softly. "How you doing, girl?"

She grunted, then stretched out her neck so her big soft muzzle nudged his shoulder. And Cody, the most self-conscious kid ever born, forgot to be self-conscious. He rubbed her nose, and her bristly chin, and her neck, murmuring soft nonsense. She sighed with contentment when he scratched her between the ears.

The foal kept watching them, tail flicking, ears pricked forward. Cody held out his hand, low with the palm open. "C'mere, little one. I won't hurt you. C'mere . . ."

The foal lurched to its feet. Cody went down on one knee, moving slowly so he wouldn't startle her. She sniffed his hand, nose twitching, and jerked her head back. He held his hand steady, keeping up a low-voiced monologue. The foal sniffed and pulled back a couple more times. Finally, she allowed Cody to give her a rub between the eyes. She pressed forward in clear acceptance, letting him rub her muzzle and head. He laughed out loud when her small pink tongue came out and licked his hand. She latched on to his finger, sucking away. She was so damned cute, shiny as a new penny, cuddling up to him like a regular pet. Completely lost in the moment, he looped his arms around the foal's neck and pressed his cheek to her warm, smooth face.

He heard a noise behind him. The mare, thumping her foot on the floor, he told himself. Please let it be that.

He stood up and turned, knowing goddamned good and well it wasn't the mare that he'd heard. Someone had just caught him red-handed at his most ridiculous.

"Hi, Cody," she said. "I came to see the new foal."

"Um, Molly, yeah." He could feel his face filling up with a blush like a thermometer rising. "That's your name, right? Molly?" As if he'd forgotten. As if she'd be fooled.

She grinned at him, and the sun through the skylights seemed to get brighter for a second. She was amazing, her long straight black hair so shiny it was like water. Her face was the type of face you never wanted to look away from.

"That's my name."

His ears were on fire. He could feel the flames rising from them. "I was, um, making friends with her myself."

She let herself into the stall, expertly stroking Sylvia to put the mare at her ease. But her eyes never left the foal. "Ooh, she's such a little beauty." She dug in her pocket and pulled out a treat for Sylvia. "It's okay that I saw you doing that," she said as the mare crunched down the carrot.

Cody nearly choked with embarrassment. "I was just—"

"I usually kiss 'em on the lips," she stated, then squatted and held out a hand to the foal.

He stood back, feeling a tad superior that the filly wouldn't have a thing to do with the girl. He didn't care how long she spent trying to coax it. He'd be happy to stand here all day staring at Molly. Barn clothes looked just right on her. At his school in Seattle, the tight leggings and paddock boots, oversize sweater and puffy down vest would draw comments of dork and dweeb. But here in Sam's barn, she looked natural and comfortable. He found himself wondering what it would feel like to hold her slender form close to him. He wondered what her hair smelled like, and if her cheek was as soft as it looked, and if her lips—

Whoa. His thoughts were way out of control. He owed Claudia his loyalty, not this skinny backwater stranger. Claudia was the one who had pulled him out of obscure mediocrity at school. Because Claudia was his girl, he was suddenly someone, suddenly important. People knew his name when he walked down the halls at school.

The trouble was, when Molly Lightning looked up at him with shining eyes, she made it real easy to forget all that stuff.

"She's a perfect filly," Molly said. "Just perfect. I knew she would be."

"How'd you know that?"

"She's by Calyx, out of Sylvia. The perfect combination."

"By Calyx. You mean that's the father?"

"Uh-huh. Or the stud, you could say. Breeder talk, I guess."

"Whatever." Awkwardness stole over Cody. "Um, do you want to get a Coke or something?"

She stood. "Sure. We should leave the baby alone, anyway."

It turned out she was right. Practically the second they left the stall, the foal curled up and fell asleep. They raided the beat-up old refrigerator, filled with shots and wormer and soft drinks. The Border collie thumped her tail, then went back to sleep. They stood in the barn office, sipping from the cans as unease settled over them again.

"So my mom heard you got kicked in the head." Molly eyed the knitted gray cap Cody had pulled on that morning.

He felt a little swell of pride as he touched his forehead where the edge of the bandage showed. "Yeah. I got in the way of Sylvia's hoof at the wrong time."

She regarded him with such admiration that he felt inches taller. "I'm glad you're all right."

He liked the way she sipped her Coke from the can. He liked the way her fingernails were cut, short and plain. Claudia painted hers a different color practically every day, and on special occasions she painted tiny designs on each one. He had never seen the point of it, but it was a girl thing, he supposed.

"So how'd your mom hear about the accident?" he asked.

Molly rolled her eyes comically. "My mom hears everything. She teaches English at the high school. I bet Edward Bliss told her."

"Did he tell her the other stuff?" Cody felt a strange lightness in his chest, as if he'd inhaled cigarette smoke and was holding his breath.

"What other stuff?"

"About . . . Sam McPhee."

"What about Sam?"

"That he's my dad." He made sure he sounded totally blasé. "My biological dad." He didn't look at her, but he felt her stillness, her dawning amazement.

"Wow," she said at last.

"So I guess your mom doesn't hear *everything*."

"Guess not. Did Sam know about you?"

Something that felt uncomfortably like shame touched Cody. It pissed him off that he had been conceived so carelessly and then dismissed, no more important than a foal to a stud. "Nope. He and my mom lost track of each other."

"Do you have a stepdad?"

He thought of Brad, with those clean hands and that fat wallet. And those eyes that didn't trust him. "Nope." He poked the toe of his boot at a coil of rope on the floor.

"So are you happy about it or what?"

"He's just some guy my mom used to know. It doesn't change anything."

Molly put her empty can in the recycle bin. "Are you sure?"

"What, you think they're going to pick up where they left off and fall into each other's arms?"

"What if they do?"

"They won't," he said quickly, fiercely. "We live in a different state. We're here temporarily."

"I really like Sam. Everybody does."

"I don't even know the guy."

She paused. "He was seeing my mom last summer."

Cody's head jerked up; he narrowed his eyes. "Yeah? Are they still together?"

"Nope. They're good friends and all, but they don't really go out. I heard he sees a lot of different women." Her cheeks glowed pink. "That's what I heard, anyway."

"What about your dad?"

She shrugged. "Ditched us when I was little. I barely even remember him."

"I guess you know Sam a lot better."

"I guess."

Cody waited, wishing she'd say more. Since learning about Sam, he'd been on fire with curiosity. There was so much to wonder about. Where was Sam from? How had he grown up? Did he have any brothers or sisters? What did he eat for breakfast?

Why didn't he come looking for me?

He slammed his can into the recycle bin and stalked out of the barn office. "I better get to work," he said, growing short-tempered with all the thoughts swirling through his head.

"Want some help?" Molly asked.

"Nope."

"I could—"

"No." He turned and faced her. She stood in the doorway, backlit by sunlight. He wished she'd leave in a huff, but she stood her ground. "There's not much to be done," he said lamely.

"See you around, then." She walked out of the barn. A tall Appaloosa with a shaggy winter coat stood tethered to the paddock rail. She untied the horse and swung up into the saddle, turning him and walking him away with unhurried dignity.

Chapter 22

The illness was the enemy. The moment he had been diagnosed, Gavin had envisioned it as a living thing, a monster stalking him through the dark. Initially, he'd wasted a lot of time in denial and rage. Humiliated by the disintegration of his body, he had cursed the universe, embraced a death wish. A binge of drinking and tomcatting had nearly brought him to his knees. He had awakened one morning in an emergency clinic in Kalispell to find that they'd dragged him back from the edge of a coma—temporarily. The rest was up to him.

He went home and got down to the business of survival. He waged a battle against his disease, planning strategy with the precision of a film director blocking out a scene.

Yet he was losing ground. Hiring a special nutritionist, participating in special therapies had only postponed the inevitable. His kidneys were useless. Dialysis wasn't getting the job done. He was slowly poisoning himself. If the transplant didn't work, he'd be dead in a matter of months.

Driving down the highway away from town, he flexed his hands on the steering wheel. Part of his strategy for dealing with this was to act as if everything was fine, as if he didn't carry around a bag of dialysis fluid connected by a tube sticking out of his side. He still went to the feed store, still placed his stock orders and gossiped with the cow buyers and rodeo directors who came through town. Still stopped in at the diner for a cup of tea—coffee had been banned long ago.

He was a fixture in Crystal City. Even now, years after his last film, he was regarded as the town celebrity. People liked coming up to him and saying hi. They liked telling their kids he was the guy on all those tapes at the video store.

They kept his movies in the Classics section.

He drove along the empty road, thinking about Michelle and wishing like hell for some alternative to the surgery. Christ, she didn't owe him a thing, least of all a frigging *kidney*.

But the minute she'd figured out the score, she'd latched on like a tick, and she wasn't about to let go.

Why was that? Filial love and devotion didn't explain it. A sense of duty—maybe. The trouble was, they were doing this ass-backward. Forgiveness should come first. *Then* the transplant. Sad to think it took a crisis to bring them both to the table.

He pondered the long gap in their relationship, a gap that spanned the years of Cody's life.

I'm pregnant, Daddy.

I'm not surprised. Your mother was careless, too.

Christ. What the hell had he been thinking, speaking to his young, frightened daughter that way? Worse, Gavin had made sure she didn't have Sam McPhee to turn to. No wonder she had left, erecting a wall of silence that had endured for years. He didn't blame her.

He had responded to her departure by finding a mistress nearly as young as Michelle and becoming the resident playboy of Crystal City. He threw himself into work, producing a few small-studio independent films and giving the rest of his attention to the rodeo stock breeding program on his farm. There had barely been time to come up for air. And he sure as hell hadn't been inclined to let her know her old boyfriend had made good and moved back to town.

He'd salved his guilt about Michelle in equally typical fashion—by setting up a massive college fund for her child. He knew better than to suppose he could buy her forgiveness, but at least the boy would never have to worry about paying for his education.

Many times since his diagnosis, Gavin had picked up the phone, even dialed the number. It was a terrible thing, a pathetic thing, to use pity and compassion to bridge the gap. He'd held off telling her as long as he could. Michelle caught on when Gavin had set up a new trust fund in Cody's name. Within hours of receiving the papers to sign, she had called.

On some insane level, he was grateful for the illness that had brought her to him so swiftly and unquestioningly. If the transplant didn't work, he'd feel like a failure. But that was asking for a guarantee, and for once in his life, he knew better than that.

The sight of a breakdown at the side of the road startled Gavin from his musings. He recognized the beige Chevy Celebrity parked on the shoulder with its hood propped up. He eased off the road and parked behind the car.

"Car trouble?" he asked the woman bent over the engine.

She straightened up. Instant recognition froze her face. Tammi Lee Gilmer was in her fifties and looked it, with tired skin and overtreated hair teased high. She was slender and pale-eyed, a wary smile playing about her mouth. In the years since she'd moved back to Crystal City, she had lived a quiet life, never showing any signs of the out-of-control partying that had once made her the talk of the town.

She worked in a fabric shop—Gavin had never set foot inside it. On the rare occasions that he saw her, they dismissed each other with a nod and a murmured hello. Now he was trapped.

"It just died on me," she said. "I can't think what happened." Her voice was husky. As far as Gavin could tell, she'd given up drinking, but the habit still haunted her voice.

He opened the passenger door of his truck. "I'll give you a lift."

She slammed down the hood and grabbed her purse off the seat. "Thanks, Gavin. I was on my way out to Sam's. I can call McEvoy's Garage from there."

It was a tall step up into his truck, and he held out a hand to steady her as she climbed in. Her arm felt small and bony, but she was spry enough as she settled into the passenger seat. She smelled of cigarettes and drugstore perfume, and he found the fragrance unpretentious and therefore slightly welcome. He came from a world where women donned formal dress to go to the mailbox. He didn't miss that world at all.

He walked around the truck and got in, easing back onto the highway.

"You know the way to Sam's?" she asked.

"Yeah, I know where Lonepine is. I've been out there once or twice." Gavin had bought a couple of horses from Sam. Beyond that, they hadn't spoken.

Tammi Lee crossed one leg over the other, adjusting the wool cuff of her snow boot. Gavin kept his eyes on the road, but he found himself remembering, almost against his will, one of the meetings he'd had with his transplant team. The psychologist had pretty much guaranteed him he'd have no interest in sex for a good long while—maybe never again. The antirejection meds had a motherlode of side effects.

"But it's life," Dr. Temple had said, his painfully earnest face animated by optimism. "Preferable to the alternative."

Gavin hadn't smiled. "Shoot me now," he'd grumbled, and the psychologist had scribbled something on his clipboard.

Gavin missed Carolyn, who had lived with him until he'd been diagnosed. A former first-runner-up Miss California, her favorite things were riding horses, watching movies, shopping, and having imaginative, recreational sex.

When he told her about his illness, she had looked at him in horror, left that same day, sued him for eight thousand a month in palimony, and sold her story to a magazine.

His attorney had negotiated a much cheaper settlement, and Gavin had set up the second trust fund for Cody.

"I guess you know why I was headed out to Sam's," Tammi Lee said, bringing his thoughts around full circle.

"To see the boy, I imagine."

"I've been told the boy's name is Cody." Her voice held a gentle censure. "Cody Jackson Turner. So it's lucky I ran into you. Now you can tell me all about him, sort of prepare me."

"I haven't seen much of my grandson, Tammi Lee."

"Yeah, well, he's my grandson, too, and I've *never* seen him."

"A word to the wise. Don't expect a bunch of hugs and kisses."

"From a sixteen-year-old boy who doesn't know me from Reba McIntyre? Don't worry, Gavin, I'm not that stupid." She was pensive for a few moments. "When Sam was that age, he acted more grown up than me. Quit school and went to work for you. I took that boy's childhood away from him. No. I never let him have a childhood in the first place."

The frank regret in her voice made him wince. "Hey, take it easy on yourself. Sam's fine. Not every mother raises a boy to become a doctor."

"He did it all on his own. I never forget that. Never."

"You have a right to be pretty proud of Sam," Gavin remarked.

She laughed briefly, shaking her head. "I keep thinking he was left with me by mistake, that he was actually meant for some couple with a nice house full of books and a piano and supper hot on the table every night."

"I bet that would have made him too soft to do everything he's done." Gavin wished she'd drop the subject. He knew what she'd been like when Sam was coming up. Though she'd been his full-time mother, in a way she had been as absent from Sam as Gavin was from Michelle. Because when you were a drunk, you weren't there. Simple as that.

"Okay, here we are." He turned down the drive to

Sam's place. It wasn't a showy spread, not like Blue Rock was. A battered mailbox was the only indication that it had a name; LONEPINE was stenciled on the side and the flag was up. In the middle of the front pasture, the huge old lodgepole pine tree that had given the place its name stood draped in snow.

A slim girl on a tall Appaloosa rode in the opposite direction, leaving the ranch. Gavin recognized her as Ruby Lightning's girl.

"Wonder if she was keeping Cody company," Tammi Lee murmured. "If the youngster's anywhere near as good-looking as his dad, he'll have no trouble in the girl department. How about that daughter of yours?" she asked suddenly. "I hear she's some big-shot ad executive in Seattle."

"Uh-huh. But I didn't have anything to do with that."

"Nice she came back after all these years."

He pulled up to the barn and parked. A Border collie scampered out, barking and leaping in the snow.

Turning to Tammi Lee, Gavin forced himself to level with her. "Michelle didn't come back to be nice."

"Oh . . . ?"

"I've been sick." He hated saying it, nearly gagged on the words. "You probably heard that."

"There was talk of it in the shop."

"I've been on dialysis, but it isn't doing it for me. I could go toxic anytime. I need a kidney transplant. Michelle's going to be the donor."

"My God—"

"I'll never be able to thank her."

"Just get yourself healthy, Gavin. That'll be thanks enough. I know that for sure."

Sam's partner, Edward Bliss, came out hefting an extra

large Havahart wildlife trap. Gavin opened Tammi Lee's door for her.

"Hey, folks," Bliss said, his greeting light, his stare heavy with curiosity.

"Hey yourself, Eddie." Tammi Lee tucked her knitted hat down over her ears. "My car broke down. I'll use the phone in the barn office."

"Sure. Sam's at work today."

"I know. I came to see Cody."

Bliss's interest was so intense it was almost comical. "He's in the barn."

Gavin said, "You want some help with that trap?"

"No, thanks." Bliss shuffled away on reluctant feet. "I've got it." He deposited the trap on a flatbed sled hitched to a snowmobile. "Better be going. We've had a cat prowling around lately."

"Let me know if that thing works. I've had trouble with mountain lions myself the past couple of years," Gavin said as Bliss started the engine and rode off. Gavin stood between the truck and the barn, undecided. There was no need for him to stay, but he didn't feel like going just now either.

Tammi Lee hesitated at the barn door. "Hey, Gavin?"

"Yeah?"

"Maybe you could, um, introduce us."

For the first time since finding her on the side of the road, he smiled. He didn't blame her, feeling nervous about meeting a sixteen-year-old grandkid she never knew about. Cody was enough to make anybody nervous. "Sure," he said. "Of course."

They went into the barn together. The fecund smells of hay and molasses oats and manure filled the air and, somewhere, a radio played terrible music designed to drive people crazy.

"I'm no square in the music department," Tammi Lee whispered to Gavin. "Does this count as music?"

He made an exaggerated show of covering his ears. "Welcome to Cody's world."

They spotted him cleaning a stall. Oblivious to the visitors, he had a pretty good rhythm going with the shovel, bending to load, then swinging up to deposit the load in a wheelbarrow.

"Too bad Sam got to the kid first," Gavin commented, surprised to see him working so industriously. "He would be pretty useful around Blue Rock."

"You should give him some chores," said Tammi Lee, her stare devouring Cody. "I bet he'd work for both of you."

"When I first laid eyes on the boy, I didn't think he'd turn out to be good for much of anything. To me, he looked like every reason I never watch MTV."

Tammi Lee crossed her arms in front of her, leaning against a post. "Then you forgot the cardinal rule of kids."

"What's that?"

"Underneath the most terrible attitude and the most terrible clothes, he's just a kid."

"I don't have much experience with kids."

"Me neither." Apprehensive as a nervous filly, she took a step toward Cody.

"You okay?" he asked, surprised by her hesitation.

"Look, I didn't do so hot with Sam," she said. "I don't want to blow it with Sam's son."

Gavin's heart took an unexpected lurch. Suddenly it struck him that getting off the bottle had been a struggle for her, a battle, a war. And that she was never really safe from a relapse.

Without thinking, he took her hand. "Come on. I'll introduce you."

Reaching for the radio, he switched it off.

Cody's uncertain tenor voice kept singing, then broke off. "Hey, what the—" He stopped himself again when he saw Gavin and Tammi Lee.

"Sorry about that." Gavin grinned in a friendly fashion. But he'd screwed up already, embarrassing the kid.

"You shouldn't sneak up on people like that." Cody set aside his shovel and peeled off one glove, inserting his finger up under his cap where the edge of his bandage showed.

"Your head all right?" Gavin asked.

"It itches."

"I brought someone for you to meet. This is Sam's mother, Tammi Lee Gilmer."

He felt her give his hand a squeeze before she took the final step toward Cody. For someone Gavin barely knew, she was easy to read. The woman was petrified. And moved—he could see that in the tremor at the edge of her smile, in the extra sparkle in the corner of her eye.

"Hey, Cody," she said in her cigarette voice. "This is such a surprise. I couldn't wait to meet you."

He quit scratching. After a second, he held out his hand. She took it briefly.

"Hi," he said.

"I guess you'd better call me Tammi, or Tammi Lee," she said.

"Not Granny or Grandma?" Gavin asked in a teasing voice, trying to lighten the moment.

"I sure wouldn't mind," she said in a rush of honesty that left her flushed. "But 'Grandma' is a name that has to be earned, don't you think? Cody and I have only just met."

She folded her hands in front of her and studied his face. "You're probably going to get sick of hearing this, but you look exactly like Sam did when he was young. Sam was just about the best-looking kid in town."

The boy shrugged. He was a little lacking in the poise department, Gavin observed. Too much time plugged into Nintendo? He didn't know. There was too much he didn't know about this boy.

"Cody," Tammi Lee said, "I don't want to embarrass you. I don't want to push myself on you. But if you don't mind, maybe we could spend a little time together sometime."

"I have to work," he said bluntly.

"Oh," she said. Her fingers knit together. "I make a mean homemade pizza," she added.

He nodded noncommittally and pulled on his glove. "I'd better get after it then."

"See you around, maybe," Tammi Lee said.

"Maybe."

Gavin walked away with her. The music came back on. They stopped to look in on the mare with the new baby, leaning against the half door and admiring the little one. Gavin chanced a look at her, and wasn't surprised to see a tear tracking down her cheek.

"Hey, he's just a jerky little kid," he said, handing her a bandanna from his pocket.

"I didn't expect him to fall into my arms. But Jesus Christ, I wanted to hold him." Her hands shook as she grasped the top of the stall door. "How I wanted to hold him."

Her stark, honest yearning touched Gavin. "I think we both missed out on that stage with Cody."

She blotted her cheeks and handed back the bandanna. "I guess what makes me so sad is that I missed out on a lot of that with Sam, too. Some things you just learn too late."

An old twinge nagged at Gavin. Seventeen years ago, he'd made up his mind about Tammi Lee and Sam—and he'd been wrong.

"I better go call about my car," she said.

As they reached the barn door, the loud music cut off. Tammi Lee and Gavin turned back. Cody stepped out into the breezeway.

"Hey . . . Tammi Lee." He sounded uncertain as he spoke her name.

"Yeah?"

"What kind of pizza?"

A smile broke across her face. "Whatever you like, hon. Whatever you like."

Chapter 23

Sam's snow tires crackled on the drive as he turned into his farm. He was surprised to see Gavin Slade's Ford 350 parked outside the barn. Damn, what was Gavin doing here?

Sam pulled up to the house and spotted a light on in the kitchen. He stopped on the back porch, amazed to see his mother offering a steaming mug to Gavin Slade.

Sam paused to collect himself. His first meeting with Gavin Slade had set in motion events no one could have predicted. When Sam was seventeen, his mom's car had died in the parking lot of the Truxtop Café in Crystal City. The owner, above average in the decency department, had arranged a tow to McEvoy's Garage and had given Tammi Lee a job. A few inquiries steered Sam to Blue Rock. Good reputation, rodeo stock contractor. The kind of operation a cowboy dreamed of.

Gavin's foreman had taken one look at Sam in the saddle and summoned the boss. Sam's physique had always worked in his favor. He was tall and rangy with long hands and a relaxed way that gave people—and horses—confidence.

"Well, you look like a cowboy. Can you ride like one?" Gavin had wanted to know.

Digging in his heels, Sam had demonstrated on the borrowed quarter horse.

"How'd you get here?" Gavin had asked.

"Walked."

"From town? That's six miles."

Sam made no comment. Gavin hired him on the spot.

Sam had been quietly fascinated by the parade of glitterati that came to call on the famous actor. He recognized faces from old movies, late-night talk shows, celebrity game shows. Beautiful women and well-dressed men came seeking favor, for after retiring from movies, Gavin Slade became a respected producer, picking and choosing his projects with care.

Gavin had entered Sam in a few local roping events. The purses at the small shows didn't amount to much, but Sam had a taste of something he hadn't sampled before—possibility.

Fate had worn a yellow ponytail, expensive riding clothes, and a soft-eyed, dreamy look that made him forget his place in the world.

Damn. The boss's daughter.

Could he have been more stupid?

Sam yanked open the kitchen door. Gavin was a charmer, a ladies' man. What the hell did he want with Tammi Lee?

"Hey, Mama." Sam took off his hat, holding out his hand. "Gavin."

"Good to see you." Gavin flashed a smile, but his eyes stayed cool, wary.

"I had car trouble," Tammi Lee explained. "Gavin gave me a lift out here."

Sam relaxed a little. That seemed innocent enough. But he didn't kid himself about Gavin Slade. The old man had considered him ranch-hand scum, not good enough for his daughter. That in itself might have been forgivable, but Gavin had played hardball. Even the ruse with the missing money had been understandable, if not forgivable. What Sam couldn't ever forget, though, was that Gavin's schemes had knocked Tammi Lee in the dirt when she was already down.

"I wanted to meet Cody," Tammi Lee continued.

"He was feeling well enough to come to work." Pride touched Gavin's voice. "Frankly, I was glad to see it. A little work sure can't hurt the kid."

"So you met him, Ma?" Sam studied the lined and faded face, and he sensed the sadness that always seemed to linger at the edge of her mood. For as long as he could remember, he had felt responsible for that sadness. He knew it wasn't his fault, but he'd give anything to banish it.

"Gavin introduced us," she said. "I won't bullshit you, Sam. We're not the Waltons."

"I hope he was civil, at least."

She waved her hand. "I don't think we'll find much in common, but I'm glad we met. He's a good-looking boy, Sam. Reminds me of you at that age."

Sam wondered if he'd had that same screw-you attitude. Maybe he had. Maybe bonking the boss's daughter had as much to do with his attitude as his hormones.

"Speaking of Cody, we'd better head out." Gavin picked up his hat from the rack behind the door. "It's getting dark."

Sam shot his mother a look. Had she been hanging out with Gavin Slade all afternoon? Telling himself it was none of his business, he went out to the barn. While Gavin warmed up his truck, Sam found Cody standing at the far end of the row of stables, his shoulder propped against the door. Sam was pleased to see all the equipment had been washed down and put up. He was a lot less pleased when he saw that Cody was smoking a cigarette.

He tried to sound casual as he remarked, "Those things'll kill you."

Cody turned quickly. A rebellious look shadowed his face. "It's just something I do sometimes. I can quit anytime."

"How about now?"

"I'll choose the time."

"Well." Grabbing a water hose, Sam twisted the spray nozzle and doused both Cody's gloved hand and the cigarette. "I choose now."

"Hey!" Cody jumped back, shaking water from his hand. "That's cold as hell."

"So don't smoke around here anymore."

"I'll do what I—"

Sam held up the hose. "Don't push me. I'm armed."

Cody flung off his glove in disgust. "You could have just asked me to put it out."

"I'm *telling* you to quit."

"And I'm *telling* you to get off my case."

They faced off, glaring like a pair of rival dogs. Sam refused to flinch, but so did Cody.

"How's your head?"

"Itches. I better get going. 'Bye." He stalked away, muttering under his breath.

Welcome to parenthood, Sam thought. Christ, how did Michelle do it?

Thursday

Thursday

Chapter 24

W aking up was hard for Michelle at home. She had done her bedroom in soft aquas and golds, spent an absurd amount on bedding from Nordstrom's, and invested in an imported eiderdown, the kind you sink into like a cloud. Her bedroom exuded comfort and luxury, and she responded by sleeping too long and too hard there.

In Montana, she woke up at the crack of dawn and hurried like a child to the window to look out at the long fields and pastures of her father's ranch. The sides of the mountains corrugated by the blue ripples of glaciers. The fall of light from the rising sun.

And God knew what was going to happen each day.

She got a clue when the early light glinted off a car parked in the circular drive in front of Gavin's house.

There was probably only one lime green Volkswagen bug in the Northwest.

Michelle paused to check on Cody—dead asleep, a benefit of hard physical labor—then pulled on her old gray sweats, stuffed her feet into boots, and hurried across the compound to the main house. She entered through the kitchen, greeting Tadao in passing. The aromas of coffee and kidney-friendly roasted green tea wafted over her, but she was not hungry, just on fire to know what the hell was going on.

Gavin and Natalie sat in the sunken living room before a roaring blaze. Gavin spotted Michelle first; he was in the middle of laughing, and the smile on his face lifted her heart. He stood up. "Hey, Michelle. Morning."

"Hi, Daddy. I see you've met Natalie."

"I certainly have."

"At about five o'clock this morning." Natalie's bangle bracelets and hoop earrings, silken head scarf and tie-dyed leggings, and especially her warm smile, were familiar and dear to Michelle.

"Hey, you," she said, holding out her arms.

"Hey, you," Natalie said back, standing up to give her a hug. "I tried to get here last night, but the old Volkswagen wouldn't cooperate. I had to take a breather in Coeur d'Alene."

"You should have called, Nat."

"We talked, remember? You knew I was coming."

"Yes, but—" Normal logic didn't work with Natalie Plum. Michelle sat down on the big leather sectional with them.

Natalie's eyes twinkled. "I acted as though I'd never seen a movie star before—"

"You haven't," Michelle reminded her.

"Well, that explains why I kept staring and stammering." She sipped from her mug of coffee. "Your dad got all squirmy on me. You'd think he's never been awakened at five in the morning by a crazed fan before."

Her father leaned back, crossing his booted feet at the ankles. "I admit it's been a while."

He was loving this, loving every minute of it. His need to put his face in front of millions of people was nearly as strong now as it had been at the height of his career in the movie business. There were those who hungered for recognition, even though it didn't necessarily mean anything to them except recognition. She thought it was true in her father's case. Anyway, he was far from annoyed by Natalie's breathless admiration.

"So we've been up talking for a couple of hours." Natalie sent him a look of melting sympathy. "You should go back to bed now. I feel so guilty getting you up."

"I'm an early riser. And this visit was worth it." He patted his hand on a stack of fat photo albums on the coffee table.

"You brought those from Seattle," Michelle said, sounding slightly accusing.

"You bet I did, girlfriend." Natalie sent her a smile. "I can't believe you forgot them."

Guilt stained her cheeks. To be honest, Michelle had never even thought of bringing the photo albums to show her father. Never even thought he'd be interested in snapshots of Cody's first birthday, or the bike Santa brought him one year, or his first day of school.

"I loved the pictures, Michelle," her father said quietly. "More than you can know. I'm proud of you for the life you've built for yourself and Cody."

She blinked, startled. Since she arrived at Blue Rock, they had avoided talking about certain topics. Dr. Temple and the social worker on the transplant team had been saying how important it was to discuss personal stuff, family stuff. They gave Michelle and Gavin some little blank books for writing down thoughts and feelings. Michelle's was still blank. She bet Gavin's was, too. So his statement about being proud of her took her by surprise.

Putting his hands on his knees, he got up, his thick heather gray sweater looking warm and comfortable on his big, lean frame. The bulkiness of the knit camouflaged the dialysis bag. "Chores," he explained. "I've got a meeting with the arena director."

"See you around, pardner," Natalie said in an exaggerated, corny drawl.

"Jake turned on the heat in the bungalow next to Michelle's. If you need anything, holler."

"It's all perfect, Gavin. Thank you for welcoming me."

"My pleasure, ma'am." He went out through the kitchen, and Michelle drummed her fingers on the arm of the couch, trying to figure out if he was flirting with her best friend or not.

Natalie and Michelle sat alone in the living room, watching morning sunlight steal across the hand-painted tile floor. Michelle picked up a plaid pillow, tossed it at her, saying, "You bitch."

She caught the pillow, laughing. "You have no idea."

Suspicion stole into Michelle's radar range. "I don't?"

Natalie propped her sock feet on the leather-bound albums. "I figured your dad would want to see the old family photos. But I really brought them for you to show Sam McPhee."

"God, you really are a bitch."

"You have to show him. You have to let him in on Cody's whole history."

"I don't have to do squat."

"Legally, probably not, unless he sues for visitation."

A chill skittered down Michelle's spine. "He wouldn't dare."

"Who knows? But he'll want to see the pictures."

"You know what makes you such a bitch?"

"What?"

"It's that you're right."

She grinned. "I know. So when are you going to show him?"

"I guess I could today, when I drop Cody off to work at his ranch. Sam's on split shift." It was amazing how quickly Michelle had memorized his schedule. He'd explained how he split the clinic duties with his partner, how his on-call situation worked. He'd only told her once, yet she had absorbed it like a sponge. Funny.

"You don't have any more . . . appointments and stuff with your father?"

"It all starts Saturday." She took a shaky breath, silently blessing Sam for intervening with Dr. Temple.

Natalie held Michelle's cheeks between her hands. "Do you know how special this is?"

Michelle swallowed a sudden painful lump in her throat. "I can't seem to look at it as anything more than a fairly complicated surgical procedure."

"It's so much more than that." She stood up, tossing a glance outside at her car. "I've been naughty."

Michelle picked up the heavy leather albums. "True."

"I mean, not just the photos. For once in your life, you've got time to get back into painting."

Not you, too. Michelle got the feeling Natalie had colluded with Sam about this. Or maybe her secret wish was absurdly obvious. "Give me a break," she said flatly.

"As if." Outside, Natalie lifted the front hood of the Volkswagen, revealing the trunk. In addition to her luggage, there were shopping bags from Madrona Bay Art Supply in Seattle.

Michelle's heart lurched. Madrona Bay was a Mecca for fine artists all over the West. The store was one of the first things she had discovered when, newly pregnant, she'd moved to Seattle. She used to save every last scraped-together dime to buy art supplies. It was a magical place, filled with all the things she needed to give life to the images burning inside her.

She hadn't been there in years, though.

"You bitch," she whispered, her eyes glazing over with yearning and frustration. "I don't need any of this."

"Oh, honey." Natalie grabbed her flowered bag and hefted it over her shoulder. "You do. You absolutely do. What else are you going to do while Gavin recovers?"

"I—" Well, really, thought Michelle. Natalie had a point. The studio was still there, untouched, as Sam had showed her the other night. "I guess I could mess around in my spare time."

"Good girl. So let's get a move on. We've got to bring poor Camille in out of the cold."

Camille was her cello, a 1968 Juzak concert instrument from Hungary. She never went anywhere without it. She kept it in a hard shell case plastered with stickers from all the places she'd visited—places like Sri Lanka and Lake Lucerne and Montreal and Rio de Janeiro.

They walked across to the bungalows, and Michelle stowed the photo albums in the Rover. She wondered if she would dare to show them to Sam. Natalie was right, Michelle conceded reluctantly. He needed and deserved to see what Cody's first sixteen years had been like.

They toted the paints, brushes, and Belgian linen canvases into the studio. Then Michelle helped Natalie carry her stuff into the guesthouse. It was already warm and cozy inside, and Natalie sighed with satisfaction. "Let me freshen up a little, and we'll go together."

"Go where, Nat?"

"To Sam McPhee's. Didn't you say Cody's working there? He needs a ride, right?"

"Yes, but—"

"Do you think I could stay away?" Natalie rummaged in her bag and found a brush, which she used to draw upward through her spiked hair. "I'm dying here, Michelle. You're my best friend, and you've got a scarlet past I know nothing about. Do you have any idea how crazy that makes me?"

In spite of herself, Michelle grinned. "I sort of like this."

"Bitch," Natalie said, and gave her a hug.

Chapter 25

S am walked out onto the front porch with Edward Bliss as the Range Rover pulled into the yard. Sam felt a now-familiar lurch in his chest when Cody got out of the car.

My son. I have a son.

Yet other than stitching his wound, Sam had never touched him.

"He's doing a little better in the wardrobe department." Edward sipped from a mug of coffee. "Starting to dress for the weather and the job, eh?"

Cody still appeared a little ragged, though he had abandoned the studied slouchiness of his city garb in favor of old jeans, work boots, a fleece-lined denim jacket. A warm hat covered the new haircut and the bandage.

"Who's that in the car with Michelle?" Edward asked.

Sam squinted, but the glare of the sun off the windshield blinded him. "Not sure. Gavin again?"

The passenger door of the car opened and out stepped the strangest woman Sam had ever seen. She resembled a butterfly, wearing a long multicolored shawl, crazy purple boots, and a Sherpa mountain guide's alpaca hat. With her skirt and shawl flowing, she skimmed over the snow toward the house, gabbing with Cody the whole time. Michelle went around to the back of the car, lifting the rear cargo door.

"*Ai caramba,*" Edward said under his breath. "Who's the babe?"

". . . so unbelievably cool of your mom," she was saying to Cody as they reached the porch. Barely pausing for breath, she tilted her head back, revealing earrings in unexpected places, and said, "Okay, Cody, shall we play *What's My Line?* Which one's your dad?"

She took off her hat to reveal spiked hair with purple and green streaks. She had slightly uptilted eyes and the face of a pixie—impish, animated, and sly. Tinkerbell on acid.

Red-cheeked but clearly enjoying himself, Cody said, "Sam and Edward, this is—"

"Wait, wait!" The imp held up a hand, impractically covered in fingerless black lace gloves. "Don't tell me. Let me guess." She grew very serious, looking from Cody to Sam to Edward to Cody. "No contest," she said. "It's the tall one. So introduce us, numb-nuts." She elbowed Cody in the side.

"This is my mom's friend."

"Not your friend?" Tinkerbell looked wounded.

"Yeah, mine too." Cody stuffed his hands in his pockets. "Natalie Plum."

"Actually, I'm his fairy godmother." She stepped up onto the porch. "He didn't tell you about me?"

"I better get to work," Cody said, hurrying toward the barn.

Sam was gratified by his haste to check on the mare and foal. He wanted to believe the kid could get interested in the horses. Maybe that way they'd find some common ground.

Natalie stepped up onto the porch and shook hands with Edward, then Sam. "You'll have to excuse me," she said. "I've had about nine gallons of coffee. You might find me a tad talkative. Hope you don't mind."

"We don't mind a bit," Sam said.

Edward put the full force of his charm into a comical bow. "Welcome to Montana."

Natalie's face lit up. "Thank you."

Michelle arrived, lugging an armload of large, thick books.

"Here." Sam jumped down from the porch. "Let me help you with those."

"Michelle, you bitch," Natalie burst out, turning on her friend. "You didn't tell me he was George Clooney!"

Sam took the top two books from Michelle. "I'm not George Clooney."

Natalie Plum raked him with a frankly assessing glance. "Close enough."

"But I'm friendlier," Edward cut in. "And I have better work hours."

"Perfect," she said with a dazzling smile. "Then you can show me around the place. Cody wouldn't shut up about the new baby."

Edward took her hand and led her toward the barn. "My pleasure."

As they walked off, Sam heard her say, ". . . every last thing, do you hear? I want to know absolutely *everything*."

Michelle watched them go. The morning light was soft on her face, nose and cheeks tinged by the cold. She held two of the books against her like a shield. "And does Edward know everything?" she asked.

"If he doesn't, he'll make it up."

"I'm serious, Sam."

"Okay, he figured out about Cody even before I did. The second he saw him. But he didn't say anything until I told him. Edward doesn't lie, and he doesn't hurt people. Ever." He indicated the books. "So what's all this? Photo albums?"

"Uh-huh. You got a minute?"

"I'm guessing this will take more than a minute. But as a matter of fact, I've got all morning." He glanced down at the pager clipped to his belt. "So long as the beeper stays quiet. Come on in."

In the living room, he added a couple of golden larch logs to the fire crackling in the woodstove and cleared a spot on the coffee table. "Can I get you something to drink?"

She didn't answer. He glanced at her to find her staring at the painting over the mantel.

"My God," she said. "I had no idea what happened to this."

The picture had occupied a place of honor over the mantel ever since he had settled in Crystal City. It was the only gift Michelle had ever given him. The painting had a life of its own; it glowed with the sheer wonder expressed in every brushstroke, echoing the underlying tenderness of a very young, very talented artist.

"I'm glad you kept it," she said, her voice soft, husky. "It's a good picture."

"I've always thought so. Everyone who sees it says so."

She shivered, though it wasn't cold. "I thought I had so many more pictures in me."

"I still can't believe you don't paint anymore."

"Painting took more out of me than I had to give. Life comes first, then art."

"I bet your pal Natalie doesn't agree."

"Natalie's different."

"I noticed."

Her manner became brisk, almost businesslike as she seated herself, as if her show of vulnerability had embarrassed her.

"You should still be painting, Michelle."

Her chin came up. "What, in all my spare time?"

"You make time for what's important."

The anger that flashed in her eyes was new to him. The Michelle he'd known years ago had a temper, sure. But her anger had never been cold like this. Or strangely directed at herself.

"What's with the books?" he asked, changing the subject.

"Natalie brought these from home."

Sam lowered himself next to her. His heart thumped; until now he wouldn't have thought a moment like this was important, critical. "Pictures of Cody growing up?"

"Yes. You interested?"

Here it was, then. The past, staring him in the face. Here in these four fat books lived the history that had left him out. The years he had lost with his son.

"Hell, yeah, I'm interested."

She picked up the top one. "I haven't had time to go through these and edit them, so what you see is what you get."

"What would you want to edit?"

"You'll see when we get there." She took off her shoes and tucked her feet up under her on the sofa. Sam, who had seduced a decent number of women on this very sofa, found the gesture almost unbearably sexy. He forced himself to focus on the photo album.

She flipped open the front cover. "My first apartment in Seattle. Natalie and I shared a place on Capitol Hill when I first moved there." Unremarkable, a snapshot of a sunny room with sliding glass doors and overstuffed furniture. Neat, nicer-than-average student housing.

"I studied painting while I was pregnant," she said. "I tried to keep it up after the baby was born, but life just got too hectic."

His gaze dropped down the page to a picture of Michelle. It wasn't a very good shot, but it moved him. She stood at the rail of a ferry boat painted white and green. Blue water and forested islands and a distant mountain range in the background. She wore her hair in a silky blond ponytail, and she had on a denim jumper.

A breeze plastered the blue dress against her round, ripe abdomen. She was the picture of a healthy young woman in the last trimester of pregnancy. Sam stared, fascinated by the knowledge that only months before the shot was taken, he had held her in his arms. He had planted that baby in her.

He lightly rubbed his thumb over the girl in the photo. "I hate it that I missed this."

"Right." She seemed to be working to keep her voice in control. "I was fat and cranky all the time. I think this is the only picture of me pregnant."

"Who took it? Natalie?"

"Yes." She turned the page. "Ah. Here we go."

The next photo showed a black-haired imp with thickly mascaraed eyes peering over a surgical mask.

"Natalie again?" Sam asked.

"She was my birth coach."

He set his teeth. Then, when he could trust himself, he said, "Should've been me."

Michelle shook her head. With the motion, a light drift of her fragrance hit him, and his body heated with the need to touch her.

"Sam," she said, "you were eighteen. You weren't ready to go through childbirth—"

"You were only eighteen, too. Were you ready?"

"I didn't have a choice."

"I wasn't *allowed* a choice. I would've stuck with you, Michelle. You know damned well I would have."

"I didn't know a thing. You were gone so fast, I didn't even have a chance to tell you I was pregnant." She pointed to a poorly focused photograph. "And there he is, hot off the press."

There was nothing unique about the picture. As a physician, Sam had seen his share of moments-after-birth shots, and this one wasn't particularly well done. But because it was Michelle, holding his son, his mouth dried. He couldn't speak; he couldn't even swallow.

Cody's wet red face lay against her chest, clad in a dotted hospital gown. The baby's tiny foot flailed, and Michelle wore a look of complete, exhausted relief.

"You had the glow," he remarked.

"The glow?"

"The new-mom glow. Some people deny its existence, but it's a very real thing." Gently he outlined the shape of her face and the baby's.

"Very scientific, Dr. McPhee," she said, though a soft edge diluted her sarcasm.

And then, step by step, page by page, she took him through the lost years. It was like opening a door and stepping into a world whose existence he hadn't even suspected. A parallel universe, hidden from him for seventeen years.

He saw Cody as a round-faced baby, doted on by Natalie. A toddler in overalls and a Seattle Mariners cap waved at him from a wrenching distance of years.

"See that blue thing in his hand?" Michelle rubbed her finger over the photo. "He never went anywhere without that thing. It's one of your old work shirts."

Sam felt a powerful jolt of emotion at the sight of his shirt, clutched in that chubby little hand. "Yeah?"

"When I left here, it was one of the few things I brought with me. Your—" She broke off and bit her lip.

"Your what? What were you going to say?"

"Your smell. It had your smell on it."

He put his arm around her. This was why things never worked out with him and women. He couldn't handle their softness, their fragility, the way his heart twisted in a knot when sentiment struck. "Aw, Michelle, damn it—"

For a moment she leaned into his shoulder. Then she seemed to get a grip and turned her attention back to the album. A first-day-of-kindergarten shot revealed a kid who was becoming his own person as he stood by a redwood fence with a Power Rangers lunch kit and a Looney Tunes backpack. Sam viewed school portraits, Little League team photos, excursions to the zoo, the aquarium, ski trips, summers at remote beaches.

What struck him about Cody was the kid's smile. It was the kind of smile that made the sun look dim—it covered his whole face and lit his eyes. Joy radiated from every photo of him.

Cody didn't seem to smile much anymore.

Natalie Plum appeared in a lot of the pictures. Every so often, there would be a picture of Cody with a guy.

"So who's this?" Sam indicated a man in a Hawaiian shirt, roller-blading with a six-year-old Cody.

"Someone I used to date. I haven't seen him in years."

Sam hoped she didn't hear him let out his breath. He found a couple more interlopers—Cody's third-grade teacher: "He was the gentlest man. Cody really loved him."

"And you? Did you love him?"

"He wanted a full-time wife. I had no idea how to be that, so we stopped seeing each other."

"And this other guy?"

"Someone else I used to see. We met at a commercial-art convention."

"Did he want a full-time wife, too?"

She gave a humorless chuckle. "As it turned out, he preferred several part-time lovers. What a jerk."

"So did you date a lot?"

"Did you?" she shot back. "You're digging for dirt, Sam. And trust me." She drummed her fingers on the photo album. "You won't find it here."

Sam spotted a good shot of Cody at about twelve, frozen in the midst of executing a perfect soccer kick. His face was intent, his gaze focused like a laser on the ball.

"He scored a goal with that kick," Michelle said.

Sam would have traded anything—*anything*—to have seen that kick in person. "Looks like he was a good little athlete."

"He was, but he lost interest in team sports."

"Do you know why?"

"Because he turned sixteen?"

"Plenty of sixteen-year-olds go out for sports."

She drew a quick breath. "I told myself I wouldn't get defensive. I'm working really hard not to."

"Sorry." He touched the photo. It was a five-by-seven, covered with the gluey cellophane of the album page. "This is a good shot."

She hesitated. "Brad took it."

"Ah. Brad."

"The year I met him. He was a community sponsor for the soccer club. His pharmacy franchise was, actually. Med-Plan Pharmacies." She flipped ahead a couple of pages. "Here we are at our ski place in Whistler."

It showed the three of them in front of a modern condo. Cody smiled his winner's smile. Michelle's gaze seemed curiously off focus, as if she was searching for something beyond the camera. The guy called Brad was tall, probably six-two, and thick-set, with a tanned face and a white-toothed grin, designer logos splashed across his ski outfit.

Sam had no doubt this was a decent guy, well-heeled, caring.

But as he regarded the picture, he felt such a stab of complete hatred that he had to look away.

As Cody grew older, the pictures of him were sparser, taken at infrequent intervals. "I think that's always the way," Michelle confessed. "When they're little, you want a picture of them every time they sneeze. But by the time they're in high school, a Christmas picture is about all you remember to take. Here he is with his girlfriend," she said. "Claudia Teller. They didn't want me to take their picture, but they figured it was the only way I'd get out of their hair."

"What are they dressed for, Halloween?"

She laughed. "A school dance. This is formal attire."

The girl was somberly pretty, with anorexic shadows under her eyes and cheekbones. Her hair was too red to be natural, her smile too sly to be genuine. Standing next to her, Cody looked tall and fiercely proud.

"Is she still his girlfriend?"

"As far as I know. Her parents are upper management at Microsoft, and she's supposedly the most popular girl in the school."

"She looks like a barrel of laughs."

Michelle grinned. "I'm glad it's not just me, then. But—" She looked away.

"What, Michelle?"

"It's awful."

"So be awful. I won't tell anyone."

"I'm hoping our stay here will cause his relationship with Claudia to chill. Is that awful?"

"Cody would think so."

She pressed her hand down on the picture. "I want him to have a girlfriend. Just not *this* girlfriend."

Sam studied the pale girl in the photo. From the perspective of years, could he still blame Gavin?

"Face it, Michelle," he said, "the days of arranging your kid's social life are past."

"But I *know* she's bad for him. He's completely blind to that. He thinks they're totally in love. Just like—" She stood up quickly. "We'd better see what Natalie's up to. She's a bit unpredictable."

"Finish what you were saying."

She went to the front window and stared out at the long white fields and mountains. He stood behind her. He wanted to clamp his hands around her shoulders, draw her back against him.

What did her hair smell like? What would her hips feel like, cradled against his?

"Were we wrong, too, way back then?" she asked softly. "Were we blind?"

"Your father thought so."

She turned to him, worrying her lower lip with her teeth. "My father never knew about us. At least, not until I told him I was pregnant." She moved past him. "You were gone by then."

"He knew, Michelle." Sam couldn't believe she thought otherwise.

"He never knew, not until I—that last day. We were careful," she insisted.

"You ought to ask him sometime."

Something like panic flickered in her eyes. Her relationship with her father was complex, unfathomable to Sam. He sensed that she was afraid it might crumble under scrutiny.

"It's lunchtime already," she said in a rush. "I'd better get Natalie out of Edward's hair." She went to the door and got her jacket from a hook. "I'll leave those albums here in case you want to look at them some more."

The moment had twisted, turned, changed. He had connected with her briefly, but she was slipping away again, eluding him. She seemed agitated as she stuck her arm in her jacket and fumbled with the zipper. "Damn," she swore between her teeth.

Sam took hold of the zipper and pulled it up. "Easy, Michelle." When the zipper reached the top, he didn't step away, but placed two fingers under her chin, holding her gaze to his. Her skin was as soft as it looked. Maybe softer. "Thanks," he said, his entire awareness fixating on her lips. "Thanks for bringing those pictures. It meant a lot to me."

"Thank Natalie." She ducked away, bending to put on her boots. "Why are you looking at me like that?"

"Maybe I still carry a torch for you, even after all these years."

"Men like you don't carry anything that long."

"You don't know me, Michelle."

"No, I don't." She went out onto the porch. "I guess that's my point."

"We can fix that," he said.

"If something in my life needs fixing, I'll take care of it myself." She seemed flustered, disconcerted by his attention.

It made him mad, the way she held him at a distance. "Oh yeah? From what I can tell by looking through those photo albums, you sure as hell haven't found what you want with . . . what's his name? Brad."

"How would you know that?"

"It's obvious. You're like this picture-perfect icon—a lover he doesn't really have to love, a partner who carries more than her share of the weight, a Barbie doll that looks good on the arm of his Armani tux."

"You don't know anything about me and Brad."

"Tell me I'm wrong."

"You're trivializing us. Trivializing a relationship that's been building—"

"Building toward what, Michelle? A marriage, or a business merger?"

"Oh, and you're the expert on relationships, right?" She marched outside without waiting for him to reply.

He felt a stab of guilt because maybe she had pegged him right. Certainly his track record bore it out, more than she could possibly know. *Tell her. Tell her now about the marriage.* But the moment passed, and he followed her outside.

Against the unrelieved white of the snow-draped paddock, Natalie Plum's tie-dyed skirts and leggings made a wild splash of color. She and Edward stood at the loading gate. She was talking a mile a minute, making fluttery gestures with her hands. When Cody came out of the barn leading the mare, even Natalie fell still. Sam and Michelle hurried over, stopping at the opposite side of the paddock. "What's going on?" Michelle asked.

"Edward and I decided the mare and filly could come out today," Cody answered.

"That's the one that kicked Cody in the head," Michelle told Natalie.

"She's dangerous," Natalie said, aghast.

"All females in labor are. But she's fine now. Watch."

Edward must have been giving Cody pointers. The bridle was buckled on correctly. Cody walked the horse with the proper amount of lead, her steam-puffing nose at his shoulder. She followed him like a big docile dog. Across the paddock, Natalie's coos of admiration carried on a light, cold wind.

The foal stood on stick legs in the open breezeway, whickering nervously as Cody led its mother slowly away. Unwilling to let its mother out of its sight, the baby took a tentative step into the snowy yard, then another. Its front legs splayed apart and it stumbled, then righted itself. Its muzzle came up covered in snow. It sneezed, shaking its head. Cody looked back and laughed, a ringing sound that made Sam think of the pictures he'd just seen, of a younger Cody. A happier Cody.

It made Sam's heart hurt to watch them. His son and his favorite horse, and the foal they'd helped bring into the world. There was something special and right about the fact that they were all here together.

"She's a beauty, Sam," Michelle said. "A perfect little filly. No wonder I can't keep Cody away."

Cody unhooked the bridle lead to let the mare walk around at will. The foal stuck close by her side, though it veered over to inspect Natalie, probably drawn to her flowing garments.

"I hope he doesn't get too attached," Michelle said softly.

"Would that be so bad?"

She lifted her face to his in a way he remembered from many years before. No other face, no other eyes had that particular softness, that vulnerability. "He'd never get to see the filly."

"Never?"

She blinked, long lashes sweeping down with a tragic knowing that chilled Sam to the bone. "After the transplant, I don't see us coming back here too often. Before long, Cody'll be off to college, and I'll—" She broke off and her gaze slid away from his.

"What'll you be doing, Michelle?"

She was quiet for a long time. The only sounds came from Natalie and Edward's chattering and the occasional blowing of the mare.

"When I first came out here," she said, "I had some wild notion that my father and I would finally connect. That we'd finally get to know each other the way a father and daughter should know each other. Maybe I bought into some of that cellular memory stuff, thinking that if we shared our own flesh and blood, a perfect relationship would surely follow." She loosed a small, bitter laugh. "Instead, I think we're proof that there's nothing particularly special about a living related donor except maybe a few antigens in common."

"You're making up your mind about a lot of things in a short period of time," Sam pointed out. "Slow down, Michelle. You—" A snowball exploded square in the middle of his chest. "Hey!"

Edward and Natalie were both armed, hurling snowballs as fast as they could make them. Cody jumped the rail of the paddock and joined the attack. "Be careful of your head," Michelle called.

Cody barely acknowledged the warning. Sam aimed low with a snowball, missing. The kid was quick, a hard target.

Michelle took one in the shoulder before ducking to make some snowballs of her own.

The war drove off all thoughts of lunch. Natalie's wild squeals filled the air. Sam got in a few good shots, glad to ease the tension. Michelle, complaining of snow down her neck, grabbed his shoulders and held him in front of her like a shield.

"Wait a minute," he said, though her grip on him felt eerily right. "What's wrong with this picture?"

Cody took advantage, pelting him in the face and laughing so hard that Sam laughed, too.

Sam scooped up another handful of snow. The pager clipped to his belt went off.

"What's that?" Michelle held up her hand to signal a truce. Her face was wet from snow and beautifully flushed. Sam felt a strong surge of desire. If they were alone, he knew just where he'd kiss her, taste her. . . .

He checked the digital readout on the pager. His skin chilled at the code. "Michelle, your father's gone to the hospital."

Chapter 26

"I hate it that I know the way to the hospital," Michelle said as the landscape whizzed past. She ran a finger around her collar, feeling the damp spots from the snowball fight. "It's sort of ghoulish, knowing the way to the hospital."

"Not if you work there." Sam's voice was calm, doctorly.

She pressed her knuckles to her mouth to keep the questions in. *What happened? Why? Does this mean the transplant has to be postponed?*

She didn't want to ask those questions yet. She was not ready to hear the answers. She wanted to see her father. Wanted to hear his voice again, take his hand in hers. Wanted to let him know she loved him.

I love you, Daddy.

How hard was that to say? Why hadn't she said it before? Because she wasn't sure she meant it, or was she afraid it would be one-sided?

"Almost there," Sam said, his truck veering around the snow-covered Salish statue in the middle of the town square. They arrived at the hospital, and under the awning she jammed her shoulder against the car door and opened it, feet racing as they hit the ground. The electronic doors hissed open.

"Gavin Slade," she told the clerk, the same one who was there for Cody's accident. "I'm his daughter, Michelle."

"In the exam room."

She rushed in to find her father with a stocky, gray-haired physician. Gavin looked haggard, a yellowish cast to his skin and the whites of his eyes.

"I'm Michelle Turner," she told the doctor, not taking her eyes off Gavin.

I love you, Daddy.

"Hey, Michelle. This is my doctor, Karl Schenk." His voice was gravelly, tired, thin.

"What happened?"

"Toxemia. The dialyzing fluid failed."

"But it's going to be fixed, right? He's going to be fine?"

Schenk stayed busy with the monitoring equipment.

Sam walked in, bringing the smell of snow and wind with him. She thought about what he'd said to her earlier, that her father had known about them as kids.

Is it true, Daddy? Are you the reason Sam disappeared?

She cast away the thought. This was hardly the time or place. She wanted to touch her father, but she didn't know where. He had an IV stuck in the top of one hand and another in the crook of the opposite arm. Tubes snaked from his midsection. She settled for laying her hand on his leg, covered in a thin aqua-colored sheet.

Time for the questions. She took a deep breath. "Will this have any effect on the transplant?"

Schenk regarded her with a level look. "I've got a call in to his nephrologist."

"And?"

"If Gavin stabilizes, he can proceed."

She looked her father severely in the eye. "So stabilize."

He tried to smile. She could tell he felt crummy, but the attempt encouraged her. "I'm trying."

Then Sam took charge. It didn't surprise her. In the past few days she had come to realize that the attractive, serious boy she'd once known had turned into a calm, decisive—still-attractive—man. So when he started going over the tests Schenk ordered, then switched to making sure someone called Edward to tell him to send Natalie and Cody home in the Rover, and then called her father's nutritionist, Tadao, she just stood back and let him work.

It felt good. Sinfully good. To have someone else in charge for a while. To have someone else say, "This is how it's going to be," was a luxury.

She watched Sam with a phone cradled on his shoulder and a metal clipboard in hand. Why did it feel so good when he took charge?

She felt vaguely disloyal, having such thoughts. Brad was a take-charge guy, too. But the things he took charge of were . . . different. The vacation plans, his next real-estate investment, country-club dues. He never burdened her with that sort of thing, because he knew it wasn't that important to her.

But there were burdens she had never asked him to share.

The sorts of things Sam was helping with, and she hadn't even asked.

As the afternoon headed on toward evening, she stood back in a daze of dissipating worry. Gavin's tests came back, indicating that he was stabilizing. Orderlies arrived to take him to a private room, and she stood by his bed while attendants checked all the monitoring equipment.

"Don't scare me like this again, Daddy." She tried to sound stern.

"Go on home to supper. I'll call for Jake when they decide to release me."

"I'd rather stay—"

"Michelle, I'm trying to tell you politely that I'm tired as hell, and as soon as you leave, I'm going to sleep. Okay?"

She peered at his thin face. It was a wonderful face, full of character and experience. He had such a stunning aura of charisma that even lying sick in bed, he still qualified for *People* magazine's "most beautiful" issue.

"Okay." It was awkward to kiss his cheek because of all the tubes and monitors. The cool, medicinal smell hung thick in the air. " 'Bye, Daddy. See you tomorrow."

"First thing in the morning, I'm out of here."

"I hope so."

Sam was waiting in the corridor as she came out, quietly closing the door behind her.

"Never a dull moment," she said, trying to lighten the mood.

"That's Crystal City, all right."

They walked outside to find that it was sunset already. A glaze of orange tinted the mountains, and the temperature had dropped a few degrees. A gleaming black sport-utility vehicle drove by, slowing down as it passed the hospital. "Someone you know?" she asked Sam.

"Nope. Car's too new. Probably a rental." He opened the truck door for her. "You'd be a great candidate for primal-scream therapy."

"Why do you say that?"

"The tension. You're so damned tense even I can feel it. I think it's contagious."

"Sorry. You think it'll affect my kidney tests if I drink myself into oblivion tonight?"

"Most definitely."

"That's what I was afraid of."

"I'm not a big fan of drinking to oblivion on any night."

She climbed into the truck, shivering against the chill vinyl seat. "Sorry, Sam. I know it was awful for you, dealing with your mother's problem."

The streetlights blinked on, just a few along Main and Aspen. There was a certain coziness to this town that tugged at her. Some people thought it would be oppressive to live in a place where everyone knew everyone else's name. But after years in the big city, she understood the appeal.

"Cody mentioned meeting your mom," she said, uncomfortable with Sam's silence.

"Yeah?"

"He's curious. I think he wouldn't mind getting to know her."

"She'd like that. No idea what they have in common, though."

They passed the movie house. When they were teenagers, they had gone to the movies there. She remembered sitting in the popcorn-flavored darkness with Sam, holding hands and watching *An Officer and a Gentleman*.

"Too bad the Lynwood folded," she said, bothered by

the sight of the unlit marquee. The movable letters gaped like rotting teeth, spelling out the imperfect message, "CL SED."

"I think it had its last season about three years ago."

"My father wants to reopen it, but everything's on hold until after the surgery."

Sam pulled around to the side of the old building. "Want to go in?"

"Can we? It's not locked?"

In the lowering light she could see his smile as he rummaged in the glove box for a flashlight. "I've sneaked into a few picture shows in my day. Come on."

She felt a little furtive as they headed for the back of the building. She saw the gleam of headlights on Main Street, but no one was likely to notice the truck parked in the alley by the theater. As Sam had predicted, the rear fire exit wasn't locked. They went in, and he switched on the flashlight.

The shifting beam illuminated an eerie scene straight out of *Phantom of the Opera*. Michelle gazed at the old-fashioned chandeliers draped in cobwebs, peeling fleur-de-lis wallpaper, the shirred-velvet curtain over the screen in shreds.

"Creepy," she said, her breath making frozen puffs.

"You want to leave?"

"No, let's look around."

Floorboards creaked as they walked up the aisle. The box office and concession stand were dusty and deserted, the lobby empty, lined with vintage movie posters. The ones featuring her father bore his autograph. Sam beamed the flashlight on *Act of God,* a disaster epic that set box-office records and blasted her father into the ranks of the highest-paid stars of his day.

In the thirty-odd years since the poster had been printed,

Gavin Slade had changed very little. He had a classic, timeless bone structure that weathered well despite the years.

"I've always been ambivalent about his career," she confessed to Sam. "On the one hand, how could I look at something like this, or watch his performance in *The Face of Battle* and *not* be proud? On the other hand, he put his career before me—at least, until he needed something only I can give him. How can I not resent that?"

He was silent, and she hugged herself against a chill. "I'm a terrible person. I shouldn't think things like that."

Sam touched her shoulder. "You're not a terrible person. I figure it's pretty normal to feel that way, given the circumstances."

"Now you're sounding like Temple. The one who thought we had too many 'issues' to sort out."

An electric heater hung over the concession stand. Sam plugged it in, and Michelle was gratified when the coils took on a comforting red-orange glow. Evidently her father still kept up the utilities on the old place. Within a few minutes, the overhead heater bathed the lobby in faint light and a pleasant heat. She remembered the funky old furnishings from long ago: a musty club chair and chaise, marble ashtrays yellowed by the years. She took a seat on the old velvet-covered chaise lounge with rolled ends and fringe. Its springs creaked as she settled in.

"The way I figure," Sam said, turning to her, "your 'issues' will work out a lot better after the surgery's behind you."

So simple. She felt as if someone had taken a forklift and moved the weight that had been pressing on her chest. Why hadn't she thought of that? Why hadn't she made herself look beyond the surgery and understand that the real healing would take place if she simply let it happen?

"Thank you," she whispered as he sat beside her on the chaise. "Thank you for saying that."

"Feel better?"

She sensed the warmth from the heater and the comfort of Sam's presence and the dry odor of the abandoned building, and a strange and unaccountable feeling of peace and safety came over her.

"Much better."

"Good." He grinned. "It's what I live for."

Michelle drew her knees up to her chest, watching him. "I can't get over that you're a doctor."

He lifted his hand, skimmed his thumb over the ridge of her cheekbone, and everything inside her fell still, waiting, totally focused on the spot he was touching.

"I can't get over that you're a mother," he said.

He reached a place inside her no one had ever reached before—except the boy he had been so long ago. How could she have known, when they were eighteen, that he would be the only one? How could she have known that when he left her life, he'd leave a gulf of emptiness and loneliness no one else would ever fill?

"Damn it, Michelle," he said, dropping his hand, "I wish you'd told me."

She heard his anger, too, echoing her own, and the problem with this sort of anger was that it was fueled by regret—for what they didn't do, for the road they didn't take. And the problem with regret was that it had no place to *go*. It just stayed inside, turning dark and bitter.

"I tried to tell you," she said softly, picturing herself that day, frightened and excited and oh, so very young. It was November, the sunset dull in the sky, and she was wearing her riding clothes—buff-colored leggings and a big cable-knit Aran sweater. "You didn't show up for work that day."

He held himself very stiff, as though every cell in his body had come to attention. She could tell he knew which day she was talking about. She borrowed a Jeep from the ranch, and she drove slowly, terrified because of what the home pregnancy test had just revealed and nervous because she had never gone to Sam's home before.

It was a weathered, wood-frame shotgun house on the east side of town, one of a row of dwellings built for migrant cherry pickers to use in the summer. She had not missed the symbolism of having to drive over the railroad tracks to reach his house.

No lights burned in the windows, and the driveway was empty. On some gut level she could already sense the desertion, could already predict the silence that would greet her knocks upon the door. But she knocked anyway, at the front door and the back, ducking under a clothesline with a single forgotten sock hanging frozen from it. She called out, and then tried the back door, not surprised when it opened. Crystal City was a small town where people left their doors unlocked—particularly if there was nothing in the house to steal.

She had shivered, walking through the four rooms, picturing Sam there with his mother. Sagging furniture with holes in the upholstery, a dinette set from the fifties, swaybacked beds in the tiny bedrooms. No wonder he'd never invited her over.

"You were gone," she said after a long silence. "Your house was empty. I drove up to the café to see if your mom was still working there. Earl Meecham said she took off, hadn't even left a forwarding address for her last paycheck."

"Forwarding addresses are always a problem," he said, "when you don't know where you're going."

She stared into the ripening glow of the heater. "What would it have cost you to tell me good-bye?"

He was quiet for a long time, so long that she got suspicious and studied his face in the light from the heater. She didn't know him anymore, couldn't read that lean, serious face. He seemed tense, his eyes turbulent as if he was at war with himself.

"Sam?"

"I don't know why I didn't say good-bye," he said at last, his voice quiet and controlled. "It was a long time ago."

"Everything was a long time ago."

The anger drained away and brutally soft memories crept up to seize her. There was a time when they stood at the center of the world, and everything seemed possible. She remembered the laughter, the passion, and the utter belief that all their dreams would come true. She remembered the love everyone thought they were too young to feel.

He rubbed his thumb over her cheek. "I've never been good at good-byes."

She knew he was going to kiss her. He had his hand in the right place, cradling her cheek, and he had their eyes in the right place—they were both staring at each other's lips—and, most of all, he had the moment in the right place. She was not thinking of anything beyond the here and now, and how badly she wanted him to kiss her, hold her.

He leaned forward and she moved her knees out of the way, and neither of them hurried, because every heartbeat, every breath, every second was important. Their lips touched, and the taste of him rushed through her with a powerful force, memories exploding across the years, and the passion between them was fresh, alive, yet as old and familiar as something they had carried around for decades.

They didn't speak. They knew better than that. Because if one of them spoke, they'd start to rationalize, and if they rationalized, they would know this was insane, and in a tacit agreement they decided to explore the insanity. Their coats came off, then boots and sweaters and jeans, and his hands were everywhere, and so were hers, sensations tumbling faster than thought. Hard muscle, soft flesh, his mouth mapping the topography of her body until instinct and remembrance converged and they knew each other again. Finally, the hurrying started, because there was an urgency, a need that wouldn't wait. She leaned back against the curve of the chaise and he braced his arms on either side of her, and he came down and she came up, and there was a moment of union so perfect that she saw stars.

Afterward he stayed on top of her, and she wanted to keep him there forever, because as soon as one of them moved or spoke, life had to start up again. She felt his back warm beneath her palms, listened to his heightened breathing, touched her lips to the pulse in his neck.

"What are you thinking?" he asked, and he remembered that thing with her ear, the way it made her tingle all over when she felt the heat of his intimate whisper.

No one but him had ever discovered that about her.

"That we shouldn't move or talk," she whispered back.

"Good idea."

But after a while, she couldn't help it, and she asked, "What are *you* thinking?"

"Oh, honey. Dirty thoughts. Really dirty thoughts." And he told her in explicit detail, shoving her back against the chaise, whispering into her ear in the way only he knew how to do, and all of a sudden they were making love again, his kisses and the strokes of his body harsh the way she needed them to be, bringing her to a soaring climax that had her crying out, her voice echoing through the gloom of the empty building.

"*Now* what are you thinking?" he asked, long afterward.

"That I'm glad for the dark." She kissed him briefly— that inventive mouth that had just done such unspeakably exquisite things to her—and forced herself to sit up, pull on her sweater.

"Why?"

"Because—" she stood up, hurriedly pulling on panties and jeans "—I'm not an eighteen-year-old girl anymore. I'm thirty-five, and I look it."

He laughed in disbelief, zipping his jeans. "You're worried I'll be disappointed in how you *look?*"

She fumbled with the buttons of her fly. "Well, maybe not worried, but—"

"Listen." He took her busy hands and put them against his bare chest, his unbelievably muscular, sexy bare chest.

"I'm listening."

"Of course I remember the way you looked back then. How could I not? I was eighteen, too. Your body used to drive me nuts. Yeah, I remember that." He traced his finger down her throat, over her breasts, waking them up again. "But what I was thinking about when I was holding you just now was how I used to love you."

She felt dizzy, suddenly, sick and dizzy with guilt and confusion. "We'd better go."

He hesitated, as if he was going to say something else. But then he buttoned his shirt, turned and unplugged the heater, and flicked on the flashlight.

They left through the door they had come in. It had started to snow, big thick flakes, the kind pictured on

Christmas cards. In the sodium vapor glow of the corner streetlamp, the swirling snow looked glorious, magical.

Halfway between the door and the truck, a shadow fell across the alley.

Sam put his arms around her, catching her against his chest. "What the—"

A flash exploded in their faces, and although Sam didn't realize it, she knew exactly what had happened.

They'd found her. The dirt diggers. The paparazzi. The kidney-patient stalkers. The princess-murderers.

Tires spun on the salted and sanded road, and then the sport-utility vehicle sped away, leaving Michelle and Sam frozen like a pair of coyotes caught in a bounty hunter's searchlights. The familiar glowing ache from the flash filled her head. She should have recognized them. She had seen their Explorer pass the hospital earlier this evening. She should have known the buzzards were circling.

"What the hell was that all about?" Sam asked.

"You'll read it in the papers," she said dully, feeling her insides coil up with dread. "Could be as early as tomorrow." Digital file transfers had made the process as swift as a phone call.

"I don't read that kind of paper."

"You'll be amazed when you see who does."

Friday

Friday

Chapter 27

Michelle stood in the hall of the hospital feeling weak with relief. Her father had stabilized and he was back on the pre-op meds he'd been taking in preparation for the transplant. Barring any other crisis, they were back on track for the procedure. In a few minutes, he'd be discharged.

But she felt as if all the other parts of her life had careened off in different directions. Last night, in the mysterious darkness of a half-forgotten place, she and Sam had made love. She'd wanted him with a wildness and a hunger so uncharacteristic of her that she had begun to think she was becoming someone else entirely. A stranger to herself. A traitor to the life she had built so far from here. She should be feeling shame, regret, guilt . . . but she couldn't.

Restless with her thoughts, she wandered to the small

waiting lounge by the reception area. No one was around, so she helped herself to coffee. Nurse O'Brien came in, smiling a greeting.

"Michelle, right?" she asked.

"Michelle Turner. I'm spending way too much time at this hospital."

The nurse sat down on a vinyl-covered sofa and gave a weary sigh. "Tell me about it. There's a flu going around, so I've been working overtime for the past week. Your boy doing all right?"

"He's fine. But that head wound was a big scare." She paused, wondering how much the nurse knew about them. Everything, probably. This was a hospital, after all. "Did you happen to notice a reporter or photographer snooping around last night?"

"Uh-huh. I'm afraid your father was seen checking in yesterday." She sent Michelle an apologetic look. "We didn't let anyone in to see him."

"Good. It's a constant worry," she admitted. "I've tried to keep Cody anonymous for years." She took a deep breath. "Um, so are people here talking about it? About Sam and Cody?"

"That they're father and son?" she said easily. "Oh, yeah."

"I was afraid so." Michelle was dying to ask what they were saying, but she was not sure she wanted to know.

"I never could picture Sam with a kid of his own."

Something in Alice O'Brien's tone, in the deep knowing of her observation, caught Michelle's attention. "Have you worked with Sam long?"

Alice O'Brien lifted her eyebrows in surprise. "He didn't tell you?"

Michelle felt a strange shift in the atmosphere and instinctively braced herself. "Tell me what?"

The nurse waited, clearly weighing her options. Then she said, "Sam and I used to be married."

The atmosphere silently exploded. "Oh." *God.*

"It appears you and Sam must have a lot of catching up to do."

"He should have told me," Michelle said, mortified by the situation he had put her in.

"It's all old history, but it's no secret." Alice O'Brien spoke straightforwardly. "When he came here five years ago, I took one look at him and fell like a ton of bricks." She grinned. "Most of the staff did. Sam and I got along great, decided to get married. I think Sam just drifted into the relationship, and I was fool enough to mistake it for love." Tugging her pink sweater close around her shoulders, she added, "I have the classic nurse personality— nurturing, caretaking—and he wanted love and sex and a woman."

"Alice," Michelle said, "you don't have to explain this." *Sam should have.*

"I don't mind. You're bound to hear the story from somebody or other. It wasn't too dramatic. I fell hard, and Sam—well, he sort of came along for the ride, I suppose. When I said I wanted to start a family, that was my wake-up call." She pushed back the sleeve of her sweater, checked her watch. "He had a bad reaction to that. Said he saw enough unwanted kids in his practice. And I realized he was never going to give me what I needed. Hell, what I *deserved*. So we split up." A tolerant smile tilted her mouth. "He felt bad about it, but I stuck to my guns. It's better this way. We're still friends, colleagues."

Michelle leaned back in her chair, her thoughts spinning. Though younger than Michelle, Alice spoke with the wisdom of a much older woman, and her words reverberated in the silence. *He was never going to give me what I needed.*

"In his way, I think he loved me for a while. Just wasn't meant to last," she concluded, standing up and checking her watch again. "He's a complicated guy, had a rough life. He learned to love fast, he learned to love hard, and he learned to let go. No one ever taught him how to hold on."

Mounted on a line-backed dun mare named Daisy, Michelle rode along a track that wound to the south and west of Lonepine. She felt the cold slice of air in her lungs, the numbing lash of the wind on her face. The afternoon sky was overcast and tinged bronze by a stingy leak of sunlight.

After Alice's revelation, Michelle had taken her father home; then she drove straight to Lonepine. Sam had gone off on horseback to check a wildlife trap. "He'll probably stop at the hot springs on the way back," Edward had informed her. "He generally likes to do that when he's in a mood."

In a mood. She didn't ask Edward what he meant by that. She'd find out for herself soon enough.

The trail was easy to follow, just as Edward had said it would be. She rode up past an abandoned slash pile from an old logging operation, then angled down toward a low field where the snow had melted away to reveal steaming mudflats. A herd of elk shied away as she approached. At a rock-bound natural pool, a tall roan horse was tethered, but she couldn't see Sam. Dismounting, she wound the reins around a low alder branch and climbed up to the pool. Thermal springs abounded in the area, and the wispy steam softened and obscured everything, adding a faint tinge of salt and sulphur to the air.

"Fancy meeting you here," said a disembodied voice.

Michelle peered through the steam, and there he was, sitting chest-deep in the pool, wearing nothing but a smile. She tried not to think about that smile, or the way the dampness curled his hair, or the beads of water on his shoulders. "I had a little talk with Alice at the hospital today," she said.

His smile disappeared. "Then I guess you'd better have a seat."

"Maybe you could get dressed, Sam—"

"Or you could join me." The smile sneaked back across his lips.

She sank down on a flat rock, covering her face with her hands. "I can't believe you didn't tell me you were married."

She heard a trickle of water, and suddenly he was gliding toward her, taking her hands away from her face. She should leave now, just get up and ride away, but she felt stuck here, unable to move.

"I would have told you, Michelle, but we haven't had that much time to talk."

"We've had time to do a lot more than talk."

"Yeah." His hands—damp, warm, insistent—peeled off her gloves and unzipped her jacket. "Yeah, we have."

The rising steam and the heat and his touch filled her with a strange and helpless lassitude, and everything she'd planned to say simply evaporated. With slow and deliberate care he removed her boots and socks.

"It's my fault my marriage to Alice didn't work out." His whisper rasped in her ear, and then he kissed her in a leisurely way, imprisoning her by her own desire. It was a powerful drug, the taste of him, the taste of passion.

"She claims her needs . . . weren't met." She forced the words out even as she surrendered, peeling off sweater

296 / Susan Wiggs

and jeans, letting the delicious shock of cold air and hot water race over her bare skin.

"She's right. I couldn't give her what she needed." Long slow slide of his hands down over her body as he drew her deep into the silky water, secretly heated in the heart of the earth. "Because I gave it all to you."

Sam had always been one to think on a matter before deciding what to do. But the thing was, all the thinking in the world never seemed to do a damned bit of good. He always came around to what his gut told him to do in the first place. The second he had figured out the truth about Cody, he had been consumed by fascination. He wanted to know the boy, be near him, be with him. Circumstances had handed him a way to do that—if he could get Michelle to agree to it.

Still sitting in the thermal pool and squinting through the thick wisps of steam, he watched her getting dressed. His body reacted as fast as it had when he was eighteen— maybe faster. Because now he knew from experience that sex like they'd just had didn't come along every day.

He figured he ought to be dressed when he broached the topic of Cody, so he made himself chill out, waded to the shore, and dried off before the numbing cold hit him. Yanking on jeans, socks, and boots, he kept stealing glances at Michelle. She was beyond beautiful, always had been, but now that he was coming to know her again, he saw something more in this woman. Years ago, he had seen the promise. Now he saw the way time and caring and motherhood had molded her, softened her. Though she was slender, her breasts and belly had the sweet roundness common to any woman who had ever given birth and nursed a baby. It didn't seem to matter how much time passed. The mother-shape was always there.

"What are you smiling about?" she asked, slightly suspicious, still flushed from the hot springs and from their lovemaking.

He tugged a gray UT Athletic Department sweatshirt over his head. "Do you have to ask?"

She sniffed, but not before he caught a flash of amusement in her eyes. "I didn't come out here looking for sex. I came looking for answers."

"So the sex was just sort of a bonus, I guess," he said.

"Very funny." She put on her boots and started walking toward the horses.

"Michelle, wait." He followed her, jumping from stone to stone to keep clear of the steaming mud. A few elk, only slightly perturbed by the presence of humans, sidled off toward the woods. "There's something I need to ask you."

His tone must have touched off her suspicions, for she turned to him with her eyes narrowed and her arms folded across her chest, unconsciously protecting herself. "What is it?"

He figured he'd best just get it said. "When you and Gavin go in for the surgery, I want Cody to stay with me."

He knew she was going to object before she even said a word. It was there in her narrow-eyed, guarded expression. He didn't wait for her to speak, but went on, "I've been thinking about it for days, and it's a good plan. He can—"

"I already have a plan for Cody," she said. "He's staying at Blue Rock. Tadao and Jake are there, and now Natalie. They—"

"They are not his family." Sam tried to keep his temper, his desperation, in check. "His flesh and blood. He's got me and my mother. He needs a chance to know us. The timing's right, Michelle."

She took a step back. "No."

"What are you worried about?" he asked. "I want to spend some time with my son. How can you object to that?"

"Because I don't think you know what you're asking." She spread her arms. "You just dismissed your marriage to Alice with a shrug, more or less. You split up with her after a year. And now you want to take on a son?"

The barb dug deep, but Sam wouldn't let his pain show. He knew what she was doing. She was trying to make him mad, hurt him, so he'd back off. Suddenly, he saw her so clearly that he wanted to hug her. "Aw, Michelle, you don't need to be afraid."

Her chin came up. "I'm not afraid."

"You are. You're scared Cody and I will become best friends and he'll forget the person who walked the floors at night with him, and fixed him birthday cake, and stood in the rain at all his soccer games." Sam walked over to her, took her hand, pressed his lips to it, and kept hold. She tasted of the mineral springs. "You don't need to worry. A kid will always choose his mother. Trust me on this."

He stepped away and jammed on his hat. He hadn't meant to say something so revealing. "Come on, Michelle. You've had sixteen years. I'm asking for a week."

She unlooped the lead rein of her mare, then raked her fingers through the horse's thick winter coat. "Where are we, Sam?" she asked him. "I need to know that before I decide."

He knew she wasn't asking for directions home. They had come to a place where there were no more secrets, no hesitation. But with their new closeness came vulnerability on both their parts. He didn't know for certain he could become a family man overnight. His experience with his mother had taught him the tender hurts of commitment and responsibility. But he wanted to try. They were opening themselves to trouble—but also to joy, if they could make this work. Sam was sure of it.

"Well?" she asked, waiting. "Where are we?"

He held her horse's head while she mounted and stood looking up at her. "At the beginning, I guess."

The restaurant called Trudy's was one of the few good things about Crystal City, Cody decided. His meal of a giant cheeseburger and fries, followed by chocolate cream pie, had been a welcome change from the macrobiotic stuff his grandfather's nutrition specialist served.

Too bad his parents had ruined it by dropping a bomb on him right after dessert.

He scowled into the darkened display window of the Northern Lights Feed Store. He had asked to be excused after dinner, and for the past fifteen minutes had been wandering down Main Street, which was basically the only street in town. At one end lay city hall and the library, which appeared to be the only place other than Trudy's that stayed open after dark. At the other end was an old movie house with an abandoned shop adjacent to it, the glossy windows practically begging for someone to throw a rock through them.

His mom said Gavin owned the Lynwood and might do something with it one of these days, but for now it was as empty as a Sunday afternoon. A few kids came and went from the library, and the sight of them—guys pushing and jostling each other, girls with schoolbooks hugged to their chests—only lowered Cody's mood. Day after tomorrow he would be starting school, which added insult to injury.

Hunching his shoulders up, he moved along, passing the shop where Tammi Lee Gilmer worked. His mom and Sam were probably wondering where he'd gone. He pictured them sitting across the table from each other at the restaurant, maybe holding hands and looking worried. Hell, let them worry. He had promised to stick around, said he just wanted to get out for some air. Fat chance—the Greyhound bus was idling across the street, puffing diesel fumes into the night. The lighted header over the bus bore enticing destinations: MISSOULA-SPOKANE-SEATTLE.

Man, what he wouldn't give to hop on that sucker right now. Digging in his pocket, he found a flattened pack of Camels. Two left. When those were gone, he didn't know what he'd do. How did kids get their smokes in a town where everyone knew everyone else? He lit up, letting the match burn for a minute while reading the matchbook cover: "Alone? Scared? Broke? Dial 1-800-RUNAWAY . . ."

"I should be so lucky," he muttered under his breath, then took a deep drag of the cigarette. Around the first of the school year, he had taken up smoking in order to hang out with Claudia, and it had worked. She'd noticed him, bummed a cigarette, and within a few weeks they were going out. He wondered what she was up to now. They'd only been apart for a week, but he was already worried she wouldn't wait around for him. The thought pissed him off so much that he nearly plowed down a couple of kids coming out of the library. He said a brusque, "Excuse me" and propped his hip on a cold steel bike rack in front of the building. There were only a couple of bikes chained to the rack. Must be hard to ride on these pitted, icy streets. Why did people live in Montana anyway? he wondered, blowing out a stream of smoke.

"Hey, Cody," said a familiar voice.

He looked up to see Molly Lightning, her arms laden with books. He held his pose at the bike rack. "Hey."

Her gaze fell to the orange-tipped cigarette in his hand, and he felt stupid all of a sudden. Stupid and self-conscious, the way he had when he'd first learned to smoke. Trying to act nonchalant, he dug for the nearly empty pack. "You want a smoke?"

"No."

He'd known without asking that she didn't smoke. Ah, well. At least she wasn't going to be all sanctimonious about it.

She seemed ill at ease as she glanced up and down the street.

"You waiting for someone?" he asked, trying to be discreet as he dropped the cigarette and ground it out in the damp snow. Good move, he thought peevishly. Half of a perfectly good smoke, and now it was gone.

"My mom's supposed to pick me up at eight." She gazed at him with unmistakable interest. She might have a crush on him, he thought, and the idea pleased him.

At the other end of the block, three guys in baggy pants and big parkas made a racket, laughing and shoving each other. One of them picked up a rock or a chunk of ice and hurled it at the marquee over the awning of the Lynwood, punching the air in victory at the sound of shattering lightbulbs.

"Jerks," Molly said softly.

Cody felt a little better to hear her echo his own thoughts. "Who are they?"

"Guys from school. Billy Ho, Ethan Lindvig, Jason Kittredge." The threesome crammed themselves into the cab of an old El Camino and roared off into the dark. "Everyone thinks Billy is so cool, but I think he's a jerk.

He was on juvey probation last year for stealing, but that only made kids think he's even more cool. He didn't even get kicked off the football team." She fell silent, looking worried, as if she had said too much. She shifted uncomfortably from one foot to the other.

"Um, can I take those books from you?" Cody asked, hoping he didn't sound too dorky.

She smiled the way she had the first day they'd met. Sort of shy, but also a little bit sexy. "Thanks," she said, transferring the stack of library books to him. "I didn't want to put them down in the snow." She smelled really good, like soap and fresh air. Cody hoped the cigarette smell didn't cling in his jacket. "So what are you doing out here?" she asked.

He nodded toward Trudy's in the middle of the block. "My mom and . . . Sam McPhee took me to dinner. I just wanted to walk around a little." She didn't say anything, but listened with an expectant quality. "My mom's going into the hospital to donate a kidney to my grandfather," he blurted out.

He braced himself for her shock and disgust, but she surprised him. She simply smiled again, and said, "Cool."

"I guess." For the first time, Cody started to think maybe it *was* kind of cool. "But," he added, his rush of candor continuing, "while they're in the hospital next week, they want me to stay at Sam's. They sort of left the decision up to me."

"So what are your choices?" she asked.

He liked it that she seemed genuinely interested. He had planned to call Claudia tonight and get her take on all this, but she didn't know the people involved. It was easier standing around talking to Molly, face-to-face. "I can stay at Blue Rock with Jake and Tadao—they work for Gavin." He rested his chin on the top book. "Or I can go to Lonepine."

She grinned and put her hands on her hips. "Are you kidding? Like there's a decision to be made? Sam's your dad, and he's got a horse farm. It's a no-brainer."

Saturday

Chapter 28

Tammi Lee Gilmer didn't usually get Saturdays off work, but she had arranged to be off in order to pick up her car at McEvoy's Garage. Setting a freshly lit cigarette on the cluttered bathroom counter, she took a round brush and teased some loft into her hair. No one teased their hair anymore; she knew that. Hell, no one smoked anymore. But that sure didn't stop her.

She knew Sam didn't like her smoking, but he never said a word. He had stood by her, helping her break so many other habits that the cigarettes probably seemed minor in comparison. She picked up the cigarette and took a drag, scowling at the amber burn mark it had made on the edge of the faux marble countertop. It was disgusting, really. She should quit.

Tomorrow.

Today, she wasn't going to beat herself up over it. This

was something it had taken her years of AA to learn. She had to forgive herself, to avoid sinking into regrets about the past. It was an everyday battle for her.

She did her makeup and put on a pair of jeans and a loose sweatshirt. She still fit into her size-eight Wranglers, and she was proud of that. Yet deep inside her dwelt a strange longing that seized her at the oddest of times. It was a longing to be soft and doughy, maybe like LaNelle Jacobs, who owned the quilt shop. She secretly dreamed of being like LaNelle: plump and bespectacled, with forearms that jiggled and a double chin, wearing a housedress and a bib apron and sensible shoes. Smelling of talcum powder and Jergens lotion and freshly baked bread.

Tammi Lee walked outside, lifting her face to an overcast sky and feeling the tingle of the nineteen-degree temperature on her face. Yeah, it was insane, but she wanted to be one of those plus-size blue-haired women. Because when you looked like that, it told folks you knew your place in the world. It meant you'd raised a family, making pancakes for them on the weekends and reading bedtime stories to the kids. It meant you'd made a house into a home, putting up curtains and picking out the right color for the walls and buying flats of petunias for the garden every spring. It meant you had grandkids who came running up the walk to the front door because they couldn't wait to see you. It meant you had a husband who had several annoying habits, but you loved him anyway because he was your whole world.

God, what she wouldn't give to fit into a life like that, instead of into her size-eight Wranglers.

She felt a familiar buzzing heat inside her and started walking down the street toward the center of town. The buzz was a warning; it was the craving, the dark desire that had consumed her for so many years. One drink, that was all it would take. One drink, and the buzzing would quiet and she'd feel normal again.

She quickened her pace, clenching her hands into fists inside her jacket pockets. Maybe she'd better give her sponsor a call. This was a weak moment; it had come out of nowhere. They always did.

Yet as she walked, the cold had a calming effect on her, and the sick, thirsty moment passed. She had the life she had. God knew it was more than she deserved. By the time she got to the garage, the craving had settled to a dull roar. "Hey, Tom," she said, stepping into the overheated, grease-scented office. "Am I all set?"

"New water pump did the trick," he said.

She paid him in cash. She used cash for almost everything these days, because writing checks had never brought her anything but trouble. Sam had given her a debit card drawing on his own account, but she avoided using that. Giving her her life back was enough; she didn't want to take more from him than she already had.

A block from the garage, she pulled into Ray's Quik Chek to get a cup of coffee and the latest *Enquirer*, hot off the press. Sam gave her grief about all the gossip rags and movie magazines she bought, but she loved them.

The new *Enquirer*s were still wrapped in plastic binding. As she poured herself a cup of coffee, Ray opened them up and sold her one, along with *People* and her own reserved copy of *Country Billboard*. She went to her car and sat there sipping the coffee, waiting for the blower to heat up and paging through the magazines.

A giant picture of a 108-year-old *Titanic* survivor occupied the front page of the *Enquirer*, but a small inset at the top caught her eye.

"Ho-ly shit," she muttered, nearly dropping her coffee. Her hand shook as she set the cup in a holder and opened the paper to page two. A file photo of Gavin Slade and Michelle, looking as golden and fit as Peter and Bridget Fonda, caught her eye. Next to that was a blurry shot of someone on a stretcher being wheeled into County Hospital. On the same page, a grainy black-and-white picture showed Michelle Turner and Sam, caught in an embrace in the middle of a snowy street. The headline read: *Daughter of Dying Movie Idol Seeks Solace with Lonesome Cowboy.*

The Chevy fishtailed out of the parking lot. One of the few good things about her rambling lifestyle was that she had probably driven more miles than a long-distance trucker, and she was good at it. Negotiating the icy patches on the highway, she raced home and picked up the phone.

Sam was on duty today, but his service took the message. "No emergency," Tammi Lee said, "but it's important."

Next, she tried Blue Rock Ranch. The guy who answered the phone said Mr. Slade was "unavailable." Tammi Lee had no choice but to try the hospital. Maybe the *Enquirer* was right about something for a change.

She reached the hospital in five minutes, and the first thing she saw was Cody Turner sitting hunched on a concrete bench outside the attached professional building where Sam's office was. He wore a knitted black cap and little wiry headphones. His foot jiggled in time to the music only he could hear.

My grandson. That's my goddamned grandson, she thought wonderingly.

He looked cold, sitting there, restless and sulky. And a bit like Sam.

She got out, boots crunching on the sand-and-salt surface of the parking lot. "Hey, Cody. Remember me? Tammi Lee Gilmer."

He took off the headphones. "Hi."

"So what's up?" She kept her voice casual.

"My grandfather drove me over to get my stitches out. And he had some kind of checkup."

"So how's the cut?"

He took off his black knit cap. "Okay, I guess."

She studied the curved wound. "Some week, huh?" she said. "All this hospital stuff."

"Yeah, it sucks."

She indicated his Discman. "What kind of music do you like?"

"Alternative, some heavy metal. And some older stuff," he said vaguely.

"Ever heard of rockabilly?"

"Sure." He put his hat back on.

"I know something about rockabilly. Used to sing in a band."

"Nuh-uh," he said, regarding her with dubious interest.

"I did. A group called Road Rage. Had a big hit single called 'Dearly Departed.'" She hummed the melody line.

His eyes grew wide. "No way. I've heard that song."

"A lot of folks have. It was on a Dodge truck commercial." She steadied herself. "Listen, maybe you could come over for a while today."

He was quiet, scuffing his toe against a lump of ice on the sidewalk.

"If you get bored, you can go right home, promise."

He looked her straight in the eye, and she realized he had a great face, a beautiful face, the face of a boy who was turning downright handsome. But in addition to hand-someness, Tammi Lee could see insolence, difficulty. Michelle Turner must be having quite a time, raising this kid.

"I saw that thing in the paper," he said.

She forced herself not to drop her gaze. "I was hoping you hadn't."

"Sam saw it, too. All the nurses were waiting to show it to him when he got to work this morning."

"The paper's a rag. They print lies and innuendo." She took a deep breath, wishing for a cigarette. "That picture doesn't mean a thing. Your mom probably slipped on the ice and Sam grabbed her so she wouldn't fall."

"Maybe," he said. "I hate those damned tabloids."

"Me, too," she lied.

"When I was little, my mom was always worried they'd come after us because of Gavin."

"And did they?"

"No, but she'd always say, 'Look at Lisa Marie Presley. You want to end up like that?'" His mouth hinted at a grin.

"So what do you say? Want to come see where your old grandma lives?"

He hesitated. "I guess."

"Wait here, then. I need to make sure it's okay."

He replaced the headphones and Tammi Lee went to the clinic entrance of the brick building. She usually got a big kick out of seeing Sam in his long white coat, but today she was worried. "Got a minute, Sam?" she asked him quietly.

He held open the door to the staff lounge. It was empty, a clutter of coffee mugs and well-thumbed medical manuals and clipboards on the table.

"So how much truth was there in that tabloid story?" she asked. No point in beating around the bush. "Are you taking up with a girl you went nuts over seventeen years ago?"

It was hard to read her son's mood. He had always been a stoic. In one of her many recovery sessions, she had admitted to taking shameless advantage of his calmness, his willingness to forgive her, no matter what. When she'd said so to his face, he had given her a sweet-sad smile and said, "You are who you are, Mama. You don't forgive the clouds for raining."

The memory touched her, and she took Sam's hand. "So is this just a fling," she asked, "or—"

"It's not a fling," he said.

She wished she could be the kind of mother you saw on TV, the one who could pat his arm, say a few wise words, and make everything work out fine before the next commercial. "Well, I'm no expert, but you'd better be sure you know what you want out of this. Because there are three of you involved, and one's just a kid."

"I realize that. Cody's going to stay with me while Michelle and Gavin go in for surgery."

"Yeah?" She rinsed a coffee mug at the sink and poured herself a cup, trying to picture her son being someone's father. "So are you excited?"

"Sure. Nervous, too. He's got to start school on Monday. I never heard of a sixteen-year-old starting mid-year in a new place and actually liking it."

She sipped the slightly stale coffee. "Builds character." She set down the mug and glanced at the door, making sure they were alone. "What are you going to do about the tabloid story?"

"Ignore it."

"Is Michelle ignoring it?"

"We haven't had a chance to talk." His face looked taut with frustration. "She and Gavin just left for Missoula to prep for the surgery."

"Maybe you'd better get on down to Missoula and talk things over with her." Something—fate, destiny, pure chance—had brought Sam and Michelle together again. Lord knew, they'd never had much of a chance as kids. "Don't second-guess her, Sam. You know, this morning I was having regrets, wishing I'd done things differently, made better choices. I don't want you to do that. I don't ever want you to have regrets."

"I can't get away until tomorrow morning."

"Then go tomorrow morning," she said. "I swear, for a doctor, you're pretty dense sometimes."

He sent her a fleeting grin. "Okay. I'll offer to drive Cody down in the morning."

Cody was quiet on the way to her house. As she let him in the front door, she wished she had put out some potpourri. The house smelled of stale cigarette smoke and yesterday's coffee. She wouldn't blame the kid if he turned and walked out.

He stepped inside hesitantly, looking around.

Tammi Lee couldn't stand it anymore. She grabbed a cigarette from a pack on the counter and lit up. Belatedly she asked, "You don't smoke, do you?"

He shrugged. "Sure."

"Well, I'm not offering you one. Your dad would kill me. How about a Coke?" She went to the fridge. "I understand Monday is the big day. For the transplant."

He popped open the can. "Yep." He drank his Coke while a long, awkward silence spun out. Tammi Lee finished her cigarette and lit another one. Cody's gaze wandered around the room like that of a trapped animal looking for escape. And suddenly his expression changed from wary to wondering.

"Wow," he said under his breath. "Is that a Stratocaster?"

"Yeah. Just like Dick Dale used to play." She took the vintage electric guitar from its stand in the corner. The old instrument was a classic. She'd pawned and rescued the thing countless times, and in the end she still had it. She rarely played these days, but she knew she'd kept it for a reason.

As she looked at Cody's face, she finally figured out what that reason was.

"Do you play?"

"A little," he said. "Do you?"

She took the guitar, adjusted the tuning, strummed a few riffs, her fingers surprisingly nimble. Glancing at Cody, she laughed at his expression. "What, you didn't believe me?" She stuck a cassette tape into the console. "This is a demo tape called 'Hand-Me-Down Dreams.'"

She hadn't heard it in ages, and the sound of her own playing and singing startled her. She remembered laying down the tracks in a Reno studio they'd rented by the hour. She'd left Sam wailing in a playpen in the control room. After the final cut, they'd all gone out to get wasted, Sam sleeping in his carseat under a table in the dim, smoke-filled club.

"It's a good song," Cody said when it was over.

"You think so?"

"Sure."

"Feel like making pizza?"

"I could eat, I guess."

Amazing. A teenage grandson who actually wanted to spend time with her.

And she didn't even have to wear a housedress and sensible shoes.

Sunday

S am had no privileges at St. Brendan Hospital in Missoula, but he used his credentials to inquire about Michelle's procedure, and learned that everything was still on schedule. She was staying at an old Arts and Crafts–era hotel built for timber barons early in the century. Now, because of its proximity to the hospital, it was always occupied by families of patients and visiting doctors. Early in the morning, he stood outside her door, trying to collect his thoughts, but they refused to be collected so he knocked.

"Who is it?" Her voice was small, but not sleepy.

"It's Sam."

"Come on in," she said, opening the door. Bathrobe. Bare feet. A look of apprehension on her face. On the bed lay a paperback novel and several newspapers spread across the rumpled covers.

"Hi." He bent and kissed her, aiming badly, his lips grazing her temple. She smelled of toothpaste and pHisoderm disinfectant.

"Is Cody all right? Did he drive down with you?"

"He's fine. I left him downstairs in the coffee shop with Gavin, eating pancakes."

"So you think this arrangement—him staying with you—is going to be all right?"

"Sure, Michelle. We agreed."

"If he gets to be too much for you, I want to know right away."

"Your confidence in me is so gratifying."

She sent him a fleeting smile. "I think you believe it's easier than it is."

So far, it *had* been easy, but he and Cody had only been together one night. Cody had been quiet, probably thinking about the surgery and school. Sam almost felt sorry for the kid. "How did your angiogram go?" he asked, deliberately changing the subject. The procedure was the last and most physically invasive of all the testing done on a living donor. He knew it to be a fairly scary and uncomfortable procedure. She had been treated to a mild sedative. Through a small incision, a tube was inserted into a vein and a dye injected so the transplant team could study her kidneys and all the related connections.

"It was great. A barrel of fun. Natalie and I laughed for hours."

"Ah, a sense of humor. That's always a good sign."

"That's what the nurse who shaved my groin said."

"You feeling all right now?"

She sat down on the bed, leaning back against a bank of pillows. "I felt all right five minutes after the procedure, but they made me lie motionless for six full hours. They picked out a lovely kidney for my father, so I guess everything worked out. They're going to take the one from my left side."

She paled a little as she spoke, and Sam's heart constricted. Who did she tell her fears to? Her hopes and her dreams? Natalie? The elusive Brad? Was Cody old enough to understand?

"So do you want to talk about it?" Unable to ignore the issue any longer, he indicated the paper on the bed.

She picked it up by her thumb and forefinger. "I've seen worse. When I was twelve, they printed a photo of me dancing with one of the Kennedy cousins at a wedding, with a caption about a child bride."

The paper was folded open to the story. The headline and text were filled with blatant suggestions and outright lies, but the camera had caught . . . something. The falling snow softened the focus, and there was a suggestion of movement in the way Sam's arm went around her and her head was tucked against his chest. It was a picture of two alone, absorbed in each other. The invasion of privacy made him sick.

"When I saw this rag," he said, "I wanted to hurt somebody."

"Welcome to Gavin's world." She gave an unapologetic shrug. "You get used to it by learning to ignore it."

He didn't want to get used to this. Didn't want to ignore it. But he felt himself being drawn to her, just as he'd drawn her into the hot springs. The first time he'd lost Michelle, he had built a hard wall around his heart, and that wall had protected him from the very things he was starting to feel now.

She worried her lower lip with her teeth. "So did Cody see the story?"

"Yeah."

"Did he say anything?"

"Not much. Just that you made out better than Lisa Marie Presley."

"So you don't think . . . he's reading anything into it?"

"I don't know. He didn't say much about it to me or my mother."

Her eyes widened. "He was with Tammi Lee? By choice?"

Sam felt a twinge of annoyance. "What, you don't approve of my white-trash mother?"

"Oh, Sam. Damn it, you know that's not what I meant. I have trouble picturing Cody hanging out with anyone over sixteen. I hope he was civil to your mother."

"They seemed to get along okay. Talked about music, I think."

She drew her knees to her chest. "I guess I don't really know her myself."

"She's changed a lot," Sam said.

"We've all changed a lot."

"Some things don't change at all." He took a deep breath. "After all these years, I still want you."

"Sam—"

He gestured at the papers. "There's something going on between us."

"Don't believe everything you read," she shot back, her pale cheeks turning red.

He stepped closer to the bed, touched her shoulder. "I didn't have to read it in the paper. But you know, I'm kind of glad it's out in the open."

She shifted away from him. "Do you know how incredibly bad your timing is?"

"What, because I didn't show up at a soccer game when you were feeling lonely?"

"Screw you." She glared at him. "I never thought I'd

see you again, Sam. Ever. And now I'm just supposed to make room in my life for you?"

"Why are you so testy?" he asked.

She took a deep breath, closed her eyes briefly. When she opened them she appeared more composed. "It's nerves," she admitted. "I've never been much good at dealing with . . . unforeseen circumstances. I'm letting Cody stay with you this week. What more do you want? What?"

He paused. Put away his frustration. "It's not just Cody. I want to know you again. I want . . . what we had Thursday night, and Friday at the hot springs."

"We got carried away. It's not like me to lose my . . . perspective like that." Her hands twisted into a knot of nerves in her lap. "I have a good job, I'm up for partner, I have a perfectly fine life in Seattle. Shall I chuck all that because you've got those great eyes?"

"I never knew you thought I had great eyes."

"There's a lot you never knew about me. If you knew me, you'd understand that I can't have a fling with you for old time's sake."

"What makes you think it's a fling?" He watched the agitated pulse leaping in her neck, and he traced it with his finger. Soft. So soft, like dry silk.

"We have no business getting involved no matter what our hormones are telling us."

He threaded his fingers up into her satiny hair. The years swept away, and everything he had felt for her, everything he had kept inside him all his life, rose up, seeming to push the air from his lungs. "Michelle, I'm not listening to my hormones. I'm listening to my heart."

Her lower lip trembled, and she caught it in her teeth, looking away. "What on earth," she asked with tears in her voice, "makes you think this could work?"

He drew her around to face him. "What makes you think it can't?"

A sharp knock on the door interrupted them.

"Michelle," a voice called. "It's me."

"Oh, God," she whispered. "Brad."

Chapter 30

D on't get up." Sam walked over to the door, cool and calm, as if he had not just turned Michelle's world inside out. He opened the door, and in walked Brad.

He was good-looking in a clean-cut J. Crew way. He had a "yachty" air about him. One of the things that first attracted her to him was that settled refinement. There could be no chaos in the life of such a man.

"Brad." She tried to compose herself. "I wasn't expecting you." She was dying to know why he was here. Earlier they had agreed he wouldn't come unless she asked him to. But he was here. Was it because of the tabloid, or had he decided she needed him?

Her voice deserted her as he and Sam regarded each other like a pair of rival stags about to tangle their antlers. Then he brushed past Sam and came over to the bed, bending to kiss her forehead. Expensive aftershave and a shirt that crackled with starch. Altoid mints. *Brad*.

"Hi, babe." He stood back, regarding her critically.

She shifted nervously on the bed. Was she blushing? Could he see where Sam had been touching her cheek, her hair—

"So how'd it go? You okay?" Brad asked.

"Great. We're all set for tomorrow. Brad, I want you to meet Sam McPhee. Sam, this is Bradley Lovell."

"You're the guy," Brad said, his voice controlled. "The guy in the paper." He patted the side of his Louis Vuitton flight bag, stuffed with folded newspapers. "Michelle told me all about you."

"Yeah?" Sam looked over at her, lifting an eyebrow. "She didn't tell me squat about you." There was nothing—*nothing*—J. Crew about his looks. It was obvious he hadn't shaved today. He had on time-worn jeans that had custom-tailored themselves to his long, lean body. A gray athletic sweatshirt and a baseball cap. And he was asking her with his eyes: *What did you tell him, Michelle? Did you tell him we made love? Did you tell him you saw stars? Did you tell him you cried yourself to sleep that night?*

"Michelle said you used to be . . . what, some sort of hired hand at her dad's place?" Brad spoke nonchalantly, as if it really didn't matter to him. A small muscle tensed in Sam's jaw.

"That was years ago, Brad," she said, breaking in. "Sam's a physician now. I told you that, too."

"So what are you doing here?" Brad's gaze was blunt and challenging as he glared at Sam.

"Wondering why a guy would let Michelle go through this alone."

The testosterone was getting thick, she thought wryly. "I'll tell you what he's *not* doing. He's not getting into a pissing contest with you." She scowled at Sam, then at Brad, daring them to defy her. "In case you've forgotten, this is about my father."

Sam went to the door. She knew he was not retreating. It was clear on his face that he wasn't through with her yet. "I have to get back. I'm on call this afternoon. So I guess . . . I'll see Cody after school tomorrow." He stared at her for a moment, and she felt strange soft echoes of the way he had touched her when they made love. He adjusted the bill of his baseball cap. "Your transplant team's the best. Everything will be fine."

Michelle felt compelled to explain to Brad, "Cody's going to stay with Sam this week."

Brad let out a low whistle. "More power to you. Don't let him pull the wool over your eyes. The kid's bad news."

Sam's eyes narrowed. "My son is the best news I've ever had. See you around, Michelle."

Brad turned to her before Sam was even out the door. "Hey, I didn't expect a three-ring circus," he said. His easy grin relaxed her. This was the Brad she knew, the one who charmed her clients at office parties, the one who took her out to dinner every Friday night, the one who attended swing-dancing lessons just because she asked him to.

Even as she welcomed his familiar presence, she felt Sam's absence, a dark and gaping hole in the day. A sense of unfinished business. And the terrible, wonderful words echoing through her: *I'm listening to my heart.* She should have let him go on, but she hadn't dared.

"God, what a week it's been." She deposited the papers and magazines on the floor.

One week. In that short span of time, the world had been transformed. Everything she used to believe was being challenged, pushed, reshaped. Everything she thought she had planned out was starting to unravel.

Even the idea of family. When she was growing up, "family" was something she and her mother lacked. When she was bringing up Cody, it was something she insisted they define for themselves. "Family" included Natalie, who was the sort of aunt every kid wanted, the sort of sister every woman should have, related by something much more potent than blood. And it was Brad, who tried to get along with Cody because of her, an effort she knew not many men would make. Cody hadn't been making it easy for him.

Now the circle widened to encompass her father, and Sam, and even Tammi Lee, who—wonder of wonders— had spent the day with Cody yesterday. She had to fit them into her life now. She *needed* to.

"So did he spend the night here, or what?" Brad asked bluntly.

For a second, she was too stunned to answer. "I can't believe you asked me that."

"I can't believe I showed up at your hotel room at ten in the morning and found some guy with you."

"He's not some guy. He's Cody's father."

"Then he should be with Cody."

"He was worried about the bullshit story in that tabloid. He wanted to talk to me about it."

"Yeah, he looked real worried to me." Brad took a tin of Altoids out of his shirt pocket and offered her one. She shook her head, and he said, "You didn't answer me, Michelle."

"Answer what?"

"Did you sleep with him or not?"

Sleep? She could safely deny that. No sleeping had taken place. "I had a surgical procedure yesterday. I ordered a tuna sandwich from room service and watched

HBO last night." She folded her arms defensively in front of her. "Why did you show up without calling first?"

"I wanted to surprise you. Wanted to do something spontaneous."

"You've never done a spontaneous thing in your life."

"Okay, so maybe that tabloid thing made me curious."

As he lowered himself to the bed and put his arms around her, she realized she had a lot of things to explain to Brad. A huge confusion swirled through her. She knew she should confess, but she had no idea how to begin.

"Have you had breakfast yet?" she asked him, chickening out.

"A cold bagel and weak coffee on the early flight."

"We could join Cody and my father downstairs, or maybe call for room service."

"Room service sounds good." He went over to the desk, picked up the hotel guide with the menus in it.

While he was reading off the selections, the divider door to the adjoining room opened. Natalie, who had driven down to be with Michelle during yesterday's procedure, waltzed in. Her bright hair was damp from a shower, her skirts and shawl shimmering around her. "Beat you to it, buddy." She crossed the room to give Brad a kiss on the cheek. "I already ordered breakfast." Her smile was full of mischief as she winked at him. "But I'll let you buy it, okay?"

"God, it *is* a circus," he said, standing back to look at Natalie. "We've got the tattooed lady and everything."

She touched a spot just above her left breast. "You're not supposed to know about my tattoo."

"You weren't supposed to go topless in my hot tub, either," he reminded her, laughing.

Michelle laughed, too, remembering that night last summer. Natalie had come over, weeping because she'd just dumped her current boyfriend, a timpani player named Stan. A few tequila slammers later, they had stripped down and jumped, giggling, into the hot tub on Brad's deck. Michelle hadn't realized back then that he'd noticed the tattoo.

Natalie stuck her tongue out at him and came bounding over to the bed, sitting on the end. "Okay, so give me a report."

"I'm fine. Had a great night," Michelle told her.

"Really?"

"Really. I'm dying for a shower."

"I thought you weren't supposed to get that incision wet."

Brad rifled around in his bag. "I'm way ahead of you, babe." He brought out a packet of DermaSeal, something from the pharmacy to keep wounds dry during bathing.

"You're a lifesaver." She hiked up the hem of her nightgown. "Have at it."

"This is too kinky for me," Natalie declared, hurrying to the window and looking out.

In the shower, Michelle took longer than she should, standing in the steamy tub, feeling the water needle down on her neck, shoulders, back. After a long time and plenty of soap, she got out of the shower and put on leggings and a loose sweater, wrapped a towel around her head. When she walked out to the bedroom, there was Natalie in the lotus position on the floor, her eyes closed and her lips moving soundlessly. It was a bizarre start to a day that promised only to get more bizarre.

Beginning with the breakfast Natalie had ordered— cheese blintzes, fruit compote, scrambled eggs, smoked salmon, and a pot of herb tea. Michelle sat on the edge of the bed, nibbling a croissant, and it hit her. Brad had barely mentioned Cody. The kid had just found the father he never knew, and Brad hadn't even asked about what the experience had been like for Cody.

She wondered why. Was it because he felt threatened?

"So I was talking to the concierge, and he gave me a list of recommendations for tonight." Natalie passed her a folder with the hotel logo on it.

"What's tonight?" Brad asked.

"The night before the big event, numb-nuts." She sampled a spiced apple from the fruit compote. "I decided we need a party."

"A party? You can't just have a party—"

"Watch me." She rolled her eyes. "God, Mr. Wet Blanket, can't you for once in your life be spontaneous? I bet you schedule your bowel movements."

"You're a real charmer, Natalie. You really are."

"Just listen, okay? Tomorrow, Michelle and her dad are going to make a miracle. Don't you think it would be good karma to mark the occasion in some way?"

Michelle expected him to argue, but instead he softened. "A kidney party. It would be a first for me."

"Wait till you see the menu," Michelle warned him, giving Natalie a hug.

Monday

Monday

Chapter 31

*M*ichelle stared at the glowing red digits of the hotel-room clock: 4:45 A.M. She was supposed to be asleep, resting up for the big event that loomed only hours away.

The truth was, she had barely slept at all. Natalie's party had been as strange and wonderful as Natalie herself. The group, consisting of Gavin, Brad, Cody, Natalie, and Michelle, had occupied a corner of the restaurant. Somehow, Natalie had managed to get Dr. Kehr, Donna Roberts, both surgeons, and Dr. Temple to show up. Natalie and Cody hung up balloon people with incisions drawn on them. Some of the balloons bore terse instructions: *Please close carefully after opening. Did you leave anything behind? Please check in the overhead compartment for personal belongings.* Lave los manos.

The laughter and toasts ranged from silly to sentimental. Her family, Michelle had thought, regarding them with a powerful surge of affection. They were not exactly a Norman Rockwell painting, but they were hers, and her love for them burned strong and steady. The doctors, acting officious, broke up the party by eight o'clock, sending Gavin to sterile isolation and advising everyone to get a good night's sleep. Michelle wanted to feel grateful for Brad's closeness, for the familiar feel of his arms around her as they lay in the dark of the hotel room. But it felt awkward being with Brad again. In Seattle, she had become accustomed to a predictable schedule, making plans together, letting herself in and out of his house at will, confident of her place in his life. Now she didn't know anything at all.

She moved restlessly in the bed. Brad awakened, squinting at the clock. "Hey, stranger."

"I didn't mean to wake you," she said.

"I sure wouldn't mind making love to you," he whispered.

She froze, her throat locking shut. Dear God.

"But we need to watch that incision." Brad's pronouncement rescued her from having to answer. "Besides, I bet that's the last thing on your mind."

Had he always done that? Made up her mind for her? Idiot, she told herself. He was a stable, responsible man who knew her well. Most women would kill to have that.

He turned over, mumbling, "Go back to sleep, Michelle."

Sleep. He was telling her to sleep when she needed him to listen. Really listen—to her fears and apprehensions about the surgery, her guilt and confusion about Sam. She sat up in bed, looped her arms around her drawn-up knees, moving gingerly to protect the incision. "Brad?"

A long-suffering sigh. "Yeah?"

"If something goes wrong with this surgery——"

"Hold on," he said, reaching over and snapping on the lamp. "We've discussed this. As a donor, your risk is completely within reasonable limits."

"Of course," she agreed. "But I thought you should know. If anything happens to me, I'm leaving Cody in the custody of Sam. I had the papers redrafted yesterday."

"Makes sense, since he's the kid's father. But it's a moot point. You're not in any danger. You'll be home before you know it, and all this will be behind you."

"No." She barely spoke above a whisper. "I don't think it's going to turn out like that."

"So do you want me to stay?" he asked.

She knew he'd wait through the surgery if she asked him to. But was that what she had been doing with Brad the past couple of years?

Making him stick around?

"No," she said. "Everything is going to be fine. You don't need to stay."

He was quiet for a long time. Then, with a small, curious smile on his lips, he got out of bed and slowly, deliberately got dressed.

She got up, feeling ill at ease. "Do you want to talk about it?"

"Michelle." His voice was quiet, firm. "I know what you're going to say."

It had been a long, strange week, she was an emotional wreck and a ball of anxiety, but she got it. She finally got it. They'd had a good run, she and Brad, three years of a relationship that went no deeper than the epidermis. And they didn't even have to discuss this. Just by watching his face, she could see that they had come to the same conclusion independently. But it was time to move on. He deserved more. She deserved more. Sam hadn't made her any promises yesterday, but she didn't need promises. She simply needed to be free.

"I feel like crying," she admitted.

"I hate when you cry."

"I know." A very slow smile formed on her lips. "That's why I never do it around you." She sat quietly on the bed while he finished packing and phoned to check on the early commuter flight to Seattle. A brief, awkward peck on the cheek, a wish for luck, and then he was gone.

After Brad left, she crossed to the glass doors that led out onto a second-story balcony. The heavy drapes were shut, but she could hear the sounds of the road outside, trucks' air brakes hissing, the scrape of snowplow and sander.

There was a table in front of the window, and on the table was a telephone. She could take it outside, sit in the cold predawn, and call Sam on the pretext of last-minute instructions about Cody.

She hated it that she wanted to call him.

Fighting the impulse, she stared at a narrow gap in the curtains. The sky was getting lighter. And something started to happen in her head. She couldn't look away from that space. Almond-shaped, it framed nothing but the sky, yet her mind transformed what she was seeing. The slender gap in the drapes became a round, ripe, pregnant shape. Or an eye. Or a raindrop. Or the space between two praying hands.

It was a space that she suddenly wanted—*needed*—to fill.

On the table lay the flat folio box with the art supplies Natalie had brought from Seattle. Almost without thinking, Michelle grabbed a pencil and began drawing in the half-light, her heart guiding her hand. Something inside her had come unstopped, and it gushed over the paper, and she filled page after page, her hand barely able to match the speed with which the images and emotions overtook her.

By the time the sun tinged the sky with a pink blush, she sat at the table with tears streaming down her cheeks. Maybe it was only for a moment, maybe it wouldn't last, but for the past hour she had glowed with an inner light she thought had burned out. She didn't know what had sparked the change; it was probably a combination of everything that was happening: being back in Montana, saying good-bye to Brad, facing the surgery, finding Sam again.

With shaking hands, she looked at what she had done. She had no judgment. Trash or treasure, she couldn't tell. But the work was hers. She knew where it came from, and it was a place more honest, more deep, than anything she had recognized in herself in more years than she could count.

She felt a certain quiet reverence as she gathered up the drawings and slipped them into the zipper compartment of her suitcase. And for the first time as she faced the surgery, she thought, I can do this. *I can do this.*

When the radio clicked on at precisely 6:00 A.M., she was ready.

As ready as anyone could be for an organ transplant.

The final preparations felt almost surreal. Forms being checked and double-checked. Signatures in triplicate. Meetings, IV drips, paper gowns and caps. Cody and Natalie hovering, chattering nervously. Michelle looked in on her father and found him waiting with a patience and a stillness that broke her heart. When an orderly came to take her away to her private room, Gavin turned to her.

Neither of them said anything. Gavin put his hand on

his heart. She did the same, afraid to speak, afraid she might cry. *What do I do?* she wondered. If she said her good-byes, did that mean she was afraid something would go wrong, that she'd never see him again? If she said nothing, what would they have to hang on to if something *did* go wrong?

In silence, with all the unsaid things screaming inside her, she walked away, following the orderly to her room.

She hovered wildly between acting like this was the most mundane of procedures and feeling convinced, as Natalie was, that it was a spiritual event. Natalie and Cody came in. Each bent to kiss her, to murmur "I love you," and to hear her whispered echo of the phrase. Cody looked pale, unable for once to cover his apprehension with attitude. She hadn't said much about Brad—just that he'd taken the early flight to Seattle. Explanations would come later.

She was glad Cody was starting school. He needed the distraction. Rather than pacing the halls during the procedure, Natalie would be driving him back to Crystal City in time for first bell.

"It's going to be all right, Cody," she said from her hospital bed.

"What if it's not?" he asked, his voice breaking as it sometimes still did.

"You have to believe it'll be all right." Michelle watched his face, loving him with all the fullness of her heart. "For months the doctors have been telling us that attitude is everything. That includes your attitude."

"You didn't answer my question. What if something goes wrong?"

"Nothing will—"

"Mom, cut it out."

She took his hand, noticing with mild surprise that he

had calluses from working at Sam's. "All right. Yes, there is a risk that something could go wrong. But it is a tiny, calculated risk that's hardly worth considering when you think of how this is going to help my father live again."

"Why wasn't I tested?" he demanded suddenly, anger pushing through his fear, redness rising in the pallor of his face.

"What?"

"When you started in on all these tests to find a donor, why wasn't I tested?"

"Right from the start, it looked as if I was the best match, Cody. There was no need."

"You didn't even bother testing me."

She was stunned. He actually resented her for overlooking him as a donor.

"Hey, sport." She forced herself to sound calm. "I did you a favor. How'd you like to be in my position right now?" She gestured at the thin, printed gown, the wheeled bed, the cold tile walls.

Natalie came hustling in. "We'd best get going, kiddo. School today."

"Aw, man," he said, genuine distress in his face. "Why can't I go back to Seattle with Aunt Natalie—"

"Hey," Natalie cut in, her voice uncharacteristically sharp. "We went over this last night. You're going to school today. You'll knock 'em dead."

"Yeah, right."

Michelle's heart sank at the misery in his voice. She had never felt more helpless in her life. Cody had to go to a new school, and she was too out of it to be of any use at all.

He glared at her. "You should have tested me for the kidney."

"I love you for saying so, Cody. Remember that. I love you."

A pair of orderlies came in. "Time to go to pre-op," one of them said.

"One more kiss, for luck," she said to Cody.

He kissed her cheek and squeezed her hand, and she closed the sweetness of the moment into her heart. "I'll see you soon," she whispered.

"'Bye, Mom." His eyes flooded with brightness, and then she lost sight of him as they wheeled her around a corner of the corridor.

"You got a nice kid, ma'am," an orderly said.

A gentle cottony calm, augmented by the sedative she was given, washed over her. Doing the sketches this morning had been cathartic, and the last moments with Cody had set a seal of serenity upon her. The orderly had called her kid "nice." What a concept.

They reached the pre-op area, and she was amazed to see a second gurney there.

"We've got to stop meeting like this." Gavin winked at her.

Reaching out, they could touch hands. "I didn't know I'd see you here, Daddy."

"Me neither."

Their respective anesthesiologists came in and chatted with them, telling them what to expect.

Then the oddest thing happened. The orderlies and the anesthesiologists left. Gavin and Michelle found themselves alone for long, quiet minutes.

"They gave me a pre-op sedative," she said. "You?"

"I'm not sure. They've been prepping me all night." He rubbed his finger over hers. "So here we are, just the two of us."

"Here we are." She didn't know what to say. They'd

had plenty of time to express their regrets, proclaim their commitment, acknowledge the love that lay at the center of everything. But had they said it? *Had they?*

Michelle's mother had died during surgery. She tried to keep her mind from going there, but she couldn't help herself.

"Daddy?" The word came out on a high note, sounding juvenile, but she didn't care.

"Yeah, honey?"

"I'm scared."

She could feel him smile, could feel it somewhere in the region of her heart. He squeezed her hand. She had forgotten they were still touching.

"Me too, Michelle. I'm scared, too."

"I don't think it's something we're going to get over, do you?"

"Not likely. But we'd better not let Temple hear us. He'd put the brakes on this whole thing."

"He was a pain in the ass, wasn't he?"

"Yeah. Listen, I know I only showed up in your life every once in a while." He took his hand from hers and touched his chest. "But you've always been here, right here in my heart."

She wanted it to be true so badly that she held her breath.

"Michelle?"

"What?"

"You're giving me my life back. I wish I could tell you what that means to me."

Emotion came in a warm rush, driving away the chill of the tiled pre-op. They lay side by side, helpless in their hope and love and fear. She swallowed hard and tried to keep from crying.

"Don't cry, sweetheart. I don't ever want to make you cry."

She felt it flowing, the smooth warm river of light that she had felt earlier, and she finally believed that maybe there was some merit in what Natalie had said about this bond, this invisible connection between father and daughter, between mother and son.

"I don't mind crying for you, Daddy."

"Everything's done, Michelle. I fixed my life as best I can. I played my hand the best I know how. I don't know what more I can do."

The doors swished open. "Showtime, folks," someone said. "Ladies first."

Michelle kept thinking she should say one more thing to her father, something hopeful and profound, but the only words that came out were, "See you around, Dad." Then they were both wheeled away, passing the glass-enclosed scrub area where surgeons and nurses readied themselves like postulants in some strange cleansing rite.

The operating room looked smaller than she had pictured it in her mind. Too many doctor shows on TV. In the real world, operating rooms were chilly and crammed with monitoring equipment. Blue-green tile and stainless steel. Glare from the observation dome overhead—dear God, she thought, someone might be watching this?—and the transplant team assembled in a semicircle around her. Masked and capped, miner's headlamps strapped to their heads, plundering hands in skintight gloves. The nurse stood on a stool to tower over the rest.

Their questions came fast, floating disembodied from behind the anonymous masks: Did she remember them from the meetings? Did she feel all right? Did she know each person's role and what was happening? Did she have any more questions?

Michelle shook her head, mute with terror. Now it was real. Now it was happening. No turning back.

The mask came down, the sharp lemony taste of the drug invaded her air passages, and images swam and stuttered before her eyes—the blue-green tile, the monitors and masked team, and then all that was gone and she saw faces tumbling through her mind: Cody and Gavin and Sam and finally the slender space formed by a gap in the draperies, a hole in the world, a shape she had to fill in, had to fill and fill with everything that was in her.

The You I Never Knew / 309

Michelle shook her head, more with terror. How it—
Now a vast hunger in his turning back.
—lowed her for minutes. Shelby knew, face of the
faced her in pleasure. into images them had sur-
tered before her even—the blue-gray line. He smothing
and masked terror and that all that was true and she saw
faces tumbling through her mind. Cody and Cody and
Sam and finally the tender space formed by a gap in the
draperie, a hole in the world, a shape she had to fill all
has to fill and fill with everything that was in her.

Chapter 32

Quit driving yourself nuts, son, and go on down
to Missoula."

Sam kept shoveling. It had snowed last
night, and he was clearing his mother's front walk and
driveway. "I'm not driving myself nuts."

Tammi Lee sat down on the porch step and regarded
him with a knowing sympathy. "Well, you're driving the
hospital down there batty by calling every fifteen minutes."

"I'm not calling every fifteen minutes."

"Yes you are. And Karl's on call, Cody's at school,
and if you shovel any more snow, you'll end up having a
coronary right here in my front yard. So get your butt in
the truck."

"I should be around when Cody gets out of school.
See how his day went." It felt strange thinking about a

kid's school schedule. He had never imagined himself in such a role. The thought led to a flash of memory. When he was a kid, riding the school bus home, he used to observe kids getting off at their stops, eagerly awaited by their smiling mothers. Watching them used to make Sam sick with envy.

"You can get to Missoula and back before school's out," his mother said.

"I'm not needed in Missoula," he said after a long, ponderous silence. He kept telling himself that. Maggie Kehr had promised she'd page him the minute each surgery was over.

"How do you know that?"

He sliced the blade of the shovel into the new-fallen snow and thought about Brad Lovell. Serious, sure-of-himself Brad Lovell, who had a 401(k) plan, who had seen Cody play soccer before Sam even knew his son existed. Lovell was the perfect example of someone a woman *needed*, pure and simple. He was steady and clean-cut, practical and predictable. A regular bachelor of the month.

How did a guy get like that? Sam wondered, deliberately ignoring his mother's question. He wished he knew, because he ought to try it himself. Try listening to common sense. After surviving a chaotic childhood, struggling through school, and failing at marriage, he'd finally put his life in order. His mother was sober. He had his practice, his horses, a respected place in the community. Did he really want more than he had? He was wary of taking on more. He didn't know if he had what it took.

Michelle Turner had only been back for a week, and already people were starting to talk.

He shoveled at a furious rate, scraping the driveway down to bare concrete. He was fighting to stop the knowledge building inside him, but he couldn't run from it, couldn't hide from the truth.

In all the years he'd lived and all the miles he'd traveled, he'd never loved anyone the way he loved Michelle.

When he had taken her into the empty theater, he'd felt a harsh desperation to possess her, even if it hurt them both. At the hot springs the harshness had softened, reminding him that he still had tender places deep inside him, places only she could touch. In that moment, he'd known with a certainty he hadn't felt in years that they needed a second chance. They needed to get to know one another, to look at one another through adult eyes and see if the passion they shared as teenagers really meant something.

At least, that was what he'd thought.

Now he had no idea what to think.

When his pager went off, he stabbed the shovel into the snow and pressed the readout button.

His mother stood up on the porch step. "Any news?"

"The surgery's over."

"ichelle. Michelle, wake up." A woman's voice reached like ghostly fingers through a fog.

"Mmm." Her mouth felt welded shut. Taste of rust and clay. She supposed what she was feeling was pain, but it was so huge, so overwhelming, that she couldn't call it pain. It was a vast red cloud, pulsating in the middle, holding her in a grip of such power she couldn't think.

She moved her jaw from side to side. "'S'it over?" No saliva in her mouth. Completely dry. The crimson fog throbbed, intensified, punishing her for her effort.

"You're all done. You did great, just perfect." Donna. That was the woman's name. Donna Roberts, the nurse.

Michelle didn't feel perfect. She felt inches from death. The pounding in her head blotted out all sound. She forced her eyes to focus on the nurse's mouth, made herself listen carefully.

Donna checked a green-and-black monitor. "We'll be transferring you to your room pretty soo—"

"My father. I want to see my father."

"He's all right, Michelle. He's in post-op, too."

I want to see him. But she couldn't get the words out. The pain surrounded her, clouding her brain, lifting her up and swirling her far, far away, and she couldn't see anything except that tiny slit of space opening up to the paintings she hadn't done. Two hands, parting a curtain. Giving her a glimpse of something she hadn't created yet. Now it was clear to her. She had to learn to do it anyway, even though it hurt.

She sank deeper and deeper into the formless red morass of pain, and she let herself go, a victim of slow drowning, too weak to fight her way back to the surface.

Chapter 34

There was something wrong with the clocks in this frigging school, Cody decided.

They didn't move like normal clocks. They must be from another dimension where a minute equaled an hour and a day lasted forever.

Because that was how long his first day at Crystal City High School had lasted—forever.

And it was only lunchtime.

Feeling like a complete dork, he had shown up in homeroom with a "New Student" folder under his arm and this enormous zit on his forehead. He hadn't had a zit since September, and he'd woken up that morning looking like he was about to sprout a unicorn horn.

No sympathy from Aunt Natalie, who had driven him up from Missoula. "Nobody will notice. It just feels obvious to you. Act like it's not there."

"Oh, right, like no one's going to notice Mount Vesuvius in the middle of my face."

"Sweetie, if this is the worst thing that ever happens to you, consider yourself blessed." In his mom's absence, Aunt Natalie played the part of the expert on all things.

At least Brad had gone back to Seattle. Cody had been worried that he'd hang around asking a bunch of questions. Brad liked to act all buddy-buddy, and Cody didn't feel like answering stuff like how did it feel to meet his father and all that crap.

Coming in new mid-year was a special torture that should be reserved for convicted felons. First there had been the homeroom teacher's "Class, we have a new student" routine. Then the issuing of books and supplies. The stack of forms to be signed.

The Assignment of the Seat.

The teachers all thought they were doing him this big favor, putting him right up front in the middle so he wouldn't miss a second of their fascinating lectures on the Voting Rights Act or phytoplankton. What they were actually doing was making him vulnerable to the whispers. This was the equivalent of blindfolded torture, because he could hear bits and pieces of the conversation, but couldn't see the speakers.

". . . like some skater from the inner city . . ."

". . . he's got a pierced *what?*"

"Well, *I* think he's cute . . ."

". . . acts like hot shit because his grandfather's a movie star . . ."

". . . wait till you hear who his *father* is . . ."

The hissed speculation, through civics, trigonometry, and science, had hit him like spitballs to the back of the neck. When he'd try to get a look at the speakers, dropping a pencil or something and twisting around, he was met by mute, blank stares.

Losers. Everyone in this frigging school was a loser.

After third period, he had trouble with his locker—of course—and once he got it open, couldn't cram all his books in along with his coat, so he kept the coat on even though he was sweating like a hog in the overheated building.

Lunchtime. In his regular school it was his favorite period of the day, because he sat at the table where everyone was cool and where everyone else only *wished* they could sit. Claudia would be at his side, eating like one potato chip and then saying she was full, and talking and laughing the whole time.

He was a long way from that lunchtime, a long way from Claudia.

Shit. Shit. Shit.

He went through the fast-food line and ordered a burger and a Coke. Safe choices. Picking something different for lunch was risky, even at his school in Seattle. If you had something like tofu or Thai noodles, you were in danger of being Different. There was a guy named Sujit at his other school who brought the weirdest stuff because of his religion. During certain times of the year, he couldn't eat meat or dairy products or anything normal. The kids had made a big deal of it, holding their noses and gagging when he walked by, sometimes playing keep-away with his falafel burger or hummus. One time, Sujit had lost it totally, calling them all pig-eating infidels, which had only made them laugh harder.

Cody wasn't laughing now. He wished he hadn't teased Sujit. Because now *he* was the one surrounded by pig-eating infidels.

He took a long time getting his napkin and straw, lingering at the counter while letting his gaze dart frantically around the busy, noisy cafeteria. Where to sit? *Where to sit?*

Though fewer in number, the tables were segregated exactly as they had been at his old school. The popular kids occupied the middle. Just as in Seattle, these kids were uniformly good-looking, relaxed, laughing while the whole school revolved around them. Nearby sat the football players and cheerleaders. The jocks were like jocks everywhere—food fights erupting, body noises followed by a chorus of "eeeeuw . . ."

Around the busy inner sanctum tables, there was a neutral buffer zone of regular kids with no distinguishing status. And of course, on the fringes of all the activity were the dweebs, geeks, and losers.

They had plenty of room at their tables. Some hid behind comic books or thick-lensed glasses. The fat ones ate furtively, pretending they didn't eat but were just fat because they had unlucky glandular activity. The totally clueless ones acted as if they had no idea they were dweebs. They just gabbed away and had lunch—lots of nerdy thermoses and Tupperware kits. These kids didn't give a rat's ass that they were the scum-sucking bottom-dwellers of the school population.

Maybe he could just hunker down at the end of a geek table, scarf his burger, and slip out to the Commons, an outdoor spot for hanging out during break.

But man, a *geek* table.

If he didn't do better than that, he'd be a goner for sure.

He sucked in a deep breath and went to one of the neutral zone tables. Like all of them, it was crammed. He spotted one possibility. A gap at the end of a table of mostly boys who were talking loudly about snowboarding. Hey, he could talk snowboarding. Keeping his eyes focused on the empty spot, he moved in, trying not to hurry, determined to make it look as if he'd arrived there almost by accident.

"Sorry, that's my spot." A kid scooted in fast, grabbing the seat.

Cody felt his face redden, though he shrugged nonchalantly. But now he was trapped, standing like an idiot with his tray in the middle of the lunchroom.

Somebody jostled him from behind, sloshing his Coke on the tray.

"Hey, look out," he muttered, but not loud enough to be heard.

The bun of the burger was soggy with Coke. If he didn't find a place to sit in a minute, people were going to notice. But the only seats he could see now were at the geek table. Sweat trickled down his back. Damn, he wished he'd taken his coat off. A feeling of impending doom pressed at him, and he felt as if he was about to lose it. The geek table. The goddamned geek table.

"Hey, Cody!"

At the sound of his name, he looked up, and there was Molly Lightning.

It was like seeing an angel, watching her stand up with one knee propped on a bench, waving her slender arm at him.

"Hey, come have a seat." She was at a neutral table where the kids weren't particularly geeky or particularly cool. Just regular.

He nodded, nonchalant as you please, but inside he was exulting. She'd saved his butt, no doubt about it.

*   *   *

Feeling like an ex-P.O.W., Cody exited the loud, gym-bag-smelling school bus and stood at the side of the highway. Breathing. A survivor after a disaster. Man, he felt as though he'd been holding his breath all day, expecting an ambush. They'd promised to get him out of class if anything bad happened at the hospital, but there had been no interruption of the slow torture of school. He had to feel grateful for that, at least.

Swinging his backpack over his shoulder, he trudged up the frozen gravel drive toward Sam's house. Another bonus, he thought sourly. On top of everything else, he had to stay here all week.

In spite of his thoughts, his heart lifted when the Border collie came careening down from the field and leaped at him, long pink tongue reaching for his face. For a minute, Cody couldn't help himself, and he laughed aloud. Then he saw Sam coming out of the house.

If he asks me how school was, I'm going to hurl, I swear it.

"Hey, Cody." Sam swung a canvas bag into the back of his old pickup truck. He put a cooler of drinks and a bag of tortilla chips in the cab. "I guess you want to get on down to the hospital right away."

The guy had read his mind.

They were both quiet as Sam pulled out onto the highway and headed south. The old Dodge truck smelled of timothy hay and motor oil, and the column shift rattled with the bumps. Sam McPhee sure wasn't like any of the doctors Brad played golf with, Cody reflected. But then again, he pretty much wasn't like any other doctor, *period.* Or maybe Cody just thought he was weird because he was his dad.

"My mom taught me to ride a bike when I was five,"

he said suddenly, for no particular reason. His breath fogged the window.

Sam flexed his hands on the worn, shiny steering wheel and kept his eyes straight ahead on the road. "Yeah?" Another long silence. And then, "We're a little short on bikes around here. Plenty of horses, though. You could do some riding."

Cody felt a spark of interest, but forced himself not to show it. The truth was, he really did want to ride a horse, but he thought he'd feel stupid. Most of the kids at Crystal City High had been born knowing how. They were all goat ropers and cutters and stuff. "Maybe," he said guardedly.

"You could fool around on a snowmobile, too."

"That'd be cool, I guess."

"Can you drive a standard shift?" Sam asked. "A car, not a horse, that is."

Cody's mouth twitched. "Sure. I learned on one."

"There's an old Jeep in the pole barn I could let you use for getting to and from school. That way, you wouldn't waste time waiting around for the school bus. You'd have more time for chores in the morning."

Cody carefully weighed the merits of the offer. It was really no contest. The bus that smelled like a locker room or chores and his own wheels. "That'd be good," he said. Then, reaching through reluctance, he said, "Thanks."

Sam acted like it was no big deal. He opened the chips and passed the bag to Cody. They were silent again until Cody spoke up without even thinking. "This morning really sucked," he said, feeling stupid but unable to keep quiet.

"The transplant, or school?"

"The transplant. School—well, that sucked all day. At the hospital, everybody was like, really nervous." He made a face in the side mirror. "I kept thinking how totally gross the whole thing was."

"Gross, huh?"

He stared out the window at the scrubby landscape swishing past. "You must think I'm really selfish." He immediately wished he hadn't said that. It was none of this guy's business what was going on in his head. But it was so strange. Cody just kept wanting to *talk*.

"Why would I think that?"

"Because I didn't make them test me to see if I could be the kidney donor."

"I suspect they would have tested you if your mom hadn't turned out to be a near-perfect match."

"Nobody even asked me."

"And that's a problem?"

Cody scrubbed the side of his hand at the fogged-up window. "They should have checked me out instead of treating me like I didn't exist."

"Did you say you wanted to be tested?"

"My mom didn't even tell me what was going on until a few weeks ago. And then it was like, 'Well, we're moving to Montana so I can give this guy a kidney.'"

Sam cleared his throat. Cody thought he might be grinning. For some reason, Sam was pretty easy to talk to. He didn't push, didn't try too hard. He was just . . . there. Quiet. Cody's mom was always nagging him about "opening up." She didn't seem to understand that he was not going to open up if she kept talking all the time.

"So anyway," he said, "it was like, really intense. They had my mom in this room with one of those paper hair things on her head and a bunch of tubes and wires all hooked up to her, and I had to go in and say good-bye, like she was going to another planet and I wouldn't ever see her again. And all that was *before* I had to go to Hicksville High."

"I can see how that would suck."

Though Sam didn't take his eyes off the road, Cody could feel the full force of his attention, his fascination. It was a new experience, having an adult be this interested in what he had to say. Why? Because Sam was a doctor? Or his father, or just a guy? Or because he'd been hanging out with Cody's mom and they put that stupid picture in the *Enquirer*?

"Since nobody called from the hospital while I was at school, I guess everything went okay. But I was wicked nervous all day."

"Uh-huh," said Sam in that lazy way of his. "So was I."

Chapter 35

"Mom. Hey, Mom." *Cody*. More powerful than any drug, her child's voice drew Michelle out of the fog.

"Cody . . ." She could feel her lips move, but only a whisper of sound came out. She had the sense that time had passed; she remembered hearing that her father was all right. The pain-cloud still surrounded her, but this time she wanted to fight her way out of the fog.

"Where . . . am . . ."

"In your room, Michelle." A deeper voice. A man's voice.

"Brad—" No. Sam. *Sam*. "Hurts," she said.

"She's miserable." Sam spoke to someone in a clipped voice. "I want her to have a self-administered morphine pump."

Bless you, Sam.

"Yes, we've ordered one—"

"Now, okay? Not in a minute, but now."

Typical doctor. That aggressiveness, that obnoxious, abrasive personality. His staccato order worked. She couldn't open her eyes or count the minutes, but in a short while she felt the drip, and someone guided her thumb to the button that would deliver the gentle, numbing surge of narcotics to her system. She pushed the button, and almost instantly felt the wavelike swish of morphine curling in, then rolling back out, taking some of pain's fury with it.

"'S'working," she said. Dry. Mouth was so dry.

"That's good, Michelle," Sam said. "You rest now."

She couldn't remember if he'd touched her or not since she awakened. Probably not. Doctors didn't do that so much, not anymore. She tried to recall what had passed between them the last time they'd been together. Hotel room. Something big, important, interrupted. She couldn't think.

"School." She formed the word carefully with her lips. "Cody. How was school?"

"I survived," he said simply.

She wanted to hear it all, every detail, but she couldn't stay focused on one subject. "You've seen . . . my father?"

"I'll take Cody in a minute," Sam said. "Gavin's on this floor, different wing. He has to be quarantined in ICU for a while, but we'll look in on him."

Michelle drifted in and out of pain and consciousness. Heard the TV news, and smiled when she felt Cody come over to the bed and awkwardly, hesitantly, touch her head.

Floating in the morphine fog, she listened to them getting ready to go back to Crystal City. She mouthed *I love you* and when they left she turned her face to the wall and wept for no reason she could name.

When she woke up again, the room was empty except

for the drips and equipment. The space between the drapes showed a night sky.

She pressed the button on the morphine pump. Gentle swish of drugs.

The sky grew red around the edges as if it had caught fire.

Later, someone put something around her ankles. Helpless but resentful, she mumbled, "What's that?"

"Air cuffs. You'll hear the electric pump come on about every twenty minutes."

"Too loud. Won't get any sleep at all."

"You have to keep these on until you can get out of bed."

With that powerful motivation, she was up at sunup, clinging to the arm of a nurse's aide as she took one step, then lowered herself gingerly to the chair by the bed.

"Okay," she said. "Off with the cuffs already."

The aide touched a buzzer. "You win. Your husband warned us that you were a fighter."

Husband. Sam. No way. He wasn't her husband. He was ... too damned complicated to explain to the nurse's aide.

Later she forced herself to get up again and wait patiently, staying in the chair, even eating something. Rice pudding. Too sweet, not enough nutmeg. Then it was back to bed, feeling as if she'd run a marathon. At one point Donna checked in on her, face wreathed in smiles.

"Just wanted to be sure you heard—your kidney is working great."

Michelle squeezed her eyes shut and felt a powerful rush of gratitude.

We did it, Daddy. We did it.

Tuesday

Tuesday

G od, these are incredible. When did you do these?" Natalie's voice pried into a strange dream Michelle was having. In the dream, she floated through the wisps of steam that curled off the surface of the hot springs where she and Sam had made love. Only she was alone in the fog, searching, calling out, but no one could hear her.

"Michelle?" Natalie was insistent. "I was asking about these drawings."

She gave up on the dream and dragged her eyes open. "What . . . drawings?"

"Here." Cody held a plastic bottle with a flexible straw to her lips.

Michelle drank gratefully. "Thanks. What drawings?"

"I found them in your suitcase." Natalie held up one

of the sketches Michelle had done before the surgery. "These are wonderful."

"They're pretty cool, Mom."

She took another drink. Didn't want to think about the drawings and what had happened the morning of the transplant. Truthfully, she had no idea if the experience meant anything at all. "I feel as if I've been away forever," she said. "What day is it?"

"Tuesday."

She studied Cody. He seemed . . . different. She supposed that working outside a lot added color to his usually pale face. He might be eating better, too. He looked bigger. Filled out. When had that happened? she wondered with a clutch of apprehension. Changes don't happen overnight. Why hadn't she noticed?

"Is school going all right?" she asked.

"Yeah."

She didn't believe him. Someone had probably coached him not to say anything to upset her. "Are you and Sam getting along okay?"

He shrugged. "I guess."

"I've been keeping tabs on the situation," Natalie reminded her. "They're getting along fine."

"He doesn't know me," Cody pointed out. "He's just some guy. Ow! Quit kicking me, Aunt Natalie."

"Now the big question," Michelle said. "How's school going?"

"Sucks," he said predictably, then winced as Natalie kicked him again. "I'll survive, Mom. But I really want to get back to Seattle."

"Speaking of getting back, I have to leave, sweetie," Natalie said. "That is, if you'll be okay without me."

Michelle smiled, feeling her lower lip crack with the

effort. "I'll be okay without you. Just not nearly as entertained."

"Call me, all right? Anytime, night or day."

"Sure, Nat. You've been a peach."

"Take care of yourself. I'll keep the home fires burning."

After visiting hours were over, the nurses let Michelle walk in the hallway, wheeling her IVs. She made them take out the catheter at the first opportunity. Pain flamed through her, but she kept walking, concentrating on the scuffing sound of her slippers on the linoleum tile floor. She found her way to Gavin's room.

Her father was asleep, zippered in a sterile cocoon of clear plastic. He looked terrible, a waxen corpse. *No.* She wanted to scream it. *Daddy. Oh, Daddy.* We're not finished, she thought frantically. We just found each other again. The very air around her suddenly felt unnatural, noxious. Everything was broken.

But his coloring was remarkable—a healthy flush to his cheeks, hands and fingernails pink. Everyone assured her that the transplant was a success, the kidney was working.

Please let it be true. Please please please let it be true.

She lifted her hand, pressed her fingertips lightly to the plastic bubble, and said, "I love you, Daddy." Her words sounded muffled and small in the machine-snarled room. His chest gently rose and fell, rose and fell.

As she shuffled slowly back to her bed, she wondered if she'd ever told him that when he was awake.

She hadn't.

But if he didn't know it after this, he'd never catch on.

Chapter 37

Sam cleared away the Styrofoam remnants of Trudy's takeout. Never much of a cook, he felt lucky Cody had taken a shine to Trudy's burgers and pizza. Cody picked up his backpack and headed for the stairs. The two of them had been circling each other like a pair of wary dogs, giving a little here, taking a little there. In some moments, Sam felt a connection, but usually they were strangers. He kept telling himself to be patient. Most fathers had years to get to know their kids. He had only days.

"There's a Sonics game on tonight," he said. "You a Sonics fan?"

Cody paused at the bottom of the stairs. "Sort of."

Sam went into the den and flicked on the TV, filling the room with bluish light and the rapid-fire monologue of a basketball commentator. Without looking at Cody, Sam took a seat and gave his attention to the game. Cody sat on the end of the couch, poised to spring up and flee any minute. When a beer commercial came on, his attention wandered, touching on the stack of journals Sam didn't have time to read, the beige drapes, the photos of horses. Alice had tried to spiff the place up when they were married, but Sam had never put much effort into it. He didn't know diddly about fixing up a house to resemble a home.

Then Cody's gaze fixed on the large painting that hung over the fireplace. "Did my mom do that?" he asked.

"Uh-huh." Sam reached up and turned on the mantel light. "Have a look."

Cody stood with his hands dug into his back pockets, studying the winter scene. Sam kept his face neutral, remembering the day Michelle had given him the painting. They had done everything teenagers are lectured *not* to do. They had unprotected sex, they believed love would be enough, they dared to cross the invisible-but-rock-solid barrier of class and privilege. The result had been a pair of broken hearts . . . and this boy.

"It's pretty awesome," Cody said, staring at the signature and date in the bottom corner.

Sam tried to imagine what was going through the kid's head just then as he stood looking at something his mother had done before he was born. He wondered if Cody was able to picture the girl she had been, to think of her as someone other than his mother. Probably not. That just wasn't the way a kid's mind worked. "Your mom says she doesn't paint anymore."

"She does stuff for work, mostly on the computer." He sat back down on the sofa. His expression gave no clue to his thoughts.

The game came on again, and Sam couldn't think of

anything else to say. But he wanted to fill the silence, so he asked, "Did that Jeep run okay?"

"Yeah, it ran fine." Cody hesitated. "I gave Molly Lightning a ride home after school today."

Sam wasn't sure how to respond to that. Should he commend the boy for giving a ride to a friend? Admonish him to drive carefully and wear seat belts? Chastise him because he hadn't asked permission to give rides to passengers?

He said, "You should have checked with me before offering rides to people."

Cody stared him straight in the eye. "Why?"

"Because I'm responsible for you."

Cody snorted. "Right."

"This week I am, damn it—" Sam stopped, amazed to find that his pulse had sped up. This kid had a killer instinct when it came to pushing buttons. "Okay, look," Sam said, pressing the mute button on the remote control. "I should have told you not to take on passengers unless you check with me first."

"So why didn't you?"

"Because I'm new to this, that's why. I'm making it up as I go along."

"That's obvious."

"You're not making it easy, Cody."

"Why should I?"

Sam clenched his teeth until he brought his temper back in check. In a slow drawl, he asked, "Are you enjoying this?"

"What, being here? Hell no," Cody said bluntly. "You're not having any fun, either, so maybe you should just send me back to Seattle to stay with Natalie." He patted his shirt pocket. "I have a copy of the bus schedule."

"Not an option," Sam said, his gaze flashing to the painting over the mantel. "I said I'd look after you this week, and that's what I'm going to do. We could probably have an okay time together if we could get past the bickering stage. What do you say?"

Cody picked up a thread on the arm of the sofa. "I don't see the point."

"Maybe there doesn't need to be a point. Look, you're a teenager. It's your job to question every rule and push at every boundary. It's my job to tell you the rules and boundaries. By not telling you about passengers in the Jeep, I fell down on the job. So here's the rule—number of passengers cannot exceed the number of seat belts. Got it?"

"Yeah. Whatever."

"It's your job to tell me where you're going when you leave and what time you'll be back."

"I don't see why—"

"So if you don't show up, they'll know where to look for the body," Sam snapped.

Cody got to his feet. "Jeez, I didn't mean to start World War III. I just mentioned I gave a girl a ride home. She likes me. Is it so hard for you to believe someone likes me?"

"Christ, no, Cody. *I* like you. I want you to be safe. I want us to get along, okay?"

"Whatever," he muttered one last time, stooping to pick up his heavy backpack and heading for the stairs. "I've got some homework to do."

Crossing his arms across his chest, Sam scowled at the TV screen without really seeing it. The conversation had exposed glaring inadequacies he never knew he had, and it bugged the hell out of him. As a parent, you had to figure out when to say yes and when to say no. When to praise and when to upbraid. And getting it right was harder than it seemed.

Wednesday

*I*t wasn't until he pulled up to the barn at Lonepine after school the next day that Cody realized he'd forgotten to call Claudia—again. If he didn't keep in touch with her better, she was going to think he'd died or fallen off the planet or something.

But the days kept rolling along, the distance between here and Seattle seemed endless, and time got away from him.

Still, he should have phoned her. But he'd been so eager to get away from that frigging school that he'd roared off in the old Jeep without even remembering he'd meant to stop at Blue Rock and call Claudia. He didn't want to use Sam's phone for long-distance. Sam would probably let him, but Cody didn't want to ask.

He just didn't know where he stood with Sam. It was so weird being in his house, knowing the brand of shaving cream he used and what magazines he subscribed to, learning personal stuff about a stranger. Sometimes they had normal conversations and everything seemed fine, and then they'd rub each other the wrong way and argue. Cody kept trying to tell himself it didn't matter. He kept telling himself he didn't want to know this guy. He'd done fine without a father and he didn't need one now.

Sam McPhee was a hard guy to know. He sure as hell wasn't a guy Cody wanted to ask favors from, like phone permission.

Ah, well, he thought, swinging down from the driver's seat, he'd call Claudia tomorrow.

The Border collie came racing across the yard, barking her foolish face off. She knew Cody by now, having slept at the foot of his bed the past few nights. She launched herself like a missile at him. He caught her in his arms, staggering back a little with the motion, and laughed as she licked his face. It felt good, having someone greet you with this level of enthusiasm.

When they got back to Seattle, he'd talk his mom into getting a dog or a cat, maybe.

"That's loyalty for you," Sam said, ambling across from the house. "The minute I turn my back, I find my best girl in the arms of another man."

Cody tried not to grin as he set down the dog. "How's the new horse doing today?"

"Come on back and see for yourself." Sam didn't spend a long time looking at Cody, studying him. He just turned, totally casual, and ambled away.

Cody wondered if Sam was just naturally cool, or if he didn't care, or if he didn't want to get involved with a kid he didn't know. Maybe Cody was trying to read too much into Sam's attitude. It was hard as hell not to ask a bunch of questions, but he'd be damned if he'd make the first move.

Seeing the filly wiped out all his worries for a while. She acted as if she was happy to see him, frisking around the stall and thumping the walls, butting up against the mare. When the mare tried to eat, the filly kept trotting back and forth in front of her. With a quick, exasperated motion, the mare shoved the filly bodily away.

"Hey, why'd she do that?" Cody asked.

"The filly got in the way of what the mare wanted. She didn't hurt it." Sam drummed his fingers on the stall door, catching the filly's attention to distract it while Sylvia ate. "I was thinking she'll need a name one of these days. I have to register her papers."

"Yeah?"

"What do you think we ought to call her?"

Cody looked at the horse, and everything that crossed his mind was hokey and cute. Brownie. Blaze. Socks. He shrugged. "I don't know. Whatever."

Sam crossed his feet and propped his shoulder on the side of the stall. "A good horse might be around for twenty, thirty years. You have to make sure you pick the right name."

"So pick one."

"How about you pick it?"

"Why me?"

"You brought this animal into the world. I thought you might like to be the one to name her."

Cody shrugged again. Shit. He didn't know how to act. How did kids act around their fathers, anyway? "I can't think of anything."

"Maybe something will come to you. You let me know, okay?"

"Yeah. Okay."

The foal got tired and curled up in the straw for a nap. The mare fussed and licked at it for a while. It was amazing how she seemed to know exactly what to do.

"Do you have homework?" Sam asked. Then he shook his head. "Feels strange asking that."

You think you *feel strange,* thought Cody. "I did it in study hall."

"Okay, then you can get started on chores." Before Cody could reply, Sam held out a shovel and said, "It's good having you around."

Cody glanced at him sharply. What was good? His company? Or his manure-shoveling skills? Sam didn't say, and Cody didn't ask. They went to the tack room, put on quilted coveralls and gloves. Cody was mildly pleased to see Sam pick up a shovel, too. After the usual stall duties, today's task was to clean out the oat bins, getting rid of the moldy stuff on the bottom, scouring the galvanized metal bins, and replacing the oats.

"Ever given any thought to what you want to do after high school?" Sam asked.

"Some. I haven't made up my mind, though."

"You interested in college?"

"Sure. Most people go to UW. That's probably where I'll end up."

It helped that they were working as they talked. For some reason, it felt more natural to talk during the rhythm of the shovels. This week had to be the strangest time of Cody's life, starting a new school while his mom and grandfather did the kidney transplant. Talking didn't make things any better, but it didn't make things worse, either.

"You'll probably like college," Sam remarked. "I liked it a lot."

Cody wondered what it had been like for Sam and his mom, years ago, making a baby together and then never seeing each other again. He pushed away the thought and got back to work. Even though the chores were a drag, Cody sort of liked being out here, messing around with the horses and going all over on a snowmobile.

"What do you think of horse ranching?" Sam asked, reaching for a hose.

Cody snorted, chagrined that he even *looked* as if he might be enjoying himself. "It's a barrel of laughs." He stabbed his shovel into a mound of manure. The strange dance of uncertainty between him and Sam McPhee made him nervous.

At sunset, Sam and Edward were in the pole barn, replacing the spark plugs in a snowmobile. Two car doors slammed. Sam walked out to the drive to see Cody and Tammi Lee going toward the house.

"Almost suppertime," Tammi Lee called. She gestured at the two pizza boxes Cody balanced in his hands.

"We'll be in shortly." Sam grinned with the fine pleasure of seeing his mother and his son together. Family had always been in short supply for him. This was a new sensation for him. Did he like it, or was it something a guy like him was better off without?

"I think he likes it here," Sam said. "I think he even likes my mother."

Rummaging in a tool box, Edward regarded him sharply. "So you getting attached to the kid?"

"He's my kid." The wonder of it still swept through Sam each time he said the words. "What, I'm not supposed to get attached?"

"I didn't say that. But what happens when they leave?"

A blunt question, one that had been nagging at Sam. "It's not like they live on another planet," he said.

A faint yelp echoed down from the hill beyond the paddock. Edward shaded his eyes. "Hey, check this out."

Sam followed his gaze and felt a cold churn of fear in his gut. It was Scout, hurrying toward them—but not with her usual swift and joyous abandon. "She's hurt," he said, breaking into a run. He reached the collie halfway down the hill. A smear of blood marked her trail. It came from a long slash down her foreleg. Four scratches furrowed her muzzle.

"Hey, what's the matter with Scout?" Cody asked, jumping down off the porch and hurrying toward Sam.

Scooping up the dog, Sam hurried to the tack room. In one corner was a stainless-steel table and a couple of exam lights. He set her down, eyes and hands scanning her injuries.

"She need the vet?" Edward asked.

"Let's have a look." While Sam took off his gloves, Cody went around the other side of the table and murmured the dog's name, stroking her. Sam met the boy's eyes. "Keep her calm. I need to check out this cut." Edward opened the large first-aid wall station, stocked with instruments and supplies, and Sam used the clippers to trim away the long white-and-black hair, exposing a wicked gash.

"What happened?" Cody asked. "Is that from barbed wire?"

"Cat, more likely," Sam said. "A mountain lion. See the scratches across her nose? Scout's been known to tangle with a big cat if it wanders too close."

"Is she going to be okay?"

"Yeah, we'll fix her up."

Cody looked at the indigo sky through the small square window. "Are there a lot of mountain lions around here?"

"A fair number," Edward said, bringing some medicine from the office fridge. "We put out a trap, but they're street-smart. Last season we caught three, sent them down to Yellowstone to be turned out in the wild." Muffled thumps came from the stalls, the horses settling in for the night.

Sam snapped on a pair of surgical gloves. He and Cody worked together, Cody soothing the dog while Sam disinfected the superficial scratches. Edward stood back watching them thoughtfully.

"Hand me that syringe of lidocaine," Sam said to Cody. "Don't break the seal until I tell you." He cleansed the site and injected the topical anesthetic. The dog whimpered, and Cody hushed her. While he waited for the lido to work, Sam caught himself studying his son's hands, gently splayed across the collie's silky fur.

Wow, he thought, the kid's got my hands.

"You okay?" he asked Cody. "This is on the gory side."

"I can handle anything after pulling that foal," Cody assured him.

Sam used a double-ended needle and surgical thread to stitch the gash. At one point he glanced up and caught the boy looking at him, and the expression on Cody's face nearly bowled him over. Having a son was a fine thing. Having a son who admired you made you feel like a god.

"Go ahead and spray her with the Furex," he said, nodding at the plastic bottle. "That's right, up and down the wound." With intense concentration, Cody applied the yellowish antiseptic.

"Ever give an injection?" Sam asked.

"No."

"Want to learn?"

"I guess."

Sam prepared a dose of anti-inflammatory and penicillin, then coached Cody through the injection. As he worked, Cody's face wore an expression of complete absorption. Scout whimpered and took advantage of the extra attention she was getting. Walking tall with a sense of accomplishment, Cody carried her across the yard to the main house, putting her down gently in the kitchen.

"You guys make a pretty good team," Edward said, as they washed up at the sink in the mudroom. A certain quiet ease pervaded the atmosphere, and it felt good to Sam. A hell of a lot better than coming home to an empty house.

That evening after supper, Tammi Lee hung on Cody's every word as he described the treatment. She made a good listener, and he responded to that. Absently, he kept his hand on the dog's head as he spoke, and the sight evoked echoes of that rare warm feeling that had come over Sam earlier. Then Tammi Lee glanced at the clock.

"Better go," she said. "I've got some videos to return before closing time. You know what folks say." She winked. "Crime doesn't pay."

Sam was pleased to see that Cody stood up when she did, out of courtesy. She turned to him. "You looking forward to your mom and granddad getting home?" she asked.

"Yeah." Yet the reminder seemed to agitate him. He lifted a shoulder, just this side of insolent. "The sooner they get better, the sooner we go back to Seattle."

"You miss your friends?"

"Sure."

"I figured you'd make new ones here," said Tammi Lee, heading for the door. "Nice kid like you."

Cody looked startled. He was probably trying to recall the last time someone had called him a nice kid.

Thursday

Chapter **39**

With a weary motion, Cody shrugged his backpack over one shoulder and made his way to the main door of the school. Somehow, another endless day had ended.

Somehow, he had survived another day at this armpit of an institution.

He was sort of glad to be going to Sam's rather than the hospital this afternoon. His mom was lots better, but that meant she'd ask the usual questions about how his day went, and what were his teachers like, and did he make some more friends, and all that crap, and he didn't want to talk about it.

The only bright spot in this godforsaken place was Molly Lightning. She was great, not making a big deal of him but making sure she introduced him to a couple of her friends each day. They were way different from his friends in Seattle. Who would have thought he'd be sitting around at lunchtime talking about goat roping and 4-H Club?

At least it wasn't the geek table.

Maybe he'd call Molly tonight, pretend he needed a homework page or something.

"Cody?"

A voice behind him. Female, but not Molly.

He stopped at a heavy door with wire mesh through the glass. He recognized the girl from homeroom, the one he was already thinking of as the Blond Bombshell. Shiny yellow hair, huge tits.

He smiled. "Yeah?"

"It's Cody, right? Cody Slade?"

"Turner."

"Oh." She stuck her thumb in the top of her jeans pocket, tugging the waistband down to show a little of her bare stomach. "Someone said you were related to Gavin Slade."

"I am, but I've got a different last name." He pushed the heavy door open, stood to one side to let her pass. She smelled like bubble gum and shampoo. Her sweater was tight. Really tight. "He's my grandfather. I'm staying at his place."

Her face lit up, pretty and bright. "I think that's so cool." She ducked her head and looked up at him through long eyelashes. "I'm Iris York. We're in homeroom together."

"And English." Color flooded his face. "I noticed you in English class last period." He'd noticed her in the lunchroom, too, at the inner sanctum table, but she hadn't called out to him.

She made a face. "I can't stand the teacher, Mrs. Lightning. She's picky, picky, picky. I can't wait until the term's over and I can take drama instead."

Cody had actually thought Mrs. Lightning—Molly's mom—wasn't too bad. She was the only one who hadn't made him sit in the front, and she didn't act all chummy with him just because she was friends with Sam McPhee.

"Can I give you a ride somewhere?" he asked boldly, gesturing at the Jeep.

"Um . . ." She looked from side to side, then shrugged. "I don't see my usual ride, so I guess I'll take you up on that. I live up in Windemere Hills, on the golf course."

"Great." They headed across the parking lot.

"So tell me about your grandfather. I think his old movies are sooo bitchen—"

A Bondo-colored El Camino came around a corner and lurched to a stop in front of them. Cody jumped back, flinging out his arm in an instinctively protective gesture. Slush from a filthy puddle sluiced over his feet. Ice-cold water trickled into his shoes.

"Hey, Iris." The driver got out and came around the car, opening the passenger door. "I thought I'd missed you, but here I am."

Iris bit her lip. "Hi, Billy. This is Cody Turner. Cody, this is Billy Ho. The guys in the back are Ethan Lindvig and Jason Kittredge." Gangsterlike, they nodded at him from the rusty bed of the truck.

Billy was one of the coolest guys in school; Cody could tell. Good-looking in a Native American way. Outside the library Molly had pointed him out, said he was big trouble. But he was just cool. Molly probably couldn't see that.

"Cody offered me a ride home," Iris explained. "I thought you'd left without me," she hastened to add, pushing out her lower lip.

"Today's your lucky day." Billy opened the door wider.

When she hesitated, Cody knew it was now or never. Speak up now and get the cutest girl in the school on his side, or forever hold his peace . . . and sit at the dweeb table.

"The offer's still open," he said.

Billy didn't speak, but his glittering black eyes and go-to-hell expression said it all. Cody was trespassing, and Billy didn't like it one bit.

"Maybe another time," Iris said.

"Maybe never," Billy snapped.

Billy grabbed for Iris's arm. Cody didn't think, he just stepped between them.

"Maybe she can make up her own mind," he said.

"Out of my way." Billy shoved him. Hard. Cody stumbled back, putting out a hand behind him, but there was nothing to catch him, so he plopped, ass-first, into a puddle of muddy, half-frozen slush.

He came up swearing, ready to fight, but it was a stupid move. He wasn't cut out for fighting, and Billy Ho was built like a dump truck. Cody laughed and hoped he sounded convincing. "Hey," he said, trying not to let his teeth chatter. "No big deal, right?"

At that moment the El Camino coughed and died.

"Balls." Billy reached in and tried the ignition. "This has been giving me trouble all day." He tried several more times, but the heap wouldn't start. "We better push it out of the way."

Iris got behind the wheel. The guys went around to the rear. Billy tossed his long black hair out of his eyes. "Yo, Cody. You gonna stand there, or you gonna help?"

Cody threw off his backpack and his anger. Here was his chance to get in good with these guys. Being one of their crowd might even make school bearable.

Once they'd moved the car to a parking spot, Iris pouted at Billy. "*Now* where's my ride home?"

Just for a second, Cody recalled his conversation with Sam about passengers in the Jeep. Only if there were enough seat belts to go around. They were one short, but Cody didn't even hesitate. Screw Sam. He'd never find out. "I'll give all of you a lift,"

"Excellent, man. I need to get to the auto-parts store." They all piled into the Jeep. Cody's jeans felt squishy, making him wish for a hot shower and clean towels. As he pulled out of the parking lot, he heard a faint "Hey, Cody!"

"Who's that?" Billy asked.

"Ugh, Molly Lightning." Iris wrinkled her nose. "The *cowgirl*."

Molly emerged from a knot of students. "Can you drop me by the arena?"

"No!" Billy said, putting his hand on Cody's shoulder. "Jeez, the teacher's kid. Her mom's flunking me."

Cody had a split second to decide. He made eye contact with Molly as she approached the Jeep. Taking a deep breath, he said, "Sorry, kid. Car's full." At least he didn't have to lie. He punched the gas pedal too hard, sending up a plume of mud and slush.

"Good move, man!" Ethan thumped him on the back.

Cody glanced in the rearview mirror to see Molly standing on the curb, shaking out her book bag. He felt something icier than the parking lot slush. Something that wouldn't come off with a shower and a stack of towels.

Friday

Chapter 40

An old El Camino, pockmarked by rust, came fast up the drive to Lonepine, spitting a rooster tail of gravel and ice in its wake. Favoring her wounded leg, Scout had to dart to the side of the road to avoid getting hit. Annoyed, Sam walked out onto the porch. He was still in his office clothes, having just got home after a long day of clinic visits.

Behind the El Camino came Cody in the Jeep. Patience, Sam told himself as he crossed the yard to the horse barn. No one ever said this fatherhood gig was going to be easy.

But as four disreputable-looking kids tumbled out of the vehicles—the most disreputable of all being his son—he gritted his teeth into a forced smile for the introductions. With a decided lack of grace, Cody gestured at each boy in turn—Billy, Ethan, and Jason. He recognized Billy from providing his school sports physical every year. The kid was wearing a jacket that looked brand-new and unaffordable. Sam grew annoyed at himself for having the thought. He was turning into a pretty judgmental s.o.b. lately.

A throaty screech, far off but distinct, echoed down from the veil of trees above the meadow. Scout growled and crouched in close to Sam, too smart to run off after the predator a second time. Sam shaded his eyes, studying the blue-shadowed distance, but he saw no movement in the field.

"Hey, guys," Sam said to the boys. "How was school?"

They rolled their eyes in unison. "Sucked," Cody said.

"Yeah?" Sam asked, tugging his tie loose. "You might consider the alternative."

"What, no school? That'd be awesome."

Sam shook his head. "When I was sixteen, I was working ten hours a day unrolling frozen bales of hay. Trust me, it's not awesome."

They didn't trust him, of course. Kids never fell for that "in my day" stuff. He ought to know better.

"I brought the guys over to show them the filly," Cody said.

"Fine. Take it easy around the mare. Don't get between her and—"

"I know, I know," Cody waved a hand. "Always face and acknowledge the mare, blah blah blah."

"You got it."

"Can we use the snowmobiles?"

Sam hesitated. "All right. But they're working vehicles, not toys. So don't screw around—" He stopped. Christ, he was talking to them like an old schoolmarm. "Okay, so you're going to screw around. But be careful. Use the helmets."

"We will," Cody said.

Sam nodded to Cody's friends. "Nice to meet you, but I can't stick around. I need to shower and shave." He rubbed his jaw.

"Big date tonight?" Billy Ho asked with a sly wink.

"I guess you could say that." If you counted a hospital visit as a date.

Cody regarded him with narrow-eyed suspicion. He'd made it clear he didn't favor Sam and Michelle getting to know each other again. Probably a natural reaction—kids raised by single mothers tended to feel threatened by any interloper—but it annoyed the hell out of Sam.

"C'mon." Suddenly in a hurry, Cody headed into the barn. His friends trailed after him, and Sam went back to the house.

He had no idea how to judge what kind of job he'd done with Cody this week. He was a difficult kid. They weren't all like that, Sam thought as he got into the shower and raised his face to the hot needles of the spray. Take Molly Lightning, who lived down the road. Bright, athletic, good student. She had prospects. You could look at her and picture her in a good place in ten years. As for Cody, it was hard to imagine where he was headed. Sam sensed that he'd never been tested. Never been forced to the wall, because Michelle had been so concerned about insulating him—from photographers, from hurt, from want. It wasn't her fault, but everything had come so easy to Cody that he had never learned to work for what he wanted. He maintained a sense of entitlement that bugged Sam. It was a hell of a thing.

So far, the father-and-son bond had eluded them both. There had been moments, here and there, when something, some connection, could be felt. Sam supposed that was all he could hope for at first. Deep down, he still wondered if he wanted more, and his own hesitation bothered him. Above the hiss of the shower, he could hear the nasal whine of snowmobiles being ridden fast. Too fast. He had to force himself not to go yell at them to take it easy. They'd just blow him off anyway, he knew. These kids were like creatures from another planet. He felt awkward around them, as if he had never been that young himself.

He scrubbed himself hard and efficiently, cleaning off the remnants of a rough day. Too many patients, too much red tape, not enough time. At least when he went to see Michelle at the hospital, it would be as a visitor, not a doctor. He was just drying off when he heard someone pounding at the door.

Pulling on a pair of jeans, he hurried downstairs.

Billy Ho stood on the back porch, his eyes wide, looking different from the go-to-hell kid who'd climbed out of the El Camino. "Um, Cody had sort of a . . . problem. With the horses."

Sam was already stuffing his feet into a pair of snow boots by the door. He grabbed a parka from the mudroom and put it on over his bare, damp chest. "What kind of problem?"

"Well, the little horse—the foal—got out."

"No big deal," he said, relaxing. "She'll come back in once we put the mare up. A filly that young won't stray far from her mom."

"No, man. I mean *out*. Like outside the paddock. Then it kind of panicked and took off."

Sam broke into a run. Billy trotted alongside him, breathless, trying to choke out an explanation. "We were just goofing around. No one knew the horse would take off. Cody went after her."

"Where's the mare?"

"She tried to follow the foal out, but Cody put her up. She's pissed, man—"

Sam could hear her. Frantic whinnies and stomping hooves echoed down the breezeway of the barn. He could see the snowmobile trails slashing and crisscrossing the broad slope of the meadow leading up to the woods. Shit. A filly that young would never leave her mother or the familiar terrain of the paddock unless she was truly terror-stricken. The boys had probably herded her uphill on the snowmobiles. As he put on a pair of gloves, he tried to remember what Cody was wearing. School clothes. If he got lost, he'd freeze to death in no time flat.

Sam harnessed a utility sled to one of the snowmobiles. He shot out of the yard, following a crooked line of footprints up the rise behind the barn. The panicked foal had traveled fast; he could see the stretch of its stride in the snow. Despite its young age, it could outrun Cody, especially if it was scared and lost without its mother.

The footprints disappeared into a cover of larch and fir trees. Sam drove into the woods, feeling a shower of golden larch needles rain down on him. He had to slow down to dodge the trees. Before long the density of the trees stopped him altogether. The sled behind the machine was too wide to negotiate the forest. Turning off the snowmobile and cursing through clenched teeth, he continued on foot.

In the silence after the engine's rumble, he heard a sound midway between a cough and a snarl. His blood ran cold. It was the distinctive call of a mountain lion. A big cat didn't usually bother things it couldn't easily kill, but if it felt cornered or hungry enough, it might take a swipe at a young horse. Or a kid. The eerie screeching escalated, a deadly rasp that echoed through the winter woods.

Sam climbed to the top of the ridge. There, he spied

a bitten-off section of snow that had crumbled down the opposite face in a small avalanche. Pressed against the curve of the scarp was Cody, waist-deep in snow, the horse floundering, its skinny legs sunk uselessly into the bank.

A livid smear of blood stained the snow.

Crouched on a bare rock above the boy and the foal was the cat. This one was big, maybe ninety pounds.

Its paw slashed out, claws extended, lips peeled back in a snarl. Cody had grabbed a branch and held it out, trying to fend off the reaching paw.

"Yah!" Sam yelled, waving his arms. "Yah, beat it, you old bitch!"

The cat froze and faced him with glittering eyes.

"Stay calm, Cody, and don't crouch down or turn your back, okay?" Sam called.

The boy's face was gray with terror.

"These cats like small prey," Sam said, praying the kid wouldn't panic. "Don't run, or you might trigger her instinct to attack. Keep waving the branch. You have to act aggressive."

He walked steadily toward the cougar, and his gut twisted as she swung her tawny gaze back to the boy and the horse. "Don't look it in the eye," he yelled, cupping his hands around his mouth.

The long tail switched slowly, rhythmically, nervous as a rattlesnake. The horse fell still, its stamina gone.

"If she attacks, you fight back, Cody," Sam hollered, hurrying as fast as he dared. "You hear me, son? Fight back!"

"O-okay," Cody said, his voice thin, snow-muffled. He brandished the branch like a sword.

The mountain lion coiled like a spring. For a sickening moment, Sam feared it would attack. A cougar always went for the head and neck. He reached the top of the bank and waved his arms, kicked up snow. The mountain lion retreated a few steps, turned, snarled. He yelled and waved his arms again, close enough now to see a string of drool drip from her mouth. Sam grabbed a chunk of ice and hurled it as hard as he could. Grumbling low in her throat, she slunk into the woods.

"Cody!" Sam half ran, half tumbled down the bank. "You okay? What's all this blood?"

The kid's bare hand kept its hold on the mane of the horse. "I'm okay. Let's get her up. She's stuck, see?" His face was dull white, his voice shaking.

"What's bleeding?" Sam demanded.

Cody held up his free hand. "Hit it on something on my way down." His chin trembled; maybe it was a shiver; Sam didn't know. "Help me, Dad."

It just seemed to slip out, the *Dad* part. Probably didn't mean a thing, but it had an incredibly powerful effect on Sam. "Okay, keep hold of the mane, you've got it. She's in a panic because she can't get her footing. We'll help her up the bank." Inch by inch, they pulled the foal upward. She was terrified, her eyes rolling, her hooves kicking out every which way.

"Watch the feet," Sam said through his teeth. They had no bridle, no way to control the horse except by brute strength. The minutes seemed to crawl as they struggled up to the top of the escarpment. The snow crumbled beneath them, sending them back a foot for every few feet they gained. Cody was panting, almost sobbing, when they reached the top, then staggered, pushing and pulling the horse to the snowmobile. She flailed every step of the way, twisting and snapping, hooves slashing out, impossible to contain.

"I'll hold her on the sled and you drive," Sam instructed. Using his teeth, he peeled off his gloves and tossed them to Cody. "Put those on. You'll get frostbite." He wrestled the foal onto the sled and Cody held her in place. Off they went, a smooth ride down the mountain, then into the paddock. The El Camino was gone. He wasn't surprised the kids had hightailed it at the first sign of trouble.

Sylvia had practically torn a hole in the stable door. The little one trotted inside and Sylvia was on her immediately, sniffing and licking her from stem to stern. Cody stood in the breezeway, teeth chattering, his nose bright red.

"Thanks," he said in a quiet voice.

"I'm just glad I found you."

The boy hesitated, then looked him in the eye. "I'm glad I found you, too."

And then without even thinking about it, Sam hugged him. It could have been awkward, but it wasn't. It was the most natural thing in the world to let a sudden wave of love for this boy spill out and over, to gather him in his arms in a hug that tried hard to make up for all the years of hugs he'd missed. Sam's throat felt tight as he stepped back. He didn't know if he was cut out for this. He'd never felt anything like the icy burn of terror that had ripped through him when he'd seen Cody in danger. His nerves were shot.

Cody was shuddering violently now. "Are you going to tell my mom?"

"Your mother's got enough to worry about." Sam grabbed his arm, pulling him toward the house. "We need to warm you up, have a look at that hand," he said.

A minute later they sat at the kitchen table, Cody's arm propped on a towel while Sam used tweezers to clean the grit out of the cut.

"When was the last time you had a tetanus shot?" Sam asked.

"Not sure." Cody winced as the tweezers dug deeper. "I had a bunch of shots before going to camp two summers ago. Ow!"

"Sorry. Don't watch. It's making you tense up."

Cody turned his head away. "Who's Alice McPhee?" he asked, focusing on the stack of junk mail on the table. The top item was a lingerie catalog with a label bearing Alice's name.

Sam hesitated. "My ex-wife."

Cody drew breath with a hiss. "Man, I didn't know you had a wife."

"I don't."

"It's bogus not to tell me you were married before."

"I was married before."

"I mean it's bogus that you didn't tell me right off."

"Cody—"

"Does my mom know?"

"She knows." Sam tweezed a sliver of dirt from the wound. "Hey, cut me some slack. I'm new at this."

"Yeah, well, so am I," Cody muttered.

Sam wanted to take the focus off him and Alice. She represented a failure he didn't like to talk about, so he changed the subject. "So what happened?" he asked, concentrating on the deep gash.

Cody shrugged, some of that old screw-you attitude slipping back into place.

"Hold still," Sam said through his teeth. "What happened?"

"We were just goofing around, man. We let the mare and the foal out into the paddock. Then we started riding snowmobiles and . . . the filly got out and took off. The noise confused her, and she went up the hill."

"Because you left the paddock gate open."

"Somebody did. I don't know who."

"Do you think that matters? You were in charge, Cody."

"Everything worked out okay, no harm done. Back off, man."

Sam's hand didn't falter, his gaze didn't waver as he cleaned the cut. But inside, he froze. "Everything *didn't* work out. A valuable filly almost died or broke a leg. Sylvia could've injured herself going ballistic in her stall. You almost got killed. What if I hadn't been around to come after you?"

"Man, you haven't been around for sixteen years, and I survived." Contempt dripped from his voice.

Sam stopped working. He set down the tweezers and regarded the sullen, defiant face so like his own—and yet so strange to him. "Well, I'm back now. And the bullshit is over. I figured putting you in charge of the filly would be good for you. Don't prove me wrong, Cody."

"Yeah, well, maybe you *are* wrong about me."

Sam got out a bottle of disinfectant. "This'll sting."

"Ouch. Hey, man." Cody tensed the muscles in his arm.

"Maybe you'd better choose your friends more carefully. You could use a few more responsibilities—"

"Hey—"

"—don't interrupt. You screwed up, and there are consequences. If you thought the work around here was hard before, you—"

Cody snatched his hand away before Sam was finished. "You're not my frigging jailer." He stood up fast, his chair legs scraping the floor. "What do you want with me?" he demanded.

Sam didn't have an answer for that. *Did* he want a

kid, or was it a concept he liked better in the abstract? No matter, he told himself. The reality was, he had a kid—and a difficult one at that. He had no idea if he knew how to be a good father. He picked up a length of gauze. "Let me wrap that wound."

Cody grabbed it from him. "I'll take care of it myself." He backed away, pausing in the kitchen doorway. "I know what you want with my mom, and I can't do anything about that, but stay the hell away from me."

Saturday

Chapter 41

It seemed like half the population of Missoula found some reason to stop by Gavin's room. They were timid at first, asking if he needed anything, making small talk. As the week wore on and he was moved from the SICU to a private room, their numbers increased. Nurses, aides, orderlies, residents, volunteers. The timidity fell away and then finally, on a rush of hard-won courage, they started asking for his autograph.

The mistake had been in giving out that first one, to a brown-eyed aide who looked a little like Carolyn.

"You remind me of the last woman who dumped me," he said, scrawling his signature on the back of a work-order pad. "No, on second thought, you're prettier."

She must have alerted the whole ward, maybe the whole floor, because all through the week he had to deal with furtive fans. He'd given the hospital strict instructions that the transplant was to be kept private, but strict instructions only went so far.

"They're wearing me out, Doc," he said to Maggie Kehr when she stopped in. She wore a shamrock in her lapel and a little leprechaun clinging to her scope. "You've got to let me go home and get some rest."

She smiled down at the chart she'd been writing on. "I want to keep you at least a week."

"It's St. Paddy's Day, fer chrissake," he said in an exaggerated brogue. "I've been lying around on my poor arse long enough."

"A week, Gavin."

"Aren't you the one who said it's the best kidney transplant you've ever seen?"

"Yes, but—"

"Didn't you say we set some sort of record, getting the kidney to work? Didn't you remove the catheter forty-eight hours sooner than you thought you could?"

"I did, Gavin—"

"Didn't I just take the healthiest piss you ever saw a man take?"

"Now *that*," she said, "is debatable."

"Only because guys piss for you all the time."

"One of the great perks of my specialty."

"I'm going home, Doc. With or without your blessing, I'm checking out when Michelle leaves here." She was being discharged today, and he was bound and determined to go with her. There was something vaguely horrifying about being left behind while his daughter went back to Crystal City. If he stayed, he'd feel like the loser in some battle or race.

"Never say whining doesn't work," Dr. Kehr said, signing a sheaf of forms.

"What do you mean?"

"You're a free man, Gavin. You've got the luck of the Irish on your side."

"I love you, Maggie, I really do."

"You're an old coot. Take care of that kidney now. They're a little hard to come by."

"My body is now Fort Knox."

"Just make sure that body doesn't miss a single follow-up appointment or a single pill. A pharmaceutical therapist will stop in to go over your meds and your daily log with you."

"Again, huh?" He didn't argue. From the very start, they'd impressed on him the importance of taking the antirejection medications. With a decided lack of sympathy, Maggie had warned him that the drugs would make him itch and sweat and suffer from impotence. He'd probably gain weight, and it would show in the cheeks and gut.

Not a pretty picture. Still, given the alternative, he'd settle for night sweats and chipmunk cheeks. But if this didn't work and he died, what the hell. It had brought him and Michelle together. It was up to them to find the things that mattered. Maybe they hadn't quite found that just yet, but they would. He knew they would.

The discharge was nicely choreographed so that he and Michelle were both wheeled into the main lobby at the same time from opposite wings. Smiling volunteers gave them green carnations for St. Patrick's Day. Gavin looked around suspiciously, thinking maybe the media had managed to barge in. He'd hate having this moment captured by some shutterbug who'd get five grand for the photo.

But what a moment it was.

Michelle. His daughter. She had always been incredibly beautiful, blond and luminous, with a way of looking at the world that was completely original, completely

unique. It was something he had seen even in the cray-
oned Father's Day cards she'd dutifully sent him as a small
child. Seated in the wheelchair, smiling at him, she touched
his heart.

He felt his throat fill with thick emotion, and the acting skill that usually came so naturally deserted him. He
held out his hand. "Thank you, honey," he said, suddenly
reaching forward to touch her cheek. "You know, you're
the best thing I ever did."

For a moment she just blinked at him, almost comically speechless. They'd seen each other now and then
through the week, visiting, talking quietly, but this was
different. They had done what they'd set out to do. They
were going home now.

She took his hand and pressed it against her cheek.
"All set, Daddy?"

"Yes. I want to tell you, I haven't felt this good in
two years. I'm not sick anymore. No matter what I'm doing
or thinking, I just stop in the middle of it and say to myself, 'I'm not sick anymore.' "

"That's the point." Her smiled widened. "Ready?"

"Past ready." He signaled to the orderly pushing the
chair and put on an English accent. "Driver, to the eleva-
tors."

"Feels good to be going home."

Gavin wondered what she meant. "Home" as in Blue
Rock, or "home" as in Seattle? He didn't know much about
her life there, had only met two of her friends. Natalie
was great. Brad Lovell was . . . adequate. The sort of solid
guy you'd want for your daughter. Except that you wanted
a guy to look at your daughter with worship, pure and
simple. Not pride of ownership, which was what Gavin
had detected in Brad's manner.

Gavin's burgundy Cadillac pulled up beneath the

awning. He expected his foreman, Jake, to get out, but instead, it was Cody. He sent Michelle a questioning look, narrowing his gaze suspiciously. "Did you know about this?"

She laughed. "Uh-huh."

He gave a low whistle. "I think I'd rather wheel this chair home."

"Be nice, Dad. The drive's nothing. A straight shot up the highway. It hasn't snowed, so the roads are clear. And he's worked really hard. Sam said he was practicing all week."

Gavin saw her knuckles tighten on the arms of her chair. "So how did the week go, him staying with Sam?"

She watched the suitcases being loaded into the trunk. "I don't know. He hasn't said much." Finally, she turned to him. "Daddy, what if he does better with Sam than he did with me?"

Gavin wished he was close enough to touch her. "It's not a competition." It was all he had time to say, when she needed so much more from him. She needed the years he couldn't give back to her, when pride and anger had kept them apart. "We'll be all right," he said, and vowed to make it so even if it killed him. "We're going to be fine."

The doors swished open, and out they went. Cody looked a little out of place, but very determined behind the wheel. Probably gave the kid a charge, driving Gavin's Caddy. Something about driving two people who were full of stitches and drugs probably made him feel particularly important.

"Here goes nothing," Gavin pushed himself up out of the chair.

The electric doors opened, and he stepped out into the bracing cold air. He wore a shirt and slacks that hadn't been cut to fit over a dialysis bag, and his blood sang. He wasn't nervous about the kid's driving. How could he be? Something magical had happened to him in the hospital, and now he was going home.

"I do love the occasional miracle," he said.

Sunday

Sunday

Chapter 42

Cody was pretending he wasn't nervous about school in the morning, Michelle observed that evening. It made her nuts that she'd been so out of it the past week, unable to be there for him every second, helping him through the ordeal of starting a new school. She had been there for every moment of his life, big and small, but last week, he'd been on his own.

And—wonder of wonders—the world had not come to an end. She was thankful he'd survived that first week, but she could tell he was anxious about the days to come. She knew that look, the shifting of his eyes, the jiggling of his foot against the chair as he ate dinner—a feast prepared by a beaming Tadao. They had eaten in the huge den of the main house, with Gavin and Michelle reclining like Romans on sofas. She had asked Cody if he liked his classes, if he'd made any friends, how he'd liked staying with Sam, but he'd only given her one-syllable answers. That was all she'd heard all week. She'd questioned him about the bandage on his hand, but all he'd said was he'd cut himself working at Sam's.

Gavin drank a glass of wine, his first since he was diagnosed, and he got almost teary-eyed as he tasted the Jordan Cabernet. With both Tadao and Michelle supervising, he took his evening meds and noted them in his daily log. Though he didn't whisper a word of fatigue, Gavin excused himself to go to bed early.

After an extralong shower, Cody went to his room, leaving Michelle lying on the sofa, fiddling with the TV remote. She was oddly manic and restless on her first night away from the hospital. She felt fragile and vulnerable from the lingering pain of an invasive procedure. She worried about bumping into things, worried about sleeping, worried about her father, worried about how she'd feel seeing Sam again.

But when she looked out and saw the snow begin to fall, her worries seemed to have no more substance than the weightless snowflakes settling over the yard. That was the gift that had been given back to her the morning of the surgery. She hadn't recognized her old friend at first, but it was just as Joseph Rain had said, so many years ago. *The gift comes to you in secret. If your heart and your mind are not open to inspiration, then it passes you by.*

Now, finally, in the midwinter of her life, she understood. It was the space she had glimpsed between the two parting curtains. That was the offer. What she did with it was up to her.

She didn't allow herself to think. Ignoring her doctor's orders, she bundled up and walked through the blowing snow to the small dwelling at the end of the compound, the studio she had abandoned seventeen years before. There, she turned on the heat, rubbed her hands together, and took a deep, steadying breath. Physically, she felt dead tired. But she couldn't quell the restless need inside her. Time enough later for sleep, she decided.

Natalie—bless her—had set up stretched and gessoed Belgian linen canvases and laid out new paints and brushes. But even if these had been the crudest of supplies, it wouldn't have mattered, because at last she was ready. She lowered the legs of the easel and positioned it in front of the old red couch so she didn't have to stand up. Then she rolled up her sleeves and began.

She worked at a fever pitch from a vision that had been hidden inside her for years. It was a painful emergence, a birthing of sorts. For someone so conditioned to look outside herself, to emulate the hard lines and precise angles of that which could be seen and quickly grasped by someone paging through a magazine, it was a difficult transition. But for once that didn't stop her. After enduring what she had endured this past week, nothing could seem hard.

The transplant, confronting mortality, and coming face-to-face with her past had forced her hand. From her slumbering subconscious emerged the inspiration, the sense of awe and wonder, that had once meant everything to her.

The shapes and colors of her soul exploded onto the canvas. She didn't think, didn't evaluate. She just worked. And inside her, something happened. Something magical and true and luminous. She felt free, racing above the earth, elation pouring over her, out through her hands and her heart, becoming something wholly original, wholly her own.

She had no sense of time passing. She simply sank

into a strange beta state where nothing mattered except the painting, where the colors and emotions came from, and what the images were. The urge was sensual, predatory, dangerous, seductive, and in a leap of faith, she gave herself to it utterly.

When Sam McPhee walked into the studio, she should have been surprised, but she was not. It made a terrible, wonderful sense that he would come here alone, searching for her.

He stood in the dim foyer, his shoulders dusted with new snow, his face unsmiling, his eyes filled with a look she recognized from long, long ago.

"I saw the light on," he said.

Suddenly nervous, she grabbed a linseed rag and wiped her hands. "I . . . couldn't sleep."

"You sure as hell ought to be. You're recovering from surgery—"

"I'm all right, Sam. Don't doctor me. I've had enough doctors hovering over me, okay? I'm on the couch, see?"

"You're supposed to be flat on your back."

"That would make it hard to paint."

"Worked for Michelangelo." He studied her, and she braced herself for further argument, but he didn't pursue it. Taking off his coat, he hung it on a hook behind the door. He wore jeans and a thick flannel shirt.

"You're staring," he said.

"Am I?" One Christmas, she had bought Brad a shirt exactly like that. It was still in his closet, still folded with the pins in it.

"Michelle. Are you feeling okay?"

It was a question from Sam the doctor. Not Sam the ex-boyfriend. Not Sam the father of her child.

"Yes." She settled back on the old sofa. "I'm fine, really. My father and I are fine. We had a nice dinner to celebrate coming home. And I'm glad you came over. I want to thank you for keeping Cody last week."

He lifted the corner of his mouth in a half grin. "He's a barrel of laughs. We're going to have to do something about him being so accident-prone."

We. Did he really mean that? "He never did explain how he hurt his hand."

He tucked his thumbs in his back pockets. "Barn chores," he said dismissively.

"It was sweet of you to take care of him, Sam."

"I didn't do it to be sweet." He crossed the room and sat down beside her, very close, and the unique smell of him was achingly familiar. He touched her chin. "So you're fine."

"Uh-huh."

"Been painting."

"Yes." She held her breath while he regarded the tall, spattered easel with the halogen lights shining down. "It's not finished."

She watched him, still not daring to breathe. She saw the impact of the painting go through him as if he'd touched an electrified fence. His arms, legs, shoulders, neck stiffened; then he turned to her quickly.

"Wow," he said.

"Is that good wow or bad wow?"

"You mean you don't know?"

"Sam, the paint's still wet. I barely know my own name."

He held out his hand. She hesitated, then took it, studying the broad canvas. She saw an abstraction of pure emotion. It was no use. She had no objectivity.

"It's the first time in years I've done a painting that wasn't for work," she admitted.

"It's about damned time, Michelle."

"But what do you *think*, Sam?"

"Hell, I'm no art expert. To me, it's amazing. I look at this, and it makes me think differently. Makes me want to stare, fall into it, I don't know. I don't have the vocabulary or the expertise."

She tried to see the picture as he saw it. The composition was classical, straight out of Art 101. But so were van Gogh's compositions. The principal motif in the middle came from her vision—the mysterious space between the parted curtains. Within that space dwelled an abstract study of color, light and shadow. She saw pain and passion and depth, and realized she was looking at a painting that expressed precisely what she wanted it to express. Whether or not that had any particular value didn't matter.

"You know what?" she said suddenly. "You don't have to tell me if it's good or not. It's the painting that came out of me."

"I think it's incredible."

"Do you think it could be the drugs? I'm on Percocet."

"It's not the drugs, Michelle."

They sat together for long, silent moments, staring at the painting. She felt drained in a good way—the tension had flowed through her. She was the crucible. All the feelings, emotions, good and bad, had melted down inside her and then emerged in a new form, a thing of power and beauty, this painting.

She looked out the window, weighing her thoughts. What if she asked him about Cody's week? Then Sam would know Cody had barely spoken to her. But then she remembered her father's words: *It's not a competition.*

"What?" Sam asked, regarding her reflection in the blackened window. "Are you all right?"

"Just . . . thinking. I'd like to hear how last week went from your perspective. With you and Cody."

"It was fine, Michelle. Not every second, but we got along all right." Lord, just like Cody. He wasn't telling her a thing.

"What does he think of school?"

"Sucks," Sam said, emulating Cody's sullen manner. "But what else is he going to say?"

"Has he made any friends?"

"Hard to say. He was hanging with some guys. I don't know if you'd call them friends. He spent some time with Molly Lightning, too."

It felt . . . normal, talking over her son with Sam. Maybe this was what married couples did. She recoiled from the thought. "I feel so bad, making him go to a strange school."

"You ought to try to get over feeling bad on the kid's behalf."

"I'm a mother. It's what I *do*." She fell silent.

After a while, Sam said, "I was surprised Brad didn't stick around for the surgery."

Michelle felt a stab of defensiveness. She didn't know how to tell him about Brad. It was too . . . embarrassing. And he might read something into Brad's departure that wasn't there. *Would* she have broken off with Brad if Sam hadn't been in the picture? She wanted to believe she would have, but the truth was, she didn't know for certain.

"His job is incredibly demanding," she said evasively. Color heated her cheeks. She had let Sam make love to her. Did he understand that she hadn't given herself to him lightly? Did he understand she had never done anything remotely like that before? Did he understand that she'd been swept away by yearning and nostalgia and a passion that she needed more than air?

Or were those just excuses?

"If you're so committed to some other guy, then why is he in Seattle while I'm sitting here doing this?"

"Doing what?"

"This."

He cupped his hands over her shoulders and kissed her long and searchingly just then. His embrace caught her, supported her, and imprinted the texture and taste of his mouth on her, and when it was over, she felt stupid and dazed.

She wanted to speak out, to stop him, but she held a hush in her throat, trusting the knowing tenderness of his hands as he caressed her. He drew from her a shameless and powerful wanting.

"We can't do this, Sam." Guilt shuddered through her. If she let him make love to her again, she was a goner.

He pulled back and gave her a look. "Only because you're still recovering. Otherwise, we'd make friends with this old couch again."

Laughing at her blush, he helped her turn off the lights in the studio and walked her back to the guesthouse. At the front door, he kissed her again, like a suitor dropping her off after a pleasant date. She went inside and stood at the window in the darkened living room, watching his headlights illuminate the snowy night and letting the tears come, feeling her heart shatter. What sort of life would she have had if they had stayed together?

If only.

The big burning issue in her life.

If only she had believed in Sam, if only she had worked harder to find him and tell him about the baby, her life would have been so different. They might have supported each other through the hard years, and now they'd be a family.

No. If Sam had known about Cody, there would have been no rodeo circuit for him, no medical school, no Yucatán. Burdened with a family, he might not have become a doctor at all, and all the lives he had saved would be lost, all the wounds that he'd healed and all the illnesses he'd cured might have gone untreated. Perhaps everything happened for a reason. Perhaps their estrangement was some sort of preordained event, designed to make their lives work out the way they had.

The thought nagged at her. She was back in Crystal City, wasn't she? Beyond the obvious, what could be the reason for that?

It was idiotic to speculate. Gavin's illness wasn't part of some cosmic plan. It was something that had just . . . happened. Meeting Sam again was pure coincidence. She shouldn't make any more of it than that. Certainly she shouldn't be having these thoughts just because Sam McPhee had a way of kissing her until she couldn't see straight, because he made love like a form of worship.

She had failed with Brad. Sam had failed with Alice. Maybe the two of them just weren't cut out for the long haul.

The thought followed her to the edge of sleep.

Monday

Monday

*M*ichelle spent the day lost in thoughts of Sam. Her father was in bed, on the phone trying to arrange the renewal of his pilot's license, and Cody was at school. Michelle tried reading, watching television, sketching a plan for a painting, but after a while she simply gave in to memories of Sam. She felt herself being sucked back into the past, dredging her heart through memories that burned. He was the first boy she had ever loved, and that one long-ago summer stood out vividly as a magical time. Each sunset burned brighter, more beautiful than the last. Each moonrise glowed with a promise she had felt certain was meant for her, only for her. She had been so naively young back then. She thought her love was like a river, ever flowing, never ceasing; nothing and no one could stop it—not even the granite boulders that divided the stream. She used to tell Sam her wildest dreams, and he would confess his deepest secrets. They were so open with each other, so trusting. She had thought she would remain in that dream-state of bliss all the rest of her life. She hadn't understood that those golden days were rare, never to be lived again.

The hours passed so quickly that she felt startled when she heard someone drive up. Getting out of bed, she saw Cody getting out of the Jeep Sam had lent him. It was a cranky old thing, one that would have caused Cody acute embarrassment to be seen driving in Seattle. But here it was different. Her son was different, she thought, observing his assurance as he hefted his backpack over one shoulder and headed for the barn complex.

She put on a jacket and went outside, finding him with the farrier and a bright sorrel horse in the crossties. The hot smell of the blowtorch pervaded the air.

"Howdy, ma'am." The farrier spoke past the wad of snoose that bulged in his lower lip.

"Hey, Mom." Cody sat with a box of shoeing nails in his lap.

She couldn't help smiling. "I guess this is something you don't see every day."

The farrier aimed a stream of tobacco juice into the waste trough. "Hand me one of those sixes," he said, all business.

Michelle was surprised that Cody could distinguish a six-nail from a five or an eight. When the horse shied, she was even more surprised to see her son help out while the farrier worked.

"Let's see what's going on in the arena," Michelle suggested when the shoeing was finished.

They stood at the rail, watching some of the hands work with the broncs. The horses wore flank straps to irritate them so they'd kick up their back legs, the higher the better. Raising rodeo stock was serious business. A good bronc or bull could become famous in its own right, and many Blue Rock animals had, but it required constant care and training.

"Until we came here, I never even knew they trained bucking broncs," Cody said, lapping his elbows over the top rail. "I just thought they were wild horses."

"Some cowboys have been known to ride their broncs home after a show. They just take off the flank strap and the horse turns into a kitten."

They watched for a while, and Michelle took in the clear bright air, the sound of hoofbeats and equine snorts, the sharp profile of white mountains against blue sky. The ranch hands and horses worked together with a rhythm that seemed ancient, timeless. And in some way, crucial.

"You were a bit late getting home from school," she said to Cody. "Did you stay after?"

"I gave some kids a ride."

"I'm glad you've been making friends." She took a long, slow breath and stared straight ahead at the jagged line of mountains. She didn't want her expression to sway her son's response in any way. "Hey, Cody?"

"Yeah?"

"Uh, Brad and I aren't going to be seeing each other anymore."

From the corner of her eye, she saw him stiffen. "Yeah?" he said again, this time with a different inflection.

"He's a good guy, but we weren't really going anywhere." She hesitated. Cody didn't seem to have any comment. Michelle asked, "Do you ever wonder what it would be like if we lived here instead of Seattle?"

"Hell, no, Mom," he said, almost panicking as he jumped down from the fence and backed away. He touched the healing wound on his head where the stitches had been. "There's *nothing* here. Nothing! We live in Seattle. It's where we belong." He paced up and down in the snow. "No one moves in the middle of high school. It sucks here." Eventually he slowed down, then stopped, leaning against a fence post. "You're not really thinking about moving here, are you?"

"I've been thinking about a lot of things, Cody."

He picked at the gauze bandage on his hand.

"I wish you'd tell me how it really went last week, with you and Sam," she said, frustrated.

He stuck the bandaged hand in his pocket. "It didn't *go* any particular way. He's just some guy to me. We got thrown together because of you, that's all."

Could it be? No chemistry, no magic, just circumstance between them?

"It's too early to tell."

"There's no point. We're going back soon. Right, Mom? Right?"

She didn't answer him.

Tuesday

S ome days, it was the emptiness that hit Sam hardest. It didn't happen often; long ago he had taught
himself to survive without support from another
person. Yet every once in a while, it caught him, that
emptiness. Especially after having Cody around the week
before.

To make things worse, today had been one of those
days in doctoring that made him wonder why he thought
he could help anyone. First there was the forty-year smoker
who had decided to hold Sam personally responsible for
his inoperable lung cancer. Followed by a harried mother
whose HMO benefits had just been cut—she could no
longer bring her asthmatic son in for therapy. She had to
lie awake at night, crying helplessly while he wheezed for
breath. Then there was a guy with a broken hand—claimed
he'd done it on a hay baler, but when, shortly afterward,

Deputy O'Shea showed up, Sam knew the cowboy had done it on some other guy's face. He had seen Mrs. Duckworth for imaginary aches and pains, turned away a drifter who came looking for a prescription for narcotics, and listened as a teenage girl wrestled over whether or not to terminate her six-week pregnancy. Given the recent changes in Sam's life, her dilemma took on a painful, personal edge.

As he drove home, he felt tension building in his neck and shoulders, and he knew it was one of those days when the empty house would echo with the void that existed, usually hidden, in his life. He used to visit Candy on the rez for some uncomplicated sex, but that wasn't what he needed. He had to quit fooling himself. What would it be like, he wondered, to walk into a house that was warm and glowing with evening lights? That smelled of dinner and the presence of another human being?

What would it be like to talk about his day, really talk, not just complain or vent his frustration but to explain what went on in his heart, in his soul, when he had to look a good man in the eye and tell him he had cancer or when he lost a patient to the absurd vagaries of the health-insurance system?

He had attempted, long ago, to create that sort of life. It hadn't worked. He and Alice had both tried, but their marriage had felt wrong, artificial. The end-of-work conversations were strained. The affection felt both false and forced. He was always pulling back when he should forge ahead.

The thing about it was, Sam knew how to take care of a needy person. He'd done it all his life, and never knew any other way. But he didn't know how to love a woman who didn't *need* him. A woman who could stand strong without support. Life had taught him that relation-ships were hard work, not a quest for joy and completion.

Ordinarily there was nothing Sam couldn't get over by sitting down and having a beer with Edward, tossing a rope at a dummy steer, or taking one of the horses on a long, solitary ride up to the hot springs. But now that Michelle was back, he wanted more.

More than talk.

He wanted a connection, and he wanted it with Michelle. God knew, he'd seen enough other women over the years to understand that it only worked with a certain person.

Christ, she must think he was a maniac, coming on to her while she still had a healing incision. He wondered if she was pissed about that.

He swore between his teeth, and when he reached the turnoff for Lonepine he drove right on by. Kept going until he got to Blue Rock Ranch, its imposing gates and the dark boulders at the entrance as ostentatious as a castle drawbridge.

A glare of lights burning in the window of the stu-dio beckoned him. He didn't pause to think, just parked the truck and walked to the door. Through the sidelight he could see her on the sofa, and he paused, waiting for the nervous energy churning through him to calm down.

She was in another world; he could tell by the look on her face. He knew that look. It was the expression she had worn as a girl, totally absorbed by the images on the big canvas in front of her. Michelle was a beautiful woman, there was no doubt about that. But Michelle in the act of creation was beyond beautiful. As she painted, there was an incandescent quality about her that made him believe in her with all that he was.

He knocked at the door, but didn't wait for her to answer it. "It's me," he called, letting himself in. "Don't get up."

"Sam." She sounded pleased. But cautious.

"Where's Cody?"

"He's over at the main house, doing homework. He needed to do an assignment on a computer, so he's working in my dad's study."

"How's Gavin doing?"

She squirted something on her hands and scrubbed them with a rag. "He's amazing. Stronger and healthier every day. He complains about the medications he has to take, all the side effects, but he's faithful about it. We had a checkup today, and my staples are gone." Drying her hands, she pulled her knees up to her chest. "I'm so glad it's over." She caught his expression. "The doctor in you probably feels compelled to point out that we're not out of the woods yet. The transplant team warned us about rejection episodes, but I've already put my father on notice. He wouldn't dare reject my kidney."

She smiled and spoke lightly, though he could tell she worried. Rejection episodes were always devastating. Between Michelle and her father, more than the kidney was at risk.

"These days, the episodes are treatable," he said. "I recommend you quit worrying about something that hasn't happened and might not."

"Okay. Thanks, Sam."

"Michelle, about the other night—I was damned pushy."

Her face darkened with a blush. "Was that an apology?"

"Well, I'm not sorry I kissed you like that."

She ducked her head and fell silent.

"Can I see what you're working on?" He hung his coat on a hook behind the door.

"Um, sure." She angled the easel toward him. "I'm in advertising, remember? I'm used to people looking over my shoulder. Breathing down my neck, even."

He walked over to the easel. It was the abstract painting she had been working on before. The big, violently emotional images hit him on a visceral level. Maybe he was reading a lot into it, yet he thought he could see the rage and the melancholy, but more than that, the sense of hope radiating through a distorted, two-sided structure near the center. It was a strange and moving work, startling and possibly disturbing.

"Michelle, this is no advertising art."

"I thought I'd work on some things for the firm, but I keep wanting to paint." She shrugged apologetically.

Her attitude bothered him. "Don't apologize for doing work like this."

"I'm not apologizing. I'm just—"

"Don't explain this or rationalize it, either. Not to me."

She glared at him. "I wasn't."

"And don't get defensive on me. It's a bad start, especially when you consider what I came to say."

She eyed him warily. "And what's that?"

He took a deep, steadying breath. Held her gaze with his. "For seventeen years you were dead to me," he said. "I had to live my life as if you'd never existed. Then, out of the blue, you come back here."

Her hands twisted in the hem of her painting smock. "I didn't come to torture you."

"True. But your coming here made something happen. Something new and good."

"Sam, that's all in the past."

"Look, if it was just a youthful fling, we would have

forgotten, would have moved on. I know, because in seventeen years, I never forgot you, and believe me, it's not for lack of trying. It's because I never stopped loving you, Michelle."

She tore her gaze from his, shaking her head. "How do I know I didn't just catch you between 'tryings'? How do I know your sudden interest in me isn't because of Cody?"

"He's a part of this, too. And you know better than I do that he's not an easy kid. But he makes me want to try like hell to work this out."

She went to the long worktable by the easel and started cleaning up, her hands moving nervously as she put the caps back on tubes and swirled paintbrushes in jars of cleaner.

"What is it you want from me?" she asked.

"For starters, I want you to sit back down. You're supposed to be resting."

"I'm sick of resting." She worked faster, finishing her cleanup with an air of defiance. That was her way. Finish one thing before starting another. Finish cleaning up the paints before you give your attention to a man baring his soul.

He waited for her to finish. When she finally did, he said, "I've been thinking about you a lot, Michelle. You don't seem happy, and your happiness matters to me."

She wadded up her smock between her hands. "Don't pretend this is about me and my happiness, Sam. It's about you—"

"Let me finish, damn it." He knew he was stepping out on thin ice, but he'd already decided to take the risk. "You asked what I want from you. Why didn't you ask what I want to *give* you?"

"Why should I think you have anything to give me?"

"You've trained yourself not to expect anything from anyone. You're the giver, Michelle, not the taker. You give Cody every last thing he needs and expect nothing in return."

"It's called parenting."

He ignored that. "You give your friend Natalie a roof over her head when she needs it, a shoulder to cry on. You give your father complete forgiveness for anything in the past, and just in case the world needs a symbol of your daughterly devotion, you give him a damned kidney."

"I think you'd better go. Before we both say things we regret."

He shook his head. This wasn't coming out right at all. "I'll regret the things we *haven't* said, Michelle."

"What hasn't been said?" She stood there, beautiful, challenging, vulnerable.

And he thought back over his life, and the years that had gone by, the path he had taken, and where everything had brought him. In all the places he'd been and people he'd met, he had learned and moved on. But there was one person in his past from whom there was no moving on. Someone he was destined to carry around in his heart for the rest of his days. The truth of it stood out like a scar on pale flesh.

"I love you." The words sounded so inadequate for the size of what he was feeling. "I never stopped."

She sat down and hugged her knees up to her chest as if she'd felt a sudden chill.

His gut churned, and he realized he was scared, scared in a way he hadn't been in a long time. He'd been doing fine, his life had been set, and suddenly she had him walking off the edge of a cliff. "I mean it, Michelle. It's not hard to love you. It's one of the only things that came easy when I was young. And it's still easy."

She looked terrified. "But it can't mean anything. It can't change anything."

He put out his hand, cradled her cheek in his palm. "It already has."

"No, not in the way you're saying. That night at the theater—"

"What, you're saying that didn't change anything? The hot springs didn't mean anything?" He took his hand away. "Does that mean you're in the habit of cheating on your boyfriend?"

"I believe that's my cue to smack you across the face."

He raked his hand through his hair. "It was a shitty thing to say. But you've got to do better than tell me 'it can't work' or 'it hasn't changed anything.' Because we both know it can. And it has."

She sat silent, pale and tight-lipped with anger. And fear, too. He saw that in her eyes, and he hated being the reason for it.

"Just what do you expect from me?" she asked at length.

"I want you to be completely honest. Do you have the life you want back in Seattle? Or is it just something you settled for?"

"I worked damned hard to get my act together in Seattle—"

"That's not what I asked." He gestured at the canvas. "Do you do that in Seattle?"

She waved a hand dismissively. "When I'm home, I *work*. This time I'm spending here, Sam, it's not real. I'm not on a sabbatical from work. I'm on a sabbatical from my life. But that's the thing about sabbaticals. They're temporary. And you still haven't been straight with me. What do you expect? You want me to ditch everything

I've built for fifteen years and move out here? Be your 'woman'?"

"Now you're talking."

"How about the other way around? How about you drop everything here and move to the city?"

"Is that what I should do, then? Sell my place, set up practice in Bellevue or some nice suburb?"

"You'd do that?" Her voice was small, disbelieving.

"Haven't you been listening? This kind of love doesn't just happen every day. Believe me, I know that. Took me a while to figure it out, but now I know. I loved you when we were young, and I lost you. After all these years, we've found each other. I'm not about to lose you again without a fight."

"This is not a fight." Panic flashed in her eyes. "You haven't thought this through. Say Cody and I decided to live out here. I'd turn into some beatnik studio artist selling my paintings at county fairs. Cody would never forgive me for ripping him away from his school and his friends in the middle of high school. The difference is, he'd have two of us to blame for his misery. Two of us to torture."

"I'm not about to let the kid torture either of us, Michelle. Or dictate my life for me."

"Oh, Sam. It's what kids *do*. It's what they're about. Until you're a parent, day in and day out, facing every crisis and triumph and dealing with him moment by moment, you won't get it."

"Then give me a chance. Give me a chance to 'get it.'"

"What if you decide it's not for you? Then you just move on? Send us back to Seattle?"

"You aren't listening. I'm not saying let's give this a try. I'm saying let's do it. Let's be a family, Michelle."

She shut her eyes. "Don't you think we should give this a little more time?"

"Time's not going to change my mind."

"*I* need the time. It's late, Sam. You'd better go."

He stood, forcing himself to walk away from her. "See you, Michelle." He left before she could answer, and stepped out into the cold, clear night. "By the way," he said, turning to see her framed in the warm light of the doorway, "what I said earlier about us being a family— that was a marriage proposal."

Wednesday

Chapter **45**

A *marriage proposal.* Michelle kept her eyes straight ahead, watching the vanishing point of the trail framed between low bramble and bunchgrass trying to push up through the snow. She had gone AWOL. Her surgeon wouldn't approve of her taking a walk so soon, but she couldn't help herself, and she'd picked a day when spring felt like a certainty instead of an empty promise. Physically, she felt fine. Emotionally, she was roadkill.

A marriage proposal. With those three words, Sam had taken her world, her life, and turned it upside down, and then he'd gone home, leaving her stricken by doubts . . . and aching with hope.

After a restless night, she needed to get out into the wild spaces of Montana, to watch spring arrive on a sudden gust of warm chinook wind. Moving slowly and gingerly, she walked a short way to a ridge top. A timberline of towering Douglas firs skirted the mountains. Layer upon layer of snowy peaks stretched out against the endless bowl of the sky. An eagle circled, then dived, and she watched the silent fury of its descent. The mystery and magnificence of the place gripped her. She felt infinitely small and insignificant, yet at the same time a sense of vastness and possibility expanded her soul.

The silence gave way to the sound of a stream. Rounding a bend, she came to a snowbound creek. Awakened by the chinook, the sun beat strongly on the south face of the mountain, and chunks of melting snow and ice littered the trail. Even as she watched, the thaw escalated. The irrepressible power of the flowing water and the relentless glare of the midday sun worked at the stingy trickle. She stooped to drink the icy, numbing water from her cupped hands. The constant, steady swish of the current echoed the flow of blood in her veins.

In the corner of her eye something glittered and instinctively she turned to look. As a trio of hawks spiraled against the blue sky, a ledge of snow gave way above the stream. The avalanche boiled down a natural couloir that curved away from the trail. In its wake, the stream was unleashed. A whitewater cataract sprang from the heart of the mountain, shooting out and down over the rocks, making the sound of someone exhaling after holding a long breath. A rainbow, thrown up by the sun-shot water, dazzled her eyes.

Inside her, something rose up like the rise of the hawks, kettling and then moving off in a different direction.

It was the artist—Michelle recognized her exuberance and her darkness. For years she had kept this creature imprisoned, icebound, but she was free now. She was home.

All her life, Michelle had tended to hide from things

that scared her. Losing her mother and being estranged from her father taught her to avoid facing the rocks and relics of emotional entanglements. But now she had changed; the hurt was still there but not the fear. She let all the feelings in like the cataract tumbling over the rocks, and the exultant pain cleansed her, reminded her that she was alive. Awakened her to old dreams that had never really died. Like the icebound stream, she had been silent, but the current never stopped coursing through her.

Sam's words had hung over her head all night long, and now they nagged at her, unanswered, impossible to ignore. She had been haunted by their last conversation. *A marriage proposal.* He'd left her stunned, speechless, her tongue numb with the inability to reply to him.

No one had ever proposed to her before. She had tried to savor the novelty, but instead it scared her. Brad had never proposed, even though they had been together, neighbors and lovers, for three years. They had both been extremely adept at avoiding that level of intimacy.

But Sam didn't know the rules. He didn't know how she operated. He didn't know she tended to hide from things that scared her, surrendering her dreams in order to keep herself safe.

As marriage proposals went, his was a doozy. It had done everything it was supposed to do. Gave her chills, made her blush, kept her awake at night, stopped her from thinking about anything but him.

His schedule gave her the gift of this new spring day all to herself, to gather her thoughts and steady her nerves. He was working at the clinic and then at the Flathead reservation, so she wouldn't be seeing him until tomorrow night at the earliest. Maybe by then she would know what to say.

Perhaps the reason she hadn't given Sam an immedi-

448 / Susan Wiggs

ate answer to his proposal was that on some level she didn't really trust that he'd meant to ask her. It could be a way of saying he wanted to spend more time with Cody.

As for herself, she had to figure out the secrets of her own heart. Watching the spring thaw, she thought she was beginning to hear what her heart was telling her. Sam McPhee made her feel as starry-eyed as a girl again. Yet in the end she had to acknowledge that she was a big girl now. The grown-up part of her knew the truth—that asking was the easy part.

It was what came after that was so hard.

That was why she was still resisting him. She could look beyond the dizzying whirl of passion and see that there was work to be done—and it wasn't the sort of work she and Sam had proven themselves to be good at. After the passion, there was struggle, sometimes disappointment, the daily grind of living—could they survive that, year after year?

She tipped her face up to the dazzling brightness of the sun. In that moment she realized that she knew the answer. She'd always known.

Chapter 46

*T*ammi Lee Gilmer's car reeked of cigarettes, but Cody didn't mind, because she was letting him drive it. He'd pretty much slacked off smoking because cigarettes were too hard to get in this one-horse burg. The clerks at Ray's Quik Chek knew all the kids by name—and by age. They were anal about not selling to minors.

Cody probably could have sneaked a pack or two from Tammi Lee, but he would have felt too shitty, stealing from her. She was pretty cool, and he didn't mind hanging out with her now and then. If anyone would have told him he'd actually *like* having a recovering alcoholic rockabilly grandmother, he would have snorted in disbelief. But the fact was, he and Tammi Lee got along more like friends than relatives, and that was fine with him.

He'd had supper with her tonight because the ranch

Jeep was in the shop and wouldn't be ready until McEvoy's Garage closed at eight. It was a gas, driving around here. Cody didn't have to worry about traffic and winos and one-way streets like in Seattle.

Tammi Lee had made fried chicken for dinner, with chocolate mud pie for dessert. After dinner, Cody had to go to the library to get a book on Montana state history for some bogus assignment, and his grandmother had offered her car. She also asked him to return a rented videotape she'd left at the shop. She hated being late. It wasn't just the fines, she'd explained, but the whole idea of being forgetful.

It was kind of spooky, thinking about her lonely existence, and how she stayed up late watching movies and reading paperback novels to keep from wanting to drink again. She'd told him that some days, it wouldn't take much to set her off, make her take another drink.

"While I'm out, I'll get the tape from the shop and return it for you," Cody had offered.

She hadn't hesitated a single second. "Here's the key to my car, and this one's to the shop. I left the tape in the storeroom in the back. Little cubby with my name on it."

Cody was getting too used to this small town. He realized, as he drove along Main Street past the Indian statue in the square, that it was becoming as familiar to him as the palm of his hand. He passed the darkened Lynwood Theater, thinking that a movie house would be a huge improvement around here.

In the library, he found the book he needed and applied for a card, the whole transaction only taking a few minutes. Under "Home Address" he had written Blue Rock Ranch, wincing as he did so. When his mom had asked him what he thought of moving here permanently, he'd instantly hated the idea. If she was just checking, she had her answer.

In the parking lot, he spotted some kids coming out of the library, backpacks on their shoulders, shoving each other as they skidded along the icy sidewalk. One student walked alone, slim and straight. Cody leaned across the seat and cranked down the window.

"Hey, Molly," he said.

She tensed, reminding him of Sam's filly. He didn't blame her. They hadn't spoken since the ride incident because he couldn't figure out a way to apologize. He'd never been big on explaining his behavior or apologizing.

She came to the car, tucking a silky black lock of hair behind her ear as she bent to peer into the passenger-side window. "What's up, Cody?" She didn't look at him the way she had when they'd first met—the sideways, kind of shy-but-interested way he liked. She was neutral now. Guarded.

"I'm running an errand for my grandmother," he said. A ride, yeah, that would do it. He'd offer her a ride home. That would give them a chance to talk. "Hey, you want a lift—"

"Yo, Cody!" a familiar voice called. "Where'd you get the wheels?" Without waiting for an answer, Billy Ho and his sidekick, Ethan Lindvig, jumped in, one in front, one in back. "My El Camino's wasted again. Couldn't get it to start." Billy sent an "aw-shucks" grin to Molly. "You want to come along, cowgirl?"

She shook her head and stepped away from the car. Her face went all hard, her eyes flat and glossy. "See you, Cody," she said, her tone dismissive.

He couldn't very well call her back with Billy and Ethan breathing down his neck. "Where to?" he asked them.

"My house," Ethan said.

"I've got to make a quick stop." Cody eased away from the curb. "Then I'll give you a lift." He glanced in the rearview mirror. Molly stood on the sidewalk, slender and straight as a young tree. She watched the car for a moment, then turned and walked away.

Damn.

He didn't listen to Billy and Ethan yakking away as he drove a few blocks and stopped at the quilt shop. "Be right back. I need to grab something for my grandmother," he said.

He used the key to let himself in. The shop smelled of dry goods and old ladies. A dim light over the counter cast its glow on an old-fashioned brass cash register.

"Cool," Billy said. "I've never been in here before. What *is* all this shit?" He took a bolt of fabric and draped the loose end around him, strutting in the aisle and singing the wedding march off-key.

"Hey, you shouldn't be in here," Cody called. "I just need to get something from the back room."

"Chill out," Ethan said, honking the breast of a mannequin. "We're having a little fun."

Losers, Cody thought as he went to the back room. He didn't know why he put up with them. It wasn't like they liked *him,* they liked who he was—Gavin Slade's grandson, the one with the big allowance and the reliable wheels. He couldn't believe he'd left Molly Lightning freezing on the sidewalk for these two clowns. He'd make it up to her, he decided. He'd ask her out, maybe invite her over to Sam's to ride some of his horses. She'd like that.

He could hear the guys goofing around in the shop while he retrieved the rented video from a cubby with Tammi Lee's name cross-stitched over it. Then, closing the storeroom door behind him, he said, "Okay, let's go. Did you put back whatever it is you were messing around with?"

Ethan and Billy exchanged a glance. "We didn't mess with anything, man," Billy said.

Cody didn't like the furtive glee on their faces, but he was in a hurry. He wanted to get them out of the shop before they wrecked anything.

Thursday

Chapter 47

The way the morning light cut down through the skylight of the big kitchen of Blue Rock reminded Michelle of those old murals in church, the ones she used to stare at when she was little. They went to All Saints on Camden Drive in Beverly Hills, her mother wearing white gloves and Michelle in lace-edged socks, gleaming Mary Janes, and an outfit bought on her father's I. Magnin account. She used to sit beside her mother, studying the little girls seated securely between two parents, swinging their legs and bumping their toes against the soft foam-covered kneelers. Mom on one side, Dad on the other, a pair of bookends to prop her up no matter which way she leaned. Michelle used to lift her eyes to the back wall where a pair of gigantic pre-Raphaelite angels soared, the sun pouring over them like

458 / Susan Wiggs

melted butter, and when mass was over, she would go home and draw what she had seen.

Fixing herself a bowl of raisin bran, Michelle realized she hadn't thought about those moments in church for a very long time. Something about the angle of light and the quiet of the house brought back the memory.

And of course, it was easier to think about the past than the future.

She owed Sam an answer, but they hadn't had any time alone together. Yesterday he'd worked out of town, and last night he was on call. He had office hours today, and she had to go to Missoula with her father for another checkup. She supposed they could discuss it on the phone, but this was the sort of thing to talk about face-to-face.

Her confidence faltered. It was fun playing two-crazy-kids-in-love, but when real life intruded, it intruded with a vengeance. Already, outside events were conspiring to keep them apart.

Her father came into the kitchen just as the alarms on both of his wristwatches beeped. Medicine time.

"Hey, Daddy." She got up from the stool at the counter and poured him a glass of water.

"How's my girl?" He grinned, and the flush of health on his face was so welcome it made her want to weep.

But she felt compelled to ask, "You feeling okay?"

"Fine."

"Really? I'm not making idle chitchat here."

"Okay, the side effects of the medicine can get annoying." He held out his hand, and for a second she noticed a tiny, brief tremor. "Cyclosporin does that. Prednisone and immunosuppressants are their own kind of fun." He grinned again. "Enough whining. All I have to do is consider the alternative, and it shuts me right up."

She handed him the water and waited while he took

out a massive plastic pill box with dividers for each day. He swallowed his meds, the radical cocktail of stabilizers and antirejection pills that were so critical after the transplant. So far so good. The transplant team had declared that their speed of recovery was one for the record books.

Gavin set a stack of mail on the breakfast bar and slowly picked up a thick envelope. Michelle saw his hesitation and the slight shaking of his hand as he broke the seal and took out a packet of official-looking papers. He studied them for a minute, then shut his eyes and kissed the certificate with beatific reverence. "My pilot's license has been renewed," he said. "I'm back in the game, honey."

"Daddy, no kidding?"

"No kidding." His legendary blue eyes shone. He poured himself a bowl of raisin bran and then methodically proceeded to pick out all the raisins. Michelle watched for a second, hiding a grin. She and her father were alike in ways that startled her. An occasional gesture, a look, a quirk of taste. She didn't eat the raisins in raisin bran, either.

Her father seemed unaware of his thoughts. He ate some cereal, then drummed his hand on the stack of papers. "This is the second-best thing that's happened since I got sick."

"What's the first best?" She held her breath.

"Finding you and Cody again, honey. Didn't you know that?"

She couldn't speak for a moment. This, she thought as her heart soared. This was the essence of life. A moment of joy and triumph so sweet that her entire being filled up with happiness. How long had it been since she'd allowed herself to feel this much, this deeply? "Ah, Daddy," she said, and something in her inflection made him look up. "I did know."

Simple little words. An ordinary conversation. But she had waited a lifetime to share a moment like this with her father. They finished their breakfast; then he helped himself to coffee, shutting his eyes and smiling as if he had just seen God. "I've missed drinking coffee."

They sat in companionable silence for a while, sipping their morning coffee and watching the play of sunlight over the polished-granite countertops and gleaming copper cookware hanging from the range hood.

"You going to work on your painting today?" her father asked.

"Yep. I have no idea what I'm doing over there, but I'm loving it."

"That painting you've been doing. It makes me damned proud of you."

His words filled her with warmth. Just for a second, she wanted to ask him where that belief in her came from, why he had never expressed it until she gave him a kidney. But the second passed, and she knew there was no answer, and no point trying to get one.

"Thanks." She indicated his clipboard, covered with pink phone message slips. "You've been busy."

"As a matter of fact, I have."

"What is all that?"

He paged through the notes. "Here's one from Carolyn." He winked, though buried in his cynicism was an almost-hidden hurt. "She's ready to kiss and make up now that I don't have a dialysis bag hanging out of me."

"So are *you* ready?"

"I told her to piss off." He crumpled the note. "Pun intended. Here's one from a contractor in Polson. I'm going to reopen the Lynwood on Memorial Day."

"Really?" She felt a rush of excitement. The old theater was filled with memories for her, memories of that long-ago summer, but even more important, memories of a snowy night not so very long ago. "I'm glad. This town's more than ready."

He pushed a fax across the counter to her. "This is what we really need to talk about."

It took her a minute to assimilate what he was showing her. "Daddy?"

"It was on the fax machine when I got up this morning. It's from the same contractor who's going to be renovating the Lynwood."

Michelle swallowed, but she couldn't banish the dryness from her mouth. "Daddy," she whispered, "what the hell's going on?"

He beamed at her. "Keep reading."

It was a bid for restoring the vacant retail space in the shop next door to the old theater. At Gavin's request, the space would be converted into an art gallery. Picturing the vintage storefront, the old plank floors, the hammered tin ceilings, Michelle felt a giddy light-headedness. A buoyant sense of wonder.

"A gallery," she said.

"Might bring some culture to Crystal City." He touched her hand. "You've never had a showing, Michelle, and God knows, you deserve one. That is, if you think this is something you want."

It was something she hadn't even dared to want—until now. Maybe that was what the whole ordeal of Gavin's illness had been about. It was a kick in the pants. A way to jolt her out of the comfortable monotony her life had become. She got up slowly, walked around the counter, and put her arms around him. "Dad—"

The phone rang, and he grabbed it. "This might be the contractor." But then he handed her the receiver. "It's Sam."

"Sam!"

"Did I catch you at a bad time?"

"Um, no."

"I've missed you." His voice was low and sexy.

A shiver ran through her. She could feel her whole body start to smile. "Same here." She stared at the fax on the counter. She thought about what he had said the last time they were together, and all the things they had to talk about. What would it mean if she decided to marry Sam? So many questions. They had so much to discuss. It was too much, too big to explain to him right here, right now. "Have dinner with me tonight, Sam," she managed to say. "I have something to tell you."

A pause. Then she could hear the grin in his voice as he said, "Honey, wild horses couldn't stop me from seeing you tonight."

Chapter 48

*I*t's okay to grab the apple," Molly said.

Cody looked down at her from the dizzying height of the horse's back. This was a terrible idea. It was the worst idea he'd ever had, inviting Molly over to ride horses at Sam's after school.

"What apple?" he asked, mortified when his voice broke on the last syllable.

She didn't seem to notice. "The saddle horn," she explained. "If you feel a little unsteady, you can always grab hold of the saddle horn, pull a little leather."

"Oh." He clutched it, two-handed, white-knuckled. "I thought that was against the rules."

"Are you competing?"

He liked the laughter in her eyes. It almost made him forget he sat atop fifteen hundred pounds of bone and muscle and hoof, a sorrel gelding called Ace. "No," he said.

"Just try to relax, okay? If you're tense, he can feel it." It was pretty great, the way she instructed him. She had lots of patience and didn't make him feel inferior just because he'd hardly ever ridden a horse. She started him out really slow, and before long he actually began liking the rocking motion of the horse, going round and round the fenced arena, listening to the creak of the saddle and the heartbeat of hooves. Thanks to Molly, he was feeling pretty good, all things considered.

This afternoon during study hall, he'd gone right up to her, looked her in the eye, and apologized for being a jerk. Instead of making him squirm like a bug on a pin, she had forgiven him with more generosity than he deserved. He would always remember her words: "I like you, Cody, no matter what." No one had ever said such a thing to him. When he'd said he'd like to try his luck riding a horse, her smile had lit up the day.

After about an hour, Ace had worked up a sweat, so Cody got off and put him up, carefully hanging the saddle and pad and all the gear. They went into the barn office, where he washed his hands at the sink and got some soft drinks from the fridge. They sat together on an old couch with lumps in the seat, and it felt perfectly natural to put his arm around her. She made it clear that she liked it, setting her head easily on his shoulder. For a while, they just listened to the whistle of the wind through the barn, the flutter of swallows high in the eaves, and the occasional low-throated sound of a horse stomping and muttering. They had the whole place to themselves. Sam was at work, and Edward was doing errands in the city.

He turned on the radio and couldn't find anything but country western. But he didn't mind.

Molly didn't say a word, just took his can and set it on the floor next to him. When she turned her face up, he kissed her, softly at first, then longer and harder. She tasted like Dr Pepper, chilly and sweet, and everything about her was perfect. She pressed close, clearly liking the kiss as much as he did, and when he eased back on the sofa so he was half-lying down, she came with him. He put his tongue in her mouth. His hand strayed. He really, *really* wanted to touch her.

She lifted her mouth from his just a little. "It's okay," she whispered, and undid the top two buttons of her denim shirt. "I've been thinking about this a lot, Cody. I don't mind."

She spoke as if she'd read his thoughts, and her honest desire touched off a forest fire inside him. Yet despite her words and the excitement shining in her eyes, he realized that she probably hadn't done much fooling around at all. But she wanted it, he could tell, and she took his breath away. Her kisses were open and searching and inviting, her hands like a pair of inquisitive kittens crawling over him. Quickly enough, things got away from them—shirts undone, and then the top button of his jeans, and she held him and made a nervous, excited sound in her throat. It struck him then that she was not going to tell him to stop. What happened next was totally up to him. He pulled back and looked down into her face. "Girl, you're driving me crazy."

Her eyes shone. "Really? I wasn't sure you wanted me."

"Hell, yes, I wanted you."

"I'm glad, Cody. I'm real glad about that." She lifted herself toward him, and he couldn't help himself. He kissed her again, opening his mouth over those soda-sweet lips.

She was soft and willing, her touch honest and warm. For the first time since he'd started dating girls, he'd found one who made him feel something tender and new, something that had more to do with feelings than with sex. Amazing.

And so, at the crucial moment, Cody astonished himself. "You're a nice girl, Molly," he said. "But I think we'd better stop."

"I don't want to stop," she said quietly, pressing her open hand to his chest.

"I don't either," he admitted. "I like you, and maybe one day it'll be right for us. Just not now. We should wait. Okay?" Man. It *hurt*. He couldn't believe he managed to get the words out.

"I'm not a baby. I know what I want."

"Then waiting a while won't change that." He ground the words out through gritted teeth. Faintly he heard a car or truck, but it sounded very far away, and he had more immediate concerns. He had Molly right where every guy dreamed of getting a girl—ready and willing—and he was blowing his chance. How stupid was that? Still, it was the right thing to do, and by some miracle, Cody still knew what the right thing was.

As he drove home from work, Sam caught himself pushing hard on the accelerator. Unlike most days, he was eager to get home, to get cleaned up, and go see Michelle. Tonight it would begin. The love that had started more than seventeen years before kept growing stronger every day. It was a scary thing, to love someone like that. But scarier still to think of life without her.

He drummed his fingers on the steering wheel and tried to shrug the day off his aching shoulders and back. He had set a bone this morning—a sheep rancher's tibia. He'd seen four flu patients, an infant in respiratory distress, treated a dog bite, and had gone over a special diet with Earl Meecham, who had an ulcer. The last appointment was with a mentally handicapped ranch hand. Sam had to show him how to use a rubber and he wasn't sure the lesson would stick. The kid was slow, but his body was that of a man. Bad combination. Sam still had some of the rubbers in his back pocket.

The day just wouldn't go away until he filled his mind with Michelle. That was the magic of her. Before she'd come back to him, his bad days and hard thoughts had no place to go. He tried to picture her in this house, in his bed, in his life. And the worrisome thing was, the picture wouldn't form. She was so damned sophisticated. Could she really be happy here, a ranch wife, of all things?

It was almost as ludicrous as picturing himself living in some suburban sprawl outside of Seattle. Then there was Cody, who needed things Sam didn't know how to give.

Details, he told himself, loosening his tie. That's all they were. Details. They'd work things out. He saw a shadow in the sky over the highway and looked up. He thought it might be Gavin Slade's little P-51 Mustang, banking through the breaks and draws of the valley over the country air park. Sam grinned in spite of his complicated feelings about Michelle's father. So Gavin was flying again. He was truly on the mend now.

When Sam pulled up at Lonepine, he noticed the Jeep parked outside the barn, and country music wailing from within. Curious, he went over to the barn and saw a horse from the Lightning place tethered to a loop. Good, he thought. He'd rather see Cody making friends with Ruby's daughter than those punks who had spooked the horse. Sam decided to go in and say hello, let them know he was home.

When he walked into the office, Cody and Molly Lightning were as stunned and embarrassed as he was.

They both jumped up from the sofa, brushing hastily at their rumpled clothes. Molly's hair was mussed, her face red as a beet. She clutched the front of her unbuttoned shirt.

"I, um, I was just leaving," she said in a strained voice. She was gone before Sam could think of a single thing to say.

He swung around to glare at Cody. Still no words. His earlier thoughts mocked him. He was totally unprepared for this situation.

Cody tried to brush past him. "I'd better get over to Blue Rock," he muttered.

"The hell you will," Sam burst out, planting himself in front of him.

"Hey, man—"

"Don't you hey-man me," Sam said, flexing his hand. "What the hell were you thinking, groping her like that?"

"We're both sixteen," Cody pointed out. "And you might not believe this, but I wasn't going to do anything."

"Yeah, sure," Sam said. "I *don't* believe you."

"I wasn't." Cody jutted his chin out. "But that's between me and Molly, not me and you."

"Under my roof, it's my business."

"Hey, I didn't ask to come here. I'll go back to Seattle anytime, just say the word. But if I'm stuck here, the least I can do is try to make friends."

"Looks like you were trying to make more than that. You've grown up thinking you're entitled to every goddamned thing in the world." Sam's anger wasn't rational, the way a wildfire wasn't rational. It flared and flamed with a life of its own. "Smart-ass like you ought to know better than to have unprotected sex."

"We were just fooling around," Cody snapped. "Not having sex."

"Only because I happened to show up before things got out of hand."

"You don't know that. You always want to think the worst of me."

Something inside him snapped, and he blew up with anger. "Did you even think for one second what you're risking? Bringing another unwanted baby into the world—"

Sam stopped himself. Too late, he realized what he'd just said. Too late, he recognized the source of his anger. And the deep red flush on Cody's face meant he recognized it, too. Neither of them said a word, but a silent storm howled between them.

And Sam knew in that moment that he loved his son. He knew, because it hurt so bad to hurt him.

The phone rang, shrilling into the tense quiet of the office. Holding Cody with a raised hand, Sam grabbed the receiver from the wall. "Sam McPhee." He frowned as an automated message instructed him to press 1 to accept the collect charges from the incoming call. With a shrug, he pushed the button.

"Hiya, hon. It's your mama."

He didn't move, but at the unmistakable slur in her voice, he could feel everything inside him curling up, burning down to nothing. "Mama. Where are you? What've you been drinking?"

Cody's pale face sharpened, but Sam couldn't think about the boy now. "Mama? Talk to me."

"Lessee. Made it to Kalispell. They got a honky-tonk here, the Roadkill Grill. Think they'll lemme be in the band? I used to sing real good. 'Member when we cut that album in Reno? You were in your playpen still . . ."

He could hear the lazy slide of liquor through her

voice. Jesus, five years. She'd been sober five years, and now this. "Mama, slow down. What happened?"

"That old cow LaNelle fired me from the shop."

"LaNelle Jacobs fired you? Why?" From the corner of his eye, Sam could see Cody edging toward the door. He pinned him in place with a fierce stare. The boy flattened his lips and squinted defiantly, but he didn't leave.

"They said I stole all the money from the cash register. All forty-two bucks of it. A staggering fortune. Jussst . . . staggering."

"That's absurd, Mama. LaNelle knows you wouldn't steal from her shop."

"Someone saw my car parked there last night. 'S'morning, the cash was gone. 'Course she's gotta blame me. Who else could it be, son? Who the hell else could it be?"

"Mama—"

"You never really outgrow what you are, do you son? Folks' opinions of you never really change."

"I'm coming to get you," he said. "Don't move. Get a cup of coffee and sit tight."

She wasn't listening now. He could hear someone asking her if she wanted another tequila sunrise, could hear her cackle with harsh glee. *Oh, Mama. Not again, Mama.* He slammed down the phone.

"What's going on?" Cody asked, his face strangely still. "Someone's saying she stole from the shop?"

"When I find the son of a bitch who did, I'll kill him, swear to God I will."

Cody paled. "Hey, it's not the end of world, man."

"I don't have time to deal with you now," Sam snapped. "I have to go." He grabbed his parka and his keys. "Tell your mom I can't make it tonight. Tell her—" He broke off. "Ah, hell. Tell her I'm sorry."

Chapter 49

"How was school today?" Michelle's hairbrush hit the carpet with a *thunk*. Klutz, she thought. She was a bundle of nerves.

"Okay," Cody mumbled into the refrigerator. He stood in the white glow of the interior light, scanning the contents.

Michelle picked up the brush and studied her son. He wore his black jeans and leather jacket, and she felt a frisson of unease. For some reason, it struck her that he looked exactly as he had when they'd first come to Crystal City. He wore gloves, concealing his bandaged hand. A knitted hat covered the scar on his head, so there was no evidence of the wound Sam had mended.

She walked toward him. "Is something wrong?" she asked.

He twisted away from her, ducking his head as if to

avoid getting an unwanted kiss. "Just the usual." He dropped his backpack on the floor and took out a carton of milk.

"Uh-uh," she said automatically as he put it to his lips. "Use a glass."

He eyed her over his shoulder as he got a tumbler from the cupboard. "Can I ask you something?"

"Sure, Cody."

He sloshed some of the milk on the counter. Without thinking, she grabbed a paper towel. Annoyed, he took it from her and wiped up his own spill. "I was wondering. Did you . . . want me? I mean, did you ever think of getting rid of me?"

He had never, ever asked her before. Michelle wondered how long he'd held the question inside him, unasked, festering. Tears gathered thickly in her throat, and she touched his cheek. "Oh, Cody. Not for a single second. You were so wanted. You were my life." She swallowed and hoped she wouldn't cry. He had almost never seen her cry. She remembered, with startling clarity, every sensation of being pregnant, and pain was no part of that sensation, no part at all. She had gone for natural childbirth, and she had felt his entire journey from her womb into the world, and seeing his tiny face for the first time had filled her with a fierce sense of purpose. "Having you saved me," she said. "You were the best part of my life, and you still are."

He seemed a little embarrassed by the display his question had incited. "Cool," he said, and took a deep gulp of milk. "What're you all dressed up for?"

She laughed, wanting to hug herself with glee. "Well, I've got some news."

He narrowed his eyes in distrust. When had he learned to do that? To conclude that her good news meant bad news for him? He leaned against the counter, drinking his milk, waiting.

"You know I've been painting lately." It felt good to voice the notion that had been at the back of her mind for days. Saying it aloud made her heart soar. It was impractical, impulsive, but she was determined to reclaim herself. "Like I used to, years ago. I've been thinking about making some changes. Gavin and I are looking into opening an art gallery in Crystal City." She felt almost fearful about how badly she wanted this. How much it meant to her.

His gaze flicked over her—black cashmere trousers, black angora sweater, her good pearls. "So what's with the outfit?"

"Sam's coming over for dinner." She tried to keep the tremor from her voice as she told him the *real* news. The one thing she wanted more than the next breath of air. "Sam asked me to marry him. I haven't said yes yet, but I'm going to. Tonight."

"Shit." He set down his glass and brushed past her, flopping down on the sofa.

She tasted lipstick as she bit her lip. "I was sort of hoping for a more supportive reaction from you." Don't do it, she wanted to beg him. Don't take this happiness from me. But on the heels of that thought came the thoughts any mother was conditioned to think: How can I do this to my child? How can I rip him out of the middle of his life and plunk him down amid strangers? Isn't there some compromise? Can I have what I want and keep him happy, too?

He was quiet for long, long moments. She was dying to know what was going on in that head of his. Finally, he took a deep breath, looked her square in the eye, and said, "Don't bother waiting for Sam to show up. He took off."

"What do you mean, he took off?"

"He's gone, scram, vamoose."

A chill of disbelief snaked through her. "Gone where?"

"Out of town. He said to tell you . . ." Cody hung his head.

"What? What did he say? What happened?" Disbelief hardened into a horrible dread. She had to know. She needed a reason. She was inches from shaking this kid's teeth right out of his head.

"I guess he didn't want to be my father after all."

"Oh, for Pete's sake, that's ridiculous. Sam loves me. He wants to love you, Cody—"

"Not anymore." His head hung lower. "Something, um, happened."

She pressed herself against the counter until she felt her surgical scar. What occupied the space where the kidney used to be? she wondered irrationally.

"Talk, Cody," she said, fixing her attention on him with a will. "Start at the beginning."

"Molly and I were hanging out at his place this afternoon, and he . . . he acted like I was molesting her or something. We weren't doing anything much, Mom, we weren't."

Michelle took a deep breath, trying to assimilate everything he'd just told her. "Let me get this straight. You and Molly were at Sam's."

"Yeah." He glowered at the toes of his shoes. "I was riding a horse, and it was great, and then we went into the barn office. We were like, fooling around a little bit, no big deal—"

"Fooling around." Her stomach knotted.

"No big deal," he repeated sullenly. "We're not babies. We know the score. We were fully clothed, Mom, every second. But Sam scared Molly off and started yelling at me."

Overnight, she thought. Overnight her son had changed from a little boy with grass stains on his knees to practically a grown man ... with a man's desires. "Look at it from his perspective. She's a neighbor. The daughter of a friend. Can you blame him?"

"I should've known you'd take his side."

"I'm not taking sides—"

"But you don't believe me. You didn't hear the things he said, Mom. He went into this big insane lecture about safe sex and unwanted babies." Cody folded his arms across his chest. "Then he said he ... he doesn't want me for a son."

The pain was sharp, hot. "He can't have said that."

"Call him. Just try it. He won't answer. Swear to God, he doesn't want me, and good riddance, I say. I don't want him either."

She studied his pale, worried face. And deep in the center of her, a core of ice formed, grew bigger, colder. "Why would you say a thing like that?"

"Because I mean it, Mom. Sam has the hots for you, but that doesn't mean he gives a shit about me."

Michelle went through the motions even though her horrified certainty hardened with each creeping moment. She called Edward, who had been in the city all day and had seen neither hide nor hair of Sam. She called Sam's service only to be told Dr. McPhee would return calls when he checked in for his messages. No answer at his mother's. His partner Karl was brusque, telling her to try the service or, if it was an emergency, to go to County.

Her hand was ice-cold and shaking as she hung up

476 / Susan Wiggs

the phone for the last time. A terrible sense of déjà vu broke over her. She remembered exactly how she had felt that long-ago night, sick and exhilarated with the knowledge of her pregnancy, rushing over to Sam's house only to discover that he'd left without a word.

He took off. He took off. He took off. Disappeared into the night just like before.

Friday

Chapter 50

Almost dizzy from lack of sleep, Michelle dressed in the gray quiet of the dawn. Cody's bedroom door was firmly shut, and not a sound came from within. She wondered how well she knew her son anymore. She could only guess at what was going through his head. The emotional roller coaster of finding his father so unexpectedly, then having the big quarrel with Sam, was a lot for a kid to handle. A lot for *anyone* to handle. Yet beneath the hurt and anger, she had detected something a little harder to put her finger on. Evasiveness. Shame, perhaps.

Resolving to talk to Cody about it when he got up, she put on a pair of boots and went over to the main house. She walked into the great room, stood before the fire, and thought of that first night when she and Gavin had sat together in this room. It seemed long ago that they had been so awkward with one another. She'd gone to him because, at long last, he needed her. The irony was that she had needed him just as much.

She pressed a wadded Kleenex to her cheeks. Her father came in, took one look at her, and opened his arms. It felt so right to collapse against him, and the tears spilled again. She knew her father now, and she needed him in a way she never had before. "Sam's gone, Daddy. He and Cody had a fight last night," she said. "It was bad. Cody thinks Sam doesn't want him."

"Cody's wrong. Sam wants his kid. Trust me," Gavin said, bringing her to the sofa and sitting down.

"How do you know?"

Lines deepened in his craggy face. "I did a stupid thing years ago, letting you leave. Before you came to me when your mother died, I didn't think I wanted a kid. I didn't know how to be a father. I sure as hell wasn't much good at it. When you left, I convinced myself it was for the best. But I was wrong. I wanted my daughter. I just didn't know how to bring you back. Anyway, that's how I know Sam wants his son. Whatever went on between them won't change that."

"But if Cody doesn't believe Sam wants him, then we've got problems. And something tells me they won't just blow over."

"If he's gone, there's bound to be an explanation. He's not some no-account drifter. He'll be back this time."

"True. But how can I get Sam's side of the story if he simply takes off at the first sign of trouble? He should have called me."

"Don't jump to any conclusions."

"I'm trying not to. But I just feel so . . . stood up. Maybe I'm not cut out to be with a guy like Sam. People don't really change, Daddy. He took off seventeen years ago, and he's done it again." She felt the chilly ghost of the old feelings of abandonment. In different ways and for different reasons, she had lost her mother, her father, Sam . . . and now she felt Cody slipping away from her. "Maybe," she admitted, "I don't have it in me to love them both in the way they need."

Gavin turned to her on the sofa. "You know better than that. You have the most generous heart of anyone I've ever known, Michelle. You came to me in spite of my failings. You came even though you knew it would be hard for you. Things turned out to be even harder than you imagined, and you stayed, honey."

A long silence stretched out, and the sun broke over the mountains. Michelle turned to her father. "The first time Sam took off, I never even tried to find him." She took a deep breath and finally admitted something about herself, something she wasn't proud of. "There was probably a part of me that saw him as a delinquent, no good, a guy who would never amount to anything. I was wrong back then. The failing was mine, not his. That's what I don't know, Daddy. I don't know if I'm better than that now."

"About the first time." Gavin put his hand on her arm.

His touch made her pause. She looked up into his face, a little puffy now from the meds, but still so expressive, so anguished.

"He and his mother left town because I arranged it," Gavin said quietly.

Michelle stared at him. Her fist tightened around the Kleenex. "I don't understand."

"There was money missing from the foreman's office. Maybe Sam took it, maybe he didn't. I wasn't really thinking about that. I was thinking about you, Michelle. I'd just found out you were seeing Sam, and I wasn't thrilled with the idea. I thought the boy and his mother were trouble, and I didn't want you hurt. So Deputy O'Shea and I confronted him with the missing cash. He denied taking it, of course. For good measure, O'Shea also reminded Tammi Lee of her rubber-check habit and several outstanding warrants. She was given a choice. Disappear, or do time. Sam really didn't have a choice."

"My God." She drew away from her father.

"He never told you about that, did he?" Gavin asked in a pained voice.

"He never said a word."

"I'm sorry as hell, honey. I didn't know what to do. I was afraid you'd go running off with him."

"And I did run off. Only not with him." She pulled her knees up to her chest.

"I wish I could undo what I did. But I acted out of desperation because I loved you, and I was so damned scared."

Her throat stung. "Why——" she said, and had to pause. "Why didn't you just say so? Why didn't you tell me you loved me? You never said it."

"I thought you knew." He was silent for a long time, staring down at his hands. "You're a parent yourself now. The love happens whether you talk about it or not. You've made choices for Cody—some good, and some bad. But you always acted out of love for him."

The stark truth struck hard. He was right. She didn't approve of Cody hanging out with Claudia Teller. Every once in a while, Michelle would "forget" to pass on a message that Claudia had called. Or manage to schedule Cody for a dental appointment when she knew he and Claudia had plans. Michelle was uncomfortably certain she would resort to devious means if she thought she could keep them apart.

"Sometimes a parent does the wrong thing for the right reasons," Gavin pointed out. "I'm so damned sorry, Michelle. I should have trusted your judgment."

"Are you saying I should trust Cody's?"

"Maybe. Yeah, I am. Look, I failed with you. But you have a chance to succeed with Cody."

"Right now it's Cody's judgment that he doesn't want Sam in his life."

"I suspect he'll come around. He's a kid, thinking about himself first and foremost. He doesn't want to move in the middle of high school—what kid would? But he's also your son. He wants you to be happy, Michelle. Do what's right for you. He'll come around."

"I can't do it, Daddy. I can't force the two of them together and pretend it will be fine."

"You don't know how it will be. Maybe it won't be fine, maybe not all the time. But what is? What the hell is in this life?"

Restless, she got up and opened the doors to the front porch, feeling the harsh chill of the morning air on her face and hearing the sounds of the ranch coming to life— diesel vehicles firing up, the foreman's whistle, the hydraulic hiss of a dump truck. Horses blowing and stamping, the tinny sound of the farm and ranch report on someone's radio. She needed to clear her head, had to think about what it would really be like to marry Sam—a man who had just taken off without a word of explanation.

It scared her when she considered how hurt she was by that. How vulnerable she was when it came to Sam. "I'd better go wake Cody for school," she said.

Returning to the guesthouse, she knocked lightly on Cody's door. No response. "Cody?" she said, and pushed the door open.

Reality registered slowly. The bed that hadn't been

slept in. Closet door carelessly open to empty space. The big duffel bag gone.

Terror broke over her in a dizzying wave. Gone.

Her son was gone.

It was every mother's nightmare. She tore out of the room, screaming for her father, her mind filled with visions of Cody broken, bruised, abused by someone who had picked him up hitchhiking.

Gavin met her halfway across the yard, holding out the cordless phone. "It's okay," he said.

His words barely penetrated her icy, heart-freezing terror.

Her father closed her hand firmly around the phone. "It's okay. He's in Seattle. Here, let Natalie tell you."

Standing in the blanketed yard, her hand shaking, she put the phone to her ear. Natalie was calm, uncharacteristically subdued, as she explained that Cody had taken the all-night bus from Missoula. Dear God. Her son had run away from home last night. No, he'd run away *to* home. He had run away from *her*.

"Let me talk to him," Michelle said. Tears threatened to melt the ice of terror, but she held them in, afraid that if she started to cry, she'd never stop.

"He's on his way to school. He wanted to get there early to re-enroll."

"You let him go to school without calling me?" She wanted to jump through the phone line and throttle Natalie.

"I told him he should call you. He said he would. Later." Natalie hesitated. "Michelle, he didn't explain why he showed up here alone, but I can guess. He's safe. Let him cool off, okay? If you don't give him time to realize on his own how much he loves you and misses you, he might never figure it out."

She was still trembling when she hung up. Her first impulse was to phone Garfield High School, demand that they find him, bring him to the phone. Then she looked across the white mystery of the fields of Blue Rock, and a small, surprising voice inside said No and then louder: *No*. She handed the phone to her father.

"You want me to fly you to Seattle?" he asked.

"No." The word formed of its own accord. "Natalie just said something to me that makes perfect sense. He's got to fix this on his own, Daddy. It's time he made his own decisions and figured out how to deal with the consequences."

Gavin looked at her for a long time. "When you were young, you went away, too. And like a fool I just let you go. I was too stubborn. Are you being stubborn or is this the right thing to do?"

She spread her arms. "Who knows what the right thing is? I just know that what I've been doing lately isn't working. Maybe I was too much of a perfectionist, too demanding. That's probably what made him turn into a rebel in the first place."

Now, with a lurch of her heart, she suddenly understood. It was only natural to distance himself from her expectations. And it was her job to let him find his own way.

"I was smothering him with love, getting him out of scrapes when I should have let him fall and pick himself up again." The decision hurt, but it felt right. She realized that what she really had to do was make the painful choice of letting Cody go. He might discover the answers on his own, or he might not. It was no longer up to her.

At six-thirty at night, Cody stood on the rain-slick sidewalk in front of the town-house complex in Seattle. It was weird, but he missed the dark of Montana, the inky purity of the night in the mountains. Here in Seattle it was never all the way dark, not with the yellow shore lights, the busy ferry docks, and the ribbons of reflected neon snaking along the wet streets. The high bluff framed a view of Elliott Bay, a glittering necklace of lights along the shore.

Today had definitely been one of the strangest days of his life. He had gone to school, handing a re-enrollment slip to the clerk in the office. After the initial paperwork it had been like a regular day. Same classes, same kids.

Same Claudia.

He'd found her at the usual place, a wooded area everyone called the smoke spot. Unobserved, he had stood at the fringe of the woods and looked at her, expecting a theme song to start up or something. He'd watched her throw back her head and blow out a cloud of cigarette smoke, and he'd felt . . . nothing. Not the rush of excitement that used to keep him awake at night, not the heady pride that made him walk tall through the school halls. No theme song, just the boring hiss and spatter of the incessant Seattle rain through the alder and cedar trees.

When she'd seen him, she had squealed and flung herself at him, but her questions had all been about Gavin, and what it was like to have a celebrity grandfather, and why hadn't he ever *told* her that his grandfather had played Lucas McQuaid, and had he saved any of his prescription painkillers . . .

He had tried hanging out with his old crowd after school, but nothing felt right. There was nothing different about them, but it *was* different. The energy had gone flat, like a Coke left out too long. Their jokes sounded stale, their laughter rang hollow. He couldn't share their reminiscences of the Phish concert last weekend. It was as if he had been away for years rather than weeks.

He planned to call Claudia tonight and break up with her. Then, if he could get up the nerve, he'd call Molly Lightning. It was shitty, the way he'd left without explaining anything to her. She probably thought he'd been shipped off to reform school. It wouldn't be the toughest call he had to make, though. He had to figure out what to do about his mom and, tougher still, Tammi Lee. It was his stupid fault she'd lost her job. His stupid fault for chickening out and not telling the truth about what had happened. His stupid fault she'd gone out drinking.

Through the window of the gated entrance, he spotted a movement. A shadow. His heart thumped. Behind him, a wino shuffled along the sidewalk, muttering to himself. Noticing Cody, he said, "Hey, gotta smoke?"

"Nope," Cody said. "I gave it up."

Slowly, his backpack feeling like a load of bricks, he trudged up the walk toward his house. For a few more minutes, he stood listening to the low hum of the hot-tub pump and feeling the moist chill of the Seattle evening on his hair. Then he took a deep breath, punched the security code into the keypad, and let himself in.

The place smelled vaguely of patchouli oil and Natalie's experimental Middle Eastern cooking. She had a performance tonight, and so she'd left dinner in the fridge and a note in fat pink magic marker—*Call your mother.*

"I know, I know," Cody murmured under his breath. He set down his backpack with a thunk and went to put on some music. It was too quiet in the house. He found himself wandering around, feeling more alone than he'd ever felt before. Without really planning to, he found himself in the study, a neat-as-a-pin room with a glass-topped desk, a big angled drafting table, and two computers, their black faces gathering dust. He went to the closet and folded the louvered door aside, and then he realized what he was looking for.

His mom's paintings.

They were stored in the very back of the closet in a large, flat portfolio with three clasps. Working carefully, he took out the canvases and sketches and leaned them against the walls. There weren't very many of them, and he'd only seen them a few times.

He supposed he'd always known the pictures were good—great, even—filled with color and life and movement. They seemed to say something important. Like the painting that hung in Sam's house. But up until today he had always regarded these pictures as something created by a stranger, someone he never knew.

For the first time, he managed to connect the paintings to his mom. He pictured her in the studio at Blue Rock, lost in her work, not harried and tense like she was at the agency. Pacing in agitation, he thought about how she had looked yesterday when he'd told her he and Sam would never get along. In his heart, Cody didn't believe he was wrong. Sam *didn't* want him.

But maybe Cody had twisted the truth . . . a bit. It was pretty obvious Sam was pissed at him, but he'd never actually said he didn't want a son. It was a fine distinction. But if Sam was pissed about Molly, he'd go ballistic when he learned who the real culprit was in the quilt-shop incident.

Cody felt a rank lump of guilt in his throat. He didn't blame Sam for not wanting him.

The reason Sam had left Crystal City didn't have a thing to do with Cody or his mom. That phone call Sam had received . . . In his mind's eye, Cody could still see rage and fear on his face. And something worse—the hurt.

Sam had to take off in order to save his mother, and Cody had done the only thing he could think of. He'd fled.

Now he knew how the filly had felt, driven up to the woods in terror of the snowmobiles. He'd run away, but maybe he'd wound up in a place of greater danger. Hell, he didn't know. He should just stay away from Montana, where he didn't fit in. He'd never fit in.

Feeling restless and unsettled, he grabbed a yogurt from the fridge and scarfed it down, then drank half a quart of orange juice. Then he picked up the phone and jabbed in Claudia's number. Might as well get the easy call out of the way before he decided what to do about the rest.

In the middle of the third and fourth ring, the sound of the buzzer from the security office nearly made him jump out of his skin. Frowning, he hung up the phone. He wasn't expecting anyone.

He was amazed when the guard announced the name of his visitor. *Gavin Slade.* Switching on the lights over the entranceway, he opened the door.

"Hey," he said tentatively.

"Hey yourself." With a jangle of flying-ace buckles and straps, an unsmiling Gavin Slade strode into the house.

Cody followed him inside. "Um, how did you get here?"

"Flew the Mustang to Boeing Airfield. I wasn't planning on taking her out for a long haul so soon, but here I am." The bluewater eyes inspected Cody. "I expect you know why I came in such a hurry."

Cody eyed him warily. The angry energy of defiance coursed through him. "If you came out to lecture me because I blew it with my mom, you wasted a trip. My mind's made up. I don't fit in there."

Gavin scanned the room and Cody realized he was

seeing where his daughter lived for the first time. "Actually," he said, "it's more than that. I guess I came because, a long time ago, *I* blew it with your mom. She needed me, and I wasn't there for her, and she took off." His eyes looked deep and sad. "For seventeen years," he added. "I'm here because this is what I should have done for my daughter all those years ago. I should have come after her."

"This is different. Sam can't stand me, and the feeling's mutual."

Peeling off his leather jacket to reveal several more layers of clothing, Gavin studied a big studio photograph of Cody and his mom, done about five years before. He walked right up to the framed picture and pressed his palm to it. "How old were you in this picture?"

"Maybe ten or eleven." Cody remembered the red Izod shirt, and the feel of his mom's open hand on his shoulder, and the way the photographer had tried to flirt with her.

"I wish I'd known you then," Gavin said. "I feel lucky to have met you at all, Cody. Look at all the time we lost, with us being so stubborn." He turned to face Cody. "I don't know what went on between you and Sam, but the one who's getting hurt is your mom."

Cody's throat felt dry as sandpaper. Gavin was right. She had been happy and flushed and calm up until last night. Up until Cody's big lie.

"It took a kidney failure to get us back together," Gavin said. "What's it going to take this time? A heart attack?"

"You don't understand," Cody said. "You don't understand how bad I am." He felt too miserable to be embarrassed when his voice broke.

"Then make me understand, Cody."

The genuine caring in Gavin's quiet voice reached out to Cody. "You're not going to like it," he said. And then his voice steadied, and he told the truth. He told his grandfather what he had done.

Gavin gave a low whistle. "That's pretty damned bad."

"See? Sam'll never forgive me, and who can blame him?"

Gavin was quiet for a long time. Cody's stomach knotted. He hated what he'd done. Hated what a jerk he'd been. Finally, Gavin spoke. "I think I get the picture. You know, Michelle doesn't have the sort of troubles your grandmother does, but that doesn't meant she doesn't need you."

"What does she need with a screwup like me?" Cody demanded.

"You're only a screwup if you don't know how to straighten out the mess you've made," Gavin pointed out. "Nothing'll ever feel right again until you do. You know that, don't you, son?"

"You're right," said Cody, filling up with elation and terror.

Sam stood in the shower, letting the too-hot water pound down on his head. There was nothing, he thought, *nothing* worse than dropping your mother off at rehab. He felt as if a bomb had gone off in the middle of his life, and pieces lay scattered about, unrecognizable.

He'd had to pry her away from the dim, smoky cocoon of the honky-tonk; he'd listened to the familiar protests and promises; he'd hardened his will to her desperate pledges. Then he'd spent most of the day getting her checked in at the facility in Missoula.

"We did it again, di'n' we?" she had said, staring woozily out the truck window. "Stepped over the line.

Tried to fit in with respectable folks, where we don't belong. We're still on the wrong side of the tracks, Sammy. We always will be."

During the drive home, the rage had struck Sam hard, as it always did. What the fuck had LaNelle Jacobs been thinking, blaming the robbery on Tammi Lee? All the slights and slurs of years past had suddenly come back on a wave of resentment. Five years of peace and quiet in Crystal City had lulled him into thinking the past didn't matter.

Sam turned off the shower. Slinging a towel around his waist, he picked up the phone and stabbed his fingers impatiently at the numbers.

"Blue Rock," said a familiar and unwelcome voice. Jake Dollarhide.

"Sam McPhee here. I'm looking for Michelle."

"I'll see if I can get her on the intercom." Sam heard an unpleasant sneer in Dollarhide's slow drawl, and suddenly the years peeled back to expose the gaping wounds of the past. He remembered all the times he had tried to call her long ago, all the times Gavin and his staff had put him off.

"On second thought," Sam said brusquely, "never mind." Without further explanation he hung up and got dressed.

Screaming gusts of wind kicked up a ground blizzard, and everyone with a lick of sense stayed indoors. Not Sam. Not tonight. He was exhausted to the last inch of his shadow, but he had to see Michelle.

He wasn't sure what he'd say to her. He'd never had anyone to talk to in the middle of a crisis; he was used to going it alone. Still, he owed her an explanation. After all, he'd stood her up.

Have dinner with me tonight. She had sounded so excited. Fresh and alive, the Michelle he had known as a young man. But a lot had happened since her breathless invitation. He had lost his cool with Cody, and the incident made him wonder just what sort of father he would be. His mother's fragile sobriety had been shattered, reminding him that loving someone carried hazards that could crush even the stoutest of hearts.

It did not escape him that the other time he had disappeared from Michelle's life had been on his mother's behalf. The reason had not changed. Michelle was strong. She knew how to keep herself safe and secure. No matter how much Sam loved her, he also loved his mother, who could not survive without him. Michelle's very strength was her Achilles' heel. She had trained herself not to need, want, desire. And perhaps the habit was so ingrained that now she no longer remembered how to want something.

But when he saw her through the window of the studio, standing and staring at her canvas, he knew there were mysteries inside her he could not guess at. They would reveal themselves to him gradually—but only if he knew the right way to unlock them.

When he knocked at the door and stepped inside, she folded her hands in front of her. "Sam."

"I had an emergency," he said. "This was my first chance to call."

She stood quietly in the warm glow of the studio lights. He told himself to explain the rest, yet the words wouldn't form. When it came to his mother, he was private and intensely protective. And even a little ashamed, as if his mother's disease were due to some weakness in him. The silence opened a gulf between him and Michelle.

Last time they were together, he had proposed to her. Now he couldn't even make small talk.

The ground blizzard pounded at the windows and doors. Michelle shivered, and he saw that the fire in the woodstove had dwindled to embers. To occupy himself, Sam wrenched open the iron doors and added a quartered log.

"Cody told me what happened when you found him and Molly in the barn," Michelle said.

He crushed up a wad of old newspaper and stuck it under the log. "He told you his version. Molly's the daughter of a good friend. A nice girl."

"According to Cody, they weren't doing anything that risky. Sam, they're sixteen. It's what teenagers do. We can't stop them. We can just hope they don't do anything rash."

He grabbed a bellows and pumped at the banked embers. "The trouble is, sometimes hope isn't enough to stop them, and the consequences are pretty far-reaching." The air wheezing from the bellows sparked the yellow edge of a flame under the new, raw log.

"You made that clear to Cody. You made it clear he was an accident, an unwanted child. When he came home, he asked me if I'd ever considered having an abortion or giving him up for adoption. That's the first time he's asked me that, Sam. Ever."

Sam shut the stove door and stood to face her. A cold chill hardened in his gut. Doubts buzzed through his mind. He *had* lost it, overreacted. How was it that he'd been so sure of himself only two days ago?

Now he didn't know a damned thing, except that loving someone carried a commitment that could crush you. All his life, he had borne the responsibility for his mother.

The price of that had been that he'd had no parental guidance of his own.

"Well, what should I have said, finding him like that?" he asked.

"There's no oracle that lays it all out for you. You just have to pray you get it right most of the time. When it comes to sex, Cody knows the decision is his to make, and all I can do is hope that whatever he decides, it will keep him on course with who he is and what he wants to become."

"You didn't answer my question, Michelle."

She held out her hands to the stove, warming them. "I suppose I would have told him to wait, to be careful. I would have reminded him that he has all the time in the world." She fixed her gaze on Sam. "I would have told him I know it's damned hard to wait when you're sixteen."

"That's naive as hell. The kid is a bundle of raging hormones—"

"He knows when to stop, Sam. I have to trust that. If I can't, what sort of a mother am I?"

Sam envied Michelle her conviction. He realized now that he doubted his own ability to be a good father. God knew, he wanted to be, but he was afraid he'd screw up.

"I'm sorry I made that remark to Cody," he said. "Maybe I just don't have enough patience and understanding to handle him—I guess I proved that by blowing up at him." He gestured toward the door. "I should stop in and talk to him."

She was quiet for a long time. Shadows sculpted her face, and he couldn't read her thoughts.

"Michelle?"

"You'd better go, Sam. This isn't a good time for a discussion with Cody."

His heart lurched. "He's taking it that hard?"

More silence strained between them. Michelle bit her lip, hesitant to speak, and pushed her hair out of her eyes with a weary motion. "This just isn't a good time," she repeated. "I don't know what to think, except that you and I don't work until you and Cody figure out a way to get along." She opened the door to the howling night. "I won't let myself be torn to pieces by the two of you." Her good-bye was as brief and painful as the cauterizing of a wound.

He drove home, the chill inside him expanding. Damn it. Last time he'd seen Michelle, he'd asked her to marry him. Two days later, she was practically throwing him out. Sam squinted at the dry, blowing snow. He was tempted to turn back, but the doubts—and the remembered words of his mother—held him back.

"Don't go chasing after her again." Only yesterday, his mother had admonished him in a tequila-harsh voice. "Don't go getting your heart stomped into the ground."

He told himself not to jump to conclusions. They'd work out their problems. But no matter what he told himself, he still remembered that Michelle hadn't tried to find him years ago.

Saturday

Chapter 51

The next morning, Michelle was still wearing the
sterling-silver earrings she had put on for her big
night with Sam. The night that never happened.
It seemed like ages ago. Miles ago. A lifetime ago. With
Sam, she had known a love so deep that it left her gasping and haunted her still. Watching him leave last night
had crushed her, and it was far worse now than it had
been years ago, because now she understood exactly what
she had lost.

She took off the earrings and made a fist around them.
Something had broken down between her and Cody and
Sam, and she didn't know how to make it right. She didn't
know if it could be made right. Maybe she should have
told him Cody had disappeared. The fact that she hadn't
was revealing in and of itself. Regular couples would discuss the issue right off, up front, and confront it together.

Instead, she had resisted telling Sam that after his quarrel with Cody, their son had taken an all-night bus to Seattle.

That was important, overwhelming. She should have told him. Yet she hadn't. Why?

Because it would make her look like a failure. A mother who lacked control of her own son. She was tired of feeling like that. She was embarrassed. She imagined people saying, "Her son took off on her." People's opinions shouldn't matter, but to Michelle they always had.

She hadn't seen her father since breakfast the day before. He'd gone to the air park. She had spent the day painting and worrying and waiting for Cody to call.

He hadn't.

It was all she could do to keep from jumping in the Rover and racing across three states to him. But she forced herself to stick by her decision. The old Michelle would have done that, and the old Cody would have expected it. But things were going to be different now. Different and new. Until Thursday night, she had thought Sam would be a part of it, but now she wasn't so sure. The child they had made together should be a part of their love. Instead, he had become a symbol of their doubts and differences.

It was just as well that she had come to see those differences now rather than sinking even deeper in love with Sam. The thing to remember was the hurt. The sense that, when all was said and done, the past few weeks had been an interlude. By nature, an interlude had to end.

Sam McPhee was all her heart wanted. But she was so scared. Was she to spend her life with this ache of yearning in her chest, the walking wounded of failed love?

She had made a studious effort not to try to second-guess Sam. Who knew what he was thinking, blowing up at Cody and then disappearing like that? Maybe everything got a little too real for him. Maybe he started thinking about what it would be like actually to be married, to be the father of a difficult teen. Maybe it was not what he wanted after all.

And so she couldn't look to him for comfort. Her wounds had to stay private. The pain was too raw, too sharp to show anyone yet.

The past weeks must have happened to someone else, she thought. Her giddy happiness with Sam felt surreal, a fairy tale made of myth and spun sugar. No one's life could actually turn out like that, she realized. But her hopeful, foolish heart reminded her that at the center of every fairy tale lay a truth that gave the story its power.

Lord. Even now. Even after last night, she was still dumb enough to hope. It was a shock to realize that even though she loved Sam with everything that was in her, it wasn't enough. Her throat filled up, and her eyes swam, and she blinked frantically. She decided to go riding, work on her painting, try to feel normal for a while.

And maybe, please God, maybe, wait for the phone to ring.

The crisp edge of winter kept its hold on the ranch even though a dazzling sun kept trying to warm things up. On her way to the barn, Michelle passed the calving shed, hearing sounds of bovine distress and a few well-chosen swear words. In the lot adjacent to the stockyard, protesting steers were being loaded for shipping to some rodeo or other. A dark-skinned young man, carrying a bucket of oats for the horses, tipped his hat in greeting. She remembered how enchanting she had found all of this when she had come to her father, eager and shy, to live as his daughter for the first time. They couldn't have known then the turns their lives would take, and she had never dreamed she'd be back here again, loving this place even more, if that was possible.

On a day like this, Blue Rock was the idyllic place in the imagination of everyone who had ever dreamed of the West. The rim of mountains, the fields of snow with bunchgrass showing through, the clusters of buildings and ranch vehicles spoke both poetry and permanence.

She heard a grinding of tires and saw a car turn in from the main road. Sunlight glared off the windshield of her father's Cadillac as it parked in front of the old building she used as a studio. Shading her eyes, she watched two people get out of the car. Her heart seemed to drop to her knees.

Cody and her father didn't see her as they went around back to the trunk. They were both wearing leather flight jackets and weary grins. She couldn't believe it. Couldn't believe her father had gone after Cody, and that Cody had come back to Blue Rock. Yet it made perfect sense. Gavin had done for Cody what he should have done for Michelle—brought him back to the place he belonged, whether he knew it yet or not.

Her throat stung as she watched her father and her son facing each other—Gavin tall and white-haired and distinguished, Cody slender and intense. They spoke for a moment, then Gavin clasped Cody's shoulder in a way that was so awkwardly male that she couldn't help smiling through her tears.

For so long, she had thought Gavin had been no father at all to her. But last night, she had sat down with the blank book the transplant team had given her months ago, when she had first agreed to the transplant. The pages had stayed blank, as empty as she had been before coming to Montana. Then last night, she had lain in bed and written in the book, and by the time she finished, she understood that Gavin had been her father in the only way he knew how. She had written of the precious time she and Gavin had spent together seventeen years ago. An early-morning ride on horseback. Lazy afternoons on the porch, watching the mountain wind ripple through the fields of avalanche lilies. Evenings by the fire, sketching while he read his mail. That was what he had given her. And it was, she suddenly knew, enough. Enough. *Thank you, Daddy.*

She blotted her cheeks while Cody lifted the lid of the trunk. He took out something she hadn't seen in a very long time—her portfolio case.

The tears threatened again, and Michelle pressed a hand to her mouth. Cody went into the studio, and she was dying to know what he was up to, but she had something to do first. She went and got the journal and took it to her father.

Gavin's expression indicated that he recognized the book.

"Read it," she said, kissing him on the cheek. "I think you'll like it."

"I love you, honey," he said, taking the gift. "Now go see your boy. He's got a lot to say for himself."

"Thanks, Daddy. Thanks for bringing him home." She kissed him again, then hurried to the studio to find Cody. "Hey, stranger," she said from the doorway.

His shoulders stiffened, and the reaction stung her. Lately it was automatic, the way he braced himself for the worst. He turned to face her. "Mom," he said. "Mom, I'm really sorry I took off."

She tried to say something, but no words came out. She stepped into the main room of the studio, and her heart soared.

Cody had taken out the paintings and lined them up against a wall. The light flowed over bold splashes of color, and she thought about how long it had been since she had looked, really looked at her own work. The paintings were honest and painfully beautiful, filled with truth and emotion. She could see the evolution of frustration, grief, joy. When she regarded the paintings now, they seemed to have been done by someone else. Someone more emotional. More tender. With more of her soul to give. It seemed a miracle to Michelle that these images had come from her. There was one significant painting missing, she realized. It was the snow scene—the one that hung over the mantel in Sam's house.

Sam.

Pushing away the ache of regret, she opened her arms. Cody hugged her, and she marveled at how tall he was, tall and wiry and stronger than she remembered.

"Hey, Mom—"

"Cody—"

They both spoke at once. She gave a little laugh and stepped back. "I'm so glad you came back," she said.

He picked at the bandage on his hand. "I never should have left like that, Mom. It was so stupid."

"We'll get over it," she said, and was pleased to feel actual conviction behind the words. "Cody, I owe you an apology."

His face paled. "Mom, no. I'm the one who—"

"I do." She held up a hand to quiet him. She felt a sting of regret for the way things had been between them lately. She'd always thought it was her job to protect him from being hurt, but she'd wound up teaching him to shy away from emotion. "I was awful to you sometimes, Cody, and it was my own frustration making me pick at you and fuss at you. That was wrong, and—"

"Mom, there's some stuff I need to tell you."

Struck by his tone, she went over to the cushioned

window seat. Cody was somber and tense as he sat beside her. In Gavin's bulky flight jacket, he looked strange and poignantly familiar. His hair was combed, there were no headphones in sight, and when he looked up at her, she saw both Gavin and Sam in his face. "I screwed up, Mom," he said. "I screwed up big-time."

"What do you mean?"

He rubbed his hands on his thighs. "Um, I don't blame you if you get mad at me."

"So just say it, Cody. I can't read your mind."

He picked at the fraying gauze bandage on his hand. "I didn't tell you the whole truth about Sam taking off Thursday night." His voice was low but steady. "His, um, mother—Tammi Lee—got in trouble. Sam didn't say, but I think she was drinking. So he had to drop everything and go help her."

Michelle's stomach lurched. Sam hadn't said a word about this. He had kept it from her, just as she had kept Cody's disappearance from him. She had never known much about Sam's life with his troubled mother. How hard it must be for him, for them both, every day. And her son had held his silence. Her son . . .

"Why didn't you tell me?" she asked Cody, more baffled than angry.

"I didn't know what to do. Everything happened so quick—Sam was yelling at me about Molly and he made me feel so bad, and then he had to go help his mother. She got fired from her job, see? And I'm the only one who knows the real reason why." His cheeks flamed, and Michelle was shocked to see tears in his eyes. "Some guys from school took money from the shop, and Tammi Lee got the blame. Instead of speaking up, I just let Sam go running off to help her, and then I started thinking how much he'd hate me when he got back, so I didn't tell anyone . . . it just got away from me."

She detected a hint of his old sullenness. But she wouldn't stand for evasion, not anymore. "Those are excuses, Cody. What's the real reason?"

He didn't speak for a moment, and she felt a little shock of disorientation as she watched him fighting tears. "I got scared, Mom," he said.

"Scared of what? Cody, tell me."

"I got scared, thinking about what it would be like to have Sam for a father." The admission was squeezed out of him along with the tears he had been struggling to hold back.

Scared. Michelle's heart skipped a beat. She knew then what Sam had tried to tell her the last time they were together—that Cody was in danger of becoming like her. Holding back and hiding from love because it was frightening. Overwhelming. All her life she tried to buy emotional safety at the risk of feeling only half alive.

"I saw how happy he makes you," Cody added, "and I guess I was afraid you'd love him more than me."

"Oh, son." She touched his face. "It's totally different. You have my heart, all of it, and that will never change."

"I'm sorry, Mom. I'm sorry. I'm sorry." His arms went around her. He still smelled like a boy, of soap and outdoor air, and he still needed his mother. As much as she needed *him.*

"I'll make everything right with Sam and Tammi Lee," he said. "I swear I will. I just hope they forgive me." Cody straightened up and scrubbed at his face with the back of his hand. Then he put his arm around her, and the universe came back into balance.

She gazed at him, and in his eyes, she saw Gavin's

eyes. Her father and her son. It took both of them to make her understand that life was short; who knew how long anyone had? When she got to wherever she was going, she wanted to have painted her paintings. She wanted to have loved with a passion beyond reason. She wanted to know that Cody was not just her son, but her friend.

She used to look at him and wonder where her little boy had gone. Now she realized she'd found him. She'd found him in this hurting, confused, and ultimately good kid who was becoming a good man. She paused, drew a breath, tried to think of the right thing to say.

"You know what's even more scary?" she asked. "It's that I almost lost you, Cody. But I think we're going to be okay." She realized that she'd almost lost Sam because she hadn't trusted herself with him. What she should have done was fling herself into the relationship the way she had flung herself into painting. Because it wasn't just the painting that came back to her after its long sleep in the frozen tundra, but life. And Sam had awakened her to that.

She thought about the transplant. Fear and love were sometimes the same thing, both necessary, unavoidable. Now she understood that it was okay to bleed if you know how to heal.

"So we'll call Sam, right?" Cody said. "He'll give me another chance, won't he?"

She put her hands on his shoulders. Lord, but it felt good to hold him again. She had never felt closer to her son. At sixteen, Cody was learning what she wished she had known long ago—that you have to love even though it hurts, even though there are no guarantees. You have to spend it all even though you never know what you'll get in return.

"Oh, Cody." She wanted to reassure him that of course

Sam would forgive him. But how did she know that? She'd had sixteen years to love and understand Cody, to learn who he was. Without all that groundwork, Sam's forgiveness would have to be a leap of faith.

Chapter 52

I t snowed later that day. An oppressive quiet shrouded the land, and flying snowflakes pocked the colorless sky. Michelle rode beside Cody in the Range Rover with headlights shining in the bleak day. The heartbeat rhythm of the windshield wipers, batting at the snow, punctuated the silence.

This was nuts, she thought. This was asking for heartache. When Cody had phoned Lonepine, he'd spoken to Edward Bliss, and the news was not good. Sam had taken his mother to detox, then brought her back to the house for a day or two while she found her footing. No, Edward wasn't any too sure they wanted company. And yet here she was, driving her son over to Lonepine, just as they had that first day—Lord, was it only three weeks ago?—before Sam and Cody had any idea they were father and son.

Why did she ever think this was a good idea? Barging back into Sam's life, hoping and praying he would let her back in.

Self-doubt and sheer terror pounded in her gut. In the past, the fear would have stopped her from taking this step. She would have chosen emptiness over pain and joy. Now she knew better. For a short and glorious time she had found the essence of all she desired in the arms of Sam McPhee. It was something she wouldn't get another chance at, something most people didn't even experience in a lifetime.

Parking at Lonepine, she stared out the window at the white-quilted landscape that was starving for spring to come again. Tammi Lee stood out on the porch wearing a big jacket with the collar up and smoking a cigarette.

"You want me to come with you?" Michelle asked Cody.

"Nope. I'm on my own."

He got out of the car and walked toward the house. She realized he didn't need her to prop him up as she had so often in the past, even when it would have been better to leave him be.

Tammi Lee tossed out her cigarette and sat very still, waiting for Cody to come to her. She felt drained, wrung out, as if she had just run a marathon. She hated having her grandson see her like this, but this was who she was—someone who had flown high and crashed-landed more times than she could count. She hovered in a low gully, wondering if she'd rise or fall this time.

"Can I talk to you?" Cody asked. His face looked pale and tight, hands jammed hard into his pockets.

"Sure," she said, her breath freezing in the air. She could listen. Yeah, she could do that.

"It's about . . . what happened with the shop and stuff." He stepped up onto the porch. "That night I borrowed your car, something happened."

Tammi Lee's head began to buzz, craving her meds. She focused sharply on the nervous young boy. He was so good-looking. And right now, he looked as wrung out as she felt.

"It's my fault the money in the cash register went missing," he blurted out. "I didn't know—I—it's my fault."

Tammi Lee sat very still. She was so used to getting kicked in the teeth that she braced herself.

"The cash disappeared when I went into the shop after hours," he said. "It's all my fault."

"Did you take the money?" she asked quietly.

His hands dug even deeper into his pockets. "That doesn't matter. I was responsible. And I blew it. I went to see Mrs. Jacobs today, and I explained it all to her, paid her what was missing. She feels real bad, and she's going to ask you to come back to work. That is, if you want to." He scuffed his foot at a frozen lump of snow on the edge of the porch. "I'm real sorry," he added. "I'll do whatever I have to do to make it right. I just—I'd like to have a second chance."

Tammi Lee felt herself rising a little, hovering above the abyss. Her head pounded, but the pain meant nothing. This was it, she realized. She could forgive this boy and go on from here, or she could let anger and resentment drag her down.

When she looked into his eyes, she saw Sam's eyes. Sam, who'd given her more second chances than anyone had a right to expect. Sam, who deserved a chance of his own. There was really no choice to be made. She stood up and opened her arms. A tentative smile started in Cody's eyes as he hugged her. Over his shoulder she saw Michelle

Turner standing by her car, watching them, one hand pressed to her mouth.

"I think we're going to be all right," Tammi Lee whispered, and she started to soar, lifted by hope. "I think we're going to be just fine."

Sam came out of the main barn and started walking toward Michelle. Her knees felt liquid, threatening to buckle. She was aware of the bruising cold, the snow coming over the tops of her boots, her incision aching.

She used to think healing meant stitching up, scarring over, turning a mess to neatness. Now she understood that she had to let things melt down, unravel, and then come back together in the way they were meant to be.

She had to quit looking for a reason that things happened. This was life, it was messy, and now she knew better than to expect a guarantee. Her heart pounded, she had never felt more alive. She had no idea what the expression on her face was, but she didn't care. When she looked up at Sam, she saw everything she wanted her future to be.

And no matter what that was, it was bigger and brighter than her dreams had ever been.

Hope and fear were locked, unspoken, in her throat. She and Sam walked to the edge of the snow-covered driveway and stood beneath the twisted skeleton of a crabapple tree.

"Cody blames himself for everything that happened," she said at last. "He wants to make things right with you and your mother."

He looked over at the house, where Cody and Tammi Lee stood very close, talking. "I guess I'm glad to see that."

"Can he?" she forced herself to ask. "Can he make

things right? Can *we*?" She twisted her gloved fingers into knots.

"I've been asking myself the same thing."

"Last night, we were both still hiding things. You didn't tell me about your mother, and—" she swallowed hard "—I didn't explain to you that Cody had run away." She forced herself to meet his disbelieving gaze. "He took the bus to Seattle. I wanted to tell you, Sam, but I didn't know how. My father brought him back this morning."

"I guess I'll just let Cody do the explaining, then." Sam held her gaze for an endless moment. "We'll give it our best shot, honey. Okay?"

She managed to choke out his name, and the dam inside her broke like the thawing mountain streams. The sobs of relief came from the deepest part of her, a part she couldn't discipline or control. Sam was a wall of warmth, silent and steady as he absorbed the brunt of her tears. She found a sanctuary, not a threat, in loving him.

"I was so afraid." Her hands clutched at his jacket. "I was so afraid you'd decided Cody and I were too much for you."

His arms slid around her. "Ah, Michelle. Everything's not going to be perfect all the time. But we can survive the mistakes. You know that. You *know*."

"Sometimes I think I'm just not good enough at this," she whispered.

He held her away from him, and dear God, he had the most magnificent face, so full of hardness and soul, weathered by life's joys and sorrows. Snowflakes landed and disappeared on his cheeks, his shoulders. "We'll work it out. You and me and our son."

"*Our* son. It sounds just right." There was a catch in her throat, and she swallowed hard. "I love you, Sam." It was time to say it, long past time. It was so easy. It had turned from impossible to effortless. "I always have, and I always will."

He pulled her against him, pressed his lips to her hair. In that moment, the last of her doubts slid away, and Sam said, "I know, honey. I know."

"You do?"

"Oh yeah."

Michelle closed her eyes as joy settled over them, as silently powerful as new-fallen snow. And like the snow over a stubbled field, it covered everything else—all the flaws and ruts and bruises of the past—with its perfection and purity.